THE FOYLES BOOKSHOP GIRLS' PROMISE

ELAINE ROBERTS

Boldwood

First published in Great Britain in 2024 by Boldwood Books Ltd.

Copyright © Elaine Roberts, 2024

Cover Design by Colin Thomas

Cover Images: Colin Thomas

The moral right of Elaine Roberts to be identified as the author of this work has been asserted in accordance with the Copyright, Designs and Patents Act 1988.

All rights reserved. No part of this book may be reproduced in any form or by any electronic or mechanical means, including information storage and retrieval systems, without written permission from the author, except for the use of brief quotations in a book review. This book is a work of fiction and, except in the case of historical fact, any resemblance to actual persons, living or dead, is purely coincidental.

Every effort has been made to obtain the necessary permissions with reference to copyright material, both illustrative and quoted. We apologise for any omissions in this respect and will be pleased to make the appropriate acknowledgements in any future edition.

A CIP catalogue record for this book is available from the British Library.

Paperback ISBN 978-1-80549-711-0

Large Print ISBN 978-1-80549-712-7

Hardback ISBN 978-1-80549-710-3

Ebook ISBN 978-1-80549-713-4

Kindle ISBN 978-1-80549-714-1

Audio CD ISBN 978-1-80549-705-9

MP3 CD ISBN 978-1-80549-706-6

Digital audio download ISBN 978-1-80549-709-7

This book is printed on certified sustainable paper. Boldwood Books is dedicated to putting sustainability at the heart of our business. For more information please visit https://www.boldwoodbooks.com/about-us/sustainability/

Boldwood Books Ltd, 23 Bowerdean Street, London, SW6 3TN

www.boldwoodbooks.com

*To my late husband and a promise of love we made and kept.
I will always love you.*

PROLOGUE
AUGUST 1914

Rosie Burrows and Fran Wilson joined others leaning against the wrought-iron railings, soaking in the view of the Southend seafront and all the talk of war because of some archduke from Austria getting shot.

Rosie tucked her brown hair behind her ears, before glancing at Fran. 'Should we be worried? It's all everyone seems to be talking about. Well, that and the possibility of unions calling a general strike.'

Fran shook her head. 'My pa says the general strike won't happen now, and the suffragettes have called off their demonstrations to get behind the men going off to war. He said the country has got to pull together for us to stop the killing of innocent people.' She squinted into the sunshine. 'I expect Sam will be worried about his brother going off to the front line.'

Rosie frowned as she glanced over at the brothers walking towards them. 'Yes, Alfie was certainly keen to enlist straight away.'

Fran followed Rosie's gaze. 'As was Frank. He joins his regiment tomorrow. I expect I'll see him later but he's spending the day with his family.'

Rosie studied her friend. 'I'm sorry. You two were getting on so well, and he's certainly very handsome.'

Fran smiled. 'Yeah, well, I said I'd write to him and that's the best we can hope for now. I take it you'll write to Alfie, what with him being your boyfriend?'

Rosie nodded. 'I've said I will, although I'm not sure how I ended up being his girlfriend.'

Fran giggled. 'Well, let's face it, your families have known each other for years so if it hadn't been Alfie, it would have been Sam.'

Rosie chuckled. 'You make it sound like I couldn't have met anyone else.'

Fran laughed. 'I'm not sure you would have done; you don't exactly thrust yourself into enjoying other people's company, and especially not men's.'

Rosie raised her eyebrows. 'You mean like you do.'

'Well, as my gran used to say, "You only live once," and now with this war on, we must make the most of every day.' Fran nudged her friend. 'Thankfully we're only sixteen and our brothers are too young to go to war, so let's not think about it any more today. Today we're going to have some fun, chips, ice cream and feel the sun on us.'

As Alfie and Sam drew closer to the girls, Rosie freed the chips from their newspaper wrapping. 'Come on then, they smell good, so let's tuck in before they go cold.' She waved them under her friend's nose. 'Mmm.'

Alfie leant against the black railings, standing next to Rosie before peering at his brother. 'According to the chippy, they reckon the war will be over by Christmas, so I'll be back in time for my presents.' He slipped his arm around Rosie's waist.

'And some Christmas kisses; that's if I don't meet some nice French girl. You should be kind to me because I'll be off fighting for king and country tomorrow, keeping you all safe.' He squeezed Rosie close. 'I'll need some good memories to keep me going, so we need to make the most of today.' He winked at her. 'Aren't you going to share those chips with the love of your life?'

Rosie eyed him soberly before saying teasingly, 'That's exactly what I'm doing, and they're very nice, aren't they, Fran?'

Alfie grinned. 'And there was I thinking how happy I am to be in Southend, in the sunshine, with two beautiful girls.' He rested his other hand on Fran's waist, pushing himself between them.

The warm breeze caught at Fran's loose brown curls, sending them across her face as the colour crept up her neck.

Rosie offered Alfie and Sam the chips. 'You can't beat them. We're lucky the chippy gave us a huge portion.'

Sam shook his head. 'No, thank you.'

Alfie helped himself before winking at them both again. 'Of course, we'll have to toss a coin to see which one of you gets lumbered with poor old Sam at the end of the day when the fun really starts.'

Sam said nothing but turned to stare at the waves rolling in on the beach.

Rosie frowned. 'Alfie, stop being mean to your brother, and I'm enjoying myself now, never mind at the end of the day.' She stepped away from him. 'And I don't need you to hold on to me so tightly, you're not my father. You're only two years older than Fran and me, and three years older than Sam.' She glared at Alfie. 'I've never known a time when you've acted brotherly towards him.'

Sam gave a wry smile. 'Don't worry, Rosie, I'm quite used to it.'

Alfie reached out and wrapped his fingers around Rosie's

arm. 'I just want to have a good day and evening before I go off in the morning; after all, you might never see me again.'

Rosie stared at Alfie before pulling her arm free and turning to wave the chips under Sam's nose. 'Come on, Sam, have a chip, there aren't many left.'

Sam nodded and helped himself. 'They taste as good as they smell.'

Alfie watched Rosie mothering his younger brother. He threw his head back and laughed. 'Stop taking it all so seriously; someone has to toughen him up. Ma treats him like a baby and now you're doing it as well.' He grabbed Rosie's hand and lowered his voice to barely a whisper. 'And the last person I want to be compared to is your father; my thoughts are far from that direction, if you know what I mean.'

Flushed with colour, Rosie stepped away from him again. 'Come on, Fran, let's go.'

Alfie frowned. 'Remember, I'll be going off to war after my training, so you'd better start showing me some love, never mind poor old Sam.'

Ignoring him, Rosie turned her attention to the brick-built archway that led onto the pier and to the pavilion. She watched the small sailing boats bobbing up and down on the waves. Children screamed with delight as the sea lapped around their feet. Dads and grandfathers were helping to build sandcastles, while the mums and grandmothers unpacked the picnics. Rosie smiled. 'Isn't it beautiful? I could stay here forever.'

Fran straightened up, scanning the beach in front of them. 'It certainly is; there seem to be a lot of happy families.' She clapped her hands together. 'Look, look, there's a Punch and Judy show, let's go and watch it.' She turned and grinned at Rosie. 'Then we'll have an ice cream.'

Rosie smiled. 'Let's. It all has to be done when you're at the beach.' She crumpled the chip wrapping into a ball and they both lifted their ankle-length skirts up before laughing and running towards the beach. 'Come on, Sam.'

Sam beamed as he ran with them.

Alfie shouted after them, 'Aren't you too old to sit with the children listening to "That's the way to do it"?'

Rosie giggled as she peered over her shoulder. 'You're never too old.'

They leant against the railings listening to the puppet show and laughing along with the children who were sitting on the beach.

Everyone groaned when the show finished.

Fran turned to Rosie. 'That was good fun, but I suppose we'd better get home before the family send someone out to find us.'

'Yes, I suppose so, but I've really enjoyed today.'

Sam chuckled. 'We're all just small children at heart.'

Alfie scowled. 'Speak for yourself.'

Rosie stared at Alfie. 'Stop being grumpy; we did enjoy it as much as the children.' She looked round at Fran. 'Come on, we might just catch the next train if we're quick.'

They ran to the station just as the steam train pulled in, and the four of them jumped into the nearest carriage.

Rosie sat down, trying to catch her breath.

Alfie sat next to her and rested his hand on her leg. He leant in and kissed her cheek, letting his hand slowly rise up her leg as he did so.

Rosie brushed his hand away.

The four of them sat in silence until just over an hour later, when the train pulled into London. There was the clicking of doors opening, followed by the thud of them closing again.

Fran and Sam were the first two to step down on to the platform.

Alfie grinned. 'Don't wait for us; Rosie and I are going for a walk as we have things to talk about.'

Fran's eyes narrowed. 'I'll see you tomorrow, Rosie. Stay safe, Alfie.' She walked off quickly, followed by Sam.

Sam glanced over his shoulder. 'Will you be all right, Rosie?'

Alfie's lips curled. 'Of course she will be. It's our last night together and, as I said, we have things to discuss; just get yourself home.'

Sam turned to walk away. He stopped, giving a last glance over his shoulder before stepping in line with Fran.

Rosie stepped away from Alfie. 'I should get home; my ma will be worrying.'

Alfie grabbed her arm. 'Ahh come on, Rosie, your ma won't be concerned; it's not like she doesn't know you're with me, and this might be our only chance to be on our own before I go off to war. There are things we need to say and do while we can. You know I'd like a proper goodbye kiss; after all, you might not see me again. We'll find somewhere private; there must be plenty of alleys around here.'

Rosie's heart was pounding. The palms of her hands were damp. 'Can't we say what we've got to say here?'

'No, it's an important moment – as I said, you might not see me again after tonight.' Alfie tucked her arm in his and squeezed it tight against his body as they walked along the platform and out of the busy Liverpool Street train station towards The Railway Tavern. The door of the public house opened, and noise filled the air around them, along with the stench of beer and cigarette smoke.

Rosie wrinkled her nose and held her breath, trying hard not to cough as the smoke hit the back of her throat.

Alfie pulled her down an alleyway next to the public house and pressed her against the wall.

Rosie had always known he was a ladies' man, but surely he wouldn't force himself upon her, would he? Wasn't he raised to be better than that? Rosie's fear took hold and tears pricked at her eyes. She wondered if she could find the strength to push him away, but she was trapped.

Alfie grabbed her arms and pulled her closer to him.

She stumbled.

His hands roamed over her body. A deep groan escaped from him. 'I've waited a long time for this.'

Rosie yelled, 'You're hurting me.'

Alfie tightened his hold. 'I need something to remind me of you, memories to keep me going while I'm fighting the enemy and keeping you all safe. I could die in battle and we would never have been together, is that what you want?' He pushed Rosie back against the wall. 'You know if I wanted to, I could take you right now.'

Rosie stayed silent as the tears tripped over her eyelashes.

Alfie held her tight. 'I'm sorry, I didn't mean to frighten you, I really didn't. We are meant to be together; will you wait for me to return?'

Rosie was tense with fear. Was this his marriage proposal? She wondered how she could say no to him; she knew she couldn't reject him before he went off to war. What if he did die? She would never forgive herself. Rosie took a deep breath. 'I *will* wait for you, but tonight isn't how it's meant to be; I'm not ready.' She wiped away her tears with her sleeve.

Alfie shook his head. 'Stop crying, you are quite safe, I would never hurt you. I will find someone who wants to be with me tonight, but don't forget – when I return, we will be together.' He pulled her to him and stroked her hair before stepping back to take her hand. 'Come on, let's get you home.'

Rosie shook her head and stepped farther away from him.

Alfie shrugged and turned to walk away.

Rosie stood hunched up, sobbing as he walked off. She slid down the wall, weeping into her hands.

Someone reached out and gently pulled her up. She screamed and began hitting out, but Sam held her tight. 'It's all right, Rosie, you're in safe hands now.'

Rosie shuddered as the sobs wracked her body.

Sam hugged her close while she cried.

1

Rosie Burrows pulled up the soft woollen collar on her coat as the freezing March wind bit through it. The air was cold and crisp. She shivered and let her mind drift back three and a half years to the lovely hot day she had spent in Southend with Fran, Alfie and Sam. She remembered that someone had said the war would be over by Christmas in 1914, and yet here they were in 1918 with no sign of it ending. A lot had changed in that time.

Shaking her head, Rosie tried to shrug off the melancholy that had wrapped itself around her since she'd woken up that morning. She normally enjoyed the walk to Foyles Bookshop on London's Charing Cross Road as it gave her time on her own, which was very sparse at home with a younger brother, a grandmother and her mother all living in the same house. Not for the first time, she wondered when this so-called Great War would end; it was all her twelve-year-old brother David could talk about. Her thoughts quickly turned to her father whom she loved and missed so much. Was it really just over a year ago that he'd died in the munitions factory explosion in Silvertown? It felt like yesterday that the house was rocked by the explosion and her ma had peered out of the window to see the flames in the distance licking at the sky. They hadn't known then that the explosion had happened where her father had worked and that he had still been there. For a while the heart of the family had been ripped out, but they were gradually learning to cope without him. Sighing, Rosie missed her father's voice of reason and, at twelve, David now needed his firm hand more than ever.

Her thoughts turned to Alfie, her fiancé, and to when – if ever – she would find out whether he was still alive or not. Like many young men, he had rushed to enlist when the king had given his speech on the balcony of Buckingham Palace. That had been almost four years ago. Nearly two years ago, Alfie's mother had cried on her doorstep when she had opened her front door to see the telegram boy standing there. He had silently handed over the envelope and, without waiting, had cycled off. Mrs Bennet had told Rosie it had taken her a while to open it and when she finally had, she was relieved to read Alfie was missing and presumed dead, which meant there was still hope he was alive and would come home again – but there had been no word from him or anyone else since then.

Rosie turned left onto Tottenham Court Road; the overnight frost glistened on the pavement, making it slippery underfoot. The Horseshoe Brewery came into view. Sniffing in the cold air, she was glad the weather had kept the familiar pungent smell of the spent grain left to ferment in the storage bins at bay.

'Rosie, Rosie!' a woman's voice yelled.

Rosie stopped and turned around to see Mrs Bennet waving as she paced towards her. She forced herself to smile. 'Good morning, Mrs Bennet. Don't rush, I'll wait, I don't want you slipping on the snow and breaking something.' She pushed up her coat sleeve to reveal her small wristwatch. 'You're out and about early today, it's only eight thirty.'

Was she rushing towards her because she finally had news about Alfie?

Mrs Bennet frowned as she tried to draw breath. Her hand rested on her chest as she gasped for air. 'I want to be near the front of the queue at the butcher's; it's too cold to be hanging around.'

Rosie nodded as they stepped forward together. 'It's certainly bitter this morning. How is Mr Bennet doing?'

A young woman, huddled up against the cold, brushed past Rosie. 'Sorry.' She didn't look round or reach out.

Mrs Bennet sighed. 'I don't suppose he's ever going to get better again, and I just have to accept it.'

Rosie frowned as she watched the young woman's pace slow down but not stop. There was something familiar about her, but she couldn't put her finger on what it was. She looked like someone down on her luck though.

Mrs Bennet cleared her throat, bringing Rosie's attention back to what she was saying. 'Sorry, I was a little distracted by that woman. How did you say Mr Bennet was doing?'

Mrs Bennet looked round but didn't say anything. She lowered her eyelashes. 'He's wasting away. I mean, he's eaten very little for the last few months, and even that has to be almost forced down him. It's this damn war; sorry, I shouldn't use such language, but he hasn't been the same since Alfie went missing, and he hasn't worked since the explosion at the munitions factory. He lost friends like your father that day, and he's never got over it. It would help take his mind off things if he got himself another job. I keep telling him he has to keep going for when Alfie comes back, but I think he's given up. He seems to have forgotten that he's got another son, who works so hard at the school. Sam deserves better from his father.' Mrs Bennet blinked quickly as a tear dropped over her lashes. 'He's a good boy and it won't be long before he gets called up too, and then where will we be?'

Rosie rested her red-woollen-gloved hand on Mrs Bennet's arm. 'I expect Mr Bennet finds it hard after all this time, but I'm sure Sam understands.'

'I know.' Mrs Bennet gave her a tearful smile, wiping her fingers under her eyes. 'You're a good girl, Rosie, unlike that so-called friend of yours, Fran; she should have kept her legs crossed and that would have saved a whole lot of shame and embarrassment for her and her family.'

Rosie immediately thought back to the duress Alfie had put her under on his last night at home. 'It's not her fault; some men put girls under a lot of pressure to give them what they want.' Alfie's words echoed in her head. 'You know, things like "I might not come back" and "This might be my only chance before I die", and yet it's always the woman that carries the shame.'

Mrs Bennet glanced up at Rosie. 'That sounds like the voice of experience; thank goodness my boys aren't like that. Alfie's lucky you've been here waiting for him to return.'

Rosie squeezed Mrs Bennet's arm, but she wondered how long she was expected to wait without any news. 'It must be hard for you both, I mean, not knowing what's happened to him.'

Mrs Bennet raised her eyebrows as she peered at Rosie. 'I know Alfie's still alive; I like to think that, as his mother, I would feel it if he were no longer here.' She paused. 'I keep telling that to that husband of mine but he thinks I'm mad.' She forced a smile. 'I was saving his army pay so you two could buy a house together, but once he was declared missing, the pay stopped. That would have set you both up and let's face it, your ma has already got a houseful, and Alfie won't want to live with me and his father.'

'That was very kind of you, Mrs Bennet, but I'm sure we'll work things out when he gets home.'

Mrs Bennet nodded. 'I'm sure you will, but we all need a little help along the way. I've been meaning to ask whether you've been buying things for your bottom drawer. You know, things like bedding, crockery, cutlery and saucepans. It's a lot of money to put a home together, especially when you're first setting out on a life together.'

Memories of that last evening with Alfie raced into Rosie's mind. Her chest tightened: was that the type of man she wanted to marry? Suddenly aware that Mrs Bennet was looking at her, she shook her head. 'No, no I haven't.'

'Well, you're probably right to save your money instead. Anyway, I had better get going, otherwise I'll be last in the queue at the butcher's and then there'll be nothing left.' Mrs Bennet reached out and wrapped her arms around Rosie. 'You have a good day at Foyles and take care after all that business with the spy. Who knew a bookshop could be a dangerous place to work.'

Rosie chuckled. 'That wasn't a normal day so don't worry, I'll be perfectly safe as long as the Germans don't bomb us. Anyway, enjoy your shopping and stay warm.'

Mrs Bennet waved as she turned and walked away.

Rosie raised her hand. Mrs Bennet was so certain Alfie was still alive, but if that were so, why hadn't he written to let them know?

Rosie continued to walk briskly along Charing Cross Road, the cold wind blowing the tendrils of her hair around her face. She lifted her hand to move them away just as the large Foyles Bookshop sign came into view. The black sign with large white lettering always stood out above the other shops; it permanently advertised to customers that they could get a tuppence refund on any books they returned, so many books were sold several times.

It was a busy shop, as it had come to be the place to go for books, for a chat, or just to get out of the cold. She was thankful that the Germans had missed Foyles on the many times they had bombed London.

Cars chugged slowly past her along the icy road and a couple of men in uniform marched along, passing other people who were walking tentatively in the snow. A car tooted its horn as a woman stepped off the pavement. Rosie spun round in time to see her step back again. Barrows were being set up on the pavement, the sellers starting to shout out their wares, and the tantalising smell of vegetable soup and fresh bread invaded her senses along with the fresh flowers on the stall she was walking past. Rosie tilted her head as she drew level with Foyles to glance at the spines of the books sitting on the rack under the awning outside the shop. She spied the suited Mr Leadbetter watching her and knew she didn't have time to read them properly.

'Good morning, Miss Burrows, it's another cold day.' Mr Leadbetter pulled at the bottom of his black waistcoat as Rosie walked through the open door of Foyles Bookshop. 'I trust you enjoyed your week off, and have got over the excitement of Albert thrusting heavy books at the spy to save Miss Beckford.'

Rosie grinned. 'I'm glad to be back, Mr Leadbetter, and Albert was definitely a hero that day. It was fortunate he came up from the basement when he did, although I did worry when he fell; he's no longer a young man. Do you know if Ellen is all right after her ordeal?'

Mr Leadbetter nodded. 'Yes, and she's now going to be working here full-time, and it will take a lot to keep Albert down, even at sixty-nine. He hasn't taken a day off; in fact, I think he's been enjoying the attention he's getting from all the ladies here, but you can rest assured we've all been visiting the basement to check on him.'

Rosie giggled. 'That's good to hear; he's like everyone's father or grandfather.'

Victoria Appleton, Mr Leadbetter's assistant floor manager, smiled as she saw Rosie and came over to speak to her. 'Hello, Rosie, it's great to have you back. I have some good news for you: as you've worked here for some time, we've decided to take you off permanent shelf and book-dusting duties and train you on one of our counters. I might put you with Molly for a while; she knows how this shop is run so there's nothing you can't ask her that she won't be able to answer.'

Mr Leadbetter sucked in his breath. 'That's true. Mrs Greenwood is very knowledgeable about the shop – but she can be a little mischievous at times.'

Victoria laughed. 'I think it's the best option, at least until Alice comes back to work permanently.'

Mr Leadbetter nodded. 'I'm not sure if Mrs Leybourne will come back full-time; she's enjoying having some time at home with her two boys.'

Victoria tilted her head and frowned. 'If that's the case, that's all the more reason to train someone to take over her counter; there's always Ellen as well.'

Mr Leadbetter looked thoughtful for a moment before smiling. 'I suppose it won't do any harm to train her too, then.'

'I quite agree, sir.' Victoria smiled. 'Come on, Rosie, let's find Molly and we can start your training straight away.'

The two girls nodded at Mr Leadbetter and headed towards the back of the shop to clock in. As they got nearer to the staff room, the sounds of chatter and laughter spilled out into the shop.

Rosie grinned as she walked in. 'Morning, ladies.'

'Hello, Rosie,' everyone chorused.

Vera, one of the mother figures amongst the shop assistants, stepped forward. 'It's good to see you back. I hope you're well and raring to go after your week off.'

Rosie laughed at Vera. 'It's always good to get out of my house and away from my younger brother who talks of nothing but the war. I think he finds it exciting and can't wait to go off himself.' Rosie shook her head. 'I don't think he realises what's going on, but then again, he's old enough to know now.' She sighed. 'I'm just sick of hearing about it.'

Vera threw her arms around Rosie and gave her a hug. 'Don't think about it, lovey, that's how I'm getting through life at the moment.'

Molly bounced into the room. 'Morning, everyone!' She walked towards the clocking in machine, picked out her card and listened for the clicking sound before pulling it out again.

'Morning, Molly!' The ladies beamed at her as they shouted as one.

Victoria stepped forward and rested a hand on Molly's arm. 'Mr Leadbetter has agreed for you to train Rosie and, if possible, Ellen to work behind the counters.' She shrugged. 'I know it's a lot to ask because the children's section is always so busy. There won't be as much time for you to spend reading to the little ones, and of course there will probably be longer queues than normal. But hopefully it won't take them long to get the hang of things and you being a more experienced shop assistant, you're the best person for the job.' Victoria giggled. 'That's obviously apart from me and Alice.'

Molly tried to suppress her smile. 'Blooming cheek; everyone knows I'm the fun one out of us three.'

Victoria chuckled. 'That's my exact point.' Her laughter faded as she lowered her voice. 'Just make sure you teach the girls how to do a good job; we're too busy to carry anyone.'

Molly raised her eyebrows. 'Of course. Is Alice in today? Now she's working odd days, and not in every week, I struggle to keep track of when she's going to be in.'

'Not today, but she will be later in the week.' Victoria smiled. 'It's like the old days, when she's in, and we get to eat lunch together and have a good old chat.'

Molly nodded. 'Yes, it is. I tell you what, we should book Monico's; we haven't had tea and cake there in ages.'

'Now that's a good idea. When Alice comes in, we'll sort out a date.'

* * *

Rosie sighed as she sat in the armchair opposite her grandmother, her gaze drawn to the flickering flames of the fire in the hearth. The small front room was inviting with its heavy dark green floor-length curtains drawn against the draughts that blew through the closed windows. A small wooden dining table stood in the corner of the room with six slatted chairs tucked under it. A couple of rugs were scattered under the furniture.

Rosie shivered. 'It's freezing out there; even my bones feel cold, and I'll be glad when the street lights can come back on.'

'Move your chair nearer to the fire; it'll soon warm you through.' Mary grinned at her granddaughter. 'Another busy day at Foyles?'

Rosie flopped her head against the soft back of the armchair and closed her eyes for a moment. 'It's always busy.' Chuckling, she opened her eyes again. 'But I'm being trained on one of the counters. You know, how to fill out the bill payments, where to put the books, and get proof of payment before handing them over.' She raised her hand and rubbed it across her face. 'And then there are the returns to deal with.'

Mary tilted her head. 'My, that sounds like a lot to remember.'

Rosie nodded. 'It is, but I'm sure I'll soon get used to it.'

Ivy, Rosie's ma, strolled into the front room, wiping her hands on her apron. 'Ah Rosie, I thought I heard the front door.'

Rosie smiled at her mother. 'Hello, Ma. Sorry, I should have come and said hello.'

Ivy peered closely at her daughter. 'You look tired, is everything all right?'

Mary's gaze travelled between her daughter-in-law and her granddaughter. 'Rosie's been promoted.'

Rosie giggled. 'I wouldn't say that, Gran, but I'm learning about what happens at the counters so I can work behind one of them at Foyles.'

Ivy clapped her hands together. 'That's wonderful, Rosie, they obviously trust you to do a good job.'

'Let's hope I don't let them down.' Rosie hesitated. 'I saw Mrs Bennet this morning; she still hasn't heard anything about Alfie, but she's convinced he's alive.'

Ivy frowned. 'All she has is hope.'

Rosie shook her head. 'It's more than that.' She sucked in her breath. 'Mrs Bennet asked me if I had started a bottom drawer and when I said no, she thought it was a good idea to save my money for when Alfie gets back, because she's been saving some of his army pay so we can buy a house or something.'

Mary studied her granddaughter. 'You look quite downhearted about it all; are you not excited to be marrying him?'

'Gran, I don't even know if he's alive, and if he is, why isn't he writing to his family?'

Mary shrugged. 'I'm sure there'll be an explanation for it; perhaps he can't.'

'Maybe. I struggle to believe he's still alive, but I can't say that to Mrs Bennet; she's so adamant that he is.'

Ivy rested her hand on top of Rosie's. 'We don't have the answers, Rosie.'

'I know, I'm sorry, it's just Mrs Bennet was talking about something that feels like it happened a lifetime ago.' Rosie paused. 'None of us will be the same people now; I was only sixteen, and he was eighteen when he went off to war, and a lot has happened in those four years.'

Mary glanced over at her daughter-in-law before looking back at Rosie. 'I'm sure you'll both work it out when he returns.'

'That's just it, Gran. How long do you wait to find out whether someone is still alive or not?'

'Have you met someone else?'

Rosie shook her head and laughed. 'Of course not, it's just Mrs Bennet was so certain, and I don't know what to think any more.'

Ivy studied her daughter for a moment. 'A mother has to have hope.' She sighed. 'I don't know how I'd fare in her situation.'

Rosie half smiled at her ma. 'You'd be strong; you always are.'

Ivy gave a little laugh. 'I don't think that's true; I just keep my worries to myself.'

Rosie sighed. 'By all accounts, Mr Bennet isn't doing so well. From what Mrs Bennet said, he's forgotten he has another son. I feel sorry for Sam; it seems like he's always been overshadowed by Alfie and that hasn't changed.'

Mary pursed her lips. 'It may not be that bad; all families are different, and I don't suppose Sam thinks anything of it.'

Rosie shrugged. 'Just because he doesn't complain, it doesn't make it right. He has a good heart and was a great comfort to me when Alfie went away.' She sighed. 'Actually, thinking about it, I must try and speak with Fran again. I've tried writing to her several times, but she doesn't write back. I haven't seen her for ages, despite sending her son a birthday gift every year, and he must be three now. She's another strong woman bringing up her son by herself, despite all the gossip when she fell pregnant, and the baby coming early. I can't say I understand what's going on, but it feels like the older her son gets, the less she wants to see me.' She shook her head. 'It's very confusing; after all, the four of us had a lovely day in Southend before our lives changed.'

Ivy furrowed her eyebrows. 'She was foolish to let a man take advantage of her at sixteen, love or no love. I'm glad you weren't taken in like that.'

Rosie took a deep breath. 'I know, Ma, but she told me when she found out she was pregnant that she really loved him – not that she will tell me who the father is. All she has said is that she wanted to give him what he wanted before he went off to war.'

'He hasn't been back though, has he?' Ivy sucked in her breath. 'Anyway, I came in to say dinner is ready; we have a vegetable casserole with a little bit of chicken thrown in as well.'

Rosie and Mary pushed themselves up out of their chairs.

Rosie put her hand under her grandmother's elbow to guide her across the room to the hall. 'I'm quite hungry, Gran; what about you?'

Mary chuckled. 'At my age, I don't need much food.' She squeezed her granddaughter's hand. 'You can have my share.'

Laughter bubbled from Rosie. 'I'm sure David will be first in the queue.'

Mary nodded. 'That's true; that boy doesn't sit still for one minute.'

They both chuckled as they followed Ivy to the kitchen in time to see her placing a bowl of boiled potatoes next to the casserole dish.

David came running into the kitchen and sat down at the worn, scrubbed table.

Ivy looked at her son. 'You know the rules. Wash them hands before you sit down to eat.'

David smiled at his mother and scraped back the chair on the tiled floor. Walking over to the sink, he turned on the tap and picked up the soap.

Rosie frowned as she looked at her mother. 'When I was talking to Mrs Bennet this morning, someone bumped into me; she didn't stop or look round, but she did say sorry as she walked away.' Rosie shrugged. 'I didn't see the woman's face because she was well wrapped up with a woollen hat and scarf against the cold, but I can't lose the feeling there was something familiar about her.'

Mary sat listening to her granddaughter. 'Maybe it's someone you helped in Foyles.'

Rosie nodded. 'Maybe.'

Ivy raised her eyebrows. 'You don't think it was Fran, do you?'

Rosie shook her head. 'No, Fran would have had her son with her. I expect I'm just letting my imagination run away with itself.'

* * *

Mrs Bennet and Sam helped Mr Bennet to the kitchen table.

'Pa, you've got to start eating; it feels like you're starving yourself and you're getting weaker every day.'

Mrs Bennet dragged a wooden chair away from the table.

They slowly lowered him on to the chair and lifted the table, so Mr Bennet was tucked in.

Mrs Bennet stared at her husband. 'Why are you doing this? Why are you starving yourself?'

Sam took a deep breath. 'Look, Pa, I know you're worried about Alfie, but you can't slowly fade away. You have me and Ma to fill your life, and one day you will have grandchildren to make you smile. Don't forget Alfie will need you when he comes back so you'll need to be fighting fit, especially if he has any injuries.'

Mr Bennet stared straight ahead.

Sam glanced at his mother. 'There's no response. I don't even know if he heard me.'

Mrs Bennet shook her head. 'I don't know what to say; he has to want to be with us, we can't *make* him eat.' She sighed. 'Sit down, Sam, and eat your dinner; we can't afford to waste the food. I'm sorry it's sausages again but there's not much in the shops, and the prices have gone up.'

Sam's eyes widened. 'Ma, you should have said! I can try and help out more. I'm sorry, I should have thought about the repercussions of Pa not working, on top of losing Alfie's pay.' He thrust his hand inside his trouser pocket and pulled out a crumpled ten-shilling note. Smoothing it out, he passed it to his mother. 'Next week I'll see if I can give you more.'

Mrs Bennet smiled. 'No, you keep it, we can manage; I've always been careful with money, so I have a little put by for these occasions.'

Sam waved the money at his mother. 'Ma, I insist, and if you truly don't want it, save it for me for when I need it later; you know, when I have to buy a suit or something.' He chuckled as his mother took the note.

'All right, now eat your dinner before it gets cold.' Mrs Bennet sat down next to her husband and began cutting up his sausages into mouthfuls. She put a small amount on a fork. 'Right, come on, Les, I want you to eat something, even if it's only a little. Open your mouth.' He didn't move. 'Come on, Les, please, just a mouthful.' She sighed when he didn't respond. She put the fork down on his plate. 'I don't know why I keep trying, I really don't. You're so selfish; don't you think we'd all like to give up and sit back feeling sorry for ourselves? We're not the only family to have someone missing in action; at least we haven't had a telegram to say he's been killed. Look at Mrs Burrows, she lost her husband, and he didn't even go off to war, but she's still getting up every morning and trying to help men like our son at the hospital.'

Sam put a mouthful of sausage and mash in his mouth and chewed quickly. 'Ma, eat your own dinner and I'll sort Pa out; he might eat something for me.' He moved to sit nearer to his father. 'Come on, Pa, it'll help stop us worrying and nagging if you eat something.' Sam picked up the fork with a little sausage and mash on it and held it near his father's mouth. He raised his eyebrows as his father opened his mouth a little, and Sam gently inserted the fork. 'Well done, Pa; see, you can do it.' He lowered the fork and loaded it with more sausage and mash.

Mrs Bennet shook her head. 'Oh, I nearly forgot to say I saw Rosie this morning. She's a lovely girl; Alfie was lucky to find someone like her.'

Sam tightened his lips but remained silent.

Putting her fork down on the side of her dinner plate, Mrs Bennet watched Sam patiently feeding his father. 'I worry that if Alfie doesn't write soon, he could end up losing her to somebody else.'

Sam frowned. 'Ma, I know you won't like me saying this, but maybe he's changed his mind and doesn't have the courage to let Rosie know. After all, a lot has happened since this war began.'

Mrs Bennet scowled. 'It's easier to let someone down by letter than it is in person, and that doesn't explain why he isn't writing to me.'

'I know it doesn't, Ma, but I just want to prepare you for things you haven't thought about. After all, no one is coming back from the front the same person they were before they went.'

Mrs Bennet sighed. 'I know, but can you imagine the embarrassment if he's asked her to wait for him and then he turns his back on her? That's almost as bad as what Fran has put her family through.'

Sam laughed. 'I don't think so, Ma; it depends on how Rosie feels about it all. I mean, she was only sixteen when he asked her to wait for him and in that situation, how can anyone say no? Imagine if she had and something had happened to him. How would Rosie be able to get over it and not carry the guilt and blame for him dying?'

Mrs Bennet looked at her son. 'I suppose you're right, but I shan't forgive Alfie if he messes her about. She deserves better than that.'

2

Ivy pulled her hat further over her ears as she walked along Mortimer Street towards Middlesex Hospital. The large stone pillars holding the black ornate lamp high above them came into view. She glanced at Rosie. 'It doesn't seem to be getting any warmer. I'll be glad to get indoors. I really don't like this time of year, what with the dark evenings and the cold. I can't wait for March to be over with.'

Rosie laughed.

'What are you laughing at?'

'Nothing, Ma. Well, I was being childish.' Rosie looked sheepish. 'Seeing your breath in grey swirls as it hit the cold air reminded me of when David and I were younger, and we'd pretend we were smoking.'

Ivy chuckled. 'That seems a long time ago now.' She pushed open the hospital door with one hand and loosened her red woollen scarf from around her neck.

The foyer was busy, and heads turned as the cold air rushed in. Men, women and children occupied the chairs that sat along the grey walls. There were scuff marks and chips taken out of the walls in places. The foyer looked in a sorry state, but then so did the people waiting there to talk to someone.

Rosie followed her mother inside, her gloved hand closing the door behind her. The smell of disinfectant and carbolic soap hung in the air, causing her to cough as she breathed them in.

Ivy turned to her daughter before looking back at the people. 'Let's go to the desk and see where we're needed today; it looks like it's going to be a busy Monday.'

Rosie nodded as she pulled off her gloves and began unbuttoning her coat. Her flat shoes were silent on the grey floor as she followed her mother to the reception desk. 'I expect they'll want me to do the usual and take the trolley of books around, as I'm not a nurse, whereas you are of more use to them.'

Ivy paced towards the desk. 'Yes, it's daft that I'm not allowed to continue nursing as a married woman, yet I can volunteer to help at the hospital.'

Rosie stroked her mother's back. 'It's lucky the matron knows you, and so is aware of what your experience is worth.'

Ivy smiled. 'Yes, we started out together.'

A little boy sobbed as he sat down on a wooden chair.

Rosie swivelled round and stared at the boy, then arched her eyebrows when she noticed Alfie's brother, Sam, sitting on the chair next to him. She watched Sam for a moment; it had been a while since she'd last seen him. She had avoided him as much as possible after Southend, but often thought about being in his arms that night. She shook her head; she was promised to Alfie, so she couldn't allow her thoughts to go there.

Sam patted the boy's arm before clearing his throat. 'Don't cry, it'll be all right. It's only a graze; someone will take a look at it and then I'll get you home to your mother.'

'Hello, Mr Bennet.' Rosie frowned as she took a couple of steps nearer to the boy.

Sam raised his eyebrows. 'Mr Bennet is very formal; when did I become my father?' He chuckled. 'You've always called me Sam, what's changed?'

'Nothing, but I'm assuming you are from this young man's school.' Rosie stooped down in front of the boy and forced herself to smile as she spoke to him. 'Are you all right? I can see you've hurt your leg; did you fall over?'

The boy sniffed and nodded.

Rosie glanced at Sam before smiling at the boy as she peered down at his grazed knee. 'I'm sure the nurse will clean the dirt out of the graze; it looks like you have a little cut there as well, so it might sting a little, but I'm sure you're a brave young man.'

The corner of Sam's mouth lifted. 'It's nothing to worry about. I've only brought him to make sure; after all, you can't be too careful. He'll be fine once I get him home and his mother's looking after him.'

Rosie didn't look at him. 'I'm sure he will be, but at the moment he's looking for sympathy.' She peered over her shoulder and saw her mother walking towards her. She smiled when she looked back at the boy. 'My name's Rosie, can you tell me yours?'

'Tom.'

Rosie beamed. 'Hello, Tom, and how old are you?'

Tom looked up at Sam, who nodded. 'I'm six.'

Rosie squeezed his hand. 'My goodness, you *are* brave for a six-year-old.'

Ivy nodded at Sam. 'Hello, Sam, I haven't seen you for some time; is everything all right?'

Sam grinned. 'Hello, Mrs Burrows. Yes, I don't know if you are aware or not, but I was fortunate enough to be given the opportunity to be a pupil-teacher at All Souls Primary School in Foley Street, until I qualify. Especially as the head there is very good at guiding me, and gives a lot of her time for training me. Of course, in the last few years they've changed how you become a teacher, but I managed to get in at just the right time.'

'That's good news, and I expect it's keeping you busy then.' Ivy glanced at Rosie before looking back at Sam. 'Let's hope the war ends, or you qualify, before you get your call-up papers.'

Rosie peered up at Sam. 'I knew you were working at the school, but your ma never mentioned you were training as a teacher when I saw her the other day.'

Sam shrugged. 'I expect she forgot. Everyone's preoccupied, worrying about Alfie – although knowing him, he's probably fine.'

Rosie's lips tightened. 'That just makes him heartless then.'

Sam looked horrified. 'I'm sorry, I didn't think about what I was saying. I truly didn't mean it the way it came out.'

Rosie stood up. 'It doesn't matter.'

'Yes, it does. I'm old enough to know better, I'm sorry.'

'Everyone is entitled to their opinion.' Rosie had no desire to discuss Alfie, or to admit that Sam was probably right. She looked at her mother. 'This little man, Tom, has had a fall.'

Ivy looked down at his knee before ruffling his short hair. 'I can tidy that up for you; you can tell your friends you have your own war wound.'

The boy beamed at Ivy.

'Right, I'll go and get something to clean your knee with. I'll be right back.'

'Thanks, Ma, I had better get going or they'll think I'm not coming.'

Tom reached out for Rosie's hand. 'Wait, don't go.'

Sam frowned. 'Tom, Rosie has a job to do.' He glanced up at her. 'I hope you don't mind me using your first name, but that was how you introduced yourself to Tom.'

'Of course not.' Rosie stooped down in front of Tom. 'How about I wait until my ma gets back and then I'll have to go, otherwise I'll be in trouble.'

Sam nodded. 'Thank you, Tom has taken quite a shine to you.'

Rosie studied him for a moment. 'He just wanted a bit of a fuss made of him.'

Ivy returned carrying a metal bowl with a small amount of liquid in it. She patted Rosie's back. 'Right, Tom, let's get you cleaned up.'

Rosie stood up. 'You take care, Tom; my ma will look after you. Bye, Sam.' She waved as she walked away and smiled as Sam and Tom waved back. Within minutes, she had climbed the stairs and was pushing open the doors to Percy Ward. It wasn't a large room but there were beds on either side. The pale green walls were broken up by the daylight coming through the windows, which helped lift the gloomy atmosphere. Small clipboards holding sheets of white paper hung at the end of each neatly made bed. Some men were lying still, and groans escaped into the air, while others were more upright. A bedside cabinet and a wooden chair, not dissimilar to the ones in Rosie's home, filled the space between each bed. She forced a smile to her lips, as she had done many times before. 'Good afternoon, everyone, I shall be back in a moment with the book trolley.'

* * *

Rosie's heart was pounding as she stood behind the counter in Foyles Bookshop. She couldn't decide whether it was unexpectedly seeing Sam last night at the hospital and spending half the evening remembering the feel of his arms around her, or if it was because this was her first day standing behind the Foyles children's book counter on her own. Shaking her head and taking a couple of deep breaths, Rosie couldn't deny she loved the smell of all the books that surrounded her; she had never been able to pinpoint what it was – it was like a woody, musty, print smell. Rosie started moving things around the counter.

Molly watched Rosie nervously picking up paper and pens before putting them back down again. Her eyes scanned the area around her. 'Rosie, you look terrified. It will be all right. We will work together until you're completely comfortable with everything; it's not complicated, but it's always extremely busy in the children's department.' She laughed. 'The children are adorable and usually want us to help them, perhaps by reading the first few pages of a book before they decide it's the one for them.'

Rosie nodded. 'Yes, I've heard you're very good with them.'

Molly smiled. 'I don't know about that, but I think it's important to remember that children usually adore the funny voices of different characters when you're reading to them. I tend to think we are here to bring some sunshine into their lives, so for a time they are not worrying about family and this war.'

'That's a lovely thing to say.' Rosie beamed. 'I shall remember that. Let's face it, we all need to escape our thoughts at times, even innocent children.'

'That's true, but please enjoy your being here because in my eyes, it doesn't get any better.' Molly patted Rosie on the back just as several children burst noisily into the children's section.

A young man's voice boomed. 'Come on now, remember your manners; there will be other people in this shop.'

Molly glanced over at the man and laughed as she stepped forward. 'Good morning, Mr Bennet, I see you are still trying to keep your children in order.' She looked down at the boy holding his hand. 'Hello, Tom, how are you today?'

Tom gave Molly a sad look and pointed down to his leg. 'I

hurt my leg yesterday. Mr Bennet took me to the hospital and a nice lady cleaned it.'

Molly took his hand and squeezed it. 'Were you brave?'

Tom nodded. 'Mr Bennet took me home after and my ma made me my favourite dinner.'

Molly grinned at the boy. 'Oh, and what was that?'

Tom giggled. 'Sausage and mash.'

Molly smiled. 'Oh, you know what, that's my favourite too.' She glanced round and beckoned Rosie to come forward.

Rosie took a breath and stepped closer. 'Hello, Tom.' She nodded to Sam.

'Hello, Rosie.' Sam didn't take his eyes off her.

'Hello, Miss, I saw you at the hospital; you came over and asked if I was all right.'

Rosie nodded. 'That's right, and my ma told me you were very brave when she cleaned your leg.'

Tom stared wide-eyed at Rosie. 'It did sting a little, but your ma did say it might, and I held on to Mr Bennet's arm.'

Sam grinned. 'You held on very tight; it's a wonder my arm wasn't black and blue with bruises.'

Rosie stooped down in front of the boy. 'How's your war wound now?'

Tom beamed. 'As me ma says, "I'll live".'

Rosie giggled. 'Well, that is good news.'

Molly turned to Rosie. 'Rosie, I take it you know Mr Bennet; he tells me he's training to be a teacher at All Souls Church of England Primary School in Foley Street.'

Rosie laughed nervously. 'Yes, I've known Sam and his family for a few years. I hope you are well, Sam, and have got over your unexpected hospital trip last night.'

Sam nodded before thoughtfully staring at her. 'Yes, and I

learnt a valuable lesson: to think before I speak.' He began to undo the buttons of his black coat.

Molly chuckled. 'It's good to hear I'm not the only one who gets into trouble for that.'

Sam moved his gaze to Molly. 'I don't know if you are aware, but we are looking for volunteers to help us at the school.'

Molly shook her head. 'No, I didn't.'

'The thing is, a lot of teachers enlisted. That means our classes have more children in them than usual, and that makes it difficult to always give them the attention some of them need.'

Molly tilted her head to one side. 'I've never thought about how the schools could be short of teachers. What sort of thing will the volunteers have to do?'

Sam glanced across at Rosie again.

Molly cleared her throat.

Startled, Sam shrugged as he turned his attention back to Molly. 'I haven't thought it through yet, but we could at least do with someone to listen to the children read. Then of course there's helping with other things like their sums. I thought I might make some toy money to teach them about how far a pound, shillings and pence go. There's also teaching them about kindness, and how to clean any grazes they might get while they're running around—'

'That's quite a list you have there.' Molly laughed, her gaze moving to watch the children searching through the books. 'I'll mention it to the staff here, but I know a lot of them volunteer at the hospitals and other places.'

'I understand, I just thought I'd mention it as you and Rosie are very good with children.' Sam glanced again at Rosie. 'Maybe you could mention it to your mother for me.'

'Of course, I'm sure she would love to help.'

Molly looked back at Tom. 'Would you like to go and find a

book with Rosie? Mr Bennet will still be here when you get back, and Rosie will read you a story with those funny voices you like.'

Tom peered up at Sam, who gave him a reassuring nod.

Rosie bent down to speak to Tom. 'Let's go and find some books, shall we?'

Tom grinned and looked at Sam.

'Go on then, but please be careful.' Sam smiled broadly at Rosie. 'He's a little accident-prone so you might want to keep an eye on him.'

Rosie nodded. 'Don't worry, he's in safe hands.'

Molly laughed. 'Well, we had better see how your class is doing hunting down books.'

Sam nodded as he stared after Rosie. He suddenly turned to Molly. 'I've been meaning to thank you for letting the school know about Father Christmas being here; I understand you were responsible for organising it. The children loved it; in fact, some of them are still talking about it even though it was three months ago.'

Molly beamed. 'That's lovely to hear; everyone in Foyles loved doing it for the children. We all need some joy and excitement in our lives.'

'Talking of which, I had better get on and find the children. I don't want their mothers accusing me of losing them.' Sam smiled and stepped away, following the excited children's voices.

* * *

Rosie swirled the dish cloth around the soapy water in the bowl before picking up a plain white dinner plate that was soaking in the sink and rubbing the cloth over it. It chinked as she placed it on top of another plate on the draining board. 'Sam came into Foyles today with his class.'

Ivy smiled. 'Did he say how Tom was?' She chuckled. 'I can tell you he had a tight grip on Sam when I was cleaning his graze.'

Rosie laughed. 'Yes, Sam said as much, but Tom is proud of his war wound and his mum made him his favourite dinner of sausage and mash.'

Ivy beamed. 'Bless him.'

'Apart from letting the children choose a book, Sam was asking for volunteers to help out at the school.' Rosie tilted her head. 'You know, listening to them read.'

Ivy gave her daughter a sideways glance as she picked up the dinner plate to dry. 'Are you tempted?'

Rosie shrugged. 'You know me, I love books, but I can't fit in doing that, working at Foyles, and helping out at the hospital.' She paused. 'He asked me to tell you because I think he wants them to learn about first aid. I'm not sure, but I think they are all under ten. Tom definitely is, so it will be very basic stuff.'

Ivy finished drying the plate before placing it on the wooden kitchen table. 'I don't mind popping in a couple of times to teach them.' She glanced over her shoulder. 'What about you?'

Rosie didn't answer.

Ivy watched her daughter closely. 'You know, I think Sam likes you quite a lot.'

Rosie sighed. 'And what is that based on?'

Ivy chuckled. 'Call it mother's intuition and the fact he never took his eyes off you at the hospital.'

Rosie felt something flutter inside her stomach. 'I think you're letting your imagination run away with you.'

Ivy laughed. 'Maybe. Anyway, are you going to help out at the school?'

Rosie shook her head. 'I don't think it's a good idea if you're right about Sam.'

Ivy ran her palm up and down Rosie's back. 'But this isn't about you or Sam, it's about the children having a good start in life, and God knows they need it with this war going on.' She paused. 'Doesn't it excite you to know you could be part of that?'

'Of course it does, but I don't want Alfie or his family feeling like I'm leading Sam on when I'm promised to his brother.'

Ivy sighed. 'Do you like Sam?'

Colour flooded Rosie's cheeks.

Ivy smiled. 'That answers that question.'

Rosie knew she couldn't tell anyone about the feelings she harboured for Sam, not even her mother. The feelings she hadn't known she had until he had kept her safe in his arms after Alfie had left her crying in that alleyway. 'He was a great comfort to me on Alfie's last night, he held me while I sobbed. He was a good friend.'

Ivy nodded. 'We all need good friends, Rosie, you just need to be careful you don't break his heart.' Pain trampled across her face. It was quickly chased away as a smile began to play on her lips. 'You know, I was only sixteen when I met your father. He was such a kind and gentle man, he never pretended to be something he wasn't. I think that's why I fell in love with him. He always made me feel loved and safe.'

Rosie turned round and put her arms around her mother, letting her wet hands hang loose. 'I know it's hard, Ma; do you miss him terribly?'

Ivy blinked away tears. 'All the time; life will never be the same.' She stepped back. 'I have to be braver now, and not be frightened to try and make the right decisions on my own. We always used to discuss everything together, especially when it came to family things.'

Rosie wiped a tear away with the sleeve of her jumper. 'I

know it isn't the same but you're not on your own, you can discuss anything you want with me.'

Ivy took a deep breath. 'I know, and thank you.' She stepped away and picked up another dinner plate. 'So what are you going to do about helping out at the school?'

Rosie gave a wry smile, as she recognised her mother didn't want to discuss her own pain and grief. 'Well, I suppose you're right. It's not about me or Sam, and it would be nice to try and give something back to the school I went to, no matter how little that is. Although I'd have to speak to the matron at the hospital to let her know I'd need to drop some of the hours I spend there.'

Ivy nodded. 'I think that's a good decision and I don't mind telling her.'

3

Sam Bennet removed his suit jacket and draped it across the wooden-armed chair behind his large desk at the front of the classroom. It had only been a couple of days since he had taken the class to Foyles Bookshop, but he had hoped someone – Rosie in particular – would have offered to help out. Maybe he needed to think of another tactic to try and spend more time with her so she could get to know him as more than Alfie's little brother.

Sam watched the children laughing, enjoying their innocence even with the war going on, before clapping his hands to get their attention. 'Now, now.' He rubbed his hands together, feeling the heat taking effect. They all looked in his direction. 'You've been sitting still for a long time today, so do you need warming up before we start singing our times tables?'

'Does that mean running around the playground?' A little voice could be heard from the back of the room.

Sam chuckled. 'If you're cold and stiff, it's the best way to get your blood flowing through your body and get your brain working.'

'Then no thank you, sir, it's too cold.'

Sam raised his eyebrows. 'Right, we'll see how we go but it doesn't mean we won't be running around if we have time, although that seems to be flying by.' He glanced down at the sheet of paper on his desk, which had his lesson plan written down for the day. 'It's been a cold day and it's nearly over, so let's sing our times tables together.'

The classroom door-handle grated as it was turned. Everyone fell silent as their attention settled on the door. Sam moved nearer to it and pulled it open. He stepped back, unsure how to react.

Rosie gave a nervous smile. 'Hello, Sam – I mean Mr Bennet – I came to help with listening to the children read, and anything else I can do to be useful.'

Sam nodded before stepping aside and Rosie hesitantly walked into the classroom. He coughed to clear his throat and shut the door behind her.

Colour flushed Rosie's cheeks as she looked around the room and saw the many eyes staring back at her. 'Maybe I should come back at a more convenient time.' She turned towards the door to make her exit.

'Hello, Miss!'

Rosie turned back to face the class and saw a boy waving at her. 'Hello, Tom!'

Tom beamed at her. 'Are you going to help Mr Bennet? He says we're quite a handful so it will be a tough job for you. My ma says she don't envy Mr Bennet, whatever that means.'

A smile spread across Rosie's face when she glanced at Sam; he looked uncomfortable with Tom's words. She looked back at Tom. 'I'm sure Mr Bennet copes well enough, but I have come to offer to listen to you all read.'

Tom clapped his hands. 'Will that be all right, Mr Bennet?' He beamed as he turned towards his friends. 'Rosie's really nice, she looked after me at the hospital.' The children all started chattering at the same time.

Sam clapped his hands together. 'If Rosie – I mean, Miss Burrows – does help in class, you will need to show some respect and call her Miss Burrows and not Rosie.'

Tom's arm shot up in the air. 'I'm sorry, sir, I didn't know her proper name, Miss told me her name was Rosie.'

Sam opened his mouth to speak but Rosie's voice filled the room. 'That's all right, Tom. It's different at the hospital because we are looking after people who are sick or unhappy, so I told you my first name so you wouldn't be frightened or upset.'

Tom grinned and nodded. 'That did work.'

The school bell rang out several times in the hall. Sam glanced down at his watch. 'Well, thanks to Miss Burrows, you've been saved from practising your times tables.' He glanced around the classroom. 'Collect your coats and anything else you brought to school today, and we'll go out and find your families who can take you home.' He turned to Rosie. 'Do you mind waiting? We'll talk when I get back.'

Rosie shook her head. 'I'm sorry I arrived before school had finished.'

Sam shrugged. 'It's not a problem, I just need to match these children up with their families, then I'll be back.' He ushered the children into a straight line before leading them out into the playground where snow was thick on the ground. Many of the mothers started waving at their children.

Rosie looked around the classroom before sitting at Sam's desk to wait for him.

A few minutes later Sam took a deep breath and strode back in. 'Making yourself comfortable?'

Rosie jumped up. 'I'm sorry, I wasn't doing anything, but this chair is the only one that's the right size.'

Sam smiled. 'I didn't mean to make you jump.'

Rosie giggled. 'There's something about being in a classroom, and with teachers, that takes you back to being a child and feeling like you've been naughty, even when you haven't.'

Laughter burst from Sam. 'I know exactly what you mean, but the more you're here, the more that feeling gradually disappears.' He walked over to his desk and gathered his papers together. 'Shall we go somewhere more comfortable for a chat? Let's see, we can either go to the staff room, a cafe, or just walk.'

Rosie looked pensive. 'Maybe a walk will be good. I don't fancy sitting with the teachers. I won't be able to form a sentence and that won't give a very good first impression, will it?'

Sam eyed her for a moment before grinning. 'I don't think you have to worry about first impressions, but there's always the cafe if you want to be inside in the warmth.'

Rosie shook her head. 'If we get seen, people will think we're on a date or something, and Alfie or your ma wouldn't like that.'

Sam laughed. 'Who cares? We have known each other for years, so let the gossips have their day. Anyway, would that idea be such a bad thing?'

Rosie shrugged. 'I promised Alfie I would wait for him; you know I sobbed in your arms when he left.'

Sam stared down at the papers he was holding, remembering the smell of her hair as he'd held her tight in his arms. 'Yes, I remember you – and then later Fran – crying as you waved him goodbye; he was obviously very popular. But you haven't heard from him for quite a while so maybe it's time you stopped waiting and got on with your life. I mean, how long are you prepared to wait? Five years, ten years – the rest of your days?' He frowned, immediately regretting that he had allowed himself to be so outspoken. He had no desire to frighten her away. He forced a smile. 'And let's face it, if – er, when – you do marry

Alfie, I'll be your brother-in-law, so it won't matter if we're seen out together.'

Rosie remained silent, not wishing to keep talking about any possible future with Alfie.

'Well, how about we wrap up warm and have a walk around Regent's Park?'

Rosie nodded, hoping he had picked up on her silence and that they could talk about something else – anything else. 'I can't be out too long. I want to give Fran a knock; perhaps this time she'll answer the door.' She thought about how she hadn't seen Fran since it was obvious she was pregnant. Was she deliberately hiding herself away? *Maybe it's time I stopped knocking and accept she doesn't want to see me.* She grimaced, knowing she couldn't do that as she was genuinely worried about her.

* * *

Rosie and Sam were silent as they strolled into Regent's Park, slowing down to admire the green shoots just visible above the ground.

Rosie stared straight ahead. 'I can't believe we are at the end of March already, and this weekend is Easter Sunday.'

Sam sighed. 'I know. I don't know where the time goes; it feels like it was only yesterday we were celebrating Christmas.' He shook his head. 'Well, there wasn't much celebrating going on in my house; my father doesn't really say or do anything now, and all my ma talks about is Alfie and the day you two will be married.'

Rosie shook her head. 'I'm sorry, Sam; I find those conversations difficult. After all, we don't even know if he's coming back, so I don't see the point in keeping talking about it. It must be harder for you.'

'Don't be sorry, I've never known it to be any different. Alfie seems to have never done wrong; I've long since got used to it.'

'When I'm in church on Sunday I'll say a prayer for us, and maybe ask God to guide us through our troubles.' Rosie smiled up at Sam. 'I think give it a week or two and this park will be an array of colourful spring flowers.'

'Are you cold? I'm happy to put my arm around you to warm you up a bit.'

Colour filled Rosie's cheeks. 'No, I'm fine, thank you. It's just the wind – it's quite biting at times.'

Sam nodded. 'Well, my arms are here if you change your mind.' He gazed around. 'This park is beautiful; we're lucky to have it in the middle of London. The wet weather has given the grass a new lease of life and it's a luscious green. Maybe we should have headed for the lake in Hyde Park?' Sam smiled. 'Have you ever been there on Christmas Day?'

Rosie raised her eyebrows and gave a little laugh. 'No, but I've heard you can watch people swim in the Serpentine. I believe it happens every year on Christmas Day.'

Sam frowned. 'That's not for me; the water must be freezing.'

Rosie laughed as she gazed up at him. 'I think that's the whole point of it.'

Sam shook his head. 'They must be mad.'

'You don't fancy giving it a go then?' Rosie giggled.

'I shall assume that isn't a serious question.' Sam looked at her as if she were mad before chuckling, his eyes sparkling with mischief. 'No, I don't, but I will if you will.'

Rosie giggled. 'Definitely not.' She paused. 'Are you enjoying working at the school?'

Sam looked thoughtful. 'It's rewarding, although some of the children are struggling with their fathers being away – but hopefully that's where I can help.'

Rosie nodded. 'I can see that; it must feel good to be needed.'

Sam gave a hearty laugh. 'You mean after years of Alfie…'

Rosie's lips tightened.

Sam gave her a sideways glance. 'You know, none of us have heard from him for so long, I think we should just assume he's not coming back.'

Rosie stared wide-eyed at Sam. 'Just like that?'

Sam shrugged. 'I know it sounds heartless but what else are you meant to do, wait forever?'

Lowering her eyelashes, Rosie sighed. 'Everything has changed since this rotten war began. We were so carefree at Southend, and next thing you know, Alfie has gone off to war, and Fran is pregnant and won't say who the father is.'

Sam stopped to look at the buds on the trees around them. 'You know spring is a chance for new beginnings, new starts in life. Nature brings back what you thought was gone, then colour and smells fill our lives.' He took Rosie's hand in his before tucking it under his arm and resting his hand on top of it. He took a breath, letting her floral perfume fill his senses. 'Fran will tell you when she's ready; I suspect she's holding onto a little shame.'

Rosie pondered on moving her hand away from his arm but decided she liked the feeling of closeness it gave her. 'But we were best friends, and now I get the feeling she avoids me most of the time. I don't understand it, I don't understand what went wrong.'

Sam squeezed her hand. 'As I said, I suspect she's holding onto the shame she has been made to feel.'

'But not by me; I would never do that to her,' Rosie said. 'Never.'

'I know, I was just talking generally.'

'I'm sorry, it's just I don't know what to do about it.'

Sam held her gloved hand. 'Don't worry, it will all work out in the end.'

Rosie nodded. 'I suppose so, but I miss her.'

Sam looked thoughtful as he peered down at her. 'Perhaps I'll try and talk to her.'

'I'd appreciate that, Sam.'

Sam smiled. 'Now let's talk about you helping with my class.' He paused. 'How much time can you give and what help are you happy giving?'

Rosie laughed. 'Ooh, is this my interview?'

Sam chuckled. 'No, of course not. I'm sorry, did I sound very formal?'

'Only for a minute; I just wasn't expecting it.' Rosie glanced up at him. 'I can probably do most afternoons. I work part-time at Foyles and that tends to be mornings, and I also help out at the hospital, but that's not every day, so I'd need to juggle it around.' She looked thoughtful. 'As for what I can do to help, the obvious one is reading, but I don't mind helping out with other things; you've just got to let me know what you want.'

Sam peered down at Rosie and spoke in a whisper. 'If only it were all as simple as that.'

Rosie's eyes widened as she stared up at him. 'What?' She could feel the heat rising up her neck. 'Sorry, I didn't quite catch what you said.'

Sam lowered his eyelashes. 'It's me who should be sorry for mumbling.' He took a breath and his words tumbled over one another in the rush to escape. 'I was just saying if only it were as simple as that. I mean sometimes the help is needed in unexpected ways, like if we're doing a project or something.'

Rosie squeezed Sam's arm. 'Don't look so embarrassed. I tell you what, how about I come in after Foyles and you can tell me on the day if you need me to do something specific and if not, I'll listen to the children read.'

Sam nodded. 'That sounds like a good idea.'

* * *

'I'm home,' Rosie shouted into the empty hall. She stopped to sniff the lavender plant on the narrow consort table and smiled. The deep purple flowers were a contrast against the pale green walls. She didn't know much about flowers, but she felt sure this one shouldn't be in bloom in winter. Her mother definitely had a way with plants, although she would correct her and say it was now spring and not winter. Rosie smiled as she unbuttoned her woollen coat and hung it on the coat hooks with the rest of the family's. She blew her warm breath onto her hands and rubbed them together before slipping her feet out of her heeled shoes and into her slippers.

'Hello, Rosie, you're later than usual,' Ivy called from the kitchen. 'I'll make you a cuppa; go and sit with Grandma and I'll bring it in.'

'Thanks, Ma.' Rosie walked into the front room to see her father's empty armchair next to the fireplace. She bit the inside of her bottom lip as she held back the tears. She flopped down on the sofa next to her gran. 'Everything all right?'

Mary smiled. 'Of course. You're later this evening.'

'I went to All Souls Primary School to offer my help in listening to the children read.'

Mary looked up at the carriage clock. 'It's six o'clock; the school would have shut hours ago.'

Rosie chuckled. 'Sam Bennet and I went for a walk. We walked from Foley Street up Great Portland Street to Regent's Park to talk about how I could help at the school.' She paused. 'I feel sorry for him. I get the impression he's almost invisible at home; Mr and Mrs Bennet only seem to think about Alfie, and yet Sam is a lovely man.'

Mary looked across at Rosie. 'That might explain the colour in your rosy cheeks.' She studied her for a moment. 'You're not falling for him, are you? You don't want to come between two brothers; that's never a good thing.'

Ivy walked in carrying a cup and saucer, the teaspoon clattering against the crockery. 'What's never a good thing?' she asked as she passed the drink over to her daughter.

Rosie laughed as she reached out to take the tea. 'It's nothing, Ma, just Gran getting carried away with herself. It's quiet in here; where's David?'

Mary chuckled. 'You're not changing the subject, are you?'

Ivy glanced at her mother-in-law and her daughter. 'He's spending the evening round his friend's; one of us can collect him later.'

Rosie smiled. 'That's good, I don't mind going to get him, it'll save you a job.'

Ivy nodded. 'We'll see. So, what's never a good thing?'

Rosie shook her head. 'I told you, it's just Gran getting carried away.'

Mary peered over at Ivy. 'Rosie was just singing Sam's praises while feeling sorry for him, and I just said she needs to be careful because no one should come between brothers.'

Ivy chuckled. 'Mary, Rosie's known Sam for most of her life; they were in the same school albeit he's a couple of years younger than her. She's bound to have a soft spot for him.'

Rosie nodded her agreement. 'Thank you, Ma, I've always said Alfie wasn't very nice to him and now it sounds like Sam's invisible at home.' Sam's words bounced into her head, but she chose not to repeat those about his mother and their wedding.

Ivy nodded. 'Why don't you invite him round for dinner one evening?'

Rosie shrugged. 'I could, but I don't want anyone getting the wrong idea because Alfie wouldn't be too pleased if he found out.'

Mary curled her lip. 'Such nonsense; he should be happy you're looking out for his brother and he's looking out for you,' she snarled. 'I've never liked Alfie; I don't know why you agreed to wait for him.'

Rosie frowned. 'You never said.'

Mary shook her head. 'It's not for me to pass an opinion.'

Rosie laughed. 'But you just have.'

Mary tilted her head. 'Yes, well, I didn't mean to. I'm sorry, there's something about him that I don't trust. He's too much of a ladies' man for my liking and if it hadn't been for the war, I don't think you'd be entertaining him at all. In my opinion you are too good for him.'

Rosie stayed silent but wondered if her gran was right; would she still be with him if the war hadn't happened?

4

Rosie walked into the staff area. There was a constant clicking of the clocking in machine as everyone took it in turns to insert their card. There was a lot of chatter and laughter with the women trying to keep one another happy by telling funny stories.

'Morning, Rosie,' Vera shouted across the room.

Rosie smiled. 'Morning, Vera. It's noisy in here this morning.'

Alice followed Rosie and clocked in. Several women yelled out, 'Morning, ladies.'

Vera nodded. 'It's good to have you back, Alice, you've been missed.'

'Thank you, it's good to *be* back.' Alice turned to Rosie. 'I think everyone's trying to keep their spirits up; one of the girls isn't in because the family got news of her brother being killed on the front line.'

Rosie gasped. 'Oh no, I'm so sorry to hear that, it must be so hard to keep going when you get those telegrams.'

Alice nodded. 'I know. We were all devastated when we got one about my brother Robert. It rips everyone apart.'

Rosie nodded. 'I'm so sorry, I didn't realise you had lost a brother because of this war; I must admit to being pleased my brother is too young to enlist.'

Alice touched Rosie's arm. 'I didn't mean to drag you down; you know, whether we like it or not, life goes on.'

Rosie smoothed her hands down her black skirt. 'I know Mrs Bennet is going through something similar with Alfie missing in action. She's living on hope he's going to return but I can't live like that – it's been so long without any news, and all it does is stop you from grieving and moving on.'

Alice shrugged. 'Hope is all some people have and they can't face the alternative.'

Rosie frowned. 'That's true. I don't mean to sound so heartless, and I know it's happening to many families right now.' She sighed. 'I don't suppose it will be long before Sam will be called up.'

'You're not heartless, this war is dragging everyone down.' Alice reached up and patted down her hair. 'As they say, there are no winners in this situation; both sides are losing loved ones. I'm just glad my Freddie was able to come back and return to being a policeman; at least I know he's all right.'

Victoria and Molly walked towards Alice.

Molly reached out and wrapped her arms around her. 'It's lovely to see you; are you looking forward to your day working?'

Alice hugged Molly and stepped back, beaming. 'I love this shop and I don't see it as coming to work; how can anyone who loves books?'

Victoria stepped forward to embrace her friend. 'Before you go home, we must make a date for a trip to Monico's for tea and cake; it's been ages.'

Alice laughed. 'That's a good idea. You do know I'm always full of good intentions, but then I don't get round to doing half the things I plan to. To be honest, I don't know where my time goes.'

Molly smiled. 'It's those two wonderful boys you have.' She frowned for a second before chuckling. 'I expect you are making the most of them.'

Alice noticed the frown and wondered if Molly and Andrew wanted children and it just hadn't happened for them. It was not something they had ever discussed. She forced a smile. 'They do take up a lot of time but I'm lucky they have a doting family who can't seem to get enough of the two of them.'

The girls laughed.

Mr Leadbetter poked his head around the doorway and raised his voice above the chatter. 'It's time, ladies.'

Victoria smiled at Alice. 'I've put you working on your old counter?'

Alice checked the buttons on her white blouse. 'I wouldn't have it any other way.' Her eyes were shining as she looked at Victoria. 'I know it's only been a couple of weeks since I last stood behind the counter, but it feels like it's been ages.'

They both walked into the shop. Alice took a deep breath. 'Oh, don't you love the smell of books!'

Victoria laughed. 'Come on, I've missed seeing you and having lunch together every day, and I know Molly has too.'

Rosie watched them. Their friendship and love for each other wasn't hidden away; it was there for all to see, just like hers and Fran's once was – so what had gone so terribly wrong that Fran couldn't or wouldn't talk to her about it?

A grey-haired lady gave Alice a toothless smile. 'Hello, dearie, it's good to see you.' She tried to pull herself more upright over her walking stick. 'Will your wonderful husband be in later? You know how I love a man in uniform.'

Alice beamed at the stooped lady. 'I'm afraid not, but I'll tell him you were asking after him.'

The old lady giggled. 'Bless you, you've made an old lady very happy.' She waved and hobbled away, chuckling. 'If only I were forty years younger, then these men in uniform wouldn't stand a chance.'

* * *

Rosie stood by the classroom door as she watched Sam standing on the platform where his large desk and chair sat. He moved in front of the blackboard with a stick of white chalk in his hand and he began to write the two times table on the board. Rosie smiled as she noticed he had a line of white dust along the side of his hand as he moved along the board, smudging the chalk. Her heart was pounding. She glanced around at the boys and girls staring at Sam and stiffened. How could she be so frightened of them? A voice in her head rang out: *They are just children.* She could do this; after all, she told herself, she had been reading to little ones most of the morning in Foyles and they were just children. What could go wrong?

Sam glanced over his shoulder at his class, all sitting on their benches staring at him. He cleared his throat and carried on writing on the blackboard. 'Right, I want you to use your chalk to copy these tables down on your boards, and then we'll read them together.' He turned to look at them before pointing his index finger at a child near the back of the class. 'Charlie, I want you to read to Miss Burrows first, and then you can write your tables down. I shall leave them on the board for a while.' Sam's arms swung by his sides and he stepped away from his scribblings, leaving a trail of white dust on his dark trousers.

Rosie took another deep breath. This was it. A tremor ran

through her as she scanned the class, wondering who Charlie was. She watched a boy stand up and walk slowly towards her. His trousers had several patches on them and were too short for him. His scuffed shoes had seen better days. Rosie studied him and fleetingly wondered if he had an older brother. She made a note to ask Sam the ages of the children in his class because some were definitely older than others. Running her damp palms down the side of her black skirt, she forced a smiled to her lips. 'Hello, Charlie, can I ask how old you are?'

Charlie scuffed the toe of his shoe into the floor. 'I'm nearly seven.'

'Well, Charlie-who-is-nearly-seven, are you ready to have some fun?'

Charlie stared at her but remained silent.

'Don't look so worried, I don't bite.' Rosie smiled. 'I love reading books and, in my head, I use different voices for each person in the story. Is there anything you like to read?'

Charlie shrugged.

Rosie held out her hand to the quiet boy. 'Come, let's go and sit in the corner where no one can hear us.'

Charlie placed his small hand in hers and they walked to the back of the class.

Rosie beamed at him. 'I wasn't sure how much reading you have done so I've brought with me *The Tale of Peter Rabbit* by Beatrix Potter.' She held up the book to show him. 'Look, that's a picture of Peter and he's wearing a coat to keep warm.'

Charlie smiled as he gazed down at the cover.

Rosie opened the book on the first page. 'Now, can you let me hear what you can read? Don't worry if it's difficult for you because we can read it together and next time, I'll bring something else.'

Charlie stared down at the words on the page. He frowned at them.

Rosie ran her hand over his back. 'Don't worry, Charlie, I'll read the first line and then maybe you could try and read it afterwards. We'll take it slowly.' She placed her index finger under the first word. '"Once upon a time there were..."' Rosie's finger moved along as she spoke the words out loud. She glanced at Charlie. 'Right, shall we read those words together and see how we get on?' She returned her finger to the beginning of the sentence.

Charlie was hesitant but then slowly nodded his head.

'Good, let's start. Ready? Take a deep breath.' Rosie watched as the boy's chest expanded and flattened again. 'Right, "Once..."' She waited for Charlie to say the same word before carrying on.

Rosie and Charlie spent thirty minutes reading the first page.

Charlie beamed. 'They're funny names, Flopsy, Mopsy and Cotton Tail.' He giggled.

Rosie laughed. 'They are, but maybe not so if you're a rabbit.' She looked up and saw Sam strolling towards them.

'It sounds like you two have had fun.'

Charlie frowned as he looked up. 'Sir, I've been trying to read but was laughing at the rabbits' names.'

Rosie smiled. 'Charlie has done very well.'

Sam grinned at Rosie. 'That's good news, well done.' He turned to look at Charlie. 'It's time you went back to your seat and wrote your times tables down as we will be singing them soon.'

Charlie stood up. 'Yes, sir. Thank you, Miss Burrows. You were right; it was fun.' He took a step before turning back to face her. 'Can we do it again?'

Rosie nodded. 'Of course.' She watched as the boy walked back to the narrow bench he shared with two other boys. She peered up at Sam before speaking in low tones. 'I don't think Charlie can read at all.'

Sam's eyes narrowed as he watched the class. 'No, I'm sorry, I should have said. Not many of them can, that's why I need help. I was frightened that if I told you, I'd scare you off.'

Rosie shook her head. 'Obviously I'm not a teacher, and I don't know if what I'm doing is right, but Charlie had fun and that's an important step to enjoying books.' A smile slowly crept across her face. 'And I must admit I had fun too, but it's a big job if none of the children can read.'

Sam chuckled. 'Some can read a little, but I didn't want to tell you. I thought it was best you found out for yourself, and if I'm honest, I was hoping once you got to know the children you wouldn't mind it being such a big job.'

Rosie giggled. 'Now that's a bit sneaky, if you ask me.'

* * *

Rosie stifled a yawn as she pushed open the ward door. The smell of disinfectant rushed at her. She pushed the trolley of books and newspapers in ahead of her. She glanced around the Middlesex Hospital ward; there wasn't a free bed, and a couple of the men waved as they caught her looking around. The concentration of working with the children at school after working in Foyles was taking its toll, and then coming to the hospital made her wonder if she could manage all three jobs every day.

'Ah, Rosie, would you take this water to bed six, please.'

Rosie peered over shoulder at the sound of her mother's voice. She smiled. 'Of course I will, let me just move this trolley to one side so it's not in anyone's way.' She moved it to the foot of an occupied bed before going back to collect the glass of water. 'Bed six?'

Ivy chuckled. 'Yes, please, but she's quite fragile so be careful. I've got to change the dressing on the leg injury in bed three and the head injury in bed nine.'

'Of course.' Rosie smiled. 'I don't mind what I do, I'm here to help so just shout if you need anything.' She took the glass and walked down to bed six. 'Did you want some water?'

The lady opened her eyes before she spoke in low tones. 'Yes, please.'

Rosie placed the glass in the woman's hand. 'Would you like me to tidy your bed or plump your pillows?'

The lady shook her head. She took a sip of the water and passed the glass back to Rosie, who placed it on the bedside cabinet.

Rosie gave her a thoughtful look. 'I shall be along in a moment with a trolley full of books and newspapers.'

The lady frowned. 'I don't want anything.'

Rosie wanted to say something but decided to just smile instead. 'If you change your mind, let me know.'

The matron was just walking on to the ward as Rosie reached her trolley. 'Hello, Rosie, how are you?'

'I'm well, thank you. I've just given the lady in bed six a glass of water, but I sense she's very despondent.' She paused. 'Is there anything I can do to help her?'

Matron pursed her lips. 'It's very difficult; her husband was killed on the front line and the shock brought about a miscarriage, so I don't think she has any desire to live. She isn't sleeping or shedding the tears that need to fall for the healing to begin. At the moment she is deep in grief, so we just have to keep a close eye on her.'

Rosie nodded. 'I could read to her; I know she won't say yes to that but if I just carry on regardless, she might end up reading the book herself or talking to me about it all.'

Matron gave Rosie a sideways look. 'I don't have a problem with you reading to her but if she wants to talk about things, we need to get someone in who knows how to deal with what she's feeling. Grief is a terrible thing that almost never ends.'

Sadness flooded through Rosie. She thought about her father and how she missed him every day; she knew it wasn't the same as losing a child or a husband because that was the wrong order of things. 'I'll see what I can do.' She took the trolley and called out as she pushed it slowly along the ward. 'Would anyone like a newspaper or a book to read?' She reached bed six. 'Can I leave you a book? I don't mind coming back and reading it to you.'

The woman stared at Rosie. 'Please, just leave me alone.'

Rosie tilted her head slightly. 'That's just it, I don't think I can.'

The woman's voice took on a higher pitch. 'I don't need your sympathy or charity; I just want to be left alone.'

Rosie took a step away. 'I'm sorry, I wasn't offering sympathy or charity – just my company, in whatever form.'

'Well, I don't want it.' The woman's eyes were red and watery. 'Go away and give it to some young man who will appreciate it.'

Rosie pulled up the wooden chair and sat down.

The woman scowled at her. 'Did you not hear me?'

Rosie's heart pumped furiously. 'I did hear you, and I truly don't want to upset you any more than you already are, but we should all be there for one another.'

The woman sighed. 'Really, do you know how patronising you sound?'

Rosie closed her eyes for a second; she must let the harsh words bounce off her. 'That was never my intention, so I'm sorry if that's how it came across.'

The woman stayed silent.

'Is there anyone – a friend or family member – that I can fetch for you?'

The woman remained quiet.

Rosie persisted in a calm voice. 'You know, if it were your friend or someone from your family lying in this bed, I'm sure you would feel hurt or upset that you hadn't been contacted to help them through their difficult time.'

The two of them stared at each other but neither said anything.

Rosie stood up and smoothed down her skirt. 'I'm going to take these papers and books around the beds and then I'll come back to you.' She bit her lip. 'You need to know that I won't give up; I can't change what's happened, but I can make sure you're not going through it on your own.' She took a step away and glanced over her shoulder as the woman sniffed and wiped away her tears. She was pleased to see the long road to healing had begun.

5

Molly picked up a couple of books from behind the counter in Foyles's children's section. They looked like they hadn't been collected from the previous day; she would check the payment pad before putting them back on the shelves. She glanced over at Rosie. 'How are things going at the school with Sam?'

Rosie laughed. 'It's wonderful to listen to the children read and hopefully pass on my love of books.'

Molly chuckled while straightening the payment pad and pen. 'It sounds like you got as much fun out of helping out at the school as the children would have done learning to read.'

Checking the small pearl buttons on her white blouse, Rosie peered down at them. 'I've got a couple of loose buttons so if you notice any of them hanging off, please can you let me know? I'd hate to lose them; I'll sew them on tighter tonight.'

Molly nodded. 'If Alice were here, she'd be able to give you a needle and thread; she's the only one of us who's prepared for anything.'

'Well, hopefully they'll be all right until I get home later.' Rosie smiled. 'I really enjoyed helping at the school yesterday. I'm going again today. I'm hoping the rain will have stopped by then. I like April with the colourful spring flowers, but the rain gets me down a bit.'

Molly had a glint in her eye when she studied Rosie. 'There's nothing like trying to discuss the weather to change the subject, but you need to know it will take more than that to throw me off the scent of a potential romance. So, is it the children or Mr Bennet that's the attraction?'

Rosie's mouth dropped open. 'There's no potential romance between us; we are just friends.'

Molly gave a hearty laugh. 'Are you sure about that? I saw the way he watched you when he brought his class to the shop; he barely took his eyes off you.'

Heat rose in Rosie's face, and she fought the strong urge to fan herself. 'I think you are imagining it, Molly. As I said, we are friends and have been for a long time, and you're forgetting the most important thing of all: I promised his brother I would wait for him to return from the war.'

Molly shook her head. 'I'm sorry, I can't resist teasing, but I do think he feels something for you, and so would you if you saw the look on his face when he's watching you. I tell you, he's smitten. Mind you, he comes across as a gentleman so he probably won't do anything about it, but that doesn't mean you shouldn't be aware of it.'

Rosie gave a wry smile. 'That sounds rather spooky. I'm not sure I like the idea of someone watching me.'

Molly laughed. 'I didn't mean it in a creepy way, I just meant he obviously has feelings for you.'

"ello, ladies.' Albert's cheery voice greeted them. 'I 'ave some children's books that 'ave been returned.'

Molly reached out to take them from him. 'Hello, Albert, it's good to see you. How are you?'

'I'm as I always am, 'appy to be working.'

Molly smiled. 'And your lovely wife?'

Albert beamed. 'You mean the trouble and strife.' He chuckled. 'She's getting 'er barnet cut today.'

Rosie frowned. 'Barnet?'

'Barnet fair, 'air, she's getting 'er 'air cut today.' Albert shook his head. 'I thought you were all doing well learning the cockney slang, but I'm obviously not doing enough.'

Rosie turned and picked some books up from behind the counter. 'It's not your fault, we're just slow learners.'

Molly put her arm around Albert's shoulders. 'Victoria no longer says stairs, it's always apple and pears.' She giggled. 'So, some of it is sticking.'

Albert chuckled. 'It's good to know my work 'asn't been wasted.'

Rosie laughed. 'We have some books for you too; they've been returned this morning.'

Albert nodded. 'Let me get rid of these others first and I'll come back for 'em, otherwise I'll get confused over which ones 'ave been checked.'

Rosie nodded as she placed them back behind the counter.

Albert frowned. 'I've got to see Mr Leadbetter before I take any more books into the basement.'

Molly dropped her arm from Albert's shoulders. 'Is everything all right?'

Albert nodded before glancing down at his black shoes. 'I think so, but I need to check with 'im because there was some water on the floor this morning, so I don't know if there's a leak somewhere. I've taken all the books off the floor just in case, but Mr Leadbetter might want to get it checked out. I expect it's nothing serious, but I don't want it flooding and ruining all the books down there.'

Molly gasped. 'Right, you go and find Mr Leadbetter.'

* * *

Rosie stood next to Sam at the front of the classroom, thirty pairs of eyes staring back at them. Her mouth was dry. She tried to lick her lips but failed as she realised teaching one to one was very different to looking out at so many faces. The children were still wearing their coats as the beginning of April hadn't yet brought the promise of spring sunshine. The classroom had a damp odour about it that she hadn't noticed before. Rosie glanced at the misted windows and noticed the paint flaking from the rotten wooden window frames. The bright yellow and red of the spring flowers were just visible in the garden near the school.

Sam smiled at the children. 'Right, I've decided to put you into groups of four for your reading lessons with Miss Burrows. The groups might be swapped about depending on how well everyone is doing. So one group will read with Miss Burrows, two others will write out their times tables from the board, two will practise their handwriting as we've done before, and the remaining children will do some drawing. I shall walk around you all so if you have any questions, put your hand up and I will come and talk to you.'

Rosie peered back at the children and was drawn to two girls sitting together. She wondered what they were thinking about that made them glance at each other with an almost secret smile and a little giggle. It reminded her of her own school days with Fran, the secrets they held for each other and never repeated to anyone. Not even when they liked the same teacher and pretended to be his girlfriend. Rosie wondered if Sam knew he had some admirers. She would keep their secret. All the fun and laughter she and Fran had shared seemed a lifetime ago now. Frowning, Rosie realised she couldn't let her friendship with Fran just disappear, no matter what had happened in the past; surely their friendship was more important than Fran's embarrassment at getting pregnant four years ago.

'Miss Burrows.' Sam coughed and nudged her at the same time. 'Miss Burrows.'

Startled, Rosie automatically smiled. 'Yes, Mr Bennet.'

Sam gave her a thoughtful look. 'If you'd like to take the first group to the classroom next door until the school bell is rung, and then we'll change over.'

Rosie frowned as her gaze travelled from Sam to the children staring at her.

Sam cleared his throat. 'Right, will the children in group one please follow Miss Burrows, and I want to hear that you've all tried hard for her. After all, she gives up her time to help us.' He clapped his hands. 'Right, come on then, let's move to where we should be.'

Rosie nodded at Sam as four children scraped their chairs on the floor. She turned and waited by the classroom door.

Beaming, Tom ran over to Rosie. 'Me ma says me pa's coming home soon.'

Rosie stooped down in front of Tom. 'That's wonderful news; I can see you're excited.'

Tom nodded his head vigorously. 'Me ma said he may need a lot of rest so we're not to bother him at first, but I don't care, he's coming home.' He threw his arms around Rosie, who almost lost her footing.

Rosie wrapped her arms around him too. 'I am so happy for you.'

Tom giggled as he pulled back. 'Will I still have to come to school?'

Laughing, Rosie nodded. 'I'm afraid so but if you work hard, you'll be able to show your pa what a good reader you are.'

Tom stared at Rosie. 'Do you think he'll be proud of me?'

Rosie ruffled his hair. 'Of course he will be.' She stood up. 'Come on, let's get reading.'

* * *

Rosie stared at the splintered wooden front door of Fran's building. She entered to find a hallway dull and yellow from the smoke of many cigarettes. A stench of urine mingled with the smoke, and Rosie thought for a moment she was going to be sick. She placed a handkerchief over her nose and mouth and sucked in her breath. Closing her eyes, she concentrated on her breathing for a moment. She pulled up Fran's door knocker and let it drop with a thud. Rosie listened carefully but could hear nothing. She wondered how Fran could live in such a run-down place. Did her parents know where she was living? Anger surged through her; how could they turn their backs on her when she needed them the most? Didn't they care they had a grandson that Fran might need help with? How was she managing for money? Rosie shuddered at the thought of Fran begging on the streets with her baby, or worse – selling her body so they could eat. Why hadn't Fran confided in her? Why hadn't she turned to her for help? She sighed. There must be something she could do. Rosie raised her hand and thumped hard on the door. 'Fran, I'm not going away this time. I'm going to sit here until you open your door to speak to me. I am your friend and I've tried to step back, thinking you would eventually want to see me, but it's been three years and I'm not going to wait any longer.' Her voice was greeted with silence. Perhaps Rosie was talking to herself because Fran wasn't in.

Rosie scanned the area around her. The hallway floor was sticky underfoot and the walls were scuffed and stained. She looked at the stairs and wondered if they would be any better for sitting on while she waited for Fran to open her door. Perhaps she could talk to her mother again and see if they could fit Fran and her baby in their small house. She shook her head; she already knew there wasn't room for two more. Rosie thought about the day Fran told her she was pregnant. Rosie had pushed as hard as she dared to find out who the father was, but she had got nowhere; all Fran would say was that she loved him. Maybe she had pushed her too hard and that was why Fran didn't want to see her.

Rosie had managed to persuade Fran to tell her family because she felt sure they wouldn't kick her out on the streets, but she had been wrong. They had let her stay until the baby was born, but she wasn't allowed to leave the house in case the neighbours saw her. When the baby was a week old, they had given her five pounds and told her she wasn't allowed to return to their home unless she gave the baby up. Rosie shook her head as she remembered her shock when she went round to see Fran and found they had made her leave. They had written down Fran's address for her, but not before ranting about the shame she'd brought on their family and how she had brought it all on herself because she wouldn't give the baby up.

The main front door to the building was flung open. A wild grey-haired man with weathered features and a long, thick, curly beard and moustache, stepped through the open doorway.

Startled, Rosie stepped back, her imagination immediately kicking in. Could she protect herself against this man?

'You want young Fran? She doesn't open the door to many people, so I hope yer a friend.' His hand formed a fist and he thumped on her door hard, twice, and waited. 'She'll know that's me 'cos I always knock the same way, and I got 'er some sausages for the little 'un.' He gave a toothless grin. 'Yer need to know I won't let yer upset 'er; she's a good girl.'

'I promise I'm not here to upset her. I've known Fran since we were children.'

He eyed her suspiciously. 'Well, we'll see in a moment, won't we.'

Sure to his word, footsteps could be heard getting nearer. Bolts scratched as they thudded across the top and bottom of the door. The handle turned, screeching as it did so. Rosie gasped; this strange-looking man had managed to get the response that she couldn't.

Fran smiled up at the tall man standing near Rosie. 'Hello, Cyril.' Her smile faded as she looked across at Rosie.

'I got yer some sausages from the butcher; I did a couple of jobs for 'im and 'e offered to pay me in food, so I grabbed it with both 'ands.' Cyril beamed at Fran and reached out with a wrapped paper package. 'Go on, these will last yer a few days.'

Fran looked back at Cyril. 'That's very kind of you but you need to eat as well.'

Cyril shook his head. 'Don't yer go worrying yerself with that. Now come on, take 'em, yer need to keep yer energy up 'aving a little lad running round.' He beamed as he thrust the package into her hands. He turned to look at Rosie before gazing back at Fran. 'Now, this young lady claims to be a friend of yers. If she isn't then I'll get rid of 'er.'

Rosie gasped. Was he some kind of gangster? Should she be worried? Would a gangster bring Fran sausages?

Fran frowned as she glanced from Cyril to Rosie. 'No, Cyril, she *is* my friend but I'm afraid now isn't a good time, Rosie. Maybe we can chat another day.'

A child's laughter could be heard inside, and Fran quickly

looked over her shoulder before her wide eyes looked back at both of them. 'I'm sorry, I have to go.' Fran pushed the door to close it. 'Thank you for the sausages, Cyril, you're very good to me and James.' The door clicked shut as mumbled voices reached the hallway from within.

Rosie frowned; she had strained to hear the voices, but it was all to no avail. Did she have a man in there? She shook her head, knowing she would have told others off for jumping to conclusions, but James wasn't giggling by himself, so Fran had let someone in – just not her.

Cyril turned to Rosie. 'It looks like yer've 'ad a wasted trip, but Fran doesn't usually let anyone in so don't take it personally.'

Rosie peered up at the man. 'Thank you. At least I know you're looking out for her.'

Cyril smiled. 'She needs someone looking out for 'er.'

Rosie nodded. 'I was beginning to think I had the wrong address, and she didn't live here.'

Cyril eyed Rosie. 'She's lived 'ere for some time, but if yer really friends yer would know that.'

Panic began to rise in Rosie. 'Oh, we are friends but since she's had the baby we sort of lost touch.'

Cyril growled. 'Yer not one of the gossips giving 'er a 'ard time, are yer?'

'No, no, definitely not, she's my friend.' Rosie stared wide-eyed at Cyril. 'It's just this war that's got in the way. Anyway, I'd better go, my ma will be wondering where I am.' She stepped towards the main door. 'Thanks again for looking out for Fran.' Sighing, Rosie stepped outside, realising she had let her imagination run riot. Cyril might look frightening, but he clearly cared about Fran and the baby. She shook her head and tried to remember not to judge someone because of the way they looked; that was not how she had been brought up.

6

Sam glanced at Rosie. 'Thank you for your help with the children today, I really appreciate it.' He looked down at his feet and fidgeted from one foot to the other. 'They seem to have really taken to you, so that's good.'

Rosie blushed. 'Thank you, I enjoy listening to them read and helping out where I can. They clearly adore you.'

Sam sucked in his breath. 'I think I'm the nearest some of them have to a father figure, so I always have to be careful that I don't say anything that could be misunderstood.' He ran his fingers along the inside of his collar, trying to loosen it from around his neck. 'It's getting too hot to wear a tie, but I feel it's expected of me.'

Rosie smiled. 'It is getting warmer, but you look very smart in your shirt and tie, with your jacket. Your mother must be very proud of you.'

Sam gave a nervous laugh. 'Good job Alfie isn't here to hear you say that.' He shook his head; he wanted his brother to be alive but dreaded him coming home. He wasn't ready to give Rosie up yet, even though she had never been his to lose.

Rosie frowned. 'I never understood why you let your brother put you down all the time; why didn't you stand up to him?'

Sam shrugged. 'I suppose I never noticed it as much as you because he had always been the same.' He paused for breath. 'Anyway, that's your fiancé you're talking about.'

'I'm beginning to think he isn't coming back. I know your ma is very positive he will, but I haven't heard from him for so long I'm not so sure.'

Sam clenched and unclenched his hands by his sides. He took a couple of deep breaths. 'Maybe it's time you got on with your life. After all, how long can you wait without hearing from him?'

'I've been having similar thoughts, but then I feel incredibly guilty for those very thoughts. To make it worse – and if I'm being really honest – I'm not even sure I love him. I was only sixteen when he went away and let's face it, he liked to flirt with the ladies.' Rosie looked at Sam. 'Tell me truthfully, does that make me a bad person?'

Sam shook his head. 'You could never be a bad person to me.'

'That's very sweet of you, Sam, but I'm not sure your ma, or mine, would agree – or Alfie, if he returned.' Rosie paused. 'I said I'd wait so that's what I must do.'

Sam raised his eyebrows. 'Are you saying you will marry someone you don't love because you promised when you were a girl to wait for him? Alfie had no right to ask you to wait, and I don't mean to be horrible about my brother, but I'm not convinced he could love anybody because he enjoyed the thrill of the chase too much.'

Rosie chuckled. 'Sam Bennet, you're not trying to put me off your brother, are you?'

Sam gave her a sheepish look. 'I just don't want you throwing your life away. He doesn't deserve that kind of sacrifice.'

Rosie's eyes narrowed as she stared at Sam. 'Do you know something I don't? Has he written to you? Did he say something before he—'

'So many questions!' Sam held up his hands and laughed.

'Sorry, for a moment there I thought you knew something I didn't.'

'Trust me, Rosie, I don't.'

'I'm sorry.' Rosie's fingers entwined in front of her. 'I feel so bad thinking I should start living my life again and stop worrying about him. After all, if he is alive, why hasn't he written to me? I mean, the telegram I saw didn't say he was a prisoner of war... I don't know, my head goes round and round in circles. I think I'm going mad.'

Sam reached out and covered her hands with his. 'Why don't we go out one evening? We could go to the pictures or for something to eat; it might take your mind off things, at least for a little while.' He gave her hand a gentle squeeze and took a deep breath. 'You know I've always had a soft spot for you, don't you?'

Rosie blushed. 'I never knew for sure because Alfie was always saying things about you and the way you followed me around.'

Sam dropped her hand and stepped back.

Rosie reached out for him. 'Look, I've always known Alfie was mean to you, but I was not much more than a child then, and I just thought it was one brother teasing a younger one. It's only as I've got older and thought about our last evening together that I've looked at everything differently.' She paused. 'I believe Alfie is quite selfish; he wanted what he wanted and was determined to get it no matter what.'

Sam studied her for a moment. 'And yet you are still prepared to marry him.'

Rosie shrugged. 'I gave my word.'

Sam stepped nearer and pulled Rosie into his arms.

Her eyes widened as she looked up at him.

He slowly lowered his head until he felt her soft lips touching his.

Rosie rested her hands on Sam's back as she pulled him closer. Her body pressed against his as his fingers touched her hair. Something in Rosie's stomach was doing somersaults and her body was tingling; was that excitement? She had never felt like that before, not even with Alfie. Panic suddenly took hold and she stepped back.

Sam let go of her and watched confusion run across her face. 'I'm sorry,' he stammered, 'I shouldn't have done that. I don't know what came over me. Let's face it, I'm old enough to know better.'

'I... I...' Rosie turned and rushed out of the classroom.

'Rosie, wait!' Sam ran along the corridor until he caught up with her. 'Please, let's walk, I don't want to lose your friendship, and I promise to try to behave myself.'

* * *

Rosie and Sam strolled along Foley Street, heading towards Rosie's home in Bedford Avenue.

Rosie peered up at the grey sky, wanting to fill the strained silence that hung between them. 'I do believe it might be getting warmer. The trouble with April is it's so wet; mind you, we'll soon be in May so I suppose I shouldn't complain.'

Sam glanced across at Rosie. 'Am I forgiven? I meant what I said about your friendship being so important to me.'

'There's nothing to forgive, you're important to me too.' Rosie hesitated. 'Let's just pretend it never happened.'

Sam peered at Rosie's mouth as she spoke, trying not to think about those lips touching his.

Rosie smiled. 'I love the first signs of spring; it's all about new beginnings. You know the new cycle of life is starting again.'

Sam chuckled. 'You should write poetry.'

Rosie giggled. 'Oh, I could never do that but it's true; spring is about life starting again.'

Sam nodded. 'You're right, I must admit I'd never thought of it in that way. I suppose I've just taken it all for granted.' He looked around him before glancing back at Rosie. 'You're making me see things through different eyes.'

Rosie nudged him. 'Nonsense, you're just flattering me.'

Children ran past, shouting at each other and laughing as they went.

Rosie smiled.

Sam looked around for someone who might be with the children.

A woman's voice yelled, 'Wait, you two! I don't want you racing too far ahead.'

Sam noted she had her arm through a soldier's, and they had eyes only for each other. 'They look like a couple in love.'

Rosie followed his gaze and was silent for a moment. 'Yes, they do. It must be wonderful to feel and to be able to show so much love to each other.'

Sam took Rosie's hand and thrust it under his arm. 'You sobbed when Alfie left; wasn't that a sign of love?'

Rosie raised her eyebrows. 'That's a good question, and one I don't have the answer to. I was only sixteen when he left, and I didn't know what love was. When I look back, I think it was more about losing a friend. Although he was pretty mean to me that evening before you came along.'

Sam frowned. 'And yet you still intend to marry him.'

Rosie glared at Sam. 'I gave my word I would wait for him and that's exactly what I intend to do. My word is important; I don't want people to not trust what I say.'

Sam nodded. 'I can see that. I'm sorry, I shouldn't have questioned you like that.'

The corners of Rosie's lips lifted slightly. 'That's all right, it's a bit of a sore subject for me.' She kept her gaze forward. 'Let's talk about what you want me to do at the school; that's if you still want me to continue helping?'

Sam chuckled. 'There's nothing I would like more.' He took a breath. 'The main help I need is teaching the children to read, which I think you've shown you can do very well. I'm afraid I can't give them the individual attention they need and deserve. If your ma doesn't have time, you could teach them some basic first aid, like how to clean a grazed knee. You have good qualities that would also be something for the children to learn, like caring for one another, and honesty.'

Rosie blushed. 'You are definitely flattering me now.'

Sam laughed. 'No; you notice things that most people don't, like the flower shoots, and you're loyal—'

'All right, all right, you'll give me a big head if you carry on. I'm far from perfect as you probably know, you just don't want to admit it.'

Sam squeezed her hand and chuckled as she gave him a scornful look.

* * *

Mrs Bennet picked up the letter off the floor in the hallway, hoping it would be from Alfie. Turning it over to read her address, she sighed as she recognised her cousin's handwriting. She dropped it on the console table without opening it. Mrs

Bennet rubbed her hands across her face, wondering how she managed to keep going, but she knew she had to for Alfie; he would need her when he finally came home. She couldn't give up on him, hope was all she had.

A key rattled in the front door and when it swung open, Sam was standing there. 'Hello, Ma.' He frowned as he took in her pale features. 'Are you all right? Is it Pa, or Alfie? Have you had news?'

Mrs Bennet held up her hands. 'No, I haven't had any news, but you know what they say, "No news is good news."'

Sam looked at her with a critical eye and shut the door behind him. 'You don't look too good, so talk to me.'

Mrs Bennet shook her head. 'It's nothing. A letter arrived today, and I thought it might be from Alfie, but it wasn't; it's from my cousin.'

Sam stepped forward and wrapped his arms around his mother. 'Ma, I know it's difficult, but you've got to stop this; it'll be the death of you.'

Mrs Bennet pulled back and smoothed down her floral overall. 'I know, but I can't help myself. I just need some news. Surely they should have found him by now, and as if I don't have enough to worry about, look what it's doing to your father.'

'I know, Ma, I know.' Sam took her hand and led her into the front room where his father was sitting, staring blankly ahead of him. 'Hello, Pa, I'm going to make a pot of tea so while I do that, you can talk to Ma; she needs cheering up.' He frowned and turned to his mother. 'Sit down for a moment and I'll bring in a pot and you can have a lovely cuppa, even if I say so myself.'

Mrs Bennet chuckled. 'Thank you, you're a good boy.'

There was a thud at the front door. Sam strode towards it. 'I'll get it, Ma, then I'll make the tea.'

The door handled screeched as Sam turned it. He pulled the door wide open; his jaw dropped as he gasped.

'Well, aren't you going to let me in?'

Sam couldn't believe it as he stepped aside. 'Ma... Ma's in the front room with Pa.'

'Aren't you going to say hello, or give me a hug? After all, you haven't seen me for a very long time.' Alfie stood there; Sam noticed his army uniform hung off him where he'd lost weight.

Sam gave a wry smile as he stepped nearer to his brother. 'Of course. You've just taken me by surprise; I wasn't sure I'd ever see you again.' He threw his arms around his brother and momentarily held him close. He shook his head as he pulled back. 'I'm sorry, it was a shock seeing you standing there, I thought you were dead. Ma will be very happy to see you, and it might just save Pa's life.'

Alfie patted Sam on the back before stepping away. 'Is he that bad?'

Sam lifted his chin. 'We can't get him to eat anything, but I expect he will now you're home.'

Alfie looked Sam up and down. 'Well, the war doesn't seem to have treated you too bad.'

Sam's lips tightened. 'We've all had our crosses to bear.'

Mrs Bennet walked out into the hall and looked like she was going to pass out.

Sam and Alfie rushed forward to her, catching her before she dropped like a stone.

'Alfie, is that really you?'

'Yes, Ma, it's really me. Let me take you into the front room so you can sit down.'

Mrs Bennet reached up and stroked his bearded face. 'You're real, it's really you.' She put her arms around both her sons. 'Let's not talk war. I'm just glad you're alive and well, we've all been worried sick. One thing's for certain, I need to feed you up a bit, but you've made your Pa and me very happy.'

7

Rosie was standing in Foyles Bookshop with an armful of books, wondering where she could squeeze them in on the shelves, when she picked up on the conversation of two of the customers. It had been all hands on deck when the water had been discovered in the basement – to get as many books as possible out of there while the leak was being located and fixed. Most of them had been carried to the staff area and Albert was doing his best to get them moved on to the shelves.

'You wouldn't guess who I saw today; at least, I'm almost positive it was him...'

'Who? Who did you see?'

'Alfie Bennet; I saw him going into his ma's house.'

Rosie stood rigid as she concentrated on the women's voices. Was it true? Was Alfie home? When did he get home? It had only been two days ago that Sam had said they hadn't heard from Alfie in a long time. She closed her eyes as she relived his lips on hers, then she gasped and opened her eyes wide. Had Sam lied to her because he didn't want her to marry Alfie? Rosie looked around her, trying to identify who was talking, but there were only a couple of young women with small children in the aisle she was standing in. She stepped nearer, listening as they chatted about their families. Shaking her head, she walked to the end of the bookshelves and looked around. John Williams was chatting to Ellen. They both looked so in love, and weren't worried about who knew it. To think, if Ellen hadn't got the part-time job in the local newspaper office, they would never have met. Rosie gave a faint smile as she watched them, pushing down and crushing the jealousy that was threatening to rise to the surface.

'He was in his uniform, although I thought he looked like he'd lost weight, but I suppose he's not alone in that.'

Rosie turned around at the woman's voice. She scanned the aisle; it was so busy she couldn't see anyone she recognised.

'That's true, but I expect the Bennets were so happy to see him after all the worry they've had.'

Victoria walked over to Rosie. 'Are you all right? You look a bit confused; do you need help?'

Rosie jumped. 'No, I'm fine, honestly, it's just that we have so many books there's not enough room on the shelves for these.'

Victoria stepped back and looked up at the rack of books, trying to seek a space they could be squeezed into. 'I think you're right; we need to look at how we do these books because we definitely have more than we have shelf space for, despite the number we sell. Perhaps the best thing to do for now is take them back to Albert, and he can leave them on the higher shelves in the basement until we can find room for them.'

Rosie drew in her breath. 'Victoria, you live in Percy Street, don't you?'

Victoria nodded. 'I do, why do you ask?'

Rosie's lips tightened. 'I probably have no right to ask you, but I just wondered if you knew the Bennets and whether you had heard anything about Alfie?'

Victoria studied Rosie for a moment. 'I wouldn't say I know them well. Is something wrong?'

'I don't know, I've just heard two ladies talking about Alfie Bennet coming back from the front. Apparently one of them saw him going into the family home.' Rosie shook her head. 'I haven't had any letters from him for ages, years, and I know there's a war going on, but everyone I know seems to get letters from their men folk, so I suppose I'm just trying to work out what it all means.'

Victoria frowned. 'It may not mean anything; we don't know what the men are going through at the front. He may have been stuck somewhere. It's hard for us to understand what it must be like for them standing in the trenches up to their ankles in water, and from what I've heard, there are rats as well. Then there's a lack of food, let alone all the bombs and the shooting going on all around them.' She paused. 'I think you need to have a conversation with him before you upset yourself too much; don't let your imagination run away with you.'

Rosie nodded. 'You're right, I was just shocked to hear he was home.' She forced a smile. 'I'm sorry, I shouldn't have bothered you with my thoughts.'

Victoria reached out and touched Rosie's arm. 'Nonsense, at Foyles we're like a family, so we're all here for one another.'

'Thank you.' Rosie shifted the books in her arms. 'I'd better go and see Albert; these are getting heavy.' She turned and walked back to the staff area. Sam's kiss jumped to the front of her thoughts; what did it mean? Did it mean anything? She wasn't sure how she felt about him; after all, he had always been there for her as a friend, or at least that was what she had thought. Was Sam taking a leaf out of Alfie's book and just trying it on? Rosie shook her head. Sam wasn't the same as Alfie, they were nothing alike, so what did the kiss mean? And, to add to the confusion, Alfie was back. Where had he been? Her thoughts chased each other around in her head.

'Rosie, are you all right?'

Startled, Rosie turned.

Ellen frowned. 'I've been calling you.'

Rosie forced a smile to her lips. 'Yes, sorry, I'm lost in my own world these days. Did you want me for any particular reason?'

Ellen smiled. 'No, not really, it's just that… I don't wish to pry but it's just that you seem deep in thought today, so I wanted to check you were all right?'

Rosie studied Ellen's concerned expression. 'How do you know if you're in love? I mean, *you* clearly are; I saw you chatting to John just now and you both looked so happy, and even now you have a sort of glow about you.'

Ellen giggled as colour rushed into her cheeks. 'A glow?'

Rosie shook her head. 'It doesn't matter, I'm sorry, I'm overthinking things.'

Ellen stopped laughing. 'No, I'm sorry, I shouldn't have laughed.' She paused. 'I can only tell you how I feel about John, but I expect everyone is different.' She took a breath. 'I want to be with him all the time and my stomach does somersaults when he kisses me. He makes me laugh and is so caring, I know there's nothing he wouldn't do for me, or I for him. You've caught me off guard so these are just my first thoughts, but I hope it helps.'

Rosie nodded. 'Thank you, I didn't mean to put you on the spot.'

Ellen touched Rosie's arm. 'We can talk anytime about anything, and I mean that.'

'Excuse me, I'm looking for something for my sister.'

Ellen and Rosie both looked round at the customer.

Ellen smiled. 'I'll get this while you get rid of your books.'

* * *

Rosie turned the key and strode through the open front door. The wind caught it and it slammed shut behind her. 'Ma? Ma, where are you?'

David ran into the hall, his face smeared with dirt. 'What's all the shouting about? Are you all right?'

Rosie shook her head. For a moment she had forgotten how David had lost his carefree innocence since their father had died. Like all young boys, in the beginning he had found the war exciting, but now he was terrified of something happening to anyone he cared about.

'Has a bomb gone off? I didn't hear an explosion; you're not hurt, are you?' David's words tumbled over one another in their rush to escape.

She bent down and pulled him close. 'I'm sorry, everything is fine, I didn't mean to scare you.'

David pulled away and shrugged. 'I wasn't scared.'

Rosie eyed her younger brother. 'Why is your face covered in dirt?'

David looked at her as if she were mad. 'Me and me mates have been playing war games so this is so they can't see me.'

Rosie closed her eyes for a split second before forcing a smile. 'Of course, I should have known.'

Ivy rushed into the hall, her face flushed from cooking over the stove. 'What on earth is the matter?' She turned to her son. 'Look at the state of you; tuck in your shirt and wash your face and hands ready for dinner.'

David eyed his ma and sister before turning away to do as he was told.

Rosie's fingers fumbled with the buttons of her coat as she tried to undo them. 'I overheard a couple of customers chatting in Foyles today and they were saying Alfie's back. Have you heard anything? Has he knocked, or has his ma been round to let us know?'

Ivy shook her head vigorously. 'No, Rosie, I haven't heard anything, and I've been in all day. Are you sure?'

'Obviously I'm not positive, but it's what they were saying; they saw him going into the house.'

Ivy frowned. 'Have you been to the school to see Sam? He must know if his brother's back home.'

Rosie gave an exasperated sigh. 'I've come straight from Foyles to here. Besides, if Alfie is home, I expect Sam isn't at work.'

Ivy shook her head. 'Sam is a teacher, he can't just not turn up for work; what about all those children who rely on him? You need to calm down and start thinking rationally.'

Mary stepped into the hall; her gaze travelled from her daughter-in-law to her granddaughter. 'What is all the noise about? What's going on?'

Rosie lowered her eyelashes and shrugged. 'I'm sorry, Ma, I just can't believe that we've heard nothing from him for a couple of years and then he just comes home as if everything is all right – and what's more, he hasn't bothered to come and see me.' She walked past her grandmother and into the front room where she flopped down on the sofa. She closed her eyes for a moment, her head thumping. She took a couple of deep breaths before opening her eyes to see her mother and grandmother staring at her.

Mary gradually lowered herself into the armchair, gripping the arms as she went down. 'Is this about Alfie?'

Rosie nodded. 'Apparently, he's home. I heard two ladies talking about it in the bookshop this morning.'

Mary studied Rosie for a moment. 'Did he come back today? I suppose that's a silly question.'

Rosie shook her head. 'I don't know, I assumed it was today, but maybe it wasn't.' She paused. 'But that just makes it worse if he's been back for longer and hasn't bothered to come round, or to let me know in some way that he's home.' She paused and took a calming breath. 'But Sam would have told me Alfie was back when I saw him a couple of days ago if that were the case, I'm sure of it.'

Ivy stepped forward and rested her arm across Rosie's shoulder. 'It might not be as bad as you think; he might not even be home. I think we need to find out for certain before you make assumptions and judgements.'

Mary leant forward in her seat. 'Your ma is right; you need to find out the facts first. After all, it wasn't long ago when you were saying that Mr Bennet wasn't in good health, so maybe that's what's brought him home, and in all fairness, if that is the case, that would be his priority.'

Rosie closed her eyes again and patted her mother's hand on her shoulder. 'Of course, you're right, I've blown it all out of proportion; the trouble is, I've thought of nothing else while I've been at work. I expect I've come across as quite selfish in wanting to know why he hasn't contacted me, especially if his father is ill. The trouble is, I don't recall Sam saying his father was that ill or that it was a worry; he did say he seemed to have given up on life with Alfie missing, but he didn't say he thought he was dying.'

Ivy stepped away from Rosie to sit in the chair opposite her. 'Maybe Sam doesn't know the full story of how ill Mr Bennet is.'

Rosie's eyes darted from one side to the other. 'Or maybe Alfie's avoiding me and if that is the case, you have to ask yourself why. Why would he be avoiding me?'

Mary pursed her lips. 'Well, if he's avoiding you, it clearly bothers you, so maybe you should be asking yourself why that is?'

Rosie jumped up out of the chair and paced around the room. 'Gran, it bothers me because I've waited like I said I would, and yet he hasn't written to me for a couple of years, or to his mother, and then he turns up as if nothing has happened. Am I now expected to just wait until he deigns to knock? What happens if he doesn't? What happens if he then goes back to the front without contacting me at all? Am I then meant to wait for another two, three, five or ten years?'

Ivy peered up at her daughter. 'I think you need to stop pacing and calm down because you're in no fit state to see anyone at the moment, and you're likely to say something you might regret.'

Rosie nodded. 'I know you're right, Ma, I just didn't think this was how it was going to be when I found out he was back home.'

Mary raised her eyebrows. 'You don't know that he is home yet.'

David came running into the room. 'Are you all arguing?'

Ivy looked at her son. 'No, of course we're not.'

David glanced across at Rosie. 'That's not how it sounds to me. And if it's about Alfie and you marrying him, well, you shouldn't bother.'

Rosie stared at her brother. 'Why, have you heard or seen something?'

David smiled. 'No, but Pa never liked him. I overheard him talking to Gran about what a waste of space he was, and Pa was always right.'

The three women were silent as they stared at him, not knowing what to say.

* * *

Sam pushed open the front door and laughter greeted him. He frowned; was that his father laughing? He shut the door quietly behind him, the click of the catch seeming to echo in the hall. He stood still as he undid the buttons of his coat and then he heard it, the unmistakable voice of Alfie. He quickly hung up his coat, took a deep breath and then paced into the front room. 'Oh, my goodness, am I dreaming or am I really hearing Father laugh?'

Mrs Bennet beamed. 'Yes, Sam, and Alfie managed to get your father to eat some lunch; he'll be well again before we know it.'

Sam's gaze travelled from his mother to his brother. 'Thank goodness you came home in time to save him.'

Alfie fidgeted in the armchair. 'It's good to be home, Ma, I've seen things that no man should ever see.' He turned to his brother. 'You don't know how lucky you are being at home, to not be at the front and have men dying all around you.'

Sam looked away from him and pulled out a dining chair before sitting on it. He felt the wooden slats pressing hard into his back. 'Don't worry, I'm sure it won't be long before I get my call-up papers. Anyway, where have you been? I mean, I know you've been at the front fighting for king and country, but Ma has been going out of her mind with worry, and if it comes to that, so has Rosie.'

Alfie leant back in his armchair. He didn't look at Sam but gave his mother a sheepish look. 'I'm sorry, Ma, I didn't mean to worry you. It's just... it's just everything was so bad I didn't want to write and tell you how awful things were.'

Sam shook his head and tapped his fingers on the table. His instinct told him Alfie was lying; after all, other soldiers had been home on leave, but not Alfie. He knew he couldn't say anything in front of his mother and father as they looked so happy for the first time in a long time. 'Are you going round to see Rosie?'

Alfie glared at his brother, before quickly slipping into a

smile. 'Of course, but not yet. This time is all about enjoying Ma's cooking, having a bath, relaxing at home and being with family.'

Sam's brows drew together. 'Do you not think she deserves to hear you're back from you and not from someone else?'

Alfie chuckled. 'I see you're still looking out for my girlfriend; I'm surprised you haven't tried to move in on her while I've been away.'

Sam opened his mouth to speak but his mother's voice rang out. 'Now I don't want any trouble between you two, you should be past all this childish behaviour.' Mrs Bennet stepped towards Sam. 'Alfie, your brother is teaching now and he's getting on very well.'

Alfie didn't say a word.

Mrs Bennet walked to the window and peered out at the row of houses. 'I saw Rosie, and we talked about your wedding; she hasn't been saving or buying for her bottom drawer so it's just as well I have.' She turned and looked at Alfie. 'Rosie has been very understanding so I think it would be good if you set a date while you're home.'

Alfie vigorously shook his head. 'Ma, this isn't something I want to talk about now, and I'm certainly not setting a wedding date to suit everyone else.'

Sam's lips tightened. 'What, not even Rosie? The woman you declared your love to and begged to wait for you?'

'Shut up, Sam; you don't know what you're talking about.'

'Don't I? Who do you think gave her some comfort when you went away? She sobbed in my arms when you left her to go and see some other friend on your last evening.'

Alfie scowled. 'I bet you loved that, playing the hero, holding her in your arms.' He gave a disdainful laugh. 'Let's face it, it's the only way you would ever get to hold a girl like Rosie.'

Mrs Bennet screamed at the top of her voice. 'Stop it, the pair of you, for goodness' sake! Alfie you have only been home for a few minutes and already you are arguing with Sam, and Sam, you have yet to ask your brother where he's been, even though he's been home for two days.'

The two brothers peered at each other. 'Sorry, Ma,' they answered in unison.

Mrs Bennet shook her head. 'Rosie is a good girl, not like her friend Fran Wilson who got herself pregnant at sixteen. Mind you, I hear she's doing a good job bringing up the child on her own.'

Sam scowled. 'Ma, she didn't get herself pregnant, there was a man involved as well.'

'I know, and I don't know what kind of bloke does that to a young girl; it's disgraceful, but she should have kept her legs crossed.'

Sam sighed, turned on his heels and left the house.

8

Sam marched along Percy Street, anger soaring through his veins. He could feel his pulse thumping in his temple. He shook his head, feeling tormented by Alfie, feeling like he was fourteen again. He wondered if those feelings would ever change. Sam was obviously pleased his brother was safe, but he couldn't understand how Alfie could put his family – and Rosie – through the torment of not staying in touch. He marched along with his head down, not looking left or right; he knew Alfie was about to shatter his dreams and there was nothing he could do about it. Sam had waited too long to tell Rosie he loved her, and that he had since he was a boy, but now with Alfie back he had no right to say anything.

'Sam.'

He hesitated. He knew who it was without turning around, and it was tempting to walk on and pretend he hadn't heard her, but he knew he could never do that.

'Sam.'

Sam turned to see Rosie running towards him. His heart

soared when he saw her, but he immediately tried to shut it down. He had no right to feel the way he did; this was his brother's fiancée.

'Rosie, what are you doing out at this time of night?'

Rosie laughed. 'It's not late, you know; I just wanted a breath of fresh air. What are *you* doing out, are you going to the pub?'

'No, like you, I fancied a walk. I just needed to clear my head.'

Rosie's eyes narrowed as she studied him. 'Is everything all right?'

Sam's lips tightened as he struggled with his news, and whether it was his to tell.

Rosie frowned. 'It's true, isn't it? I heard two women talking in Foyles, they said they'd seen Alfie.'

Confusion ran across Sam's face as he clenched his hands by his sides. Was that hope he heard in her voice? The kiss they shared would now be forgotten, but he knew – regardless of what Rosie did – he would keep that memory close forever. 'Yes, I didn't know he was coming home myself until I opened the front door to him today.' He took a deep breath. 'And for the first time in a long time I heard laughter; Ma and Pa were obviously pleased that Alfie was back.' Sam lowered his eyelashes; she was never going to be his now Alfie was back.

Rosie nodded. 'Of course they are, they were never going to be anything else. They would feel the same if it were you.'

Sam shook his head. 'I don't think for one minute you believe that but thank you all the same.'

Rosie reached out and rested her hand on Sam's arm. 'I know they have a strange way of showing it, but you're their son as well, so why wouldn't they love you?' She squeezed his arm through his suit jacket; the kiss they shared immediately sprung to mind. She shook her head. 'You must be cold without your coat on.'

Sam frowned. 'I didn't think about putting my coat on, I just left the house.'

Rosie hesitated. 'Would you like us to walk together? I mean, I wasn't going anywhere special, but I don't want to hold you up if you were.'

Sam breathed in her floral perfume and fought the urge to take her in his arms. Shaking his head, he realised he would rather have her friendship than nothing at all. 'I'm just out for a walk. As I said, I just wanted to clear my head.'

Rosie gave a wry smile. 'It doesn't bode well if you already need to escape, and you've only been in Alfie's company for a few hours.'

Sam laughed. 'It wasn't even that long.'

Rosie threaded her arm through his. 'Come on, let's walk; it doesn't matter where.'

They walked in a comfortable silence; the only noise was of the cars chugging past and Rosie's small heels clicking on the pavements.

Rosie cleared her throat. 'Try not to let Alfie get to you. You're a man now with a wonderful job teaching those young children, and what's more, you're very good at it.'

Sam chuckled. 'Why thank you, kind lady.'

Rosie giggled. 'You're not poking fun at me, are you?'

'Definitely not, and while we're on that subject, the children love having you in the classroom, so I hope with Alfie home you won't stop helping me out.'

Rosie peered up at Sam. 'Of course I won't; you'd have to tell me I wasn't needed or welcome any more for me to stop reading with them.'

Sam and Rosie's eyes locked for a moment. He lowered his and cleared his throat before giving a little chuckle. 'That means you will be in that classroom with me forever then, because that's never going to happen, at least not if I have anything to do with it.'

'That's good news because I love it as much as they do, if not more. It's also lovely to see you at work; the children clearly like you. I think one day you will make a good father.'

Sam shook his head. 'I can't see that on the horizon; I have to have a girlfriend first, and women are not exactly queuing up to fill that position.'

Rosie raised her eyebrows. 'Well, you have to be open to loving someone and allowing them to love you.'

Sam stared straight ahead. 'You mean like you and Alfie?'

Rosie was silent for a moment.

Sam patted Rosie's hand. 'I've upset you now, I'm sorry.'

'You haven't upset me; it just feels like Alfie and I have got complicated all of a sudden.'

'Is that because he hasn't written to you?' Sam arched his eyebrows. 'Or told you he's back?'

Rosie nodded in the darkness. 'That's some of it, but also the war has changed all of us; I was little more than a child when Alfie went off to war. Since then, I've seen and heard so many injured men who have come home; that's without the bombing we've experienced.' She paused for a moment as she took a breath. 'Don't get me wrong – I'm sure he has been through much worse on the front line, but we've also had a sense of what it must have been like for them, so none of us are the same as we once were.'

Sam squeezed Rosie's hand closer to his body, eager to know whether she had changed her mind about marrying his brother, but he knew he couldn't ask that question of her – at least not yet. But hope surged in his heart. They turned into Oxford Street.

Rosie took a deep breath. 'Let's cheer ourselves up and do a bit of window shopping, shall we?'

* * *

Rosie yawned as she crossed the threshold of Foyles Bookshop.

Mr Leadbetter stepped forward. 'Good morning, Miss Burrows. This doesn't look like a good start to the day for you. I would have thought that with the greyness of winter gone, the April sunshine and the spring flowers in bloom would have put a spring in your step.'

Rosie laughed. 'I'm sorry, Mr Leadbetter, I just didn't sleep very well last night.'

'Are you worrying about something?'

Rosie tilted her head. 'I don't think I am any more than anyone else is. Don't worry sir, I shall be fine.'

Mr Leadbetter smiled. 'I hope so; this is a wonderful shop and consequently, we are always busy.'

Rosie nodded. 'Yes, sir.' She carried on walking through the shop.

'Morning, Rosie.'

She looked round to see Victoria and Molly walking towards her. 'Morning, ladies.'

Victoria cast a critical eye over her. 'Are you all right? You look tired.'

Rosie winced. 'I must look shocking today. Mr Leadbetter just asked me if I was all right too.'

Molly stepped forward and stroked the back of her black coat. 'You look well, just tired.'

Rosie took a deep breath. 'Alfie is back.'

Victoria gasped as she studied Rosie's pale features. 'That's wonderful news, isn't it?'

Rosie shrugged. 'Of course, it's good to know he's safe...'

'But?' Molly studied Rosie before glancing at Victoria.

Rosie shook her head but said nothing.

Victoria lowered her voice. 'It'll be all right; I know you haven't seen him for a long time but look at me and Ted, we were apart for many years and yet now it's like we've never been away from each other.'

Molly turned to Victoria. 'I'm pleased everything is going well; does that mean you've finally set the date for your wedding?'

Victoria frowned. 'This isn't about me; this is about how Rosie feels.'

Molly turned back to Rosie. 'Of course, sorry, I let my own excitement take over.' She paused. 'What is it, Rosie?'

Rosie glanced over her shoulder. 'It's nothing, really. We had better get on, customers will be coming in soon. We'd better get clocked on and to work.' She marched towards the back of the shop.

Molly watched her go. 'It's all about Alfie. I wonder what he's said or done. When a woman looks as troubled as that, it's always to do with a man.'

Victoria shook her head. 'You're so cynical.'

Molly grinned. 'Unless his brother has told her he loves her and that's added to her not knowing what to do.'

Victoria tightened her lips but said nothing.

'Do you think I'm wrong then?'

'No, but she clearly doesn't want to talk about it.'

Glancing at Victoria, Molly frowned. 'She will, because she'll have to in the end; everyone has to speak to someone about their problems, otherwise they just keep going round in circles with them.'

Victoria nodded. 'But it doesn't mean she has to talk to us.'

Molly tilted her head. 'Do you think she doesn't want to marry Alfie now?'

Victoria shrugged. 'She was only sixteen when he went away

so I don't suppose she's the same person any more. I mean, when we look back at our sixteen-year-old selves, would you say we're the same people?'

Molly chuckled. 'I think I am pretty much.'

Victoria gave a wry smile. 'Which is why you are still getting into trouble.'

'True, but then it wouldn't do for us all to be the same, would it.'

Victoria nudged her friend. 'No, it wouldn't. Come on, we've got work to do.'

* * *

Rosie sighed when she saw, through the arch, the ambulances lined up outside Middlesex Hospital; they were queuing along Mortimer Street.

Ivy watched with dismay as the ambulances slowly shunted forward. 'It looks like it's going to be a busy night.'

As they reached the hospital's main doorway, the driver's door of the lead ambulance opened and Alice jumped out.

Rosie's eyes widened as she watched Alice unlock the back of the vehicle. She rushed forward. 'Alice, do you need help?'

Alice glanced over her shoulder. 'Yes, please; if you can find a wheelchair, that will help.'

Rosie ran into the reception, coughing as the disinfectant hit the back of her throat. She quickly grabbed a wheelchair and pushed it through the main doors to Alice. 'I had forgotten you were an ambulance driver.'

Ivy helped to move the wounded soldier onto the chair. 'I'll take him in.'

Alice nodded. 'Thank you.' She turned to Rosie. 'I didn't expect to see you here either.'

Rosie shrugged. 'I just help out from time to time.'

Alice smiled. 'I've just seen Victoria at Endell Street Hospital, that's where she volunteers. Anyway, I had better go because there were an awful lot of injured men at Victoria train station when I left.'

Rosie nodded. 'Take care.' She waved as the ambulance pulled away and another took the vacant spot. A man opened the door and jumped out of the driver's seat. She stepped forward. 'Is there anything I can do to help?'

The man stared at Rosie. 'You can find a doctor because I think this youngster will need to go straight into surgery, and I don't want to move him and make matters worse.'

Rosie nodded and ran into the hospital and straight to the reception desk. 'I'm sorry but I don't know if you are aware there are at least half a dozen ambulances queuing outside.'

The nurse opened her mouth to speak but Rosie carried on. 'The driver of one of them says the soldier he is carrying will need to go straight in for an operation, so he doesn't want to move him until a doctor has looked at him.'

'Leave it with me. A couple of the doctors are on their way down, so I'll let them know the importance of the one in front.'

Rosie nodded. 'Thank you. I think it's going to be a busy night.' She turned and walked back outside to the ambulance driver. 'The doctors are on their way.' She looked round and some of the ambulances were offloading the walking wounded they had on board. Rosie had to remind herself she wasn't a nurse, so she might do more damage than good if she got involved. Taking a deep breath, she walked back into the hospital and up to the ward. She hoped the lady in bed six was doing better because they would probably need her bed.

The ward door suddenly opened, startling Rosie.

A woman stood there, frowning. 'Sorry, I didn't mean to make you jump.'

Rosie smiled at her. She looked immaculate, without a hair out of place. 'That's all right, I was miles away, thinking about some of the patients we have.'

The lady eyed her for a moment. 'I recognise your voice; aren't you the one who spoke to me about reading?'

Rosie looked at her properly for the first time; it was the lady from bed six. 'Yes, what are you doing out of bed?'

'I'm going to stay at my mother's. In fact, she's probably waiting in reception for me.' She gave a weak smile. 'I can't take up a bed when there are so many injured soldiers who definitely have a greater need.'

Rosie remembered her grief at losing her baby and her husband. 'I know you won't get over your loss, but I hope whatever happy memories you have will help to ease the pain eventually.'

The lady leant forward and hugged Rosie. 'Thank you.'

Rosie smiled. 'If you change your mind about wanting a book, I work at Foyles Bookshop on Charing Cross Road, so please pop in and see us.'

The lady gave a faint smile. 'You don't give up, do you?'

Rosie laughed. 'That's because I love a good book. I love to escape into another world.'

The lady clutched her bag tight. 'I shall bear that in mind; now, I must go before my mother comes looking for me, but I'm glad we've spoken.'

Rosie watched her walk away. 'Take care.'

The lady glanced over her shoulder. 'Don't worry, my ma is really bossy so I'm not going to have a chance to feel sorry for myself.' She smiled. 'But for all of that, I know she loves me.'

Rosie nodded. 'That's mothers for you.'

A cloud momentarily passed over the lady's face, but then she waved and carried on towards reception.

Rosie shook her head, annoyed at her clumsy comment. She wasn't going to have time to think about it if the ambulances queuing outside were anything to go by; it was going to be a busy evening.

9

Rosie walked through the open school gates and on to Foley Street.

Sam ran outside while thrusting his arm into the sleeve of his brown jacket. 'Rosie!'

Rosie hesitated for a moment; should she pretend she hadn't heard him? Something was changing between them, especially since she'd begun helping in his classroom. She didn't know what; maybe seeing him with the children had given her a newfound respect for him. She shook her head. He was good with the children, but it was the kiss; she couldn't stop thinking about it. It was full of promise, of gentle passion and love. The last night with Alfie rushed into her mind. His kiss had been forceful, letting her know he was in charge, and that he wanted what he wanted; there had been no love attached to it. Rosie frowned as guilt washed over her. She had to stop thinking about Sam and the kiss they'd shared. No matter how much she wanted to be in his arms, she couldn't; her life was with Alfie. She knew she had to be strong because she still wanted his friendship and didn't want to give up helping the children with their reading.

Sam called out again as he ran to catch her up. 'Rosie!'

Rosie stopped; then, taking a deep breath, she turned around to face him. 'Hello, Sam, where's the fire?'

Sam slowed down. 'I could ask you the same thing; we normally have a chat before you go home but today, you left without even a goodbye.'

Colour crept up Rosie's neck. 'I'm sorry, I didn't think, I just have things to do.'

Sam frowned. 'Is everything all right? Is someone ill?'

Rosie shook her head. 'No... no, I'm sorry, I didn't mean to cause you concern. I just need to try Fran's again before I get home; I still haven't managed to make any real contact with her, not since just before the baby was born. Although I did see her when she opened the door to her neighbour – Cyril, I think that was his name. To be honest I was too busy being scared, but he was just a kind man looking out for her.'

'That's good. I suppose we should all try and do more to help one another.' Sam gave a wry smile. 'Can we walk together?'

Rosie nodded. 'Of course.' She hesitated for a moment, watching him. 'Can I ask you if you've had any luck getting hold of Fran?'

Sam's gaze shifted from her, and he coughed to clear his throat. His lips tightened as they strode forward together. 'I did, actually. Little James is not so little any more, he's coming up to three years old and Fran looks tired but well.'

Rosie beamed. 'That's good news. I miss her; she used to make me laugh so much and I always did things with Fran that I wouldn't ever do by myself. You know we tried to sneak into the pictures once, but we got caught. She also pinched a couple of her father's Woodbine cigarettes; we tried to smoke them, but they were so strong we couldn't stop coughing. We never tried smoking again; luckily my ma never found out, otherwise I would have been in no end of trouble.'

Sam chuckled. 'It sounds like she could have got you into trouble.'

Rosie giggled. 'Maybe, but she always had a brave spirit about her, which I loved and was even envious of, but I suppose that's why she now has a child. Anyway, what did she say when you saw her? Does she want to meet up somewhere? We could go to the park or something, and then James could run around while we talk?'

Sam balled his hands down by his sides. 'I'm sorry, but I got the impression she doesn't want to meet up with anyone.'

Rosie's heart sank. 'I just don't understand why she won't talk to me. What have I done that is so bad that she won't see me?'

'You probably haven't done anything, it's probably her embarrassment at having a child and not being married.' Sam peered at Rosie. 'Fran has been through a lot.'

Rosie frowned. 'Surely that's more of a reason to have your friends beside you. She has turned her back on me, but apparently not on you, so what does that mean?' She thrust her hands up in the air. 'What does it mean? She was – is – my best friend, so why is she avoiding me?'

Sam frowned. 'Please don't misunderstand – I wasn't allowed inside, I just saw them at the door.'

'Did you tell her Alfie's back? Fran always liked him and if anyone can get her to meet up, it could be him.'

Sam nodded.

'Was she pleased?' Rosie's voice rose in frustration. 'Did she say anything at all? You must have some idea about how she felt.'

Sam shook his head. 'No, she didn't have anything to say about Alfie, at least nothing outside of the daily niceties.'

'She must have said something.'

Sam shrugged. 'She's not the same carefree girl she was before she had James. In fact, she's very thin and quite pale.'

'I know, I only saw her for a few minutes and she wouldn't let me in, but that might be because someone else was there.' Rosie frowned. 'When the door shut, I heard muffled voices, but they weren't loud enough for me to recognise.' She paused. 'Maybe I need to just sit outside her front door until she opens it.'

Sam reached out for Rosie's hand, but she stepped away from him. He lowered his eyes. 'Why don't we go to the tearoom and have a slice of cake?'

Rosie looked despondent before shaking her head. 'I'm sorry but I'm not in the mood for cake, I just need to get home and think about what I'm going to do about Fran. I can't let her keep shutting me out; I've given her time but enough is enough.'

'And what about Alfie? What are you going to do about him?'

Rosie paced on. 'That is up to Alfie. I don't know how long he is home for, has he said?'

Sam lengthened his stride. 'Not to me, but then I haven't asked.' He peered across at Rosie. 'You do know it's not just up to Alfie, don't you? I mean, you have a say in who you marry and if you no longer love Alfie, you should tell him.'

Rosie frowned. 'I know what you're trying to do Sam, but I'm not Fran, I don't want to be called names, shunned or gossiped about because I came between two brothers.'

Sam reached out for Rosie's arm and clasped his fingers around it.

They both stopped walking and stared at each other.

Sam broke the silence between them. 'I'm not trying to do anything; I just think you should only marry someone because you love them.' He reached out and stroked her cheek before leaning in and gently kissing her on the lips. His hand moved into her hair as he pulled her close.

Rosie groaned as the kiss grew in passion.

10

Rosie pushed her chair back away from the dining table, ignoring the scratching on the tiled floor. Standing up, she began to stack the empty dinner plates one by one. Her mind full of Sam's kiss, she was shocked at herself for responding to him. She shook her head; maybe it would be for the best if she were not on her own with him.

'Are you all right, Rosie? What are you shaking your head at?'

Rosie forced herself to smile. 'Nothing's wrong, Ma; I didn't even know I was shaking my head.'

Ivy eyed her daughter before pushing back her chair to help. 'Don't carry too much; you'll end up having an accident.'

'I'm fine, Ma, you just sit and relax. I'll do the washing up and when that's done, I'll bring you in a cup of tea.' Rosie stepped out of the dining room clutching several plates balancing on top of one another. A fork slipped away and clattered to the floor in the hall. 'It's all right, Ma, it was only a fork.' She walked into the small kitchen just as the thud of the knocker rapped on the front door. Placing the plates on the kitchen side, she glanced up at the clock, wondering who it could be.

Ivy yelled from the hall, 'I'll get it.'

Rosie picked up the kettle and turned on the tap to fill it with water. The old pipes rattled as the water gushed out, playing its melody as it hit the metal.

Ivy stood in the kitchen doorway and cleared her throat.

Rosie turned round. 'Ma, go and sit down, I shall bring the tea in shortly.'

'You have a visitor.' Ivy stepped further into the kitchen. 'Alfie has come to see you.'

Colour drained from Rosie's face.

Ivy moved closer and watched the water spilling over the top of the kettle. 'Rosie, you've overfilled the kettle.'

Startled, Rosie reached out and turned off the tap. 'Sorry, Ma, you just took me by surprise.'

Ivy took the kettle from her. 'Go and see him. I've left everyone in the dining room and taken him into the front room to give you some privacy.'

Rosie took a deep breath, wondering why she wasn't more excited to see Alfie. She shook her head; was it Sam's kiss? Maybe Victoria was right, and it was just because she hadn't seen him for so long, and they'd just pick up where they'd left off. 'Thanks, Ma.' She sucked in her breath. 'I had better go and see him.' Rosie dried her hands on the tea towel and without another word, marched out of the kitchen. She was thankful her slippers made no noise as she approached the front room slowly. Taking a breath, she finally pushed open the door.

Alfie jumped up when Rosie stepped into the room. 'Rosie, it's wonderful to see you. You're beautiful and a sight for sore eyes.'

Colour flooded Rosie's face. 'It's lovely to see you too, Alfie. Please, have a seat.' She pulled out a chair and sat down. Her back was rigid as she perched on the edge of the chair. Silence stood between them for a moment until Rosie spoke in low tones. 'I didn't think I was going to see you again, but your ma kept the faith.'

Alfie gave a slight smile. 'Good old Ma, she would never give up on me.'

Rosie could feel the torment she had been feeling for a while course through her body. 'I didn't give up on you Alfie, but you haven't written to any of us for about two years; what were we meant to think?' She stared at him. 'Have you been a prisoner of war? And if you were, how did you escape?'

Alfie lowered his head. 'This wasn't the homecoming I was expecting; I thought you would've thrown your arms around me in your excitement to see me.'

Rosie shook her head. 'I'm obviously pleased you're here but why didn't you let us know you were safe? We've all been worried sick.'

Alfie raised his voice. 'Look, I'm sorry, all right? I'm not going to be home for long so it's not something I want to waste my time talking about now.' He smiled, looking like the Alfie Rosie was used to. 'Don't I even get a kiss?'

Rosie frowned. 'No, at least not in my mother's house.' She studied him for a moment, thinking about some of the gaunt, jumpy men that were in hospital, their eyes dulled with fear. 'You've lost weight but you look well, especially compared to some of the men arriving at the hospital returning from the front.'

Alfie said nothing.

'Have you seen any of our friends since you've been home?'

Alfie shook his head. 'No, this is the first time I've left the house. Is there anything I should know? I mean, is everyone well?'

Rosie shrugged. 'I don't see many people. I help out at the

hospital and at the school, mainly with Sam's class. I haven't seen Fran much; I think she avoids me, but I don't know why. Of course, she could just be caught up with being a mother.'

Alfie lowered his eyelashes. 'I expect she's a good mother, although I understand she's not married?'

Rosie's lips tightened. 'No, I don't think she's married.'

Alfie smiled. 'I bet that went down well with the old dears round here.'

Rosie scowled at him. 'It's not funny, people have given her hell and made her feel ashamed, so now she just locks herself away.'

Alfie looked sheepish. 'I'm sorry, you're right, it's not funny, but it could have been you if you hadn't sent me away on my last night.'

Rosie blushed. 'I didn't send you away, you walked away because I wouldn't give you what you wanted. If I remember correctly, you left me in tears without a backward glance, and all because I wouldn't let you do it against the wall in a side street. I've been brought up to believe my first time should be better than that.'

Alfie ran his hand across the stubble on his chin. 'You're right, but that might have been my only chance to be with you, and I wanted that so much.'

Rosie shook her head. 'I will not feel guilty Alfie. Everyone knows you see yourself as a ladies' man and I had no intention of being left in Fran's position, let alone bringing the shame on my family.'

Alfie chuckled. 'Your family would have been pleased; I'm a great catch.'

Rosie stared at him. 'The trouble is Alfie, you're the only one who thinks so.'

Alfie ran his fingers over his chin again before smiling. 'It's only a guess, but something tells me you're really mad at me.'

* * *

Rosie stood inside Fran's building, the rain forming a pool on the floor as it dripped off her. She stepped onto the doormat outside Fran's front door, trying to shake the raindrops from her coat before taking her white handkerchief out of her pocket to dab at her damp face. She looked back at the closed door of the building; maybe that should have been left open to let some fresh air in and blow the awful lingering stench out. Rosie wasn't even sure what it was that was causing it, but couldn't wait to get outside again. Taking a breath, she grimaced as she thumped hard on Fran's door before thrusting the handkerchief back into her coat pocket. She pulled off her small, brimmed hat and shook it, letting the drops of rain fall off. Was that what was causing the smell? Was it damp? Rosie sighed, guilt spreading through her as she realised she should have done that outside; her mother would have told her off had she done it at home. Rosie patted down her damp hair before knocking on the door again; as she expected, there was no response. Leaning forward, she put her ear to the door, but couldn't hear anything at all. If Fran was out, where did she go every day with a child, and if she was going out, why wouldn't she see her? Perhaps she should go to the police; maybe something had happened to her and the baby. She could ask Alice's husband to knock to make sure Fran was all right. Rosie shook her head; she was getting carried away with herself.

The main door swung open, and an elderly lady stood watching Rosie as the drips of rain ran down her face. Her grey hair was soaked and plastered flat to her head. Her patched coat had seen better days as it clung to her body. She rubbed her hand peered out at the wet pavements, thankful it had finally stopped raining. She glanced back. 'Thank you.'

The lady nodded and waved as she carried on up the stairs.

Rosie placed her hat back on her head and stepped outside, pulling the door closed after her. She was beginning to think she was never going to have a conversation with Fran – and who was this man? Was he the baby's father and if so, why hadn't they got married? Especially as it sounded like she clearly loved him?

* * *

Rosie strolled alongside her mother as they walked along Mortimer Street from Middlesex Hospital. She pulled at her black woollen scarf, lifting it to cover the back of her neck. 'It might be the end of April, but the evenings are still cold.'

'The evenings are cold but hopefully summer will soon be upon us.' Ivy glanced across at her daughter. 'I haven't had a chance to ask you, how did it go with Alfie? Are you going to go out with him now he's home?'

Rosie tightened her lips; she had known her mother wouldn't be able to not ask. 'I don't think he wants to leave his ma's house, or at least not go too far, so he will either come to us or I'm to go there.'

Ivy frowned. 'That's strange, I would have thought he'd want to make the most of being home, you know – visit a public house, the theatre or something.'

Rosie sighed. 'I don't know, Ma, war changes people.' She hesitated. 'He didn't want to talk about his lack of letters to let us know he was all right. In fact, I got the feeling he wasn't concerned about it at all, which I find a bit worrying.'

Ivy nodded. 'I know what you mean, but maybe he has seen such things that writing letters home seemed trivial.'

across her cheeks before narrowing her eyes. 'What are you doing here? You don't live in this building; I know everyone who lives here.'

Rosie stepped nervously to one side. 'I'm looking for my friend Fran, Fran Wilson.'

The lady stared at her. 'She's not here, she went out early with that young lad of hers and her man friend.'

Rosie frowned. 'Man friend?'

The lady lifted her head. 'You ain't that much of a friend, otherwise you'd know about him; best you get out of here.' She pulled the door open. The rain splashed through the doorway.

Rosie bit her lip, trying to ignore the open door. 'Do you know what the man looked like? I don't mean to be rude, but Fran has kept him a secret and I'm curious about why she would do that.'

The lady studied her for a moment. 'I don't know what I can tell you. Let's see, he's taller than her and she looks up at him with an adoring look of love.'

Rosie's eyes widened. 'Do you know if she's known him long?'

The lady tilted her head to one side. 'I think he's been around for a couple of years, maybe longer than that, but I can't be certain about the time. Lately, there's been a couple of men looking for Fran, but I don't know why she's suddenly got popular. Anyway, I'm not going to stand around gossiping about Fran, she's a lovely girl and deserves better than that.'

Rosie nodded. 'Of course, you're right, I'm sorry. Please can I ask you, if you see her, to tell her Rosie was here and she misses her.'

The lady let go of the open door and shuffled nearer to the stairs. 'I will but I don't know when I'll see her.'

Rosie stepped towards the front door, opening it again. She

'That could be so, but you and I both know from our own experience at the hospital that the men look forward to the letters and parcels from home; actually, they not only look forward to them, they need to know their loved ones are well.'

Ivy shook her head. 'It does seem strange but I'm sure he'll have his reasons and he'll talk about it when he's ready.'

They walked on in silence for a moment, the darkness of the night with the unlit streets wrapping around them both.

Ivy peered over her shoulder. 'I hate the dark streets, especially when it's this late, but I suppose with a small moon we have less chance of being bombed by the Germans.'

'That's true, Ma.' Rosie pulled her close. 'It's all right, I'll protect you.' They both burst out laughing. 'I was thinking I'm probably going to have to step back from helping out at the hospital while Alfie's home, especially as he hasn't said how long he'll be home for. I don't want to, but I need to be realistic; there aren't enough hours in the day to fit in the school, Foyles, seeing Alfie and working at the hospital.'

Ivy squeezed her arm. 'I understand, and I'm sure the hospital will too. I don't think there's a shortage of volunteers, so don't worry.'

'I will come and meet you so you're not walking home by yourself.' Rosie frowned. 'I promise I'll be back once Alfie returns to the front.'

Ivy stared out into the darkness. 'I assume Alfie hasn't been injured. He didn't look like he had, but you never can tell, and of course there's always what happens to the mind. At night, we often have men waking up screaming; they have nightmares about it all, which isn't that surprising.'

Rosie tilted her head a little. 'Maybe that's why he doesn't want to talk about it. I've been a bit harsh on him because that hadn't occurred to me.'

Ivy nodded. 'Yes, he could be trying to save you from hearing all about it.'

Rosie raised her eyebrows. 'Well, unless he's a totally different man, I can't see him enjoying staying indoors with Mr and Mrs Bennet all the time; he used to say they drove him mad.'

Ivy laughed. 'I expect that was true once, but as we know this war has changed everyone, and the men coming home in particular.'

Rosie peered at her mother. 'Then there's Fran. I went round to her place earlier and an old lady who lives in the same building told me she went out for the day with her child and a tall man. Apparently, she gazes up at him with adoring eyes and yet she still won't let me into her life.'

Ivy shrugged. 'I expect she has her reasons. After all, she was always a bit flighty. I'm surprised you didn't get into trouble with her as your friend.'

Shaking her head, Rosie glared at her mother. 'Ma, don't say things like that, we never got into any trouble.'

'No, but when she did, she really did.' Ivy paused. 'She doesn't help herself because she won't name the father; she's a silly girl.'

Rosie studied her mother in the darkness. 'But you brought us up to have faith in the Lord, and yet here you are judging her and finding her lacking. When actually it has nothing to do with anyone else; it's not a wonder Fran shuts herself away. For goodness' sake, she doesn't have to tell anybody anything if she doesn't want to, including me.'

11

Victoria walked into the staff area at the back of Foyles Bookshop. She pulled out a chair and sat at the table with Ellen and Rosie. 'Hello, girls, I'm glad it's lunchtime; I'm starving.' She placed her paper-wrapped fish paste sandwiches down on the table in front of her. 'How has your morning been?'

Ellen laughed. 'As busy as always, although I do enjoy working behind a counter and chatting to the customers.'

Rosie reached out and squeezed Ellen's hand. 'I can't believe it was only a few weeks ago that we had that run-in with the spy; I must admit I'm glad the police were around, and Albert wasn't hurt.'

Ellen nodded. 'It feels like it was a lifetime ago and I'm glad it's over with.'

Victoria was beaming from ear to ear. 'Are you and John still stepping out?'

Ellen blushed. 'Yes, we are.'

Rosie clapped her hands. 'Do you think it's serious?'

Ellen's colour deepened. 'I believe so; my family adore him, so that's always a step in the right direction.'

Victoria watched the two girls as they chatted. 'I take it you feel the same.'

Ellen blushed. 'I do.'

Molly dropped her lunch on the table and pulled out a chair. 'I think I'll join you, you all seem very happy, and I thought for a moment I was missing out on some news.' Her gaze travelled to Ellen. 'You weren't practising your wedding vows, were you?'

Ellen's eyes widened. 'No.' She giggled. 'And I'd rather the attention moved away from me, thank you.'

They all laughed.

Molly's eyes held a hint of mischief in them when she turned to Victoria. 'From what I hear, you've been grinning like a Cheshire cat all morning, so come on, what's the news? Well, actually, I can guess the news so maybe I should say, when is it?'

Colour crept up Victoria's neck as she fidgeted in her chair. 'It's going to be in June; we're going to see the vicar later to confirm the date.'

The girls around the small table squealed with delight. Others in the room glanced over their shoulders to see what all the commotion was about.

Molly looked around at their smiling faces. 'I'm going to tell you all, because Victoria won't.' She glanced at her friend who nodded. 'She's getting married.'

Everyone in the room cheered and clapped; some came over and gave Victoria a hug.

Mr Leadbetter poked his head round the door and looked at Victoria. 'I take it everyone knows now?'

Victoria giggled. 'Yes, thanks to Molly.'

Molly pulled herself upright and her gaze travelled between Mr Leadbetter and Victoria. She frowned. 'Wait, are you saying Mr Leadbetter knew before your best friends?'

Giving Molly a sheepish look, she said, 'Yes, but not because I told him; he guessed.'

Molly laughed. 'Well, good for you, sir. I had heard she'd been grinning all morning.'

Mr Leadbetter chuckled before waving and leaving their chatter and laughter behind him.

Rosie smiled as she watched the happiness that was all around her and wondered if that would be her, one day soon.

Molly clasped Victoria's hand. 'So, we'll need to go wedding dress shopping soon.'

Ellen beamed. 'How exciting; are you having bridesmaids?'

Victoria grinned. 'It will be my sister Daisy, along with Alice and Molly. We've been friends for as long as I can remember, we're almost family.'

Rosie unwrapped her sandwich, the paper crunching as she smoothed out the creases with the palm of her hand. 'Ellen's right, it is exciting and it's lovely to have something to look forward to.'

Victoria studied Rosie for a moment. 'It is, and I'm sure if Alfie is back, it won't be long before you are having the same conversation.' She smiled at the two young girls. 'I know you haven't been here very long, but I hope you will both come to my wedding and bring your boyfriends.'

Rosie gasped. 'I don't know what to say.' She glanced across at Ellen. 'Except it would be an honour, and I'm sure Ellen feels the same.'

Ellen's eyes lit up, her excitement taking over as she clapped her hands together. 'I would love to come, and I'll ask John if he would like to accompany me.'

Molly giggled at their excitement before turning to Victoria. 'We should have been in Monico's having tea and cake with Alice for this announcement.'

Victoria chuckled. 'I don't think I would call it an announcement…'

'What 'ave I missed? What's the announcement?' Albert beamed as he opened the basement door and strode into the staff area. 'Whatever it is it must be good, yer all look 'appy.'

Victoria's eyes were sparkling at everyone's infectious mood. 'It wasn't an announcement, Albert, it's more like everyone guessed about me and Ted deciding to get married, so I had no option but to let the cat out of the bag.'

Molly grinned. 'That may well be true, but it means we need to go round and see Alice to discuss when we can all go shopping for your dress, and of course ours as well. Have you decided on what style you are going to have and what colours you want for us?'

Victoria shook her head. 'I don't want to dampen everyone's excitement but I'm afraid I don't have a lot of money to spend on the wedding.'

'You're as cautious as ever.' Molly laughed. 'I'm sure Daisy will want to help as well.'

Victoria's eyes hooded over as she shook her head. 'Why do I get the feeling it's already running away from me – and that's before Alice or my family in Brighton get involved.'

Albert stepped forward and wrapped his arms around Victoria. 'I'm so 'appy for yer, it couldn't 'appen to a better person, congratulations. Yer wait 'til I tell the missus, she'll be over the moon for yer.'

Victoria squeezed Albert tight. 'I hope you'll both come.'

Albert laughed. 'Yer can't keep inviting everyone; remember, it all costs money, but we'll definitely come to the church. You deserve to be 'appy.'

* * *

Rosie absently stirred the tea in her cup, staring into the swirling brown liquid. The rustling of the waitress's long black skirt and the clip of her shoes as she walked between tables went unnoticed.

'It's lovely to see you in a summer dress and jacket, that pale blue really suits you. I've got used to seeing you in the Foyles uniform of black skirt and white blouse.' Sam sipped at his hot drink. He peered at Rosie as his cup chinked down on the matching saucer. 'Are you all right? You look deep in thought.'

Startled, Rosie forced a smile. 'You're very good with the children at school; they clearly look up to you.'

Sam chuckled. 'Thank you for saying so but that's not what you were thinking about.'

Rosie tilted her head. 'You don't know that.'

Sam studied her for a moment. 'That's just it, I think I do. You were miles away and wherever you were, they weren't happy thoughts.' He hesitated before leaning back on the wooden chair. 'Dare I ask, were you thinking about Alfie or Fran?'

Rosie raised her eyebrows. 'I've thought about Fran so much it's a wonder I can still go about my day-to-day living. Her ignoring me hurts because I don't know what I've done wrong, and trust me, I've thought about it long and hard, but I've come up with nothing that deserves this form of punishment. I've been back to her place several times but she doesn't open the door. Do you think she's making money in a way that she's ashamed of?'

'What, you mean on the game?'

Rosie could feel heat burning her cheeks. 'I'm almost certain I heard a man's voice when she shut the door telling me it wasn't a good time. I know she's trapped in her situation and must be at her wits' end trying to work out how to survive, but surely she wouldn't do that kind of work with James there, would she?'

Sam shrugged. 'I suppose it depends on how desperate she becomes; as you say, she must feel she has no one or nowhere to turn to.'

'But why wouldn't she turn to us, her friends, before doing that kind of work?' Rosie shook her head. 'I can't be certain; I mean, I heard mumbling so I can't be sure if it was even a man or a woman.'

Sam sighed. 'You would think so, but she hasn't turned to us at all in the last couple of years; she's obviously too proud to ask for help.'

Rosie stared hard at the white tablecloth; she smoothed her hand over the creases. 'I don't understand any of it, I'm obviously missing something important.'

Sam nodded. 'Well, I think we both are, and unless Fran wants to tell us what it is, then we're just guessing all the time.'

'It's all such a mess.' Rosie gave a wry smile. 'You know, I sometimes think Alfie's still angry with me for not giving him what he wanted after our day in Southend. I've never spoken about it to anybody before, but he kept telling me he didn't want to die without doing it with me.'

Sam squeezed her hand. 'You don't have to talk about it now, I don't want to know. It was enough that I found you sobbing after he had left you.'

Rosie gave a half smile. 'I was so grateful you came back to make sure I was all right.'

Sam shook his head. 'It was luck, and my instinct that something wasn't right. I had been walking slowly, not sure whether to go straight home or not, and that's when I saw him pacing towards me; he looked quite angry, and he was mumbling to himself.' He frowned. 'I stepped into someone's doorway so he couldn't see me and then I went back to find you.'

Rosie studied Sam for a moment. 'I'm glad you did; I'll never forget your kindness that night. It's hard to believe you are brothers.'

Sam hesitated. 'I was hoping we could go out together one evening, maybe to the theatre or the pictures; what do you think?'

'And what about Alfie?'

Sam laughed. 'Well, Alfie will do whatever Alfie wants.'

Rosie shook her head. 'That is true.'

Sam watched the sadness flick across Rosie's face. 'But you have a say in your own future.' He picked up his tea and gulped a mouthful of the hot liquid.

Rosie picked up her own cup, wrapping her fingers around it. 'You have spent more time with Alfie than I have, so tell me what you think his plans are.'

Sam shrugged. 'I have no idea, and I'd be the last person he would tell.'

Rosie sat in silence for a few minutes.

Sam rested his hand on top of hers. 'How long are you going to give Alfie?' He watched the conflict run across her face and took a breath. 'Look, this might not be the right time, but I want you to know I'm here for you and you're very important to me, which I'm hoping you've realised by now.'

'Thank you for asking about the pictures but I don't think it would be a good idea.' Rosie licked her lips. 'Alfie's home and I need to have a proper conversation with him about our future. Your ma is expecting us to get married and she will be very upset if we decide not to.'

Sam lowered his lashes. 'Yes, she has already mentioned it to Alfie.'

Rosie pulled herself upright on her chair. 'What did he say?'

'He refused to talk about it.'

* * *

Sam sat down on the bed in the room he shared with Alfie. The evening was closing in. He stared at his brother as he lay on his own bed reading a newspaper. A large mug of tea stood on his bedside table. He thought about the cup of tea he'd had with Rosie earlier. Frowning, Sam knew he had to keep his feelings in check while he was talking to his brother. 'So, Alfie, are you going to tell me why you chose not to write to Ma and Rosie to let them know you were safe?'

The newspaper rustled as Alfie turned the page over, but he didn't look up.

Sam shook his head. 'Did you not think they would be worried about you? Rosie had promised to wait for you, and she didn't know whether you were dead or alive; and Ma had a telegram that said you were missing in action, and Pa was convinced he was never going to see you again. Why didn't you write to them?'

Alfie dropped the newspaper on to his lap and stretched to reach his tea; he took a slurp of the hot dark liquid. He replaced his cup and stared at his brother but never said a word. He picked his paper up; it crackled as he folded it in half and resumed his reading.

Sam's lips tightened. 'Are you just going to ignore me?'

Alfie peered over the top of his paper. 'I am trying to read the news.' He lowered his head again, partially hiding his face.

Reaching out, Sam grabbed the newspaper and pulled it down. 'You can read that once I've gone to work; you can't keep avoiding everyone and their questions.'

'Can't I? I think you'll find I can do what I like.'

Anger surged through Sam. 'You've always been arrogant, but now you are taking it to a whole new level.'

A smile slowly crept across Alfie's face. 'This has nothing to do with me not writing to anyone; this is about you and Rosie, isn't it? You're still carrying that torch for her, aren't you? I bet you still look at her with those lovesick eyes, too.'

Sam clenched his fists, fighting the urge to thump his brother.

Alfie reached out for his tea again. 'You do know you're wasting your time with her, don't you?' He took another gulp of his drink before resting the cup on his bedside table. 'You should be thanking me for keeping you away from her; she's not as much fun as you think she is.'

Sam closed his eyes for a moment. He took a calming breath before snapping them open again. 'I don't know what you're talking about. You know she sobbed when you left her in the alley near the train station the night before you went away, but you don't seem to care about that.'

Alfie shook his head. 'Look at the opportunity I gave you. I bet you loved comforting her, didn't you? You'd waited a long time to hold her in your arms, but I would guess you haven't done it since, have you? You made yourself a laughing stock the way you followed her around when what she wanted was a real man and not a boy.'

'You don't care about Rosie at all, otherwise you wouldn't talk about her like that, and you wouldn't have stormed off that night while she cried.'

Alfie gave a bitter laugh. 'I gave Rosie a lot of my time and attention, but you know what, even though I said I might never come back, that I might die, she wouldn't give out. She told me she wanted to wait until her wedding night; who does that these days?'

Sam's eyes narrowed. 'Rosie does what she thinks is right and that is something to be admired.'

Alfie laughed. 'I knew you'd say something ridiculous like

that. It doesn't matter now; I used my charms elsewhere and ended up having a good night.'

Sam shook his head. 'Alfie, life isn't all about you, can't you see that?'

'I was going off to war, so yes, it *was* all about me. You have no idea what it's like on the front line.'

For a moment, Sam looked ashamed. 'I know I don't, and I'm sure it's awful, but you had no idea before you went and yet you still tried to use the situation to your own ends.'

Alfie nodded. 'And luckily for me not all girls think the same as Rosie.'

'I can't believe you. If you'd seen what Fran has been through, I'd like to think you'd have different thoughts about it all.'

Alfie frowned. 'What do you mean "what Fran has been through"?'

Sam studied his brother for a moment. 'You have no idea, do you? Her family don't want to know her; she was kicked out with hardly anything to her name and with a baby. She's been on her own. She's an unmarried mother and there's no respect or the usual love that comes automatically from others when a woman has a baby. She's had no support. Fran won't tell anyone the name of the father and that seemed to make it all worse; she's been the subject of gossip – hurtful gossip at that. She locks herself away in that awful building where she lives. She won't even see Rosie, and they were best friends. Rosie's worrying about how she's managing for money. It breaks her heart to think she might be begging or turning to prostitution.'

'But why was she a subject of gossip?'

Sam sucked in his breath. 'Are you not listening to me? She got pregnant. She managed to hide it for a while so everyone was shocked when she had her son, James.'

Alfie stared down at the crumpled newspaper.

Sam shook his head. 'As I said, Fran won't tell anyone who the father is, which is another reason why she's treated like a leper. She's protecting the father over herself. It's terrible and when I saw her last, she looked very pale and thin so I'm not sure how she's managing for money. I can't see how she's going to get out of the situation without moving away and pretending her husband died in the war.'

Alfie picked up his newspaper again. 'Maybe the father has been providing for them? That's if she's told him about the boy.'

Sam bit down on his lip. 'Then why is she hiding away from Rosie?'

Alfie shrugged. 'Who knows? That's women for you; you shouldn't try and understand them.'

* * *

Ivy gave her daughter a sideways look.

Rosie vigorously stirred the gravy, the spoon clanging against the inside of the stainless-steel saucepan.

'You're very quiet tonight, Rosie, is everything all right?'

'Yes, Ma, everything is fine.' Rosie frowned as she gave the gravy a final stir. 'Shall I pour this into a jug?'

Sighing, Ivy peered over Rosie's shoulder. 'Yes, it looks fine. Go and call your grandma and David to the table.'

Ivy frowned as she watched her daughter leave the kitchen. She wished she knew what was going on. She was sure it had something to do with Alfie, but what? Did he want to get married before he went back to the front line, and she didn't? Maybe she didn't want to marry him at all? Perhaps she had met someone else, or could it be Sam? Ivy wasn't convinced about that; after all, would Rosie want to come between the brothers? She needed to get Rosie to talk to her and make her realise that she was only concerned with her daughter's happiness. Opening the oven door wide, Ivy stooped down and pulled the vegetable pie from the oven. She placed it at the centre of the table next to the bowl of mashed potato and the jug of gravy just as David came running into the kitchen. 'Stop, David, how many times do you have to be told not to run into the kitchen? You'll end up getting burnt. And where are your slippers?'

David looked sheepishly at his mother. 'Sorry, Ma, I'm starving, and I don't know what I did with them.'

Ivy shook her head. 'You're always hungry.'

Mary chuckled as she hobbled into the kitchen. 'He's a growing lad.' She pulled a wooden chair out from the tired old table; its legs scraped along the floor, causing Ivy to wince. 'Would you like me to cut up the pie?'

Ivy nodded. 'I'm afraid it's only vegetables. It's hard to know what to cook for dinner these days.'

Rosie pulled out a chair and sat down. She took a dinner plate for her brother and began spooning mashed potato on to it before passing it to her gran for the portion of pie.

It wasn't long before they were all sitting and tucking into their meals.

Mary leant back on the hard slats of the chair. 'I don't think I've ever known a meal to be eaten in such silence.' She glanced around the table. 'David, you normally talk non-stop so what's happened to make you so quiet?'

David peered up at his grandmother; his eyes began to fill with tears. 'My friend wasn't in school today, so I knocked to see if he's ill or something.' He paused and bit down on his lip. 'When I spoke to him... he told me his ma had a telegram saying his brother had died...' He sniffed. 'They said he died a hero.'

Rosie rested her hand on David's and squeezed it tight.

Ivy gasped. 'I'm so sorry, David, I expect the family are all very sad.'

David nodded. 'He didn't want his brother to be a hero... he wanted him to come home... he misses – missed him. He talks about him every day.'

Mary nodded. 'You know, David, he's going to need a friend more than ever now so make sure you are there for him; even if you don't know what to say, it's good to let him talk.' She shook her head. 'It's a very sad day for them and not one they will forget in a hurry.'

A tear tripped down David's cheek. 'I'm glad I don't have a brother.'

Rosie lifted David's hand to her lips. 'And we're glad you're not old enough to go to war, it's not as glamorous as you think it is.' She kissed his hand.

David shook his head. 'But I've sneaked into the picture house and watched the Pathé News.' He hesitated for a moment. 'That shows men standing in the trenches smiling, laughing and smoking cigarettes. It doesn't look scary at all.'

Ivy scraped back her chair. 'Firstly, David, you shouldn't be sneaking into the pictures; the Pathé News isn't for children to watch. Secondly, they aren't going to show our men being killed, if only because they want more to join up. If I find out you have been in there again you won't be allowed to leave the house, and I'll be picking you up from school if you can't be trusted.'

David lowered his head. 'Yes, Ma, I'm sorry.'

Ivy walked round and ruffled David's hair. 'Well, there's no point in me keeping on at you but I mean everything I say.' She stooped down next to his chair. 'Are you all right? This is the first person, other than your father, that you know to die because of the war.'

David nodded. 'It's just so sad to think his family won't see or speak to him ever again.'

'I know.' Ivy pulled herself up. She glanced across at Rosie and wondered why she was so quiet, but now was not the time to ask again.

12

Rosie wrinkled her nose at the stench that surrounded her; maybe something had died in the building and hadn't been discovered. How did Fran survive in such a place? Opening her handbag, she rummaged around inside before pulling out her handkerchief and placing it over her mouth and nose. Shaking her head, Rosie didn't remember the smell being that bad when she'd come before. She glanced over her shoulder before peering up the stairs but there was no one around, so she turned back to Fran's front door. Taking a step nearer and tucking her hair behind her ears, she pressed herself up against it, straining to hear any signs of movement, but there was nothing. Taking a breath through the handkerchief, Rosie lifted her hand and rapped hard on the wood. After a few minutes she stepped nearer to the main door of the building. She opened it and squinted in the early morning light as she peered up and down the street in the mist that shrouded it, but there was no sign of Fran. She turned back into the building; surely she wouldn't be out this early with a small child. She stepped closer to Fran's door and knocked again. 'Fran, I'm going to keep coming back until you at least talk to me.'

Rosie listened, but there was only silence. She opened her handbag again and retrieved an envelope with Fran's name on it. 'Fran, I've written a note and I'm pushing it under your door. Please read it, it's been a while and I miss you. I'll come back soon and then maybe we can talk.' She bent down and pushed the envelope through the small gap under the door. 'Please read it, Fran, we need to talk.' She stood up straight and smoothed down her black skirt. 'I have to go to work but I'll be back.' Pulling her woollen jacket closer, Rosie stared at the door, hoping it would open and Fran would be standing there, pleased to see her, but it stayed shut. Shaking her head, she felt foolish talking to Fran's front door, especially if there was no one on the other side of it, but what else could she do? Sighing, she turned round and let herself out of the building. She stared down at the pavement as she paced along the road; perhaps she should give up on Fran. After all, she clearly didn't want to speak to her, for whatever reason. But it always came back to the same question: why? Distracted, she walked headlong into someone coming the other way.

'I'm so sorry.'

Stumbling, Rosie felt a strong hand grip her arm. She looked up at an older grey-haired man in a suit. 'No, it was my fault. I'm afraid I wasn't looking where I was going.'

The man smiled. 'As long as you're all right.'

Rosie cleared her throat. 'Yes, I am, thank you.'

The man nodded, tipped his hat, and immediately strode away from her.

Rosie's hands curled around her middle as her embarrassment took hold. She felt the heat of a flush creeping across her cheeks as she looked around her to see if anyone had noticed her bumping into the man and him saving her from a fall.

That's when she saw him. She gasped; was that Alfie turning into a road nearby? Taking a breath, she began to pace after him but as she rounded the corner there was no sign of him. She scanned the street, moving one way then another to see men's faces. Where had he gone? Perhaps it wasn't him. Was she going round the bend? Her stomach was churning, and something was niggling at her, but she didn't know what. She needed to talk to someone who wouldn't tell her she had to stop trying to see Fran and marry Alfie, regardless of her feelings about him. She was missing something – something important – and she was sure once she discovered that, everything would become clear. She knew in her heart she couldn't let it go.

* * *

Victoria and Rosie pulled out the racks of books, placing them carefully under the Foyles awning. Victoria looked around her. 'It's not nine o'clock yet and there are already so many people around.' As she spoke, potential customers were checking the books on the shelving. She glanced up to the grey sky as spots of rain began to fall. 'By the looks of things, it's going to be another miserable day; let's get inside before the heavens open up.'

Molly came pacing along the pavement. 'Thank goodness I made it on time. I thought I was going to be late. Andrew and I overslept this morning; I hope he won't be late getting to work.'

Victoria smiled. 'Well, you're not late but you better get yourself clocked in otherwise you'll lose some pay.'

Molly nodded and rushed into the shop, waving as she went.

Victoria shook her head; it was unusual for Molly to arrive so flustered; she'd check that everything was all right later.

Rosie's gaze followed Molly, but she looked back at Victoria in time to see a shadow of a worry cross her face. 'I'm sure everything is all right; we all have days that start off better than others.'

Victoria smiled. 'Of course.' She looked slightly sheepish. 'Have you managed to see much of Alfie since he's been home?'

Rosie's body immediately tensed.

Victoria reached out and placed her hand on Rosie's arm. 'I'm sorry, I shouldn't have asked.'

Rosie frowned. 'It's not that, it's just I don't understand what's going on with him. Apparently, he's shut himself away and isn't really seeing anyone.'

Sighing, Victoria was tight-lipped for a moment. 'It's this damn war – excuse my language – but it has a lot to answer for. If you give him some space, things might improve.' She paused. 'It isn't always good to have time on your hands; the mind can run away with itself and cause all kinds of problems.'

Rosie lowered her eyes. 'I don't see I have much choice; I just have to wait until he wants to talk about us and our future together.'

'As Molly would say, "you do have a choice; you could take control" and not allow him to make all the decisions. In fact, I think even Albert would say he sees us as his family and would do anything to look after us all.' Victoria watched as Rosie's eyes snapped open. 'I mean, do you want to marry him?'

Rosie closed her eyes and took a deep breath. 'That's just it, I don't think I do, but I'm torn because of the promise I made and let's face it, I wouldn't look very nice if I pulled out of it. You can hear it now: "Alfie's just got back from the war to be dumped by his fiancée." The gossips would have a field day with it all.'

Victoria raised her eyebrows. 'How you look to others will be short-lived against being married for fifty years to the wrong man, but it's a decision only you can make.' She hesitated for a moment. 'You know my sister, Daisy, used to follow what the suffragettes were doing and yes, the obvious thing was women getting the vote, but she also took away from it all about freedom. The freedom of choice, and that includes not just marrying because it's what someone else thinks you should do; it has to be right for you as well, because you're important too.'

Rosie nodded. 'I remember speaking to Ellen about her ma, and she told me her ma always said they should marry for love, and she wanted them to think for themselves and make their own decisions.' She paused. 'The trouble is, my ma has never talked about that kind of thing and she believes your word is everything, so I would be letting everyone down.'

'Miss Appleton.'

Victoria glanced over her shoulder at Mr Leadbetter, before turning to Rosie. 'I'm sure all your ma would want is for you to be happy; isn't that what all mothers want? Maybe you need to talk to her.'

Rosie nodded. 'Maybe you're right; thank you, I will.'

Victoria smiled. 'I'm sorry, I don't want to, but I have to go – but I'm here if you want to talk.'

Rosie smiled as she saw Mr Leadbetter walking towards them. 'Thank you, I had better get to work as well before Mr Leadbetter wants to know why I'm not at my counter.'

Victoria laughed. 'Don't worry, I'll tell him I was asking how you were getting on.'

* * *

Rosie picked up the tea towel, stopping to think about her conversation with Victoria that morning, before taking a dinner plate off the draining-board. She slowly began to run the drying cloth over it. 'Gran, do you think people should always follow their heart when making decisions?'

Mary stopped washing the dish in the kitchen sink and rested her arms on the edge. 'That's a difficult one to answer.'

Rosie frowned. 'Why?'

Mary began rubbing the dishcloth around the dish; the water swished back and forth. 'Well, it depends on the decision that has to be made.'

Rosie silently placed the dry plate on the table before picking up another one.

Mary glanced across at her granddaughter and pulled herself upright. 'I know it's not the answer you were looking for, but it's an honest one.'

Picking up another wet plate, Rosie shrugged. 'I suppose I already knew that and was hoping for something else.'

Mary frowned as she put the dish on the draining-board. 'You need to talk about the decision you think you have to make – if not with me, then with someone you trust.'

Without saying a word, Rosie carried on drying the dinner things.

Mary pulled the plug in the sink and watched the water slowly drain away, her hand rotating the water as it disappeared. She picked up a small towel from the worktop and dried her hands. 'Do you want to talk about it?' She studied Rosie. 'Is it about Alfie?'

Rosie sighed. 'It's not just about Alfie, although I am concerned about marrying a man I don't think I love. Someone said to me I should follow my heart, but I don't think it's as simple as that.'

Mary stared down at the towel and carried on rubbing her hands with it. 'Have you spoken to your ma about this?'

'I haven't spoken to anyone about it, until now that is.'

Mary looked up. 'Why now? And why is the thought of marriage disturbing you so much? If it's your wedding night...'

'It isn't.' Colour flooded Rosie's cheeks.

Mary smiled at her embarrassment. 'It's nothing to worry about, and you'll have to keep your man happy at least once a week; it's a woman's duty to put her man's needs above her own. You have to look on it like ironing; it's a chore that has to be done every week.'

Rosie raised her voice. 'Gran, it's not that, and I don't really want to talk about it.'

Mary held up her hand. 'All right, I'm just trying to help.'

'Well, you're not.' Rosie glared at her gran, then seeing the hurt flicker across her face, said 'I'm sorry, I shouldn't have raised my voice like that.' She sucked in her breath. 'There are two girls at Foyles who will probably be getting married this year and you can see their happiness; they are clearly in love. They have a look when they talk about it, you know, a spring in their step and they are all smiles. I don't have such feelings of joy when I think about marrying Alfie.' A shadow crossed her face as she thought about how disappointed Mrs Bennet would be if she called it all off; could she do that to her?

Mary nodded. 'You probably need to get to know him again.'

Rosie looked thoughtful for a moment. 'I expect that's it.' She glanced at her grandmother. 'Go and sit yourself down and I'll bring you in a cup of tea.'

Mary frowned. 'You know we all want you to be happy, so if Alfie isn't the man for you then your ma will understand. She will probably worry you are making the wrong decision, but she'll get over it.'

Rosie smiled as she leant forward and kissed her grandmother on the cheek. 'Thank you, now go and sit down and don't worry about it all, it's probably just cold feet now he's home.' She watched her gran leave the kitchen before turning on the tap to fill up the kettle.

'Rosie, you're getting water everywhere.'

Startled at her brother's loud voice, Rosie quickly turned off the tap.

David ran to her. 'What's happened?'

Rosie raised her eyebrows. 'Nothing has happened; what makes you think something has?'

David waved his hands around. 'I came in to talk to you, but you were in a world of your own because you didn't answer me and then the water spilled over the top of the kettle.' He frowned. 'Is Ma all right?'

Rosie put the kettle down and rested her hands on David's arms. 'Of course. She's at work; you know Ma sometimes works late in the evenings.'

David stared down at the floor.

Rosie placed her finger under his chin and lifted it up. 'I'm sorry if I frightened you, I was just deep in thought, but none of it is for you to worry about.' She suddenly realised David had been quieter and at home more since his friend's brother had died. 'Is your friend back at school now?'

David shook his head.

Rosie studied him for a moment. 'Have you been round to see him?'

David shook his head again. 'I don't know what to say to him; if Pa had been here, I would have asked him what I should do.'

Rosie stooped down; her tears didn't feel far away as she looked at his tired red eyes. She blinked quickly. 'I know it's hard, but you just have to let him know you're there as his friend if he wants to talk about his brother or anything else.' She took a breath. 'It's hard to explain but sometimes when people die, others stay away from the family because they don't know what to say, and they are frightened to mention the person who died because they don't want to upset them, when actually they want to hear that person's name.' She paused as she studied her brother. 'Does that make sense?'

David nodded. 'Do you think I should go and see him then?'

Rosie thought for a moment. 'Do you want to see him? It might be difficult for you and for him. I mean, there might be tears and he might need a man hug from you.'

David pondered for a moment. 'I can do that; I'll go and see him tomorrow.'

Rosie wrapped her arms around her little brother; he was growing up into a kind young man. 'I'm very proud of you for caring about him so much, and Pa would have been too. Don't forget if you want to talk about it, or anything else, just come and find me.' She kissed the top of his head.

* * *

Sam frowned as he peered down at the brown envelope his mother was holding.

Mrs Bennet remained motionless as she too stared down at it before giving it to him. 'Please God, don't tell me they're your call-up papers.' Her voice became very high-pitched. 'Please, I pray they will not take my second son as well.'

Alfie shook his head. 'I'm here, Ma, and we all have to do our bit, you know; it's now Sam's turn.' He studied his younger brother. 'You have no idea what it's like in the waterlogged trenches with rats at your feet, and that's without seeing men being shot or blown up all around you.'

Sam scowled at his brother. 'You mean unlike you, the big brother who always does what's right.'

Alfie jumped up from his armchair. 'Don't try it with me because you'll lose, just like you've done your whole life.'

Mrs Bennet looked from one to the other. 'Stop, I don't know what's going on but I'm not listening to this again. There were all kinds going on between you before this awful war started, and I didn't understand then and I don't understand now. It's about time you both grew up and started acting like men, which is about more than arguing over nonsense, getting into fights and going off to war.'

Stunned, Sam held his mother's gaze, momentarily wondering whether he should tell her how his older brother made his life hell.

Alfie smiled. 'It's simple, Ma, your little boy here never had the courage to stand up and be counted, not even where the ladies are concerned.'

Mrs Bennet looked over at her husband, who shrugged his indifference. 'Don't just shrug; you're their father, you should be sorting this mess out, whatever this is.'

Sam frowned at his mother. 'I'll tell you what this is, Ma; your brave little soldier here is in hiding, aren't you, Alfie?'

Alfie clenched his hands. 'As per usual you don't know what you're talking about.' He stared at Sam before curling his lip. 'I got a chance to come home and see Pa, so I took it; I was worried when I heard he was in a bad way, and they gave me special leave.'

The corner of Sam's mouth lifted slightly. 'Special leave? I'm sorry, but I'm finding it all hard to believe. How come you haven't been out, apart from going to Rosie's? You've always been the lad who had to be out acting the big man but not since you've been back, so don't tell me you're not hiding away.'

Alfie made a harsh sound. 'When you've seen what I've seen you wouldn't want to be out either. I don't want to be asked about it, I don't want to talk about it, but I don't expect you to understand.'

Sam shook his head. 'You're right, I don't understand; you haven't really spoken to Rosie about anything of importance.'

Alfie gave a humourless laugh. 'Ahh, I might have known this was about Rosie. Nothing has changed except now you think you're brave enough to speak up.' He sneered at Sam. 'You need to get some backbone, otherwise you won't last long on the front line.'

Sam stared at his brother. 'I'm surprised you did; you make out you're the big man but I know that's just a front.'

Mrs Bennet cleared her throat and stared at her husband. 'Aren't you going to say something?'

Mr Bennet shook his head. 'Nah, I'm not getting between brothers.'

Alfie took a packet of cigarettes from his trouser pocket and stared at them for a moment. 'You have no idea what it's like.' He flopped down on to the sofa. 'To get covered in your friend's blood as the bomb just misses you but gets men around you. Listening to screams and lying next to them, pretending you are dead for hours on end just to survive. They are all sights and sounds I will never forget, and I relive them every time I close my eyes.'

Sam lowered his eyelashes and whispered, 'I'm sorry, I know you have nightmares, but I had no idea.'

Alfie shook his head. 'And why would you? From what I've seen since I've been home, the news only seems to give good news, on the whole.'

Mrs Bennet shook her head. Glancing at her sons, she decided to change the subject. 'Alfie, Sam is right about Rosie, she's been a good girl while you've been away, and she deserves to know where she stands.'

Alfie smiled. 'I'm sure she has, but who wants to be around "a good girl"? You know, Ma, they ain't much fun.'

Mrs Bennet gasped before raising her voice. 'She'll make you a good wife, and you should show her some respect.'

Alfie fidgeted in the armchair. 'I'm sure she will.'

Mrs Bennet frowned as she turned to Sam. 'Are you going to open that and put us all out of our misery?'

Sam turned the envelope over in his hands before inserting his finger underneath the edge of the flap and tearing the paper apart. He pulled out the folded piece of paper. Opening it up, he stared down at it for a few minutes. He sighed. 'I have to go for a medical in a couple of weeks.'

Alfie nodded. 'And then you'll have to go for training and from what I hear, there's no equipment. The men are learning to fight with sticks.'

Everyone was silent. They stared at Alfie in disbelief.

He stood up and walked out of the room.

Sam stared back down at the paper and all he could think about was Rosie. She felt so good in his arms. He could still smell her floral scent. Would that be enough to keep him going while he was away fighting? He sighed; he had no right to ask anything of her, but he would write to her every day he could.

13

'Hello, Ellen, how are you?' Rosie shifted the books in her arms.

'Hello, Rosie, better now the weather is getting warmer. I don't like the winter.'

Rosie nodded. 'I know exactly what you mean. I've been wanting to ask you if your father has settled back to work after breaking his leg and all that terrible nonsense you all went through.'

Ellen beamed. 'Oh yes, he's like a different man. I'll always be thankful to Victoria, Molly and Alice for helping me through all that, never mind Albert who I'm sure saved my life that day.'

Rosie smiled. 'It was certainly a scary morning but thankfully it turned out well.'

Ellen grinned. 'It certainly did.' She tilted her head to one side. 'So much of my life is wrapped up in this shop, it's unbelievable. My mother used to bring my sister and me here most days so I can't imagine working anywhere else, and on top of that I met John here as well.'

'You seem happy; do you think you and John will get married?'

Colour rose up into Ellen's face.

Rosie rested her hand on Ellen's arm. 'I'm sorry, I didn't mean to embarrass you.'

Ellen giggled. 'You haven't, honestly. We've talked about it so unless something terrible happens, we will be setting a date soon.'

Rosie stepped forward and hugged Ellen. 'It's an exciting time for you and you deserve to be happy.'

Ellen stepped back. 'It's definitely that, especially with Victoria marrying the love of her life as well, but everyone deserves to be as happy as I am.' She paused. 'Look, I have no wish to pry but I've thought for a while there's a sadness around you. I... I just want to say – whatever it is, follow your heart and pray for the help you need, and it will present itself. I do believe we all know what we have to do, but when it's difficult, we shy away from it. At least I know I did; I allowed my emotions and worries to get in the way of facing things. If nothing else, Molly taught me to be strong and face things head on, because that's the only way you can move forward.' Ellen gave a nervous laugh. 'I'm sorry, I overstepped the mark, especially as I have no idea what the problem is; please forgive me.'

Rosie shook her head. 'There's nothing to forgive.' She smiled. 'I shall look forward to hearing that you've set a date soon.' She looked down at the books she was carrying. 'I'd better get these down to the basement; Albert needs to check them before they go back on the shelves, plus they're getting heavy.'

Ellen laughed. 'Yes, sorry, I've kept you chatting.'

Albert crept up behind them, giving an almost toothless grin. He brushed his gnarled hand through his grey hair. 'What are you two chatting about? Are those books for me?'

Rosie jumped. 'Albert, you startled me. I was on my way to the basement to see you with these returns.' She smiled at the man who was like a grandfather to the girls at Foyles. 'How are you? You must get bored in that basement all day on your own.'

Albert threw back his head and laughed. 'I'm never on my own for long; everyone pops down to say 'ello, and I get to 'ear all the gossip.' He studied Rosie for a moment. 'I 'ear yer man is back.'

'Yes, he is.'

Albert raised his eyebrows. 'Does that mean yer'll be setting yer date soon?'

Rosie's lips tightened. 'That's what everyone keeps asking me.'

He rested his hand on Rosie's. 'I'm sorry, girl.'

'You've nothing to be sorry for. The trouble is, I don't know what's happening, Albert. In fact, I don't think I've ever been more confused.'

'Take it from this old man, yer need to take control; don't let someone else make the decisions that affect yer.' Albert reached out and gave Rosie a hug. 'Don't let anyone else decide yer future, it's yer life so yer decide how yer want to live it.'

Tears pricked at Rosie's eyes. 'Thank you, Albert, I need to make some decisions.' She stepped back and wiped her hand across her face.

Albert nodded. 'Yer can do it, girl. Yer know there's no right or wrong ones, it's about yer being 'appy wiv the ones yer make.'

Rosie nodded. Was she up for the fight, the confrontation, the gossip, and holding her own against her and Alfie's families' opinions?

* * *

Fran sat cross-legged on the floor; she watched her son playing with some wooden building blocks. She smiled as he built them up and knocked them down again, while saying, 'Oh no!' She glanced over at Alfie hanging his jacket up on the hook behind the door. 'He'll do that all day. Thank you for the bricks.' Fran looked sad for a moment. 'He doesn't have many toys.' She smiled. 'Although he does play drums on my saucepans with the wooden spoons, and I can tell you it's a right old noise.'

Alfie laughed. 'I know. Not only is he happy but he's a good-looking lad as well; he'll break some hearts when he's older.'

Fran gave a wry smile. 'He takes after his father.' She studied Alfie. 'How's your father doing?'

Alfie looked thoughtful for a moment. 'Now he's eating properly, he's improving every day, but I think he still has a way to go.'

Fran nodded. 'At least he's going forwards, which can only be a good thing. Someone was looking out for you that day I bumped into Rosie talking to your mother; if I hadn't overheard that conversation, you would never have known.'

Alfie sat on the floor next to Fran. 'I suppose that's the problem with shutting yourself away and not facing things; life is still going on for everyone else.' He took a breath and studied Fran for a moment. 'So, is it time you stopped shutting out your best friend? I know you felt you had no choice in the early days – which was the time when you could have done with her by your side – but things need to move on.'

Fran shrugged. 'There's nothing I would like more than to have Rosie back in my life, but I've had a lot of nasty comments, and people cross the road rather than walk near me; it's almost as if I have something catching. I've heard mothers say to their daughters: "She ain't no better than she ought to be." Do you know how that feels?' Her eyes welled up; she blinked quickly, hoping to stop the tears from falling. 'I would have thought you of all people would know how it feels to be trapped in this place with no hopes or dreams for the future.' Tears slowly rolled down her face. 'I'm sorry, but you coming back has made everything worse because I'm now keeping your secret as well, and God only knows how that is going to end. James will probably never know his family because of the shame I brought on them, and you could end up getting shot, so he won't know you either; so forgive me for trying to protect him from the hurt that people can cause.'

'I'm sorry, but doesn't that mean you could have done with Rosie fighting your corner?' Alfie frowned. 'I know I wasn't here but surely you needed her all the more and shouldn't have turned your back on her.'

Fran gave a harsh laugh. 'No, you weren't here. What was I meant to do, drag her down with me? And what kind of friend would that have made me?'

Alfie shook his head. 'But she keeps coming back. For goodness' sake, she leaves a birthday present for James every year, and yet you're still shutting her out. You talk about protecting James from the hurt people cause and yet you are doing the same to Rosie. She's hurting and doesn't understand why a lifetime of friendship has been thrown away. I mean, when I went away, you two were inseparable.'

Fran scowled. 'Don't you think I know that? As you're well aware, a lot has happened since then, and you know why I've kept her away. I've had a lot to deal with, as well as my own guilty feelings.'

'Yes, but you should have gone through it together, like true friends.'

Fran tightened her lips. 'And how would you suggest I did that? You have no idea what I've been carrying on my shoulders. I'm not like you, I can't just pretend I've done nothing wrong.'

Alfie stared at James for a moment. 'Well, maybe it's time people learnt the truth. You can't keep hiding away; it's not good for you or James.'

Fran frowned. 'Did you just come here to moan at me?'

'No, but someone has to tell you you're not being fair to James or Rosie; don't you think he should be mixing with people, so it won't be so bad for him when he has to go to school?'

Fran jumped up. 'Since when have you been an expert on bringing up a child?'

Alfie stood up and grabbed her hands. 'I'm not, and I'm not saying I am, but I care for you, and I don't like the idea of you being on your own when it's time for me to go. I don't know what the future holds for me, but I need to know you are being looked after by friends and family.' He wrapped his arms around Fran. 'You deserve more and I'm going to put things right.' He let her go and turned back to James. Sitting on the floor, he grinned. 'Come on, James, show me how to build a tower.'

James giggled and picked up a block in each hand, carefully placing one on top of the other.

Fran watched on. Confusion and fear gripped her, yet she was enjoying watching her son playing with Alfie. She had a feeling things were going to get worse before they got better, and her only concern was to protect her son from the gossips and their hateful words. She had made the fateful decision nearly four years ago, not James, and she had to live with it. Fran smiled as she watched James knock the blocks down again. She had no regrets for her actions, except losing Rosie's friendship, but her job now was to protect him, no matter what it took.

* * *

A loud bang woke Rosie. She immediately jumped out of bed and ran to the window and peered around the edge of the thick, dark green curtains. There was a flash of light in the darkness. Panic surged through her. They were the maroon rockets she had heard about from Ellen, warning everyone the Germans were on their way, which meant bombs. She grabbed her dressing gown from the back of the door and ran out of her bedroom, shouting. She moved quickly along the landing to her gran's room, thumping on her mother's and brother's bedroom doors as she went. 'Wake up, the Germans are coming! We've got to get to the basement.' There was another loud bang followed by flashes of light. She pushed open her gran's bedroom door. 'Come on, Gran, I'll help you down the stairs.'

'I'll do that.'

Rosie swung round and saw her mother standing in the doorway, doing up the buttons to her long dressing gown.

Tension was etched on her face. 'Rosie, you collect whatever you can get your hands on from the kitchen; we don't know how long we'll be down there for. Get David to help you.' Ivy stepped forward and helped Mary put on her warm dressing gown.

Rosie nodded, dashed past her mother and immediately bumped into David. 'Sorry, David, come with me.' She hurried down the stairs, with David close behind her. 'We need to fill jugs and pans with water to take down to the basement. Also grab bread, butter and anything we can eat, plus cutlery, especially a sharp knife to slice the bread in case we end up being stuck down there for a while.'

They rushed into the kitchen and went about filling bags with food and everything they might need for the next few hours. David ran down the basement stairs carrying what he could, going back and forth several times. It didn't take long for them all to be seated in the basement.

Rosie watched Mary fidget in the armchair her father had put down there when the war began. She sighed. It all seemed like a lifetime ago. She forced a smile. 'I think we got everything down here in record time, thanks to David.' She busied herself pulling the spare covers off a couple of single beds, revealing blankets and sheets.

Ivy nodded. 'Thank goodness.'

Rosie glanced across at her mother. 'Ma, you and Gran take the beds and try and get some sleep.'

Ivy shook her head.

'Ma, after tonight you'll probably have a busy day at the hospital, so you need it the most. David and I will be all right on the chairs.'

Ivy sighed. 'Come on, Mary, Rosie's right.'

Mary wrapped a blanket over her knees. 'I hate being down here; it smells damp and musty.'

Ivy pursed her lips. 'We all hate being down here, but hopefully lighting the candles will help with that.'

Rosie nodded. 'We're lucky, Gran. At least we have a basement; not everyone does, and we haven't been through this for several weeks. I was beginning to think we wouldn't have to be down here ever again; at least, I was hoping that would be so.'

Ivy squeezed her daughter's hand. 'It must be worse for those who have to take cover under tables in their homes, or run outside to get into an underground station, especially with young children.'

'Yes, you can't imagine it.' Rosie paused. 'I hope everyone is safe.'

Ivy helped Mary out of the chair before pulling back the blankets and tucking her into bed.

Rumbling could be heard above them, quickly followed by a barrage of bangs.

Ivy looked up at the ceiling and listened. She shook her head and got into the other bed. 'I'll be glad when this war is over.'

David snuggled in closer to Rosie.

'It'll be all right, David; we're safe down here.' Rosie squeezed him tight. Resting her hand over his ear, she felt him shake. 'Take a couple of deep breaths and try to relax; we could be down here for the rest of the night, so we need to attempt to get some sleep.' Rosie thought about the children at the school and everyone she knew, sending up a silent prayer they would all be safe.

* * *

The next morning, Rosie opened her front door to see Sam standing there. 'Sorry, did you knock? I never heard it, which is unusual.'

Sam looked uncomfortable as he moved from one foot to the other. 'I... I wanted to check you and your family are safe after last night's bombing.'

Rosie turned round and called out into the empty hall. 'Ma, I'm going out to check everyone is all right at Foyles and talk to the children at the school. I'll see you later.'

Ivy's voice travelled back. 'Take care, and don't forget I'll be at the hospital, although I'll probably go in earlier in case they need an extra pair of hands.'

'I won't forget. I'll walk up and meet you when you've finished.' Rosie moved towards Sam and pulled the door closed behind her. 'Sorry, I didn't want to leave without letting her know.'

Sam nodded and stepped back. 'I didn't mean to hold you up. It's just I'm not sure where the bombs landed last night, and I needed to check you... er... everyone was safe.'

'Thank you, Sam, I'm pleased to say we're all safe and sound. Thankfully the bang of the maroon rocket going up woke me, so we managed to get down to the basement before the bombs started dropping.' Giving a little shiver, Rosie pulled up the collar of her coat. 'I know what you mean though, I'm going out earlier than usual for the same reason, but it's a bit nippy out here considering we're in May; there's also a smoky smell in the air.'

'It's a bit grey today. I don't know if last night has anything to do with that, but the smell of smoke will be from the gunfire and bombs.'

Rosie looked around her as they started to walk along. 'I'm amazed, I expected to see a lot of damage this morning. It sounded like the German Gothas were over our house most of the night.'

'I know, I thought I might be able to help with something, but I was shocked to see the only damage close to us seems to be just outside Regent's Park. Unfortunately, a soldier was injured, and a lot of houses have smashed windows around there. I also checked Charing Cross Road and Foyles doesn't appear to have any damage to it.'

Rosie nodded. 'Thank goodness.'

Sam sucked in his breath. 'I expect Kent and Essex took a lot of the bombs as their defence guns, and those along the River Thames, would have stopped a lot of the raiders from getting through. I've read before that if the Germans think they can't get through, they just drop the bombs and head back to Germany.'

Rosie gasped. 'I do hope no one died, it all sounded so close.'

Sam nodded. 'Everything seems louder and nearer in the silence of the night.'

Rosie tried to stifle a yawn. 'David was shaken by it all; he hasn't said, but it probably reminded him of Pa dying in the munitions factory explosion. We all heard and felt that when it happened, and we looked out of the window and saw the sky lit up with flames. Of course we didn't know it was the factory at the time. Since then, David has become such a worrier about losing one – or all – of us, whereas he used to be quite carefree.'

Sam glanced at Rosie. 'If there's anything I can do to help, please just say. I don't mind if he needs someone to talk to; talking to another man might help.'

Rosie frowned. 'Thank you, I'll bear that in mind.' She paused. 'Was everyone all right at your home?'

Sam smiled. 'Yes, we had the usual scurry of getting to the basement; my father was grumbling about wanting to stay in his own bed, but my mother yelled at him.' He laughed. 'I think my father is under no illusion about who's in charge at our house because he soon went to the basement after that. We've been lucky not to have had any air raids for some weeks, so one tends to think it's all over, but last night gave us all a reminder that it isn't.'

Rosie nodded. 'It certainly did that. I hope the children from school are all safe.'

Sam raised his eyebrows. 'I've had the same thoughts because I don't think they all live in places where there is a basement. In fact, one of them told me the children in his family all huddle under the dining table; I'm not sure how much protection that will give them.'

'I know it's daft, but I try not to think about it too much.' Rosie paused. 'Mainly because I've had thoughts about us being buried alive in the basement if the house gets hit, and I've never told anyone that.'

Sam reached out and stroked her back. 'Don't worry, your secret is safe with me, and you need to know that most people probably have similar thoughts.'

Rosie smiled. 'That's what I like about you, Sam, you never make me feel like I'm being daft over my thoughts and worries.' She frowned. 'How was Alfie?'

Sam shook his head. 'I don't know. He didn't say much but I think he was awake for most of the night, and I caught him looking up at the ceiling a few times. He had already gone out when I left the house, but I don't know where he was going, he never said.'

Rosie nodded. 'Perhaps he was comparing it to what he has already experienced at the front, so I imagine to him it was quite tame. Ma has told me most of the men in hospital have horrific nightmares; they are jumpier than most people and want to get under the bed when something makes a bang, like a car backfiring.'

'I expect you're right. He does have nightmares most nights, although we never talk about it.' Sam shook his head. 'I don't know, something was definitely bothering him; he seemed to be deep in thought most of the evening.'

Rosie stared ahead. 'Maybe it reminded him that he would have to go back soon.'

Sam fought the urge to tell her that he had to go for his medical soon and could be joining his brother on the front line.

They both fell silent as they walked together, lost in their own thoughts about what the future held and when – or if – the war would ever end.

14

Sam cleared his throat. 'I'm going to check on the school and I want to be there before the children in case they get there earlier than usual.' He glanced at Rosie. 'Do you have time to come with me?'

Rosie smiled. 'I was planning on going to the school when you knocked – or didn't knock.'

Sam chuckled. 'I was worried it might have been too early to be knocking on your door.'

Rosie giggled. 'It's never too early in my house; we're all early birds. Having said that, it doesn't mean we're all ready for the day to begin.'

They both turned onto Foley Street and breathed a sigh of relief.

Sam strained his neck to see more of the All Souls Primary School. 'Well, from here it looks like it's still in one piece, thank goodness.'

They reached the school gate. Sam looked up and down the road and across to the main door of the school.

Rosie watched him before breaking into a smile. 'You look

like you're up to no good.' She looked around them. 'I hope everyone knows you work here, and they aren't running for the police because they think the school is being broken into.'

Sam chuckled as he thrust his hand into his trouser pocket. There was a chink as his fingers moved coins around; he pulled out a key ring with a couple of keys hanging from it. They clattered against each other as he waved them in the air. 'Come on, let's go and check inside before the children start arriving.' They strolled up to the main door. 'Did I hear your mother say she will be going to the hospital later?' Sam inserted the key, which grated as the lock turned.

Rosie nodded. 'She'll probably go early in case they need an extra pair of hands—'

'Wait,' Sam whispered. 'Did you hear that?'

Rosie shook her head.

There was a thud that sounded like a door shutting.

Rosie grabbed Sam's arm as he stepped forward.

Sam peered at Rosie. 'Stay close, I don't want you getting hurt. Perhaps you should wait outside.'

'No, I'm not leaving you on your own.' Rosie's heart was pounding as she followed his lead but wondered how someone had got in when the door was locked. She spoke in low tones. 'Maybe it's a dog or a cat.'

What sounded like a chair scraping across the wooden floor made Rosie stop and look around. 'Where did that come from?'

Sam shrugged and carried on moving forward. 'Maybe some families broke in to feel safe last night.'

A door swung open. 'Mr Bennet, Miss Burrows – we're in here.'

They both looked around and saw Tom standing in a classroom doorway.

Sam rushed over to him. 'Tom, what are you doing here? Why aren't you at home?'

A lady carrying a toddler stepped forward. 'I'm sorry, Mr Bennet, it's my fault. I... I found an open window and Tom climbed in and let us in through the back door. We were just scared, and I wanted to keep my children safe. I don't have a basement, and my kitchen table ain't big enough for the three of us to get under, but then I remembered the big tables and the long benches here in the classrooms.'

Tom grinned at his teacher, tugging at his coat. 'We made a den, come and have a look.'

Sam looked from one to the other. 'Come on then, let me see.'

Tom took Sam's hand and they walked together into the classroom. Rosie quickly followed them. She wanted to laugh when she saw the tables on their sides butting up to other tables that were upright.

Tom's mother glanced from Sam to Rosie. 'I'm sorry, I know what we did was wrong, but I just didn't know what to do.' She paused. 'And now this little one is heavier, I can't run and carry him to the underground like I could before.'

Rosie put her arm around Tom's ma. 'Don't worry, you're safe and that's all that matters.'

Sam squinted at Tom. 'You do know it's normally wrong to break into a property; if you were older, you could go to prison.'

Tom's mouth dropped open. 'Does that mean my ma will go to prison?'

Sam ruffled Tom's hair. 'No, not this time, but I don't want you going around thinking it's all right to climb through open windows and get up to mischief.'

Tom looked serious. 'I won't, sir, I promise, we were just frightened of the bombs getting us.'

Sam nodded and looked over at the upturned desks. 'That's a great den you made though.'

Tom grinned before looking at Rosie. 'I'm sorry, I took some books off the shelves to read to me ma.' He glanced at his mother who was smiling.

'I have to say he reads very well and he made up lots of different voices as he went along.' Tom's mother paused. 'He was very brave and kept us all smiling.'

Tom chuckled. 'Miss Burrows told me to make up the voices to make the reading more fun.'

Tom's mother laughed. 'Well, it certainly made listening to it fun.'

Sam grinned as he looked across at Rosie beaming at Tom. 'All your hard work seems to have paid off, Rosie.' He looked back at the upturned desks. 'Tom, I'm going to need your help straightening up the classroom before the other children arrive.'

'Yes, sir.'

* * *

Rosie and Sam walked along Foley Street in silence, each locked in their own thoughts.

Sam let out a big sigh. 'It feels like it's been a long day, and I haven't rushed to Charing Cross Road to work in Foyles and then back to the school to work with the children like you have.' He chuckled. 'You're definitely a star.'

Rosie gave a tired smile. 'I don't know about that.'

Sam glanced across at Rosie. 'I do know. I'm pleased that none of the children seemed worse for wear after the bombing raid last night.'

Rosie nodded. 'Tom was quite resourceful turning the desks over; he'll go far in life.'

Sam laughed. 'I think you're right, although I do worry some of them are not being given a chance to be children because of the weight of responsibility they carry.'

Rosie nodded. 'I can see that, but Tom seemed to thrive on the praise he was being given; it all adds to their confidence, and let's face it, they don't have much to be happy about.'

Sam eyed Rosie for a moment. 'You're right of course, but the other thing is that some of them don't remember life before the war.'

Rosie frowned. 'Gosh, I hadn't thought of that. How sad, I can't imagine what it must be like for them. I mean, to not have their fathers or any other men around much in the last four years.' She shivered and began fastening her jacket buttons as a chill breeze blew it open. 'Sometimes I think the weather is getting colder instead of warmer.'

Laughing, Sam glanced at Rosie. 'It won't be long before everyone is moaning it's too hot.'

Rosie raised her eyebrows. 'I wasn't moaning, I was just saying, that's all – and anyway, I would rather moan about the weather than think of the children not knowing what it's like to have a father around all the time, or play and sleep carefree.'

Sam nodded as he glanced at her. 'I'm so pleased you're helping the children with their reading; it seems to be working well, especially if Tom's anything to go by.' He chuckled. 'You know the children love you, don't you? You're clearly making a big difference to them.'

Smiling, Rosie looked across at him. 'Thank you, they adore you too; in fact, I'd say you have a couple of admirers.'

Sam laughed. 'I'm sure that won't last, but I wanted you to know that I appreciate your help in the classroom, and it hasn't escaped me that you're probably doing less volunteering at the hospital because of it.'

'That's true, but I did check with them before I started helping out at the school, and I did say I would go in if they are really short. My ma is there every day, and she tells me they are managing.' Rosie paused. 'I probably shouldn't say this, but some of the men are in so much pain it's heart-rending; at least the children are quite innocent, and their smiles brighten my day.'

Sam nodded. 'I can see that, and I can't imagine anyone would judge you on those thoughts. Alfie seems to have got away quite lightly compared to some of the men you see returning.' He hesitated before taking a breath. 'I've received my call-up papers; I have to go for a medical in two weeks' time.'

Horror ran across Rosie's face. 'Oh, my goodness, not you as well? I was hoping this war would be over before you got called up. It's never going to end, is it?'

Sam reached out and pulled Rosie close, wrapping his arms around her and holding her tight. 'It has to end at some point. Will you write to me, and I promise I will reply to you? I'm going to miss you.' He breathed in her floral perfume. 'You smell lovely.'

Rosie nestled in the comfort of his arms before whispering, 'I shall miss you too.' She stepped back. 'Wait, do they know you're a teacher? I'm sure I read somewhere – or I heard someone say – that teachers don't have to go to war. The War Office must have made a mistake.'

Sam shook his head. 'I'm not a fully qualified teacher. I'm working towards it but at the moment, I'm just helping out, so I'm not sure that counts.'

'Maybe they thought you were qualified enough and that's why you were late being called up.' Rosie's eyes widened. 'We have to find out and convince them they've got it wrong.'

Sam studied Rosie. 'If only it were as simple as that; my ma would be very happy if that were the case. She's getting herself into a right old state at the thought of losing both her boys, although I told her I've got to have the medical first.'

Rosie lowered her eyelashes. 'Do you know when Alfie is going back?'

Sam shook his head. 'No, he won't talk about it. Ma has tried to push him about marrying you, but he won't discuss that either.'

'Your ma must be beside herself; I know how much she wants it to happen.'

Sam placed his finger under Rosie's chin and lifted her head slightly. 'Do you want it to happen?'

Rosie's body tensed. 'That's a conversation I should be having with Alfie and no one else.'

Sam lowered his hand. 'You're right, of course.'

Rosie stepped back. 'You won't have to worry about the children, I will do my best to look after them.'

Sam nodded. 'I know you will, you are a naturally caring person, and I'm sure they'll soon replace me at the school.'

Rosie's lips tightened. 'Well, first you have to pass the medical – not that I'm wishing you have something wrong with you – but if they found out you couldn't go because you needed glasses, then that would make me very happy.'

Sam chuckled. 'Hmm, I wonder what I'd look like wearing glasses. Perhaps I might look more intelligent.'

Rosie laughed. 'You are already intelligent. I expect your class would have something to say about it.'

Sam raised his eyebrows. 'Oh, my goodness, do you think I'd lose my admirers?'

Rosie stopped and stared up at him before smiling. 'I shouldn't think so; you'll become their hero because you're going off to fight.'

Sam stared ahead as he thought about what was to come.

Would he have the courage to tell Rosie he loved her before he left, or would that be unfair and make him as bad as Alfie?

* * *

Rosie walked through the Middlesex Hospital doorway. She scanned the reception area.

'Good evening, Rosie, are you looking for your mother?'

Glancing across at the desk, Rosie saw the matron filling out some paperwork. She walked over to her. 'I am but if it's all right, I'll sit on one of these chairs and wait until she's finished.'

The matron glanced down at her watch. 'I'll chase her up because she came in early and her normal shift should have finished at least ten minutes ago.'

'On no, please don't do that; if she's still working, there must be a reason for it. I'm not in a hurry so I'll just wait for her. Did you have many injuries come in from last night's bombings?'

'No, I think this area must have got away lightly. From what I hear, Kent and Essex took the brunt of it, along with South London.' The matron studied her for a moment. 'You look tired; I don't suppose you got much sleep last night.' She smiled. 'Are you enjoying helping out at the school? You know we miss you here.'

Rosie's eyes widened. 'Oh no, I haven't left you short, have I?'

Matron laughed. 'No, no, we can manage, although we still miss you.'

Rosie smiled. 'That's very kind of you. I do love helping the children learn to read.'

Matron nodded. 'It must be very rewarding. I want you to know you will always be welcome here if you wish to return, but try and get an early night tonight.'

'Rosie, I'm sorry I'm late.'

Both Rosie and Matron turned to see Ivy buttoning her black coat as she strode towards them.

Rosie shook her head. 'Slow down, Ma, there's no rush.'

Ivy nodded. 'I know, I just don't like the idea of keeping you waiting.' She turned to Matron. 'It feels busier on the wards tonight, which doesn't make much sense because we have the same number of patients. Anyway, I'll see you tomorrow.'

Matron nodded. 'Thank you for your help, Ivy, it's really appreciated. I'll see you tomorrow. Have a good evening – well, what's left of it.'

Ivy smiled. 'We will. Don't work too hard.' She waved before hooking her arm through Rosie's and walking towards the hospital's main doors.

Rosie glanced across at her mother. 'You look tired, Ma. When we get home, you sit yourself down, put your feet up and I'll make you a cuppa.'

Ivy chuckled. 'That's very kind of you. It's been a busy shift. I'm glad you came to meet me because it gives us a chance to have a proper chat on our own.'

Rosie laughed. 'That sounds ominous.'

Ivy nudged her daughter. 'No, it isn't. David told me about the conversation you both had about his friend.'

'Oh, I hope I didn't do wrong. Did he go and see him?'

Ivy smiled at her daughter. 'You didn't do anything wrong, and he did go and see him.'

Rosie lowered her eyelashes. 'Is David all right? I expect he found it difficult.'

Ivy nodded. 'He's growing up fast but from what he said, it sounds like he and his friend had a good chat.'

Rosie peered at her mother. 'You're right, he *is* growing up fast and sometimes I feel he doesn't want to let Pa down.'

Ivy frowned. 'I think you're right.' She reached out to her

daughter. 'I'm aware you've been troubled lately, and I want you to talk to me about what's bothering you.'

Rosie stared straight ahead. 'How come it was busier at the hospital today?'

Ivy chuckled. 'That was an obvious change of subject, not very subtle at all.' She paused. 'I understand you might not want to talk about it but if it's affecting you, then you need to talk it through, whatever it is.'

Rosie sucked in her breath. 'I know, but it's not as simple as that.'

Looking down, Ivy studied the pavement as they walked along. 'Try me.'

Rosie shook her head. 'I don't really know what's going on.'

'Well, it can only be a few things: the school, Alfie, or Fran. Or maybe Sam has ended up in the mix somewhere.' Ivy gave her daughter's arm a squeeze. 'I thought we could talk about anything, and I don't like to see you so troubled, and you know what they say: "a problem shared is a problem halved".'

Rosie laughed. 'I have to give you credit, Ma; you don't give up.'

'You're my daughter, I would never give up, no matter what it was.'

'Ma, stop worrying, there's nothing wrong.'

Ivy's lips tightened. 'I expect Alfie will have to return to the front soon; has he said when he's got to go back?'

Rosie shook her head. 'No, actually I've hardly spoken to Alfie.'

Ivy glanced at her daughter. 'Maybe I should knock at the Bennets' house and see what I can find out.'

'No, Ma, don't you dare. That would be so embarrassing. I'm not a child.'

Ivy sighed. 'Then talk to me.'

Rosie frowned. 'Ma, I know you and Mrs Bennet want the happy ever after but I'm not sure you're going to get it.'

'What, you mean you and Alfie?'

Rosie took a deep breath. 'Yes, something isn't right, but apart from him not loving me, or me him, I can't help feeling there's more to it and that's what I'm trying to figure out.'

Ivy reached out and squeezed her daughter's arm. 'Maybe there isn't more, maybe you're just looking for a reason to make it easier for you to say you don't want to be his wife.'

Rosie stayed silent. Maybe her mother had a point, but she couldn't get rid of the niggling feeling there was more to it.

* * *

Sam lounged in the front room, fidgeting on the sofa as he watched his brother open their mother's display cabinets to examine her treasures. He guessed there was nothing of value in them so he wondered why Alfie was intent on inspecting everything in detail. 'They are only Ma's little keepsakes; I don't think they are worth anything.'

Alfie glanced over his shoulder. 'I wonder why she keeps them then.'

Sam's eyes narrowed. 'I expect there are memories attached to them.' He watched as Alfie placed an ornament back in the cabinet. 'What are you going to tell Ma about you and Rosie?'

Alfie laughed. 'I'm not going to tell Ma anything; it's nothing to do with her.'

Sam sighed. 'I don't know why you're being so stubborn about it because you'll tell her eventually.'

'Maybe, but it will be when I'm ready and not because everyone is nagging me.' Alfie stayed silent and turned his attention to the street outside. 'What are you going to do about Rosie?'

Sam's eyes narrowed. 'I'm not going to do anything; she's your girlfriend and unlike you, I couldn't be so cruel to my brother.'

Alfie threw back his head as he roared with laughter. 'That attitude will never get you the girl.'

Sam clenched his fingers together. 'I can't pretend I understand you, or the game you are playing.'

Alfie glanced over his shoulder at Sam. 'It will all become clear in due course, but it's enough for you to know that Rosie and I will never get married.'

Sam stared wide-eyed at him. 'What?' He sucked in his breath. 'Does she know? I mean, have you spoken to her about it?'

Alfie turned round to face his brother. 'No, not yet, I'm just biding my time.'

Sam stood up and took a step nearer to Alfie. 'Don't you think she has a right to know? Believe it or not, life isn't just about you.' He watched as an expression fleetingly appeared on his brother's face, but he couldn't make it out. 'What? What is it?'

Alfie gave a wry smile. 'Now is not the time, and you'll find out in due course.'

Sam closed his eyes and silently counted to ten. 'Do you know when you have to go back, or is that another secret you are keeping from us all?'

'I will be here when you have to go for your medical.' Alfie laughed. 'I want to see your reaction when you have to go off for your training and the war suddenly becomes real.'

Sam shook his head. 'I know I have to go, so I'll do whatever I've got to do.'

'You can't even tell the girl you've loved for years how you feel,' Alfie sneered at Sam. 'You need to get some backbone; you wouldn't last five minutes on the front line.'

Sam stared at his brother. 'I'm surprised you did.'

Alfie took a packet of cigarettes from his trouser pocket, then stared at them for a moment. 'You have no idea what it's like.' He flopped down on to the sofa. 'The noise of the bombs going off and the gunshots all around you, wondering if you're going to survive the next few minutes, at times even hoping you won't – just to put an end to it all. The screams are the worst, that and trying to save someone but knowing you can't when the life drains out of them. All the time you're hoping your family are safe and waiting for you to come home, because you want to be with someone who cares whether you live or die. You soon come to realise you are just a number, expendable in this awful war; not just us but the Germans as well.'

Sam lowered his eyelashes and whispered, 'I'm sorry, I should know better than to sit in judgement.'

Alfie shook his head. 'The posters that fill nearly every outside wall make you feel guilty for not joining up.'

Sam shrugged. 'Not just the posters. I could make a pillow out of the amount of white feathers I've been given for not joining up. Clearly, people think I'm a coward, even though I'm trying to prepare their children and grandchildren for whatever the future holds for them.' He paused. 'Don't tell Ma because she doesn't know; I think it might have finished her off.'

Alfie shook his head. 'I didn't know.'

Sam smiled. 'And why would you? It was important you concentrated on staying alive and not worrying about us.' He moved to reach out to Alfie but pulled back at the last minute. 'Why didn't you write and tell us? If not Ma, then you could have told me?'

Alfie gave a humourless laugh. 'Life isn't as simple as that; letters get checked to make sure we're not giving any information away that could affect the war. Besides, what difference would it have made?'

Sam shrugged. 'I don't know but it might have helped you.'

'I found my own way of dealing with it.' Alfie tapped the cigarette box on his knee.

Sam frowned. 'How did you deal with it?'

Alfie sat in silence, staring at the floor.

'Alfie?'

Alfie turned and peered at his brother. 'It doesn't matter how I dealt with it, I'm sure you'll have the answer to that question soon enough.'

Sam studied Alfie for a moment. 'Why do you say that?'

'As I said, you'll find out in due course.'

15

Rosie carried the armful of books to the door marked 'Private'. Propping them up against the wall with her body, she turned the squeaking handle and tried to pull the door open without dropping the books.

Ellen came into the staff area and saw Rosie struggling. 'Hold on, I'll get it for you.' She stepped forward and opened the door. Stretching out, she pulled on the light cord and the stairs were lit up. 'Be careful, you probably shouldn't carry so many at once. Here, let me take some; I don't want you falling down the stairs.'

Rosie smiled. 'Thank you, but I'm sure I can manage.'

Ellen laughed. 'I'm sure you can but I shall worry until I see you again.' Reaching out, she took a few books from Rosie's arms.

Rosie chuckled. 'It doesn't look like I have any say in the matter.'

They were both laughing as they pushed open the basement door. Their smiles were suddenly frozen on their faces. They both dropped the books they were carrying and rushed towards Albert who was lying on the floor.

Rosie fell to her knees and felt his forehead. 'I think he's got a temperature.' She looked up. 'Ellen, we need help, Albert's out cold.'

Ellen turned and ran up the stairs.

Thinking quickly about things she saw the nurses do at the hospital, Rosie turned Albert on to his side. 'It's going to be all right, Albert, help is coming.'

She heard heavy footsteps mixed with the groaning of the stairs as someone ran down them. Rosie looked up expectantly. Ellen's pale features were staring back at her. 'Is someone coming?'

'Yes, Mr Leadbetter is going to take him to the hospital in the van. Do you think he's going to be all right?'

Rosie frowned as she peered up at Ellen. 'I hope so. Foyles wouldn't be the same without him.'

Ellen reached out for Albert's hand and squeezed it. 'Please get well soon.'

Mr Leadbetter appeared with a couple of young men in army uniform running behind him. He turned to them. 'Can one of you lift Albert's arms while the other picks up his legs? Then we'll try and get him up the stairs and through the side door, but please be careful with him.'

One man stood at his feet. 'I don't think this will take two of us, he doesn't look heavy, and it will be easier to get him up the stairs if I just lift him on to my shoulder.'

The man at Albert's head nodded. 'Let's do it.'

Rosie leant over him. 'Hang in there, Albert. Don't worry, they're taking you to the hospital. If you can hear me, don't worry about money, we'll have a collection.'

'Miss Burrows, we need to get Albert to the hospital as soon as we can.'

'Sorry, Mr Leadbetter, I was just trying to reassure him.' Rosie stepped back and watched one of the men expertly lift him on to his shoulder.

Ellen moved nearer to Rosie. She took a breath. 'He'll be back before you know it. He's a tough old man, just think of how he didn't hesitate to take on the spy.'

Rosie nodded.

They both stood in silence as they watched him being carried up the stairs. They waited until the door thudded to a close.

Rosie's tears pricked at her eyes. 'Do you think Albert's going to be all right? He was burning up, and we don't know how long he'd been lying on the floor like that.'

Ellen shrugged. 'I don't know, but I think he's always been a strong and healthy man so hopefully, whatever it is, he'll soon get over it.'

Rosie nodded. 'I hope so.'

The basement door creaked open, and the stairs groaned as someone came down them.

Frowning, Victoria stared at the girls. 'Are you two all right? How was Albert when he left?'

Rosie and Ellen glanced at each other before Rosie spoke. 'He was unconscious when Mr Leadbetter left here to take him to the hospital.'

Victoria paced for a moment, only stopping to stack books on the table. 'He's going to be all right. Mr Leadbetter will make sure he gets some good care.' She peered at the girls. 'Come on, the best thing we can do is keep busy, at least until we know more, and it'll help to stop us worrying too much.'

* * *

Rosie sighed as she stood outside Fran's front door. She lifted her arm to knock, then stopped mid-air as a child's laughter reached her, quickly followed by a man's voice. She lowered her arm. Should she leave if Fran was entertaining, whatever that meant? The giggling grew louder, and footsteps sounded on the other side of the door. Rosie stepped back, unsure what to do. The door opened and Rosie caught her breath when she saw Alfie standing there smiling.

Fran's voice could be heard behind him. 'I'll see you tomorrow.'

Alfie's smile faded but it didn't take him long to gather himself. 'Hello, Rosie, this is an unexpected pleasure.'

Rosie frowned and tried to force a smile. 'Indeed, it is; it sounded like you were all having fun.'

Alfie gave a nervous glance over his shoulder. 'One thing's for sure, you can't beat a child's laughter to bring a smile to your face.' He looked back at Rosie. 'I take it you're here to see Fran.'

Rosie gave a wry smile. 'I have been trying to see Fran since she had her baby, but she doesn't seem to want to see me. Although I don't understand why not.'

Alfie turned back to face Fran's gaze staring at them both. 'It's time you spoke to Rosie; she was – or is – your best friend and you're not being fair to her.' He stepped forward. 'I'm going to leave you two to it.'

Rosie stood rooted to the spot as she watched him walk away. There had been no kiss, no loving touch or smile that was meant just for her. She jumped as the main door to the building slammed shut. Was she really going to marry him?

'You'd better come in.'

Startled, Rosie turned back to look at her friend and walked over the threshold of her flat.

Fran closed the door behind Rosie. 'It's not much, but it's my home.'

Rosie peered over her shoulder and noticed a man's jacket hanging on the hook. Frowning, she looked around the room that was very sparsely decorated. A two-seater sofa sat opposite the open fire and an armchair sat to one side. A threadbare carpet square covered the floorboards between them and the fire. A modest dining table with three chairs stood next to the wall at the other end of the small room.

Fran watched Rosie as she took everything in. 'It's not the biggest room but it's enough for me and James.'

James looked up and placed his small hand in his mother's.

Rosie stooped down. 'Hello, James, my name is Rosie. I went to school with your ma.'

James partially hid behind his mother's leg.

Fran smiled down at him. 'Say hello, James.' She looked up at Rosie. 'I'm sorry, he's very shy.'

A small voice whispered, 'Hello.'

Fran raised her eyebrows as she looked across at Rosie. 'Would you like to sit down? I'm afraid I can't offer you a cup of tea because I don't have any milk.'

Rosie shook her head. 'I have come to see *you*, not the size of your home, nor to drink tea; none of those things matter.' She lowered herself on to the edge of the sofa. 'I'm afraid I'm just going to get straight to the point; why have you shut me out since it became known you were pregnant? We were best friends – at least I thought we were.'

Colour rushed up Fran's pale features. 'We were – are. I just didn't want everyone taking my predicament out on you. You know what the gossips are like, they've made my life hell.'

Rosie stared at Fran for a moment. 'I know, but surely that's when you need your friends the most. You know when you moved out of your ma's house, I didn't even know where you'd moved to; it took me ages to find out where you'd gone. Your ma told me in the end, and because you never answered the door to me, I wasn't even convinced I was knocking on the right one.'

Fran lowered her eyes. 'I'm sorry... but I don't think this is the time to talk about it.'

Rosie frowned. 'You mean because of your boy?'

Fran nodded.

Rosie shook her head. 'I would normally agree with you, and I certainly don't want to upset James, but I've been knocking on your door more times than I can probably count; you must see how I need to make the most of this opportunity. I've left birthday presents for your son but even that didn't get any response from you.' She glanced down at James and lowered her voice. 'Why should I believe you would ever let me in again to have this conversation?'

'I will, I promise. I know I've been a bad friend, but it felt like the right thing to do at the time. There have been many days when I wished I could have had a conversation with you, when I've needed you to make me laugh and tell me everything will be all right.'

'Fran, I want that too, just as I want to believe you now, but I don't know that I can. I mean, how come you let Alfie in? And he's clearly coming back tomorrow, too. I understand you've spoken to Sam as well, and yet I'm the one that has been shut out of your life. I do think you owe me an explanation because I truly don't know what's going on. Everyone keeps telling me to just walk away because you're no better than you ought to be, but I just can't do that. We were good friends, you were like a sister to me, and I've always defended you against any gossip I overheard, but I feel like I'm being punished and I don't know what for.'

Fran lowered her eyelashes and reached out to pull her son

close. 'I'm sorry, but I was trying to protect you.' She paused. 'We need to have a proper talk about all of it, and I should have done that a long time ago. I'm sorry, but I hope you'll understand... and forgive me... when we have a proper talk, but I don't think now is the time.'

Rosie eyed her friend and James. 'All right, but I won't give up until I get to the bottom of it, so I will be back.' She took a step nearer to the door before glancing over her shoulder and smiling. 'Next time, I'll bring some milk. Bye, James.'

James gave a small smile. 'Bye.'

* * *

Rosie perched on the edge of the armchair in the Bennets' front room. She stared down at the hot cup of tea she was holding. Her head was thumping. She closed her eyes, trying to understand what was going on.

Alfie eyed Rosie. 'Did you and Fran make up today?'

Rosie opened her eyes and looked at Alfie. 'I wouldn't say that, but we took a step towards talking things through. I was surprised to see you there, let alone looking so relaxed.'

Alfie nodded. 'James is a happy child, and his laughter is quite contagious.' He paused. 'I'm glad you're sorting things out with Fran.'

Mrs Bennet scowled at Alfie as she clinked her cup down on her saucer. 'Rosie, don't let your tea go cold, there's nothing worse than drinking cold tea.'

Alfie's eyes narrowed as he glanced across at his mother. 'I can assure you, Ma, there is.'

Mrs Bennet ignored him. 'Has Sam told you he has to go for his medical soon?'

Rosie's gaze travelled between mother and son. 'Yes, he did.' She took a deep breath. 'I'm hoping he will fail it because then he won't be able to go.'

Mrs Bennet dabbed at her eyes with a handkerchief. 'I don't think he will, but here's hoping; it's bad enough that Alfie joined up.'

Sam shrugged as he kept his eyes fixed on Rosie. 'I don't think there's any chance of me failing the medical.'

Rosie frowned. 'We'll face that together when the time comes.' She glanced at Alfie; his eyes were closed as he drew his brows together. 'Alfie, do you know when you have to go back?'

Alfie gave Rosie a wry smile. 'Soon. Please don't ask again because I don't wish to talk about it.'

Rosie nodded. 'That might suit you, Alfie, but I need to know what's going on.'

Alfie glared. 'Do you, now? Well, I can tell you nothing is going on.'

Rosie shrugged. 'That's not how it feels. I've hardly seen you since you've been home and in my head, that doesn't add up.' She peered at Alfie, but his face gave nothing away. 'I know you've probably been through a lot—'

'Been through a lot? You have no idea.' Alfie scowled. 'While you've been here being all sweetness and light working at Foyles, volunteering at the hospital and helping out at the school, men are dying out there.'

The colour drained from Rosie's face, but she could feel the anger running through her veins. 'I do know that, but I didn't start the war. I didn't tell you to be the first to join up, but I've waited like you asked me to, and now you don't even have the decency to talk to me about what our future means to you. As for everything else, I'm just trying to do my bit to help others. We can't all be heroes, and the children I'm helping will one day be looking after us, making the decisions on our futures.'

'Yeah, yeah, what makes you think there's any future for any of us?'

Mrs Bennet stood up. 'Enough, Alfie, enough. Rosie has been patient; she kept the faith even when you didn't write to any of us. I can only guess how bad it's been for you, but it was a worry for us not knowing whether you were dead or alive.'

Alfie stood up and wrapped his arms around his mother. 'I'm sorry, Ma, I just have so much whirling around in my head.'

Rosie lifted her chin as she took in the scene. 'And Fran, where does she fit into all this?'

Alfie stepped away from his mother and stared at Rosie. 'I went round to see her because Sam told me she wasn't opening the door to you, and I wanted to help.'

Rosie eyed him suspiciously but remained silent.

Mrs Bennet glanced at Rosie. 'I don't know why you keep trying; she clearly doesn't want to mix with you and let's face it, she's definitely no better than she should be.'

Sam scowled at his mother. 'Ma, no one cares what you think. Fran is a good mother and didn't get pregnant by herself. The man has a responsibility as well, and that aside, Rosie and Fran have been friends since they were children.'

Colour rose up Mrs Bennet's neck. 'And where is that man now? As for friendship, she clearly doesn't value it in the same way Rosie does.'

Alfie's lips tightened as he sat on the armchair. 'Or Fran was trying to protect Rosie from all the gossips.'

Rosie listened on, not wanting to get involved in an argument between a mother and her sons. She wondered why Alfie was defending Fran. 'She did say that when you let me into her home.'

Mrs Bennet stared at Alfie; her mouth dropped open. 'Wait a minute, I've just realised what you said – you've been round there? Why? I mean you've hardly seen your wife-to-be, but you make time for that... that... trollop?'

'Don't call her that.' Alfie scowled at his mother. 'She made one mistake, one that will affect her for the rest of her life.'

Rosie gazed at Alfie, then spoke in low tones. 'You sound quite passionate about it all; I didn't realise you two were so close, although I get the impression her son was quite happy in your company.'

Alfie fidgeted in his chair. 'It's about people being allowed to make mistakes without being judged by everyone. For all you know, she might have really loved James's father.'

Rosie nodded. 'That's true, but I don't remember her talking or mixing with anyone else other than us.' She paused. 'So unless it's you or Sam, I have no idea who it could be.'

Sam's head shot up. 'It isn't me. If it had been, I would have got married and looked after her.'

Rosie smiled. 'We know it's not you. Apparently, it was a soldier.' She paused. 'Actually, she was seeing another man who had also enlisted but I can't remember his name right now. Anyway, I'd better go, maybe Fran will tell me when we finally catch up.' Rosie stood up and smoothed down her floral calf-length skirt. 'Thank you for the tea, Mrs Bennet.' She glanced at Alfie, who remained seated in his chair.

Mrs Bennet stepped forward. 'I'll see you out, Rosie.'

* * *

As the front door thudded shut, Sam followed Alfie out of the front room and into the hallway.

Mrs Bennet turned round and raised her voice. 'Alfie... Alfie.'

'Not now, Ma, not now, I've had enough for one day.' Alfie climbed the stairs two at a time.

Sam glanced at his mother before following Alfie up the creaking stairs and into the bedroom they shared. He flopped down on to his single bed and watched Alfie sitting on the edge of his, holding his head in his hands. The heavy wind made a haunting sound as it caught and rattled the rotten window frame. The edge of the dark blue curtains fluttered as the wind blew through it. 'Alfie, aren't you concerned that Rosie and Ma will think you're defending Fran a bit too much?'

Alfie dropped his hands on to his lap and chuckled. 'To be honest, I don't care what they think. Fran should have had the support from everyone, and not be punished because she made a mistake. In what world is that right?'

'Rosie would have supported her if Fran hadn't shut her out.'

'That's just Rosie; what about everyone else? You heard how Ma was talking. Fran will never get past this without help and understanding.' Alfie shook his head. 'We all make mistakes. Even in the Bible, Jesus talks about being without sin and throwing the first stone, and yet everyone stands in judgement as though they've never done anything wrong; but we all have, and they all claim to be God-fearing Christians.'

Sam reached out and grabbed Alfie's arm. 'Since when have you read the Bible, let alone been able to quote from it?'

Alfie stared at his brother. 'I told you the war changes you. Innocent people are being killed on all sides; there won't be any winners in this war, just a lot of grieving families, so forgive me if I've tried to find comfort in the Word.'

Sam's lips tightened. 'It just doesn't ring true; I have a feeling there's more to this than you're telling.'

Alfie snatched his arm away. 'You need to spend less time worrying about my life and start sorting your own out. Stop being a coward and start living while you can; tell the girl you love how you feel.'

Sam tried to push down the anger that was rising inside him, fighting the urge to scream and shout. 'If you are talking about Rosie, then that will never be possible because you spent years belittling me in front of her, so I'm not sure she sees me as anything but your little brother.' He thought of Rosie in his arms, the smell of her hair and her floral perfume filling his senses, reminding him how Rosie had leant into him when she'd kissed him back. Did she just see him as Alfie's little brother? He remembered how she wouldn't go out with him because of Alfie.

Alfie gave a wry smile. 'Yeah, I haven't been the best brother in the world, have I? But you need to stop looking at her with your puppy dog eyes and put yourself out there; after all, she may not know how you feel about her.'

Frowning, Sam shook his head.

Alfie shrugged. 'Well, you won't know unless you try. You need to think about how you'll feel when she announces she's marrying someone else because you didn't take a chance.'

'You're forgetting something: everyone, including Rosie, thinks she's marrying you. So until you tell her you're not, she will never go out with anyone else.' Sam paused. 'If you must know, I've already asked her to go to the pictures with me, but she won't go because she's promised to you, and everyone will think she's cheating on you if she does.'

Alfie threw back his head, laughing. 'Or she's using me as an excuse not to go out with you because she doesn't want to.'

Sam scowled. 'Thanks for that. Have you not realised that Rosie will always do the right thing, regardless of her feelings?'

Alfie shook his head. 'Then neither of you will ever be happy. Sometimes you have to put yourself first or spend your life being miserable; is that really what you want?'

Sam sat in silence.

Alfie shook his head. 'You need to get a grip and go for what you want.'

Sam stared at him. 'Is that what you're doing?'

'Don't worry about what I'm doing.' Alfie lay back on the bed and closed his eyes.

16

Mary lowered her knitting needles on to her lap and peered across at her granddaughter, who was leaning back in the armchair with her eyes closed. 'Rosie, you look tired, and I know you said you didn't want to talk about it, but I think the time has come that you need to.' She paused. 'I want to say I was pleased you went to see Alfie tonight; has it helped to ease your worries?'

Rosie opened her eyes but didn't look at her gran. 'No, I'd say it did the exact opposite.'

Mary's eyes narrowed. 'I must admit you do still look troubled. Can I ask why? I was hoping that once you'd had a chat with Alfie you would feel better about things.'

Rosie sat upright. 'I don't know, I can't explain it, it's just a feeling I have. Anyway, he spent a lot of time being angry, snapping at his mother and defending Fran. There were no looks or words of love for me, and there certainly was no touch or kiss hello or goodbye. He didn't even get up to see me to the front door to say goodnight.'

Mary sighed. 'Is that because of his experience of the war? Do you think he could just be less patient with the normal day-to-day things?'

'Maybe, but how much and how long do I keep putting things down to the war? I know it sounds cold but are we just making excuses for him, or is it real? And that's the problem, I don't know. I can't help but think there's more to it than that.' Rosie hesitated. 'Gran, I think I need to follow my heart and just let it be known we will not be getting married.'

Mary was silent for a few minutes. 'I think you need to think about what everyone will say. What the gossips will say. What will Mrs Bennet say?'

Rosie frowned. 'I don't know, but I'm almost certain Alfie doesn't want to marry me.' She lifted herself out of the chair and began to pace around the front room. 'I don't understand any of it. I mean obviously the war has changed him, which is probably why he hasn't written to me or his mother for years, but I get a sense it's more than that.'

Mary rolled up her ball of wool and poked her needles through it. 'Have you asked him?'

'No, I never see him on my own and it's difficult to raise it in front of other people, particularly mothers.'

Mary stared at her granddaughter's back. 'Come and sit down, Rosie. Have you spoken to your mother or any of your friends about it?'

Rosie turned round while wiping her hands across her face before walking back to the armchair. She gripped the wooden arms and lowered herself on to it.

Mary reached out and patted Rosie's hand. 'Don't get upset; whatever you decide to do, I'm on your side.'

Rosie nodded. 'Thank you but unfortunately, it's not just about me; I don't want to hurt anyone with my decision-making.'

'And your friends, what do they say?'

Rosie gave a wry smile. 'Mostly that I should follow my heart, but then some of them are so happy at the thought of marrying their man... and that just emphasises how unhappy I am.' She paused. 'When I saw Alfie earlier, he was more interested in defending Fran. He has been round to see her and her son. I was there and heard them all laughing; there was no anger or coldness from what I could hear. What's more, he was beaming when he opened the door to leave, and yet he told me he was only there to get her to see me. I'm just very confused. I mean, why would she let Alfie in and not me?' Rosie stood up again, her shoulders hunched over as she stepped forward. 'I'd better go and meet Ma from the hospital.' She walked towards the door before stopping to look over her shoulder. 'Please don't tell, Ma, I'll talk to her myself.'

Mary picked up her knitting needles again. 'Don't worry, I won't.'

Rosie nodded. 'Thank you. I forgot to say that Albert, who works in the basement of Foyles, collapsed at work and they took him to hospital so I'm hoping to check on how he is while I'm there. I don't know what caused it, but I hope he's all right, he's a real character.'

'If not, hopefully you'll find out more tomorrow when you go to work.'

Rosie's throat tightened. 'I hope so. The place won't be the same without him.'

* * *

Rosie pushed her card into the slot of the clocking in machine and waited for the click before pulling it out again. She returned her card to its slot before moving to hang up her navy-blue hat.

Mr Leadbetter walked into the staff area and stood in the doorway. He cleared his throat before raising his voice. 'Can I have your attention, please?' He waited for everyone to stop talking.

Molly frowned. 'Is it about Albert? Is he all right?'

Mr Leadbetter held up his hand. 'I will tell you when everyone is listening.'

A chorus of shushing travelled around the room. As everyone turned and faced Mr Leadbetter, the relaxed atmosphere became tense.

Mr Leadbetter stood tall and rigid. 'Albert won't be in work today as he's not well. He's no longer at the hospital.' He coughed. 'Sorry; we took him home after the doctors examined him and his wife is looking after him.'

Victoria spoke in low tones. 'Do we know what's wrong with him and how long he's going to be off for?'

Mr Leadbetter shook his head. 'As you know, Albert's not a young man so it just depends on how well he can fight the influenza he's picked up.' He looked around the room. 'We will have to cover Albert's post for now.'

Ellen took a small step forward. 'Are we allowed to visit him?'

'The doctor's advised that he stay away from people, especially as he was running a temperature. Apparently, they've had several cases in the last few days so it's catching and apparently quite serious.' Mr Leadbetter paused. 'I know we are all very fond of Albert and I'm sure he'll be back to work soon. You know how he loves this place and all of you, so I think it's important we keep his position as up to date as we can, so he doesn't come back to loads of work.'

Victoria stepped forward. 'We'll do it on a rota until we know more about Albert's condition.' She looked around her. 'Vera, you have experience of checking the returns so I think we'll start with you, and then maybe you can show someone else what you are looking for when you're doing the checks.'

Vera nodded. 'It won't be the same doing it without Albert; he always made me laugh while we were working, but I'm happy to do it.'

Victoria frowned. 'Please don't talk about him as if he isn't coming back.'

Vera lowered her eyelashes. 'I'm sorry, I didn't mean to. In fact, that's the last thing I want to do.'

'I know, but we have to stay positive for him and hopefully he'll be back soon.' Victoria smiled. 'To quote Albert, "Vera, get yourself down the apples and pears and check out those books".'

Vera chuckled.

Victoria looked around at some of the sad faces. 'Right, come on, paste on your smiles; we have customers waiting.'

The ladies followed Rosie into the shop, some whispering to each other before parting to go to their work areas.

'Is everything all right?' Victoria sidled up to Rosie. 'You look like you're carrying the worries of the world on your shoulders.'

Rosie raised her eyebrows. 'Yes, well, life isn't always kind to us.' She turned and marched towards the children's section.

Molly watched Rosie approach their busy counter. She frowned. 'Are you all right?'

Rosie's shoulders hunched over. 'I wish everyone would stop asking me that.'

Molly raised her eyebrows. 'I'd say I'm sorry but I'm not; people only ask because they care.'

'Huh, or they want something to gossip about.' Rosie strode past Molly to behind the counter.

Molly studied her for a moment. 'Well obviously that could be true, but I'm not a gossip. I only asked because you look pale and beaten and no one likes to see that. You've always been quite bubbly – well, that is, when you haven't been worrying about Fran or Alfie.'

Rosie shook her head as tears pricked at her eyes. 'I'm sorry, I shouldn't be taking my problems out on you, or anyone else for that matter.'

Molly reached out and stroked Rosie's arm. 'Look, I don't want to pry but you are clearly upset about something, and I think you need to talk about it with someone.'

Rosie lowered her eyelashes. 'I'm just not sleeping very well; things are whirling round in my head.'

'Well, that tells me it's either Alfie or Fran.' Molly stopped talking to write out a payment slip for a customer. She smiled at the woman standing on the other side of the counter as she handed it to her. 'Take this to the payment booth downstairs and when you've paid, you then bring the slip back here to collect your book.' Molly picked the book up to put behind the counter. 'It's a lovely story; I'm sure the child will love it.'

The customer smiled. 'I hope so because it's a present.'

Molly handed the slip of paper over to her. 'Well, don't forget it can always be brought back for the tuppence on returns, and maybe another can be purchased when this one has been read.'

The customer nodded and took the payment slip. 'Thank you, I'll be back shortly.' She turned and walked away.

Molly glanced at Rosie. 'Where were we? Oh yes, Alfie and Fran...'

Rosie sighed. 'When I went round to Fran's, Alfie was there, and I heard them all laughing together.' She paused. 'I don't understand why she can let Alfie in and not me. I also went to Alfie's house last night and when Mrs Bennet was gossiping about Fran, Alfie defended her; he even got angry with his mother.'

Molly stayed silent as she watched the conflict run across Rosie's face.

'You know, there was no loving hello or goodbye; he didn't hold my hand or anything.'

Molly studied her for a moment. 'I want to ask you a question. Victoria is always telling me I need to be more tactful, so this is me trying, it really is.'

Rosie chuckled. 'Go on, ask away.'

Molly nodded. 'Are you upset because of the lack of love Alfie showed you or because he was defending Fran?'

Rosie thought about it for a moment. 'I don't think any of that upsets me. I feel there's a secret and I'm the last to know about it.'

Molly indicated for Ellen to come over and serve the customers while she walked away with Rosie. 'What do you think that secret is?'

Rosie shrugged.

Molly shook her head. 'Don't shrug. I think you know, just like I think I know, but you need to confront the pair of them, as difficult as that is, otherwise you're never going to get any sleep.'

* * *

Sam peered across at Rosie. She looked pale and miles away as she stood near the open classroom window. He watched as the breeze caught a couple of loose strands of her hair. No one could love her more than he did. Was she thinking about Alfie? He didn't dare to dream she was reliving the kiss they shared. He was too scared to hope he had muddied the waters for her regarding Alfie; he knew his behaviour was not very gentlemanly – let alone brotherly – but he had to fight for her. Rosie deserved better than the way his brother had treated her, and given a chance, he knew he could make her happy.

Rosie looked up and saw him staring at her.

Sighing, Sam quickly turned away and gave his attention back to his class, wondering how soon it would be his last day standing in front of them. He glanced back at Rosie; whatever she had been thinking about had left her as she laughed at the children surrounding her. It wouldn't be long before he'd be off fighting for king and country. Would she be single when he returned – *if* he returned – or would she have met someone else? He dropped his pad onto his desk. He couldn't bear the thought of her marrying anyone but him. The problem was he had no idea how to prevent it.

The school bell rang out in the hall announcing the day was over. Sam watched as the children gathered their bags and coats together and formed an orderly line for him to lead them outside.

The children chorused, 'Bye, Miss Burrows,' as they strolled past, some giving a shy wave.

Rosie beamed. 'Bye, try and be good, take care and stay safe.' She stood and picked up the books they had been reading and returned them to the shelves in the reading corner.

Sam turned round and saw Rosie watching through the classroom window as the children said their goodbyes. He slowly handed over the children one by one to the waiting ladies before giving a last wave to them and returning to the classroom. He knew in his heart he had to stop thinking about Rosie. He shook his head; that was easier said than done; he couldn't seem to think about anything else. He had loved her for so long he didn't know how to stop. Maybe going off to war would be for the best; it would certainly stop him from thinking about her and then maybe he would get over her, but he couldn't imagine not thinking about her every day.

'Are you all right, Sam?'

Startled, Sam hadn't realised he had walked back into the classroom. 'Yes, yes of course.'

Rosie studied him for a moment. 'Are you sure? You looked deep in thought when you walked in.'

Sam frowned. 'I was just thinking about the children, and when my last teaching day will be.'

'I can't think about you going off to war. I keep hoping it will end before that day comes.' Rosie pushed a bench under a table.

Sam bent down to pick up some papers. 'I don't think that's going to happen.' He took a deep breath. 'I just need to make sure you are all right? I know better than anyone how brutal Alfie can be, and he wasn't very nice to any of us last night, and Ma was clearly upset after you left.'

Rosie forced a smile. 'Don't worry, Alfie has always been a bit fiery.'

Sam shrugged. 'Don't tell me not to worry because I've been hearing that for years, and I can't stop now.'

Rosie stared at him. 'Sam, I know you mean well but you know how things are, so I can't get caught up in anything else.'

'I know, but I can't change how I feel.' Sam watched her for a moment. 'If nothing else, this war should teach us we need to make the most of every day.'

Rosie collected some pencils together and reached out to give them to Sam; their hands touched as he took them from her. She gasped and quickly stepped back. Heat began to rise in her face. She turned away. 'We should all be doing that anyway.'

Sam was silent for a few seconds, wondering if she had felt the spark between them that he had known for years. He cleared his throat. 'You're right, we should, so on that basis, would you like to go for a walk and enjoy the warmth of the June sunshine? Or we could go for a cuppa somewhere?'

Rosie walked across the classroom, tidying the benches as she went. 'I'm sorry I was short with you.'

Sam smiled. 'That's all right, I know you have a lot on your mind at the moment, but you do know I'm here for you, don't you?'

Rosie nodded as she stood up straight. 'I want to ask you a question; you may not know the answer, but I don't want you talking to anybody about it.'

Frowning, Sam nodded. 'I won't, and that's a promise.' He pulled out the corner of a bench seat and flopped down on it. 'What is it?'

Rosie took a deep breath. 'Do you know who James's father is?'

'No, I don't. Do you?'

Rosie studied Sam for a moment. 'I think it might be Alfie.'

'What?' Sam frowned. 'You said that before, but that can't be right.'

'Why's that, Sam?' Rosie started pacing around the classroom. 'It's the only thing that makes sense.' She stopped and stared at Sam. 'You heard how Alfie defended Fran last night and it would also explain why she shut me out. Her own guilt at sleeping with my boyfriend wouldn't allow her to let me in and be her friend any more.' She started pacing again. 'When I went round to Fran's and Alfie was there, you should have heard them laughing together. When he opened her door, he looked the happiest I have ever seen him.'

Sam shook his head. 'No, there must be another reason for it. I mean, he said he went round there to talk to her about you and your friendship.'

Rosie's lips tightened. 'You know, Alfie doesn't want to marry me. Last night there was no show of love at all, and I think that's because he loves Fran.'

Sam stood up, thrust his hands in his trouser pockets and walked around the room. 'Even if you're right, what are you going to do? No matter what you say to them, you may never get to the bottom of it, so you'll never know the truth.'

Rosie lifted her chin. 'I shall go and talk to Fran and try and find out the truth.' She strode towards the classroom door. 'I'll see you tomorrow.'

* * *

Rosie walked through the black iron gates of London's Regent's Park. As the day wore on, the heat became more comfortable. The skirt of her green floral dress caught in the breeze; she quickly lowered her hand to hold it in place. Her mind was in a whirl – she was now more confused than ever. Her only chance of getting to the truth was through Fran; she was never alone with Alfie to have a private conversation. Was that always his intention? Was he avoiding her as well?

A couple of women sat on a bench watching the children play chase; a little girl couldn't run for giggling. Rosie smiled at them enjoying the sunshine and the freedom the park gave them.

Rosie's mind wandered back to the lovely time the four of them had had in Southend and how lucky they had been to get away from London for the day. There had been plenty of laughter as they'd soaked up the sun and shared a bag of chips on the seafront. She thought hard about that day, trying to recollect the small details that might have given her a clue about what might be ahead. Had she missed some telltale signs that Fran and Alfie were attracted to each other? Had they shared looks behind her back? Had Alfie put his arm around Fran's shoulders more than around hers? Had Fran given him flirtatious looks? The trouble was, Alfie flirted with every girl he saw, so she probably wouldn't have thought anything of it even if she had noticed it. Anger soared through her. She wasn't upset by Fran's possible actions or by the way the pair of them had dealt with their emotions. No, she was angry with herself because she realised she had no feelings for Alfie at all, except possibly contempt for the way he had treated his family and her.

She flopped down on the nearest wooden bench. The slats were hard, but she tried to ignore the uncomfortable feeling as they dug into her back and legs. Was she getting ahead of herself, jumping to conclusions without having any of the facts, just like the gossips had done when Fran had discovered she was pregnant? It dawned on her that she was no better than they were.

Rosie thought back to life before the war began. Alfie had been his usual self, always flirting with her and Fran while putting Sam down. For all of Alfie's bravado, had he been worried about the competition from Sam? Rosie didn't understand it, but she knew something had changed between her and Sam. The way she had responded to Sam's kiss was like nothing else she had experienced, not even with Alfie; if she had, she felt sure they would have spent their last evening together in each other's arms.

Two girls ran past giggling. Rosie guessed their ages to be about nine or ten. She smiled at their happiness and innocence, wondering when that feeling had passed for her. She didn't remember leaving behind her carefree childhood and becoming a woman who worried about everything. Was that also lost because of the war? Everyone was right; she should follow her instinct and not worry about everyone else. All the bad feeling would pass with time, but did she have the courage to think only of her own future? And Sam, what about Sam? Everyone told her he couldn't take his eyes off her when they were in the same room, but until recently he'd never tried to hold her hand or kiss her, although he had asked her out a couple of times, so maybe they were right. She couldn't help wondering if his feelings were real or if he was just trying to get back at Alfie. Rosie shook her head. One thing at a time; she needed to be clear about Alfie and Fran, and if they wouldn't be honest with her, then she needed to take control, and then she might feel better about it all.

17

Fran opened her front door and stepped aside. 'You'd better come in.'

Rosie's mouth dropped open slightly. 'I didn't think you'd let me in, even though you said you would.' She walked inside and looked around. 'Where's your boy?'

Fran shut the door. 'James is in bed for the night.' She pointed to the worn-out armchair. 'Take a seat and I'll make you a cup of tea.'

Rosie gripped her handbag. 'No... no thank you, the tea can wait a while. I'm sorry to come this late; I've obviously been walking around Regent's Park for longer than I realised.'

Fran shrugged. 'That doesn't matter. I know this isn't going to be an easy conversation.'

Rosie stared down at her almost transparent knuckles. 'I feel quite nervous about it, which doesn't make any sense.' She took a deep breath. 'I don't understand what I did wrong. I don't understand how you could just throw away our friendship. I've missed you so much.'

Fran slowly sank down on to the sofa. 'I've missed you too.'

Rosie's eyes widened as she looked up. 'But... but that makes it worse; you were the one who refused to see me. I really don't understand what's going on.' She hesitated before continuing. 'You said you were trying to protect me from the gossips, but we were best friends, and I would have been a support to you when you needed it the most.'

Fran stared down at the wooden floorboards. 'You're right of course, but I couldn't have coped with your sympathy, and what's more, the last thing I needed was you to keep asking me who the father was.'

Rosie pursed her lips. 'Sympathy? It could have happened to any of us.'

Fran glanced up at Rosie. 'But it didn't happen to you.' She paused before taking a deep breath. 'You didn't give in to Alfie before he went off to war—'

'Wait, how do you know about that? I've never talked about it with anyone, not even you; I only recently told Sam.'

Colour flooded Fran's cheeks.

Rosie blinked quickly as tears pricked at her eyes. 'He walked off that night leaving me in tears. I felt dreadful when he walked away, but I also think I hated him for leaving me with that feeling, especially as he was going off to war. I mean, who does that?'

Fran bit down on her lip. 'I don't know what to say.'

'You can start by telling me what this has all been about; how do you know what happened that evening after we had a great day in Southend?'

Fran took a deep breath. 'Rosie, I don't want you to hate me, that's why I've tried to avoid you even though it broke my heart.' Tears slowly ran down Fran's cheeks.

Rosie rushed over to the sofa and wrapped her arms around her friend.

Fran jumped up. 'No, please don't comfort me, I don't deserve it.'

Rosie closed her eyes for a second. 'Please tell me. Let me decide for myself whether you deserve my comfort and support instead of taking that decision away from me.'

Brushing her hands across her damp cheeks, Fran took a couple of deep breaths. 'There's no easy way to say this, so I'm just going to blurt it out and hope you don't hate me – at least not for long.'

Rosie's eyes narrowed as her heart thudded. Was this it? Were her suspicions about to be confirmed? Her gaze didn't leave her friend's face. 'I can't imagine you doing or saying anything that would make me hate you.'

'Well, hold on to that thought because I truly hope you're right.' Fran looked up to the ceiling looking for divine intervention.

Rosie stood up and looked at Fran through teary eyes. 'You're scaring me, just tell me.'

Fran wrung her hands together before clenching them. 'Here goes. After Alfie left you, he came to see me... and one thing led to another... then James was born.'

Rosie flopped back down on to the sofa.

Fran stepped forward but stopped as her words tumbled over one another to finally be heard. 'It wasn't planned, it just happened. Alfie can be very persuasive. I would never have done anything to hurt you intentionally, you were my best friend.'

'And yet you did. Does Alfie know James is his son?'

Fran nodded.

'When did you tell him?'

Fran's hands gripped each other. 'I wrote to him when I realised I was pregnant, and again to let him know he had a son.'

Rosie shook her head; the hurt she felt was written all over her face. 'That's probably when he stopped writing to me.'

Fran reached out to Rosie. 'I'm so sorry.'

Rosie jumped up. 'I need to go; this is a lot for me to take in.' She marched to the door and didn't look back as the tears streamed down her face. She shook her head; she hadn't learnt anything she hadn't guessed, so why did she feel so hurt? It dawned on her that the tears weren't for her or Alfie, they were for the lost years of friendship and the knowledge that their friendship could never be the same.

* * *

Rosie pushed her front door open and pulled the key back through the letter box. It clattered against the wooden door when she let go of it. She eyed the stairs and fought the urge to go straight to her bedroom; her mother would never allow that to happen. She and David had been raised to always find the family and say hello when they came home. She checked her face in the mirror in the hall above the small console table. She looked pale and her eyes were red. Taking a deep breath, Rosie smoothed down the skirt of her green dress and walked into the front room.

Mary looked up from her knitting. 'Hello, Rosie, you're late. Has it been another busy day? You do look tired.'

Rosie forced herself to smile as she sat down in the armchair. 'I *am* tired, I didn't sleep very well last night.' She peered over at her mother. 'It's good to see you have a night off, you work long hours.'

Ivy nodded as she stared at her daughter. 'Have you been crying?'

'No.'

Ivy shook her head. 'I'm sorry, but I don't believe you. Your eyes are quite red.'

'I'm just tired, it's been a hard week.' Rosie rested her head on the soft back of the armchair and closed her eyes.

Ivy peered at her mother-in-law, who shrugged, before looking back at her daughter. She took a deep breath. 'In the last few weeks you've become more withdrawn; in fact, you've got worse since Alfie's got home, which is something I don't understand.' She paused. 'I thought you'd be really happy knowing he's safely back home.'

Rosie peered through her eyelashes at her mother. 'Ma, I really don't want to talk about it.'

'It might help you to talk; you know what they say, "a problem shared is a problem halved".'

Rosie shook her head. 'Ma, you need to let it go, and don't keep quoting that saying to me.'

Ivy frowned. 'Can't you see I'm worried about you, and so's your grandma? You're hardly eating and from the state of you, you're obviously not sleeping either.'

Rosie sighed before pulling herself upright. She rubbed her eyes before taking a deep breath. 'Alfie is the father of Fran's baby.'

Ivy and Mary exclaimed in unison. '*What?*'

Rosie's gaze travelled between them. 'You heard me; I don't think it needs repeating.'

Ivy frowned. 'That can't be true, he loves you.'

Rosie gave a scathing laugh. 'No, Ma, that's just it. I don't think he does, or ever has done.'

'But he asked you to wait for him, I don't understand.' Ivy stared down as she wrung her hands together. 'He must love you; maybe it's the war that's changed him.'

'No, Ma, when I think back, him asking me to wait for him

had nothing to do with love and marriage. In fact, I don't think he mentioned those words at all. Remember, he was always a bit of a Jack the Lad. The difference is that I was young and got taken in by it, and it sounds like Fran did too.'

'Huh, she's blaming him, is she?' Mary glanced at Rosie's pale features. 'Well, I blame Fran; she must have led him on.'

'For goodness' sake, Gran. Why is everything always the woman's fault? I expect he tried it on with her just like he did with me; the only difference is I said no, and she didn't. Her position could have been my position; you can't keep blaming Fran for everything.'

Ivy tightened her lips. 'Does Mrs Bennet know?'

'I shouldn't think so. After all, she joined in with the gossips and I'm sure she wouldn't have done that if she'd known James was her grandson.' Rosie took a breath. 'It's sad that she has missed out on those wonderful baby years with him. He seems a happy child, and he's clearly loved.'

Ivy glanced at her mother.

Rosie shrugged. 'Do you both feel better now you know?'

Ivy raised her eyebrows. 'I don't know what I thought the problem was, but I certainly wasn't expecting that. What are you going to do? Are you going to talk to Fran or Alfie about it?'

'I don't know, it was Fran who told me, but I left before the conversation was over.' Rosie leant back in the chair. 'I lost a best friend because of it and that hurts.'

'There's no doubt she shouldn't have betrayed you like that.' Mary eyed Rosie as she clenched her hands. 'Has she said whether Alfie is going to marry her?'

Rosie tutted. 'I don't know, Gran; we didn't get that far.'

* * *

Foyles was beginning to get busy as always. Rosie could hear a baby crying; she immediately swung round to see where the sound was coming from.

Victoria smiled as she approached Rosie. 'It's all right, the mother is rocking it back and forth. I did ask if she needed help, but she said no.' She glanced over her shoulder. 'Some women are amazing. I can't imagine coping with a crying child while shopping or trying to find a book I was after.'

Rosie forced herself to smile. 'No, I know what you mean, but maybe some people are just naturals.' Her mind drifted to Fran, and how she had coped on her own for so long. 'Mind you, I suppose if you're getting married it won't be long before babies come along.' She paused. 'Imagine if you had twins; how would you cope then?'

Victoria laughed. 'Don't say that. One child terrifies me enough.'

Rosie tilted her head. 'Don't you want children then?'

'Sometimes I do and sometimes I don't. Having been a stand-in mother for my brother and sister, I'm not sure I want to do it for real; it's hard work and I spent my whole time worrying about them.' Victoria raised her eyebrows. 'But then you look at Alice and she loves being a mother. Anyway, Molly's married and she hasn't had the joy of children yet, so it's her turn first.'

Rosie giggled. 'I don't think it happens like that. I get the impression it's the luck of the draw. I mean, look at Fran.'

Victoria tilted her head. 'Some would say she was unlucky, but I expect she wouldn't be without her son now.'

Rosie nodded. 'No. Anyway, I'm happy to work in the basement today and give Vera a break.' Rosie's gaze scanned Foyles as the customers began to fill the shop. 'Is there any news on how Albert is doing?'

'Unfortunately, it's not looking good for him, but we're hoping he will improve given time. This influenza seems to have dragged him down more than usual. I must admit to missing his cheerfulness, and the funny rhyming slang he keeps trying to teach us.'

Rosie nodded. 'I know what you mean; he was always making me laugh.'

Victoria studied her closely. 'I'm concerned about you because you do look very tired, but I sense you want to be on your own, so you can work in the basement. It's not an easy job; you have to work quickly, but thoroughly.'

Rosie nodded. 'I know, I've helped Albert before; he showed me what the job entailed.'

Victoria sighed. 'All right, send Vera up to see me and I'll come down and see you after, and we'll talk then.'

'Thank you.' Rosie sped off to the back of the shop. She wanted to avoid Sam if he came in to see her, as well as Alfie and Fran. She shook her head. Her imagination was running away with itself. Alfie and Fran had never come into the shop looking for her, so why would they start now?

* * *

Sam glared at Alfie as he slouched on the sofa puffing on a cigarette. 'Rosie didn't come to the school today to listen to the children read, and I can't help feeling you have something to do with it.'

Alfie chuckled. 'You would like me to be the cause, wouldn't you, but maybe she's not as sweet as you think she is, or maybe she's had enough of you and this family.'

Sam's hands clenched by his sides. 'I don't understand what your game is. You've come home and not really bothered with your girlfriend, or anyone else. In fact, you've hardly left the house except, it would seem, to see Fran, and I know you well enough to know it's not because you want to spend your precious time at home.'

Alfie smirked. 'Look at you – becoming a regular detective. Have you found the courage to tell Rosie you love her yet?'

Sam's eyes narrowed as he stared at his brother.

Alfie laughed. 'I'm guessing your silence means no.' He shook his head. 'You missed an opportunity there. Let's face it, I was out of the way with the odds in favour of me not returning at all, and yet you still didn't make your move.'

'No, I didn't, because why would I do that to my brother or – if it came to it – anyone else? Anyway, it doesn't matter, I'm expecting to go off for my army training in the next few days; I'm just waiting to hear.'

Alfie stared at him. 'Don't give me that; you haven't had your medical yet.'

Sam raised his eyebrows. 'I have and I passed.'

Alfie frowned as he stared at his brother. 'I think you're messing with me. Ma would've said, and I'm sure there would have been tears.'

'Ma doesn't know.' Sam paused. 'No one does, and I want it to stay that way.'

Alfie clasped the cold wooden arms of the chair.

Sam tilted his head slightly. 'It's my turn to fight for king and country.'

Alfie jumped up and spoke through gritted teeth. 'It's not a game, you know, seeing men and boys being blown up all around you. There's nothing glorious about it. You won't last five minutes.' He turned his back on his brother for a moment.

'You did, so why wouldn't I?' Sam stretched out and grabbed Alfie's arm to make him face him.

Alfie grabbed his hand and violently bent it backwards.

Sam slowly fell to the floor, his eyes pinched shut. 'Are you trying to break my hand?' he yelled as the pain ravaged him.

Alfie tightened his hold. 'That's exactly what I'm doing; you're not going to the front if I have anything to do with it.' He pulled back his arm and with a clenched fist he thumped his brother in the face. 'You are not going; no man should see the things I have. One day you'll appreciate this because I'm saving you and you just don't realise it.' He pulled back his arm and punched him in the face again.

Sam lost his balance as his knees buckled before falling backwards and hitting his head on the iron grate.

Alfie stared down at his brother. 'Come on, Sam, stop messing about, get up.' He nudged him with his foot but there was no movement.

'What's all the noise in here?' Mrs Bennet rushed in and stared at Sam on the floor. 'Alfie, what have you done?' She knelt down and tried to find Sam's pulse. She put her head to his chest, but panic began to sweep over her. 'Alfie, run to Rosie's and ask Ivy to come and look at Sam; she's a nurse so she'll know what to do, then ask at the corner shop if they know someone with a vehicle to help get him to the hospital. Goodness knows what that will cost but we'll find the money from somewhere.'

Alfie stood rooted to the spot.

Mrs Bennet screamed, 'Alfie, go and fetch Ivy, and hurry up!'

Startled, Alfie jolted into action and immediately ran towards the front door.

'Hurry up!' Mrs Bennet sobbed. 'Please stay with me, Sam, please; if nothing else, you have Rosie to live for. Hold on to the fact you love her and I'm sure she loves you too.' She paused. 'Well, I don't know that for sure, but I will say anything for you to come round and be all right.' She stroked his face. 'I don't tell you I love you enough, and I probably haven't said it since you were a small child, but I do love you.' Mrs Bennet leant over and kissed Sam's forehead.

The thud of the front door made Mrs Bennet jump. 'Alfie, is that you?'

'Yes.' Alfie stepped aside, breathless from running to catch up with Mrs Burrows. 'Mrs Burrows and Rosie are here.'

Ivy and Rosie immediately ran into the front room.

Rosie gasped at the sight of Sam out cold. 'What happened? Alfie, what did you do to him?'

Alfie scowled. 'What makes you think I did anything?'

Ivy put the tips of her fingers around Sam's wrist and felt his pulse. 'We need to get him to hospital. If we can get him to the Middlesex, I'll be able to keep an eye on him.' She looked up at Mrs Bennet. 'Head injuries have to be monitored closely, and this other hand looks like it's been broken. It's going to need plastering so that it heals properly.'

Alfie ran out the door. 'I'll look out for the ambulance.'

Rosie looked troubled as she touched her mother's shoulder. 'Is he going to be all right?'

Ivy shrugged. 'We won't know until we get him to the hospital.'

Rosie glared at Mrs Bennet. 'Alfie went too far this time; what the hell was he thinking?'

18

Rosie sat next to the bed and stared down at Sam. His face was ashen but calm. There were still traces of blood in his hair, which she hadn't noticed at the house. His hand and half of his lower arm were covered with plaster to support his broken hand and wrist.

Ivy walked to the foot of the bed. 'I've just come to check on him.'

Rosie looked at her mother. 'How long do you think he'll be unconscious for?'

Ivy stared at Sam. 'Head injuries are a bit unknown; it can be anything from minutes to months, but his signs are good so there doesn't appear to be any internal damage.'

Rosie took Sam's uninjured hand and squeezed it with her own.

Ivy rested her hand on her daughter's shoulder. 'Try talking to him; we don't know if someone who is unconscious can hear or not, but you've got nothing to lose by trying.'

Rosie scowled. Standing up, she stepped aside so her mother

could get nearer to Sam. 'I've noticed Alfie hasn't come to see him yet.'

'I'm sure he will; I expect he feels guilty.' Ivy gently put her fingertips at the base of Sam's thumb to check his pulse before placing his hand back on top of the bed covers.

Rosie shook her head. 'That'll be the day when Alfie feels guilty about anything.' She paused. 'Mrs Bennet said she'd be back later.'

'Mrs Bennet needs to know the hospital will probably call the police because it's an assault which has ended with a head injury.' Ivy studied her daughter's washed-out features before walking back to the foot of the bed. 'You need to go home and get some rest; I can let you know if anything changes.'

Rosie moved back to the side of the bed. 'I don't know, I'll see. Mrs Bennet will be distraught if Alfie gets into trouble with the police, but she needs to understand he's gone too far this time.'

Ivy watched her daughter stroking Sam's hand. 'He means more to you than you realise.'

Rosie frowned but said nothing.

Ivy continued. 'It's quite normal when something threatens life as we know it to suddenly realise how important people and things are to you.' She picked up Sam's notes and began to write in her observations.

Rosie kept her eyes on Sam, waiting for some movement, but there was nothing. 'Come on, Sam, wake up.'

Ivy crept away to give Rosie her privacy and moved on to her next patient.

Rosie slowly lowered herself back on to the chair she had recently vacated. 'Come on, Sam, you have to wake up, the children need you; *I* need you. Your young adoring fans in the school will be missing you desperately. Even your mother and Alfie will be beside themselves with worry.' She stared at him for a moment before leaning back on the chair. She looked around at the other patients. Some were groaning as they tried to move, others were shouting out to no one in particular. Rosie watched her mother going from bed to bed, trying to give comfort where she could.

Frowning, Rosie looked back at Sam. 'Please wake up, I want you to be all right. You are my dearest and closest friend. When I think about your kiss… oh it doesn't matter, I'm not even sure what love is, and how do you know whether you're in love or not?'

'How is he doing?'

Rosie looked round to see Mrs Bennet's anxious face staring at Sam. 'There's no change. My ma says his signs are good, so we just have to wait for him to come round; she's monitoring him every half hour or so; that way they'll catch any change early.' She looked behind Mrs Bennet. 'No Alfie?'

Mrs Bennet lowered her eyes. 'No, I think he feels dreadful for what he's done.'

Colour rushed up Rosie's face. 'And so he should, he could have killed him. I'm surprised you haven't dragged him here to see what he's done to his brother, or even called the police.'

Mrs Bennet's head dropped. 'We can't have the police involved. Alfie didn't mean it, he feels awful about it.'

'It may not be up to you. Apparently, the hospital might call the police because it looks like an assault with a head injury.' Rosie's lips tightened. 'He always feels dreadful, but it's about time he grew up. He talks about things he's seen and experienced thanks to this war, and yet he has no compassion about him.'

Mrs Bennet sighed. 'I know he has a horrible streak in him.' A tear rolled down her cheek. 'I truly don't know where I've gone wrong. I gave him everything. He never had the best because we couldn't afford the best, but he never did without. He's always been awful to Sam but that got worse as he got older, and Sam wouldn't say boo to a goose.'

Rosie glanced over her shoulder. 'It's time for you to let him know you love him and ask him to wake up.' She stood up. The chair scratched on the floor as she pushed it away from her and towards Mrs Bennet. 'Here, take this and talk to him; my ma says they don't know if it helps or not but there's nothing to lose by trying.' She sighed. 'Sam, I've got to go to work but your ma is here to chat to you. Don't worry about your class, I'll stop by the school and let them know you are in hospital.' Rosie leant forward and kissed his forehead before turning away.

* * *

Victoria and Molly placed their wrapped sandwiches on the table on either side of Rosie.

Molly nudged Rosie. 'How are you getting on in the basement? I bet it's nice and quiet after being in the shop.'

Rosie laughed. 'Yes, it's certainly that, but the returns have kept me on my toes.'

Victoria frowned. 'I'm sorry I didn't get down to see you yesterday, but I haven't known whether I'm coming or going the last couple of days.'

Rosie intertwined her fingers on her lap. 'That's all right, it wasn't necessary. I've been kept busy.'

Victoria studied Rosie. 'You look a bit better than you did yesterday.'

Molly raised her eyebrows. 'Were you not feeling well then?'

Rosie leant back on the chair, the hard wooden slats pressing into her back. 'I was just tired.'

Molly tilted her head as she examined Rosie. 'You do look peaky, is something keeping you awake at night?'

Rosie peered down at the table and shook her head.

Molly screwed her eyes together. 'I take it it's something you don't want to talk about.' She studied Rosie. 'That's all right, everyone is entitled to keep their own privacy.' She laughed. 'I've kept unnecessary secrets in the past and they've all come back and bitten me; what I've learnt is that secrets always come out eventually.'

Victoria laughed at Molly. 'Yes, when you changed jobs but didn't tell your family, that made life very difficult for Alice and me.'

Molly giggled. 'I know but look, I wouldn't have met Andrew if I hadn't changed jobs—'

'Or frightened the life out of us when you got caught up in that explosion.' Victoria sucked in her breath. 'Alice and I had never been so scared when we couldn't find you that night.'

Molly raised her eyebrows. 'Anyway, this conversation was not meant to be about discussing my shortfalls, I was just pointing out that secrets always come back to haunt you.'

Rosie's fingers tensed. 'That was an awful night. I can remember feeling the explosion at home and we never realised it was the munitions factory, otherwise we would have all been down there looking for my father. I've heard lots of stories of the devastation, so it's probably just as well we didn't get there.'

Victoria reached out and squeezed Rosie's arm. 'I'm sorry, we shouldn't be talking about something that brings back terrible memories for you.'

Rosie forced a smile. 'Well, we can't pretend it didn't happen and as they say, "life goes on", even if you don't want it to. I know my father would want us all to be as happy as we can be.' She took a deep breath. 'You're right about the secrets though, and everyone will know soon enough, so I might as well tell you.' She stared down at her hands as they gripped together. 'Fran's son is

Alfie's. He's the father.' She didn't look up, but the silence was deafening. 'I would like to be able to say that that's it, but I spent most of last night at the hospital, with my ma, because Alfie broke Sam's wrist and hand before punching him. Sam fell back and hit his head on the fire grate.'

Victoria reached out and squeezed Rosie's hands with hers. 'I'm so sorry, Rosie, I really am. Is Sam all right? Have the police been called?'

'Oh no, they haven't yet, at least I don't think so, but Mrs Bennet wouldn't be able to cope with the police arresting Alfie.' Rosie sucked in her breath. 'Sam's still unconscious, I only left when his mother arrived.'

Victoria watched Rosie whose eyes were weepy as she struggled to hold it together. 'Sam clearly means a lot to you; hopefully he'll come round soon, and he'll be all right. Would you like to take some time off to be with him?'

Rosie forced a weak smile. 'No, thank you, I need to keep busy. Besides, his mother will be with him most of the time.'

Molly glared at Victoria before tutting. 'Have you spoken to Alfie about what he did to Sam and whether he's the father of your best friend's child?'

Rosie shook her head.

Molly gasped. 'Well, don't you think you should?'

Rosie shrugged. 'And say what?'

Molly sighed. 'Ask the man outright. Look, he asked you to wait for him and then supposedly went and propositioned your best friend. I'd certainly have something to say about it.'

Victoria's gaze moved from Rosie to Molly. 'Not everyone is like you, Molly. Not everyone wants to confront situations, and it's clear Rosie is hurting.'

Molly looked away from them both. 'How can you be sure

about anything if you don't question things? It's beyond me why you wouldn't do it.'

Rosie's eyes narrowed. 'I don't think Fran has lied to me, and her avoiding me since it came out she was pregnant suddenly makes sense.'

Molly frowned. 'But don't you think you deserve to be treated better than that?'

Rosie peered at Molly. 'What do you mean?'

Molly grabbed Rosie's hand. 'You have been waiting for this man who hasn't written to you for God knows how long, and you haven't known whether he's dead or alive, but you've still stayed true to your word. And yet, apparently, he couldn't stay true to his word for one evening, so don't you think you should get the answers from the man himself?'

Victoria shook her head and opened her mouth to speak.

'No, Victoria, it's all right.' Rosie held up her hand. 'Molly's right, I need to talk to Alfie instead of tying myself up in knots.'

* * *

Rosie sighed as she left Foyles; it had been a hard day, but she had got through it, with help from the girls. She was lucky to have such a wonderful job with so many caring people.

'Rosie...'

Rosie stopped at the sound of her name and glanced over her shoulder. Fran stood by the Foyles door, her hand resting on the battered handle of a pushchair.

'We need to talk...' Fran reached down and patted her son's hand. 'I've hardly slept since we last spoke and I wasn't sure if you would come back again.' She paused. 'The thing is... the thing is, I know I've been a terrible friend to you, and there's no excuse for that—'

'Is everything all right, Rosie?'

Startled, Rosie saw Molly and Victoria peering at her and Fran. 'Yes... everything is good, thank you.'

Victoria nodded before putting her arm through Molly's and tugging her to leave them to it.

Molly frowned. 'If you're sure?'

Rosie nodded. 'Thank you, I'll see you tomorrow.'

Victoria nudged Molly. 'Come on, otherwise we'll never get to Alice's. See you tomorrow, Rosie.'

Rosie watched them both walk away.

'Can we talk, please?' Fran wheeled the pushchair nearer to Rosie. 'I've missed you and it breaks my heart that I've hurt you so much. I shouldn't have shut you out.'

Rosie watched James sitting quietly, playing with a teddy bear. 'And yet you did it anyway.'

'I should have been honest, but I was scared.' Fran looked around her. 'Can we go somewhere quieter to talk? I don't want everyone knowing my business, or yours.'

Rosie glanced around. 'I suppose we could go to your place; at least your son can run around then.'

The corner of Fran's mouth lifted. 'Thank you.'

The pair walked on in silence. Rosie's mind was in a whirl. Fran had given her a reason not to marry Alfie, and she didn't know how she felt about it. In her turmoil, she couldn't decide if she was happy she had a way out without everyone moaning at her, or hurt that Fran hadn't felt she could talk to her.

Fran gave Rosie a sideways glance as they walked along. 'I know I've said it before but I'm really sorry. It was just panic on my part; I didn't know what to say to you or anybody. No one knows Alfie's the father, except of course Alfie – and now you.'

Rosie stared straight ahead. 'Why did you decide to tell me

now? I know Alfie claims that's what he went round to see you about, but I have to say I don't believe it.'

Fran sucked in her breath. 'He wants to be a proper father to James, so that means being able to go to the park or to the shops with him, which he hasn't been able to do in the last couple of years.'

Rosie shook her head. 'Knowing Alfie as we do, it's a wonder he believed he was the father.'

Fran gave a little smile. 'He's not as bad as we all thought. It's all a front with him, he's a softie really.'

Rosie frowned. 'Are we talking about the same man? He's mean to everyone, and if he isn't mean to you, then you obviously hold a special place in his heart.' Staring straight ahead, Rosie took a breath. 'You know the man you call a softie put his brother in hospital yesterday. He's unconscious and has a broken hand and wrist.'

Fran gasped. 'What? What happened? Did they get in a fight over something?'

Rosie stared at Fran. 'Maybe. All I know is Sam's in a bad way and Alfie is responsible.'

Panic ran across Fran's face. 'I need to speak to Alfie; he will need me right now. I know he will be suffering over what has happened. There must've been a reason for him hurting Sam; there's more to this than we know. You know Alfie has trouble sleeping; he's had nightmares and flashbacks since he's been back. He wakes up sweating.'

Rosie shook her head. 'How do you know all that? The nightmares and everything.'

Fran watched James playing with his teddy. 'I could say he told me, but I don't want any more lies between us.' She took a breath and looked at Rosie. 'There have been times when he's stayed with me overnight.'

Rosie's eyes widened. 'My, you do love him, don't you?'

Fran lowered her eyelashes. 'I always have done, but I didn't think he knew I existed in the same way he did you. Why do you think I said yes when he came knocking four years ago?' She paused. 'I didn't think about what I was doing, I just thought about being with the one man I truly loved and yes, it's been hard, but I wouldn't be without James.' She glanced across at Rosie. 'When everything settled down and I discovered I was pregnant, I knew you would eventually find out I wasn't a true friend to you, but I wanted to try and delay it for as long as possible. Yes, I regret what I did to our friendship, but I do love Alfie, so I don't regret that night and my son.'

Rosie thought about Alfie and the way he talked to Sam and his mother. Maybe being a father had brought out his good side in front of Fran.

They had reached Fran's home now, and Fran pulled the string through the letter box. The key thudded against the door as she tugged on it. She jiggled the key in the lock to undo the front door. 'Come on, James, let's get you out of this pushchair and you can play with your wooden blocks, maybe build a tower.'

James ran into the room, went straight to his toy box and began collecting his coloured blocks.

Fran followed him inside with the pushchair. 'Rosie, do you love Alfie?'

Rosie was silent as she walked in and shut the door behind her. 'Why do you ask?'

Colour flooded Fran's face. 'Well, I've just told you I've always loved him, but I didn't think anyone noticed, especially as he flirted with you so much.'

Rosie's eyes widened. 'Do you think Alfie knew?'

Fran shrugged. 'I don't know, but he knew where to come on his last night to get his needs fulfilled.'

Rosie shook her head. 'You hid your feelings well; at least I never noticed. Why didn't you tell me?'

Fran shrugged. 'I don't know, I always assumed you two would get married.'

'And now you don't.'

Fran closed her eyes. 'To be honest, I don't know what to think, but I know Alfie won't be here for long, so I want to make the most of the time we have.' She looked at Rosie. 'I suppose we shouldn't be discussing this now; I expect you would rather be at the hospital with Sam.'

Rosie nodded. 'I hope and pray he's going to be all right; Alfie has a lot to answer for.'

Fran took a breath. 'You do know Sam has loved you for years, and I don't think there is anything he wouldn't do for you, but his loyalty to his brother always got in the way.'

Rosie smirked. 'It's a shame Alfie hasn't shown the same loyalty and respect.'

* * *

Rosie walked along Foley Street to All Souls Primary School. She paused at the metal gates, taking in the stillness that surrounded her. Closing her eyes, she sucked in her breath and let it out again slowly. Opening her eyes, she stared at the school building. She told herself she owed it to Sam and the children in his class to explain why he wasn't at school. Her vision became watery as tears pricked at her eyes. She sent up a silent prayer that Sam would wake up and everything would be fine.

Taking a deep breath, she reached out and opened the school gate. Its metal hinges screamed in the silence as she closed it behind her. Her small heels clipped the ground with each step towards the school entrance. She wondered what to say to the children; she didn't want to scare them, but she had to be prepared for tears from his admirers.

A man's stern voice travelled through the wooden door of Sam's classroom.

Rosie hesitated before lifting her hand to rap on it.

The man's authoritative voice called out, 'Come in.'

Rosie twisted the door handle and entered.

Several children jumped up and ran towards her.

The man stood tall at the front of the class as his voice rang out. 'Sit down!'

The children stood rooted to the spot.

'Now.' The man stepped nearer to Rosie, as the children slowly moved back. 'I'm Mr Shaw, what can I do for you?'

Tom put up his hand. 'It's Miss Burrows, sir. When Mr Bennet was here, she came in and taught us to read.'

Mr Shaw frowned as he turned to stare at Tom. 'Well, that's very nice but I'm sure we no longer need Miss Burrows's assistance.'

Tom stood up. 'But sir, she made reading fun.' His words were greeted with loud murmurings from the other children.

'Sit down!' Mr Shaw picked up a ruler from his desk and stepped towards Tom. 'For a small child, you have a lot to say for yourself and need to be taught obedience and respect.'

Panic ran across Rosie's face as she raised her voice. 'Mr Shaw, I'm sorry to disrupt your class but I thought I should come and explain to the children what has happened to Sam – Mr Bennet.'

Mr Shaw peered over at Rosie. 'Do they need to know? They are just children.'

Rosie gave a faint smile. 'I believe they do. It's important they know he'll be back in their classroom as soon as he can.'

Tom gave Mr Shaw a sideways glance before shifting his gaze

to Rosie. 'He will be back, Miss, won't he? I mean, what's happened to him? We all miss him.'

Rosie stepped further into the room. 'Mr Bennet has had an accident and he's unconscious in hospital, but hopefully he'll soon come round and be well enough to come back to you all.'

One of the girls ran over to Rosie and put her small hand in hers.

Rosie stooped down and gently brushed away the tears on her cheeks. 'Don't get upset, I'm sure Mr Bennet will be back, he's being well looked after.' She smiled and wrapped her arms around her. 'In fact, he's being looked after by my ma, she's a nurse.' Rosie took a breath before forcing herself to smile. 'I tell you what, why don't you all draw him a picture or write him a letter and I'll collect them and take them to the hospital. I'm sure when he wakes up from his deep sleep, they will make him smile.'

Mr Shaw stood watching the scene in front of him. 'There's a war going on and you children have to learn not to get attached to people.'

Rosie gasped as she heard his words. 'Mr Shaw, I don't know what age group you are used to teaching but these are young children, and they need to be shown kindness and love, as we all do – especially at this time.'

Mr Shaw pulled back his shoulders and lifted his chin. 'If you've said what you came to say, I'll thank you not to interfere with my class.'

Rosie looked around at the sad faces staring at her. 'I'll be back soon to listen to your funny voices while you read to me, I promise.'

The children ran forward and wrapped their arms around Rosie; some were clasped around her legs.

Rosie hugged them all tight, thinking how this class wasn't

the same without Sam, and she wasn't sure she was either. 'Now do your drawings, or whatever you want, and I'll come back and collect them.'

Tom gave Rosie a watery stare. 'You promise, Miss?'

Rosie ruffled his hair. 'Of course, and I'll tell Mr Bennet how you all want him to come back to school because you miss him.' She paused. 'Perhaps tonight when you kneel at your beds to say your prayers you could ask God to make Mr Bennet better because you want him to come back to school.'

The children looked at her wide-eyed.

Tom nodded. 'Yeah, I pray every night for God to keep my pa safe so he can come home to us.'

Rosie nodded.

A little girl chimed up. 'I do that too, and I thank him for the food that we have to eat.'

The rest of the class started chatting and smiling at one another.

Rosie breathed a sigh of relief. 'Right, I have to go, but don't forget to say your prayers tonight and I'll see you soon.' She turned to walk away to the sound of the children talking about their prayers.

Mr Shaw cleared his throat. 'Thank you, Miss Burrows, your love and kindness has indeed brought results.'

Rosie nodded before leaving the classroom.

19

Rosie wrapped her hands around the china cup. The warmth of the hot tea seeped through to her fingers. Her thoughts were with Sam, lying unconscious in a hospital bed. Her mind kept jumping around. Fran's words about Alfie not hurting Sam intentionally kept repeating themselves over and over again. Had love blinded Fran to Alfie's shortcomings, or was Rosie just determined to hate him for what he did to Sam, and everyone connected to him?

Ivy studied her daughter. 'You look miles away. I know you're worried about Sam, but is everything else all right?'

Rosie sat her cup on the saucer, the teaspoon chinking against the cup as she placed it down. 'I've been thinking about Fran and Alfie. In fact, I've barely thought about anything else.'

Ivy watched her troubled features. 'That explains why you look so tired; well, that and spending hours sitting with Sam last night.'

Rosie sighed. 'I saw Fran earlier; she was waiting outside Foyles for me. She regrets going with Alfie behind my back. I mean, she obviously loves her son, but she wishes she'd been honest with me. It seems she's always loved Alfie, and he probably knew it and took advantage of her feelings.'

Ivy's eyes widened. 'Had she never mentioned having feelings for him?'

Rosie shook her head. 'No, but that's because she always thought we would get married—'

'Until that last night. I don't know who I'm more disgusted with; they both showed a blatant disregard for you.' Ivy paused. 'I know it's not really anything to do with me, but have you made any decisions about it all?'

Rosie shook her head. 'Yes, no...'

'Well, you might feel better when you do make some decisions, whatever they are. It's all about taking control of things that affect you.'

Rosie gave her mother a wry smile. 'Molly at work thinks I should confront Alfie and get the answers from him.'

Ivy nodded. 'I think she's right.'

Rosie's eyes widened. 'You surprise me, Ma. I thought you'd be a keep-quiet-because-men-have-to-do-what-they-have-to-do person.'

Ivy laughed. 'That was my mother's way of thinking but remember, you're not married, so you don't have to put up with anything; once you're married, things do change because some men think they no longer have to worry because they believe they own you.'

'I've never heard you talk like that, Ma, not even when the suffragettes were demonstrating. You never said whether you agreed or disagreed with them.'

Ivy gave a small smile. 'Not all men are the same so I don't want to put you off getting married, but if you think it would be a mistake marrying Alfie, then don't do it. You know Gran and I will stand by you and any decisions you make; we just want you to be happy and that's all that matters to me.'

Rosie pushed back her dining chair, trying to ignore the screeching noise its feet made on the floor. She stretched her arms out and wrapped them around her mother. 'Thank you, Ma, it means a lot.' She stepped back. 'I've decided to go round and see him later.'

Ivy nodded. 'Good, I want to see your happy face again. I've missed you.'

Rosie smiled. 'I'm sorry, Ma, it has affected me more than I realised. If it helps, I know I won't be marrying Alfie. I don't love him and I don't think he loves me, but it would be wrong of me to say anything until Alfie and I have had that conversation.'

Ivy breathed a sigh of relief. 'I can't pretend I'm sorry about that decision. In my opinion, it's definitely the right one. I don't think you were ever right for each other.'

Rosie frowned. 'You've never said.'

Ivy laughed. 'Would it have made any difference if I had?'

Rosie shrugged as she sat back down again.

Ivy shook her head. 'The thing is, it's only a decision you could make because only you know how you feel.'

Rosie nodded. 'I think I've always known what I had to do, I just didn't want to do it, but when I saw how happy Victoria and Ellen are about the prospect of marrying their men, that reminded me that wasn't how I felt.'

Ivy studied her daughter for a moment. 'Do you think he will marry Fran then?' She paused in the silence. 'I know it's a hard question and you obviously don't know the answer to it, but how will you feel if that's what happens?'

Rosie fiddled with her blue skirt. 'I don't know if they'll

marry, but if Fran loves him, then I hope they do have a happy ending, she deserves it.'

Ivy leant forward and squeezed her daughter's hand. 'All things considered, I think that's very gracious of you. I mean, neither of them thought about you, did they?'

'That may well be true, Ma, but there's been enough bad feeling and guilt flying around and it's time to move on.'

Ivy nodded. 'And what about Sam? I know he's unconscious at the moment, but his vital signs are good, so I do think it's just a matter of time before he comes round.' Ivy stared at her daughter for a moment. 'I hear he's had his call-up papers – not that he can go anywhere at the moment.'

'Yes, he has to go for a medical; actually, he's probably had it, but he's not mentioned it.'

Ivy looked thoughtful. 'You do know he's in love with you, don't you?'

Rosie frowned. 'That's what Fran said.'

Ivy smiled. 'His eyes never leave you and when he thinks no one is looking, the love he feels is all over his face for all to see.'

Rosie blushed. 'One of the girls at Foyles mentioned that sometime ago but I thought it was nonsense.'

Ivy laughed. 'Your father liked Sam; he saw him as being more reliable and caring.'

Rosie laughed. 'That makes him sound boring.'

Ivy shook her head. 'No, he's just the opposite to Alfie – now you tell me which you'd prefer.'

Rosie gave her mother a sideways glance. 'I'm not falling for that one, Ma; I want to marry because I love someone and not because they have the right personality.' She hesitated before continuing. 'I'm not even sure I know what love is.'

Ivy tilted her head slightly. 'It's hard to put into words. I think it's about caring and wanting to be with them all the time. Putting their needs before your own; that's not the same as letting them walk all over you, though – it has to be teamwork. You pick each other up when times are hard. Getting butterflies in your stomach when you touch or kiss. I think when you love someone, they absorb your whole mind and body, and you want them with you all the time and when they're not, you feel like you've lost a limb.'

Rosie squeezed her eyes shut. 'That sounded like it was a voice of experience; is that how you felt about Pa?'

Ivy jumped up. 'I was just being a romantic fool; take no notice of me, you'll know love when it hits you.'

* * *

Rosie thudded on the Bennets' front door.

Mrs Bennet opened it. 'Hello, Rosie, is there news of Sam? Has he woken up?'

Rosie's lips tightened. 'No... there's no change.' She took a breath. 'At least, he doesn't appear to have got worse.'

Mrs Bennet raised her eyebrows. 'That's very true. Is Alfie expecting you?'

Rosie suddenly felt tongue-tied. 'No... no, he isn't, but I need to see him.'

Mrs Bennet opened her mouth to speak but said nothing. She pulled the door wide so Rosie could step inside. 'Alfie's in the front room, love.' Mrs Bennet followed her to where Alfie was sitting. 'I'll leave you so you can talk. Alfie, I'm about to go to the hospital to see Sam. When I get back, Rosie, I'll let you know if there are any changes.'

Rosie nodded. 'Thank you, I'd appreciate that.'

Alfie didn't get up or speak as he studied her. 'Hello, Rosie, I've been expecting you.'

Rosie lifted her chin and glared at him. 'I need to speak to you.'

Alfie's gaze moved to his mother. 'There's no need to go, Ma. I'm sure whatever Rosie has to say you'll get to hear about eventually, so you might as well sit down and hear it first-hand.'

Mrs Bennet peered across at Rosie as she perched on the edge of a chair. 'I don't think it's right that I'm part of this conversation; something tells me this should only be between the two of you, and anyway, as I said, I'm going to the hospital.' She walked out of the front room.

Rosie kept her gaze fixed on Alfie. 'I want to know about what happened to Sam.'

'It doesn't matter what happened, but Ma will be happy he's not going off to the front line, at least not for a while.' Alfie glanced at the front room door. 'Don't pretend you're not listening at the door, Ma; you know as well as I do you're interested in what our sweet little Rosie has to say.'

The thud of the front door slamming shut reached the front room. They sat in silence for a moment.

'Alfie, you always talk about me in such an awful way that I'm surprised you ever wanted to marry me, but then maybe you never wanted to. Maybe when you asked me to wait for you it had nothing to do with love and marriage; maybe we all got it wrong.'

Alfie smirked. 'Maybe.'

Rosie felt sick to her stomach. 'So why couldn't you have been honest with me, and with your mother? Why couldn't you have told us it wasn't about a commitment like marriage, it was just about you getting what you wanted before you went off to war?'

Alfie gave a hearty laugh. 'I see you got there in the end; no one was more surprised than me when Ma said you had been a good girl and had waited for me to return home.'

Rosie jumped up. 'Alfie—'

'Sit down. Everyone, apart from you, knows that Sam loves you, and for the love of God, I don't understand why you're the only one who doesn't.' Alfie gave Rosie a scathing look. 'You wait until I tell Sam you wouldn't put out, even when I said it might be our only opportunity to be together. No, the little princess thinks she's too good for that before she's wed, but thankfully her friend didn't think the same.'

A calmness washed over Rosie. 'If you think that news is going to shock me you couldn't be more wrong. Fran has already told me. I don't regret my decision then or now; in fact, it just proves it was the right one.' She watched Alfie, trying to gauge his reaction. 'When did you find out you had a son? It wasn't, by any chance, around the time you stopped writing to me and your mother, was it?'

Alfie laughed again. 'You've got it all worked out, haven't you.'

Rosie frowned. 'I just wished I had known earlier; this whole business has cost me dearly, but I don't suppose you care about that. Fran was my best friend, and the two of you took that and the last three years away from me.'

Alfie's laughter faded. 'Your friendship is my only regret in all of this. Well, that and the hope that Sam would have been brave enough to admit his feelings for you, but it seems you are both too honourable, and look where that's got you – nowhere.' He paused. 'I wonder if he'll ever tell you how much he loves you. I haven't been a good brother to Sam, but I think it's time I made amends to all of you.' He cleared his throat. 'Look, this isn't an easy thing for me to do, but I want to move forward and leave misery behind me.'

Rosie raised her eyebrows. 'Move forward? Do you call putting your brother in hospital moving forward?'

Alfie studied his clenched hands. 'That was an accident; I was trying to do the right thing for once, but it went wrong.'

Rosie shook her head. 'Right thing? I'm sorry, but I don't understand; what were you trying to do?'

Alfie closed his eyes and took a breath before opening them again. 'I was trying to save him, protect him from going to the front line. I didn't want him to see and be tormented by some of the things I have seen.'

'And you thought knocking him out would do that?'

Alfie sighed. 'No, that wasn't my intention, that was an accident. I know I've made a mess of things but I set out to break his hand so he couldn't hold a rifle.'

Rosie frowned. 'You know what, Alfie, just when I think things can't get any worse, they do. Have you been to see Sam at the hospital?'

Alfie shook his head. 'No, I can't go to the hospital.' He paused. 'I know you don't understand, and probably don't believe me, but for once I was actually trying to protect Sam.'

Rosie's eyes narrowed as she watched his pain flit across his face. 'Well, it seems Fran was right, she said you would've had a reason. Me, I would have argued against that train of thought, so she obviously knows you better than me.'

Alfie gave a faint smile. 'She's a good woman, and I'm lucky that she loves me so much.'

'Are you going to marry Fran?'

'I haven't asked her... yet, but I want to be a proper father to James.'

Rosie nodded. 'Do you love her?' She watched him squirm under her gaze. 'I don't suppose you've spent enough time together to know the answer to that question.' Her eyes widened and a smile slowly spread across her face as the penny suddenly dropped. 'Actually, I don't think that's true. Now I think about it, when I met James, he was quite shy, he hid behind Fran's legs, and yet when you opened the door to me, he was all smiles with you.' She took a breath. 'You've known James for quite some time, and that's why Fran stayed away from me, she was keeping your secret, about coming home on leave and spending it with her and James; that's how Fran knew about your nightmares.' She shook her head. 'That woman in Fran's building told me she had seen a man with Fran; it was you, wasn't it? Was it through Fran that you found out how ill your father was?'

Alfie shook his head. 'That's a big leap. Just because a child was smiling around me.'

'Is it? It seems my father and brother were right about you.'

* * *

Rosie clocked in before going straight down to the basement to begin checking the returned books. She glanced around and instantly thought of Albert; the place wasn't the same without him – his kind words and ready smile for everyone he came across.

The basement door banged against the wall as it flew open. Rosie spun round. 'Oh Molly, you made me jump!'

Molly smiled. 'Sorry! You're in early. Are you working down here today, or are you just hiding from everyone?'

Rosie blushed. 'I suppose I'm hiding.'

Molly eyed her suspiciously. 'Two things I want to know: how is Sam, and what did Fran have to say for herself last night?'

'There's no change in Sam, but I keep telling myself at least he isn't getting worse.' Rosie picked up a pile of books and moved them to one side. 'As for Fran, she told me how she's always loved Alfie and how he wants to be a proper father to his son.'

Molly nodded. 'Did you have a talk with Alfie?'

'Yes, I even asked him if he wanted to marry Fran and he didn't say yes, but he didn't say no either. He told me his only regret was about how awful he had been to Sam growing up and my lost friendship with Fran.'

Molly frowned. 'It sounds like he wants to make amends.'

Rosie eyed Molly, wishing she had her confidence. 'That in itself worries me because it doesn't sound like the Alfie I know, which tells me there must be more to come.'

Molly shrugged. 'Like what?'

Sighing, Rosie shook her head. 'I don't know for certain, but he knows Fran's son better than he would after meeting him only a couple of weeks ago. James was quite shy when I met him and yet with Alfie he was laughing. Well, all three of them were; in fact, I had never seen Alfie so happy before.'

'Are you saying he has been living with Fran and that's why she wouldn't let you in?'

Rosie laughed. 'I don't know why I'm laughing because it's not funny, really, and what I'm going to say will sound ridiculous, but I think he stopped writing to us when he found out he had a son.' She paused. 'I did say to Alfie he knew James better than he and Fran are saying; he just laughed and said it was a bit of a leap.'

Molly chuckled. 'Well, I have to agree with him there, but if it's true, it means he wasn't missing in action – he just went missing.'

'Perhaps the war has affected him more than we realise.'

Molly raised her eyebrows. 'What are you going to do?'

Rosie shrugged. 'I'm going to get to the bottom of it, so I suppose it will be another chat with Fran.'

Victoria's voice rang out. 'Molly, Rosie, are you down there?'

'Yes,' they answered in unison.

Victoria's small heels clipped the stairs as she came down them. 'I've been looking for you two, I knew you had clocked in, but you weren't at your counters.'

Rosie lowered her eyelashes. 'I'm sorry, I came straight down here to work.'

Molly looked expectantly at Victoria. 'Any news on Albert?'

Victoria smiled. 'That's what I wanted to see you about; apparently it was touch-and-go at one time, but he seems to have turned the corner and is on the mend.'

Rosie reached out and hugged Molly. 'Thank goodness.' She quickly stepped back. 'I'm sorry, I shouldn't have done that, not everyone likes to be held.'

Molly beamed. 'I've never heard such nonsense.' She reached out and pulled her into her arms, waving for Victoria to join them.

The three of them giggled as they held on to one another.

Victoria moved back. 'It's the best news ever.'

Molly nodded. 'I must admit I was beginning to think I wasn't going to see him again.'

Rosie looked sombre. 'Me too.'

Victoria clapped her hands together. 'Well, we are, so keep those smiles coming.' She turned to walk away. 'Oh, I nearly forgot, Alice will be working with us tomorrow, which is another bit of good news.'

Molly laughed. 'That's excellent. I haven't been a very good friend. I mean, apart from when we went together, I haven't visited her much at all.'

Rosie smiled. 'I'm sure she understands.'

Victoria nodded. 'She definitely will. Anyway, are you choosing to work down here again, Rosie?'

'I thought I would, if that's all right?'

Victoria glanced at Molly before looking back at Rosie. 'You can for today but after that, Vera can come down and do another stint; I don't like the idea of you shutting yourself away. Molly, you best get back to your counter before Mr Leadbetter realises you're missing.'

Molly laughed. 'It's probably too late for that; he doesn't miss much. Anyway, I came down here with some returns.'

Rosie giggled at the disbelief on Victoria's face. 'That's true, she did.'

* * *

Rosie walked on to the hospital ward. She took a deep breath and the usual smell of disinfectant and the overpowering smell of bleach filled her senses. As she moved in farther, some of the men shouted hello to her. She forced a smile and waved.

'Are you going to sit with me today?' a young man called out.

Rosie chuckled. 'I'm afraid not.'

'Whoever you're visiting is a lucky man.' The man beamed. 'You certainly brighten up our day.'

Rosie laughed but kept on walking towards Sam. She stood at the foot of his bed and stared at his motionless body. Stepping to one side, she smoothed down the covers before pulling the wooden chair closer and sitting down. Reaching out, Rosie clasped her hand around his. 'Sam, I was hoping you would be awake by now.' She sighed. 'I have seen the children at the school; they were quite worried about you, but I reassured them you would be back soon.' She smiled. 'They are all going to draw you some pictures, which they were quite excited to do.' Rosie leant forward to push his hair off his forehead, running her fingers through it several times. She took a deep breath. 'I think Alfie is sorry about all this; he told me he was trying to stop you going to the front line – he was trying to save you.' Rosie gave a strange laugh. 'Remind me never to let Alfie save me if this is the result.' She sat in silence for a moment. 'You know, I think Fran really loves him and they'll end up getting married, which feels a little strange, but I want Fran to be happy and I definitely don't want to marry Alfie; so that's all sorted – well, nearly. I just want you to wake up so we can talk, you know – have a proper conversation about things.'

'What sort of things?'

Rosie's eyes widened. Did she imagine it? It was only a whisper, but she'd heard it, hadn't she? She squeezed Sam's hand while staring at him intently. She was dumbstruck, she didn't know what to say. She needed to say something that would get a response from him. Alfie's words jumped into her head; if Sam did love her, maybe talking about it would help bring him round. 'I thought we could talk about us; you know, our future.'

Sam's eyelashes fluttered.

Rosie's heart jumped in her chest; it was working. 'I mean, do you ever want to get married? Would you like children? How do you feel about your wife working, particularly in a bookshop?' She kept her eyes fixed on Sam.

Sam groaned. 'So many questions.'

Rosie stood up and frantically looked around. 'Can someone help, please? Sam's awake.'

A nurse came rushing over, quickly followed by a doctor. Rosie stepped back so they could get to him.

Sam slowly opened his eyes.

The nurse placed her fingers on his wrist. 'How are you feeling, Sam?'

'Dry.'

'I'll get you some water to sip but you must make sure you don't gulp it.'

Sam gave a slow nod.

The doctor took his stethoscope and listened to Sam's chest before shining a light in his eyes. 'I think you are finally on the road to recovery; I don't know what brought you round, but it seems to have worked. We'll be keeping an eye on you for a bit longer. I want to make sure your brain and memory haven't been affected so we'll do some memory tests over the next couple of days.'

Rosie smiled. 'Don't worry, doctor, I'll keep an eye on him.'

The doctor smiled. 'I'm sure you will, Rosie.'

Rosie took the glass of water from the nurse and held it against Sam's lips. 'You can only have a little, especially until you can sit up, otherwise the water will end up getting spilled on the bedclothes, and then you won't be happy.'

Sam opened his eyes. He blinked quickly before staring ahead for a moment. He moved his head to one side. 'Rosie, you're a sight for sore eyes.'

Rosie smiled. 'And so are you; you've scared us all in the last few days, even Alfie!'

Sam frowned. 'I don't remember what happened.' His gaze shifted from side to side. 'I remember him bending my hand and arm but then I must have blacked out.'

Rosie put the glass down on the bedside cabinet. 'Don't think about it now. You need to rest and get well so you can go back to your young admirers at the school.' She chuckled. 'I'm sure they have missed you.'

Sam smiled and closed his eyes.

Rosie squeezed his hand. 'I'm going to leave you to rest but I shall pop in and let your ma know you have come round.'

'Are you talking to yourself? You know, they'll be locking you up soon.' Mrs Bennet's voice sounded behind Rosie.

Rosie spun round on her small heels. 'Mrs Bennet, how

wonderful to see you, I was just leaving to go and let you know about Sam.' She beamed. 'He's come round, although he needs to rest, but the doctor said everything looks good. Sam's got to take things slowly for a while, so he will stay here where the staff can keep an eye on him.'

Mrs Bennet rushed forward and threw her arms around Rosie. 'Oh, thank God.' She sniffed as she started weeping. 'I was so scared we were going to lose him.'

Rosie wrapped her arms around Mrs Bennet. 'I know, I felt the same but he's going to be all right.'

20

Rosie let the knocker fall hard on Fran's front door. She waited. There was laughter inside; did that mean Alfie was there? The laughter stopped and the door was opened.

Fran frowned. 'Hello, Rosie, I wasn't expecting to see you again any time soon.' She stepped aside and waved Rosie in.

Rosie glanced over her shoulder at Fran. She noticed the man's jacket was still hanging on the back of the door but there was no sign of Alfie. 'No... I don't suppose you were.'

'Is it Sam? Please tell me he's going to be all right?'

Rosie stared at Fran. Tension and worry were written all over her face. 'Sam came round while I was at the hospital this afternoon.'

Fran closed her eyes. 'Thank goodness. I know Alfie didn't mean him any harm.'

Rosie smiled. 'Yes, well, Alfie aside, we are all relieved that he's come round at last, as I'm sure Alfie will be. They are keeping him in to monitor him just to make sure he's all right, but at least it all points in that direction.'

Fran clapped her hands together. 'I shall keep everything crossed that he can go home soon.'

Rosie nodded. She took a deep breath. 'That wasn't why I came to see you. I'm afraid I want to ask you a couple of things.' She watched James playing on the floor. 'Hello, James. Can I play with your bricks with you?'

James stared at her before looking across at Fran.

'It's all right, James, Auntie Rosie is a friend of ours.'

James's face lit up as he gave her a smile. He handed her a brick and then another.

Rosie placed one on the floor and the other on top of it.

James kept passing them on until they were all balancing on top of one another. He squealed with delight before giving Rosie a mischievous grin and knocking them over. James stretched out his arms. 'Oh no, what happened?'

Rosie giggled at his disbelief. 'I don't know; shall we build it up again?'

James grinned and began passing her the bricks again.

Fran chuckled. 'If you're not careful, he'll have you doing that all day.'

Rosie smiled as she took another brick from him. 'I don't mind, he's a lovely lad, you should be proud at how well you've raised him on your own.'

Fran frowned for a moment. 'I'll put the kettle on.' She walked into the kitchen. 'You'll be pleased to know I have milk today.'

Rosie could hear the water splashing in the sink and then the kettle. She glanced around the room, looking for signs of Alfie living there, but there was only the jacket that she had seen before. The whistling of the kettle broke into Rosie's thoughts; maybe she had it all wrong.

Fran came into the front room carrying two cups. Colour

flushed her cheeks. 'I'm sorry, I don't have any saucers, and I only have four cups. I got them because someone in the building was going to throw them away.' She passed one of them to Rosie.

Rosie took it. 'That's not a problem, it looks like a good cup of tea.'

Fran nodded. 'Thank you, I'm afraid there's no sugar in it.'

'That's all right, I don't take it.' Rosie smiled. 'I don't think many do since this war began and created all kinds of shortages.' She hesitated; her heart was pounding. Rosie took a deep breath. 'I want to ask you something, and I instinctively know you won't want to answer it, but I need to have the truth before I can move on with my life.'

Fran gave her an anxious look. 'Go on.'

Rosie studied Fran for a moment. 'There's no easy way to say this so I'm just going to say it.'

Fran nodded.

Rosie took another deep breath to calm herself. 'Has Alfie been living here all the time we thought he was missing in action?' She frowned. 'Did he spend that time with you, without a thought about how his family were worrying about him?'

Fran stared at Rosie. 'Have you asked him? You know Alfie; nothing is ever straightforward.'

Rosie gave a wry smile. 'I told him I thought he knew James better than we were being led to believe; he said that was quite a leap just because a child was laughing with him.' Rosie paused. 'Which I can't deny. After all, James is giggling with me and he hardly knows me, but my instincts tell me I'm right and if I am, I should at least be told the truth.'

Fran nodded. 'You do deserve the truth.'

The bedroom door opened. Rosie's jaw dropped. 'Do I take it I was right then?'

Alfie smirked. 'I knew we couldn't keep it a secret forever, but we had a good run of it.' He put his arm around Fran's shoulders. 'Don't blame Fran, she wanted to come clean, but I told her I could get shot for desertion so that's why we kept it quiet, and I couldn't write because you'd know I wasn't in France.'

Rosie shook her head. 'But I don't understand how you have been managing; for money, I mean.'

Fran sighed. 'Some of it has been handouts from places like the Helping Hand in Seven Dials; they will give you bread and a cup of something to eat. The lady who runs that has a friend who owns a restaurant called Breaking Bread, and she offered me some hours, mostly in the evenings, doing whatever had to be done – you know, washing up, clearing tables and changing the tablecloths – and that helped to pay the bills. Alfie was always here to look after James because he couldn't go out for fear of being seen.'

Alfie watched Rosie as the conflict she was feeling ran across her face. 'I don't expect any forgiveness from you, Rosie, but I've tried in my own awkward way to make up for the terrible things that I've done, and it's important you know she hated not seeing you, but we couldn't risk it getting out and me being shot.' He paused as he glanced at Fran. 'Fran has shown me what a good person is. I know I've been unkind to you and I'm about to be so again, but it's important you hear it from me: if I don't get shot, I want to marry Fran, if she'll have me.'

Fran gasped and grabbed his hand in her excitement.

Rosie's eyes widened. 'What do you mean if you don't get shot?'

Alfie gave a nervous laugh. 'Well, there is a war on, and I could get shot for desertion.'

Fran dropped Alfie's hand as though it had burnt her fingers. 'Is that likely to happen?' Tears spilled over onto her cheeks. 'I mean as hard as it is living like we do, I'd rather you stayed in hiding than get shot.'

Alfie wrapped his arms around Fran. 'People know I'm home now, so I have to face the music. Besides, I want to be a proper father and husband and not have James growing up thinking his father is a coward.'

Fran pulled back and ran her hand across her cheeks. 'I know you're right; it just frightens me.'

Alfie reached out and squeezed her hand. 'It scares me too but I'm hoping if I hand myself in, I will just get prison time and then we can get married, unless they'll allow it before I get sentenced.'

Fran moved in closer to Alfie and clung on to him.

Rosie wanted to give her friend a hug but stayed where she was. 'You won't be on your own this time, Fran. Now you've let me back in, I'm not going anywhere.'

Fran nodded. 'Thank you, I don't want you to leave my life again and as excited as I am about marrying Alfie, I wouldn't do it if you didn't want me to.'

Rosie smiled. 'You don't have to worry about me, Fran; I don't think I ever wanted to marry Alfie. I wish you both every happiness, although I do wish you hadn't kept me in the dark all that time.'

Fran ran forward and threw her arms around her friend. 'Thank you. Your blessing means so much to me.'

Alfie grinned and fell to his knees to play with James and the bricks before looking up at the girls. 'It's my turn to ask you a question.'

Fran stepped back and stared at Alfie.

Alfie watched Rosie closely. 'I heard you say Sam had come round, which I'm very happy about, but has he been brave enough to tell you how much he loves you?'

Colour flushed Rosie's cheeks.

Alfie laughed. 'I hope that colour means you've both stopped being honourable.'

Rosie smiled as she watched James knock down the tower of bricks again. 'Have you told your mother you're James's father?'

Alfie chuckled. 'Ahh, changing the subject is your way of telling me to mind my own business.' He took a breath. 'In answer to your question, no, I haven't told her; we wanted you to know first.'

Rosie nodded. 'Thank you for that, but you do know your ma won't be very happy, don't you?'

Alfie reached out and started tickling James, who instantly filled the room with laughter. 'Perhaps not at first, but once she realises she has an instant grandson, she'll get over it.'

* * *

Rosie stood in front of the cooker, stirring the gravy and making sure there were no lumps before it was to be poured over the vegetable pie her mother had made for dinner. She glanced over her shoulder. 'Ma, this gravy is done, shall I lay the table?'

Ivy opened the cupboard door and lifted out some dinner plates.

Rosie took them from her. 'Do you want to eat in the kitchen or in the dining room?'

Ivy shrugged. 'We might as well eat in the kitchen, unless you would prefer the dining room.'

Rosie laughed. 'No, the kitchen is fine, there's not so much back and forth with dishes.' She gave the gravy a last stir before taking it off the heat and pouring it into a small jug.

David came running into the kitchen.

Ivy yelled at him. 'How many times have you been told not to run into the kitchen? One of these days you're going to get burnt.'

David lowered his eyelashes. 'I'm sorry, Ma, I'll try and remember in future. I just came in to see if dinner was ready; it smells like it is.'

Rosie tilted her head. 'David, go and tell Gran we're dishing it up.'

David nodded and disappeared back into the hall.

Ivy shook her head. 'That boy will be the death of me.'

'Aw, come on, Ma, he's a good lad really.'

Ivy took the pie from the oven and placed it in the middle of the wooden table. 'You certainly seem happier today.'

Mary hobbled into the kitchen with David close behind her. 'Who's happier today?'

Ivy glanced over at her mother-in-law. 'Your granddaughter is.'

Mary pulled out one of the chairs and sat herself down. She leant back against the wooden slats before shifting her position slightly. 'Does that mean you've sorted things out with Alfie?'

Rosie smiled. 'Yes, I have.'

Mary frowned. 'Is that it or do we get to hear the details?'

Rosie giggled. 'You will not hear all the details, but I can tell you Alfie and I will not be getting married.' She looked at her gran's amazed expression before continuing, 'He is going to marry Fran who loves him dearly.'

Mary eyed her for a moment. 'And you don't mind?'

Rosie shook her head. 'No, I definitely don't. He is James's father, and he is very good with him and with Fran. When they are together, they look so happy. Alfie has apologised for everything and the only people he now has to tell are his family. I must admit I didn't ask Fran about hers.'

Ivy shook her head. 'Mrs Bennet won't be happy about it at all, she was very fond of you.'

'I know, but that's not a good reason to marry someone. Anyway, as Alfie said, she'll soon get over it when she realises she has a grandson who is absolutely delightful.'

David grinned at Rosie. 'Pa will be happy; he always said you picked the wrong brother.'

Rosie giggled. 'Look at you – you keep quoting Pa.'

David looked across at their grandmother. 'It's true, isn't it, Gran? It was you he was talking to, wasn't it?'

Mary shook her head. 'I can see you listen more than we realise.'

Rosie frowned. 'So it's true then?'

Mary nodded. 'Yes, it's what he said to me, at a time when we thought we were in the house by ourselves.' She leant over and nudged David before glancing back at Rosie. 'I don't think your pa would have said anything to you; he was hoping you would come to that conclusion by yourself.'

David nodded. 'And you did, so it's all right to tell you what he thought. He'll be smiling down on us from heaven.'

Rosie laughed. 'That he will, that he will.'

Ivy reached for the knife and began cutting the pie into quarters and balancing each slice on a plate. 'Come on, let's eat before it gets cold.'

Rosie reached over and placed her hand on her mother's. 'It's good Pa is still with us, guiding us with his words and love.'

Ivy nodded. She reached into her apron pocket and pulled out her handkerchief. She dabbed at her eyes. 'I know.'

Mary picked up her knife and fork. 'What happens now, Rosie?'

Rosie gave a small smile. 'Who knows? Time will tell.'

* * *

Mr Leadbetter stood in the Foyles Bookshop doorway; he pulled his fob watch from his waistcoat pocket. He clicked the button on the side and the lid flew up, revealing the time.

'Good morning, Mr Leadbetter.' Alice beamed. 'It's lovely to be back in the fold again.'

Mr Leadbetter smiled. 'I'm hoping one of these days you will tell me you want to come back on a regular basis; you are missed, as I'm sure Miss Appleton will tell you.'

Alice laughed. 'Actually, I would like to talk to you about coming back to work but only for, say, three days a week.'

'Now that has brightened up my day. We'll talk about the detail of it later and maybe somewhere more private.' Mr Leadbetter chuckled. 'I think today is going to be a good day.'

Alice frowned. 'I hear Albert has been quite poorly; do you know how he is?'

'Thankfully you can't keep a good man down and he's itching to come back to work, but I've insisted he take his time. After all, none of us are getting any younger and I don't want something happening to him.' Mr Leadbetter paused. 'When he does come back, we'll have to keep a close eye on him; it was quite scary to see him unconscious in the basement. It was lucky there were two young men in the shop who helped to get him out of there so he could get to hospital. With hindsight, we probably shouldn't have moved him in case he had any broken bones, but I just wanted to get him some help. That's where we missed your cool head, but the main thing is that he is definitely on the mend and should be back – with his rhyming slang – soon.'

Alice grinned. 'That's wonderful news. He's a lovely man and makes everyone smile so he'd be missed if he weren't here.'

Molly rushed to the Foyles doorway and immediately threw

her arms around Alice. 'It's wonderful to see you, I'm so glad you're here!' She pulled back a little. 'I'm sorry, Mr Leadbetter, did I make it on time? I don't know what the matter is with me lately, but mornings are suddenly not my thing.'

Mr Leadbetter glanced down at his fob watch. 'You have five minutes to spare, Mrs Greenwood.' He studied her for a moment. 'Are you unwell? You do look pale.'

Molly closed her eyes for a split second. 'I feel a little out of sorts but I'm sure it will pass. Anyway, I had better clock in, otherwise I'll lose fifteen minutes' pay.'

Alice frowned as she looked at Molly. 'I'll come with you.' She turned back to Mr Leadbetter. 'Perhaps we can talk later.'

Mr Leadbetter smiled. 'Of course.'

Alice studied Molly. 'Are you sure you should be at work? You do look quite pale.'

Molly gave a weak smile. 'I'm sure once I'm busy with the children I won't have time to think about feeling ill.'

They walked through to the staff area and shouted good morning.

Victoria stepped forward as everyone shouted their hellos back. 'Alice, how lovely to see you.'

Molly found Alice's clocking in card as well as her own and put them both in the slot, one after the other.

Alice turned at the sound of the machine clicking. 'Thank you, Molly.' She turned back to Victoria. 'Molly's not feeling well so you might want to keep an eye on her today.'

Victoria laughed. 'I'm sure Mr Leadbetter would tell you he has to keep an eye on her *every* day.' She peered past Alice to take in Molly's ashen features. 'Molly, you don't look well at all; are you sure you wouldn't rather be at home?'

Molly shook her head. 'It'll pass, it usually does.'

Alice and Victoria quickly looked at each other.

Alice pulled out a chair for Molly to sit down. 'How long have you been feeling like this?'

Molly shrugged. 'I don't know, a couple of weeks I suppose, but it's not all the time. I'm probably eating something that disagrees with me, I've just got to figure out what that is.'

Victoria glanced again at Alice whose eyes lit up. 'Maybe you should see a doctor.'

No one noticed Mr Leadbetter poking his head round the corner, listening to their conversation as staff walked past him to start work.

Molly frowned. 'I'm not wasting my money on a doctor for an upset stomach.' She stood up. 'Come on, we've got to get to work.'

Victoria rested her hand on Molly's arm. 'What if it's something more serious?'

Molly raised her eyebrows. 'Like what?'

Alice smiled. 'Like you're pregnant.'

Molly's eyes widened as she flopped back down on the chair.

* * *

Ivy stood at the foot of the hospital bed and watched Sam closely before collecting his board and reading his notes. She wondered why Mr Bennet and Alfie hadn't come to visit him, but then some people didn't like hospitals, and even more so with the number of injured soldiers they had. She was thankful that David was too young to go to war and prayed he would never have to experience the things she had been told about by some of the patients she looked after. She hung Sam's notes back on the foot of the bed. 'I think you'll probably be going home later, if for no other reason than they need the bed.'

Sam laughed. 'I'm more than happy with that. I feel a fraud

taking up the bed when there is really nothing wrong with me and there are plenty of injured men who need your help.'

Ivy nodded. 'I thought you'd be happy.'

Straightening his bed covers, Sam looked up. 'I want to get back to the classroom and teach my wonderful children. I've missed them.'

Ivy studied him carefully. 'I'm not sure you can do that just yet; the doctors will want you to take it easy.'

Sam chuckled. 'Going to school is taking it easy, especially compared with being at home with everyone.'

Ivy smiled. 'Things might settle down now that Rosie and Alfie have sorted things out, and she seems quite happy that Alfie and Fran are going to get married, as I hope your ma is.'

'I'm not sure my ma will ever be happy; she loves Rosie, and she will find Alfie's behaviour unforgivable, but I suspect she has to move forward or lose her son.'

Ivy suddenly gasped. 'I'm sorry, I forgot you probably don't know everything that has been going on because you have been in here. Rosie's going to kill me when she finds out I said something because I don't think your ma knows yet. I'm so sorry.'

Sam rested his hand in the middle of his chest. 'Don't worry, I won't say anything, your secret's safe with me.'

Ivy clenched her hands together. 'You'd think being a nurse I would know better; my job is all about confidentiality.'

Sam shook his head. 'Don't punish yourself, I'm sure all this business with Alfie has taken over your family life so it's not surprising that it's all got confusing.' He smiled at Ivy. 'I promise I won't say anything.'

Ivy smoothed her hands down the skirt of her uniform. 'Thank you, you are being very kind to me, but I do feel dreadful.' She stepped aside. 'I'll see if I can find a doctor to discharge you.' She nodded and walked towards the nurses' station.

Rosie almost collided with her mother as she pushed open the door to the ward. 'Oh, sorry, Ma, I wasn't looking where I was going.'

Ivy smiled. 'That's all right, neither was I.' She looked back at Sam's bed; should she tell Rosie she had spoken out of turn? She glanced around the ward, checking the amount of work she still had to do, including changing dressings, cleaning wounds, handing out medication, checking the patients' observations and writing up notes. She sighed, deciding this wasn't the time or the place. 'In fact, your timing has been quite good because I think Sam will be able to go home today. We need the bed and it's not ideal for him to go home by himself.'

Rosie beamed. 'That's good news; I'm sure he'll be happy about that.'

Ivy nodded. 'He's got to take things easy though, which means not overdoing it. I've already told him that, but he seems to think going back to his class is taking it easy.'

'Ma, I think it *is*, for Sam, but I'll have a talk with him so don't worry.' Smiling, Rosie walked over to Sam. 'Ma has just said you will probably be sent home today.' She sat on the edge of his bed. 'Isn't that wonderful news?'

Sam grabbed her hand. 'I can't wait to get out of here and back to the classroom.'

Rosie laughed. 'She said you have to take it easy for a while.'

Sam chuckled. 'If it makes everyone feel better, I'll teach sitting down.'

Rosie shook her head before bursting with laughter.

21

As Rosie and Sam opened the main door to the school, they could hear singing coming from Sam's classroom.

Sam smiled; they were singing their times tables. He stepped forward and tried to open the door quietly. The children stopped singing and grinned as he and Rosie walked in. The teacher standing in front of the class was not one Sam knew. 'I'm sorry to intrude, I've just got out of hospital, and I just wanted to see my class.'

The teacher nodded. 'They have been quite worried about you.'

The children sat eagerly waiting for the school bell to ring out.

Sam watched them; they were all smiling at him. 'I shall be back tomorrow if that's all right with everyone.'

The children cheered just as the bell rang out. They all jumped up and ran towards Sam and Rosie. 'I'm glad you're coming back, sir, we missed you – and Miss Burrows.'

The teacher laughed. 'It looks like they are pleased to see you – and I thought I was doing so well!'

Sam chuckled. 'Don't take it personally, it's not me they're happy to see, it's Miss Burrows. She teaches them to read using different voices for the characters.'

Charlie tugged at Rosie's skirt. 'Can you read to us now?'

'Yeah!' the children chorused as one.

Rosie opened her arms and hugged as many of the children close as she could. 'I can't today because your mas are waiting outside for you, but I promise to be back either tomorrow or the day after and then we'll have a good old reading session.'

Sam wrapped his arms around the children who were nearest to him. 'Come on, let's take you to your families and I will see you all tomorrow.'

Rosie clapped her hands together. 'Can I have your attention please?' The children all stopped talking and stared at Rosie. 'Mr Bennet is not meant to be working tomorrow so can you please make sure he's all right; he will probably be sitting down taking the class.'

The children all looked very serious as they fixed their gaze on Rosie.

Charlie put up his hand.

Rosie smiled. 'Yes, Charlie.'

Charlie smiled back. 'Don't worry, Miss, we'll all be watching him.' He looked serious for a moment. 'Of course, it will be while we do our work as well.'

Rosie grinned. 'Thank you, thank you all; now let's go and hand you over to your families.'

Sam beamed. 'I'll take them.'

Rosie's gaze followed them as they left the room in single file.

The teacher frowned at Rosie. 'You do know you can be too close to these children; it doesn't do them any good to get attached to you.'

Rosie studied the teacher for a couple of seconds. 'I have to say I strongly disagree with you. I'm not a teacher but I would have thought during these hard times, no one can have too much love and happiness in their lives.'

The teacher's lip curled. 'As you say, you're not a teacher so you're not trained to be detached and to not get involved with them.'

Rosie lifted her chin. 'No, and if that's what's involved then I'll never take up the training.'

Sam frowned at the teacher from the doorway. 'I think that part of the training is open to interpretation; let's face it, a happy child is more likely to come to school and to want to learn.'

The teacher gathered up the papers on the desk. 'Well, this is your class, so how you teach is up to you.' She stomped out of the classroom.

Rosie smiled. 'Sorry, I think I upset her.'

Sam laughed. 'Don't worry, she's old school – you know, don't speak unless you're spoken to.'

Rosie chuckled. 'It's still like that in some homes.'

'That may well be but it's not how I work, and when my wife has children, it won't be how it is at home either.'

Rosie stared at Sam. 'It sounds like you've given it some thought.'

Sam gave a slow smile. 'Oh, I have.'

* * *

Alfie pushed himself out of the armchair and walked over to the dining table, and then to the window to stare out on to the busy street. The June sunshine was throwing shadows on to the road and pavements, and he watched a woman dab her forehead with a handkerchief while two children ran past her, oblivious to the heat. He sighed and turned round to face his mother and father, just as Sam walked into the room. Alfie cleared his throat, and all eyes were suddenly upon him. Tension rippled through his body; all his usual bravado had gone. 'Er... Ma, there's no easy way to say this so I'm just going to blurt it out.'

Fear gripped Mrs Bennet as she stared at her eldest boy. 'Please don't tell me you have to go back?'

Alfie's eyes widened. 'No, at least not yet, but who knows what's ahead.' He coughed. 'That wasn't what I wanted to say, anyway. Look, I want you to know I'm not marrying Rosie.'

Mrs Bennet jumped out of her seat. 'What? You're almost leaving the poor girl at the altar.'

Alfie closed his eyes and silently counted to three; he had promised Fran he would be gentle with his family. He took a deep breath; this was going to be more difficult than he'd realised. 'No, Ma, I'm not leaving her at the altar—'

'Does she know?' Mrs Bennet screamed at her son.

Alfie sighed. 'Ma, I don't wish to be rude, but can you sit down and let me finish without interrupting me after every other word?'

Mr Bennet's gaze travelled from Alfie to his wife. 'Do as Alfie says.'

Mrs Bennet's face was flushed with anger. 'Oh, so you've finally found your voice, have you?'

Mr Bennet tightened his lips. 'If you don't shut up, woman, we'll never get to hear what's going on.'

Mrs Bennet glared at him, but then slowly lowered herself on to her chair. 'Go on.'

Alfie looked over and nodded his thanks to his father before taking a breath. 'I don't love Rosie so it would be wrong for me to marry her.' He glanced across at Sam. 'She would be better off with Sam who would take a bullet for her.'

Mrs Bennet frowned but said nothing.

Alfie took a couple of deep breaths. 'You're not going to like it, Ma, but I love Fran and we will be getting married.'

Mrs Bennet scowled. 'I didn't take you for a fool Alfie. What has she done, convinced you her child is yours?'

Alfie gave a warm smile. 'The child *is* mine; I was the soldier who persuaded her to spend the evening with me on my last night before going to the front. I was the reason she's been through hell because she kept my secret, which I truly didn't deserve.' He gave a disgusted laugh. 'I tried to bully Rosie into doing the same thing in an alleyway near Liverpool Street train station, but she was having none of it, even though I said I might not come back, but you have to take your hat off to her, she stuck by her decision. I left Rosie crying and went to find Fran.'

Mrs Bennet shook her head. 'Oh no. Well, *she* didn't say no, did she?'

Alfie chuckled. 'She tried. The difference is she loved me, and I knew it, so I took advantage of that.' He sat in silence for a moment. 'I'm not proud of myself, Ma. You haven't raised a very nice man but I'm trying to put things right now.' He glanced over at Sam. 'I know I wasn't a good big brother to you and I'm sorry, but I'm hoping by breaking your hand I have saved you from seeing some of the things I have, and maybe even saved your life.'

Sam rubbed the plaster on his wrist but said nothing.

Alfie shook his head. 'James is a lovely boy, Ma; you'd love him if you gave him a chance.'

Mrs Bennet wiped a tear from her eyes. 'And what about Rosie?'

Alfie shrugged. 'We've spoken at Fran's, and she gives our wedding her blessing.'

Mrs Bennet sniffed. 'That's because she is a good, kind girl.'

Alfie laughed. 'It's also because she didn't want to marry me either, but she didn't want to let anyone down, not even you, Ma.'

He peered at Sam. 'Anyway, if Sam sorts himself out, she might still be part of this family; she knows he loves her, but she had all the mess with me hanging over her so she couldn't think about the future with me or anyone else.'

Mrs Bennet looked at Sam. 'Is that true?'

Sam smiled. 'Ma, I've loved Rosie for as long as I can remember, but I won't be pushing her into a situation she doesn't want to be in; I value our friendship too much.'

Mrs Bennet nodded.

Alfie cleared his throat again.

Mrs Bennet eyed him suspiciously. 'Don't tell me there's more.'

Alfie jutted out his chin. 'There is, but I want to be honest with you all; I'm tired of hiding everything.'

Mr Bennet looked at his eldest son. 'Everything?'

Alfie took a deep breath. 'Yes, Pa, I stopped writing to everyone when I came home.'

Sam frowned. 'What do you mean, "came home"? You stopped writing a long time before that.'

Alfie stared down at his feet. 'When Fran wrote and told me she was pregnant, and again to tell me I had a son, I decided to come home, but it took me about a year to get here.'

Mrs Bennet shook her head. 'No, wait, you've only just got here.'

Alfie ran his hands over his face. 'I've been hiding out at Fran's for the last couple of years, so I expect I'll be going to prison, or be shot, when the powers that be realise I'm back home. I'm hoping it will be time in prison so Fran and I can still have a life together. Anyway, I looked after James while Fran did some work, mainly in the evenings, so we had money to feed ourselves and pay the rent, but it's been tight.'

Sam's mouth dropped open. 'So, you were just trying to sound like the big man as usual when you told me about your friends being blown up all around you?'

Alfie's face turned crimson before he shouted. 'No, that *was* what it was like; why do you think I decided to come home and try to be a father to my son while I could? I know everyone will see me as a coward but I don't care, you had to be there to know how bad it was. Why do you think I wanted to stop you from going?'

They all sat in silence for a few minutes, each not knowing what to say.

Alfie shook his head. 'When Fran overheard Ma talking to Rosie in the street about how sick Pa was, then I had to come home, I had to see for myself. I'm sorry, Ma, you deserved to know I was still alive, but I thought that if you didn't know, you couldn't be accused of being involved in my actions.' He paused. 'I want you to meet James. After all, he is your grandson, and I have no right to ask, but I would like you to be there for Fran.'

Mrs Bennet sucked in her breath. 'What do you mean, "be there for Fran"? Where are you going?'

Alfie closed his eyes for a moment before opening them again and staring at his mother. 'I'm going to hand myself in.'

Mr Bennet shook his head. 'Is that wise?'

Alfie tightened his lips. 'I want to live a normal life with my son; you know, take him to the park and things. I want to get a job so I can support my family, but I can't do anything if I keep hiding away and anyway, I expect they'll catch up with me sooner or later. I'm daring to hope if I hand myself in, I will just go to prison. I don't expect you to understand but I already feel like a prisoner hiding away. Obviously I know there's a chance I could be shot, but I'm hoping it won't come to that.'

Sam studied his brother for a moment. 'Does Fran know what you're intending to do?'

Alfie gave a wry smile. 'Not all of it, I think I've made her a nervous wreck by running away. It's all been very hard on her and that's why I'm hoping you will all look after her while I'm gone, and I'm truly hoping I won't get shot for desertion.' He stared directly at Sam. 'Again, I know I'm asking a lot, but can you please help look after Fran and James, take them under your wing.'

Sam nodded his agreement.

* * *

Westminster Bridge at night was very different to the atmosphere of the day. There weren't so many boats chugging along the river and there weren't any children leaning over the black railings waving at the men steering them. There were only a few vehicles spluttering over the bridge, and no horses to avoid.

Rosie leant over the railings and stared into the darkness of the River Thames. She turned and looked at Sam. 'The river has a different feel about it at night. The darkness makes it seem more dangerous. It feels like you could lose yourself in its depths.'

Sam smiled. 'That sounds poetic.'

Rosie laughed. 'It's just my imagination running away with itself, but there is a different feel about this bridge to when it's busy during the day with children giggling and waving at the boats.' She looked up at the dark sky. 'We probably shouldn't be out, in case the Germans come.'

Sam's eyes followed her gaze. 'I think we could be all right because the moon is quite bright, and I read somewhere that they are less likely to strike when it's like that.'

Rosie smiled for a moment before she dropped her gaze to look at him. 'How are things at home?'

Sam frowned. 'Well, it's been a bit fraught but hopefully

things can move on now that everything is out in the open.' He paused before choosing his words carefully. 'I haven't had a chance to ask you how you feel about everything?'

Rosie shrugged. 'I'm happy for Fran, especially as she clearly loves Alfie, and he's obviously a better man than I thought he was; hiding away for the last few years must have been hard on them both.'

Sam frowned. 'What about all the worry he put you and Ma through by not writing to you?'

Rosie bit down on her lip. 'I'm not saying what he did was right. There are a lot of men with children fighting this war and they don't all have the luxury of hiding away, but I can understand his and Fran's reasoning and that makes me feel a lot better.' She took a breath. 'Especially about Fran because I never understood what I did wrong, and it turns out I didn't do anything.'

'What about Alfie marrying Fran instead of you?'

Rosie giggled. 'That's a huge relief. When I look back, I don't think I ever wanted to marry Alfie. So now that I know I'm definitely not going to, I can get on with my life guilt-free.' She paused. 'How did your ma take the news?'

Sam shook his head. 'Oh, she wasn't happy, and my father actually told her to be quiet, which is unheard of.' He chuckled. 'I can laugh now but it wasn't funny at the time. Anyway, the short story is Alfie told us everything.'

Rosie lifted her head. 'I don't suppose that went down very well.'

'No, but she'll get over it.' Sam gave her a sideways glance. 'I'm happy that you feel relieved everything has been sorted out.' He took a deep breath. 'Can I ask, now that you are free of Alfie, if you would consider going out with me? I don't know where but to be honest, it doesn't matter to me as long as I'm with you.'

Rosie blushed.

'I'm sorry, have I said too much? Is it too soon? I didn't mean—'

'No, you haven't, and it isn't. I would love to go out with you.'

Sam lifted Rosie's chin before slowly lowering his head so his lips could caress hers.

Rosie lifted her arms to hold him close, and slowly their bodies moulded together as one.

* * *

Rosie hummed quietly as she moved the books from her counter to the table behind her.

Molly smiled as she approached Rosie. 'You sound cheerful this morning. You look the happiest I've ever seen you; can I assume everything has been sorted out?'

Rosie turned to face Molly. 'Have I been really bad?'

Molly tilted her head. 'No, I never said that, but you've often looked like you were carrying the weight of the world on your shoulders, and I know what that feels like.'

'Do you?'

Pain momentarily flitted across Molly's face.

Rosie shook her head. 'I'm sorry, I didn't mean to pry.'

Molly gave her a small smile. 'You're not prying, it's the guilt I carry with me every day.' She took a deep breath. 'When this war first started, and all the men were volunteering to fight for king and country, my boyfriend didn't want to. I was embarrassed because I thought he was the love of my life, but he wasn't; that honour goes to my husband, Andrew.' Molly sighed. 'He was a ladies' man, but I just couldn't see it at the time and that might be because he was always so nice to me. Anyway, I kept on about the shame that he wasn't volunteering like everyone else's boyfriends and family members, so he went. If I hadn't gone on the way I did, he would never have enlisted until he was forced to.' Sadness ran across her face. 'He was only on the front line for a week or so when he died.' Molly could feel the tears pricking her eyes, so she blinked quickly. 'I've always felt like his death was my fault.'

Rosie reached out and took Molly's hand. 'It wasn't your fault. You weren't to know what he was going into; no one knew, especially not when the war first began. Remember, it was only supposed to last a few months and here we are almost four years later, knowing the harsh reality of what war means.'

Molly shrugged. 'No, you are right about that, but it was my pride that pushed him to his death, and I find that hard to forgive myself for. I tried to make amends by becoming a Canary Girl and working in the munitions factory at Silvertown; that's where I met Andrew. I was there when the explosion happened. That was an awful time; I thought Andrew had died in it, and I now know from our chats that your father did.'

Rosie nodded.

Molly raised her eyebrows. 'And that conversation was a typical one of me putting my foot in it and not thinking about whether other people had been involved in similar situations; it's something Alice – and particularly Victoria – are always telling me off for.' She paused. 'You know, at the time, I never realised your father worked there. I didn't really know any of the men, but a couple of the older ones were nice to me, and of course there was Andrew. He pursued me, despite my saying I wasn't going to be the boss's plaything, or words to that effect.'

Rosie gave a faint smile. 'Well, if you came across my father, he would have been one of the good ones. He was a lovely man and would have done anything for anybody.'

Molly stared at Rosie. 'He sounds like he was, and I wish I knew whether I had met him or not.'

Rosie straightened the paper pads on the counter. 'It was a horrendous night, one that will stay with me forever.'

Molly nodded. 'And me, that's for sure. I'm sorry, I didn't mean to wash your happy mood away.'

Rosie smiled. 'Don't worry, you haven't.'

Molly laughed. 'Good, so come on, what's the latest?'

Rosie placed her hand on her chest. 'Alfie is going to marry Fran, isn't that wonderful news? I mean, the baby is his and that's why Fran was too guilt-ridden to see me. There's more to it than that, but I won't bore you right now with the details because I'm sure Mr Leadbetter will be along soon to tell us off for talking.'

Molly gave Rosie a hug. 'That's wonderful news, if you're genuinely happy about it.'

Rosie squeezed Molly before taking a step back. 'Oh, I am. I feel like my execution day has been lifted.'

Molly beamed. 'And Sam?'

Colour rushed into Rosie's cheeks. 'He's asked me out.'

Molly clapped her hands. 'You do know he's madly in love with you, don't you?'

'So everyone keeps telling me. I never knew that, but I like being with him; he makes me smile.'

Molly shook her head. 'There's no doubt, and if you hadn't been so caught up about Alfie you would have seen it for yourself. When the pair of you are in the same place, he doesn't take his eyes off you.'

Rosie wondered if it was true. After all, Alfie had said more or less the same thing. The memory of the kiss they'd shared made her shiver and her stomach churn; what did that mean? Did she love him too?

22

Alfie studied Fran; tension was etched on her face.

A tear of perspiration started to roll from her forehead, and she wiped it away. 'The sun is hot today.' She moved from one foot to the other while looking around her.

Alfie grabbed her hand. 'Stop, it's going to be all right. You are not doing this alone, and I won't let anything happen to you, or let anyone say anything they shouldn't.'

Fran gave him a weak smile. 'I know, and I've wanted this for so long, but now it's here I am so scared it's going to go wrong. What if they think I trapped you into this?'

Alfie squeezed her hand. 'It's not going to go wrong. We are going to be together regardless of what they think, and if it comes to it, I shall make that very clear. You didn't trap me. In fact, I'd say the opposite; you told me many times I didn't have to be part of your or James's life, but the thing is, I want to be.'

Fran gave him a pensive glance before nodding. She glanced down at James sitting in the pushchair. 'I don't want him listening to arguments or raised voices; I've tried so hard to protect him from all of that.'

Alfie put his finger under her chin. 'I know, now stop worrying. It can only go one of two ways; they'll either accept the situation, or we'll be leaving here never to return – and that's now up to them.' He looked up at the front door. Taking a breath, he put his hand in the letter box and began pulling at the string that was holding the key.

The door flew open.

The edge of the letter box scratched Alfie's hand in the process; he gasped and stared at the red welt that had spots of blood seeping from it. He looked up and saw his mother standing there. 'Ma, you could have done some serious damage there; as it is, it hurts like hell.'

Mrs Bennet stared at Fran before peering at her son. 'I didn't think you were ever going to come in. Is there a problem?'

Alfie sighed. 'No, Ma, everything is all right, but it would be better if we could get off the street so people can't hear our conversation. We know how bad the gossips can be.'

Fran took a deep breath. 'I'm sorry, Mrs Bennet, I was naturally nervous at meeting you again. We haven't seen each other since before Alfie went off to fight.' Her words tumbled out. 'I also worried about my little boy, James. I don't want him to be part of a bad situation.'

Mrs Bennet nodded, looking down at James for the first time. 'There's no mistaking he's Alfie's; no wonder you kept him hidden, but if I'd known, I would have helped you.' She stepped aside to let them in. 'Best you leave the pushchair in the hall. Did you bring any toys for him to play with? If not, I'll get a couple of saucepans and a wooden spoon for him to make a noise on. I remember my boys loved banging on them; mind you, it was a right old racket, but they loved it.'

Alfie beamed as he placed his arms around Fran and gave her

a squeeze. 'We brought a bag of square building blocks; he likes to build them up and knock them down again.'

Sam strolled into the hall. 'Hello, Fran.' He stooped down in front of the pushchair. 'Hello, James.' He glanced at Alfie. 'Do you need some help bringing anything in?'

Alfie smiled. 'No, thank you, I can manage; besides, you've only got one good hand, remember?'

Sam moved away. 'Thanks for the reminder.'

Alfie lifted the pushchair across the threshold and Fran followed him in.

She lifted her son out and he stood next to her, hiding behind her leg.

Alfie knelt down next to him. 'Would you like me to carry you in, so you are tall like everyone else?'

James nodded.

Alfie whisked him up and James giggled as his legs flew out behind him. Alfie pulled him in close, holding him with one arm and putting his other around Fran.

Sam watched on. There was no doubting Rosie was right; Alfie was a different man with Fran and James. 'Go through, and I'll put the kettle on while you all have a chat.'

Alfie nodded and led the way into the front room. 'Hello, Pa, I'd like you to meet James, my son.'

Mr Bennet smiled. 'Hello, James, it's lovely to meet you.'

Alfie smiled at James. 'Say hello to your grandad.'

James clung to Alfie before whispering, 'Hello.'

Mrs Bennet strode into the room. 'Take a seat, we don't stand on ceremony here.' Her gaze travelled from Alfie to Fran. 'Right, I need to get this off my chest otherwise I won't be able to relax.'

Alfie studied his mother, waiting for her scathing comments about Fran and his plans.

Mrs Bennet wrung her hands together. 'Fran, I owe you an apology. Alfie has told me everything and anyone who loves my boys enough to try and protect them is fine by me.'

Fran blushed. 'Thank you, Mrs Bennet, I do love Alfie, but it has been hard keeping his secret.' She shook her head, reaching for Alfie's hand. 'There were times when I really felt he should go back, but he was suffering with terrible nightmares every night, and when a car backfired, he would drop to the floor. I wanted him to get help, but he was having none of it.'

Alfie's lips tightened. 'Fran, you don't have to tell them everything.'

Fran nodded. 'I'm sorry, I just think it's important that they know it isn't about cowardice, it's more than that.'

Mr Bennet lowered himself on to the floor and tipped the building blocks out of the bag. 'James, would you like to build a tower with me?'

James giggled as Alfie lowered him to the floor.

Alfie watched proudly as his son passed his father a square block.

Mrs Bennet cleared her throat. 'Alfie, your father and I have been talking and we would like Fran and James to move in here with us. We'll make the back room into a bedroom for them both and that way we are here to support them while you're away. Fran can carry on working without worrying about not having anyone to look after James.'

Alfie's face lit up. 'That's wonderful, Ma—'

'Wait, where are you going?' Fran's eyes welled up as she stared at Alfie.

Alfie wrapped his arms around Fran and pulled her close. 'It's time I handed myself in, Fran. I want us to lead a proper family life. I should be the one working, looking after you and James, and you must know they will catch up with me sooner or later. I thought if I hand myself in the judge might not be so hard on me.'

A tear rolled down Fran's cheek. 'But, what if—'

'There are no "what-ifs".' Alfie gently wiped away her tears. 'You know we can't keep hiding; it's not fair on James.'

Fran nodded. 'I'm scared. I'm scared of what might happen.'

'I know, but let's just enjoy today and we'll worry about it later.' Alfie glanced over at his mother. 'If Fran is all right with it, then I'm more than happy for them to move in here; it'll be one less thing for me to worry about.'

Mrs Bennet stepped nearer to Fran and squeezed her arm. 'You can trust me, Fran; nothing is more important to me than family, and you are now family.'

* * *

Sam had got up early and walked to Rosie's home. He leant behind a lamp post, staring at her front door, wondering with each minute what to do. The front door thudding shut alerted him to Rosie leaving the house, and he watched her walk towards Foyles on Charing Cross Road. His stomach churned. He had been hiding outside the house for what felt like ages, his confidence drifting away with every passing moment. It had seemed like a good idea when he'd got up this morning but now he wasn't so sure. Should he be doing this without talking to Rosie first? What would her mother say? Would she laugh at him, or worse, be angry? Especially after everything Alfie had put Rosie through.

Sam jumped as he felt a prod in the small of his back.

'What are you doing here?'

Sam turned round to see David staring at him. 'How did you know I was here?'

David grinned. 'You've been going from standing still and staring at the house to walking up and down the road.' He frowned. 'If you're waiting for Rosie, she's gone to work.'

Sam peered over his shoulder. 'You could see me?'

David chuckled. 'Of course. I was watching you from my bedroom window.' He glanced past Sam. 'If you're not waiting for Rosie, what are you doing here?'

'Er... er... I want to speak to your ma, if she has time and isn't going to work.' Sam shook his head; this wasn't how it had played out in his head this morning.

David nodded. 'Well, you'd best come in then.'

Sam gave a faint smile. 'With your pa gone I expect you've become the man of the house?'

David looked serious for a moment. 'I suppose so. As you said, my pa isn't here and I'm the only man living in the house.' He laughed. 'Though my ma will probably tell you I'm too young to be the man of the house.'

Sam studied David, remembering how Rosie had told him of her brother's fear when they were in the basement. He grinned. 'I think all mothers have something to say about where they see us in the family, no matter how old we are.'

David nodded. He looked pensive for a moment. 'Come on, I'll take you in to see Ma before you back out of it.'

Sam frowned. 'What makes you think I'll back out of it?'

'Because you've been out here for ages.' David paused. 'Are you wanting to speak to my ma about Rosie?'

Sam wondered for a moment if he should be honest with him. He told the children at school that they should always tell the truth, so he needed to practise what he preached. 'Yes, although if you're the man of the house, maybe I should be talking to you before I speak to your ma.'

David nodded. 'Well, if you want to speak to the man of the house then I think I know what you want to talk about.' He took a breath as sadness washed over his face.

Sam reached out and touched David's arm. 'We don't have to do this.'

David gave a small smile. 'No, but my pa always told me: "if you're going to do something, you should do it the best you can so you don't let people down", so tell me what you want to talk to my ma about.'

Sam could feel the respect for this young boy rising in him; he was trying to fill some big shoes. 'Well, I'm... er, quite nervous and I haven't spoken to Rosie about this yet, so I don't know if she even feels the same.'

David stared wide-eyed at Sam but said nothing.

Sam cleared his throat. 'The thing is... the thing is, I want to ask your sister to marry me but first I want your permission, and your ma's.'

David tilted his head. 'Shouldn't you have checked with Rosie first?'

Sam gave a nervous laugh. 'Yes, that would have made more sense, but she's been through a lot and I wanted to give her some space to decide what she wants, and I thought if I had the family's blessing, I could ask her when the time is right.'

David nodded. 'Do you love her?'

Sam beamed. 'Since the day I met her, and you need to know there's nothing I wouldn't do for her; she's all I think about from the moment I wake up until the time I go to sleep.' He laughed. 'And then I'm dreaming about her.'

David shrugged. 'So why did you let Alfie get in the way?'

Sam fidgeted from one foot to the other. 'I thought Rosie

wanted to be with Alfie and all I wanted was for her to be happy. To be honest, I'd rather have her in my life as a friend than not have her in my life at all.'

David nodded. 'You know my pa never liked Alfie, and he couldn't understand why Rosie was drawn to him; he always felt you were the better brother.'

'Thank you, it means a lot that your pa thought kindly of me.'

'Well, as long as you look after Rosie properly, and it's what she wants, then I'm happy to say yes.' David laughed. 'Now you've just got to get past my ma, but don't worry, I'll tell her I've already said yes.'

'Thank you.' Sam tried to hide the tension he felt rumbling inside him. 'You won't tell Rosie about this, will you? I don't want to put her off if she's not ready.'

'No, I won't. Come on, let's go and talk to Ma.'

* * *

Rosie sat on the bench showing some of the children how to write the letters of the alphabet, joining them up, and sounding each one out as she did. The children looked at the paper, enthralled. 'Now, if you get a chance, I want you to practise doing this at home. I don't want you to worry about it being perfect, it's just about practising it.'

The school bell rang out in the hall. The children groaned. 'Can't we keep going, Miss?'

Rosie laughed. 'I'm afraid not, your families will be outside waiting for you. Come on, get your things together and don't forget you can still do this at home. Mr Bennet will take you outside.' A wave of sadness washed over her as she watched them sort themselves out and leave the classroom in single file. She loved spending time with them as much as they seemed to love being with her. Rosie got up and began pushing the benches under the tables.

A short while later, Sam watched Rosie from the doorway before clearing his throat.

Rosie's head snapped up. 'You startled me, creeping about; I didn't hear you come back in.'

'I wasn't creeping about; you were obviously lost in your thoughts. Is everything all right?'

Rosie gave a small smile. 'Everything's fine. I'm going to see Fran when I leave here. I'm hoping she and Alfie are happy with the way things went with your ma and pa.'

'It seemed to go well. In fact, Fran and James are moving in with us. Pa and I will be helping her to move her belongings.' Sam hesitated. 'Alfie went to the police and handed himself in.'

Rosie's eyes widened. 'I can't believe that, although I think he's done the right thing.' She scowled. 'Do you have any idea what will happen to him?'

'Ma spoke to the police, but apparently it's not up to them, although they said the most he'll probably get is three years in prison, which Ma wasn't happy with until she thought about it; then she was pleased he wasn't being shot, either as a coward or on the front line.'

Rosie nodded. 'That's true. I must go and speak to Fran; it'll be a terrible time for her, but I know your ma won't take any nonsense from anyone. She'll look after her and James and it'll be good for your pa to have a grandson around.'

Sam grinned. 'I agree with you, and you're also right about Alfie being a different person around them, and that little lad is a joy to be with. When Alfie gets out, they are going to get married; he really cares for them.'

Rosie shook her head. 'I really hope it works out for them; Fran has been through a lot in the name of love.'

Sam stepped nearer to her. 'I think we need to talk, especially after everything that's been said lately.'

Rosie stopped what she was doing. She sat on the nearest bench. 'I've been wanting to ask you how you are since you came out of hospital? You haven't rested like you were told to, you came straight back to work even though the hand you write with is the one that's broken.'

Sam frowned as he looked down at his plastered hand. 'I know, but I love being with the children, I feel like I'm doing some good. Alfie might have broken my hand under the guise of getting me out of going to war; if I recall correctly, he said he was saving me. The one thing I can say is that he has given me the gift of time to spend with the class, and to see you and Fran become friends again, and for that I'm grateful.'

Rosie's lips tightened. 'It seems a bit drastic though, as do most things Alfie does – well-intentioned but a little awry. Although I'm grateful you can't go now, but it strikes me that it's just putting off the inevitable.'

'I agree, but I suppose it gives me a few months' grace and then I'll have my training after that so we can live in hope the war will be over by then.' Sam smiled, then shook his head. 'I want to talk about us.' He stepped nearer to Rosie. 'I've always been a little bit scared to talk to you about my feelings, mainly because I'd rather have your friendship than nothing at all, but now Alfie has thrown it out there, I feel I have no choice.'

Rosie watched him; she wanted to speak but didn't know what to say.

Sam wrung his hands together. 'The thing is, he wasn't wrong. I have loved you for what seems like forever, but you only seemed to have eyes for Alfie, and it would have been wrong of me to come between you, regardless of my feelings.'

Rosie opened her mouth to speak but no words came out.

Sam gave a wry smile. 'Let me finish. If I stop, I may not find the courage again.' He took a deep breath. 'I could be wrong, but I got the feeling, even before he had his say, that you didn't want to marry him because you didn't love him; and now you and Alfie have said you are definitely not getting married – at least not to each other.' He sucked in his breath like a man starved of oxygen. 'You know, when I kissed you, it felt so right; the smell of your hair and your floral perfume has stayed with me. Sorry, I'm sounding like an idiot.'

Rosie's stomach churned and her skin tingled as she remembered his kiss. She stood up. 'No you're not, you sound like a man in love.'

Sam's eyes widened. 'Am I hoping beyond hope that you could come to love me in the same way?'

'I must have driven you mad, always waiting for Alfie and moaning about Fran not wanting to see me, instead of getting on with my life and leaving them all to it—'

'No, you haven't, and I hate to say this, but Alfie is right. You have shown that you're honourable, you keep your word, and friendship is important to you. You are always kind and careful about what you say in front of my mother, which is probably why she loves you so much.'

Rosie held up her hand. 'Stop, I'm not sure I deserve all those compliments.' She smiled. 'But they are good for my soul.' She walked over to him. 'I don't know where this leaves us.'

Sam's gaze soaked up Rosie's face. He reached out and stroked her cheek. 'Can I kiss you?'

Rosie nodded.

Sam leant in and caressed her lips with his own.

Rosie pulled him closer and wrapped her arms around him. Her whole body felt on fire. She gasped and stepped back.

Sam frowned. 'Did I do something wrong?'

Rosie shook her head. 'No... no, it's... it's just that I've never felt like this before and it's a little bit scary.'

Sam smiled. 'You can trust me. I love you so much and I would never, ever, do anything to hurt you – and that's a promise.'

Rosie ran her fingers across her lips, swollen with passion. 'I know.' She stepped forward and into his arms again.

ACKNOWLEDGEMENTS

I would like to thank the many people, past and present, who have not only encouraged and supported my writing but my day-to-day life as well. In the last few years, I have lost friends and family, and they are all sorely missed.

A big thank you to all my readers; your loyalty, readership and reviews are always appreciated. I belong to a couple of reader Facebook groups and their friendship and kindness to one another is wonderful and very inclusive. It's lovely to know that in today's world, there are still people who care.

My publisher, Boldwood, their editors, marketing team and all the people behind the scenes deserve a huge thank you for helping to fine-tune the stories I write.

Last, but not least, I want to thank my children and grandchildren for their patience and encouragement as I lock myself away to write.

I hope you all enjoy the latest in the Foyles Bookshop series.

ABOUT THE AUTHOR

Elaine Roberts is the bestselling author of historical sagas set in London during the First World War. She joined a creative writing class in 2012 and shortly afterwards had her first short story published. She was thrilled when many more followed. Her home is in Dartford, Kent and she is always busy with children, grandchildren, grand dogs and cats.

Sign up to Elaine Roberts' mailing list for news, competitions and updates on future books.

Visit Elaine's website: www.elaineroberts.co.uk

Follow Elaine on social media here:

facebook.com/ElaineRobertsAuthor
x.com/RobertsElaine11

ALSO BY ELAINE ROBERTS

A Wartime Welcome from the Foyles Bookshop Girls

The Foyles Bookshop Girls' Promise

Sixpence Stories

Introducing Sixpence Stories!

Discover page-turning historical novels from your favourite authors, meet new friends and be transported back in time.

Join our book club Facebook group

https://bit.ly/SixpenceGroup

Sign up to our newsletter

https://bit.ly/SixpenceNews

Boldwood

Boldwood Books is an award-winning fiction publishing company seeking out the best stories from around the world.

Find out more at www.boldwoodbooks.com

Join our reader community for brilliant books, competitions and offers!

Follow us
@BoldwoodBooks
@TheBoldBookClub

Sign up to our weekly deals newsletter

https://bit.ly/BoldwoodBNewsletter

Milton Keynes UK
Ingram Content Group UK Ltd.
UKHW020132131124
2794UKWH00007B/57

9 781805 497110

HOLISTIC ANATOMY

This book is dedicated to Hugh, the love of my life,
in honour and praise of All Our Relations

HOLISTIC ANATOMY

FOR HEALERS, HERETICS & ALTERNATIVE FOLK

AN INTRODUCTION TO ANATOMY, PHYSIOLOGY, PATHOLOGY, AND DEEP HOLISM

Pip Waller

Illustrations by Rachel Lloyd

The Dreaming Butterfly
Corwen

Copyright © Philippa Jean Waller 2008

First published in Great Britain in 2008 by
The Dreaming Butterfly
Hafotty Gelynen
Maerdy
Corwen
LL21 9PA
www.thedreamingbutterfly.com
www.holisticanatomy.com

Philippa Jean Waller has asserted her right under the Copyright, Designs and Patents Act 1988 to be identified as the author of this work

A CIP catalogue record for this book is available from the British Library

ISBN 978-0-9560757-0-3

All illustrations by Rachel Lloyd
Text design and layout by Andy Garside www.andygarside.com
Cover design by Pip Waller and Andy Garside

Printed and bound in Great Britain by CPI Antony Rowe, Eastbourne

HOLISTIC ANATOMY
FOR HEALERS, HERETICS & ALTERNATIVE FOLK
AN INTRODUCTION TO ANATOMY, PHYSIOLOGY, PATHOLOGY, AND DEEP HOLISM

How the body works, mixed in with spirituality, ecology, quantum physics, sociology, theology, philosophy, psychology, ethnology and more…

"At last, a thoroughly accessible, thought provoking and completely enthralling journey through the technicalities of Anatomy & Physiology! Pip's enthusiasm for her subject literally jumps off the page, as she guides you through the terrain of the human body, mind and spirit; missing none of the fascinating side tracks along the way. I would whole heartedly recommend this book to anyone who is even vaguely intrigued by the 'how' and 'why' - and more importantly the 'what if' – of their existence…"
Karen Chagouri *Editor, In Touch Magazine, Holistic Therapist & Doula*

"This startling book looks at anatomy, physiology & pathology in a refreshing new way, holistically & in the context of life & culture. Drawing on a broad range of influences & her long experience, & using ordinary language, Pip demystifies the understanding of the body and its processes, & gives considered insights into some of the influences upon us which we have the power to change… Highly recommended."
Kath Antonis *Medical Herbalist, Registered General & Sick Children's Nurse, Clinical Teacher*

"Coming from a background of being a Physiotherapy student I have spent a lot of time reading Anatomy and Physiology textbooks, also being dyslexic I feel like I have struggled a lot of the time to understand the information in them. This book is written in a style that is very easily understood and flows, instead of just being factual information. It feels as though Pip is there with you explaining things to you in a way that really makes sense. I was lucky enough to have a copy of the draft version when I was studying, which was great, but the finished book is even better – really fantastic."
Phil Pepin *Massage Therapist*

Warning! **This is not a conventional textbook** – *it roams around through all kinds of subjects, weaving them into anatomy, physiology & pathology. If you are studying a course of some kind, you will still need your recommended books. This is meant more as an appetizer to get you going*

CONTENTS

Introduction xi

Section One – How the Body Works

Chapter One – An Orientation to the Human Body 1
Chapter Two – It's the Chemistry of Life 11
Chapter Three – Cells & Tissues – The Basic Materials (Histology) 23
Chapter Four – Between Within and Without (The Skin or Integumentary System) 39
Chapter Five – Them Bones Them Bones Them… Dry Bones (The Skeletal Sytem) 47
Chapter Six – Movement (The Muscular System) 62
Chapter Seven – Transport/The Heart of the Matter (The Cardiovascular System) 69
Chapter Eight – Drainage (The Lymphatic System) 89
Chapter Nine – The Army and the Cleaners (The Immune System) 94
Chapter Ten – Breathing (The Respiratory System) 107
Chapter Eleven – Eating and Food Processing (The Digestive System & Diet) 116
Chapter Twelve – The Liver 138
Chapter Thirteen – Waterworks (The Urinary System) 144
Chapter Fourteen – The Wiring (The Nervous system) 150
Chapter Fifteen – Hormones (The Endocrine System) 168
Chapter Sixteen – The Birds and the Bees (The Reproductive System) 179
Chapter Seventeen – Experiencing the Outside World - The Special Senses & Touch ... 202
Chapter Eighteen – An Overview of Aging 211
Chapter Nineteen – Interrelationships -
   How the Systems, and Everything, are Interconnected 217
Chapter Twenty – Dropping the Robe - Death & Dying 227

Section Two – Health and Disease

Chapter Twenty-one – Western Pathology – an Introduction 238
Chapter Twenty-two – Further Towards a Holistic Paradigm 246
Chapter Twenty-three – Emotional Health – Connecting the Mind and Body 254

Appendix A – A Completely Holistic System – Five Element Medicine 265
Appendix B – The Spiritual Cause for Disease – the Shamanic Perspective 275
Bibliography 280
Acknowledgments 287
Index 288

INTRODUCTION

In a sea of anatomy and physiology books, why write another? Mainly to help contradict the notion that anatomy and physiology are dry and boring, and to share more widely my particular style of introducing adults to the miracle of the body, Spirit made flesh, with the many opportunities of philosophizing, chewing the breeze, enjoying the apparent ridiculousness, and otherwise observing how to live well, that this subject abundantly offers.

I will assume that you have very little knowledge, beginning by introducing the body very simply and building on this knowledge later to add layers of understanding. The goal is to leave the reader truly understanding something of how the living body works, rather than to cover every detail of current knowledge on anatomy, physiology and pathology. It seems that many people study A & P to considerable depth – even managing to pass quite detailed exams on the subject – without ever gaining a real understanding. This book aims to remedy that.

I will attempt here a 'holistic' – and in places more than slightly heretical – anatomy and physiology; that is, an exploration of the mechanisms of action of the body mixed in with interesting thinking about emerging sciences such as quantum physics and the new biology, human 'emotional anatomy', ecological principles and spiritual and energetic paradigms. You will see that the study of human biology can be linked to broader considerations of how a human exists within, and interacts with, the environment, and experiences their existence in emotional and spiritual, as well as physical, terms. Some of what will follow is accepted 'scientific fact', some will challenge such facts, and some is just my own ideas and philosophies – based on both my own and borrowed observations. I will conclude with a brief overview of various paradigms of health and disease, including beginning a discussion of what total healing of body, mind, spirit and global society could mean. There are some forms of natural medicine I am very familiar with; these are the ones I mention most as examples. The absence of mention of other systems is in no way indicative of their lack of value – only of my own lack of knowledge. I hope that students of these disciplines will forgive this lack and still find this book helpful as an aid to their understanding of the medical sciences.

As this is *not* intended to be an academic work, I am referencing with almost entirely secondary references, intending where I can to point the reader on to further study. At times I repeat information to aid the learning process.[1] You can take it all with a large pinch of salt

---

[1] The main way human beings learn is by repetition, repetition, repetition…

(after all, our bodies are swimming in salt water), and enjoy the mental meandering which will help you to remember the plain facts. Actually, I advise you to be vigilant against adopting a fixed position – keep thinking for yourself, and rather than getting attached to one viewpoint, have an open mind and be prepared to adapt your thinking as new information emerges. Modern orthodox medicine offers many examples of what happens when you don't do this. Take anti-depressants, for example: this week, early March 2008, the headlines are full of how they only work for 30% of people. But did you know that the entire premise that depressed people have low levels of serotonin in their brains, first theorized in 1967, has never actually been proved, despite many attempts to do so? This theory has been accepted by many medics, including those in the mental health field, and is widely believed publicly, yet it seems very likely to be wrong![2]

The actual physiology herein is at a fairly basic level, without being oversimplified. In places it is more technical than the interested lay reader or healer would need (or like); these readers can skip over the bits that are too detailed and stick to taking in the juicy bits. Students who are required to go deeper will gain a practical understanding of how the body works and then return to their more in-depth textbooks with renewed vigour.

The human being, in body, mind and spirit, is a beautiful and complex entity – there is always more to be learnt. In this spirit, I have included some contradictory ideas which could all be true. I would be very pleased to hear from you with new ideas, information which debunks my own ideas and any other feedback which adds to understanding our bodies, minds and existence in this way.

Please contact me via the book's website, www.holisticanatomy.com

This book is intended for:
- Anyone studying, or with an interest in, holistic medicine, *particularly those with less than 100% enthusiasm for the anatomy and physiology side of things*: this book will light your fire!
- People who want to know more about how their body works but don't want to read a straight textbook.
- Those who enjoy science, but feel it can be a little disjointed.
- Healers and energy workers who need to bone up on how Spirit looks when it's in the flesh.
- Anyone with a body and a thirst for knowledge about it, who likes to look at life sidewise.

Please feel free to quote from this book, subject to acknowledgment of the source.

---

[2] 'What Doctors Don't Tell You' Vol 18 no 12 March 2008

Chapter One

AN ORIENTATION TO THE HUMAN BODY

SOME BASIC ANATOMICAL LANGUAGE,
AND A GENERAL ORIENTATION

Just as the universe is a gigantic dance of stars and planets, spinning and turning in mysterious space, so the human body is an incredibly beautiful and complex creation, with millions upon millions of cells[3], functioning in their different ways to make an integrated whole. Groups of similar cells are found joined together to form tissues. Different tissues together form structures with specific functions, called organs. Organs are associated with various tubes and supporting structures in things called systems. These carry out types of work in the body, like the different departments in a company or the various goings on in a community: communication, control, energy input, waste disposal, transport, production and so on.

The body exists in a state of constant change and movement. There is an internal balance, known as **homeostasis**, which is constantly monitored and maintained. This is the Western way of explaining what the Chinese call 'yin and yang': the complementary opposites which in life are always moving and dancing together in and out of balance (although in Western physiology, homeostasis relates to physical functions only).

In life there is no stasis - all is continually moving and changing. The chemicals in the body are kept at optimum levels. They move up and down these levels, and by so doing keep our bodies functioning well.

For the purposes of study (and following the Western scientific tradition which loves to separate in order to analyse and classify), we divide the functioning of the body into systems and look at each one individually: the skin; the skeleton; joints and muscles; the heart and circulation; the circulation's companion: the lymphatic system; the lungs; the gut; the kidney and bladder; the nervous system and the special senses; and the reproductive system.

Remember however that the parts cannot and do not function alone - all are connected together in their intricate dance to maintain homeostasis. Even though each cell has its

---

[3] Just thinking about the word 'cell' I realised it kind of sums up the separatist, mechanistic approach to life of Newtonian science which gave birth to modern medicine, which is brilliant in its way, yet lacking in connectedness – between the different bits of the body, between the body, mind and spirit, between a person and their environment.

individual life and functions, there is an over-all coherence. The endocrine and nervous systems are key in this, but not the end of the story; there seems to be an intelligence which runs through the body and mind, connecting and somehow orchestrating it all, which goes beyond what is currently understood by science.[4]

Connected to each other and to all life...

We humans also cannot-and do not-function alone. Our modern world allows the illusion of separateness. I can live in my house, go to work in my car, sit at my desk and work, buy food to cook alone or with my small immediate family (at home), with very little contact with other humans. Recent political trends in Britain positively promoted this idea, with the philosophy 'there is no such thing as society; there are only individuals'.

The reality is, we are not independent. We are absolutely and completely dependent on each other (interdependent) for our survival, just as we have been since the beginning of time, and just as our cells are dependent on each other for the survival of our body.

Long ago (about three and a half billion years) our ancestors were still in simple chemical form hanging out in the primordial soup, when they noticed that if they hung out together they were better at surviving. Hence the first creatures formed, who then noticed (about a billion years ago) that getting together with each other created yet more opportunities for multiplying. We still carry within our cells **mitochondria**, which were once smaller cells (**bacteria**) that became part of a bigger cell; were swallowed by it, or invaded it. The partnership[5] was successful for both parties and survived to be the building block of our bodies, the modern **cell**.[6]

When I awake in the morning, an alarm clock made in a factory across the sea wakes me. I get up and dress in clothes made somewhere else. I eat food grown by people of many countries; packed, transported and sold to me. Before I even leave the house in the morning I have been touched by thousands of other lives. It is impossible for a human being to be separate. We are connected to each other and to all life, to the earth we live on, as intimately as our cells are part of us. Likewise in creating this holistic anatomy, physiology and pathology book, I am roaming through body, culture, society, Earth, politics, healing and spirituality.

---

[4] Lynne McTaggart *The Field – The Quest For The Secret Force Of The Universe*.

[5] It turns out that bacteria often behave in a way that turns the Darwinian 'survival of the fittest' paradigm on its head. Not only do they not compete with each other, bacteria actively co-operate, exchanging important information about their environment (this is why they so quickly become immune to antibiotics, even those who haven't themselves been exposed to a particular antibiotic). These distant ancestors of ours are masters of adapting to their environment. (Stephen H. Buhner's *The Lost Language of Plants*). Actually, fifty years before Darwin, the man who first put forward the theory of evolution, Jean-Baptiste de Lamarck, emphasized in his presented theory the 'instructive' cooperation between organisms and their environment (Bruce H. Lipton *The Biology of Belief*).

[6] Or so one rather convincing story goes; that of evolution. There are ancient bacteria which do look quite similar to mitochondria – but let's remember that this can only ever remain a theory. We do need to be careful to not just pick the evidence we like to fit the story we like. Rather, the story should form around the unbiased facts, and we should be willing to change the story if necessary. Consider the creationists: they like their story and so only listen to evidence that supports it, and dismiss evidence to the contrary.

Anatomy and physiology: structure and function

The word **anatomy**, from Greek for 'cutting away', refers to the study of *structure*: what does it look like, where is it, how is it put together? The word came about through the process of autopsy (cutting up dead bodies), through which much of anatomical knowledge arose. This may account for some of the weaknesses of Western medicine – study of dead bodies cannot give us entirely reliable information about living anatomy.

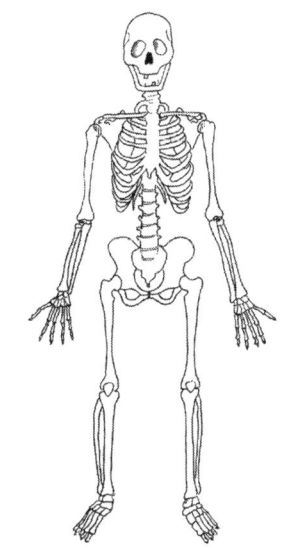

Take a look at the pictures of the skeleton in any anatomy book (including this one!); see how big a gap there is between the top of the ilium (hipbone), and the bottom rib. Now have a feel of your own body; see how much space there is between these two bones. You'll find it's considerably less. This is due to the way the skeleton is held and pulled on by the muscles, which makes it different in life and in death. This is not meant as a criticism of traditional anatomical study - but it is important to be aware, as we attempt a study of living anatomy, of the basis of much of this knowledge.

Physiology is the study of life, or *function*: what does it do, and how does it do it? Most of the knowledge modern physiology has gleaned has come from countless experiments on animals.

Anatomy and physiology naturally go together: we say that there is a *complementarity of structure and function* (e.g. blood flows in one direction: in the veins it flows towards the heart [physiology[because of the one-way valves [anatomy]).

Pathology is the study of what can go wrong: *disease*.[7] There are many different approaches here. This book will introduce some very basic Western pathology, which is extremely good at describing what is happening in the tissues during disease states. We will also briefly explore various holistic models of the causes of disease.

A hierarchy of organisational levels

There is said to be a hierarchy of **organisational levels** in the body. We love to make a pyramid out of a circle! Here they are:

The simplest level is **chemical**. Everything is made of atoms[8], combining to form molecules, which combine to form organelles...there is much more on this to come – brace yourselves!

---

[7] Which means 'dis-ease', a lack of easy functioning.

[8] Which are made of 'sub-atomic particles' which, according to modern quantum physics theory, are made of pretty much nothing but some kind of mysterious energy...yes, really! They are made of energy – incredibly fast moving vortexes of photons and quarks, which when you look really closely – disappear! (Heinz R. Pagels *The Cosmic Code: Quantum Physics As The Language Of Nature*).

Next comes **the cell**, bound by a highly intelligent, semi-permeable membrane, and containing fluid called cytoplasm. All cells have some common functions, but there is enormous variation between different cells in the body. Inside the cytoplasm are found 'organelles' which carry out the basic functions of the cell – including the mitochondria, nucleus, Golgi body and endoplasmic reticulum.

Cells and 'extracellular material' (this is stuff which cells make, is not a cell, and is found outside a cell, such as collagen fibres), get together to form **tissues**. There are four basic types: the lining **epithelial** tissue; **muscle** tissue for movement; **nervous** tissue for communication and control; and **connective** tissue for…connecting. The four tissue types are arranged in various ways in the body, forming its organs, tubes and supporting structures.

Organs are discrete structures carrying out particular functions. There are many organs in the body: the heart, lungs, brain, liver, gall bladder, pancreas, kidneys, bladder and uterus. They are made up from all the different tissue types. Hollow organs, for example, the heart, have an inner lining of epithelial tissue, a middle layer of muscle and an outer covering of connective tissue. The tubes in the body, such as the blood and lymph vessels, ureters, fallopian tubes, windpipes and gastrointestinal, tract, have the same basic structure: an inner lining of epithelial tissue, a middle layer of smooth muscle and an outer covering of connective tissue.

Organs and supporting structures (like the tubes of the gut and blood vessels) get together to perform whole areas of function in the body, and these are known as **systems.** Systems carry out the functions necessary for life, e.g. the heart and blood vessels make up the cardiovascular system, responsible for transport in the body. All the systems work together.

The whole thing is called the **organism**. It's good to remember that, although we break it down into separate parts for study, actually the organism (us!) is a complex being in which all parts work together harmoniously. The maintenance of harmony and balance within the organism is known in Western physiology as **homeostasis** (although this relates only to the body). Uniquely in world cultures, modern Western science does not recognise the existence of Spirit, and is just barely beginning to understand the Mind.

Can you see yourself as a part of a highly ordered world – universe even – with its own control systems and homeostatic balancing mechanisms? This seems far-fetched to modern Westerners, brought up with a purely mechanistic view of the world on top of the Judeo-Christian paradigm of the world being put here for the use of humans, but it is A B C (or rock, tree, stone!) to many tribal people living in close harmony with the earth. How would it change things for you to consider yourself related to all, to remember every bacteria as your close kin, to know the rightness not only of *your* existence as a beloved child of the universe, but of every single other, be it human, creature, plant, rock, whatever? This is how the remaining tribal peoples of the earth – keepers of the old ways – live.

Water water everywhere...

The human body, like the surface of the earth, is 60-70% water. This water is found all over the place: inside cells (where it is called **intracellular fluid** or **cytoplasm**), and outside cells (**extracellular fluid**). Extracellular fluid (outside of cells) is found both in and out of the tissue spaces. In the tissue spaces it is called tissue fluid or **interstitial fluid**, and this bathes every cell in the body. There is a kind of glue here that holds the cells together and makes a gel of the tissue fluid, called **hyaluronic acid**[9]. There is also extracellular fluid which is *not* found in the tissue spaces; this includes the blood plasma, lymph, and cerebrospinal fluid.

The necessary functions for life

Maintaining boundaries – this is done by the skin, and on the cellular level by the 'selectively permeable' membrane of each cell. In Chinese medicine, there is the 'Wei level' – a protective energy which circulates along the meridians at the most superficial level. All energy healing systems have a way to describe a protective energy around the body.

Movement – in animals, muscle tissue allows for movement in the body – not just of our whole body by the skeletal muscles, but also in the digestive tract, cardiovascular, urinary and reproductive systems. Interestingly, plants move too, albeit much more slowly than us. Many grow towards the light and will move as the light moves. Some catch insects, many have ways for their seeds to move across huge distances. Even whole populations can move, in response to changing conditions. For example, with global warming causing increased dryness in the South of England, beech woods are threatened there. However, they are now growing further North than ever before – so in time, the entire forest will move north.[10]

Responsiveness – this is the ability to sense changes and react to them. All cells are responsive, but the nerve cells are particularly so and this is what allows them to carry out their functions of communication and control of body activities. Responsiveness is also called 'irritability' – nice to know it's an essential life function to be cranky!

Digestion – this is the breaking down of food into usable parts.

Metabolism – this actually means all chemical reactions occurring within cells – breaking things down (catabolism) and building things up (anabolism). This is how we get energy.

Excretion – getting rid of the leftovers, the toxins and the stuff we can't use.

---

[9] Some bacteria and viruses make an enzyme called 'hyaluronidase', which breaks down this glue to allow them to move around more freely. The well known plant Echinacea has an action of being 'antihyaluronidase' – in other words, it can halt the spread through the body of invading organisms by preventing them from un-gluing our tissue fluid. Research has found that Echinacea (*Purpurea* and *Angustfolia* are the active species) also increases phagocytosis of foreign matter by white blood cells, increases lymphokines and cytokines which stimulate immune function, is antiviral at least externally (in vitro), is anti-inflammatory and yet improves wound healing and has some antimicrobial activity (Simon Mills & Kerry Bone *Principles And Practice Of Phytotherapy – Modern Herbal Medicine*).

[10] Royal Horticultural Society website: www.rhs.org.uk/research/climate change/trees (Accessed Feb 2008).

- **Reproduction** – some say this is what it's all about! On a cellular level it happens daily as many cells continuously reproduce themselves, and are replicated to replace old worn-out ones. Then there is the more challenging task at the organism level, where whole new organisms are made.
- **Growth** – this refers to the increase in size, as well as number, of cells within the organism. Many cells start off simple and grow in complexity, changing their make-up as they develop. For example, blood cells all come from one great-grandmother cell which divides and differentiates to become the very different red and white blood cells and platelets. There is also growth outside of cells, as structures such as hair are built up, and fibres are made (in connective tissue, for example).

Where everything is – body cavities and organ location

The skeleton makes areas of bony protection for squishy internal organs to hide within: the cranium of the skull protects the brain, and the vertebral column protects the spinal cord as it passes down that bony canal. The chest cavity, or thorax, protects the heart and lungs and the pelvic cavity protects the bladder and **gonads** (sex glands) ovaries, in women. (Men's gonads (known as testicles), as you are no doubt aware, reside outside of the abdominal or pelvic cavity). The thorax is divided from the abdomen by the **diaphragm** muscle, which domes up from the bottom of the ribs to a central flat tendon.

Beneath the diaphragm, the ribs protect the upper part of the abdominal cavity, and here nestle the kidneys, liver and spleen. The two kidneys are found either side at the back – if you put your hands back there on the bottom few ribs, you are directly over your kidneys. The liver takes up the rest of the right side, front and back, with the gall bladder attached to its underneath. The spleen is found towards the back on the left. The muscles of the abdomen at the front and sides, and the spine and back muscles at the back, protect the less vulnerable guts, or intestines. The lower part of the abdominal cavity is called the pelvic cavity, containing the reproductive organs and the bladder.

Location of Organs

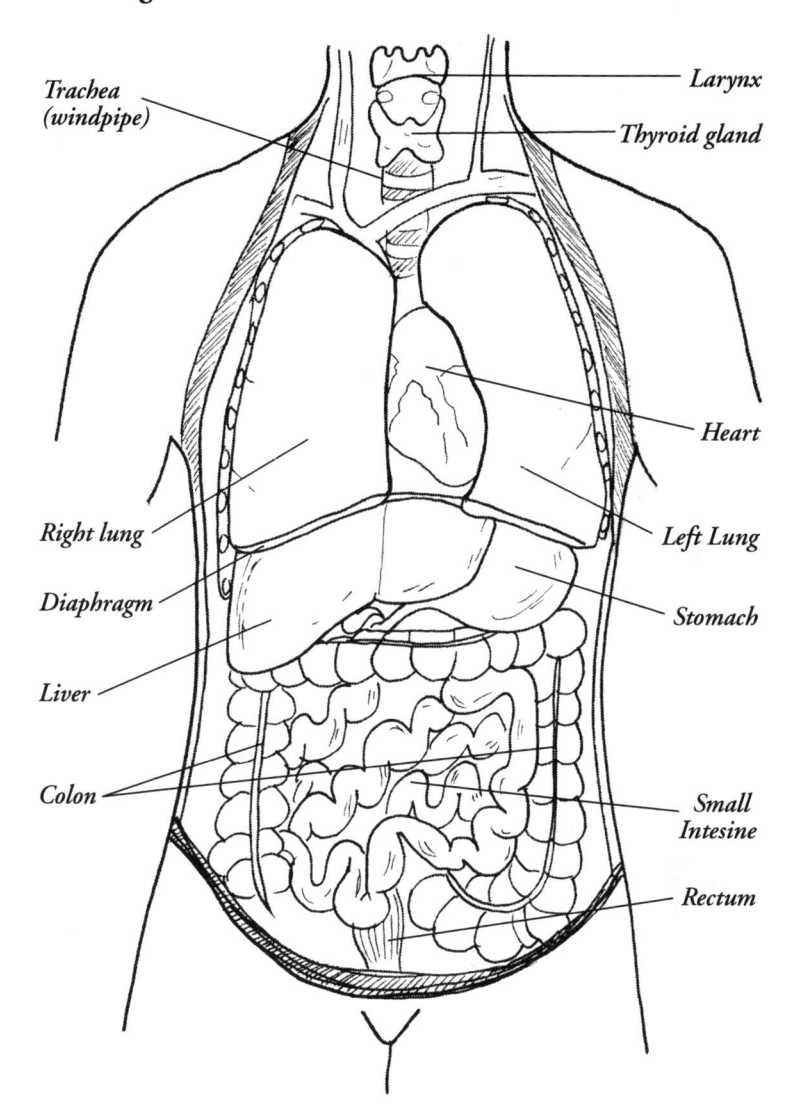

Trachea (windpipe), *Larynx*, *Thyroid gland*, *Heart*, *Right lung*, *Left Lung*, *Diaphragm*, *Stomach*, *Liver*, *Colon*, *Small Intesine*, *Rectum*

An Overview of the Body Systems

Just take a moment to be aware of your body; be aware of your bones and muscles supporting you, holding you up, turning the page, scratching your head. There's probably an ache here and there, drawing your attention to particular muscles. In fact, we often have the habit of noticing our bodies most when they are giving us trouble.

Find a friend and put your head on their chest – you can hear the 'lub dupp' of their heart beating. Feel your friend's pulse: put a couple of fingers inside their wrist on the thumb side, just outside the big tendon you can feel there. This is their radial 'pulse' – a surge of movement in the blood vessels as blood is pumped around the body. Listen to their heart and feel the pulse at the same time; you'll hear the heart beat, then right afterwards, feel the pulse as the heart and blood vessels work in concert with each other. This **cardiovascular system** is the means by which things are transported through the body. Nutrients, waste products, hormones, and in traditional Chinese thinking, chi energy – all rely on the circulation to get around.

The circulatory system is backed up by the **lymphatic system**: a collection of tubes called lymph vessels which begin in the tissues and, like the veins, drain waste products and water. This lymph fluid is filtered and cleaned by lymph nodes, and eventually returned to the blood. The lymphatic system is also heavily involved in **immunity**; protecting the body from outside organisms, and cleaning up toxins and destroying abnormal cells.

Focus on your breathing for a few moments. Can you feel your thorax (chest) expanding front and back, sides, top and bottom? Place your hands one on each side of your upper chest, with the fingertips touching your collarbone, and your elbows held in to your sides. This is the location of your lungs – are they smaller than you thought? The lungs are one of the most delicate organs in our bodies, part of the **respiratory system**; a series of pipes ending in tiny air sacs, or 'alveoli', which are surrounded by a network of minute blood vessels. Oxygen is passed from the alveoli into the blood, and carbon dioxide is passed from the blood into the alveoli to be breathed out.

The oxygen is used by your cells to 'burn' sugar and fat to make energy.[11] We've seen that the respiratory system is how we get the oxygen into the body. What about the sugar and fats? Put your head on your friend's belly and have a listen. Within moments, you will hear gurgles and pops, signs that the **digestive system** is working to break down your food into small, usable parts. When they are small enough, these molecules that made up the food you eat are absorbed into the blood stream. What you don't need is left inside the gastrointestinal tract to be excreted.

Go and take a drink – a large glass of water. What will happen to this water? First it will cross the gut wall and enter the blood. If it was allowed to stay in the blood indefinitely, the blood pressure would go up, and the blood would become too diluted. We need to keep the right amount of water in our body all the time. This process is controlled by hormones – which are chemical messengers – and by the brain. The brain also controls hormone secretion, e.g., antidiuretic hormone is produced by special neurosecretory cells. Hormones from the kidney, heart and brain control water balance, and the brain controls thirst. We can either preserve water, keeping it inside our body, or bail it out when there is too much. We bail it out using our **kidneys**. These amazing organs filter the blood and produce varying amounts

---

[11] See Chapter Two.

of urine. As well as water, this contains the nitrogen from old worn out proteins in the form of urea, and other waste products and excesses. Every minute, the kidneys filter 125 ml of blood; which means that an amount of blood equivalent to all the blood in the body passes through the kidneys in less than an hour.

How do you make a hormone? …….steal her chips![12] Seriously, hormones are very important (kind of homemade drugs), crucial to the way the body communicates with itself and controls its activities. They are not only made in the specialized places called endocrine glands, which anatomists mapped out in the 19th century, but in various other organs, tissues and cells all over the body. They are secreted directly into the bloodstream, so travel everywhere. The **endocrine glands** are the pineal and pituitary in the head; the thyroid, positioned like a bow tie around your neck; the thymus, found behind your breast bone; two adrenal glands, one on top of each kidney; the gonads or sex glands; and the Islets of Langerhans in the pancreas, making insulin. The Islets of Langerhans are not strictly speaking an endocrine gland but are one of the other cells and tissues making hormones; these include, amongst others, the heart, liver, kidneys, stomach and fat cells.

The endocrine system doesn't do all of the communicating and controlling. It is assisted by the **nervous system**: the brain, spinal cord and nerves. This system runs its wires all over the body. Close your eyes, and wiggle your fingers. What are you *doing*? Your brain is telling your fingers to wiggle: this is the motor nervous system. How do you know you are doing it? Because of your sensory nervous system you can *feel* it. That's basically it – your sensory nerves gather information of all kind and feed it to the brain, which decides what to do, and the motor nerves carry out those decisions by telling your muscles to contract or your glands to secrete. Simple!

Then there's sex………more of that later! (What a tease…)

More on homeostasis

As I said earlier, in Western physiology, the word homeostasis relates purely to physical functions, especially the control of temperature, blood sugar and body fluids. The internal organs require a fairly constant temperature for optimum functioning. When the environment is cold, we maintain heat by the blood vessels in the skin constricting (thus we look pale), and by shivering – much of our body's heat is generated by muscles contracting, so shivering is an involuntary way of getting us moving. The heat is transported around the body by the blood, rather like central heating. When we are hot, our skin reddens as the blood vessels in it dilate, allowing heat to leave the body. Also we sweat, which cools us because some of the heat energy in the skin is dissipated making the sweat evaporate.

For everything to work well, we need the right amount of water in our bodies – too much or too little can cause problems and eventually kill us. Fluid is maintained by the kidneys,

---

[12] As they say in Cork, Ireland. The rather ruder UK version is 'refuse to pay her…'.

which filter the blood for nitrogenous wastes (toxic to us, food for plants), and excrete this, along with varying amounts of water, through the tubes of the ureters, into the bladder and out of the body through the urethra.

Most of the energy we need in the body comes from the sugar called 'glucose': we digest food and absorb its molecules into the blood. We need different amounts of glucose depending on our activity: less at rest; much more during exercise (or intense thinking such as you are doing now – time for a snack?). The sugar in the blood gets into the interstitial fluid, and the cells take what they need. The right amounts in the blood are maintained by careful storing of excess glucose (as glycogen by the liver and as fat), or releasing of these stores. The process is controlled by the endocrine and nervous systems using a **negative feedback mechanism**. This basically means that as something rises in the body, whatever caused it to rise will then be decreased. For example, eating food causes your blood glucose to rise, which will also decrease feelings of hunger – although of course we can usually manage to enjoy chocolate anyway by disregarding this!

More negative feedback

In the world of physiology, negative feedback means that when *rising* levels of a certain thing (say heat or glucose) are detected by the body (specifically, by some kind of nerve receptor), that information is sent to a control centre (usually in the brain), which then sends a command to put something into motion to *decrease* that thing. If it's heat, for example, the commands will be to make the skin flush and to sweat in order to lose heat. If it's glucose, this may be taken from the blood by putting more of it into the cells, and transforming more to its stored form, glycogen.

It's rather like the thermostat in a house: if it is set at 18°C (65°F), when the temperature rises above this, the heating is switched off automatically. If the heat goes below the set temperature, the heating is switched on, thus maintaining a constant temperature.

I'd like to suggest that this is the *only* useful type of negative feedback in the universe, negative feedback in the sense of criticism not being something which encourages human beings to flourish at all.[13]

There are a few things in the body which work by physiological positive feedback, which basically means the more there is of something, the more it is stimulated. Childbirth happens like this, with oxytocin (a hormone from the pituitary) causing the uterus to contract, and this then causing more oxytocin to be released in a cascade, leading to birth. Another example is blood clotting, when a clot beginning to form actually causes more blood to clot. Maybe love works in a positive feedback kind of way too – the more there is, the more there will be!

---

[13] Of course, constructive criticism given and received in the right spirit can be very helpful indeed. However, even though negative criticism can sometimes result in positive reaction and motivation in the recipient, it can never result in the kind of deep inner flourishing that comes about as a result of really feeling completely good about ourselves.

Chapter Two

IT'S THE CHEMISTY OF LIFE...

The life of the body all starts with the fusion of two cells to make one – the tiny zygote from which all of the amazing cells, tissues, organs and systems of our brilliant bodies grow. Or is it sex it all starts with? The egg, or the chicken? We'll save sex for later, sprinkling it about here and there to spice up our anatomy life...

Actually, when you get down to it, it's about *chemistry*. Groans often ensue when people hear this word. But chemistry is just the language of the physical world. Chemistry is about how energy arranges itself to form matter. An endless dance of atoms, forming and reforming molecules, which get together with other molecules, which get together with other molecules to make – everything! Here is where modern Western science and mystical/religious/shamanic/energetic traditions agree:

Everything that exists is made of energy!

What is energy? It's a word we apply in all sorts of ways – oomph, zest, life-force, physical energy, mental energy, emotional energy, spiritual energy, kinetic energy, chi, agni, prana, pneuma, nuclear energy... the stuff which allows other stuff to happen.

Of course in Western science, the definition is narrower: energy is defined as the capacity of a system to do work, and is measurable by instruments. This definition of Newtonian origin (17th century) really came into its own in the 19th century, the Industrial Age, and perfectly reflects the work ethic of that time.

Interestingly, in the last fifty years, science has also realized that energy is the stuff that drives the universe, drives every event in the universe, and is in fact the basic constituent of the universe. Although it can be measured and quantified, we have no real idea what it actually is. Physics finds that energy is the most fundamental property of the universe; everything can be created by or dissolved into energy, including matter itself.[14] There is a background buzz of energy everywhere – the 'Zero Point Field.'[15] More on this later.

Consider Einstein's famous equation $E=mc^2$ (energy is equal to matter times speed squared).

---

[14] Heinz R. Pagels *The Cosmic Code: Quantum Physics As The Language Of Nature.*
[15] Lynne McTaggart *The Field.*

It kind of means, energy cannot be destroyed, only move or change from one form to another. The movements and changes in energy are produced by forces – such as by the push and pull of electrical force, and the pull of gravity, which is produced by all the local matter being attracted to all the other local matter (we experience this by being attracted to, or pulled, to the earth). [16]

Ancient spiritual systems throughout the world – including Vedic knowledge in India, shamanism or Earth-medicine (of which all tribal peoples have a version) and spiritual healing methods – all agree with modern physics on this business of energy being everything, but give this a different slant. Everything that exists is made of energy, including us. Because of this, we can communicate with everything – there is a place within us that can experience and in a very subjective way understand and use this energy. This approach is not separable from living in close harmony with what is all around us: nature.[17] Vedic practice is about realizing one's true nature; realizing that one is pure consciousness, therefore knowing everything, having access to all knowledge from within. Shamanic practices using this principle include weather-working (affecting the weather by dedicated relationship with the Weather Gods); remote viewing to find animals or plants needed for survival; and uncovering the causes of illness.

Of course 'subjective' is a bit of a dirty word in Western science, which prefers things to be objective, to know how things are in and of themselves. However, more and more data is emerging about the profound effect the experimenter has on the experiment (an experiment being something which looks for objective facts); just the fact that someone is experiencing an experiment (subjective) can change the result that actually occurs (objective). Therefore a truly 'objective' result seems impossible.

Many people working in the field of holistic medicine consider that totally new research paradigms are needed to properly research the field. Perhaps, in attempting to be totally 'objective' we may be in danger of cutting ourselves off from the depth and power of our subjectivity, and have it rule us by our ignorance of it.

Some of the 'energy' that powers us humans, enables us to think and move and learn and love and play and work, is **electricity**. Our cells are powered by electric fields, generated by

---

[16] To do the great Albert Einstein justice, he in no way saw the universe as empty and mechanistic. To quote him,
'The most beautiful and most profound emotion we can experience is the sensation of the mystical. It is the power of all true science. He to whom this emotion is a stranger, who can no longer wonder and stand rapt in awe, is as good as dead…'

[17] The Hopi people have long understood the interconnectedness of life forms, warning 'if you kill off the prairie dogs there will be no one to cry for rain' – "amused scientists, knowing that there was no conceivable relationship between prairie dogs and rain, recommended the extermination of all burrowing animals in some desert areas planted to rangelands in the 1950s 'in order to protect the sparse desert grasses'. Today the area (not far from Chilchinbito, Arizona) has become a virtual wasteland" (Bill Mollison in 'Permaculture'). It turns out that all the burrowing animals, from gophers to spiders, create a network of tunnels under the earth that then allow the water deep within the earth to rise and escape as moisture laden air which forms clouds and thus provides rain. Stephen Harrod Buhner says in '*The Lost Language of Plants*' "…indigenous peoples have always had access to the finest probe ever conceived, one that makes scientific instruments coarse in comparison, one that all human beings in all places and times have had access to: the focused power of human consciousness."

the positive and negative charges of the particles within atoms, which drive currents of protons through the tiny molecular machines within them. These positive and negative charges are derived from the breakdown of glucose, the body's fuel of choice.

Everything is made of energy, but there are also these things called 'particles', which seem to be there if you don't look too closely at them! We'll take a quick look at them now...

The smallest particles are tiny – even atoms are made of very little actual stuff – energy which just whizzes about and 'acts' solid. An atom has three types of particle: protons and neutrons, which are found together in the centre of an atom, forming a kind of nucleus, and electrons, which whiz about around the nucleus.

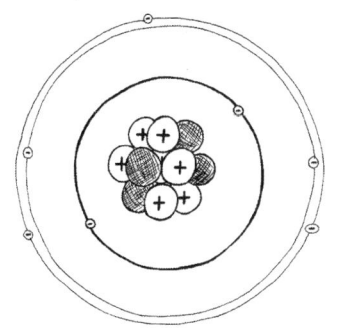

An atom looks a bit like this. The balls in the centre are protons and neutrons, the negatives orbiting around them are electrons. However, real atoms are mostly empty space. If we wanted to make an accurate drawing, we would have to draw the electrons about a mile away!

In this drawing, it looks like the electrons neatly orbit the nucleus, when in fact they don't. In reality, it is not possible to tell exactly where an electron is at a given moment or where it is going. Scientists can calculate the probability that an electron will be found in a given volume of space, but that isn't the same as knowing where that electron is. Spooky, huh?!

Electrons, which have a negative electrical charge, are the smallest particles of matter. Then there are neutrons and protons, being neutral and positive respectively. The electrons whiz around the proton and neutron centre of each atom incredibly fast.

What feels solid to us is really not so solid on a particulate level. There are particles called *neutrinos* that can move at speed straight through large solid objects – like the Earth – and out the other side without being changed at all. These particles form the basis of the universe and modern physicists are discovering some really amazing and weird stuff about them. For example, they appear and disappear *AND NO ONE KNOWS WHERE THEY GO...* This is all to do with the zero point field; so-called because physicists cool things down to absolute zero to study particles, so making them are much slower moving. Another fascinating phenomenon is that if you completely isolate two particles of the same type that are in relationship to each other (known as 'entrained') and do something to one of them, its relative in the other isolation chamber behaves as if that same thing has just been done to *it*....

It kind of looks as if quantum physics is beginning to catch up with the ancient shamanic wisdom of all cultures, and say, 'hmmm, the universe really is made of energy, everything is connected, and human consciousness has the power to affect reality'.[18]

Well, that's life the universe and everything. Now back to atoms. Atoms get attracted to other atoms, come together and 'share' their outermost electrons – this makes what is called a 'chemical bond'. As soon as two or more atoms are bonded, we call the resulting thing a 'molecule'. Some molecules are very small, for example, oxygen gas (O_2) which consists of two oxygen atoms, or water (H_2O) which consists of two hydrogen and one oxygen atom. Some molecules are comparatively enormous and consist of thousands of atoms bonded together, for example, large protein molecules.

Some atoms particularly like to get together with other atoms – if they were people, they'd be the gregarious party-going types. A prime example of this is oxygen, which loves to mingle.

When a chemical bond is made, it takes energy – you could say, energy is locked up in the bond. When a bond is broken, energy is released.[19] This process, of breaking down (catabolism) and building up (anabolism) is what we mean by 'metabolism'.[20] More on this later.

Atoms are classified into discrete chemicals called **elements** (remember the periodic table from school? Don't worry – we're not doing that now!). These are seen as the basic building blocks of all the molecular compounds in the world. The traditional view is that an element cannot be changed into anything different, at least not without huge energy input, but when they get together with other elements all sorts of startlingly different substances are created.[21]

There are 112 (to 116) elements in the known universe – and, lets face it, not all that much of it *is* known by us humans. The entire human body comprises mostly only a few of these, arranged in various ways to form molecules, which are arranged into cells and 'extacellular' stuff such as fibres and body fluids.

In fact, we are mostly water (60-70% of our body weight). When on their own, the

---

[18] Lynne McTaggart *The Field*.

[19] This is sometimes the other way around. Think of water: if you want to separate water you need to put in energy, e.g. an electric current. However, if you get a load of hydrogen and oxygen together, and put in a little activation energy, you then get loads of energy out (and lumps of metal end up on the moon!). So oxygen and hydrogen are initially in an unstable state and then give up energy to join together in a very stable, but lower energy state.

[20] Chemical reactions occur all the time in the body. All chemical reactions involve energy use or release. In the body these are part of 'metabolism' meaning a 'state of change'. There are two opposing forces in metabolism, which must remain in balance. These are ANABLOLISM (building up) & CATABOLISM (breaking down). Both activities are speeded up by 'enzymes' - protein catalysts that speed up chemical reactions without themselves being changed in any way.
1. anabolism uses free energy (e.g. when glucose is clumped together to form glycogen in liver and muscles).
2. catabolism releases free energy (e.g. glycogen being broken down to glucose).

[21] At least, this is the case in a test tube; however, according to some research done in the early 1960s by French scientist Louis Kervran, living organisms can and do transmute some elements into others! For example, chickens make eggs with shells almost entirely of calcium, even when their diet is devoid of calcium, as long as they can access potassium which is but a simple step away from calcium in its atomic structure.
You can read about this on http://www.cheniere.org/books/aids/ch5.htm   Kervan's experiments are convincing, but this work is not accepted scientific fact (yet) – it was seen as so way out that few scientists even tried to repeat the experiments, though others have since done similar work.

elements of H and O – hydrogen and oxygen – tend to exist as gases. When they get together a miraculous liquid, water, is created. Water is the perfect medium for the constant flow and ebb of chemicals; water and the other chemicals which make us up are always moving in and out of the body, in and out of the cells and tissues, and from place to place within the body. Water will allow most things to dissolve in it; it is the 'universal solvent'. We will be hearing much about this amazing substance, which is the basis for life as we know it. Water can be a liquid, or, when very cold become a solid – ice. When water is boiled, the molecules move so fast they become a gas – steam.

Water molecules have charged ends – they are 'polar'. The hydrogen and oxygen atoms in it share electrons, but the oxygen tends to hog them, so the 'H' end has a slightly positive charge and the 'O' end a slightly negative charge (electrons being the negatively charged particles in an atom).

To be more precise, the water in us is like seawater – a solution of salts in a base of water.[22]

Electrolytes

Salts are interesting molecules; they are a joining of atoms known as **ions**, which have an overall positive or negative electrical charge in their outer orbit, depending on whether they have lost or gained an electron.[23] As they can be positively or negatively charged, they follow the universal law of opposites – they attract each other – to form a salt. An example is **sodium chloride** (NaCl), a marriage of positively charged sodium with negative chlorine.

When sodium chloride is in contact with water, the polarity of the H_2O pulls the NaCl molecules to 'disassociate' into individual positively charged sodium atoms ($Na+$) and negatively charged chloride atoms ($Cl-$). All other salts behave in this way in water, and are then called **electrolytes**. The positive 'cations' are attracted to the negative 'anions', and this attraction is used by the body for marvellous purposes, including the electrical impulses of the nervous system.

One especially interesting thing about chemistry is how completely different stuff can become when it combines with other stuff. Sodium on its own is a silver-white solid substance, whereas chlorine is a (highly poisonous) gas. Amazing! It's like cooking – you take a bit of this and that and end up with all sorts of other stuff.

---

[22] Basically, the human body exists in a sea of water and electrolytes – a very similar composition to seawater. The body's internal environment of salty fluids makes it largely electrically charged, as it contains the polar covalent water molecules with many ions – positively charged cations and negatively charged anions. The charged cations, $Na+$ (sodium) and also $K+$ (potassium) and $Ca++$ (calcium), have important roles to play in making the **resting membrane potential**, which allows for nerve conduction and muscle contraction. More on this to come.

[23] Ionic bonds mean there has been complete transfer of one or more electrons between atoms, so that ions are produced. Ion means 'goer to'. e.g. sodium chloride, NaCl: when an Na (sodium) atom gets near the Cl (chlorine) atom, the Na atom transfers one of its electrons to the Cl atom, forming an ionic bond, with the sodium end being positively charged and the chloride end negatively charged. When a lot of them join together, which they like to do, they form an elegant crystal lattice structure – a salt cube or crystal like you see in coarse sea salt.

Most major spiritual traditions in the world agree on this basic similarity – everything is made of All-That-Is, or everything *is* God. Allah'ch ba. There is nothing that is not G–d. Great Spirit is everywhere and everything. You can substitute 'energy' or 'life energy' for the word *God*, and assume that the two words are in fact interchangeable. Of course, religion with its accompanying bigotry and war has given God a very bad press. Not to worry. This energy, the stuff of life cannot be destroyed – only changed.

Our bodies then are a parcel of salty water wherein various tides ebb and flow, chemicals move around, interact with each other, change and change again. The major element in us is **carbon**. This is found in every being we consider to be 'organic'[24] (which doesn't mean 'no artificial pesticides' in this instance). Pure carbon can look like coal – or diamonds. Remember Superman squeezing the coal to make a rock for Lois?

'Organic life' is basically plants and creatures – carbon based life, and their remains. In the West we consider 'alive' only those creatures who:
- require food of some sort to make energy
- eliminate waste materials
- use energy to grow
- reproduce themselves
- are sensitive to their environment and can move within it

Many other cultures in the world recognise the living energy of everything: plants, animals, rocks, air, mountains, the Earth itself and all the planets and stars, and even plastic and other man-made stuff. These tribal cultures, which have been and still are seen as 'primitive' by the dominant Western culture, consider all-that-is to be part of a whole; related and connected. Thus the idea that even as our cells, although having a kind of independent existence, are part of us, we are part of the great vast universe (which perhaps in turn is part of...).

If life is seen in this way, it is clear that creating huge piles of toxic rubbish and polluting the seas and rivers of the Earth is as irrational as filling our own bodies with toxins – particularly the kind that are no fun at all, like mercury, aluminum and formaldehyde, all found for example in vaccinations.

Slugs and snails and puppy dogs tails? What we are made of...

We are mostly made of carbon, and in addition to this and our 70% H_2O, we contain small but vital amounts of other stuff; our body is made of oxygen (65%), carbon (18%), hydrogen (10%), nitrogen (3%), calcium (1.5%) and phosphorous (1%). The remaining 1% is a mixture of potassium, chlorine, sodium, sulphur, magnesium, silicon, vanadium, copper, zinc, iron, selenium, molybdenum, fluorine, iodine, manganese and cobalt (nowadays we may also contain lithium, lead, aluminum, strontium, arsenic and bromine).

---

[24] Organic chemicals like carbon are non-polar. Unlike water and electrolytes, which are called 'inorganic', carbon forms bonds in which the outer electrons are equally shared between atoms. There is no electrical charge present in such molecules.

The main chemical groups

These atoms are arranged into molecules of the main chemical groups in our bodies, including proteins, fats, carbohydrates, vitamins and minerals. What follows is a closer look at these different types of chemical – what they are, and how they tend to function in the body.

Proteins

Proteins are very large molecules which actually form most of the structure of the body. They are made of **amino acids** of which there are 20 common types.

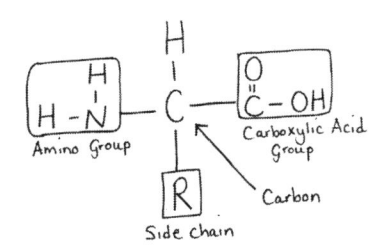

Amino acids contain a nitrogen-containing 'amine group' (NH_2), and an 'organic acid' group (COOH). They may act as a 'base' or an 'acid'.[25] On average, there are 19-20 atoms in one amino acid molecule.

Proteins are the main structural materials of the body, also having the most varied functions of any molecules in the body. Proteins make enzymes, haemoglobin, contractile proteins of muscle (actin and myosin), immunoglobulins, hormones and more.

All amino acids are the same except for one part, called the 'R' group. It is differences in the R group that give each amino acid its unique properties. Proteins are formed when the amine end of one amino acid links to the acid end of the next. (And a water molecule is formed as a result – this is called **dehydration synthesis**). There are thousands of different proteins in the body; all made from these various combinations of the 20 amino acids.

Proteins are classified by their appearance as 'fibrous' or 'globular'. Fibrous proteins are quite stable, but globular proteins are not and break down or change in certain conditions, including when the temperature, or the pH,[26] rises. This denaturing may be reversible, but if the disruption is extreme, it can irreversibly damage the protein – for example, what happens to the white of an egg (made of albumin) when cooked. In this case it is an irreversible process.

---

[25] Acids are H+ (hydrogen ion) donors – they have a tendency to give off their hydrogen ions. H+ are corrosive and dangerous to the body. Bases are H+ acceptors – they accept H+ donated by acids. A weak base accepts just a few; a strong base accepts many. Very strong bases are called Alkali. They include lye (used in soap making) and ammonia. They are powerful detergents and dissolvers of greasy, lipid material – can you think how this makes them harmful to the body?

[26] pH is measured by a notation of the potential number of H+. A 'neutral' solution is neither acid nor base, e.g. pure water has a pH of 7, which is a notational way of saying $1 \times (10)^{-7}$g of H+ per litre: i.e. 0.0000001, or 1/10 millionth – the decimal point is 7 places to the left of 1. So a stronger acid is less than 7 - i.e. 6, or 0.000001 or 1 millionth, or $1 \times (10)^{-6}$ of a gram of H+ per litre. MORE THAN 7 IS A BASE; LESS THAN 7 IS AN ACID!!!!
The normal pH of the body is 7.4 - i.e. slightly alkaline. The pH may normally fluctuate between 7.3 and 7.5. Beyond this limit is abnormal; too much acid in the body is called 'acidosis' and too much alkaline is 'alkalosis'. Each enzyme for controlling metabolism has an optimum acid base balance, or pH, to work in, as well as a permissible range of pH, which it must have in order to function at all.

Fibrous proteins include collagen (which is found in all connective tissues including bones, cartilage, tendons and ligaments), keratin (which waterproofs the skin, hair and nails), elastin (which gives elasticity where it is needed in ligaments and elastic connective tissue) and actin and myosin which allow muscle contraction and cell division, as well as transport within the cell.

Globular proteins are 'functional proteins' and play crucial roles in almost all biological processes. They include:
- Protein enzymes e.g. salivary amylase (which starts starch digestion in the mouth) and oxidase enzymes (amongst many others).
- Transport proteins such as haemoglobin and lipoproteins (amongst many others).
- Plasma proteins including albumin, which provides osmotic pressure to the blood, as well as being either a base or an acid, keeping pH balanced in the blood.
- Protein hormones such as growth hormone and insulin.
- Immune functioning proteins like antibodies, complement proteins and molecular chaperones.

See why it's essential to keep the pH and the temperature of the body within the correct range? Too much acid or heat irreversibly denatures these vital globular proteins, which would then interfere with virtually all of our vital functions. What is really interesting is that globular proteins' shape is not determined by DNA, but by environmental factors. The sequence of amino acids is determined by DNA, but the end shape is made by the way in which positive and negative atoms along the huge molecule are attracted to each other, and move together causing a turn or twist in the molecule. Various things can affect this, including, rather scarily, the microwaves from mobile phones and other wireless technology.[27]

Sugar: the Sweetness of Life

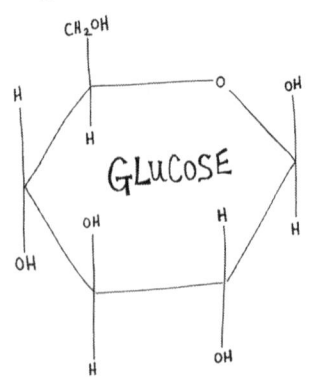

Carbohydrates provide easy fuel, which the body uses for energy and which is easily usable and easily stored. Most cells can only use a few simple sugars, the main one being glucose.[28] The brain can only use glucose and must have a regular supply.

No matter which sugars we eat, the body can convert them to glucose for the brain to use. When not needed immediately for energy production, glucose is stored as **glycogen** in the liver or muscle cells, or converted to fat. Very important, but only very small amounts, of carbohy-

---

[27] Bruce Lipton *The Biology of Belief*

[28] Glucose is broken down within cells ('glycolysis'), providing two molecules of ATP in the cytoplasm. This, not needing oxygen, is known as 'anaerobic respiration'. Then the mitochondria take over with the Kreb's cycle and hydrogen ion transfer to release 34 more ATPs (aerobic respiration). More on this later.

drate are used for construction, e.g. in the DNA/RNA of the nucleus, or attached to the cell membrane as markers.

Carbohydrates can be sugars or larger starches. **Monosaccharides** and **disaccharides** are the sugars, and **polysaccharides** are starches.

The building blocks are simple sugars or monosaccharides. These usually have carbon, hydrogen and oxygen in the ratio 1:2:1. The important ones for us can have six carbons, being called 'hexoses' (e.g. the blood sugar glucose which is $C_6H_{12}O_6$, fructose and galactose). Some have five carbons, being called 'pentoses' (e.g. deoxyribose, found in DNA – which stands for 'deoxyribose nucleic acid').

Disaccharides are double sugars – two 'monos' joined by dehydration (losing a water molecule). One such is sucrose (found in cane sugar), which is made from one glucose and one fructose. Another is lactose (glucose/galactose, milk sugar), and a third is maltose (glucose/glucose). When we digest these they are broken to simple sugars by 'hydrolysis' - (adding water).[29]

Long chains of simple sugars linked together by dehydration synthesis are called starches or polysaccharides. Such molecules are relatively insoluble, and they lack the sweetness of the simple sugars. The two important ones are starch and glycogen: starch is how plants store glucose and glycogen is how animals store it (in the muscles and liver). There are also 'oligosaccharides' – very important ones for us are the **fructooligosaccharides** (**FOS**), which are a class of non-digestible carbohydrates or sugars that occur naturally in a wide variety of foods throughout the plant kingdom. Since they are non-digestible, they pass through the human digestive virtually unchanged. When these fructooligosaccharides reach the colon, they are used by the good or beneficial bacteria found there (known as 'bifidobacteria' or 'bifidus') for growth and multiplication. A healthy population of these beneficial bacteria in the digestive tract enhances the digestion and absorption of nutrients, detoxification and elimination processes, and helps boost the immune system.

Fats

Fats, like carbohydrates, are made of carbon, hydrogen and oxygen. In the body they are used for energy, protection, construction and control. They are known as '**lipids**'.

Neutral fats are what we ordinarily think of as 'fat'. They are the most efficient and compact way for the body to store fuel. Deposits are found largely beneath the skin – this is called 'subcutaneous fat'. We also have quite a bit of fat around each of our organs. These layers of fat provide insulation from heat loss and protection from trauma. Neutral fats are comprised of one molecule of 'glycerol' – also known as glycerine[30] – plus three molecules

---

[29] Got that? Dehydration synthesis is the joining of two molecules by the *removal* of a water molecule. Hydrolysis is the opposite – splitting a molecule into two smaller ones by *adding* water.

[30] Have you ever had honey and glycerine syrup from the chemist for a sore throat or cough? Glycerol is a 'sugar alcohol', and is incredibly sweet and gloopy, demulcent (meaning soothing) to the throat as well as to other places lined with mucous membranes.

of 'long chain fatty acids'. These are made up of carbon, hydrogen and oxygen; and, yes, you've guessed it, they are 'acids' (those of you who wish to know what 'acid' actually means can read footnotes 25 and 26 a few pages ago). We can make some fatty acids in the body, but there are a few we can't make – the 'essential fatty acids' of omega-3 and omega-6 fame. More on these later in the chapter on nutrition and digestion.

Phospholipids are used in making cell membranes. As the name tells you, they are small half fat, half phosphate molecules.

Cholesterol is the essential raw material the body uses to make vitamin D, steroid hormones (including the sex hormones and cortisol) and bile salts, and it is an essential ingredient in myelin, which insulates nerve fibres.

Eicosanoids are involved in blood clotting (thromboxanes), inflammation (prostaglandins and leukotrines), uterine activity, digestive function (motility and secretion) and blood pressure (prostaglandins). They are very important chemicals – more on them when we discuss the omega oils in chapter eleven, diet and digestion.

Nucleic Acids

These are made of nucleotides, which form DNA, the largest molecule in the body. Nucleotides are made of a nitrogen-containing base, a 'pentose' sugar (do you remember what this means?) and a phosphate group.

DNA, or **deoxyribonucleic acid**, is found in the cell nucleus. It is the genetic material which directs protein synthesis and replicates itself before cell division. The sugar of the nucleotides which make up DNA is deoxyribose and its bases are adenine, guanine, cytosine and thiamine. It forms the famous double helix shape.

Interesting that the spiral has long been a symbol of eternity and continuance – for example, the Rune 'inguz' which means fertility, new beginnings and renewal.

RNA, or **ribonucleic acid**, is formed in the nucleus and copies part of the DNA[31] to carry out its instructions for protein synthesis. In other words, it acts as a messenger. Its sugar is ribose and its bases are adenine, guanine, cytosine and uracil. Its shape is a single strand, straight or folded.

Vitamins and Minerals

Vitamins are used in tiny amounts in the body for growth and maintaining good health. They are not used for energy or building blocks, but mainly function as **coenzymes** or parts of coenzymes. A coenzyme is a substance which acts with an enzyme to accomplish a particular

---

[31] A protein is a string of amino acids. The spiral DNA unwinds, copies itself to make 'messenger RNA' (transcription) which then is 'translated' into a chain of amino acids to make a particular protein.

task, e.g. some B vitamins work as coenzymes in glucose oxidation. Some, for example, vitamin D, act as hormones.

Most are not made in the body and must be taken in food - except vitamins D (made in the skin) and K (made by bacteria in the bowel).

There are fat-soluble vitamins: A D E and K; and water soluble ones: the Bs and C. They are involved in an incredibly diverse number of activities in the body, from bone formation to skin and mucous membrane development and maintenance to blood clotting and anti-oxidation. Anti-oxidants mop up free radicals (by-products of oxidation) that cause tissue damage and are implicated in cancer formation and aging.

Some are needed only in minute amounts so are called 'trace minerals' or elements. However all are essential for optimum functioning. There is a basic chart of vitamin and mineral functions in chapter eleven.

Energy and ATP

The breaking down of sugar to release a little energy is called **glycolosis**, and takes place in the cytoplasm. But the cell is also capable of **oxidising** glucose - this is called **cellular respiration** (aerobic) and occurs in the **mitochondria**, or powerhouse of the cell. As already discussed, when a chemical bond is broken, energy may be released – the addition of oxygen causes a lot of energy to be freed up. We do not use the energy released from glycolosis and glucose oxidation directly; instead we lock it up in a substance called **ATP**. You can think of ATP as being like a token or like a currency the cells of the body have to be 'paid' with in order to work. The currency they accept is ATP.[32]

ATP stands for **adenosine triphosphate**. An enzyme called **ATPase** splits one of the three phosphate bonds of ATP, releasing a large amount of stored kinetic energy and producing **ADP – adenosine diphosphate**. Phosphate is a very reactive element. Imagine one of the phosphate atoms in ATP being a person: passionate, argumentative, quick to take offence and flounce off, but with a bit of energy invested in, say, couples counselling, also quick to come back and make up. Each time the bond is broken, energy is released: when the bond is remade, energy is locked up in it.

When glucose from food enters the cell, it may be broken down and the energy used to stick a phosphate back onto ADP, thus storing the energy as ATP for later use. This energy storage release cycle is a continuous process that goes round and around for as long as the cell lives.

---

[32] Sometimes guanosine triphosphate (GTP) is used.

ADP + excess free energy + phosphate (P) = ATP (stored energy)

And the opposite;

ATP split by ATPase enzyme
= ADP + FREE ENERGY to do cells' work + Phosphate

The rate at which ATP is made by the cells is referred to as the **metabolic rate.**

Metabolism

Chemical reactions occur all the time in the body. All chemical reactions involve energy use or release. In the body these are part of 'metabolism' – which literally means a 'state of change'.

There are two opposing forces in metabolism, which must remain in balance. These are **anabolism** (building up) and **catabolism** (breaking down). Both activities are speeded up by 'enzymes' - protein catalysts that speed up chemical reactions without themselves being changed in any way.

1. Anabolism uses free energy (e.g. glucose concerted to glycogen in the liver and muscles).
2. Catabolism releases free energy (e.g. glycogen converted to glucose).

Enzymes

Most chemical reactions in the body are mediated by enzymes. Enzymes have extremely interesting properties that make them little chemical-reaction machines. The purpose of an enzyme in a cell is to allow the cell to carry out chemical reactions very quickly. These reactions allow the cell to build things or take things apart as needed. This is how a cell grows and reproduces. The cell can be described as a little bag full of chemical reactions that are made possible by enzymes. When you see a word that ends in '–ase', it is an enzyme. Enzymes are made from amino acids, and they are proteins. When an enzyme is formed, it is made by stringing together between 100 and 1,000 amino acids in a very specific order. Many of them also depend on small but vital amounts of minerals. The chain of amino acids then folds into a unique shape. That shape allows the enzyme to carry out specific chemical reactions; an enzyme acts as a very efficient catalyst for a specific chemical reaction, speeding that reaction up tremendously. Consider the possible implications of the fact that microwave pollution from wireless technology and mobile phones can affect the final shape of a cellular protein in its formation, and what this could mean when enzymes controlling all aspects of the cell's function are proteins.[33] For example, the sugar maltose is made from two glucose molecules bonded together. The enzyme malt*ase* is shaped in such a way that it can break the bond and free the two glucose pieces. The only thing maltase can do is break maltose molecules, but it can do that very rapidly and efficiently. Other types of enzymes can put atoms and molecules together. Breaking molecules apart and putting molecules together is the work of enzymes, and there is a specific enzyme for each chemical reaction needed to make the cell work properly.

---

[33] Bruce Lipton *The Biology of Belief.*

Chapter Three

CELLS & TISSUES - the basic materials.
(Otherwise known as histology)

Histology is the study of the structure and function of cells and tissues. **Cells** can be seen as the basic unit in the body – like one brick of Lego in a giant Lego castle.

These cells are grouped together to make **tissues**, of which there are four basic types. You could think of these as being like the foundations, woodwork, bricks, wallpaper and electric circuitry used in building a house. The tissue types are **connective tissue**, which supports, protects and connects; **epithelial tissue**, which lines and covers; **muscular tissue**, which provides movement; and **nervous tissue**, which is excitable and conductive, allowing for control and rapid communication of information and commands throughout the organism.

Cells

The cell is the basic unit of activity in the body. You can think of each cell as being like a factory – each one takes in raw materials, processes them and creates products and waste. Cells are amazing, and should be thought of as being individuals in their own right. An emerging model in biology is that each cell has a consciousness pervading and orchestrating it, the conciousnes of the whole organism.

Our body is made of about **50 trillion cells**. The largest human cells are about the diameter of a human hair, but most are smaller, about one-tenth of the diameter of a human hair. Look at a single strand of your hair. It is not thick, being about 100 microns in diameter.[34] Look down at your little toe - it contains 2 or 3 billion cells or so, depending on how big you are.

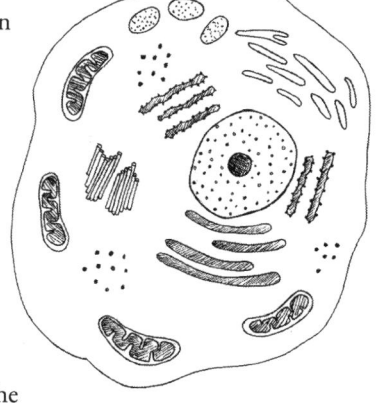

Bacteria are about the simplest cells that exist today. Interestingly, it seems that looking closely at cells may be able to tell us of our evolution. The **organelles**, or functional parts of

---

[34] A micron is a millionth of a meter, so 100 microns is a tenth of a millimeter.

each cell, look very like certain bacteria.[35] The theory is that millions of years ago some bacteria, hanging out in the primordial soup, got together with good effect – in other words, found that survival went well in co-operation with each other. Eventually the first single-celled organism – called an amoeba – was formed. Over time, amoebae grouped together successfully to make multi-cellular organisms, of which we are a wonderfully complicated example. Of course this can only ever be a theory; it is not possible to really prove by scientific methods what happened all that time ago.

Every one of the billions of cells in our body has its own kind of independent life; it has its skin or cell membrane, its own need for food, it excretes, makes energy, communicates with other cells and (in many cases) can reproduce itself. There is an old maxim used in many traditional healing systems – the microcosm in the macrocosm, and the macrocosm in the microcosm. This philosophy, first recorded in ancient Greece, means that patterns found in the largest scale – the cosmos or the universe – are repeated in the smallest – the single organism, the atom, even the subatomic level. We can see reflections of what is in the very small and the very large.

For example, imbalances in a society are the imbalances of the society's individuals writ large, and imbalances in an individual are reflections of the imbalances in society. A single leaf reveals the condition of the whole tree. Holistically thinking, every part of the whole affects every other part. We can benefit from considering the health of our cells. If the cells are healthy and getting their needs met, the whole organism will be well. This concept is gaining more and more ground in the emerging 'new biology' of such great thinkers as Bruce Lipton, who says:

"You may consider yourself an individual, but as a cell biologist I can tell you that you are in truth a cooperative community of approximately 50 trillion single-celled citizens…As a nation reflects the traits of its citizens, our human-ness must reflect the basic nature of our cellular communities." [36]

The amazing cell membrane

Each cell is enclosed in an amazing membrane made of **phospholipids**, cleverly designed to be **semi-permeable**; that is, to allow some things in and keep some out.

Phospholipids are molecules that have an electrically charged phosphate/nitrogen head, and a neutral fatty acid tail. There are two layers of these molecules arranged so that the

---

[35] A bacteria is a single, self-contained, living cell. An *Escherichia coli* bacteria (or *E. coli*) is typical. It is about one-hundredth the size of a human cell. Bacteria are also a lot simpler than human cells. They consist of an outer wrapper called the **cell membrane**, and a watery fluid called the **cytoplasm** on the inside. Cytoplasm is about 70% water. The other 30% is filled with proteins called **enzymes** that the cell has manufactured, along with smaller molecules like amino acids, glucose molecules and ATP. At the centre of the cell is a ball of DNA (similar to a wadded-up ball of string). If you were to stretch out this DNA into a single long strand, it would be incredibly long compared to the bacteria - about a thousand times longer! Very similar to our cells, in fact. On the surface of our skin alone there are ten times more bacteria than our bodies contain cells…our bodies contain about 2kg of bacteria in normal circumstances.

[36] Bruce H Lipton *The Biology of Belief.*

electrically oriented phosphate ends face outward in contact with the extracellular fluid, and inward in contact with the intracellular fluid. The lipid fatty acid tails are in the middle of the two layers.

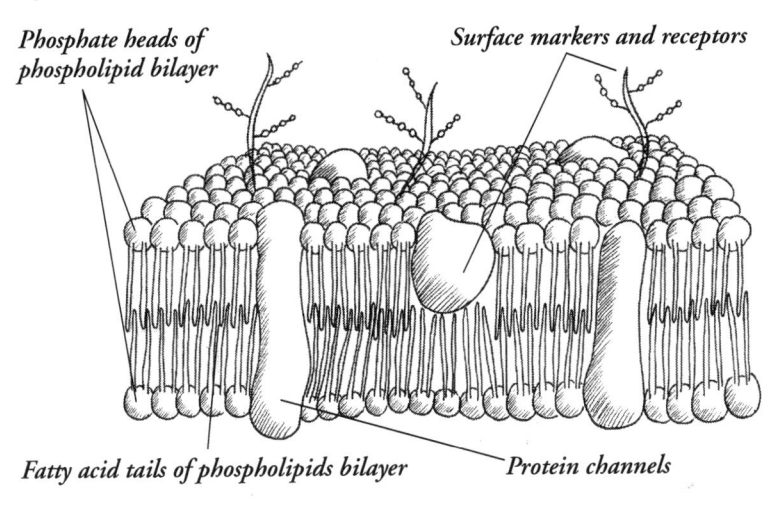

Phosphate heads of phospholipid bilayer

Surface markers and receptors

Fatty acid tails of phospholipids bilayer

Protein channels

Traditionally, the nucleus is seen as the brain of the cell, orchestrating things with its DNA, but in fact, a cell can survive for months without its nucleus, but dies instantly without its membrane. Bruce Lipton eloquently describes this in *The Biology of Belief*, which is a must-read book for anyone interested in cellular biology. He says that it looks rather like the membrane is the 'brain' of the cell, controlling what goes on, and actually switching genes on and off as needed in response to the environment. The nucleus, with its DNA, whilst seen by conventional biology as the control centre of the cell, is mainly needed for reproduction and so seems to be more like the gonads![37]

A significant portion of the lipid part of the cell membrane is made of **essential fatty acids**. You will remember that these are called 'essential' because they cannot be made by the body but must be eaten in the diet. For our cell membranes to stay healthy and functioning at optimum level, we especially need the **omega-3** fatty acids.[38]

Because of this **bipolar** attribute of the membrane, it is **selectively permeable**; some things freely cross it, others do not. Like dissolves like: because of the layers of fats in the membrane, which are non–polar, charged or polar particles such as sodium and potassium ions cannot freely cross. An exception to this is water, which is a pretty exceptional substance all round. Although water is polar it can still diffuse through the bilayer.

---

[37] Bruce H Lipton *The Biology of Belief.*

[38] Omega-3 is very long and highly flexible. When it is incorporated into the cell membrane it helps make the membrane itself elastic and fluid so that signals pass through it efficiently. But if the wrong fatty acids are incorporated into the membrane, the receptors can't react as well to their substances.

Water enters and leaves a cell according to the osmotic pressure of the fluids inside and outside: if there is more salt in a cell, water will be drawn in and the cell will expand; if there are more salts in the extracellular fluid water will leave and the cell will shrink. The business of what can get in and out of a cell is very important, as you might think. The membrane also contains structural proteins, as well as special proteins for transporting substances. Protein receptors, which are also in the cell, are being created and reabsorbed all the time, so the membrane is not static in structure but always being adapted and mended.

Getting in and out of a cell

There are various ways for substances to cross over the cell membrane and enter or leave the cell. Most of these involve the movement of water as well.

Simple diffusion involves the random scattering of very small particles from a high to a low concentration, down the concentration gradient – oxygen and carbon dioxide do this easily, dissolving through the phospholipid layer as described above. Imagine someone farts in a room full of people – at first there is a high concentration of the smelly gas around that person, but gradually it diffuses through the air in the room until eventually it is spread so far and so thinly that no-one can detect it any more…

Facilitated diffusion is a process which honours the concentration gradient, but allows bigger substances that cannot pass through the lipid membrane to cross. Carriers or channels in the membrane are used, creating a kind of gate or turnstile. Substances which cross the membrane in this way include glucose, amino acids and some ions. Each substance has its own **selective** channel or carrier to allow it to enter the cell. They may either be always open, or may open and close according to chemical or electrical signals.

Osmosis is the diffusion of water through a selectively permeable membrane, moving from where there are low levels of solutes to where there are more of those solutes – in other words, there is this tendency for equalization, seen in diffusion, when a substance will move from a high concentration to a low concentration. If the substance cannot cross the membrane, it will pull water to cross in its direction to dilute it. This pull is known as **osmotic pressure**. As well as moving through the water-filled channel or 'pore' that runs through the middle of some transport proteins, water can move by 'thrusting' through the lipid layer of the membrane – surprising, since water and fat don't usually mix. The amount of water in and around the cell is controlled by 'osmotic pressure' versus 'hydrostatic pressure'.[39]

Active transport is like facilitated diffusion in that a carrier is used, but to work the carrier must use energy (from ATP). Then it can move substances *against* their concentration

---

[39] **Osmotic pressure** is the pressure exerted by the presence of a high concentration of particles, for example proteins – the tendency is for equalization, so the strong solution will attract water into it if water can get in.
Hydrostatic pressure is like the water pressure in a hose pipe – if you squeeze the end, you make the tube narrower and so the hydrostatic pressure increases, which pushes the water out more strongly.

gradients. This is like a turnstile that takes money (or a token of ATP) to allow entrance or exit. Sodium ions (Na+) and potassium ions (K+) pass, like water, through channels in membrane proteins. Sodium ions are present at a higher concentration outside the cell, so they have a net simple diffusion *into* the cell through special sodium channels. Potassium ions are present at a higher concentration inside the cell, so have a net simple diffusion *out* of the cell through special potassium channels. A **diffusion equilibrium** of Na+ and K+ (where there is a balanced number of each inside and outside the cell), is avoided by an active transport system: the 'sodium-potassium exchange pump'. For every 3 sodium ions pumped out of the cell, 2 potassium ions are pumped in. So it is that movement of sodium and potassium is closely linked in the body.[40]

Vesicular transport transports very large particles, 'macromolecules' and fluids. The cell kind of extrudes stuff out of itself, or engulfs things that are outside and kind of swallows them. Phagocytosis is the word for cells swallowing things. As you might imagine, it takes energy (in the form of ATP as usual) for these processes to work.

Voltage difference inside and outside of the cell

An electrical charge or **membrane potential** is found across the membrane, and this makes nerve conduction and muscle contraction possible. The membrane potential is caused by a slight difference in electrical charge inside and outside of the cell. It involves sodium (Na+) and potassium (K+) ions. The effect is that the inside of the membrane is normally at about –70mV compared to the outside. This is the **resting membrane potential**. It generates our bodies' electrical field, and is utilized in nerve conduction and muscle contraction.

Membrane receptors

The cell membrane is covered with proteins called **membrane receptors**, which particular chemicals recognize and attach to, e.g. hormones, neurotransmitters, enzymes – even drugs. This binding affects cellular activity in a particular way. Only substances which a cell has a receptor for can affect that particular cell. When a substance binds with its receptor, the receptor shimmers and dances and changes shape, transmitting some kind of change or information to the cell.[41]

The health of a cell and the condition of its receptors are of vital importance. You can have a situation where a person has all the clinical symptoms and signs of a hormone deficiency, but their blood levels are normal when tested. For example, someone can have normal thyroid hormone (thyroxine) levels but have all the symptoms of an underactive

---

[40] Diuretics, which cause the body to lose fluid via the kidneys, cause loss of potassium and sodium ions too. This was discovered when the first drug diuretics killed people by upsetting their potassium balance. Interestingly, the strong herbal diuretic dandelion leaves are extremely high in potassium.

[41] Candace Pert describes this beautifully in her fascinating book '*The Molecules of Emotion*'.

thyroid. New thinking is that this could well be due to a problem with the cells' receptors for thyroxine. It is very difficult to study receptors, as there are many thousands at any one time on a cell's membrane, and the cell reabsorbs them and makes new ones in seconds.

Drug addiction and withdrawal can be connected with cell receptors; sometimes the more there is of a chemical that affects a cell, the more receptors the cell makes for it. Sometimes a cell reduces the number of receptors when more of the chemical is present so the cell doesn't get over-stimulated. This means that more of a drug is needed to get a similar response. Heroin or morphine, from the opium poppy, is identical to our bodies' own painkillers (endorphins) so many cells in the body have receptors for this drug. If a person takes the drug, a tolerance builds up hence needing more and more of it to get the same effect. Then when the drug is withdrawn, the cells are 'crying out' for it, and this is experienced as withdrawal symptoms. The good news is that in time when the drug is no longer present, the cell readjusts its receptors to a normal level, and the withdrawal period is over.

Internal environment

The cells are filled with a fluid called 'cytoplasm'.[42] Outside the cells is a similar fluid called 'interstitial' or tissue fluid. The cell exchanges nutrients and waste products with the tissue fluid. This tissue fluid and cytoplasm is what is meant by the **internal environment** of the body, which is kept in balance by homeostatic mechanisms. What's interesting is that each cell has its own independent life – taking what it needs from the tissue fluid, and putting out waste products as well as anything it makes for exportation – but the cell's primary work is to keep itself going. At the same time, the body's cells are connected and react to things together. There is more and more scientific evidence to back up what seems obvious to anyone with a body and a trust in nature – the fact that there is an innate, overall, underlying intelligence which creates a 'field of coherence' throughout the body.[43]

Holistic thinking acknowledges that we are also part of a greater whole – just as our cells can have the illusion of separateness, doing their own thing, but in fact being completely affected by the health of the overall organism; so we are part of our family, community, society, the Earth and the entire universe, completely dependent on the health of the whole for our own best functioning. James Lovelock's 'Gaia Hypothesis' describes us as an integral part of the body of the Earth, subject to homeostatic mechanisms just as our own body's are.[44] It may not be possible for us to remain completely in optimum health whilst we are part of an unbalanced and unhealthy society – but at the same time, as we become more balanced we will have a healthful effect on the whole.

---

[42] When found in a word, 'cyte' always refers to cells.
[43] Lynne McTaggert's *The Field* lays out the evidence coherently.
[44] James Lovelock *Gaia: A New Look at Life on Earth*.

Onto organelles

Within the cytoplasm are found the small components of the cell, called **organelles**, or little organs. These include the nucleus, mitochondria, endoplasmic reticulum, Golgi apparatus, lysosomes, centrioles and packages of cellular chemical products for secretion.

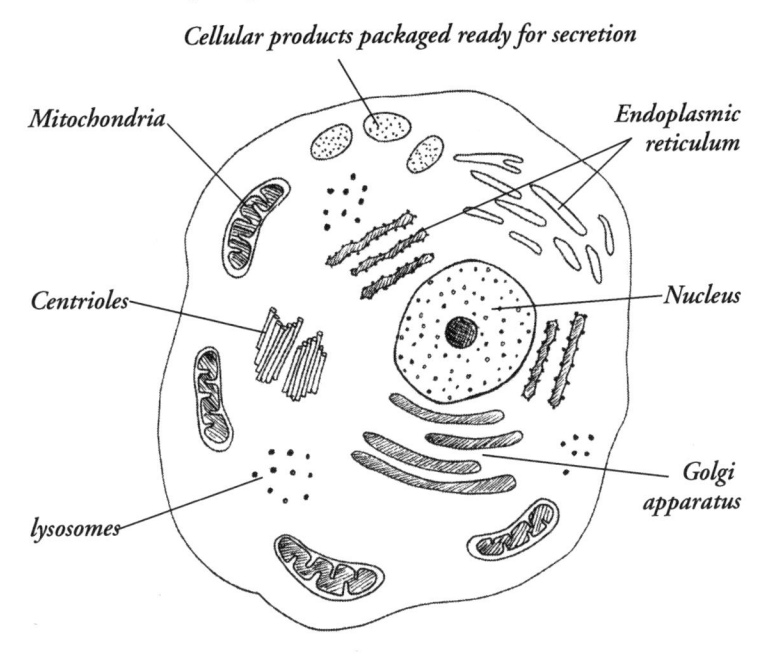

Cellular products packaged ready for secretion

Mitochondria

Endoplasmic reticulum

Centrioles

Nucleus

Golgi apparatus

lysosomes

The **cytoplasm** itself is made of proteins in water; there are about ten thousand water molecules for every protein molecule in a cell.

The **nucleus**, surrounded by a nuclear membrane and full of fluid called 'protoplasm', is where our genetic material is found. This consists of DNA (deoxyribonucleic acid). Arranged in a double helix shape, this beautiful and complex molecule contains the plans used to make all the cells and tissues of our body. Yet it is made of only four varieties of molecule, arranged in countless different ways. When cell division takes place, the DNA unravels, copies itself and is replicated into two cells. When a particular protein is needed to be made, the DNA plan for it is copied by a sister substance, **messenger RNA** (ribonucleic acid), which goes off and creates the new protein. We share DNA with all other animals – mammals, reptiles, insects, and with plants. In fact, human beings, animals, bananas and oak trees are a minimum somewhere around 42% the same in terms of DNA. There are only so many basic designs, and all the incredible variety of this beautiful Earth of ours comes from similar genetic roots; everything is our kin, our ancestor. All the other beings really are 'All Our Relations' as many First American tribes say. Human beings are actually only 95% different from our closest relatives, bonobos monkeys and chimpanzees, and the difference between two humans is a mere 0.01%. Time to wake up to our connectedness!

DNA tends to be seen as fixed and immovable; you're born with it and stuck with it. This has been the prevailing trend in mainstream science and is reflected in public perception. However, it really is not true that our genes are responsible for everything. The environment is vital. It is also now known that DNA does not just work from a fixed standpoint. It has the ability to adapt to our environment and create new chemicals as needed, for example, antibodies for a new cold virus you have just come across. The DNA does not switch itself on and off; it is the cell which seems to do this, in an as yet unknown way. Interestingly, only 3% of the uses of genetic material in our genes have so far been analysed. Who knows what the other 97% might be capable of! Also, although there are about 120,000 different proteins in our body, we have only 25,000 genes – not one gene to make each protein, as was hypothesized and would make sense if genes are really in control.[45]

The **mitochondria** are the power stations of the cell. Within them, cellular respiration happens: glucose is oxidized and ATP produced for use in energy-requiring processes.

Mitochondria have an interesting genetic twist: the DNA that makes them is separate from that of the rest of the cell. It seems that the sperm cell from our dad uses up all its mitochondria powering itself up to meet the egg. The egg, on the other hand, is full of mitochondria at conception, and it is these which are passed, mother to child, through the generations.

Through this genetic material it is possible to trace our mother's mother's mother – our female line, right back for countless generations. The remains of an ancient female human were discovered in Africa. Although she lived and died an estimated 140,000-200,000 years ago, through looking at the DNA in her mitochondria and comparing to that of all *known* races of people alive today, it is possible to see that we all come from her – way back then. She is the ancestor of us all. She is called 'Mitochondrial Eve'. Of course, we don't necessarily literally come from her,[46] but it *is* sure that the other women alive at the same time as her either had the same mitochondrial genes (in other words had a common female ancestor to her) or have no living female descendants today. Interesting stuff! [47]

The Endoplasmic reticulum is a series of tubes which carries out the general day to day business of the cell. It is made of a phospholipid membrane which encloses spaces to create sacs. It is here that nutrients are processed, and any products of the cell made. It can have a wide variety of functions depending on the particular cell. Attached to it is an area called the Golgi body.

The Golgi body or **Golgi apparatus** processes the waste or products of the cell, packaging it in parcels and sending it off out of the cell.

---

[45] Bruce Lipton *The Biology of Belief.*

[46] Also, there may well be people who haven't been genetically analysed who have different mitochondrial genes.

[47] There is some controversy (of course!) about what it all means, if you are interested take a look on the internet – do a search for 'mitochondrial eve'.

The cell is full of **microtubules**, which form a kind of skeleton within it. These are miniscule hollow tubes networking throughout the cell. Quantum events in the cytoskeleton seem likely to be involved in information arising everywhere in the body at the same time.[48] Small vesicles of powerful enzymes capable of digesting the cell, called **lysosomes**, are also present in most cells. These can destroy a damaged or diseased cell.

Cell reproduction

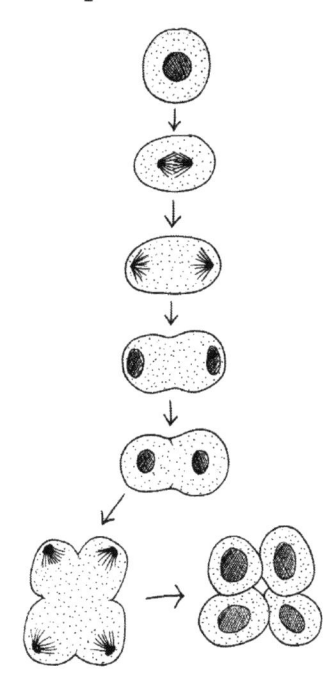

There are two ways for a cell to reproduce. One, called **mitosis**, is how a living cell reproduces or 'clones' itself. It is a continuous process throughout life. Millions of cells are doing it as you read this. Basically, the cell copies itself, becoming a kind of double cell, then splits into two, and so on.

The chromosomes that make up the DNA unravel, copy themselves, and line up on the centrosomes, which have separated onto either side of the cell. Then the cell splits into two parts, each having a full complement of genetic material.

Then there is **meiosis** - this is the very special kind of cell reproduction resulting in a new organism. It requires special 'gametes' or sex cells – the egg and the sperm. Two gametes will fuse to form a 'zygote' from which the new human grows. We will discuss this more with reproduction.

A Visualisation Treat for your Cells

Find a quiet place to relax where nothing will disturb you for 15-30 minutes. Sit comfortably or lie down and breathe gently for a few minutes, saying to yourself as you breathe in, 'I breathe in healing, relaxing energy', and as you breathe out, 'I breathe out all tension, anxiety, negativity.'

Also try 'every time I breathe out, I become twice as relaxed'.

After a few minutes like this, imagine you are floating along on a cloud of golden light, warm and safely enveloped. Begin to breathe in this healing light. As you breathe, feel the warm, loving, golden energy filling your lungs. It begins to spread through your body, up into your head, neck and shoulders, down into your arms and hands. It spreads down your back and into your belly. The warm golden healing light fills your pelvis and moves down your legs into your feet. Your whole

---

[48] The theories of Karl Pribram, Kunio Yasue, Stuart Hameroff, Scot Hagan and others, described in Lynne McTaggart *The Field* pp 91-96.

body is full of warm, healing golden light.

Imagine the cells of your body, billion upon billion, each one filled with this healing golden glow. Imagine one of your cells, anywhere you like. See it, feel it, think it filled with a warm, healing light energy. The cell is expanding, relaxing, happy and joyful as it bathes in the healing light. Every cell in your body is celebrating as they enjoy the warm and golden healing light.

Your cells know what to do; your body knows what to do. We are completely as we are supposed to be, and our bodies, minds and spirits are equipped with wonderful healing mechanisms. Allow yourself to enjoy this knowledge, allow the warm golden light to spread its glow throughout your body, and throughout your mind and spirit. All is well...

Afterwards, gently bring your attention back into the place you are in, and resume your daily activities, knowing you are filled with light and your cells are zinging with joy!

Some cells in the body normally replicate themselves, others never do. This affects their capacity for regeneration if they have been damaged. Cells that are continually replicating themselves include epithelium, bone marrow, blood, spleen and lymphoid tissue. Cells which can replicate, but rarely do under normal circumstances include the liver,[49] kidney, pancreas, smooth muscle, bone cells, and fibroblasts (which make fibres in connective tissue).

There are cells which *were* considered to be permanent – unable to replicate after normal growth is complete. This was thought to apply to nerve cells, skeletal and cardiac muscle. However, science has now found that skeletal muscles have 'limited' powers to re-grow due to satellite cells which can grow new cells, and cardiac muscle has modest ability to divide, although injuries to cardiac muscle are usually replaced by scar tissue.

Research is being done into gene therapy and stem cell therapy to enhance this process; natural healers will know that there are many ways to encourage the body's own healing mechanisms. There is a great story in Deepak Chopra's book *Unconditional Life* telling of a miraculous healing of a skeletal muscle, back in the days when this was considered more or less impossible by scientific thinking of the day – not that long ago, really.[50]

It was also believed until recently that we do not make new nerve cells. However a study on rats undertaken in the year 2000 showed that brains continue to grow well after puberty; the adult brain is capable of growth and regeneration. It is not all the downhill tumble to senility we were led to believe![51]

The implications of this knowledge for practitioners of medicine or healing are interesting; if cells are damaged, how easy is it for the body to repair or replace them? What can we do to

---

[49] The now well-known plant milk thistle (*Psylibum marianus*) has an effect of stimulating regeneration of liver cells.

[50] Deepak Chopra *Unconditional Life – Mastering the Forces That Shape Personal Reality.*

[51] MLA University Of Illinois At Urbana-Champaign (2000, April 12). Study Of Rats' Brains Indicates Brain Continues To Grow After Puberty. *ScienceDaily*. Retrieved March 2, 2008, from URL/http://www.sciencedaily.com /releases/2000/04/000406091914.htm

encourage this process? Also, do we accept that certain things are impossible, or can we hold a belief in the possibility of miraculous healing for our patients? Bearing in mind that 'accepted physiological facts' do turn out to be wrong now and then, it seems reasonable to hold out belief for optimum healing. 'Be realistic, plan for a miracle' as the bumper sticker says!

Studies have shown that our beliefs about other people are important – the power of our mind to heal applies not only to our thoughts about ourselves, but to what kind of thoughts we send to others.[52] Our thoughts are shaped by our beliefs.[53]

Tissues

As we have said, cells are arranged into tissues, which in turn get together to make the organs and systems of the body. There are four types: epithelial, connective, muscular and nervous.

Epithelial Tissue

Epithelial Tissue covers the surface of the body, lines hollow organs and tubes inside the body and forms glands. It consists of tightly packed cells arranged in continuous sheets on a basement membrane. They can be either single or multilayered (known as simple or 'compound'). Epithelium adheres firmly to the underlying connective tissue via its basement membrane. It continually renews itself; the lower levels divide by mitosis and the older cells slough off. We all have first hand experience of this with our skin, which now and then we see coming off – at least the dead top layers. Did you know that most of the dirt in the London Underground (and in your house) consists of human skin cells? Every day a new layer is made, and an old one sloughed off. The multi-layered skin takes about thirty days to be completely renewed, whilst the single-layered epithelial lining of the gut is renewed every day.

There are various types of simple and compound epithelium, named for its appearance. Examples of simple are columnar, squamous, and cuboidal.

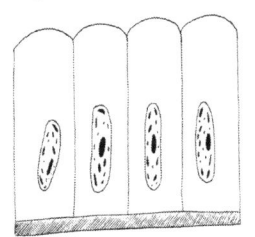

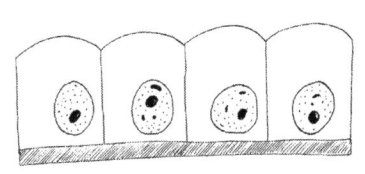

Columnar epithelium

Cuboidal epithelium

---

[52] One study looked at the power of curses – in other words, what happens when we send negative thoughts to another? In the experiment, 195 separate cultures of a fungus were 'cursed'. 77% showed retarded growth compared to the control group. J.Barry, 'General and comparative study of the psychokinetic effect on a fungus culture', Journal of Parapsychology, 1968;32(94):237-43 (from *The Intention Experiment* by Lynne McTaggart).

[53] The best thing is to try it for yourself. There a quite a lot of interesting books you might use to get you started. As well as Lynne McTaggart's *The Intention Experiment* you might like to take a look at *Creative Visualisation* by Shakti Gawain, and *You Can Heal Your Life* by Louise Hay. There are many more great books, the trick is to find one that works for you.

Squamous epithelium

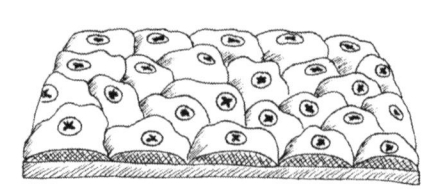

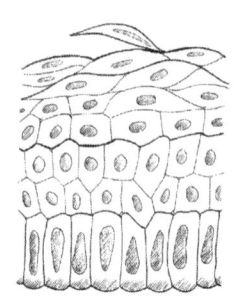

Stratified epithelium

Examples of compound epithelial tissue include stratified (the skin) and transitional (the bladder).

Sometimes epithelium is **ciliated**. Cilia are small hair-like projections of the cell membrane, which have the ability to move. They are found in the air pipes of the lungs, and in the fallopian tubes.

The epithelium of the lungs, gut, urinary and reproductive systems forms what are called **mucous membranes**. Interspersed with the epithelial cells are special mucous-producing cells called **goblet cells**. Although actually named for their shape, that of an upside-down goblet, I like to remember them by that charming colloquial British reference to ejecting mucous from the mouth – 'gobbing'!!!

The ciliated mucous membrane of the lungs is ingenious; inhaled dust and other particles stick to the mucous, which forms a lining over the surface of the epithelial cells. The cilia constantly move in one direction, shifting the mucous up towards the throat – when it reaches the throat it can be drawn into the mouth and spat out. This is known as the **ciliary escalator**. One of the injurious effects of smoking tobacco is that nicotine depresses the ciliary escalator, thus preventing the lungs from clearing themselves just when they need it most. Luckily, this effect wears off as soon as smoking is stopped – as the epithelial lining does its amazing job of renewing itself, the cilia work again. This is the reason many smokers cough in the morning – overnight whilst asleep and without the influence of tobacco, the membrane repairs itself and the lungs begin to free themselves from accumulated toxins and debris. Many a hapless smoker, on noticing that the first cigarette of the day 'cures' their cough, is able to fool himself or herself that smoking is helping them....[54]

Connective Tissue

Connective tissue is the most abundant tissue in the body. A binding and supporting tissue, it often has a very rich blood supply (although this does not apply to cartilage and ligaments; they have no direct blood supply at all, which is why they are white in colour).

---

[54] Actually the cough is not a symptom – it is the 'cure' – the bodies' attempt to remedy a harmful situation. This illustrates simply the very important fundamental holistic principle that symptoms are NOT diseases. Much more on this later!

The cells of connective tissue are widely scattered in a matrix of extra cellular material. There are many types: areolar, adipose, fibrous, elastic, cartilage, bone, blood, lymphoid or reticular. Although some of these *seem* very different from each other – blood and bone for example – if you look at the composition and formation of these tissues, they have a lot in common.

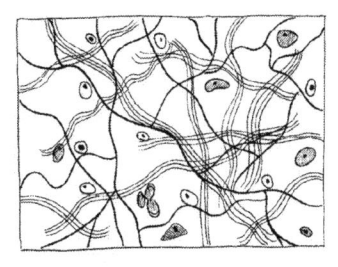

Areolar tissue is found all over the body, like a kind of packaging tissue. Sometimes it is called 'loose' connective tissue. It consists of a ground substance protein and water background, with scattered cells making collagen and elastic fibres. The dermis, found in the skin under the stratified epithelial layer known as the epidermis, is made of this type of connective tissue. What is particularly interesting about it is that it can move from a more liquid to more solid gel state and back – which affects how well substances can diffuse through it.

There is a technique called **skin rolling** which aims to loosen up the areolar tissue to get fresh fluid into it.

'Skin rolling lifts and squeezes the superficial layers of fascia underneath the skin – breaking down any adhesions, 'sticking', releasing. It can often be very painful at first, but eases with each skin roll. Lift the skin with the thumb and push underneath and against the forefinger which is anchoring skin/fascia - moving along methodically until you reach the end of the 'available' skin e.g. from the inferior edge of the trapezius to the superior (shoulder) edge. It needs to be a continual roll. Then work deeper with massage techniques.'

From Lorraine Horton of Meridian School of Massage www.lhmeridian.co.uk

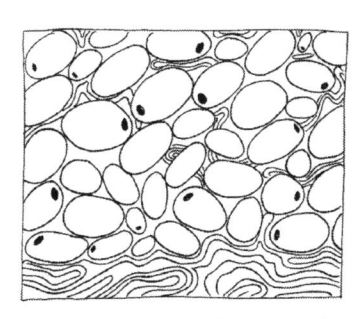

Adipose tissue is basically fat or a collection of cells which fill up with fat. It is useful for protection; padding under the skin (the subcutaneous fat) and around vital organs, and as a very concentrated energy store. And of course it gives us women our lovely curves.... One of the reasons too much of it can harm us is because it tends to collect around our organs – an excess of fat around the heart makes life a lot harder for this organ. Have you come across the 'apple or pear shaped' thing? Pear shaped people tend to put most of their fat around their bottoms and thighs. Apple shaped people tend to deposit fat around their chest and middle. It seems when it comes to carrying excess fat, the pears have the advantage, as the apples will be more prone to gathering fat around the heart, leading to a greater workload for the heart therefore increasing the risk of heart disease. Adipose tissue makes the hormone **leptin** and is involved in regulating our sensations of hunger.

Fibrous Tissue consists of collagen fibres made by cells called fibroblasts. Collagen forms thick ropes with tensile strength. The **fascia** around and within muscles, which comes together to form tendons, is fibrous connective tissue, as is periosteum, the tough fibrous covering of bone. Ligaments are primarily made of fibrous tissue, though they also contain some elastic fibres, as they need to be stretchy. The connective tissue outer coverings of organs are rich in fibrous tissue for protection and strength. Our blood vessel walls are full of it. We'll be hearing more about this important substance.

Elastic Tissue does what it says on the label – it gives stretch and recoil where needed; skin, lungs, arteries for example. The elastic fibres in the dermis of the skin give our skin its ability to snap back when stretched. There is a tendency for this to diminish with age; just like your knicker elastic, the elastic fibres don't last forever! Having said this, our bodies are of course renewable, elastic fibres which can be repaired and made new – unlike knickers which are an inanimate object…

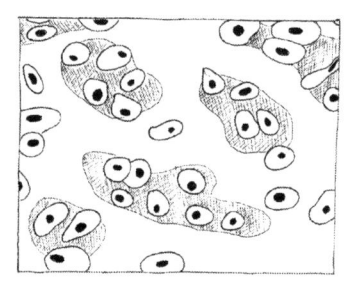

Cartilage is amazing stuff: incredibly strong, a little stretchy and totally flexible. Cartilage is found at most joints, where two bones meet each other. It allows for movement, and protects the bones from grating on each other as the joint moves. We have some in our ear lobes and nose, and an intricate assortment makes up the voice box, or larynx, which along with the vocal cords enables us to speak. Cartilage is a blue-white colour; it has no blood supply of its own, and relies on surrounding tissues to get its nutrients. Because of this, it is slow to heal when damaged. Our first skeleton, formed when we are in the womb, is made of cartilage. As developing embryos, we first make a 'cartilaginous blueprint' of our bones, then we begin to lay down calcium salts to form our bones. At birth our skeleton is mostly bone, with some cartilage left from which the bones grow. We grow throughout childhood, the bones growing from special **cartilaginous growing plates**, until they fuse in the late teens or early twenties, after which we will grow no more in height.

The body makes the background substance of cartilage, loose and fibrous connective tissue from **glucosamine** (amino acid and sugar mixed). This is made in the body by an enzyme called **glucosamine synthetase**. As we age, this enzyme becomes less effective, which is why healing is slower in the elderly. Studies have shown that taking a supplement of glucosamine daily can help arthritis, aging or slowly healing skin, ligament and tendon injuries, and possibly heart disease and IBS.[55]

---

[55] From the excellent book *Health Defense* by Dr Paul Clayton.

Bone is what gives structure, shape and support to our bodies, and protects our vital organs. It is made from cartilage with a beautiful and intricate pattern of calcium phosphate salts laid down amongst it. Bone is a vital and living tissue; it has a very rich blood supply. It can heal itself well from injuries and breaks by a process of **calcification** – repairing the breaks by laying down lots of calcium.

If you take a bone from a newly dead body and dissolve all the salts out of it, you are left with a completely flexible cartilage 'bone' that you could tie in a knot. Throughout life, our bones are reabsorbed and made anew, as we exchange the calcium salts between them and the blood. It's thought that over about seven years the whole skeleton is replaced.

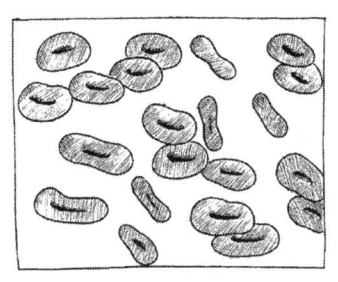

Blood is considered to be a connective tissue. It contains a background substance – the plasma – with cells loosely interspersed in it. Actually, blood cells are made in the bone marrow, so there is one obvious connection.

Lymphoid tissue, or reticular tissue, is specialized connective tissue found in the lymphatic system, in lymph nodes and vessels for example. In the lymph nodes it forms a mesh which is filled with the white blood cells of the lymphatic system. Here debris from the lymph fluid is trapped and filtered out.

A Note on Membranes

A membrane is a special covering that includes connective and epithelial tissues. Our bodies have four main types of membrane: cutaneous, mucous, serous amd synovial. The first three are continuous sheets of covering material made of an epithelial layer closely bound to an underlying bed of connective tissue, and synovial is formed from connective tissue.

Cutaneous membrane refers simply to the skin: a thick layer of compound epithelium over a thicker layer of loose connective tissue containing interesting structures like sweat glands, hair follicles and so on. The following chapter is dedicated to skin.

Mucous membranes are lovely wet slippery membranes made of either compound or simple epithelial cells interspersed with goblet cells over a layer of loose connective tissue. Mucous membranes are adapted for absorption and secretion. Some secrete a lot of mucous (the lung and the gut); some do not (the urinary tract).

Serous membranes contain a layer of epithelial cells resting on a loose connective tissue base. The epithelial cells secrete a watery fluid. They are found in the heart (the pericardium), the lungs (the pleura) and the guts (the peritoneum).

Synovial Membranes are found in synovial joints.[56] They are made of loose connective tissue, and secrete a special lubricating fluid into the joint capsule.

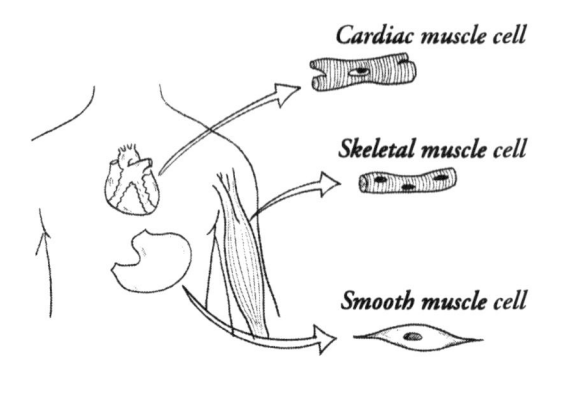

Cardiac muscle cell

Skeletal muscle cell

Smooth muscle cell

Muscle Tissue

Muscular tissue has the special property of contractibility, and so is responsible for almost all the movement in the body. There are three types: skeletal, smooth, and cardiac.

Skeletal Muscle is what you will already be accustomed to thinking of as muscle – biceps, latts, abs and the other gym favourites. As the name suggests this type of muscle moves the skeleton.

Muscle cells contain tiny **microfilaments** or myofibrils made of proteins called **actin** and **myosin**, which lie together in such a way as to be able to move over each other in a ratchet mechanism. In skeletal muscle these are arranged in lines, which makes the muscle look striped under the microscope – hence its other name, 'striated' muscle. Each movement of the fibres uses energy as ATP, and much of the heat we generate comes from muscle contraction. It is also called **voluntary** because we control it consciously and voluntarily, unlike the other two types.

Smooth Muscle is under involuntary control. Its cells are arranged in sheets, which wrap around tubes and hollow organs in the body. It moves food through the gut, and is found in all the bodies' tubes and all its hollow organs except for the heart.

Cardiac Muscle is only found in the heart. It looks striped, like skeletal muscle, but the cells are a special shape unique to it. It can never rest for long: must keep on beating all of our lives. It is under involuntary control.

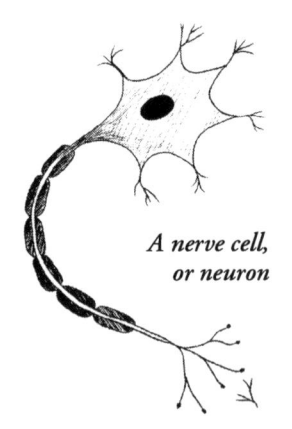

A nerve cell, or neuron

Nervous Tissue

Nervous tissue, or nerve tissue, is very specialised tissue. The cells are called neurons, or nerve cells: they are excitable and conductive. This allows for sending of messages to do with control throughout the body. It also contains special supporting cells called **neuroglia cells**, or **glial cells**. These are important in that they nourish and protect the neurons and help in regeneration. They form a scaffold all around the neurons.

---

[56] These are known as diarthroidal or moveable joints in America.

CHAPTER FOUR

BETWEEN WITHIN AND WITHOUT
(THE SKIN OR INTEGUMENTARY SYSTEM)

The largest organ in the body, the **integument**, or skin, is an outer protective layer shaping the body. It covers an area of about 22 square feet (2 square metres) and weighs about 10–11lbs (4.5–5.4kg). Our skin is the interface between within and without. It protects us from the outside world. Think of all the verbal expressions there are to do with skin - thick skinned, thin-skinned, skin deep and so on. How do you feel in *your* skin?

Feel the exposed skin on your arm – first brush the fine hairs very lightly, then stroke it gently, and then increase the pressure. Now stop and press hard on one place. Pinch it a little – ouch! Vibrate your fingers on one spot. Feel something warm such as your cat or your dog, your stomach or the radiator. Now something cold such as the wall.

Notice the sensations you feel in the skin.

Gently pinch a fold of skin. How is it attached to the tissues below? Does it come up easily in your fingers? Explore different places on your body. Is it the same everywhere, or does it vary?

Look at the thickness of the skin - find a place where it is thin. Find a place where it's thick. Take hold of it and try to get a sense of its thickness. Look closely at it. What can you see? Hairs? Small holes called pores? Wrinkles? Scars?

The skin has many important functions

Firstly it creates an obvious barrier and boundary to our bodies, it protects us from the hazards of the outside world. This protective function includes straightforward mechanical protection from injury by the outer dead layer of hard, horny skin and by the nice cushion of deep subcutaneous fat, as well as protecting us from the damaging ultra violet light of the sun. This protection is afforded by the melanin pigment in the skin, which increases with exposure to sun.

We are also protected from external microorganisms by sophisticated immune responses in the skin. Keratinocytes make interferon, a kind of protein that blocks viral infection. Other cells in the skin, called Langerhans cells, interact with germs that have managed to get through the outer layer of the epidermis. The Langerhans cells then take these antigens to nearby lymph organs and help to initiate an immune response; thus the Langerhans cells have a so-called **messenger** function. This response is disrupted by even the mildest of sunburns: UV radiation disables the presenter cells. This is probably why sun exposure triggers cold sore eruption in infected people.

The skin makes a tough waterproof barrier, which keeps out unwanted visitors and keeps water and nutrients inside. It is the oily sebum which gives this protective waterproof coating to the skin. Sebum is secreted by sebaceous glands into the hair follicles, and spreads over the surface of the skin. Without it, our skin is not supple but becomes dry and cracked. Harsh detergents in soaps and shampoos remove sebum from the skin. This can be irritating, and has the effect of making the skin produce more sebum to replace what was lost.

Toxic 'skin care' products [57]

It might surprise you to learn that chemists[58] and beauty shops are full of products to supposedly make you look beautiful which actually harm your skin as well as our environment. Some of them are considered more toxic even than some pesticides…

Sodium lauryl sulphate is in just about everything, including baby products. It is a very strong detergent which can cause eye irritation, permanent damage to the eyes, skin rashes, hair loss, flaking skin and mouth ulceration.

Combined with other ingredients, it can form nitrosamines, which are carcinogenic. Sodium lauryl sulphate easily penetrates the skin and can lodge itself in the heart, lungs, liver and brain.

Fluoride and talc are carcinogenic. Other nasties include propylene glycol, alcohol and isopropyl.

As for **mineral oil** (baby oils are usually made of this), it strips the natural oils from the skin and forms an oily film, which prohibits the release of toxins. It can also cause photosensitivity, chapping, dryness and premature ageing. Want to put it on your baby now?

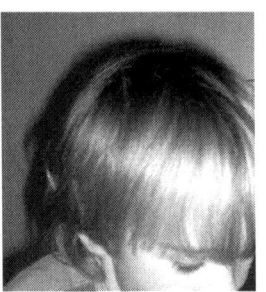

I have never used any soap or shampoo on my son, now four. He gets washed in the bath with good old water. His skin is perfect, and his hair looks great…without shampoo stripping the oils from the hair, it is self-cleaning.

The skin doesn't keep out everything however – small molecules are able to enter the body via the skin, and this absorptive function means some drugs can be administered via the skin, and essential oils applied to the skin will enter the blood stream.[59]

---

[57] There are too many references for this topic to list. If you want to look it up, do a web search on 'toxic toiletries'.

[58] Drugstores in the States.

[59] If you don't believe it, try the following experiment: apply some garlic oil to the soles of your feet, and wait. In a very short time, the garlic can be smelt on the breath. It has been absorbed into the blood, then excreted via the lungs.

The skin breathes; oxygen and carbon dioxide can enter and leave, but only a very little bit.[60] Don't try to replace breathing with your lungs entirely with your skin – it won't work!

As you will know if you have eaten a strong curry, the skin also has excretory powers – it is one of our main **organs of elimination**. Sweat can be full of all kinds of things the body wants to excrete. Herbalists use this mechanism in treatment protocols. For example, it's well known that garlic protects us from infection. When we eat garlic, the oil in it, which is the smelly bit, is excreted via the lungs and skin as well as the kidney. It is this smelly oil which is a powerful anti-microbial. Consuming lots of garlic ensures a good amount of protective oil all over our skin, and in our lungs. Many other plants which contain essential oils work in a similar way – most essential oils are strongly anti-microbial.

A team from Manchester University has carried out research on essential oils as potential anti-MRSA agents, testing forty essential oils. Two of them killed MRSA and *E.coli* straight away, and one worked longer term. The university has not revealed the names of the oils as they are trying to get funding to develop the project… A researcher from the University's Faculty of Medicine, Peter Warn, said: 'We believe that our discovery could revolutionize the fight to combat MRSA and other 'super bugs', but we need to carry out a trial and to do that we need a small amount of funding - around £30,000…We are having problems finding this funding because essential oils cannot be patented as they are naturally occurring, so few drug companies are interested in our work as they do not see it as commercially viable. Obviously, we find this very frustrating as we believe our findings could help to stamp out MRSA and save lives.'[61]

We regulate our temperature largely via the skin. When we are hot, we get red; the blood vessels in the skin dilate, allowing heat to leave from the surface of the body. The opposite happens when we are cold. Think how much paler everyone looks in the winter. This is not only because tans have faded, but also because the blood vessels in the skin are constricting, keeping the heat in the centre of the body. Sweating is also involved in heat regulation – excreting water onto the surface of the skin cools us. You know what it's like in winter when you are shopping – you need to be warmly dressed as it is cold outside, but you go into a warm place and begin to sweat. Go outside again and you feel colder as the cold air touches your sweat.

It is sometimes said that the skin is one big sense organ. We have many sensory receptors in our skin enabling us to feel light touch, pressure, temperature, vibrations, and pain. Touch is so essential for our proper development as infants and young people. Without any touch at all, babies become withdrawn, do not develop properly and even die. Therefore it is a more than reasonable assumption that quality touch throughout our life continues to be necessary

---

[60] In Chinese medicine, the skin is known as the 'third lung'.
[61] Medical Research News Published: Tuesday, 21-Dec-2004 http://www.manchester.ac.uk.

in order for a person to be in great health. Sadly many cultures – including the dominant Western one – have developed in such a way that most people receive very little touch in their lives, and often the little that *is* available is received through sex. This leaves us vulnerable to exploitation of our deepest needs; we are more dependent on sex for contact, and then this need for sex and love is used in advertising to manipulate us into buying more stuff.

Many holistic therapies involve touch. There is no doubt that intelligent, loving touch has immense power to restore and maintain health. Let's all do what we can to reclaim it for ourselves and for each other; not just as something we can get if we pay for it, or through our sexual relationships. Even if you don't usually do hugging, try it and see. Pay attention and identify someone you know who is good at hugs, then practice with them. You can soon get the hang of it if you persevere. A hug a day keeps the doctor away!

The skin cells make vitamin D by using the power of the sun. Vitamin D is necessary for healthy bone formation. Finally, the skin acts as a storage place; the subcutaneous layer of fat helps to store nutrients, the vascular tissue of the skin acts as a blood reservoir storing about 5% of the body's blood.

The skin consists of the following structures

An Outer **Epidermis** consisting of stratified squamous epithelium. Like all epithelial tissue this is continuously regenerating. The outer layer of **keratinised** cells is dead, and falls off at a rate of about 40-60 million cells per day.

The epidermis must be kept richly supplied with blood to allow all that growth to happen. The blood is supplied via the underlying dermis. The underside of the epidermis forms peaks and troughs called the **papillae**. These mean that the first papillary layer of epidermis has an increased surface area, which facilitates blood supply and allows room for lots of nerve endings. These papillae give the skin its characteristic swirling appearance and make our unique fingerprints.

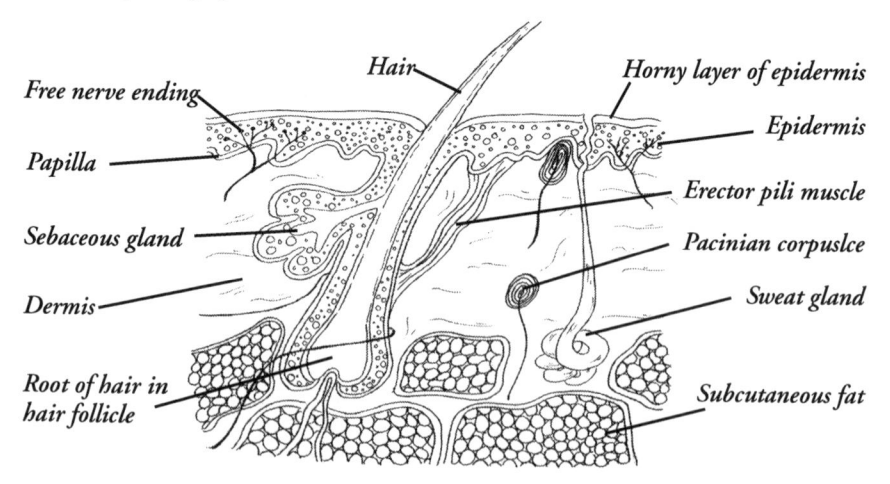

The **epidermis** consists of various layers, visible under the microscope.

From the outside, inwards they are:

Horny layer (stratum corneum). This is a tough outside layer of dead cells full of keratin. Keratin is the same stuff that our nails and hair are made of. This layer builds up more and gets thicker when used – as happens on the soles of feet and palms of hands. It also gets thicker in response to pressure, so we form a callous on an area of our skin that is used a lot. Where people walk barefoot, the soles of the feet become incredibly hard and horny, able to walk over all kinds of rough ground.

Clear layer (stratum lucidum). Just below the horny layer is a layer where the cells have almost completely broken down, which looks clear under the microscope.

Granular layer (*stratum granulosum*). This layer looks granular or speckled: the cells have started to break down, but still some parts of the nuclei remain.

Prickle cell layer (stratum spinosum/malpighian). This layer consists of living cells with intact membranes containing fibrils which interlock. Under pressure they are capable of mitosis – this is how calluses form on the soles of feet and palms of hand.

Germinative Layer (stratum germinativum/basale). This deepest layer is where the 'germination' takes place – where the epithelial cells divide and regenerate. It contains some **melanocytes** as well as **keratinocytes**. These melanocytes extend into the next layer and fill it with the skin pigment melanin. Melanin protects us from damage by UV light, and gives the skin its colour.

Below the epidermis is the **dermis**, which is basically connective tissue containing various structures. The blood and lymph supply for the skin is found in capillary loops coming up from the deeper arterioles which lie in the subcutaneous fat. There are hair follicles with hairs complete with erector pili muscles which can pull our hairs to stand on end (like happens when we are cold, scared or excited). Interestingly, women and men have the same number of hairs on our bodies, and actually humans have the same number as chimpanzees, although ours are obviously much finer!

Attached to the hair follicles are sebaceous glands, which secrete sebum into the follicles, waterproofing the skin. Without sebum the skin becomes dry and cracked and is no longer effective as a waterproof barrier. Sebum is to humans what lanolin is to sheep. Shampoo strips the hair of sebum, drying it out (and necessitating the use of conditioner). You can stop using shampoo, and keep your hair clean by washing it with water only and brushing it a lot. Brushing makes the oils move down the length of the hair. When you first do it, your hair will be extremely greasy, as due to previous shampoo use your body will be trying to make up for the extreme lack of oil on your hair. After a few months, this settles down. Actually, if you have greasy hair, you can improve it by washing it less often; constant washing of it will be continually stimulating the sebaceous glands to over-produce. An example of someone who has not washed her hair with shampoo for years and years is Patti Smith.

A cousin of sebaceous glands, ceruminous glands, is found in the ear canal and makes earwax to protect the ear. Earwax contains antibacterial substances to help protect the ear from infection.

Two little-known facts about ear wax[62]
- You can put it onto those big hard painful red spots (pimples) you sometimes get on your face and it makes them go.
- Cats love to eat it. Yes, believe it or not, most cats prefer ear wax… try it for yourself!

Also found in the dermis are coiled tubes which open onto the surface of the skin - sweat glands. There are two kinds. Eccrine glands make watery sweat and apocrine glands make thicker more pungent sweat. Sweat contains the amazing substances **pheromones**, which have a lot to do with who we find attractive and who repels us, as well as powerfully effecting the endocrine system. Interesting experiments have been done by attaching a piece of lint cotton which had been soaked in other subjects' sweat to the top lip of a bunch of women for a few hours every day, and noting the effects of this on their menstrual cycle. Yes, really! The mind boggles. Apparently, it is via pheromones in our sweat that women's menstrual cycles come into alignment with other women. Interestingly, men's pheromones affect the menstrual cycle too. Women's menstrual cycles change according to the chemical messages we are receiving from those around us.[63]

The millions of sensory nerve endings in the skin are found in the dermis, including **Merkel's cells** and **Meissner's corpuscles** for touch and **Pacinian corpuscles** for pressure. Some areas of the skin are very much richer in nerve endings than others – compare for yourself how it feels to stroke a one inch square of your leg, with a one inch square of your face, especially the skin around your mouth. The face, especially the mouth area, has a particularly high number of sense receptors.

Elastic fibres give the skin its elasticity. This wears out over time, just as your knicker elastic does. Hence the skin of a young person bounces straight back when pulled up, and the skin of an old person does not.

Hair and nails are made of tightly packed keratinised cells, the same material as the top layers of your skin. Both are alive at the root, from where they grow. It's incredible to think that keratin can be laid down in different ways to form nails, hair and hard skin.

As our first line of self-defence, the skin needs to be able to repair itself quickly if damaged. It does this remarkably well due to its rich blood supply. Remember that a good

---

[62] By the way, apparently Tatewari (Grandfather Fire) says he's here to clean the shit out of our ears…See the end of chapter seven (the heart) to explain a little more about him.

[63] Martha McClintock, Professor in Psychology, provided the first conclusive scientific evidence for human pheromones. Her findings, co-authored with Kathleen Stern (PhD.1992), were published in the March 12 1998 issue of 'Nature'.

blood supply is needed for healing anywhere in the body: without an efficient transport system, you can't get the building materials on site and the waste taken away.

The quickly dividing epidermal cells reproduce until they touch each other – a very shallow cut heals within a few days with no scar. A deeper cut takes more work to heal. The first phase of repair is the inflammatory stage, in which blood loss causes clot formation right up to the surface of the skin. The clot helps hold the sides of the cut together. The inflammatory process means lots of blood cells are attracted to the area. New capillaries form in the dermis, and epithelial cells 'migrate' to just under the clot. Fibroblasts make scar tissue, and then new epithelial cells are made and laid down with extra collagen fibres. Often a scar remains.

Various things can go wrong with the skin

There are over 1,000 skin conditions, the most common being bacterial, yeast or fungal infections. Also there are non-infective inflammations like eczema and psoriasis. More serious conditions are cancer and burns.

Skin Deep

Eczema is a very common inflammatory skin condition. It is seen as an 'atopic' or allergic type of condition. The holistic view of it is that it is a cry for help from the body, an indication of imbalance, that something is not right deeper in. It can be related to toxicity in the body such as from food intolerances. The orthodox medical treatment for eczema is the application of steroid creams which suppress the inflammation. The holistic view is that this pushes the problem deeper in. It is common for someone to have eczema as a child then later develop asthma after steroid cream use: the disease has moved further in to the body. When a person is later embarking on a healing process, very often the eczema will return as the illness is leaving their system. This is known as the 'law of cure'. We will discuss it more when we take a look at five element medicine in Appendix A.

Burns

Burns can kill us primarily because of their effect on the skin: this is largely due to a loss of body fluids containing electrolytes and proteins, resulting in dehydration; literally, the fluid and everything falls out of us. People who have been burned need an enormous amount of extra food calories daily to replace those lost through the damaged skin – it is not possible to eat enough if the damage is severe, so they are given these through IV and gastric tubes. Infection is also a major problem for people who have been burned.

In Switzerland there are people known as 'coupe feu'. Coupe feu literally means in French 'to cut fire'. These people have a special gift to stop burns and heal them almost immediately. The gift is usually, but not necessarily, passed down in the family and only one person at a time in the family possesses the gift. They never charge for their services. Most burns departments in the general hospi-

tals have a list of these people and if someone comes to the hospital with second and third degree burns they ask you if you want to phone a coupe feu. You speak to the person on the phone, give your name, where you are and where you're burnt and the pain goes away almost immediately with very little or any scarring. This is a tradition that has been passed down through generations in Switzerland and parts of France. It even works for sunburn. There's also in the same line of tradition the 'coupe sang' which stops hemorrhaging and severe bleeding[64].

Skin Cancer

Many benign tumours arise in the skin: for example warts are benign tumours caused by a virus. However some skin tumours are **malignant** – meaning that they will spread and invade other parts of the body. Risk factors include frequent irritation of the skin (by chemicals, infections or physical trauma like sun burn). It is now understood that regular exposure to the sun is not the risk it was once thought to be; it might be worse to have only intermittent exposure. Sunscreens and block use have increased enormously, but so has incidence of skin cancer. In fact, skin cancer rates have increased the most in places that people use the most sun creams, leading to speculative questions that something in the creams themselves may be carcinogenic. The three common skin cancers include melanoma, squamous cell carcinoma and basal cell carcinoma.

Interrelationships

The skin interacts particularly with the nervous, circulatory, lymphatic and immune systems in order to maintain homeostasis. There is a close relationship with the **nervous system**. Although it is actually through sensory nerve receptors that we feel things, all this experience of the outside world is mediated via the skin. As we have said, in a way *the skin is one big sense organ*, providing the brain with vital information about the world we are living and moving in. In terms of the **circulatory system** it is the skin which mediates change of temperature in the body via sweating *and blood vessel constriction/dilation*. Thermo-regulation is vital for homeostasis; heat speeds up chemical reactions, cold slows them down, so affecting **all cells and tissues** of the body. Also the skin is a vital barrier in the front line against infection being important for the **immune system.**

---

[64]Thanks to Lucy Harmer of the Innerelf Centre, Switzerland, for this information. www.innerelf.ch

CHAPTER FIVE

THEM BONES THEM BONES THEM... DRY BONES
The Skeletal System

Actually, living bones could not be more different from them dry old dead ones. In the body, bones are vibrantly alive, and continually changing. They have a rich blood and nerve supply. Bone cells continually lay down, reabsorb then lay down again a beautiful pattern of calcium phosphate and calcium carbonate salts in a fibrous network. The more weight-bearing exercise a bone is asked to do, the stronger it gets by laying down more calcium. This process is so dynamic that when we wake up in the morning after lying in bed all night, our bones are actually less dense than they were when we went to bed!

A layer of dense fibrous connective tissue called **periosteum** covers bone. It is into this periosteum that the tendons of muscles and the ligaments that support joints knit. They are essentially the same in composition: full of collagen fibres.

Beneath this periosteum is found a layer of dense **compact bone**, which gives the bones the appearance of being solid. Actually they are not. Under a thin layer of compact bone is found **spongy** or **cancellous bone**, which looks like the inside of a sponge. The holes in it are filled with **red bone marrow**, where blood cells are made. An exception to this is in the shafts of long bones, which are hollow and filled with **yellow marrow**. Yellow marrow is basically fat. It counts as a storage site in the body. (Can you say "red marrow yellow marrow" over and over again incredibly fast?).[65]

The functions of the skeleton are: support, movement (which it does by joint formation and with the help of muscles), protection, making blood cells and storage of calcium, phosphates and fats.

Types of bone

If you get your hands on a skeleton you will notice that there are different shaped bones. These are classified into **types**. Some bones, for instance the ribs and sternum and the dome of the cranium, are kind of flat. Under these are found important and vulnerable bits, hence

---

[65] Many people in the UK remember trying to say 'red lorry yellow lorry' over and over as fast as possible at daycare or the first years at school…

flat bones are seen as protective. Some bones look like the typical cartoon bone – two bulgy heads and a longer shaft between them. These are called **long bones**, and give us 'leverage', a massive range of movement and a lot of physical strength. All the bones of the limbs except the 'short' bones in the ankle and wrist, are long bones. This includes the three tiny phalanges in your little toe! The **short bones** in your wrist and ankle, called the carpals and tarsals, give flexibility and strength. The vertebrae do not easily fit into any other category, and so are called **irregular bones**. Finally there is a kind of bone called a **sesamoid bone**. These are mostly small, of sesame seed shape and size, and are formed inside tendons where they cross joints and need extra strength and support – in the ankle for instance. If you sit with your legs out in front of you and relax your thigh, you can wobble your kneecap, or patella, about. Now, tense the muscles in your thigh; notice how the patella will no longer move. It is completely inside the tendon of your quadriceps muscle on the front of your thigh – yes, you guessed it, the patella is the giant sesame seed from hell…

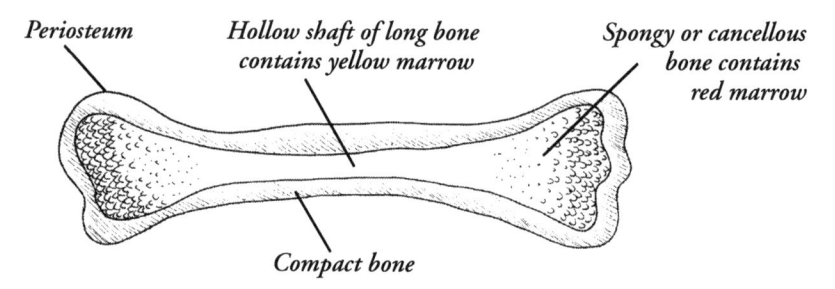

Periosteum   *Hollow shaft of long bone contains yellow marrow*   *Spongy or cancellous bone contains red marrow*

Compact bone

Bone formation – ossification

Bones form in the womb from a cartilaginous blueprint and later continue to grow by a process called **ossification**. This means that initially we make ourselves a skeleton out of cartilage. Feel your ear or the end of your nose. These are made of cartilage, an amazingly tough and flexible material. The ear and nose cartilage has extra elastic tissue, but is otherwise similar to the bone blueprint. Gradually, during the process of ossification, the bone cells take calcium from the blood (lovingly supplied from your mum's blood via the placenta and umbilical cord), and lay it down in a beautiful and intricate circular pattern to make the bones rigid. Thus inside the bones are found long tubes of calcium salts laid down in concentric circles around a central **Haversian canal**. These tubes of rigid material make the bone much stronger than it would be if it were simply solid calcium. Mature bone cells, called **osteocytes**, live in spaces, or lacunae, within the matrix of the bone they have made.

If you take a bone from a long-dead creature, what you have is the calcium salts part, after the organic cartilaginous material has rotted away. These 'dry bones' are rigid and not at all flexible – therefore they are very easy to snap. On the other hand, if you take a 'just dead' bone, and put it in acid to dissolve out the calcium salts, you will then be left with a bone that is completely flexible, but not at all rigid: you can tie it in a knot. It is made of incredibly tough cartilaginous material – you will be very hard pressed to break it or pull it apart.

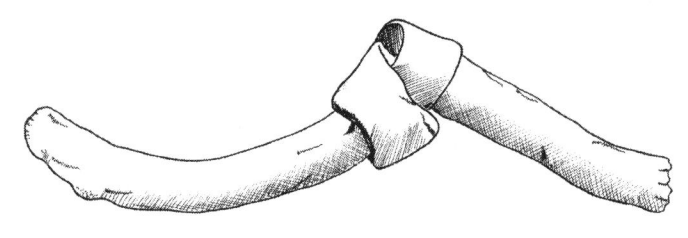

The living bones in our bodies contain both these elements – the tough flexibility of the cartilaginous blueprint, with the rigid strength of the calcium lattice. This is an amazingly successful partnership. When we are young we are incredibly juicy. Our bones are flexible and do not easily break; a young person is more likely to sustain a 'green stick' fracture on injury to a bone. To see what this looks like, literally take a green stick, a small live twig, straight from a tree, and try to break it. Later on we start to dry out, this process continuing throughout life. Another reason to live a 'juicy' life… it's good for our bones.

Bone healing

After a break, bones repair themselves by laying down lots and lots of calcium – called '**calcification**'. A bone healed in this way is stronger at the break site than elsewhere, as so much calcium is laid down. Sometimes bones take ages to heal; other times they can heal incredibly quickly. You can speed up bone healing miraculously by using the herb comfrey (*Symphytum officinalis* or 'knit bone'). Most effective taken internally as well as applied externally, comfrey contains a substance called 'allantoin' which your body also makes, using it for repair.[66]

Some anatomy jargon…

There are a lot of new words to get to grips with in the study of anatomy, and a whole bunch of them refer to where things are in the body, and how the body can move. This seems like a good place to look at them. If you have ever done any yoga, you will know that there is a

---

[66] Shamanic or earth medicine also addresses the condition of the energy body – healing the trauma or break here will vastly speed up the physical healing of the bone. There's a great story about this in *Mutant Message Down Under* By Marlo Morgan.

position called **shavasana** – literally, the corpse position. It involves lying on your back, legs loosely apart and arms by your sides, with the palms facing up to the ceiling. Translate this position to a standing one and you have what is known as the **anatomical position**. The convention in anatomy is to describe things as though the body is in the anatomical position.

Imagine a line drawn straight down the front of the body, from the middle of the top of the head. This is the **medial line**. If you sliced a body in half down the medial line, that is the **sagittal**, or **medial plane**. If you slice a body down from the top in a plane going from one ear to the other you get the **coronal**, or **frontal plane**. Slicing horizontally at 90º to the sagittal or coronal planes gives you the **transverse plane**.

The Skeleton

The skeleton consists of 204 bones. These are divided into the **axial** and **appendicular** skeletons. The axial skeleton is the axis of the body and comprises the skull, spine, ribs and sternum. Kind of hanging onto this is the appendicular skeleton: the shoulder girdle (collarbone and shoulder blade) and arms, and the pelvic girdle and legs.

The Axial Skeleton

The skull consists of the cranium, made by a number of fused bones of the face domed on top by the separate parietal, frontal, occipital and temporal bones which join to each other by close fibrous joints called sutures.

The movable part of the skull is the mandible, joined by a synovial joint, the **TMJ (temporo-mandibular joint)**. Have a feel of this: put your fingers on your face just in front of your ear. Open and close your mouth to find the joint. Now keep your mouth open and move your jaw from side to side. Is your TMJ tender to touch? Don't be surprised or alarmed if it is. This is very common. The TMJ can be out of place and cause all sorts of problems. Holistic dentists have a lot to say about your 'bite', which is the way your upper and lower jaw fit together. It seems that breast-feeding is very important here for proper development of the mouth and jaws, and therefore for the cranium. It takes a lot more pull to drink from the breast than from a bottle – so bottle-fed babies lose out on this important developmental exercising, as well as in so many other ways.[67]

Chiropractors, cranial osteopaths and craniosacral therapists can help to put right misalignments in the TMJs and the skull as well as other misalignments of the musculoskeletal system, which can cause numerous problems in any part of the body.

The hyoid bone gets a mention here being the only part of the larynx which is bone (the rest is cartilage). Like a sesamoid bone it is not joined to any other bone. You can find it on your own body by feeling either side of your voice box – find the top of it, and squeeze gently – there is a bone which you can move about a bit. This is the hyoid bone. Feel it go up and down as you swallow.

---

[67] The numerous benefits of breast-feeding will be elaborated on when we deal with the miracle of reproduction.

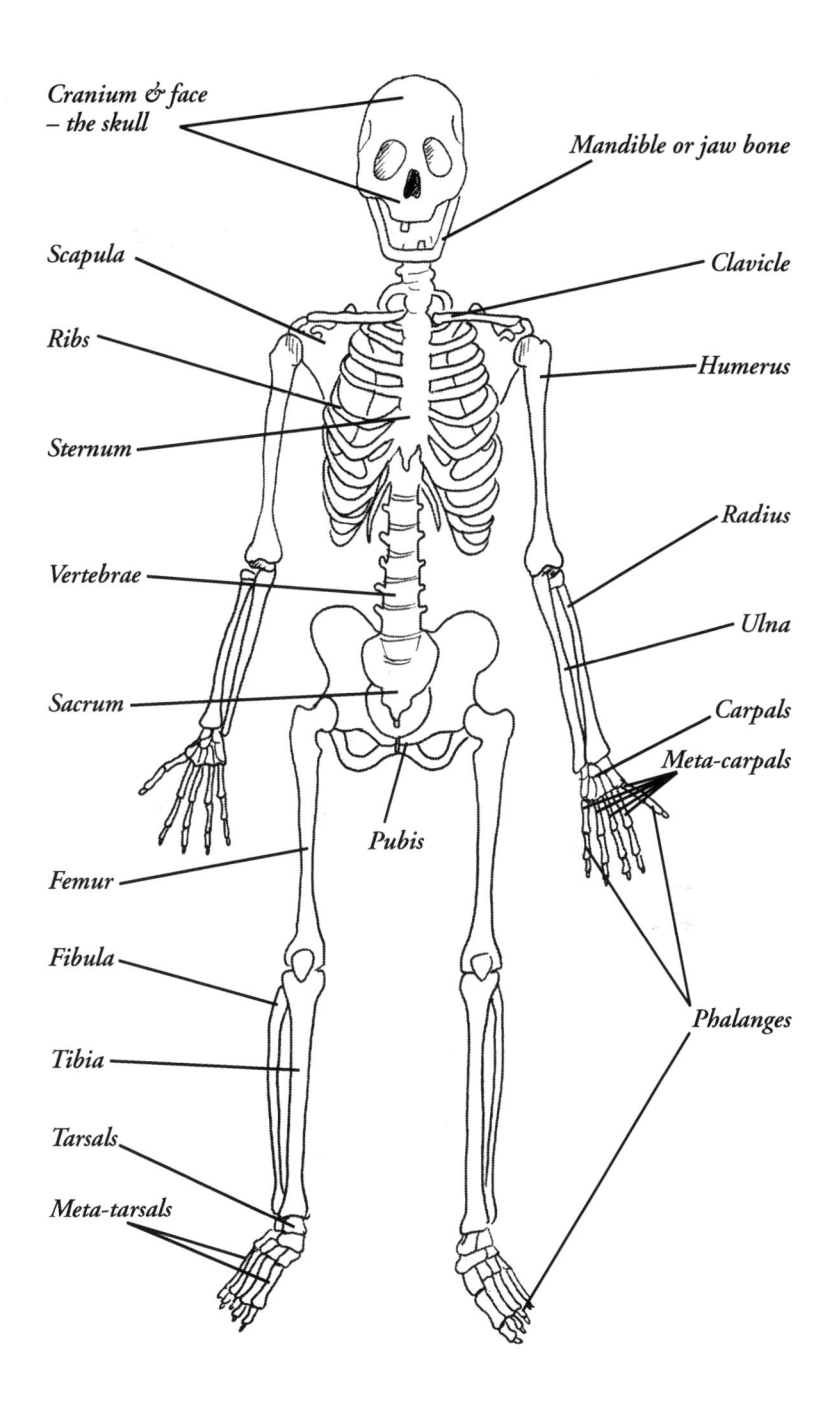

- Cranium & face – the skull
- Mandible or jaw bone
- Scapula
- Clavicle
- Ribs
- Humerus
- Sternum
- Radius
- Ulna
- Vertebrae
- Sacrum
- Carpals
- Meta-carpals
- Pubis
- Femur
- Fibula
- Phalanges
- Tibia
- Tarsals
- Meta-tarsals

Occiput

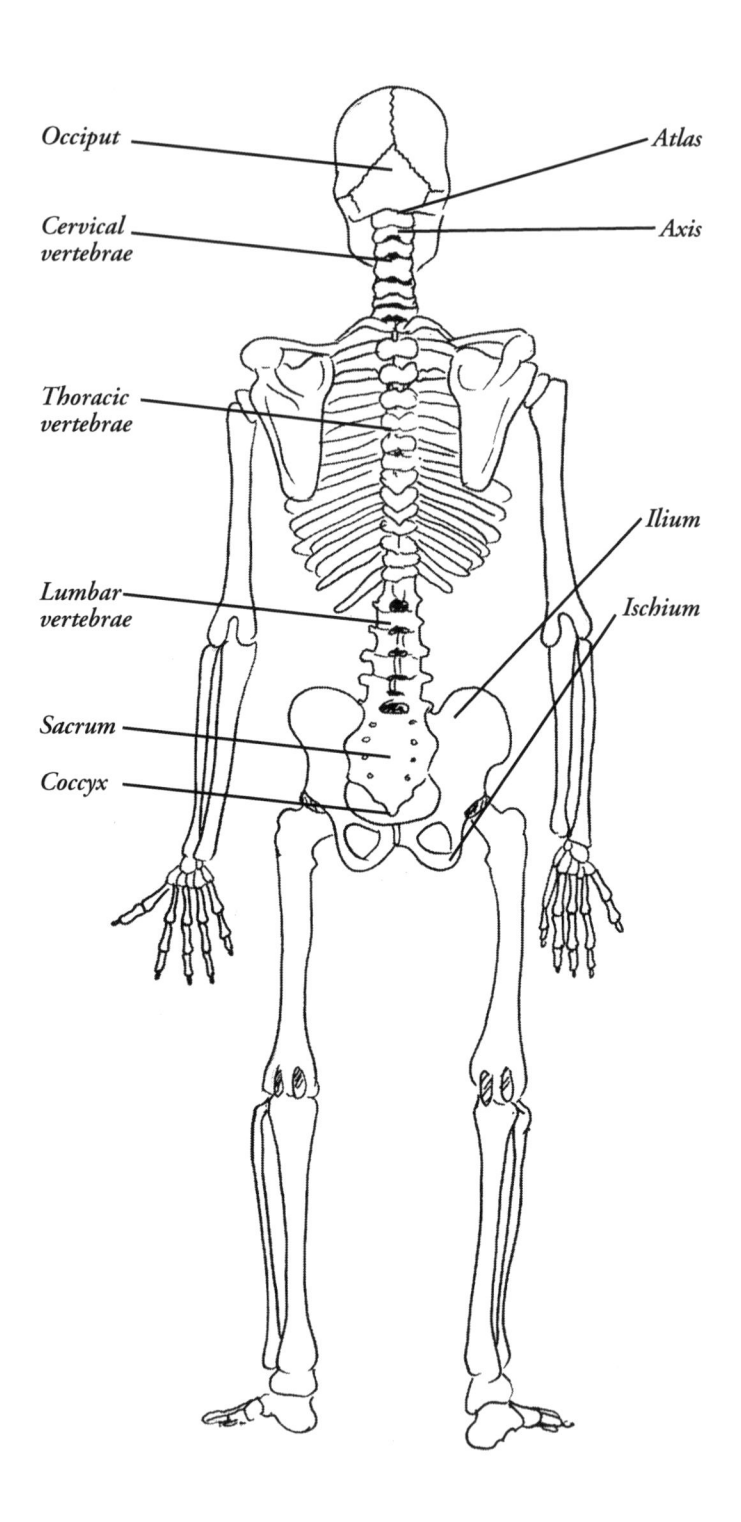

Cervical vertebrae

Thoracic vertebrae

Lumbar vertebrae

Sacrum

Coccyx

Atlas

Axis

Ilium

Ischium

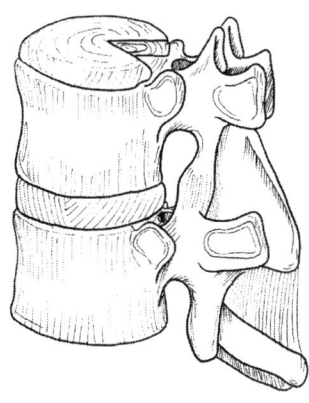

The spine consists of thirty-three vertebrae. Generally these vertebrae have a large wedge of bone called the **vertebral body**, a **spinous process** sticking out the back and **transverse processes** out the sides. The spinous processes are those sticking-out-bits you can see on someone's back. You can't generally see or feel the transverse processes, except for those of the first neck bone – the atlas. Put your fingers in the dip right underneath your ear, between the jawbone at the front and the skull at the back. Just press in, and move your fingers up and down until you feel some hard bony bits underneath them – ouch! They are probably a bit tender. Those are the transverse processes of your atlas.

Between the spinous processes at the back and the transverse processes at the sides there is a bony bridge which forms the borders of a central canal. This is called the **vertebral** or **spinal canal**, it is where the spinal cord is found, completely protected by bone. An intervertebral foramen either side at each level allows spinal nerves to exit and enter.

The **vertebral bodies** are found deeper in, and stack on top of each other with the vertebral or spinal discs between them. Generally, the bodies get bigger the lower down the spine, due to increased weight bearing.

The vertebrae are named and numbered from the top down as follows:
- **7 Cervical** – called C1 – C7
- **12 Thoracic** called T1 – T12
- **5 Lumbar** called L1 – L5
- **5 fused Sacrum** called S1 – S5
- **4 fused Coccyx**

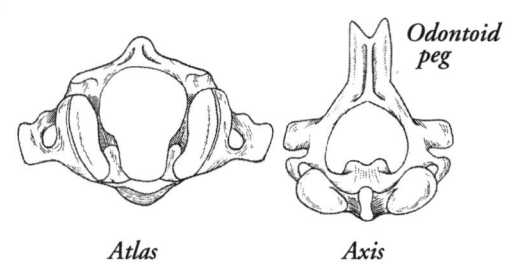

Atlas   *Axis*

Odontoid peg

The neck is called the cervical spine. (You may be familiar with the term 'cervical smear' – a screening test for cancer of the cervix – or 'neck' of the womb.)

The first two in the neck (C1 and C2) are the **atlas** and **axis.** Remember Atlas the mythological Greek guy who holds up the world? The 'atlas' holds up the head, and has a special joint with the occipital part of the skull which allows extra flexion – in plain terms, this is nodding. The next one down, called the axis, has a big peg sticking up into the round ring of the atlas, called the odontoid peg, which has a synovial pivot joint with the atlas allowing a lot of extra rotation between these two bones – in plain English, shaking the head. There is no intervertebral disc between them as there is between other vertebrae.

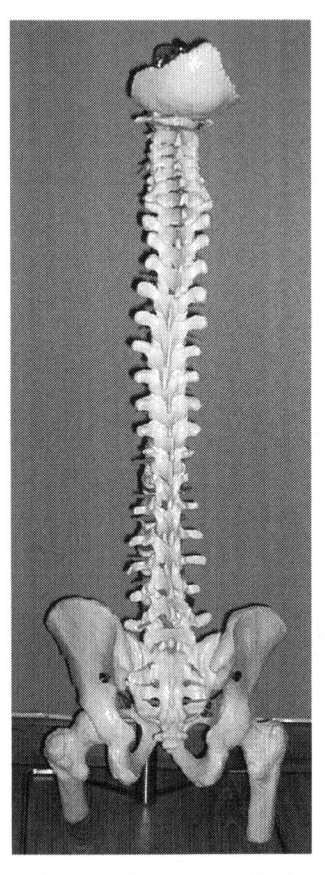

The 12 thoracic vertebrae have an extra articular surface for joining with the **ribs**.

The sacrum is one triangular-shaped bone made from five vertebrae which fused together early in our foetal development. It is interesting to look at the skeletons of mammals and compare them; there is only the barest variation between the essential designs.[68] Like us, horses and even giraffes have seven neck bones. The dolphin, with no need for back legs, has no bones fused together to make a sacrum. Four legged animals do not have the marked difference between weight-bearing legs and arms that we or other animals that spend some time on their back legs do.

If you bend your head down on your chest and feel the spinous processes at the bottom of your neck, you can probably feel at least one that particularly sticks out – this is usually C7. If you can feel two sticky-out ones, they are probably C6 and C7. It is possible to find the spinous processes from C2 all the way down to L5 with some perseverance. (On someone else, I mean – it is not at all easy to find them on yourself).

The joints of the spine include the intervertebral discs between the vertebral bodies, as well as joints between each vertebra and the ones above and below made by articular surfaces on the intervertebral arches, which are bridges of bone between the spinous processes and transverse processes. Ligaments support all these joints. As you see, the spine is designed to move. A great many of our problems in this area come about from the lack of exercise and moving we do. Each vertebra should freely move with the one above and below – for most of us, this isn't happening. Instead whole sections of the spine move together, which puts a lot of pressure on the one spot that is moving. You can find out how well your spine is moving, and consciously begin to improve its mobility, with a simple exercise:

Lie on the floor with your legs bent and your feet flat on the floor. Have a few paperbacks or a small pillow under your head if necessary. Starting with your sacrum, begin to slowly roll your back off the floor, using your legs to push up. Imagine you are moving one vertebra at a time, until you get

---

[68] Of course, we have much the same DNA as other mammals – being actually about 42% the same as a plant – a banana, for instance. It occurred to me in Bali, where the banana plant is used completely for just about everything, that people would relate to this much more easily. In the West, we have become so disconnected from nature that we have forgotten that everything we need comes from our ancestors, the plants.

to your upper back and your shoulders and legs are supporting your weight. Now do the reverse and come down.

Can you move those vertebrae one at a time? Or do you notice places where a great chunk goes up or comes down all together? Practice gently and regularly to improve your mobility. A visit to an osteopath, chiropractic, massage therapist or Bowen therapist will also help to free things up.

Some useful terminology

Imagine a line going down the middle of the body from the top of the head to the groin. This is called the **medial** line. Everything that is found towards it is called medial, everything found away from it is called **lateral**. The front of the body is called **anterior**; the back **posterior** (remember that old-fashioned polite word for your bum?).

Below is referred to as **inferior**; above is referred to as **superior.** On your arms and legs, close to the trunk is known as **proximal**; away from the trunk (i.e. towards your hands and feet) is **distal**.

Movements also have a special language. Imagine a baby in the womb, in the foetal position with everything curled up. This is called 'flexed', and movements in this direction are known as **flexion**. The opposite is called **extension**. If you take an arm or leg away from the midline of the body, it's called **abduction**. Returning it in or crossing towards the midline is **adduction**. The spine can flex forward and extend backward, and it can also bend to the side. Side bending is called **lateral flexion**. The spine can also twist around (especially the head). This kind of movement is called **rotation**. Your shoulders and hips can do it too – turn your toes out and in again; this is known as **lateral** and **medial rotation**.

Put your hands out in front of you. You can turn them so the palms face the ceiling, which is called **supination** – and makes them in a **supine** position (think of making cups of them for soup). They can also be **pronated** to face the floor.

(The whole body can be **prone** – lying on your front, face down; or supine, lying on your back, face up).

The feet can do a few things that are described in particular words. Pointing your toes – planting them to the earth, is called **plantarflexion.** Pointing your toes to the sky and keeping your heels down is **dorsiflexion**.

The rest of the axial skeleton is the **sternum** and **ribs**. There are twelve pairs of ribs, coming off the thoracic vertebrae at the back. The first seven are called 'true ribs' and they articulate directly with the sternum via long cartilaginous joints. The next three articulate with the articular cartilage of the one above. Ribs eleven and twelve are free floating; their tips can be felt. Weirdly, ribs eight to twelve are called 'false' ribs. By the way, men and women have the same number of ribs – believe it or not, this is a commonly asked question!

The Appendicular Skeleton

The Arms or 'upper limb' consist of two shoulder blades, two clavicles and two arms (usually). Each shoulder blade, or **scapula,** moves around freely on the ribs: it is not attached directly to the ribs except by muscles. The superior lateral (the top outside) part comes over the top of the shoulders, and makes a joint with the lateral end of the collarbone or **clavicle** in front of the top of your shoulder. See if you can find it. You can then follow the clavicle to the middle of your body and feel where it meets the **sternum**, or breast bone. The shoulder blade and clavicle make a shallow socket for the ball of the upper arm to join with. This joint is extremely mobile – therefore not very stable. It's fairly common to dislocate your shoulder. It has very lax ligaments to allow a large range of movement, and is supported mainly by muscles. Small children have even less stable shoulders as they have not yet built up muscle strength. This means they can be easily dislocated by, for example, swinging a small child by the arms before they are big enough (and, horribly, when a stressed and hurrying adult pulls along the young person).

The arms themselves are comprised of three bones: the terribly amusing **humerus** in the upper arms and the **radius** and **ulna** below. If you whack your 'funny bone' which is not at all funny, you have hurt the inside of your humerus at the elbow. There is a sensitive nerve very close to the surface there.

The forearm has its two bones lying together like shoes in a shoebox – the ulna is larger at the elbow end and small at the wrist. It forms the point of your elbow. Give it a feel and follow it down to your wrist – is it lateral or medial? Don't forget the anatomical position.

You will find that it lies to the inside. The radius lies laterally. It has a small head at the elbow but makes the larger part at the wrist end. Look at the back of your right wrist – you can see a big knobble on the right which is the end of your ulna, and you may not see but you can certainly feel a lump (known as a 'tuberosity') on the left. This is the **radial tuberosity**, and you can feel it at the front and back of your wrist.

If you keep feeling around your wrist you will realize that there are more lumps and bumps. Quite a lot is going on in there – the wrist itself contains eight small bones called the **carpals**, arranged more or less in two rows of four. [69] Each carpal bone forms a joint with its neighbours allowing them to slide or glide over each other a little. The radius and ulna make a joint with the proximal row of carpals, and the metacarpals in the hand join with the distal row of carpals. Phew! See what I mean about a lot going on. All these small joints together give the wrist a wonderful range of movement and a lot of extra strength. The small long

---

[69] For the sake of completeness and for those who want to know, the carpal bones are, beginning with the side of the thumb and proceeding to the little finger: in the distal row, the trapezium, trapezoid, capitate and hamate; In the proximal row, the scaphoid, lunate, triquetrum and pisiform. Pisiform can be felt on the anterior surface of the medial border of the wrist and can be moved from side to side. The hand *must* be relaxed and hanging there or you can't feel it (one of the forearm flexor muscles inserts into it and if this muscle is working you won't be able to move pisiform). The hook of hamate can be felt on very deep palpation over the medial side of the palm, 2cm distal and slightly lateral to pisiform.

bones in the palm of your hand are the five **metacarpals**, numbered 1 - 5 from thumb side. Take a look at your fingers. They are made of many small long bones called **phalanges**. How many do you have? Count them for yourself...[70]

Pelvic girdle & Lower limb – Hips and Legs

The pelvic girdle is made of two **innominate** bones, each made of three fused bones. Weirdly, 'innominate bone' means 'the bone with no name' when in fact each part has a name: the **ischium**, **ilium** and **pubis**. Apparently the bone was named 'innonimate' in the olden days when it was impolite to mention a person's pelvic area, it was such a rude place.... the weird and wonderful roots of modern medicine, eh! The pelvis is joined at the front with a wedge of cartilage between the pubic bones: the **pubic symphysis**.

At the back, each side of the ilium articulates with the sacrum, making the sacroiliac joints. All three parts of the rude bone form the socket of the hip joint. Into this deep socket fits the head of the thighbone, or **femur**. This bone, the largest and longest in the body, makes the hip joint deep in the buttocks and groin. You can feel a bone at the side of your hip, which is part of the femur called the greater trochanter. The actual hip joint is too deep inside the muscles to palpate directly.

The femur ends in the knee joint, where it articulates with the **tibia** and much smaller ('feeble') **fibula**. In front of the knee joint – protecting it – is found the kneecap, or **patella**.

At the ankle there is a similar arrangement as at the wrist – only here, seven differently shaped **tarsal**[71] bones are found. One of them, the talus, articulates with the leg bones. There is a huge bone forming the heel, the calcaneus. There are five other tarsals, four of which articulate with the **metatarsals** making the arch of the foot. Echoing the metacarpals in the hand, the foot has five **metatarsals**, numbered one to five from the big toe side. Number one is much bigger than the other four. Just like the fingers, there are fourteen **phalanges**, three on four smaller toes and two on the big toe. Take a look at your little toe – the phalanges there are tiny, yet even these are 'long' bones, because they have a hollow shaft containing yellow bone marrow and two heads whose spongy bone contains red bone marrow, which is busy making blood cells.

Joints

Bones are joined to other bones by joints, also called 'articulations'. Most joints are supported by **ligaments** - tough white fibrous tissue passing from bone to bone across a joint, knitting into the periosteum covering of the bone. The study of these is called **arthrology**. We have mentioned some as we looked at the skeleton. Here we will take a closer look.

---

[70] There are fourteen - three for each finger and two for the thumb.

[71] The seven tarsals are the talus, calcaneus, cuboid, navicular, and three cuneiforms. The cuboid and the three cuneiforms articulate with the metatarsals.

There are three basic types of joints

Fibrous, or 'fixed' joints consist of tightly strung fibres running between adjacent bones. Example of fibrous joints are the **sutures** of the cranium and the interosseous membrane between the ulna and the radius. In traditional anatomy in the UK and US, they are considered to be immovable. However, it seems that there is a very subtle and slight movement possible between, for example, the sutures of the skull. Cranial osteopathy and its offshoot craniosacral therapy developed from observation of these subtle movements of the skull during brain surgery. Interestingly, this has been known in Italy since being discovered by Italian anatomist Guiseppe Sperino in 1920. There is a slow rhythm of movement of the skull bones, assisting with circulation of cerebrospinal fluid throughout the central nervous system.[72]

Cartilaginous, or slightly moveable joints, consist only of cartilage, attached at both ends to the bone. Examples are the joints between the ribs and the sternum, the pubic symphysis and the intervertebral discs. During pregnancy, a woman's body produces a hormone called relaxin which softens up all the cartilage and ligaments. During childbirth the pubic symphysis, the join of the two pelvic bones at the pubis can open out by more than an inch to allow the passage of the baby.

Synovial, or freely moveable joints, such as the hips, knees, elbows, shoulders and so on, are the most complicated. More on these below.

Synovial joints are the most complex. They have a **joint capsule**, comprised of a **synovial membrane** secreting synovial fluid, articular cartilage, ligaments, and sometimes bursae and menisci. The 'syn-ovial' fluid is 'like egg' – crack an egg, and feel the white of it on your hands. It is viscous and extremely slippery, and this is what **synovial fluid** is like. **Articular cartilage** is white; if you have ever eaten meat, you will have probably seen the gristle on the ends of the bones in a chicken leg. This is cartilage. It being white tells us that it has no blood supply. It must get its nutrients from the underlying bone, and from the synovial fluid. Synovial fluid gets reabsorbed and made again fresh; when you move a joint, it makes more fluid. When you are not moving, the joints dry up. This is why before exercising one 'warms up' the joints by moving them; as soon as we start to move them, the synovial membranes produce more fresh fluid, containing oxygen and nutrients. Thus if we do not move much and have sedentary lifestyles, the joints dry up and stiffen. This then means our cartilage has a hard time getting the nutrients it needs to repair and replenish itself. Cartilage wearing out causes stiffness and inflammation in the joint; this is known as osteoarthritis, or **O.A.**

---

[72] John Upledger *Your Inner Physician & You – Craniosacral therapy and Somato-emotional release*. You can find out more from the Upledger Institute upledger@upledger.com

Ligaments support the joint

Hollow shaft of long bone

Spongy bone or cancellous bone at head of long bone

Hyaline cartilage

Synovial membrane secretes synovial fluid

Fibrous joint capsule

A synovial joint

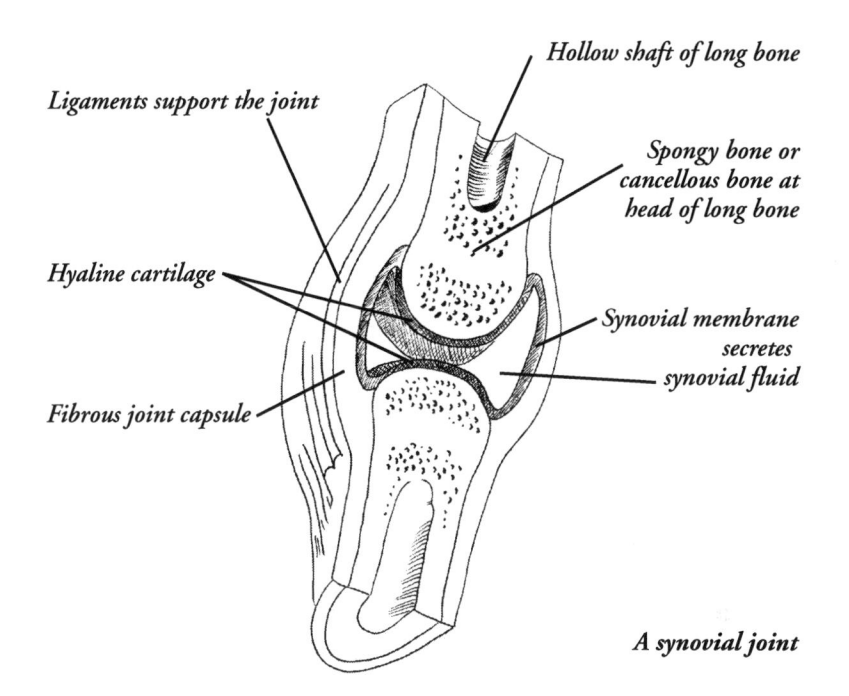

Tight muscles around a joint can cause compression of the cartilage, adding to this problem. This is why massage and bodywork can be very effective in treating arthritis and preventing further damage. To keep our joints working well we must keep them moving – use it or lose it! On the other hand, over-using the joints or putting a lot of strain on them can wear down the cartilage and hasten the development of O.A. which is a very common condition.[73]

The joint capsule is surrounded by bands of tough fibrous connective tissue called **ligaments** which attach into the periosteum of the bones either side of the joint and give it strength and stability. Ligaments contain a little bit of elastic tissue to allow them to stretch and recoil as the joint moves, but they restrict the movement of the joint and should not be stretched too far. Damage from stretching a joint too far is known as a **sprain**. Ligaments also look white – yes, you've guessed it, they do not have a good blood supply of their own. This means that injuries to them take a long time to heal. If they are badly over-stretched, the elasticity may be damaged so that they are never as efficient at supporting the joint again. This is why some people who twist their ankle (spraining it) are more susceptible to further similar injury. The joint is now more prone to over-stretching, as the ligaments are not holding it firmly any more.

---

[73] Don't forget about glucosamine to provide joints with the raw ingredients for repairing cartilage. The naturopathic approach to arthritis is to go for a detoxing and pure diet. Most people will find considerable improvement with this method. There are also many herbs which support elimination of toxins and the quieting down of inflammation. To find a herbalist contact the national institute of medical herbalists www.nimh.org

Some joints have extra little cushions inside them known as **bursae**. Bursa means 'purse'. These are made of synovial membrane and contain synovial fluid. They can become inflamed and produce lots of extra fluid, which causes huge swellings of a joint. Housemaid's Knee is an example of this.

The knee joints also have extra bits of cartilage to provide better shock absorption. Known as **menisci**, these are wedge-shaped (imagine something like the segment of an orange). Menisci fit inside the joint capsule. When you are standing up, the pressure on each knee is equal to the pressure on one car tire. Walking doubles this, running doubles it again – I hate to think about jumping! The knee has a medial and lateral meniscus, which are attached by short ligaments. These can be torn or damaged – not uncommonly from football, which as you can imagine is quite hard on the knees.

The different types of synovial joint are named according to their shape or the movements they can do.

- *Ball and socket* – shaped as the name suggests, these are the most mobile joints of all, able to do flexion/extension, adduction/abduction and rotation. They can also do a composite movement called circumduction. The two ball and socket joints are the hip and shoulder.
- *Hinge* – As the name suggests these open and close like a door – thus they can do flexion/extension. Examples include the knee and elbow joints and the joints between the phalanges.
- *Pivot* – These joints allow for rotation only. Think of the joint between your atlas and axis, the atlantoaxial joint. The atlas rotates around the odontoid peg of the axis, allowing you to turn your head and look over your shoulder.
- *Gliding*, or *Plane* – These joints allow a sliding movement in one plane. Examples are the joint between the shoulder blade and the collar bone (called the acromioclavicular joint) and the joints between the carpal bones.
- *Saddle* – These joints are shaped like a ball and socket joint but there is a little dip in them like a saddle on a horse. Thus, although they allow flexion/extension and adduction/abduction, they do not rotate. There is one at the base of the thumb, between the carpal bone (called the trapezium) and the first metacarpal. Although this joint does not allow rotation, it can do circumduction.
- *Condyloid* – These joints are shaped like a ball and socket but are oval rather than round. They are capable of flexion/extension, adduction/abduction and circumduction. An example is the knuckles – the metacarpophalangeal joints.

Interrelationships

There is an obvious close relationship with the **muscular system**; without the muscles the bones cannot move. The **skeletal system** also interacts particularly with the **endocrine system** and **cardiovascular system**, as well as the **digestive system** in order to maintain homeostasis with regards to calcium levels in the blood. Correct levels of calcium are necessary for proper functioning of the **nervous system** and the **muscular system** including the cardiac muscle of the heart. Blood cells are made in the bone marrow, so the **circulatory system** relies on the skeletal system. The **digestive system** gets into the blood the necessary ingredients for building new bone. Vitamin D, needed for bone production, is made by the **skin**. The **kidneys** help to stimulate production of bone marrow and the oestrogen of the **reproductive system** is involved in maintaining bone density.

Chapter Six

MOVEMENT
The Muscular System

Muscles can move. That's the thing about them – in fact, muscles do almost all the movement in the body.[74] This includes consciously moving the body about as well as the fine movements of the muscles which support us and help us stay upright which is done by **skeletal muscles**. These are so called because they are attached to the bones which they move about. Under a microscope skeletal muscles look striped because of how the tiny filaments inside them are arranged; hence they are also called **striated** muscles. They are under our conscious control; we can decide to move them at will, which gives them their third name of **voluntary** muscles.

Movement is also needed inside the body, in many of our internal organs and tubes. With the exception of the heart, which is made from its own unique **cardiac muscle**, this movement is carried out by **smooth muscle**, also called **involuntary** muscle. I'm sure you get the idea: we don't need to think about moving them. Smooth muscle is made up of short, spindle shaped cells arranged in sheets. It forms bands around and along tubes and organs, and can contract in segments – this is how food is pushed along the gastrointestinal tract (G.I.T.), a movement that is known as **peristalsis**. Smooth muscle in the circulatory system helps to move the blood along and also to allow varying amounts of blood into an area: if the muscle wall contracts tightly, less blood can enter; if it relaxes, the vessels dilate and more blood can perfuse into the tissues supplied by those vessels. Contraction of the smooth muscle cells is done by the movements of actin and myosin fibres. The **cardiac muscle** has to be special, since from within weeks of conception to the moment of death, the heart keeps on beating; the cardiac muscle keeps contracting, 24/7. No time off for a holiday, a sleep or a rest. The cells are all linked together with special junctions, as they must contract together in concert to produce coherent movement within the whole heart. The actual movement is again effected by contraction of actin and myosin filaments within each muscle cell.

What we know as the '**muscular system**' actually refers to the skeletal muscles (those named muscles attached to bone which cross joints and move the skeleton around). From now on this chapter focuses entirely on skeletal muscles.

---

[74] One interesting exception is the movement of spermatozoa, or sperm cells, which move using a **flagellum** (the tail of the sperm) that moves by contractile filaments within the cell making it wiggle. Cilia, the hair-like projections on the epithelium of the lungs and fallopian tubes, also move due to movements of tiny filamental parts of the cells micro-skeleton.

The composition of skeletal muscles

Skeletal muscles are made up of bundles of muscle cells, called fibres. Under a microscope they look stripy because of the straight-line arrangements of **actin** and **myosin** which lie on top of each other. Actin and myosin cause muscle contraction when they slide over each other, the myosin filaments pulling themselves along the actin filaments. Each muscle cell is wrapped in a sheath of fibrous connective tissue. A bundle of these long muscle fibres is wrapped again in fibrous connective tissue, and a bundle of bundles is wrapped again. The whole muscle is wrapped in similar stuff, which is called **fascia**. At either end, where the muscle attaches to the bone, the contractile muscle cells end and the connective tissue coverings continue and converge to form **tendons**. Tendons, as you can feel from you own body, are the incredibly tough and inflexible fibrous tissue which attach muscle to bone.

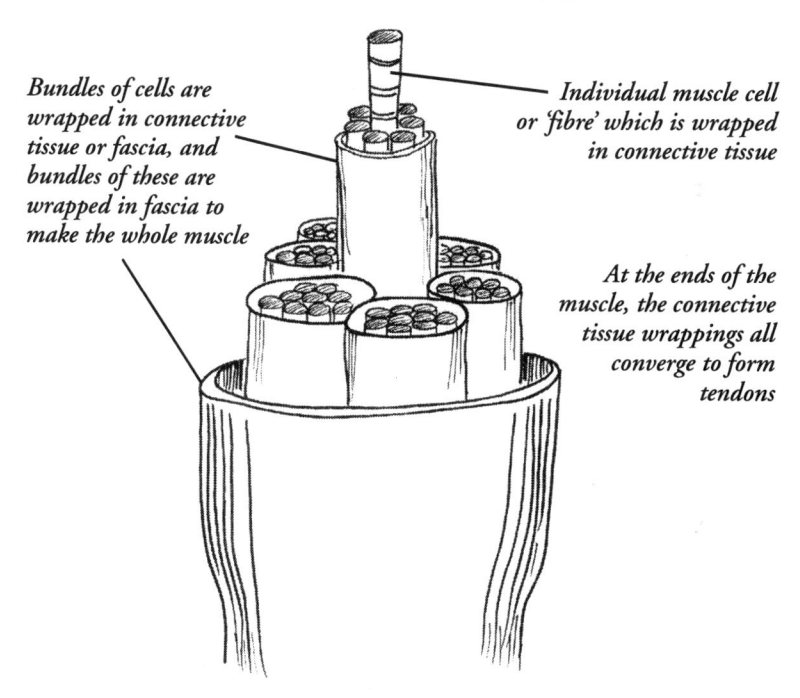

Bundles of cells are wrapped in connective tissue or fascia, and bundles of these are wrapped in fascia to make the whole muscle

Individual muscle cell or 'fibre' which is wrapped in connective tissue

At the ends of the muscle, the connective tissue wrappings all converge to form tendons

The hip bone's connected to the thigh bone...

So, fascia is the connective tissue that covers and runs right through the muscle, coming together to form the tendons at either end. The tendons knit into the periosteum – the fibrous connective tissue covering of bones that is essentially made of the same stuff as the tendons. Through this fascia, the whole body is connected. Find a friend, and ask them to lie on their back on the floor. Gently but firmly pull their toe, stretching their foot a little in the direction away from their head – and watch their head. You will see that the movement travels all the way up their body. The toe bone, through all the bones and joints and muscles along the way, *is* connected to the head bone. Fascia runs in sheets throughout our body, connecting all of our structure. It spirals around and through our muscles, covers our bones, makes up our ligaments and covers all our important organs. There is a soft tissue bodywork technique called 'fascial unwinding' in which the head or a limb is held gently supported and allowed to move in any direction it wants to.[75] The thinking is that the fascia gets twisted up over the years, and allowing the body to move in this way 'unwinds' it. This can release stored emotional baggage. Body work techniques such as postural integration and Rolfing focus on releasing deep seated emotional trauma held in the body; it is thought that the feelings are held in the connective tissue. Interestingly it looks as though meridians, the lines of energy running through the body described by oriental medicine, run through fascia.[76]

Muscle contraction

Each skeletal muscle cell can contract, or shorten, as the microscopic filaments of actin and myosin within them slide over each other with the help of calcium. This requires energy in the form of ATP. It's interesting that ATP is also required to remove the calcium and cause relaxation.

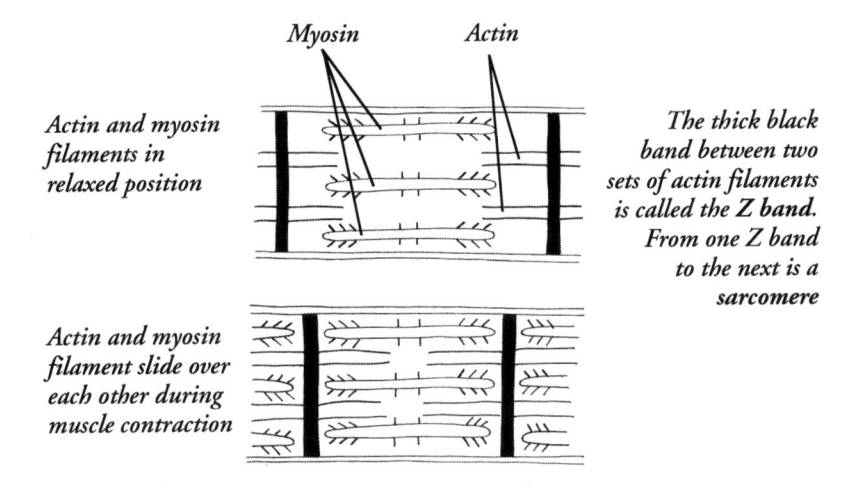

Actin and myosin filaments in relaxed position

Myosin   Actin

The thick black band between two sets of actin filaments is called the Z band. From one Z band to the next is a sarcomere

Actin and myosin filament slide over each other during muscle contraction

Each cell can only either contract or be relaxed - it's all or nothing. For a muscle to contract more, more individual cells get involved. A group of muscle cells will be innervated by one nerve fibre; in other words, one nerve cell firing will cause a set number of muscle cells to contract all at once. In some parts of the body, we have a lot of fine control over muscles; in these areas, like hands and tongue, each nerve fibre ending will stimulate just a few muscle

---

[75] Craniosacral Therapists practice this technique. College of Cranio-Sacral Therapy. 9 St George's Mews, Primrose Hill, London, NW1 8XE Tel 020 7483 0120 info@ccst.co.uk

[76] Helen M. Langevin & Jason A Yandow *Relationship of Acupuncture Points and Meridians to Connective Tissue Planes* (The Anatomical Record [Newanat.] 269:257-265, 2002). This research found an 80% correspondence between the sites of acupuncture points and the location of intermuscular or intramuscular connective tissue planes in postmortem tissue sections.

cells. On the other hand, large postural muscles like those in the legs will have hundreds of cells innervated by one nerve fibre. In other words, one nerve cell controls anything from a lot to a very few muscle cells. When the muscle cells contract, the two ends of the muscle move towards each other, causing movement between the bones they are attached too.

Whilst you are alive, the only time you could ever have a completely flaccid muscle would be if you were under a general anaesthetic, or the nerve to that muscle had been cut. In other words, there are always *some* muscle fibres contracting in a muscle at any one time. This provides what is known as muscle tone. Tone can vary between people, and from one muscle to another.

Sometimes (or should I say often!) a muscle becomes over-toned, or tense; the cells contract much more than needed while in a supposedly resting state. This can cause the muscle (and the person) to become tired as more energy is used in the contraction process. The muscle is less efficient and less effective. Also it hurts. Excess tension in muscles is so common in modern life that it has become normal; our sedentary lifestyles coupled with unrelenting stress and the lack of good emotional health generally are all factors in this. A muscle worked over its current ability can become fatigued. Tense muscles, which are already working overtime in their resting condition, are more prone to fatigue.

Aerobic and anaerobic respiration

Like other cells, muscle cells make ATP from glucose and oxygen in their mitochondria. This is called **aerobic respiration** and takes place in the absence of the absence of oxygen. By this means they can get a little ATP from glucose (by glycolysis), making lactic acid as a by-product. The lactic acid contributes to stiffness in the muscle, and will be either made into pyruvic acid (which the muscle cells can then use to make ATP), or is taken by the blood to the liver and made back into glucose. Muscle cells can also use fats for making energy. Muscles like to store their own sugar supplies as glycogen.[77]

A muscle that has gone into anaerobic respiration for a time is said to have built up an 'oxygen debt'. To repay this debt, we need to do plenty of breathing to replenish the blood's oxygen supplies.

Aerobic respiration: $O_2 + GLUCOSE \longrightarrow ATP + H_2O + CO_2$

Anaerobic respiration: $GLUCOSE \longrightarrow ATP + LACTIC\ ACID$

---

[77] Try cutting out refined sugar from your diet – many people who do this notice a change in how their muscles feel. It's likely that excess sugar puts strain on our muscles by over-filling them with glycogen they don't really need. In Chinese medicine, the Spleen Official (with some of its functions being comparable to those of the pancreas), is in charge of all movement in the body. Excess sugar damages the Spleen Official.

White and red cells

There are different types of muscle cells. Some look whiter; these do not have a rich blood supply and can operate without a constant supply of oxygen. Some look red, having a good blood supply. The **white fibres** are very fast but cannot go on and on contracting without a break. These are good at anaerobic contraction and are used for quick, occasional movements. The **red fibres** are slow, use lots of oxygen for aerobic respiration, and are used for postural support. Many muscles have a mixture of these types of fibre.

Smooth movement

Overall, muscles work together to produce movement in the body. Feel for yourself how it is to extend and flex (straighten and bend) your elbow. Biceps and triceps in the upper arm work together to make these movements smooth. Let's take elbow flexion as one given movement: there is a prime mover, or **agonist** – we'll call this **biceps brachii**.[78] The opposite movement to it – extension – is provided by triceps, the **antagonist**. To allow smooth flexion, biceps contracts, whilst triceps relaxes in a measured way. Without the opposing force of triceps, it would be difficult for biceps to make a careful and controlled movement.

So it is that muscles work together to perform movements. There is also a class of muscles called **synergists** (meaning 'go with the energy'). These are all the muscles which contribute to a given movement. For example biceps, and brachialis are synergists for flexion of the elbow. A further category is **fixators**; these are very important as they are muscles which hold some part in place in order to allow the precise movement of another part. For example in order for biceps to effectively flex the elbow, the scapula must be fixed in position. The main muscles which fix the scapula are the trapezius, rhomboids and serratus anterior muscles. So you can see that for any particular movement there are a lot of muscles involved. The coordination of muscle movements is controlled by a part of the brain called the cerebellum.

Muscles as sense organs

Muscles have sensory receptors, giving feedback to the brain about what is happening in them. In the words of Deane Juhan in his great book *Job's Body – A Handbook for Bodywork*, "muscle tissue is anything but insentient. The muscle spindles and the Golgi tendon organs are extremely sensitive monitors, and between the two of them our central nervous system is kept constantly informed about the activities of every individual motor unit…"

This sensory input is experienced unconciously, and is integral to the setting of muscle tone and reflex activity. This is key in understanding the effects of massage therapy and other types of bodywork which help tense muscles to relax.

---

[78] Biceps brachii, the two-headed one of the arm, is the superficial muscle on the anterior side of your upper arm. In fact there is a deeper muscle, brachialis, underneath, which is the prime mover in elbow flexion. Referring to the superficial muscles of the arm, this example holds well and is an easy one to grasp.

I have decided to leave out detailed descriptions of muscles from this book, although I am including pictures of the main superficial muscles. For more details you might try *The Muscle Book* by Paul Blakey for basic information, or the very excellent *Trail Guide to the Body* by Andrew R. Biel and Robin Dorn if you want something with everything in it.

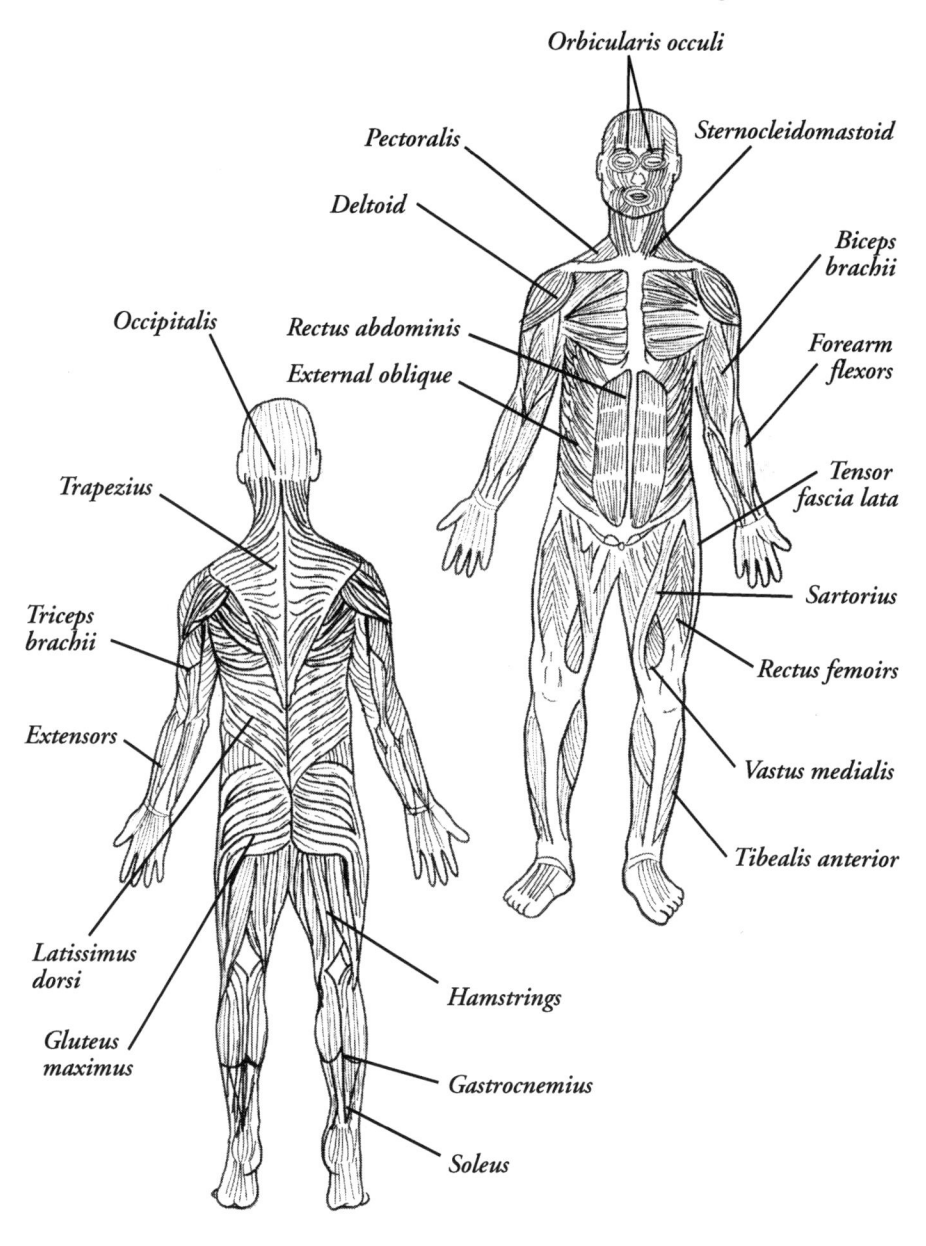

Some of the main superficial muscles back and front of the body

Interrelationships

There is an obvious close relationship between the muscular system and the **skeletal system**. Without the muscles, the bones and joints cannot move. Without the bones, there is nothing for the muscles to attach to and move. Likewise there is also a very close relationship with the **nervous system**, without which the muscles cannot move. The muscular system receives its constant supply of nutrients and oxygen via the **circulatory system**, and movement of skeletal muscles helps venous return and movement of lymph, whilst smooth and cardiac muscles form a significant part of the cardiovascular system. The oxygen needed by muscles comes into the body thanks to the **lungs**, and the nutrients they need come from the **digestive system**. The **liver**, as the 'glucostat' organ, which is involved in control of sugars, has a special relationship due to providing the muscles with glucose. There is also **endocrine** control of glycogen-glucose transformation. In order to contract properly muscles need the level of calcium in the blood to be right. This involves mostly the skeletal, endocrine and gastrointestinal systems.

Chapter Seven

TRANSPORT/THE HEART OF THE MATTER

Circulation and Blood - The Cardiovascular System

We need to be able to carry things all over the body quickly and efficiently: nutrients from food, oxygen and carbon dioxide, waste products, such as urea which ends up in urine, and the body's own endogenous (internal, home produced) chemicals, such as hormones. If there is damage to an area to repair, or building blocks are needed for routine maintenance and growth, then the necessary materials will arrive in the blood. Debris from damaged cells, toxins which have got into the body or waste products created from normal physiological processes, which would be harmful if allowed to build up in the body, are carried in the blood to excretory routes such as the kidney, bowel, skin and lungs.

Without a good transport system, it doesn't take long to get into trouble. Remember the 'fuel crisis' of a few years ago? Within a short space of time all the bread and milk was gone from the shops: how can we get food delivered if there is no transport available? If transport is interrupted, the refuse collectors cannot come and take the rubbish away. Imagine the dirt building up, the smell, and the resulting disease. People cannot get to work, newspapers can't be delivered so you don't know what's going on...a disrupted transport system causes havoc in a very short space of time.[79]

It is like this in our bodies, where the heart and circulation is the system which transports what we need. We touched on this when we looked at joints; hyaline or articular cartilage does not have its own blood supply, therefore it takes a very long to heal when damaged. I suppose it's like living in a city and not being close to a good bus route or train. Citywide travel takes longer, and the properties are cheaper. With very few exceptions, every cell of the body is in reasonable reach of a blood vessel.

There are up to sixty thousand miles of blood vessels[80] in our bodies. These are continually being repaired. We can even grow new ones, and we do so in response to increased

---

[79] A philosophy called **Physicomedicalism** was used by many herbalists in Britain in the nineteenth and twentieth centuries – and is still used by some today. An important part of this system involved diagnosing the state of the circulation and improving it, with herbs to relax over-tense arteries or tone over-relaxed veins, for example. (A.W. Priest and L.R. Priest, *Herbal Medication – A Clinical and Dispensary Handbook*).

[80] Some books put this at twenty thousand miles, but I'm going with Stephen H. Buhner who puts it at sixty thousand in his book *The Secret Teachings of Plants*.

demand. For example, if we go to a high altitude where the air is thin it is harder for us to get enough oxygen. One of the ways our amazing bodies adapt to this is by making plenty of extra blood capillaries and sending more blood around our bodies. This begins to happen pretty much straight away, as soon as the demand is felt.

As well as the sixty thousand miles of blood vessels, the cardiovascular system, or 'CVS', consists of what is usually described as a hollow, muscular, double pump: the heart. The heart has two sides, each one transiting blood into a different circulation. The right side of the heart receives deoxygenated blood from all over the body and sends this 'blue'[81] blood to the lungs, where it drops off its carbon dioxide and picks up oxygen. The blood, now bright red, returns to the heart in the veins, this time entering the left side. The left heart pumps the blood into a huge **artery** called the aorta, and branches from this artery take blood all over the body, supplying the oxygen needs of every cell. The arteries divide and divide, getting smaller each time. Small arteries are known as **arterioles**. Tiny arterioles end and open out into a network of microscopic vessels, called **capillaries**. These are made basically of a layer of epithelial tissue one cell thick; so allow in small substances (like water, gases, sugars, amino acids and other micro-nutrients) to freely leave and enter. The minute capillaries then join back together as **venules**, which join with others to form larger and larger venules, which join to form **veins**.

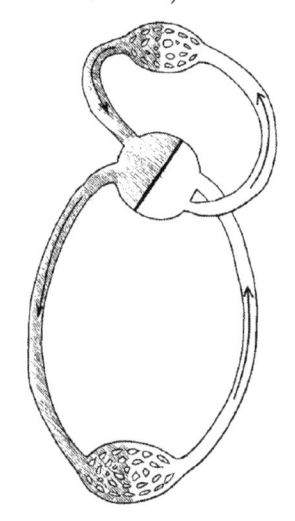

Stephen Buhner describes the system of arteries and veins, arterioles, venules and capillaries as dynamic and vibrant, moving blood along by its own contractions and by a spiraling vortex; a self sustaining movement circling around a vacuum centre, like a tornado, which exists independently of the heart. Apparently, in a chicken embryo the blood can be seen to circulate some time before the heart starts to beat; the heart, when ready, begins to beat in time with the moving blood. The heart monitors the pressure and movements in the circulating blood through sensitive receptors in itself and within the vessels, and adjusts its beating accordingly. The heart stabilizes the blood flow and makes pressure waves which move all the way along the blood vessels.[82]

Arteries take blood coming from the heart ('art the heart'[83]) at high pressure, expand with the resulting increased pressure, then shrink back to encourage the movement of blood. Their anatomy reflects this: they are very strong and their walls are

---

[81] Actually, deoxygenated blood is still red, just not as bright red as blood with oxygen in it. However the convention of colouring it blue in diagrams makes life a whole lot easier. Veins may look blue from the outside, but that isn't because the blood is; if you chop someone up (don't try this at home!) not even the veins are blue they just look blue through the skin. Largely this is due to the optical properties of skin which make the dark red deoxygenated blood look blue.

[82] Stephen Buhner *The Secret Teachings of Plants – The Heart as an Organ of Perception in the Direct Experience of Nature.*

[83] And veins show the 'vay-in' (thanks to Darien Pritchard of MTI for this one!)

rich in elastic tissue. Their inner lining is special epithelial tissue, one cell thick, known as **endothelium**. They have a middle layer of muscle, with elastic fibres, and an outer tunic of supporting connective tissue. The inner endothelial lining must be kept in pristine condition to provide a completely smooth surface for the blood to flow along. Any roughness to the vessel wall will initiate a clotting response. When fatty deposits build up in the walls of arteries it creates roughness and therefore increases the chances of forming a dangerous clot. Like all epithelial tissue, the endothelial lining of the blood vessels is continually renewed and replaced. One of the things our bodies use for this is **flavonoids**, found in many fruits and vegetables, especially red coloured ones – including grapes, bilberries and blueberries amongst others. Flavonoids are known to be anti-inflammatory and protective against clot formation. They are probably used for repairing vessels; they prevent fat deposits from building up in the arteries of people with high cholesterol, and help to maintain good health of the veins.[84] Flavonoids have many other benefits – too many to list here.

It is proven that eating plenty of fruit and vegetables daily leads to significantly reduced risk of stroke.[85] This is probably in part due to their flavonoids and in part due to their **vitamin C** content as well as to their many other constituents. There is some very interesting research connecting low levels of heart disease with vitamin C; we need vitamin C to make **collagen**, so vitamin C is essential for the proper repair and maintenance of our arteries, as well as any other tissue that contains collagen. (Collagen is found in the skin, bones, teeth, gums, tendons and ligaments, as well as giving strength and elasticity to the blood vessel walls. Even the plasma of the blood is a form of collagen – it is more or less everywhere).

Damage to the inner lining is what initiates the laying down of fatty deposits – called plaques – on the artery walls. This is the condition known as **atheroma** and is a major cause of high blood pressure, heart disease, and therefore death in the Western world. Conventional wisdom has it that having too much **cholesterol** in the arteries kind of clogs up the vessels; hence the now enormously widespread use of **statins**, drugs which lower blood cholesterol. But if it were simply a case of this, why is it the large vessels near the heart which clog up with fat, not the smaller ones? This is why: it is the large vessels near the heart which get the most wear and tear, therefore are the most in need of repair. The body is more than capable of carrying out this repair efficiently; it is an expected part of our normal functioning. However, our ability to repair blood vessels relies on us being able to make as much collagen as we need. If we cannot make good quality collagen, it looks like the body tries to repair itself with fat instead.[86]

---

[84] Mills and Bone *Principles and Practice of Phytotherapy.*

[85] An intake of 5-9 servings of vegetables and fruits daily is associated with benefit, and the public should aim toward the higher intakes. American Journal of Medicine, January 2008.

[86] This is the theory of Linus Pauling, a doctor who has been researching and working in this field for decades, and his associate Matthias Rath, M.D. The Pauling therapy for atheroma, or fatty deposits in the arteries, is to take large doses of two substances: vitamin C and lysine.

We humans are the only animals apart from guinea pigs that cannot make our own vitamin C – we must eat it daily to meet our needs. Vitamin C is highest in very fresh fruits and vegetables; if you boil your veg and don't drink the water, you won't be getting the vitamin C, but throwing it away with the water. We need a very large amount of vitamin C daily. The **recommended daily amount**, or **RDA**, is absurdly low at 70mg. If you don't have this much you develop the symptoms of scurvy within a few months and die soon after. Many people today have low blood levels of vitamin C.[87] There is research that shows that people who supplement their diets with high levels of vitamin C have significantly less risk of stroke; those with the highest blood levels of vitamin C were found over nine years to be 42% less likely to have a stroke.[88] [89]

Why, you might wonder, is vitamin C not the preferred treatment to prevent heart disease over statins? If you consider that the pharmaceutical companies, which are the richest companies in the world (they own the oil companies), put up most of the money for research, and combine this fact with the fact that vitamin C is not patentable and is very cheap to make, you can draw your own conclusions. Or is this an unfairly cynical view? Actually it doesn't do your heart any good to get too wound up about this; on the subject of heart disease, one free and fun thing you can do to help yourself is to laugh; one study found that the blood supply to the heart is increased by an average of 22% after a good laugh! More on this below.

The walls of the arteries and blood pressure

The arteries have a middle layer of smooth muscle tissue, which is thick and strong, and contains elastic fibres. An artery will retain its shape when cut. The elastic fibres allow it to be stretched when a new lot of blood enters it with each heart beat, then to recoil again, which helps to keep the blood moving along. As we age, particularly if we have poor eating habits, smoke and lead a sedentary lifestyle, the vessels lose this elasticity and become hard. You can understand how, without this elasticity, the blood pressure goes up: the artery cannot stretch as the new blood enters it with the heartbeat, so the pressure rises. The heart muscle must then work harder to pump blood into the arteries against the increased pressure and so becomes overworked. This is how high blood pressure leads to heart disease. Since one third

---

[87] A 2004 study in America found that vitamin C depletion and rank deficiency is actually widespread, affecting one person in 3. Vitamin C Deficiency and Depletion in the United States: The Third National Health and Nutrition Examination Survey, 1988 to 1994 Jeffrey S Hampl, PhD, RD, Christopher A. Taylor, PhD, RD, and Carol S. Johnston, PhD.RD Jeffrey S Hampl and Carol S. Johnston are with the Department of Nutrition, Arizona State University, Mesa. Christopher A. Taylor is with the Department of Nutritional Science, Oklahoma State University, Stillwater.

[88] American Journal of Medicine, January 2008.

[89] B vitamins (especially B6, B12 and folic acid) may also significantly reduce vascular disease, due to their lowering of blood **homocysteine**. Homocysteine is an amino acid found in the blood acquired mostly from eating meat. It is considered a heart disease risk. See *Health Defense* by Dr Paul Clayton.

of all people in the UK will die from cardiovascular disease, keeping this system in good shape is obviously important if you want a long and full life.

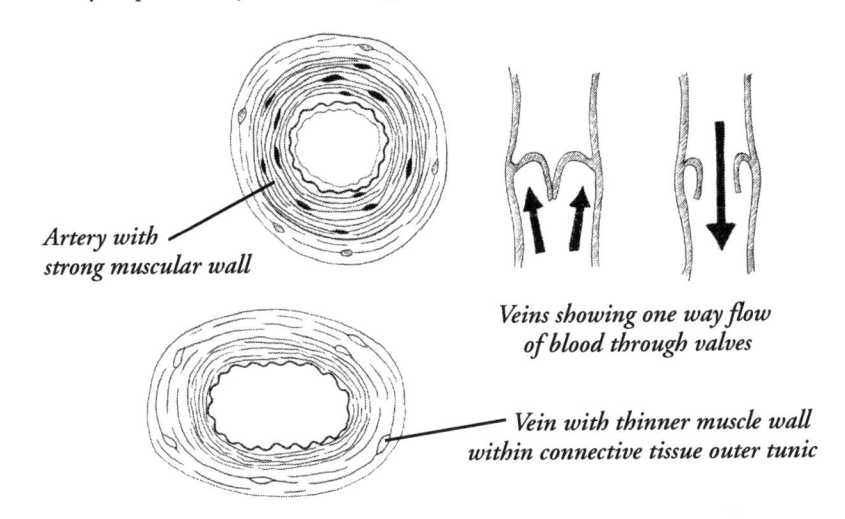

Artery with strong muscular wall

Veins showing one way flow of blood through valves

Vein with thinner muscle wall within connective tissue outer tunic

As the arteries branch they become arterioles, then capillaries

Small arteries are called **arterioles**. From the smallest arterioles, capillary beds emerge. **Capillaries** are the smallest of all the blood vessels. They have lost the two outer layers of the arteries, being made simply of a layer of **endothelium** – flat epithelial cells. Capillaries are the only part of the circulation where things can get out of the blood stream and into the tissue fluid, and therefore into the cells. Most cells in a capillary wall are pretty tightly joined together. There is just a small gap at the junctions between cells to allow some water and solutes to enter and leave. These gaps get bigger when the capillary dilates, making it more permeable. Some capillaries are more permeable, and have actual pores in their walls. These are found in the gut, where the capillaries receive absorbed nutrients, and the kidney, which is continually filtering the blood. Then there are capillaries called 'sinusoids' in places like the liver – these are particularly leaky, allowing the liver cells free access to all the contents of the blood.

Blood flow into capillary beds can be controlled; the arteriole entering a particular capillary network can shut off the blood supply by contracting a smooth muscle sphincter at the entrance. Thus we can route blood here or there in the body as needed. Blood flow throughout the entire body is also regulated. For example, after eating it's not uncommon to feel sleepy as the blood is routed to your guts and therefore away from your head. When we exercise, blood is routed to the skeletal muscles. This is why it's not such a good idea to exercise right after eating – the muscles have less access to good oxygen containing blood, so cramping is more likely (if you are swimming and you get cramp, the worse case scenario is you could drown). This kind of overall control is mostly mediated by the nervous and endocrine systems working together. There are also local control mechanisms.

Venules and veins

Just as capillaries branch out from arterioles, so they later converge and join up to form venules. Venules are the smallest of the veins. They have a different structure to arterioles because the pressure in them is much lower – the blood pressure gets kind of used up in the capillaries, so that venous pressure is next to nothing. The walls of venules and veins, whilst having the same three layers as the arteries, are much thinner; the middle muscle layer is smaller. Veins also have an ingenious adaptation; they are equipped with **one-way valves**, which open to allow blood to move through towards the heart, then close if the blood tries to go the wrong way. The blood is carried through the venules and veins to return to the heart.

This **venous return** depends on the blood entering into the venules from capillary beds and pushing the blood in front of it along, plus a kind of suction at the other end as blood enters the chest cavity on route to the heart. As we breathe, the pressure changes in the chest help to move the venous blood into the heart – one way in which deep breathing is cleansing. Venous blood is also helped to move by the contraction of skeletal muscles. The deep veins are surrounded by muscles, and as these muscles contract they push on the veins. The valves allow the blood to move in one direction only – towards the heart. So exercise, physical movement, is important for keeping the venous return going. People in jobs that involve a lot of standing but not much walking are most prone to getting venous problems like **varicose veins** (caused by incompetent valves). Standing still for long periods means there is no muscle movement in the calves and legs to help venous return, so the movement of blood slows down. When blood pools in the veins, due to standing in one spot for instance, it puts more pressure on the thin-walled veins. If the veins are in poor shape this can stretch the walls and cause the valves to become incompetent. Familial tendencies and habits issues such as poor nutrition, smoking and sedentary lifestyle are contributing factors to this condition. Like arteries, veins need to be repaired and kept in good shape. For this, the body needs plenty of vitamin C to keep collagen production going. There are also many plant medicines that help the health of the veins, perhaps the best British one is the much-loved conker[90] and bark of the horse chestnut tree. This is a wonderful internal and external remedy for the veins.[91]

---

[90] Not the spiky case of the conker, which is poisonous, but the nut you find inside (and use to hang on a string for conker battles).

[91] Mills and Bone, *Principles and Practice of Phytotherapy*.

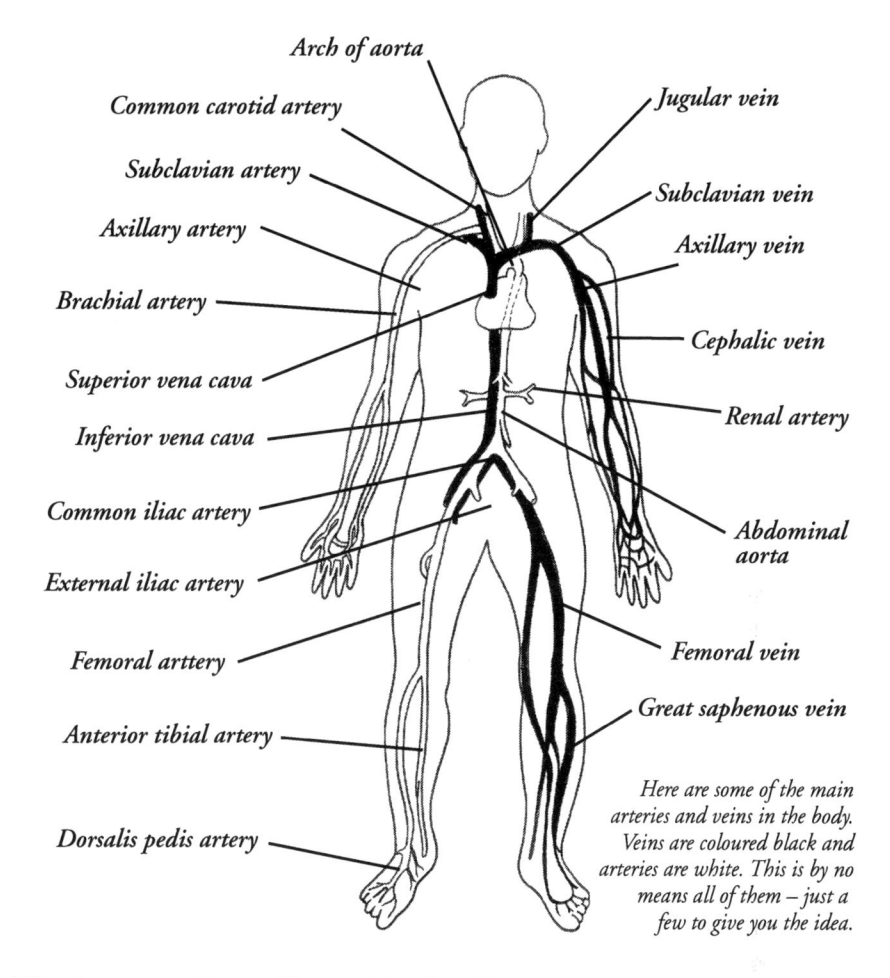

Arch of aorta
Common carotid artery
Subclavian artery
Axillary artery
Brachial artery
Superior vena cava
Inferior vena cava
Common iliac artery
External iliac artery
Femoral arttery
Anterior tibial artery
Dorsalis pedis artery

Jugular vein
Subclavian vein
Axillary vein
Cephalic vein
Renal artery
Abdominal aorta
Femoral vein
Great saphenous vein

Here are some of the main arteries and veins in the body. Veins are coloured black and arteries are white. This is by no means all of them – just a few to give you the idea.

The Supreme Controller - AKA the Heart

Found in the chest, between the lungs, being about the size of your fist, the heart is usually described as a hollow muscular organ comprising four chambers, being completely separate on the left and right sides.

When the anatomy of the heart was first being mapped and it was found that the heart is divided into two, this caused outrage amongst some physicians – to say that the heart was divided was heresy. It was a fork in the road, between the traditional 'vital forces' view and the emerging 'body-as-machine' paradigm.[92] In the past, the British system of medicine, in common with Chinese and Indian systems, saw the heart as the 'Supreme Controller'; the place of One-ness, the place of Self, or God within; the place where we connect with the

---

[92] Graeme Tobin's *Culpepper's Medicine – A Practice of Western Holistic Medicine* discusses this in its introduction.

Divine. Such a place can only be whole, never divided. It's a mistake to see the upset of these healers – which included the famous herbalist Culpepper – as evidence of their holding a primitive and ignorant view. Perhaps they could foresee the terrible division of heart and mind that the worst excesses of Western science displays, with its resulting disconnection of people from self, from each other, from rational treatment of the planet which sustains us, from Source.

Interestingly, new work on cellular memories, in particular with regard to the heart, is emerging. It seems that sometimes when a person receives the heart of a donor, they acquire some of the feelings, memories and tastes of that donor (beginning to crave beer or Fried Chicken, for example). In one case the circumstances of the violent death of the donor were played on the memory screen of the recipient, as well as other cases where names of the donor and their family were remembered.[93] It seems that the heart is indeed much more than a 'hollow muscular pump'…more on this later.

Having said that, the textbook definition of the heart is as a hollow muscular pump, completely divided into two halves by a muscular wall known as the **septum**. Each side is further divided into two by a one way **valve**, leading from the smaller entrance halls – the right and left **atria** – to the larger and stronger **ventricles**. The valves are cusped, and the cusps are anchored to the wall of the heart by tough strings (those strings that can famously be pulled on by love perhaps?). Large veins enter the atria: on the right, the **inferior vena** cava brings deoxygenated blood to the heart from the lower part of the body, and the **superior vena cava** does the same for the head and upper body.

The blood is pumped into the right ventricle by the first part of the heartbeat or contraction – known as **atrial systole**. Immediately after this, the ventricle contracts – **ventricular systole** – and the blood enters the **pulmonary artery**. This leaves the right ventricle and straight away divides into a left and right branch, taking blood to the lungs. After this, the heart relaxes as it fills with more blood during **complete cardiac diastole**. In the **pulmonary capillaries** the blood lets go of its carbon dioxide and collects oxygen, then this now oxygenated blood returns to the left side of the heart. Four **pulmonary veins** enter the left atrium, two from the right and two from the left. This oxygenated blood is pumped into the left ventricle by atrial systole (at the same time as blood is pumped from the right atria and the right ventricle), and from the left ventricle into the largest artery in the body, the **aorta**.

The aorta and its branches carry oxygenated blood to every cell of the body. The blood spirals through the body making a kind of symbolic figure of eight (the infinity symbol) with the heart at the center.[94] Actually, the blood vessels expand and contract as the blood passes through them, and without this pulse wave the blood could not travel through the circulatory system; however efficient the heart is, without the blood having its own momentum and

---

[93] Paul Pearsall *The Heart's Code: Tapping the Wisdom and Power of our Heart's Energy: The New Findings About Cellular Memories and Their Role in the Mind/Body/Spirit Connection.*
[94] This is poetic licence. It isn't, strictly speaking, a figure of eight…

being helped along by the arteries and veins, the heart would not be strong enough to force blood all the way along. As I said earlier, through studying chicken embryos scientists have learnt that in fact the blood begins to circulate even before the heart develops, making a figure of eight and traveling along like a vortex, a hurricane, through the vessels. When the heart forms it begins to beat in time with this movement.[95]

The right side of the heart contains blood without oxygen and the left side carries blood with oxygen. These two sides must be kept separate, otherwise deoxygenated blood gets into the left ventricle and is pumped round the body, this happens when there is a 'hole in the heart'. This is inefficient and can mean that not enough oxygen is available to the cells of the body, causing tiredness, fatigue and blueness. A developing foetus does not rely on its own breathing for oxygen, instead receiving oxygenated blood from mum via the placenta. Our heart is present and beating from a few weeks after conception but the septum is not fully formed, and in fact does not become so until quite late on in the pregnancy. Sometimes there is still a hole in the septum when a person is born – the baby may be blue. However, it can happen that a small hole will close over as the septum continues to grow and form after birth. With medium and large holes, more blood crosses the septum and the hole does not close on its own. Then the baby needs an operation to close the hole.

The entire heart is enclosed in a protective connective tissue sac called the **pericardium**. The outer layer of pericardium is loose-fitting, tough and fibrous, and is attached to surrounding tissues – the diaphragm below and the great blood vessels above. Inside this is a 'serous' membrane, the top layer being attached to the fibrous pericardium, and the deeper layer to the heart muscle. Between these two layers is found slippery serous fluid, which allows the membranes to smoothly glide over each other as the heart beats.[96] The pericardium protects the heart and anchors it in position in the chest.

Our heart is amazing. It starts to beat, as we have said, within weeks of conception, and continues to beat, on and on, until the time of our death. The only rest the cardiac muscle gets is a fraction of a second between each heartbeat. The heart muscle is highly specialized to allow it to work like this. It also has another amazing modification: it has an 'intrinsic' rhythm. A collection of special cells in the right atrium, known as the sino-atrial node, or colloquially as the 'pacemaker', continually and regularly initiates contraction. The contraction spreads out from here to the left atrium, and the two atria contract together. The contraction is then relayed to the ventricles and a moment later these contract. This happens over and over throughout life. The cells in the heart want to beat in concert – one cell alone doesn't quite know what to do, but two cells or more will keep a regular beat, and beat in time with each other.[97]

---

[95] Stephen H. Buhner *The Secret Teachings of Plants*.

[96] As you may recall, serous membranes contain a layer of epithelial cells resting on a loose connective tissue base. The epithelial cells secrete the fluid. They are found in the heart (the pericardium), the lungs (the pleura) and the guts (the peritoneum).

[97] Stephen Buhner *The Secret Teachings of Plants*.

Anterior Vena Cava   *Innominate*   *Aorta*   *Pulmonary Arteries*

Pulmonary Veins

Opening from Vena Cava

Opening to Pulmonary Vein

Right Atrium   *Left Atrium*

Bicuspid Valve

Semilunar Valve

Opening to Aorta

Tricuspid Valve

Chordae Tendinae

Right Ventricle   *Left Ventricle*

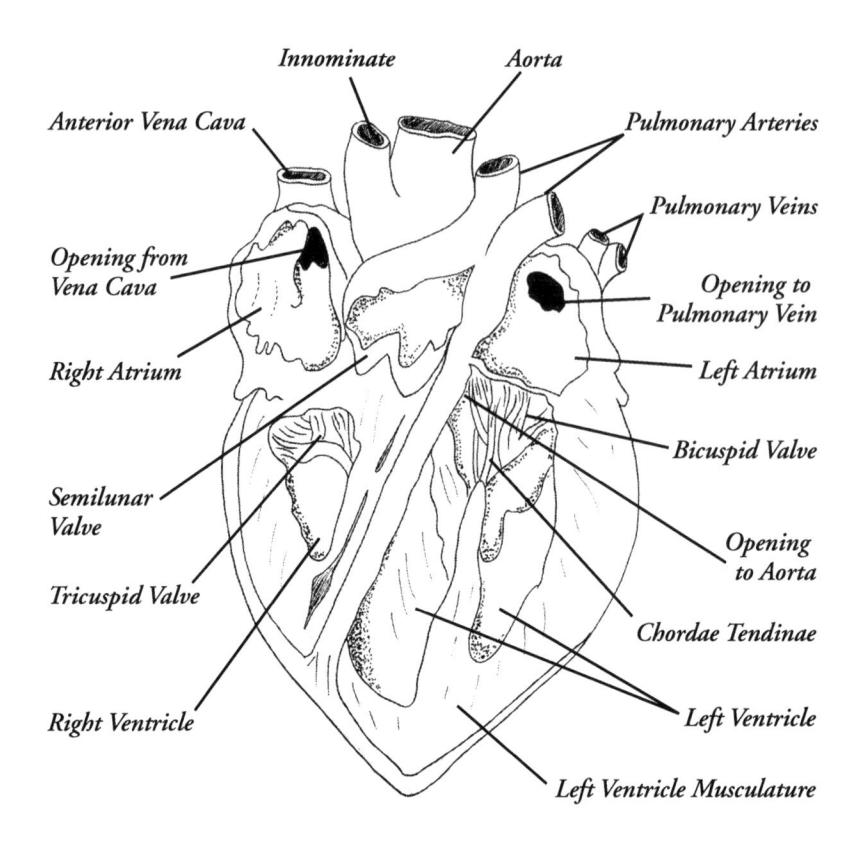

Left Ventricle Musculature

If you took a heart out of a body and put it in a bowl full of sugared and oxygenated water, (yuck…), it would continue to beat even though completely separated from the body. In fact, the intrinsic beat of the heart is faster than our normal resting heartbeat; nerves come from the central nervous system and tell it to either speed up (sympathetic nerves), or slow down (parasympathetic nerves). Sometimes people have an artificial pacemaker fitted; this is a small machine that regularly emits an electrical pulse to initiate heart contraction. You can feel the pacemaker just under the skin, kind of the shape and size of a largish watch face.

In classical Chinese medicine, the Heart Official was called the Emperor, or the **Supreme Controller**. Her/his role is to sit in the temple, in prayerful contemplation and connection with the Divine, to steer our lives in accordance with Divine Will. Our lives have a purpose, which we follow as part of the Divine plan, and it is the Supreme Controller, our heart, which keeps us on track. (You can think of him or her as being a bit like Captain Kirk, or Jean Luc Picard, in charge of all the exciting and important missions of the Enterprise). You may be as delighted as I am to learn that recent research actually backs up this view: As well as the cellular memory already mentioned, it seems the heart acts as the 'largest brain in the body'.

From 'The Intention Experiment' by Lynne McTaggart;[98]

'McCraty discovered that (these) forebodings of good and bad news were felt in both the heart and the brain, whose electromagnetic waves would speed up or slow down just before a disturbing or tranquil picture was shown *(at random to people in experiment)*...most astonishing of all, the heart appeared to receive this information moments before the brain did. This suggested that the body has certain perceptual apparatus that enables it continually to scan and intuit the future, but that the heart may contain the largest antenna. After the heart receives this information, it conveys it to the brain. McCraty's conclusion – that the heart is the largest 'brain' of the body – has now gained credibility after research findings by Dr John Andrew Armour at the University of Montreal and the Hospital du Sacre-Coeur in Montreal. Armour discovered neurotransmitters in the heart that signal and influence aspects of higher thought in the brain.'

Spiritual traditions the world over describe this by saying it's not the brain (the ego) which is making the decisions; we are moved by Spirit; Consciousness, All-That-Is, God, before the brain gets a look in. In truth the heart is so much more than a mechanical pump. It is an endocrine gland in its own right, producing at least five important hormones (so far discovered). Hormones from the heart include **atrial naturetic factor** (or peptide) known as **ANF**, and **brain naturetic factor** (or peptide) known as **BNF**, which are made in the ventricles. BNF is activated when we are under stress, leading to protection of the brain from damaging stress chemicals. ANF release is linked to blood pressure. It is a hormone which affects the blood vessels, lymphatic system, brain, kidneys, adrenal glands, pituitary gland, pineal gland, lungs, liver, eyes and small intestine, as well as reproductive function – in other words, pretty much everything. In addition to this endocrine function and heart-brain aspect, the heart is central in generating the electromagnetic field around our bodies, which allows not only communication within the body, but with all other electromagnetic fields outside.[99]

More about Capillaries

This seems a good place to take a closer look at the tube stations themselves in our underground map of the circulatory system; the capillary beds where fluid, full of nutrients, *leaves* the circulation, and fluid and waste products *enter*.

Imagine a wave coming up on the beach. Picture it whoosh up the sand, linger a moment, then retreat back into the sea. It takes with it all sorts of bits of debris: sand, pebbles, driftwood, seaweed. What happens in our tissues, where the capillaries meet the cells, is a bit like this. (Well, all right. Not much like this, but be honest, you enjoyed thinking about the sea for a moment didn't you...).

As the heart beats, a pulse wave travels along the arteries, pushing the blood along with it. As this wave of fresh blood enters the capillary bed the pressure in the vessels forces a wave

---

[98] Printed here with kind permission thanks to Lynne McTaggart *The Intention Experiment*.
[99] Stephen Buhner *The Secret Teachings of Plants*.

of water and small solutes (those that are small enough to pass through the pores of the capillary) to leave the blood circulation and enter what is called the **interstitial space**, which is always filled with fluid.[100] Large things, like the rigid red blood cells and the big, globular **plasma proteins** (which include albumin), must stay in the capillary as they are too big to fit through the pores between the cells. Oxygen, glucose, amino acids, fatty acids, vitamins, minerals, hormones and so on can all freely leave. Also, white blood cells can leave; although they are big, they can move like amoebae, and squeeze through a tight space. The tissue fluid surrounds cells, which exchange their waste products for nutrients from it.

Towards the end of the capillary bed, as the capillaries are joining up again, something interesting happens. Because the large plasma proteins stayed in the blood, they exert an **osmotic pressure**[101] on the tissue fluid, which pulls water into the capillaries. With the water comes carbon dioxide and the other waste products of the cell. Interruption of the supply or amount of plasma proteins in the blood can therefore cause oedema (water retention) in the interstitial spaces. For example, a kidney disease, which means the kidneys are allowing protein to leave the blood, or starvation which means a lack of protein is available, means that water will stay in the tissues and not get pulled back into the blood.

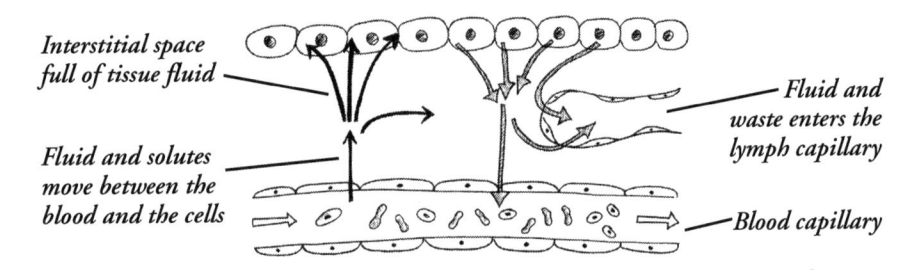

Interstitial space full of tissue fluid

Fluid and waste enters the lymph capillary

Fluid and solutes move between the blood and the cells

Blood capillary

Blood Pressure – what is it?

When you get your blood pressure measured, two figures are obtained; these are the **systolic pressure** which is higher and is given first, and the **diastolic pressure** which is lower and noted second.

The systolic pressure is the highest point pressure in the main arteries just after the heart has contracted and pushed more blood into them. The diastolic pressure is the resting pressure or the lowest pressure in the arteries before systole causes it to rise again.

The common way the blood pressure is taken is with a **sphygmomanometer**. An inflatable cuff is put on the arm and pumped up to a pressure greater than the pressure in the arteries. The thorough way of doing this is to first inflate the cuff whilst taking the pulse, until the

---

[100] Interstitial fluid is also sometimes called tissue fluid, or extracellular fluid. It is basically similar to plasma, but without the large plasma proteins such as albumin.

[101] Remember chemistry? Fluids like to be equal in strength. The blood is now 'stronger' when it comes to proteins, so tries to dilute itself by pulling tissue fluid back across the semipermeable membrane of the capillary wall.

pulse disappears. Then go above this about 20-30 mmHg. If a stethoscope is placed over the brachial artery, and the pressure in the cuff slowly let down, when the pressure in the cuff equals the pressure in the artery, some blood can again move through the artery, and this is heard as a pulse – dff, dff, dff…When the pressure in the cuff equals the lowest pressure in the artery, there is no longer any resistance to the blood pumping through, therefore the pulsing sounds cease. The two figures for blood pressure are the place where the pulsing sound started, and the place where it stops. They are measured in mmHg – millimeters of mercury – because old fashioned sphygmomanometers measured the pressure using a column of mercury.

If your blood pressure is high this is usually symptomless, but you might feel a pounding or tightness in your head, or suffer from a headache in the morning (most people have to have extremely high blood pressure to have a headache from it). High blood pressure is now judged to be a systolic over 140 and a diastolic over 90. These figures are getting lower and lower – in the eighties they were 100 plus your age for the systolic and over 100 for the diastolic. There *is* evidence that treating a person with a sustained diastolic pressure of over 105 mmHg with drugs reduces their chance of having a stroke. However for those with mild to moderate hypertension, a study by the Medical Research Council Trial (BMJ 13 July 1985) showed that if 850 people are treated with hypertensive drugs, either diuretic bendrofluazide or beta-blocker propanolol, about one stroke will be prevented in a year.[102] Common side effects for these drugs include gout, diabetes and impotence. Considering this and the yet unknown long term environmental impact of pharmaceutical pollution, the wisdom of the trend to increase the numbers of people on these drugs is questionable.

An interesting complication is that it gets more likely that hypertension is misdiagnosed with advancing age. As the arteries harden, they give more resistance to the cuff and therefore a false high is given. A study in 1985 showed that half of people over 65 showed a blood pressure of average 16 mmHg lower when measured directly in the artery as compared with a sphygmomanometer.[103]

Then there is low blood pressure, which is not acknowledged in conventional medicine in the UK, other than extreme low pressure in response to physiological shock and large loss of blood. In other European countries such as Germany, lower than normal blood pressure is recognized as a problem. The person may experience dizziness and a lack of energy and ability to concentrate. People may suffer from this if they have low adrenaline output, or inappropriate salt loss, for example.

---

[102] A huge meta-analysis in 2003 showed that none of the expensive modern drugs were any more effective at lowering blood pressure and saving lives than the older diuretics. (Journal of American Medical Association, 2003; 289: 2534- 44).

[103] Research by Dr F.H. Messerli and others from the Ochsner Clinic in Louisiana, published in New England Journal of Medicine 13 June 1985. (Taken from What Doctors Don't Tell You *The Medical Desk Reference*).

Blood

Blood has always had huge significance for people. It is the river of life, a magical liquid containing the life force. In Chinese medicine the Qi (or vital force) is thought to follow the blood in its journey around the body. Even Western orthodox medicine recognizes its importance, studying it more than any other tissue. Blood is considered to be a tissue – the only one in the body which is permanently in fluid form. It is made up of many components. Broadly separated into the liquid part, plasma (which is pretty similar to tissue fluid with the important addition of plasma proteins[104]), and cells. The blood cell types are red cells, white cells and platelets. Red cells carry oxygen; white cells are a cross between the army and the cleaners, and platelets do clotting.

Red cells, or **erythrocytes**, comprise about 45% of the blood volume. This percentage is called the 'haematocrit'. The norm for men is within 5% of 47%; for women 5% more or less than 42%. Red blood cells are small biconcave flattened discs – they look like doughnuts under the microscope. They are made in the red bone marrow (like all blood cells), but by the time they are mature and released into the blood their nucleus has degenerated and completely disappeared. Their shape is maintained by special internal protein structures, which makes them flexible enough to squeeze through small capillaries, always returning to their doughnut shape. As they age, they lose this flexibility, (a common complaint!), and after about one hundred and twenty days they pop when passing through a small vessel. They contain haemoglobin, and very little else. Haemoglobin is a globular protein bound to four molecules of a red pigment, called 'haem'. Each ring-shaped haem carries an atom of iron set in its centre like a jewel. It is these iron molecules that like to bind, reversibly, to oxygen. There are about 250 million haemoglobin molecules in just one red blood cell, so each one can carry around a billion oxygen molecules.

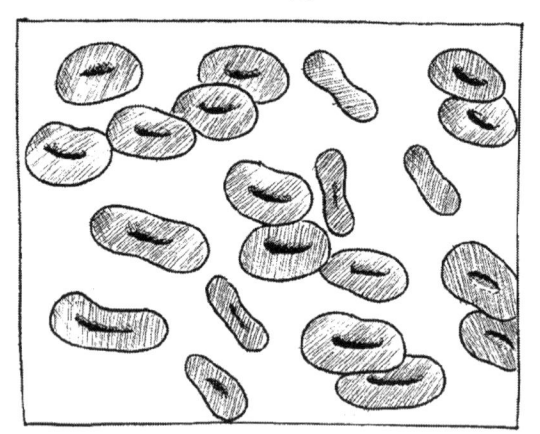

In the lungs, the blood in the pulmonary capillaries is deoxygenated before it reaches contact with the air sacs, or alveoli. As soon as oxygen diffuses into the blood from the lungs, the 'deoxyhaemoglobin' grabs it. The blood becomes ruby red. In the tissues, which are asking for oxygen, the process is reversed and oxyhaeomoglobin gives up its oxygen molecules, giving it more a purple-

---

[104] Plasma proteins are made in the liver. The most famous is albumin – the same as egg white.

red colour. Carbon dioxide is transported mainly freely in the blood, although some of it hitches a ride with the globin part of haemoglobin.

The body keeps the number of red blood cells amazingly constant. A hormone (known as erythropoietin) stimulates their development, and this is made mainly in the kidneys (a little in the liver). More of the hormone is released when available oxygen in the kidney tissues decreases. Thus low tissue oxygen stimulates the kidneys, which in turn stimulate the bone marrow.[105] Because of this mechanism people whose kidneys have failed cannot make enough red blood cells for demand, resulting in anaemia.

Anaemia

Anaemia is one of the most common conditions causing tiredness. It is a condition in which there is an abnormally low oxygen-carrying capacity in the blood. Having too few red blood cells, cells with too little haemoglobin in, or cells that are not working properly, can cause it. When you are anaemic, you feel tired, breathless, and dizzy, look pale and may be cold. If you feel your energy levels are lower than normal, or lower than they should be, suspect iron deficiency anaemia, as it is very common.

Iron is lost from the body in faeces, urine and sweat – 0.9mg daily in men, and 1.7mg in women (the extra being due to menstruation). So a woman's daily iron requirement is nearly double that of a man.

As well as iron, vitamin B12 is needed to make haemoglobin. Vegetarians need to be particularly aware of this (animal flesh is full of B12, so it is not usually an issue for meat eaters). A favourite way to get it is from yeast extract (Marmite).

There are types of anaemia that are genetic in origin and result in poorly formed red blood cells – one example is 'sickle cell' disease. The cells are sickle shaped instead of round, and are less robust, they break more easily. This disease is more common in Africa and in places where malaria is common. The sickle cell gene gives protection against malaria – the Goddess figuring out a solution to the malaria problem, perhaps? Not fully finished yet, but who knows in time…[106]

White blood cells, or **leucocytes**, are the only things in the blood that still look like normal cells, having a nucleus and all the usual organelles. They are less than 1% of the blood volume. (The white blood count is usually between 4,800-10,800 per mm³ [cubic millimetre] of blood). White blood cells are the defenders and the cleaner-uppers. They defend us against foreign invaders like bacteria, viruses and parasites. They clean up toxins and dead or diseased tissues – including cancerous cells. They can move like amoebas and get out of the capillaries into the tissue fluid. We will look at these interesting white blood cells in more detail in the chapter on the immune system.

---

[105] Interestingly, Chinese medicine has said for thousands of years that the bones come under the jurisdiction of the Kidney Official.
[106] Thanks to Diane E. Bates for this one.

Platelets, or **thrombocytes**, are not really cells though they are classed as part of the cellular component of blood. They are fragments of a very large cell called a **megakaryocyte.** They are basically a bag of chemicals involved in blood clotting. They can become very sticky, plugging up a hole in a damaged vessel wall. They circulate freely but are usually inhibited from action by chemicals secreted by the blood vessel endothelial lining cells. Clotting involves a complicated cascade of chemical reactions by proteins and enzymes which normally circulate in the plasma. They are triggered to action by any rupture or lack of smoothness in the blood vessel wall or lining. When there is damage, the vessel spasms to slow blood flow through it, then the platelets get sticky and form a platelet plug, then **coagulation** happens: chemical reactions cause the blood to change from liquid to gel form.

The two things that can go wrong with clotting are bleeding disorders like haemophilia (when the blood cannot clot) on one hand, or clotting disorders (when abnormal clots are formed with potentially fatal results) on the other. If the blood fails to clot, a person can bleed to death even from the most trivial of wounds. If a clot forms abnormally, in a deep vein of the leg, for instance (known as a **DVT**, or **deep vein thrombosis**), some of the clot can break away and travel in the blood stream until it reaches a tiny vessel where it gets stuck. This might happen with dire results in the brain or the lungs. If a clot blocks a blood vessel, all the tissues that depend on that vessel for oxygen die very soon. In the brain this tissue death causes what we call a **stroke**. In the lungs it is known as **pulmonary embolism**.

Blood groups

Like all of our body's cells, the membranes of red blood cells contain marker proteins. Some people's blood will be recognized as foreign by our immune system and some will not, depending on the similarity of our marker proteins. This is translated into what are called 'blood groups'. Generally there are AB, A, B and O, and Rhesus groups. Rhesus negative group O blood has the least proteins.[107] People with blood group A have A *antigens* on the surface of their red blood cells and anti-B *antibodies* in their plasma. People with group B have B antigens in the cells and anti-A antibodies in the plasma. Group O blood has no antigens (so can be given to any group), but has both anti-A and anti-B antibodies, so can only receive group O blood safely. O is the most common blood group in the UK. People with AB blood have A and B antigens in their cells but no antibodies in the plasma, otherwise their blood would destroy itself.

Diet and blood groups

There is an interesting nutritional idea put forward by Peter D'Adamo about blood groups; in a nutshell the theory is that we have evolved from hunter-gatherers; some of us have

---

[107] A friend of mine who has Rh-negative type O blood NEVER gets bitten by midges or mosquitoes – he puts it down to the lack of nutritional proteins available in his blood! Anyone else like this? Let me know!

nomadic herds-people as ancestors, some have agriculturists. D'Adamo's premise is that O group are hunter-gatherers and get on well with meat and veg but not so well with dairy. Group A are the agricultural types and like wheat and grains but are not as good with meat and dairy – a good vegan diet is most suitable for type As. The herdsmen or nomads have group B; they have a digestive system that can tolerate all kinds of foods, being the only group who are completely fine with dairy. Group AB is the most recently evolved group, and in terms of diet, D'Adamo recommends one between A and B. He suggests that the different blood groups react differently to compounds called **lectins** in foods.

Many dieticians, nutritional scientists and doctors say this has no scientific basis and is all hokum. They argue that D'Adamo hypothesizes based on research of various scientists, using these to make his idea, but none of the research completely supports his hypothesis. Also, no clinical trials comparing this to other regimes have been carried out. Apparently D'Adamo has mentioned trials, but not published any results.

My own experience of diets is that in practice there is no one-size-fits-all to find easily. Trial and error are often involved in figuring out a good diet – but it has to be said that a basic whole-food diet with lots of fresh vegetables, fruit, grains, pulses (such as lentils) and fish, with no preservatives, additives or other toxins, goes a long way to improving most people's health. D'Adamo's blood group diet has clearly helped many people,[108] and if it works for you, why not try it – not all useful healing methods have been, or can be, proven in currently understood conventional scientific terms.

Investivating blood

The viscosity of blood is thought to depend largely on the number of red blood cells; too many, and the blood thickens. Conventional blood tests mostly involve looking at blood which is dead – and coloured with dyes which may alter its natural appearance. There is a science of looking at living blood under the microscope, using **darkfield microscopy**, first developed in the early 1900s. This makes it possible to look at living blood and see changes which come about from illness. Interstingly, the 1930s when it was being developed[109] were before the days of processed foods, organophosphate weedkillers, artificial fertilisers, and microwaves. At that time peoples' blood tended to look either well, or ill when they had a disease. Nowadays it is apparently rare to find blood which looks healthy. This could well be a physical way of identifying changes in the physiology which indicate a disease process in the making – making it much easier to treat now instead of waiting until something very serious and nasty has turned up in the tissues. People who have their blood looked at in this way can

---

[108] Whilst there is no clinical research trial showing it to be helpful, there is plenty of anecdotal evidence (completely inadmissible in the view of science, but reasonable to encourage someone to try it out for themselves).

[109] Dr. Gunther Enderlein was one of the first pioneers in this field. www.darkfieldmicroscopy is a good place to start for more information.

be motivated to then go on a good detox programme and clean up their diet and lifestyle; after doing this, the blood is re-examined and looks better.

I find this particularly interesting because it is a very physical way of doing what pulse and tongue diagnosis[110] do – revealing an imbalance even when no **organic disease** can be found by current Western diagnostic tests. Also it is a powerful way to show the surprisingly damaging effects of the modern Western way, full of toxins of all kinds as it is.

Heart Disease

Cardiovascular disease is the number one cause of death in the UK, Ireland and the US, with one in three people dying from it. This includes heart attacks, strokes and heart failure. The medical name for a heart attack, 'myocardial infarction', tells you what happens: part of the myocardium, the heart muscle, dies. This happens due to that part having its oxygen supply cut off, for example by a narrowed vessel which can no longer supply the heart's needs.

As you know, muscular tissue is not easily replaceable, so the heart does not habitually grow new muscle, replacing the dead cells instead with scar tissue. Without a well-functioning heart, we cannot live long. So if a heart attack affects a large area of the heart muscle, or destroys an important area of the heart (say, stopping a valve from working properly), a person may die. A smaller heart attack will often leave the heart weaker and vulnerable to further problems.

Risk factors for heart disease include certain diets and lifestyle repetition, which lead to the arteries being in poor shape – including too much of the wrong sort of fats[111], low essential fatty acid diets, a diet low in fresh vegetables, smoking and alcohol. Anything which raises the blood pressure is a risk – smoking, being overweight, excess salt, stress and stored emotional tension from undischarged emotional pain.[113]

A note about salt

The excessive salt in convenience food is definitely a cause of high blood pressure. Many people are unaware of this fact, especially because the salt industry has been at great pains to suppress and deny it. The tactics over salt are much the same as those used by other sectors of industry.[114] It is not just the fact that there is lots of it in convenience foods – the salt used is

---

[110] Pulse and tongue diagnosis are used in Chinese medicine (as well as other systems) to determine underlying conditions affecting a person's health. Particular characteristics of the pulse or appearances of the tongue reveal particular kinds of problems.

[111] A lot of studies said saturated fats are bad, but these lumped saturated fats in with hydrogentated fats. It turns out that it is hydrogenated fats which are bad, while saturated fats may actually be protective.

[113] Dr Arthur Janov *The New Primal Scream*. More on this in Section Two.

[114] The Sugar Association in the United States and the Sugar Bureau in Britain have waged fierce campaigns against links between sugar and obesity and dental caries. Publication of a report from the World Health Organization on diet and chronic disease was delayed by representations from the sugar industry and 40 ambassadors from sugar producing countries who had been alerted by the industry. *BMJ* 1996;312:1239-1240 (18 May)

also refined salt, which is pure sodium chloride. Natural salt like sea salt is rich in other minerals too. On the other hand, the main problem is eating a highly processed diet which is lacking in vegetables and fruit and full of salt as well as monosodium glutamate and other additives. Salt is essential to the body. If the body is losing it unchecked, it leads to death. If we are eating a natural diet, and not confusing our palate with highly processed artificial flavours, we can more easily trust our instincts to tell us when we need salt or not.

In Finland a salt called Pansalt was developed by Professor Heikki Karppanen of the Institute of Biomedicine, University of Helsinki, to help combat heart disease, and is now used widely in the country – including in McDonald burger buns by order of the government! Pansalt contains low sodium, high magnesium and potassium, with added lysine to make it taste right. It actually leads to a lowering of blood pressure. Since its introduction, along with getting people to eat more vegetables, deaths from heart attacks cardiovascular disease and stroke have fallen by 75% in Finland.[115]

Drug problems

It also seems that the very drugs used to combat heart disease are causing it in a different way, in the US, the number of cases of heart failure are nearly doubled in Detroit because the cholesterol-lowering statin drugs given to everyone at risk of a heart condition not only suppress cholesterol production as they are designed to do (therefore decreasing fatty deposits in the arteries), but also interfere with the production of coenzyme Q10. CoQ10 deficiency causes wasting of the heart muscle, which has led to more heart failure.[116]

Looked at from the classical Chinese Five-Element perspective, most heart attacks are due to the failure of the 'Heart Protector' to do its job. The Heart Protector, called 'the Official in Charge of the Pleasures of the People', protects the vulnerable and sensitive heart by means of ensuring we have lots of good fun and loving connections with others. Science beautifully confirmed this in March 2005, when cardiologist Michael Miller M.D., researching at the University Of Maryland School Of Medicine in Baltimore, showed that laughter is linked to healthy function of blood vessels. Laughter increased the blood flow to the heart by 22% in 95% of people – similar to aerobic exercise. They got people to laugh by watching a funny film, and used ultrasound technology to measure changes in blood flow.[117] Apparently, Dr Miller got the idea to do the research after observing that his heart patients seemed to be a very serious bunch who didn't laugh much! As well as having a good laugh, other things you can do to reduce your risk of heart disease include moderate regular exercise (like walking), losing weight if you are overweight, eating a Mediterranean style diet, making sure you have

---

[115] From Dr Paul Clayton's Spring 2008 newsletter. www.drpaulclayton.com

[116] This was announced by Detroit researchers at the 2004 annual meeting of the American College of Cardiology. Statins can also damage the liver and kidneys and cause pain and wasting in muscle tissue. A CoQ10 deficiency can also come about from betablockers, some antihypertensive drugs and antidiabetic drugs.

[117] Research by University of Maryland Medical Center presented at the Scientific Session of the American College of Cardiology on March 7, 2005, in Orlando, Florida.

plenty of folate and other B vitamins to lower homocysteine, take lots of antioxidant foods - containing vitamins A, C and E - eat less salt and more magnesium, avoid hydrogenated fats and make sure you are not polluted by heavy metals.[118]

Heart fire

In common with many spiritual traditions throughout the world, the Huichol people of North Mexico have a special understanding of the importance of the heart, and the element of fire within the heart. The Huichol people name this force the God Tatewari – Grandfather Fire. The fire of love, connection, laughter, transformation; Tatewari is the force in the universe which holds atoms and planets together, the force responsible for attracting us to each other. He is the originator of jokes, fun and laughter, the keeper of stories. Tatewari's residence within us is the heart.[119]

Interrelationships

Every other system in the body relies on the **cardiovascular system** to bring needed oxygen and nutrients, and to take away carbon dioxide and waste. There is a particularly close relationship with the **respiratory system** for getting the oxygen into the blood and the carbon dioxide out. Also pressure changes in the thorax aid the venous return of blood to the heart. The **lymphatic system** is sometimes seen as a part of the CVS; without it the venous system cannot keep up with fluid drainage. The **immune system** is all about white blood cells. The hormones of the **endocrine system** are carried in the blood, and the circulation and heart function are affected by many hormones – indeed the heart itself makes hormones. It is the blood which carries the products of **digestion**, and brings glucose and oxygen to the **muscles** and all other cells for energy production. Movement of skeletal muscles helps venous return. The **kidney** filters the blood and keeps it clean. Blood cells are made in **bone** marrow, and the blood brings oxygen and nutrients to the **skin**, hair and nails.

---

[118] From *The Medical Desk Reference* Edited by Lynne McTaggart WDDTY 2000).
[119] www.sacredfirecommunity.org to connect with people working with Tatewari.

Chapter Eight

DRAINAGE
THE LYMPHATIC SYSTEM

The lymphatic system is best thought of in two sections: drainage and cleaning up which we will look at in this chapter, and cleaning up and defence, known as immunity, looked at in the following chapter.

Commonly described as an adjunct to the venous system, the drainage part of the lymphatic system consists of a series of one-way tubes that start as tiny capillaries in the tissues and join up to form bigger and bigger vessels. These pass through lymph nodes, which clean and filter the fluid (known as 'lymph'). Eventually, the lymph is emptied into the blood circulation at the subclavian veins (just below the clavicles).

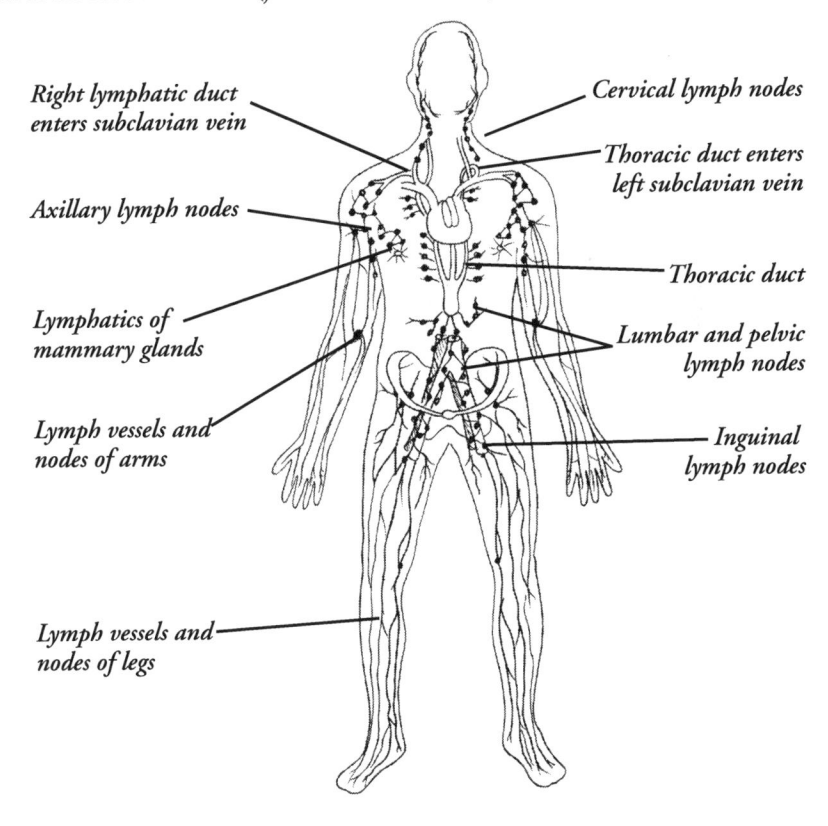

Right lymphatic duct enters subclavian vein

Axillary lymph nodes

Lymphatics of mammary glands

Lymph vessels and nodes of arms

Lymph vessels and nodes of legs

Cervical lymph nodes

Thoracic duct enters left subclavian vein

Thoracic duct

Lumbar and pelvic lymph nodes

Inguinal lymph nodes

The **lymphatic capillaries** are similar to blood capillaries in structure, but are extremely permeable. They open up and allow large amounts of interstitial fluid, containing things that are too big to enter the blood capillaries, to flow into them. Once inside the lymph vessels the fluid is called **lymph**.

Lymph is very similar to tissue fluid. Proteins that are too big to enter the blood capillaries can get into the lymph. Also, if there has been any damage or inflammatory healing processes going on, the lymph capillaries become even more permeable so that debris can enter – pus, damaged or dead cells, bacteria or other 'pathogens' (disease causing organisms), and cancerous cells. Basically the lymphatic system protects the body by making sure the lymph nodes filter out harmful stuff before returning the fluid to the blood.

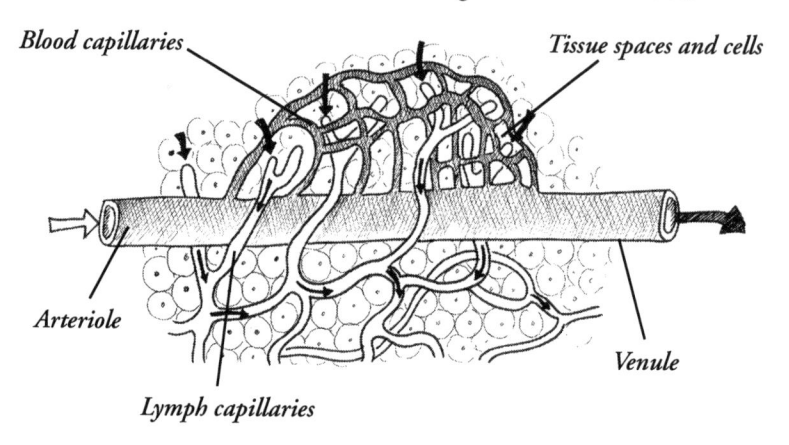

Blood capillaries   *Tissue spaces and cells*

Arteriole   *Venule*

Lymph capillaries

In the digestive system, when you eat fat it gets absorbed not into the blood like other nutrients but into special lymph ducts called **lacteals**, or **lacteal vessels**. This lymph looks milky white. It too enters the bloodstream at the subclavian veins.[120]

Unlike the blood circulation, the lymphatic system does not have a pump. Lymph is moved through the vessels slowly. The main way it moves is by the vessels being squeezed by surrounding muscles – in other words, good old exercise! The vessels have one-way valves like veins which allow flow in one direction only. Pressure changes in the thorax during breathing also help to pump the lymph; here is another cleansing effect of deep breathing. In this way, lymphatic movement is just like venous return, only much slower. Also there is some smooth muscle in the largest vessels which contracts rhythmically to help push the lymph along. In one day, about 3 litres of lymph enters the blood – this is about the same amount of fluid that leaves the blood capillaries in the tissues and does not return.

---

[120] This could be a contributing factor to the higher incidence of cancer amongst meat eaters compared with vegans. Animal foods are high in fat, which will be transported initially via the lymph, making it work harder – therefore potentially it will be overloaded and less able to carry out the general cleaning up process it is charged with. Also, animal foods are high in fat, and it is in our fat that we all store environmental toxins from pollution, so perhaps it is due more to these toxins – so many of which are carcinogenic – than to the fact of eating animals per se. Modern farming methods use a lot of pesticides and pharmaceutical drugs, so the animals most people eat are full of these.

If your lymph vessels get damaged, severe water retention, or **oedema**, occurs in the area normally drained by them. However, your lymph vessels can re-grow from vessels remaining in the area, and thus good drainage can be re-established. There is an interesting therapeutic technique called manual lymphatic drainage:

Manual Lymph Drainage is a therapy in which the practitioner uses a range of specialised and gentle rhythmic pumping techniques to move the skin in the direction of the lymph flow. It was developed during the early 1930s by Dr. Emil Vodder who created a unique range of movements which brought relief from chronic conditions such as sinus congestion and catarrh. Since then MLD has spread world-wide and has become a popular treatment in many European hospitals and clinics. It is now beginning to gain acceptance in the UK as a component in the treatment and control of lymphoedema. Manual lymphatic drainage stimulates the lymphatic vessels which carry substances vital to the defence of the body and removes waste products. MLD is both preventative and remedial and can enhance your well being. It is also deeply relaxing; it promotes the healing of fractures, torn ligaments, sprains and lessens pain and can improve many chronic conditions including sinusitis, rheumatoid arthritis, scleroderma, acne and other skin conditions. MLD may strengthen the immune system. It relieves fluid congestion: swollen ankles, tired puffy eyes and swollen legs due to pregnancy. It is an effective component of the treatment and control of lymphoedema, assists in conditions arising from venous insufficiency and promotes healing of wounds and burns and improves the appearance of old scars and minimises or reduces stretch marks.[121]

There is a particularly important movement for pumping lymph from the feet up the legs; it is the action of going up and down on your toes, as happens when you are walking. Keeping this movement going even if you are unable to walk a lot can very much help the lymphatic drainage in your legs. This is what the Queen's Guards are doing all day inside their uniforms as they stand on duty immobile.

Lymph nodes

When your 'glands are up' in your neck – when you are fighting off an infection like a cold – you can feel them as rubbery lumps either side of your throat. These are not glands in fact, but lymph nodes.

There are hundreds of lymph nodes in the body. They are discrete masses of 'lymphoid tissue' surrounded by a tough connective tissue boundary layer. They are found in clusters in your neck, armpit, groin and behind the knee. They are from a few millimetres to 1-2 centimetres in size in their resting state, but can get very big when they are working to fight an infection. Inside is a network of reticular fibres, a special connective tissue, with many lymphocytes enmeshed amongst them. B and T lymphocytes are found in the cortex (outer

---

[121] Taken with thanks from the website of MLDUK, an organisation of manual lymphatic drainage practitioners: http://www.mlduk.org.uk

layer) and medulla (inner core) of a lymph node. A few lymph vessels enter one side of the node, and one vessel leaves. As the debris-filled lymph enters the node, the white blood cells within it engulf any foreign particles, old bits of cell, bacteria, viruses, cancerous cells and such like. This engulfment (which is called **phagocytosis**) is a large part of the defensive ability of our lymphatic system. After engulfment, the cell will attempt to dissolve or break down the engulfed material into small harmless parts. These can then be released back into the lymph. Sometimes there are non-biodegradable particles engulfed (for instance, heavy metals). These would then be kept in the node, separated from the rest of body inside the lymph cells.

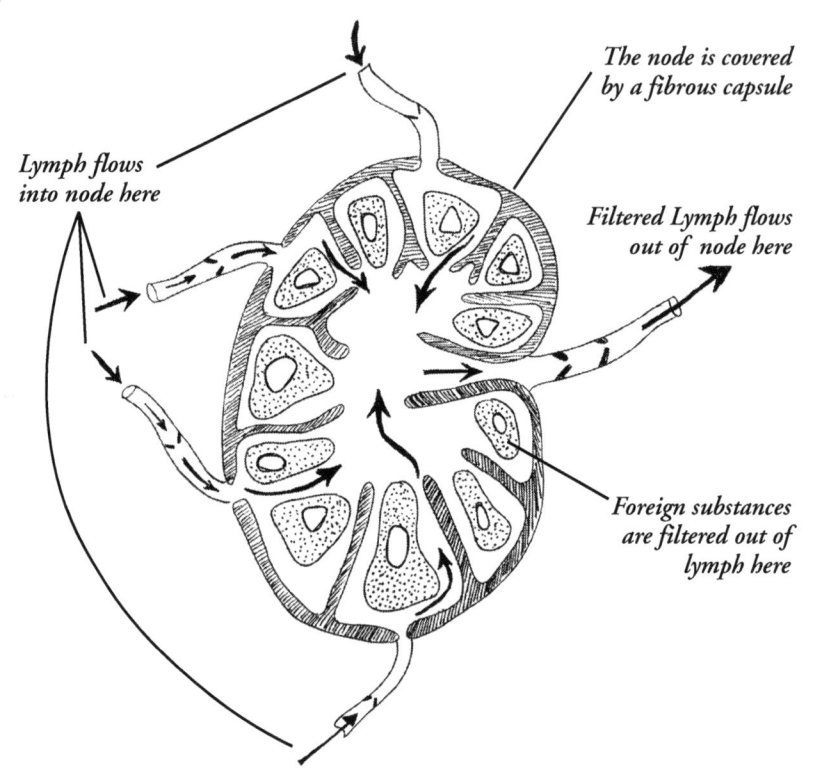

Lymph flows into node here

The node is covered by a fibrous capsule

Filtered Lymph flows out of node here

Foreign substances are filtered out of lymph here

I heard an interesting story about a person with a large tattoo who went to the doctor complaining about a lump in the armpit. They had a very enlarged lymph node, which was biopsied (a little piece removed) to check for cancer. It turned out the node was full of the dye used for the tattoo – the body had decided it was foreign and should be got rid of, but once in the lymph node there was no way the cells could break it down, so they sequestered it there in the node. Our bodies are amazing!

Interrelationships

Interrelationships of the lymphatic system are similar to those of the **cardiovascular** system, to which the **lymphatic drainage system** can be seen as an adjunct. Toxins and excess fluids from cellular processes of **all cells and tissues** in all systems (except the central nervous system) are removed by the lymphatic system. In the **digestive system** there is an extra link as fats are absorbed into the special lymph vessels called lacteals. Fluid moves through the lymph vessels thanks to the contraction of muscles of the **skeletal system**, as well as the changes in pressure in the thorax during **respiration**.

Chapter Nine

THE ARMY AND THE CLEANERS
The Immune System

The general view of the immune system is that it is the body's army, fighting off and keeping out invading hordes of disease-causing organisms (called **pathogens**).

You *can* look at it this way – particularly if your view is that life on Earth is dangerous and we are beset with enemies everywhere we turn. However, there is another approach. The immune system has many functions which can be seen as being more like tidying up and house cleaning than fighting. It *does* protect us from external threat, preventing disease-causing microorganisms from 'invading' us and multiplying too much within us. Also, it protects us from our own cells if they are dead or damaged, or turn cancerous or malignant. Yet if we remember that bacteria are our ancestors, that we have evolved together for billions of years on this planet, and hold the view that we have a safe place in this beautiful, incredible universe, along with all the other life forms we share it with, does this change things? A traditional naturopathic view is that germs are actually the cleansing agents that help us to recover from toxins or other assaults to the body. Their presence stimulates fever and increases the cleaning activities of our immune system. When their work is done, they become permanent parts of the body, in that the body can now keep them under check for optimum health. As Sara Hamo, Israeli naturopath working in the tradition of The Kingston Clinic, Edinburgh, says:

'We get sick when we (our bodies) *invite* germs (the cleansing agents) to come and make order in the polluted body'.[122]

Louis Pasteur is generally revered as being the father of modern microbiology. He was involved in early work on microbiology, though the **Germ Theory of Modern Medicine** was at least one hundred years older than Pasteur, and contemporaries of his were working away on the same lines. Bernard, one particular colleague, fought with Pasteur over the course of their careers about whether it was the germ or the state of the person that caused disease: Bernard argued for terrain; Pasteur for germs. On his deathbed Pasteur's last words were in support of the terrain theory: 'C'est le terrain.'[123] Of course, modern medicine ignored this and carried on with germ theory anyway!

---

[122] Sara Hamo *The Golden Path To Natural Healing*.
[123] You can read all about this on the internet. In July 2008 I accessed it at http://www.mnwelldir.org/docs/history/biographies/louis_pasteur.htm

When one considers what 'the terrain' means, bear in mind it is more than the state of the immune system; it is the condition of health (or lack of it) of our organs and tissues, which is related to many considerations, including diet and lifestyle. A great way to get a cold, for instance, is to be overdoing it and need a rest. Many experiments have shown that we don't get colds by being exposed to them – only 20% of people will actually catch a cold, even when the cold virus is directly painted onto the mucous membranes of their nose. **Rudolph Virchow**, known as the father of pathology, says, 'if I could live my life over again, I would devote it to proving that germs seek their natural habitat – diseased tissue – rather than being the cause of the diseased tissue, in the way that mosquitoes seek the stagnant water, but do not cause the pool to become stagnant.'[124]

There are other alternative ways of looking at the immune system too. For example, the great philosopher Rudolph Steiner suggested that before we are born our spirit chooses the body that will best fit it, then after we are born childhood illnesses help shape it to become more exactly what we need. Certainly, parents will have observed the leaps of development that come after a period of illness in a young one.

Like all the other systems in this book, we are going to considerably simplify the immune system, which really is an amazingly intricate and complicated operation. Although it is considered to be part of the lymphatic system, in fact many body systems are involved in its functioning. Unlike other systems, which have very specific tissues and structures, the immune system is made of billions of cells, and even more molecules, spread throughout the body. In addition to the lymphatic system, big contributors to immunity are the heart and circulation, the skin, lungs, kidney, gut, nervous and endocrine systems…yes, just about everything!

There are considered to be two main types of immunity: **non-specific**, or **simple immunity**, which is a generalized defence, and **specific**, or **acquired immunity**, which is a more specialised form of defence.

Non-specific immunity

There are mechanisms in the body that will clean up any irritant or abnormal substance that threatens the internal environment. This is a general protection, and includes mechanical barriers such as the skin and the mucous membranes, chemical barriers such as the hydrochloric acid in the stomach, phagocytosis by white blood cells, and generalized mechanisms like fever.

The skin is a vital barrier in the front line against infection. As well as being a straightforward physical barrier to many outside organisms and materials, the skin cells (specifically, the **keratinocytes**) make **interferons**, which are proteins that block viral infection.

Other cells in the skin, called **Langerhans cells**, interact with pathogens that have

---

[124] Dr Robert O. Young *Sick and Tired – Reclaim Your Inner Terrain.*

managed to get through the outer layer of the epidermis. The Langerhans cells then take these pathogens to nearby lymph organs and help to initiate an immune response, called a **messenger function**. This response is disrupted by even the mildest of sunburns – UV radiation disables the cells which take the pathogens to the lymph tissue. This is probably why exposure to the sun can bring out a cold sore in people who tend to get them.[125]

Mucous membranes also provide an actual barrier when intact. Those in the gut and respiratory systems can produce copious amounts of mucous which washes away debris, and also is sticky, so (for example in the nose) inhaled dust can stick to it. The mucous dries out, and the debris-filled 'bogeys' can be removed from the body (with a conveniently sized finger…!). Have you ever been traveling in London or another big city or do you live there? After a few days there you can find most interesting black bogeys coming from your nose. Great! That's a load of dirt that *didn't* get into your lungs.

Mucous is thus primarily a way for the body to be rid of toxins or unwanted visitors. It is a gel, so becomes more runny and watery when heated.[126] When we have a fever, therefore, our mucous runs freely, washing away micro-organisms and their toxins, as well as internally produced toxins, from the body. Unfortunately, the modern practice is to take antipyretics[127] like paracetamol (acetaminophen in the US) at the first hint of any fever. One effect of this is that mucous tends to thicken and remains stuck in the body. In children, the suppression of fever in this way leads to chronic mucous problems like glue ear, sinusitis or chest catarrh. Mucous can also accumulate in the digestive and urinary systems. It then can act as food for further growth of bacteria, leading to persistent recurrent infections.

If you get something in your eye, **tears** are produced to wash it out. Tears also contain a chemical called 'lysozyme' which is a strong disinfectant.[128] **Earwax** is another barrier – both physical and chemical. (Remember earwax as an anti-pimple agent? Earwax also contains the powerful antibacterial lysozyme).

Then there are some quite explosive mechanical ways to get things out of the body – **coughing**, **sneezing**, and **vomiting**. Later on, if something got past the first defenses, diarrhea can wash things out. **Hydrochloric acid** is very inhospitable to life. If there is plenty of it in our stomachs then most germs we eat are instantly killed by it.

---

[125] The herpes simplex virus causes cold sores. You get them initially by contact with someone else that has them – don't ever kiss anyone with a visible sore! Then the virus lurks in your skin cells, where your body tries to keep it down but can't always get rid of it completely. So, every time you are run down and your immunity is low, you get a cold sore. Looked at positively, you get an early warning signal that your system is suffering stress, and can take appropriate action before more serious problems evolve.

[126] As the old schoolyard rhyme goes "we have joy, we have fun, flicking bogeys at the sun, when the sun gets too hot, the bogeys turn to snot" – thanks to Mark Jack for this gem…

[127] Antipyretics are medicines which lower fever.

[128] Actually tears are amazing. As well as washing things out, and being a disinfectant, they provide the ONLY route for us to excrete stress hormones whole, without the liver having first metabolized them. So when we are stressed the chemical content of our tears changes. Crying is one of our body's helpful ways to protect us from stress. Much more on this later in the chapter on emotional causes of disease.

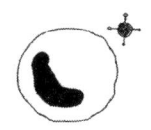

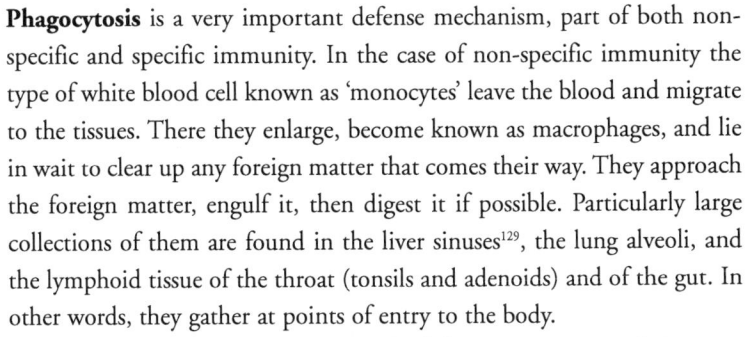

Phagocytosis is a very important defense mechanism, part of both non-specific and specific immunity. In the case of non-specific immunity the type of white blood cell known as 'monocytes' leave the blood and migrate to the tissues. There they enlarge, become known as macrophages, and lie in wait to clear up any foreign matter that comes their way. They approach the foreign matter, engulf it, then digest it if possible. Particularly large collections of them are found in the liver sinuses[129], the lung alveoli, and the lymphoid tissue of the throat (tonsils and adenoids) and of the gut. In other words, they gather at points of entry to the body.

You can see that if one's non-specific defenses are strong and vigorous, there would barely even be a need to engage specific immune defenses.

Fever or 'pyresis' is an important part of the immune response. Initially the body's thermostat in the hypothalamus is reset at a higher level. This causes the first stage of fever, when you feel cold and shivery. There is no sweating, and blood vessels of the skin constrict to keep heat inside, making you look pale, though the skin may be hot to touch. As the body temperature rises, you start to feel hot. This extra heat makes an unpleasant environment for any invading organism, which usually prefers normal body temperature, and it also greatly stimulates your own immune response. Then the fever 'breaks' and you start to sweat profusely as the body seeks to lower its temperature again. Toxins produced by infectious agents and other toxins the body wishes to be rid of are excreted quickly from the body in this kind of sweat, along with viruses. The sheets of a person ill in this way should be changed after a bout of sweating, to avoid leaving them surrounded by the very germs they are trying to get rid of.

There is a lot of fear about fever, especially in young people. Because of the easy availability of powerfully effective drugs which lower fever, there is not the familiarity with fever there once was. Even many health professionals (doctors and nurses and so forth) have not seen fever take its natural course. It is true that a small child's temperature can rise very rapidly, and as young ones are developing their immunity as they come across new bugs for the first time, there may be frequent episodes of febrile illness in childhood, but it is unnecessary to treat every childhood fever. The current trend seems to be to dose the child with Paracetamol (acetaminophen) based medicines (like Calpol or Tylenol). Many parents are encouraged to treat even mild fevers like this.[130] There are two problems with this: one is that Paracetamol will suppress the febrile

---

[129] The liver sinusoids are the extra-leaky capillaries which allow the liver cells full access to the nutrients and products absorbed in the digestive tract, which are taken straight to the liver by the portal vein. The macrophages in the liver are known as kupffer cells. There is a wonderful herbal medicine for the liver called milk thistle which, as one of its actions, increases the activity of the kupffer cells.

[130] This type of drug is routinely given to children from very small babies up. Many young ones are given it for teething, or even just for restlessness to make them sleep.

response, and therefore interfere with the activity of the developing immune system, as well as with the cleansing of mucous from the body described above; the second is that Paracetamol is a dangerous drug. Studies have found it to be toxic to the liver, even at lower than maximum dose and when given to healthy people. One study found that it caused liver damage in up to 44% of all participants who were taking it at the standard dose. Paracetamol has become the major cause of acute liver failure in the USA and Europe. Some of these cases have been the result of unintentional overdose – where perhaps one tablet too many has been taken, or people have taken too much not realising that it is in each of the several products they are taking (i.e. someone may take a cough medicine, a couple of tablets for the headache and something for a fever without realising they all contained Paracetamol). People have died after taking as little as 7g, just 3g above the recommended dose.[131] Liver failure usually kills people if they can't get a liver transplant (which is no picnic either).

High fevers in some diseases (like measles) are needed in order to discharge the virus from the body. In a clinical study of 56 children during a measles epidemic in Ghana, 1967, it was standard practice to treat every case of measles with sedatives, antipyretics like aspirin and Calpol (Tylenol), cough suppressants, and with antibiotics as needed. In the first half of the epidemic 35% of the children died. The treating doctors noticed, however, that the children who survived were usually the ones who had higher fevers and more severe rashes than the ones who died. Although the ones who died seemed less sick than the survivors at the beginning of the illness, they then later got pneumonia and died. The doctors concluded that the high fever and rash helped clear the measles virus from the body so they changed tack and stopped treating the children with sedatives, Aspirin, Paracetamol (acetaminophen) and cough suppressants. They treated only with antibiotics and blood transfusions when needed. As a result of this change of approach the death rate dropped to 17%. This fits with naturopathic and traditional thinking that diseases like measles become a problem only when they get stuck deep in the body.[132]

In common practice it is considered dangerous to have a fever of 42° C (104° F). The general belief is that this can cause febrile convulsions and even brain damage. When I was researching this book I found that actually only fever as high as 42.2°C[133] (108°F) has ever been known to cause brain damage. Therefore it makes sense to treat fevers of 42°C, to prevent them rising any higher. Fevers of 41°C (106°F) should get immediate medical attention as they are likely indications of severe infection.[134] [135]

---

[131] According to The Lancet (2006; 368: 2395).

[132] Edda West (2003) *Is Fear of Fever Hurting Our Children?* Accessed June 2008 At URL http://www.vran.org/news-art/articles/fear-of-fever.htm

[133] Is fever suppression involved in the etiology of autism and neurodevelopmental disorders? Anthony R Torres BMC Pediatr. 2003; 3: 9. Published online 2003 September 2. doi: 10.1186/1471-2431-3-9 PMC194752

[134] Bear in mind that readings under the tongue or arm are lower than internal temperature, also take care if using mercury and glass thermometers which can break.

[135] There is a shaman who 'lends' his body to Tatewari (Grandfather Fire), who comes and speaks through him. The man's temperature goes up to 106° when Grandfather is visiting.

Very few people who have a childhood febrile convulsion will sustain any lasting damage, and actually there is some evidence that people who have a very high fever in childhood are less likely to develop cancer later in life.[136] This makes sense; since cancer is a disease which can be seen as a failure of the immune system, it could very well be true that interference and repression of normal immune functions throughout childhood will affect its optimum functioning later. It is not only cancer either but other diseases which having the usual childhood illnesses seem to protect us from; measles, for example, has the ability to clear up chronic tendencies, such as recurring respiratory infections,[137] psoriasis or chronic kidney problems. Until the 1960s, the children's hospital in Basle (Switzerland) used to get young people with chronic kidney infections to catch measles in order to heal them.[138] After contracting measles, children who were susceptible to infections were found to be stronger and more resistant, needing less medical treatment.[139] There is evidence that children in the third world are less likely to get malaria and parasites after measles.[140] Hay fever and other allergies are less likely after measles.[141] There is also evidence that having had measles can protect a person from immune diseases, skin disease and degenerative cartilage and bone disease.[142]

Below are a some references about fever collected by Hilary Butler of the New Zealand Immunization Awareness Society, printed here with her permission: [143]

"Not all fevers need to be treated but many physicians do so to relieve parental concern."[144]

"There is overwhelming evidence in favour of fever being an adaptive host response to infection... as such, it is probable that the use of antipyretic/anti-inflammatory/analgesic

---

[136] For instance, having a decent attack of mumps in childhood with big, swollen 'hamster cheeks', makes a person less likely to develop ovarian cancer in later life. West –RO, Epidemiologic study of malignancies of the ovaries, Cancer 1966;19:1001-7. The risk of breast cancer is less than half for those who had measles. Albonico H.-U., Med. Hypotheses 198, 51(4): 315-320

[137] Drs Buehler and Wolff, cited by Anita Petek-Dimmer (2002) 'Does systematic vaccination give health to people?' Accessed 13/06/08 at URL http://www.whale.to/a/petek.html

[138] Chakravati V., Annals of Tropical Paediatrics, 1986, cited by Anita Petek-Dimmer (2002) 'Does systematic vaccination give health to people?' Accessed 13/06/08 at URL http://www.whale.to/a/petek.html

[139] Kummer, Der Merkurstab 1992, cited by Anita Petek-Dimmer (2002) 'Does systematic vaccination give health to people?' Accessed 13/06/08 at URL http://www.whale.to/a/petek.html

[140] Rooth I., Lancet 1985, cited by Anita Petek-Dimmer (2002) 'Does systematic vaccination give health to people?' Accessed 13/06/08 at URL http://www.whale.to/a/petek.html

[141] Lewis et al, Clin Exp Allergy 1998, 28(12): 1493-1500, Paunio M, JAMA 2000, 283: 343-346, Shaheen S.O. Lancet 1996, 347: 1792-1796 cited by Anita Petek-Dimmer (2002) 'Does systematic vaccination give health to people?' Accessed 13/06/08 at URL http://www.whale.to/a/petek.html

[142] Ronne T., Lancet 1995, cited by Anita Petek-Dimmer (2002) 'Does systematic vaccination give health to people?' Accessed 13/06/08 at URL http://www.whale.to/a/petek.html

[143] Thanks to Hilary Butler (The Immunization Awareness Society) (2002). These references were collected and published in Waves, Vol 14, No. 4. I accessed them May 2008 at URL http://www.vran.org/news-art/articles/fear-of-fever.htm

[144] Eur J Ped 1994 Jun; 153 (6): 394-402 Accessed June 2008 URL http://www.vran.org/news-art/articles/fear-of-fever.htm

drugs, when they lead to suppression of the fever, result in increased morbidity and mortality during most infections; this morbidity and mortality may not be apparent to most health care workers..."[145]

"Despite our lack of knowledge about its therapeutic mechanism, it has been claimed to be a safe drug, especially for children... paracetamol syrup[146] (presumably for children) is extensively prescribed in large volumes.. There is mounting evidence that paracetamol is not the benign drug that it was formerly thought to be... We would question the whole rationale of prescribing the drug in near epidemic proportions. If it is to be used as a placebo, then it is a very dangerous placebo... The whole place of paracetamol prescribing for children has been questioned. While there is little concern about its use in the short term as an analgesic, there is considerable controversy over its use as an antipyretic....there is little evidence to support the use of paracetamol to treat fever in patients without heart or lung disease. Paracetamol may decrease antibody response to infection and increase morbidity and mortality in severe infections...too many parents and health workers think that fever is bad and needs to be suppressed by paracetamol when, indeed, moderate fever may improve the immune response...the use of paracetamol in children with acute infection did not result in an improvement in mood, comfort, appetite or fluid intake."[147]

"The data suggest that frequent administration of antipyretics to children with infectious disease may lead to a worsening of their illness."[148]

Meningococcal Disease: "use of analgesics were associated with disease...analgesic use was defined as analgesics taken in the past 2 weeks, excluding, for cases, those taken for identified early symptoms of meningococcal disease. These analgesics were predominantly acetaminophen (paracetamol) products......because analgesics showed a stronger relationship with meningococcal disease, the use of analgesics may be a better measure of more severe illness than reported individual symptoms....*we cannot exclude the possibility that acetaminophen (paracetamol) use itself is a risk factor for meningococcal disease* (my italics)"[149]

---

[145] Infect Dis Clin North Am 1996 Mar;10(1) : 1-20.) Accessed June 2008 URL http://www.vran.org/news-art/articles/fear-of-fever.htm

[146] Known as Calpol in the UK and infant Tylenol in the US.

[147] Family Practice, Volume 13, No 2, 1996 pgs 179 - 181 Accessed June 2008 URL http://www.vran.org/news-art/articles/fear-of-fever.htm

[148] (Acta Paed. Jpn 1994 Aug;36 (4) 375-378) Accessed June 2008 URL http://www.vran.org/news-art/articles/fear-of-fever.htm

[149] (Ped Infec Dis, Oct 2000, Vol 19, No 10, 983-990) Accessed June 2008 URL http://www.vran.org/news-art/articles/fear-of-fever.htm

"Antipyretics prolong illness in patients with Influenza A.... The duration of illness was significantly prolonged from 5 days (without) to 8½ days (with)."[150]

"Taking aspirin or Tylenol for the flu actually prolongs the illness by up to 3½ days, say researchers at the University of Maryland. That is because fever may be the body's natural way of fighting an infection and taking aspirin or acetaminophen – the generic name for products such as Tylenol – may interfere with the process. "You are messing with Mother Nature," Says Dr Leland Rickman, an associate clinical professor of medicine at the University of California San Diego. "An elevated temperature may actually help the body fight the infection quicker or better than if you don't have a fever." "Whatever you do, don't give aspirin or Tylenol to children who have the 'flu or any other viral illness", Rickman said: "These results suggest that the systematic suppression of fever may not be useful in patients without severe cranial trauma or significant hypoxemia. Letting fever take its natural course does not seem to harm patients with systemic inflammatory response syndrome, or influence the discomfort level and may save costs."[151]

Parents who want alternatives to Paracetamol can look to herbal medicine or homeopathy, both of which offer many remedies to help manage fever. Herbs, for example yarrow and elderflowers, are **diaphoretic**, which means to encourage sweating therefore the lowering of body temperature via the skin's cooling mechanisms; although, it is better not to use any fever-lowering medicines unless absolutely necessary. One naturopathic approach to fever is to not bring it down too much, but to maintain it at about 38.9°C (102°F). This is thought by some to allow sufficient resolution of the important febrile phase of an illness.[152] There are other views that a higher fever is even beneficial, however – and certainly there seems to be evidence to back up this possibility. It is regrettable that there is not more research being done in this area; the idolization of vaccination, and the furious dismissal of anti-vaccination arguments by the mainstream, means the loss of good opportunities for research comparing vaccinated and unvaccinated people's long term health. (In addition there is the fact that the majority of research is driven by drug companies with the aim of increasing profits – not in proving a drug or vaccine may be unnecessary or harmful).

Specific Immunity

There are protective mechanisms that confer very specific protection against certain types of invading bacteria, viruses or other toxic stuff. This type of immunity involves lymphocytes,

---

[150] Pharmacotherapy 2000, 20: 417-422) Accessed June 2008 URL http://www.vran.org/news-art/articles/fear-of-fever.htm

[151] Take two aspirin, prolong the flu - 2 January 2001 Anne Burke, HealthScout Reporter (also reported by Reuters medical news...) the quote within the article from Dr Rickman from Arch Intern Med 2001, Jan 8; 161 121-123. Accessed June 2008 URL http://www.vran.org/news-art/articles/fear-of-fever.htm

[152] Christopher Menzies-Trull. *Herbal Medicine – Keys to Physiomedicalism.*

which have the ability to respond to particular harmful agents and then remember them for another time. Lymphocytes, like all the blood cells, start off life in the red bone marrow. Before they are ready to fight infection they have to mature, and after having matured, they must be activated. There are two basic types of lymphocyte: B-cells and T-cells. B-cells stay in the red bone marrow to mature, whereas T-cells are shipped off to the thymus to finish maturing.

Like we said before, this immunity is specific; this means that a lymphocyte will be specific for (have receptors for) just one antigen.[153] As there are vast numbers of possible antigens out there (especially considering that micro-organisms evolve and each slightly different micro-organism is considered a different antigen) you can imagine there have to be vast numbers of different T- and B-cells. The body deals with this by randomly making loads of lymphocytes with receptors that are all slightly different, like snow drops, until there are so many different types of receptors that there is bound to be one that will be a close enough fit for pretty much any antigen that exists or could exist. But there is a problem here; because there are receptors for nearly everything, this means that there would also be receptors for parts of our own bodies, and the last thing we want would be for lymphocytes to attack our own body thinking it was an antigen. So to solve this problem, during the lymphocytes maturation (training if you like), any of the lymphocytes that look like they may attack the body are weeded out till only the harmless ones remain (harmless for us anyway!).

So far, so good; we now have mature lymphocytes that are well behaved, and have been let out to wander freely (so to speak) around the body. But there is one final stage – activation. This generally occurs in and around the lymphatic system: when a few of the cells chance upon an antigen the activation process begins. While this is happening, the person experiences the disease symptoms such as fever, malaise (feeling ill), spots, cough or whatever. On a second exposure however, no symptoms are experienced because the immune response is so quick, due to **memory cells** having been formed as part of the activation process.

On activation, B- and T-cells form both memory cells and effector cells. The effector cells are the ones who go for it right now to rid the body of the unwanted guests, whilst the memory cells are the ones that hang around ready to fight another day. B-cells and T-cells behave a little differently in how they do their job. Effector B-cells swell up as they make lots of **immunoglobulins**, or **antibodies**. Then they burst releasing the antibodies into the surrounding blood or tissue fluid. Antibodies are protein complexes, which will bind to an antigen, rendering it more vulnerable to attack from T-cells, neutralizing it in some way or causing other cells or chemical processes to destroy it.

Effector T-cells can do a few things. Some, called **killer cells**, directly attack antigens – particularly cells that have been invaded by viruses. Others, **helper cells**, go to the B-cells to urge their action.

---

[153] An antigen is something which elicits an immune response – could be a virus, bacteria, fungus (infectious agents), an allergen such as pollen or house dust, or an abnormal or foreign cell.

Immunity can either be inherited or acquired. Inherited immunity is 'inborn': a genetic tendency to be immune has been passed down from our ancestors. Consider, for example, diseases that are not fatal to humans, such as distemper, but which kill dogs. A very sad way to understand this kind of inborn immunity is to look at what happened to native people in say, America, when Europeans first colonized. Ordinary diseases that are not serious in Europeans, such as measles and even the common cold, were fatal to Native Americans, who had no inherited immunity to them and died in very large numbers.

Acquired immunity can be natural or artificial, active or passive. **Naturally acquired active immunity** is what I have described above: after meeting a pathogen for the first time, an immune response is mounted, including the formation of memory cells. On second exposure, the memory cells quickly kill off the antigen so that no disease is experienced – we have 'acquired' immunity. Immunity is also naturally acquired before we are born via the placenta, and after birth via breast milk. Our mother will be making antibodies to all the germs that are around us. If we are fortunate enough to be born at home, she will already be immune to all the germs in our immediate environment, making a home birth safer (in the absence of complications). Mum's blood will be full of all the necessary antibodies to protect us, and these will be present in the breast milk she makes for us. A newborn baby's digestive tract is not yet mature; the lining of the gut is more permeable or leaky than in an adult, and allows whole proteins to cross over into the blood of the baby. This is so that immunoglobulins (antibodies) can directly enter the baby's bloodstream, giving **passively acquired natural immunity**. [154]

Artificially acquired immunity refers to vaccinations and immunizations; vaccinations being the deliberate introduction of pathogenic material, usually weakened or dead, into a person with the intention of triggering an immune response without causing the disease in the meantime. This is an active process. In practice, vaccination is never as effective as actually contracting the disease in terms of conferring life-long immunity. Immunization involves the introduction of amounts of artificially produced (usually in animal hosts) antibodies into the blood. This passively provides immunity for a short period.

Vaccination Controversy

Reading any conventional textbook, or any information from the doctors' surgery, you will see that vaccinations are heralded as the greatest single breakthrough in modern medicine, saving more lives than anything else. I have never seen any hint there could be any problems from vaccination in a mainstream textbook.

---

[154] What this also means however is that a young human is particularly designed to take only human breast milk as food. When given formula milk made from cows milk, or given the wrong sort of solid food too early (for example. wheat and cow's milk products) undigested proteins can cross into the blood and set off a sensitivity reaction or allergy. Sometimes allergies are so low level that the effects are not seen immediately, making it harder to figure out the source of the problem. More on this with the digestive system.

Anyone who questions the safety or efficacy of vaccinations is pilloried as a heretic lunatic who wants to kill children.[155] Any discussion with your doctor about the subject is along the lines of how great vaccinations are, and it seems impossible to have a relaxed discussion that includes any possibility of doubt regarding the subject.

Everyone has heard bits and pieces about the possible dangers of MMR (the triple vaccine measles, mumps and rubella), including maybe noticing how the scientists whose research seems to indicate possible problems being almost demonized, and certainly targeted by and discredited in the media. But did you know that there is a body of thought, which questions the whole premise of safe and effective vaccines? It is too complex to go into in detail here, but I will outline some of the main points, and if you wish you can look into it further.

Overburdening the immune system: Firstly, consider that the immune system is made to work overtime in a way it would never be expected to work naturally; within a few months, the developing immune system is expected to make antibodies to measles, mumps, rubella, diphtheria, tetanus, whooping cough, tuberculosis, haemophilus influenza type B, polio and meningococcus type C, all roughly at the same time. In reality, the body tends to experience one infection after another, not a whole load mixed together. These pathogens never occur all together in nature. Giving all these vaccinations over a few years means that the immune system is never given a chance to rest from having to make specific antibodies. This leads to chronic immune deficiency with respect to reacting to other pathogens – the immunity is committed to fighting the specific antigens in the vaccines, and there is no energy for fighting other infections. In effect, immunity is lowered. Children end up getting lots of other infections they would not normally have (mostly treated by more antibiotics and paracetamol).[156]

Safety: There is a massive under-reporting of adverse reactions to vaccinations, including the reporting of deaths and serious reactions. It is possible that deaths and serious injuries from vaccines may be 10-100 times greater than the number reported. In the USA insurance companies refuse to cover vaccine reactions – it is these companies who do the best liability studies.

Then there are the possible long-term effects of vaccinations, not just dramatic and obvious immediate problems. Studies have found possible links between vaccines and long term conditions such as autism, hyperactivity, ADHD, dyslexia, allergies, cancer, asthma and others.

Vaccine ingredients include mercury, aluminum, formaldehyde and phenoxyethanol (antifreeze). Considering the trend for more and more vaccinations to be given to very young babies, and for multiple delivery, there is a likelihood of adverse reactions from these added

---

[155] Dr Andrew Wakefield, for example, a scientist who found vaccine-strain measles virus in the guts of some children with autism. He was by no means anti-vaccine, but was demonized for suggesting that the findings should be looked into. www.wddty.co.uk has plenty of information about this.

[156] Dr Yubraj Sharma *Vaccination Controversy: Safety and Side Effects* (Positive Health Magazine issue 90 - July 2003).

toxins (which act as fixatives) in the future. Some vaccines are cultured on animal cells, or come from tissue originating from aborted human foetuses.

Efficacy. Medical literature is full of studies documenting vaccine failure. Measles, mumps, small pox, whooping cough, polio and Haemophilus influenza type B (known as Hib, which is seen as an important cause of childhood meningitis and pneumonia) outbreaks have all occurred in vaccinated groups. Although vaccinations are lauded for being responsible for low disease rates today, in fact childhood diseases decreased by 90% between 1850 and 1940, well before mass vaccination programs, and in line with improved hygiene and sanitation.

Take this chart, published in the British Medical Journal April 1983:[157]

Death rate of children (under 12) due to whooping cough

Year	no. of deaths (per million)
1860	1372
1910	815
1930	405
1950	5

(Mass vaccination of whooping cough began in 1952)

Also, getting a disease naturally is more helpful in terms of your immunity – often natural acquired immunity lasts a lifetime (for example contracting rubella or German measles), yet the vaccine provides immunity for only a limited time.

When I was a child, if someone had measles, mumps, chicken pox and so forth, your mum would take you round to visit them so you could get it too. Now it seems all these diseases are so scary that we need to vaccinate or die! There is evidence that getting childhood diseases is part of the development of a healthy immune system – as we have seen, people who didn't get mumps as a child are at higher risk of ovarian cancer; measles, a higher risk of some skin diseases, degenerative bone and cartilage disease and some tumours. It does seem likely that diseases our people have had for countless generations have been involved in the development of our immune system.

The immune system is incredibly complex, our understanding of it is still very limited, yet we are happily messing around with millions of people's immunity without a backing of excellent long term clinical studies and trials, and with a prejudiced system that makes proper debate and study unlikely to happen in the short term.[158]

---

[157] Found in Sara Hamo's *The Golden Path*.

[158] My main sources for this are Lynne McTaggart *The Vaccination Bible* (What Doctor's Don't Tell You 1998), Viera Scheibner – *Vaccination. 100 years of orthodox medical research shows that vaccines represent a medical assault on the immune system*. (New Atlantean Press. Santa Fe, NM. 1993) and Alan Philips – *Dispelling Vaccination Myths, an introduction to the contradictions between medical science & immunization policy*. (Prometheus, 55 Hob Moor Drive, Holgate, York YO24 4JU 2001) You can buy this booklet from Helios Homeopathic Pharmacy, 01892 537254

Auto-immunity

There is a group of diseases known as **auto-immune**. In our bodies, all of our own cells and tissues have a marker on them, like a name-tag, so that our immune system can recognise them as us. Sometimes something goes wrong with this process, the lymphocytes fail to recognize our own marker and attack particular cells and tissues, causing inflammation and damage. Examples of this type of disorder include rheumatoid arthritis, psoriasis, multiple sclerosis, some insulin-dependant diabetes and thyroid disorders.

Auto-immunity is like a civil war in the body. Literally, some part of us becomes the enemy. A theory of auto-immunity is that it is due to a so-called 'cross-sensitivity' from infection. The thinking is that often there are two infections happening at the same time – so the immune system is stretched and gets confused. What seems to happen is that some bacteria and viruses have evolved to have surface markers which are similar to the markers on certain body tissues. A person may suffer an infection, say in the lung, that the body is unable to completely resolve. Let's say the infectious agent involved in the lung problem has a surface marker very similar to those markers found on the synovial membrane of a joint. The second infection (which could be something very common like overgrowth of *Candida albicans* in the gut) upsets and confuses the immune system, and some white cells attack the synovial membrane of a joint, mistaking it for the organism infecting the lung. Now there is an inflammation of the membrane, which in turn attracts more attention of white blood cells, and so it goes on. [159] [160]

Rheumatoid arthritis and ankylosing spondylitis, an arthritic condition of the vertebrae of the neck and thorax, seem to have this aetiology (cause). There is often some damage to the gut involved, even to the extent of developing the autoimmune gut disorder Crohn's disease. People who develop sudden-onset insulin dependant diabetes often do so after having an infection which looks like 'flu. This can also be the case in those who develop an autoimmune disorder affecting the thyroid.

Interrelationships

By keeping the blood and tissues clean from diseased cells, and protecting the body from external threat, the immune system is involved with proper functioning of all systems. The immune system is particularly active via the **cardiovascular** and **lymphatic** systems, and the **skeletal system** where its active cells are made. The **liver** plays a key role with immune cells there protecting against toxins and foreign substances which gain access to the body via the digestive tract. Our immune system and **emotions** have a particularly close relationship.

---

[159] Mills and Bone *Principles and Practice of Phytotherapy*.

[160] Consider the implications to this regarding overloading the immune system with vaccinations.

CHAPTER TEN

BREATHING
THE RESPIRATORY SYSTEM

In Chinese medicine, developed over thousands of years, it is understood that people need a continuous supply of Qi, or energy, to function. Most of this is gained daily – the Qi of the Heavenly Father comes to us by the lungs and breathing. This mixes with the Qi of the Earth Mother in food to supply our energy needs.

As you know from our study of cellular processes, this is exactly what happens physiologically. Oxygen is 20% of air, and each breath takes in a quarter to a fifth of the oxygen present in inhaled air, which is brought into the body by the action of breathing, taken from the lungs into the blood from which the cells may take it to use in the oxidation of glucose (from food) for ATP production. Thus energy for cellular functions is garnered from the air and the Earth.[161]

The by-products of **cellular respiration** are carbon dioxide and water. Carbon dioxide is sent in the plasma back to the lungs and breathed out. In a wonderfully neat example of the symbiotic relationship between plants and ourselves, green plants breathe in carbon dioxide and use it for their metabolism, during which they make oxygen, which they breathe out. This is why trees are known as the 'lungs of the earth'. It's interesting that the bronchial tree of the lungs looks just like an inverted trunk and branches of a tree.[162]

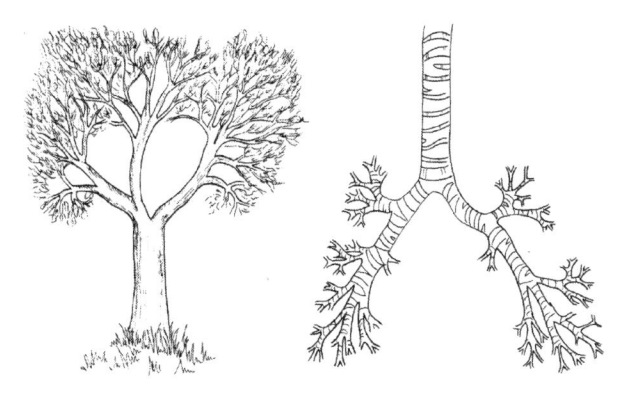

---

[161] Incidentally, the taste of the earth element is sweet. The first taste of Mother is breast milk which is deliciously sweet.
[162] Thanks to Joyce Withers for inspiration for this – from her book *The Virgin Stones*.

Airways to alveoli

The anatomy of the respiratory system basically consists of a series of tubes ending in clusters of tiny air sacs called **alveoli** where the gases are exchanged. We'll take a more detailed look from the top…

The nose and sinuses. The nose is much bigger than it looks from the outside. The sticky-out-bit on the outside is made of cartilage, and contains hairs to catch dust and debris (these are the ones that get much longer in old age…). Two large cavities go from the top of the cartilage part of the nose to deep back into the face, each being a bony cavity separated from the other by a septum. On the walls of each nasal cavity are scroll-like shapes of bone, turbines, which turn the inhaled air so that all of it comes into contact with the sticky mucous membrane that lines the cavity. Connected to the nasal cavities by small tubes are more cavities, called sinuses, embedded in the bones of the face and skull. These too are lined with mucous membranes. The mucous membranes secrete sticky mucus, so that any bits of dust or debris that gets past the hairs in the nose stick to it (this can later be removed as 'bogies'!). The membranes are also warm and wet, and this heats up the inhaled air and adds moisture to it, making it easier on the lungs. Thus it is said that the functions of the nose and sinuses are to warm, moisten and filter the air.

At the back of the nasal cavity and going down into the throat is found the **pharynx**. This is a common passage for both food and drink, and air. It contains a flap of cartilage called the **epiglottis** which blocks off the wind pipe, or **trachea**, when swallowing food or drink. What happens is that as we swallow, the voice box is pulled up and the epiglottis pushed down over the entrance to the trachea, thus sealing it off so food doesn't go the wrong way.

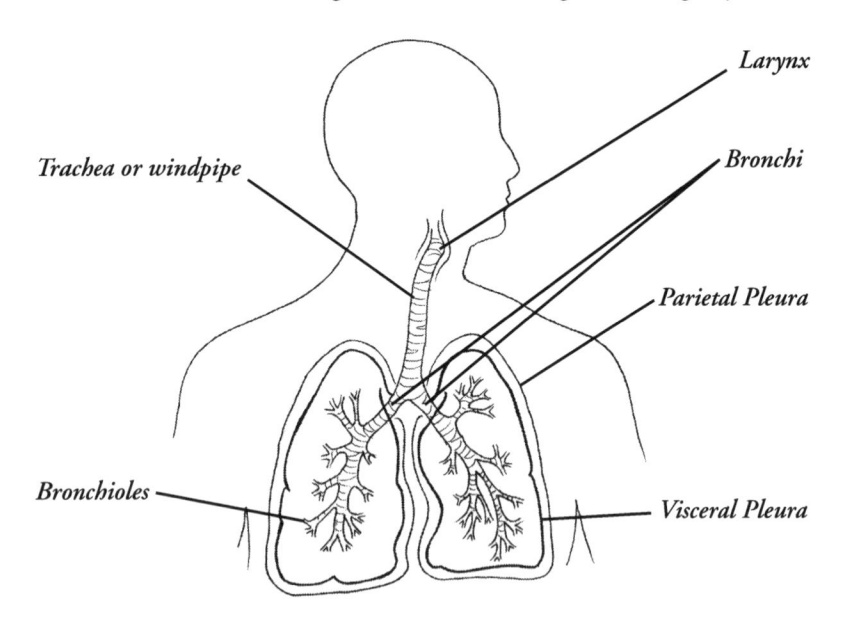

The pharynx then splits into the **larynx** at the front where the air goes, and the oesophagus at the back, which takes drink and food into the stomach. The larynx is the voice box, an amazing construction made of the hyoid bone and many pieces of cartilage, as well as the vocal cords, which are moved by muscles. The air passing through the vocal cords, each in different positions and degrees of tension, is what gives us the ability to speak and make so many different sounds.[163]

The larynx is continued below as the **trachea**, or air tube. This is a strong tube made of smooth muscle plus horseshoe shapes of cartilage, surrounded by connective tissue and lined with ciliated epithelium. The cilia (hairs) on the epithelium gently waft and move mucous up the trachea to the back of the throat, from where we can cough it into the mouth and get it out of the body.

The trachea divides at the sternal angle into the two **bronchi**. These air tubes also have smooth muscle and cartilage walls. The cartilage makes the tubes solid, keeping them open under normal circumstances. One **bronchus** goes to each lung then they further divide and subdivide into smaller and smaller tubes with less and less cartilage in their walls. When they no longer have any cartilage, but only smooth muscle in the middle layer of their walls, they are called **bronchioles.**

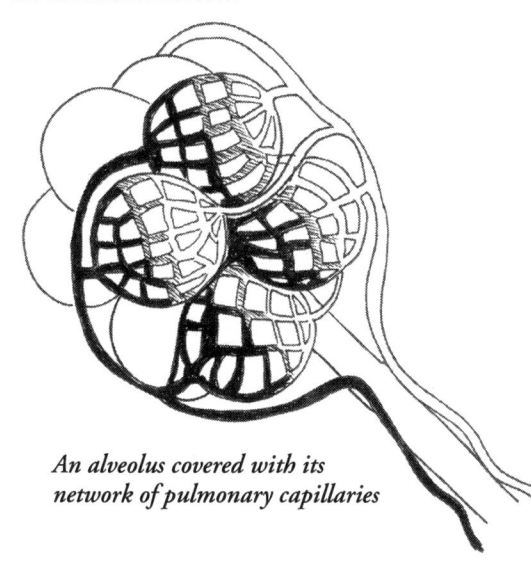

An alveolus covered with its network of pulmonary capillaries

The smallest bronchioles end in tiny delicate air sacks called **alveoli**.

These are completely surrounded by pulmonary capillaries – which have brought deoxygenated blood from the right ventricle of the heart to the lungs, and will return oxygenated blood to the left atrium. The alveoli are where gaseous exchange takes place: because the alveoli, like the capillaries, are made of one-cell-thick epithelial tissue, there is only a very small barrier for the oxygen and carbon dioxide to cross. Since oxygen is at a low concentration in the pulmonary capillaries and high in inhaled air, it crosses down the concentration gradient by diffusion from the alveoli into the blood. With carbon dioxide the

---

[163] After a tracheotomy, when an opening is made in the front of the neck over the trachea, allowing air to enter the lungs without passing through the larynx, a person must learn to talk by swallowing air and sending this through the larynx to vibrate the vocal cords. A less serious use for this ability is 'burp talking' which some school friends of mine loved to entertain with. One expert in this childhood pastime (thanks Rebecca!) tells me that an easy word to practice with is 'bollocks'…do try this at home.

situation is reversed – the blood in the pulmonary circulation is rich in carbon dioxide and the inhaled air is not, so carbon dioxide naturally diffuses across from the pulmonary capillaries into the alveoli.

The **respiratory membrane** (which comprises the alveoli wall plus the pulmonary capillary wall) is only 0.5 - 1 micrometres[164] thick in healthy lungs, making gas exchange very efficient. If this is altered by disease in any way, gaseous exchange is impaired (e.g. pneumonia causing waterlogged tissues which thickens the membranes). If gas exchange is impaired, you just can't get enough oxygen into the body, and will feel breathless and tired to the point of literally not having the energy to do things. Also, carbon dioxide can build up which makes the body too acidic. Changes in the pH of the body like this can affect many functions, as we discussed in our chapter on chemistry.

There is also a large surface area of alveoli needed to allow enough exchange - this is impaired in the disease emphysema, when the walls of adjacent alveoli break through, making larger alveoli (with less surface area), dramatically decreasing gaseous exchange. It also occurs when mucous, tumours or inflammatory materials block gas flow into the alveoli. The respiratory membranes of adult humans, if spread out, have the surface area of a tennis court. Small babies have much smaller lungs than adults – not just proportionally to their size, but because there are many less branches to the bronchial tree and many less alveoli, so their breathing capacity is much less than an adults. This is why being in a smoky environment is particularly dangerous and harmful for children.

The lungs themselves

Looked at overall, the lungs are arranged in lobes. The right lung is bigger and is made of three discrete lobes. The left lung is smaller due to the heart taking up space on the left side of the chest, and is made of two lobes. The lungs are smaller than you might expect – put your hands flat on your chest, with the tops of your fingers touching your clavicles on each side. Your lungs take up the space under your hands, more or less.

The lungs are spongy organs contained in the **pleura** – a double sack of serous membrane surrounding each lung. The inner layer of pleural membrane is attached to the lung tissue; the outer layer is attached to the chest wall at the front, sides, and back, and the diaphragm below. Like all serous membranes, the pleura secrete a lubricating fluid. This allows the two layers to slide freely over each other as the lungs expand and contract. There is no air between the two layers of pleura, so there is what is called a **potential space** – it *could* be a space as the layers are not attached to each other, but it isn't because the two layers stay together in the same way that two wet sheets of plastic would stick together. Getting air in that potential space is called a **pneumothorax**, and is very serious as it means the lung can no longer work properly.

---

[164] A micrometre is one-thousandth the size of a millimetre.

The main muscles of respiration are the **diaphragm** and the **intercostal muscles**. The diaphragm is a muscle that is attached all around the bottom of the ribs, and inserts up into a flat central tendon, making a dome shape. The diaphragm completely separates the thoracic and abdominal cavities (although, of course, there are holes for blood vessels, lymph vessels and the gullet to pass through). When the diaphragm contracts, its central tendon is pulled down, making the thoracic cavity longer. Meanwhile, the external intercostals contract and pull the ribs up and out, widening the chest. As the thorax is made bigger, intrapulmonary pressure (the pressure in the alveoli) drops. As gases like to travel from an area of higher pressure to low pressure, air rushes into the lungs until the pressure in the alveoli is equal to that in the atmosphere.

Then comes expiration: the diaphragm relaxes and rises back up and the internal intercostals pull ribs in and down, so making the chest cavity smaller and squeezing air out of the lungs – just like a pair of bellows, in fact. This getting the air in and out of the lungs, specifically the alveoli, is called **pulmonary ventilation**.

There are three things that can influence pulmonary ventilation and thus affect how easy it is to get air into and out of the lungs: airway resistance, surface tension in the alveoli and lung compliance.

Airway resistance is the friction of the air passages impeding airflow. The smaller or more contracted airways have more resistance which makes it harder to suck air through.

Surface tension in the alveoli tries to pull the walls of the alveoli together, which collapses them, making ventilation harder. To get air in you need to fight against this surface tension to open the alveoli up (think how hard it is to blow up the first bit of a balloon – once you've done a bit, it gets easier). However, a liquid covering called **surfactant** helps to minimise this surface tension. This surfactant is formed late in foetal development, so premature babies often have trouble breathing if they are born before the surfactant is properly formed.

Lung compliance is the amount of effort required to stretch the lungs and chest wall when you fill the lungs up with air; the less compliance there is, the harder it will be. So lung compliance depends on the elasticity of lung tissue and the flexibility of the bony thorax, and things that negatively affect these can impair breathing, as more energy will be required to force air into the lungs and to force air out again (this is what happens, for example, in fibrous lung disease which makes the lungs less elastic, and in arthritis which can restrict bony movement of the thorax).

When someone is suffering from a disorder which is making breathing difficult then all sorts of extra muscles get involved in the process. You can see this in someone with asthma or any restrictive respiratory disease; the muscles in the neck, back and shoulders will all be working hard to help maximize the space in the thorax. This is a vicious circle in some ways, as all the extra muscles working will require extra oxygen, thus increasing the demands on an already taxed system. You can understand how tired a person with a serious or chronic lung problem feels. Not only are they having trouble getting enough oxygen in for their energy needs, but also the disease is actually increasing their needs.

Breathing is described using a variety of lung 'volumes'

Tidal volume is the in and out of normal breathing. But sometimes you need to either take in or release extra air - so we have reserves:

Expiratory reserve volume, which can allow us, for example, to cough to remove irritants from the lungs (by applying pressured air behind the irritant to force it out). However, even after expiratory reserve volume, we still have more...

Residual volume, which you will have felt the lack of if you ever got completely winded - it's very difficult to take your first breath afterwards, rather like blowing up a completely empty balloon. Residual volume prevents us from having to inflate a completely empty balloon with every breath! That first breath we each take as a newborn is as hard as this – we have to blow up the 'balloons' for the first time. [165]

Inspiratory reserve volume allows us to inhale well beyond our tidal volumes – so we can take in extra air for swimming etc.

The placement of the lungs within the chest

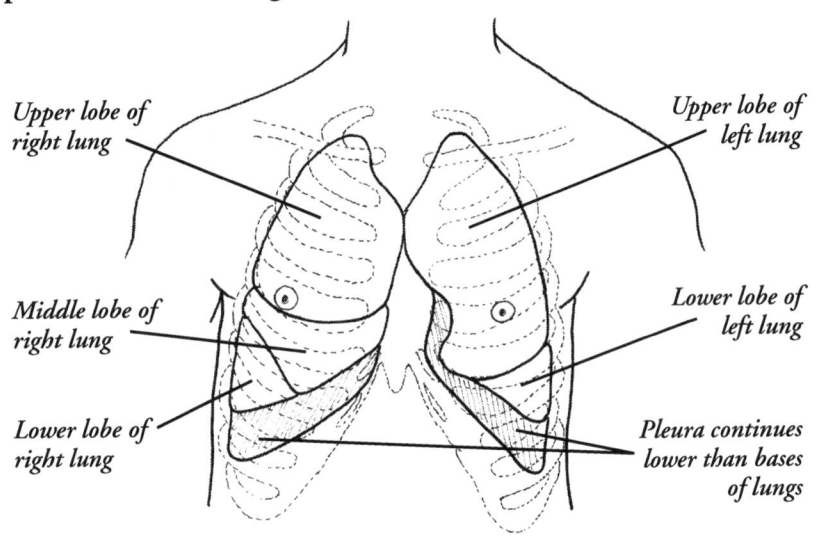

Upper lobe of right lung

Upper lobe of left lung

Middle lobe of right lung

Lower lobe of left lung

Lower lobe of right lung

Pleura continues lower than bases of lungs

Transport of respiratory gases by blood

Oxygen is carried bound to haemoglobin in the red blood cells with an additional small amount being dissolved in the plasma. (Oxygen is poorly soluble in the water which forms

---

[165] Can you comprehend the barbarity of holding up a new born human and smacking it to make it cry and take its first breath? Considered reasonable practice until frighteningly recently...

the bulk of the plasma). Haemoglobin can carry up to four oxygen molecules - when it has already taken up one, it more easily takes up two, when it has two it more easily takes three and four; when it has four it is 'fully saturated'.

Under normal resting conditions haemoglobin is 98% saturated – 100 ml of arterial blood contains about 20 ml of oxygen. The amount released when blood flows through the capillaries means venous blood is 75% saturated - and contains 15 ml of oxygen per 100ml. This is called the venous reserve – and it means that under conditions of exercise, when much more oxygen is used, more can be unloaded in the capillaries even before any increase in breathing.

Temperature, blood pH, the amount of carbon dioxide in the blood and other local chemical changes all affect the shape of haemoglobin and therefore influence haemoglobin saturation. Increases of these factors decrease haemoglobin's affinity for oxygen and therefore cause it to offload more oxygen into the blood. All these factors will be highest in capillaries of the systemic circulation, where the oxygen is used. Cells use up oxygen and release carbon dioxide, which also increases acidity in capillary blood. Heat is a by-product of metabolism so temperature goes up. Thus it is in the place that oxygen is most needed that haemoglobin's affinity for oxygen will be most decreased, therefore more oxygen will be released to be available for the cells to use in respiration. Carbon dioxide is carried mainly as **bicarbonate ions**, but with a little dissolved and bound to haemoglobin, in the plasma. Loading and unloading of it and oxygen are mutually beneficial. How neat is that? This is a great example of the kind of local regulating mechanisms which exist throughout the body.

The control of breathing

As we have already said, at different times our need for using oxygen and eliminating carbon dioxide change. The brain controls breathing via the 'respiratory centres' of the brain stem. The **medulla** has a centre which sets the pace of breathing, exciting the diaphragm and external intercostal muscles to contract, therefore causing inspiration continuously on and off, twelve to fifteen times every minute. If this **inspiratory centre** is repressed by overdose of alcohol, sleeping pills or morphine, respiration stops (with obviously dire consequences). There is another centre in the medulla with seems to contribute more in forced expiration, when more strenuous movements are needed.

Various things can affect breathing (including messages from the higher brain centres about strong emotions, and temperature). We can consciously control breathing from the cortex, deciding to deliberately speed up or slow down our breathing. The most important chemical factors affecting breathing are changing levels of oxygen, carbon dioxide and hydrogen ions (acidity) in arterial blood. Chemoreceptors[166] in the brain and the great vessels of the neck pick up these changes and relay the information to the medulla. This is how we know to increase breathing during exercise, for example.

---

[166] Sensory nerve endings which are stimulated by changes in the chemical environment of the blood. Each type is sensitive to increased levels of a specific chemical.

Chronic obstructive pulmonary disease (COPD)

This is another name for chronic bronchitis and emphysema:
- This almost always happens to people who have smoked rather than non-smokers.
- The main symptom is **dyspnoea** - laboured breathing, or air hunger - and this gets progressively worse as the disease progresses.
- Coughing and frequent lung infections are common.
- Most people with COPD (also called COAD -chronic obstructive airway disease) go on to develop respiratory failure which leads to hypoxaemia (low oxygen in the blood), carbon dioxide retention and respiratory acidosis.

*If you have COPD, you will generally have either primarily bronchitis, or primarily emphysema. Emphysema sufferers are referred to in orthodox medicine as **pink puffers** and chronic bronchitis sufferers as **blue bloaters**.*

'Pink puffers' are people who's emphysema has led them to have a reddish complexion and puff, or hyperventilate. 'Blue bloaters' are typically people with chronic bronchitis; in other words, someone with a cough with sputum for 3 months of the year or more. The person cannot get enough oxygen into the body, so begins to get cyanosis, or blueness. Ankles and legs may get swollen and neck veins may look distended. This condition leads to right heart failure. It is not a good thing to have – most 'blue bloaters' die within two to four years.

A deeper look at breathing

As we have already discussed, breathing is a powerful detoxifying process, which can be maximized by deep breathing. To clean the blood from acidic, toxic carbon dioxide which is a waste product, we need to breathe. To make this a thorough process, deep breathing is recommended. Without being fully cleansed of carbon dioxide the blood cannot carry enough oxygen. Deep breathing also creates a pressure changing pump in the thorax, which encourages venous return (of blood), and also movement of lymph, especially the emptying of the large lymph vessels in the chest back into the blood circulation (the lymphatic system is a major cleansing system of the body). When we breathe deeply, the heart, which is attached to the diaphragm via the pericardium is massaged and helped with its work. Also, deep breathing pushes the diaphragm down firmly, which massages all the abdominal and pelvic organs, helping to bring in fresh blood and energy, and keep them well conditioned.

There are many different methods and ways to work with breathing. In yoga, working with the breath is of vital importance. It is called **pranayana yoga** and is seen as not just a way to bring more oxygen to the blood and the brain, but to control the vital force or prana. It is a powerful cleansing process for detoxifying the body, mind and spirit, calming the mind and bringing spiritual growth. Like all spiritual practices, it is best followed under guidance of a teacher or Master.

There is a group of breathing exercises developed by a Russian doctor called **Konstansin Buteyko** in the 1950s to help people suffering from asthma and other breathing problems.

Its benefits were officially recognised and it was approved as a treatment for asthma throughout the former Soviet Union in 1981. Apparently, in studies of this technique, half of all asthma sufferers are able to reduce their need for inhalers in less than 3 months after beginning to practice the method. It involves a simple set of exercises alternating holding the breath with shallow breathing. You can go to a trainer to learn how to do it.[167] It works to break the cycle of panic in asthma sufferers causing more breathlessness. Asthma is a condition in which the airways narrow by muscle contraction and inflammation. As you know, when the amount of carbon dioxide in the blood rises, you will breathe more. In an asthma attack people panic, breath quickly and therefore drop the carbon dioxide level in the blood, causing the airways to narrow (as the body is aware it needs less oxygen) which makes the person panic more in a vicious cycle. The Buteyko breathing technique alternates deeply held breaths with shallow breaths, and teaches the person to control the breathing more, and also to get used to higher concentration of carbon dioxide in the blood without letting that feeling panic them.

Interrelationships

The respiratory system provides oxygen for the metabolism of **all cells** of the body, thus all the systems depend on it and could not survive without it. The **brain** and **muscles** are particularly big users of oxygen. The **musculoskeletal** system powers the mechanics of breathing with the diaphragm and intercostal muscles, and the respiratory centres for control of breathing are in the **brain**. The **circulatory** system carries oxygen and carbon dioxide from and to the lungs and around the body, including to the tissues which make up the lungs themselves. The detoxing function of this systems means all the cells of the body rely on it to keep sparkly.

---

[167] I found instructions on http://www.btinternet.com/~andrew.murphy/asthma_buteyko_shallow_breathing.html

Chapter Eleven

EATING AND FOOD PROCESSING
The Digestive System and Diet

We really *are* what we eat; on the physical level, all parts of our bodies are built from ingredients either our mums ate when we were growing inside them, or we ourselves have eaten during our life. Some parts of our body are permanent; the bits our mum made will have to do us for our whole lives, there is no replacing them.[168] Some parts of our bodies can be replaced if necessary and others are made daily as a matter of course. All is made from food. The digestive system breaks down the food we eat – protein, carbohydrate and fats (as well as vitamins, minerals and other nutrients) – into substances the body can absorb and use for energy, growth and repair. Proteins are broken down into amino acids; carbohydrates into simple sugars; fats (or lipids) into fatty acids and glycerol.

Basically it's back to chemistry: foods are large molecules, made by plants and animals make, and digestion breaks them down into small ones (catabolism) for absorption so the body can use them to make large ones again (anabolism). This breaking down and building up, and the balance between the two, is what is known as 'metabolism'. Some of what follows is similar to that found in the chemistry chapter, which you might like to re-read to refresh your memory about the main groups of chemicals found in the body.

Carbohydrates

What foods contain carbohydrates

Carbohydrates include **sugars** and **polysaccharides** (starches). Except for a tiny bit in milk sugar (**lactose**) and glycogen in meat, most carbohydrate comes from plants. Simple sugars come from fruits, sugar cane, beets, honey and milk. Polysaccharides come from grains, pulses and root vegetables.

Plants also contain **cellulose**, another polysaccharide. We cannot digest this, but it is the fibre we need to provide bulk for healthy colon function. **Fructooligosaccharides** (FOS) are

---

[168] This includes the eggs in a woman's ovaries, and it used to be thought our skeletal muscle cells, cardiac cells and nerve cells; but, as we have discussed, these do seem to have some ability to regenerate, though they do not tend to do so ordinarily. Although some cells in the body do exist from birth, it is likely that all the contents of the cells get replaced as stuff diffuses in and out, things get repaired and so forth. So our own state of nutrition is of vital importance to keep our bodies in good shape, and improving our nutrition will always begin to improve things, including in our so-called 'permanent cells'.

one type of this fibre which is called 'prebiotic'; the food for the helpful bacteria which live in our gut – the more helpful bacteria there are the less room for unhealthy ones.

Humans can be healthy with a wide variety of carbohydrate intakes, and the levels of intake considered 'normal' vary. Currently, the recommended range in the West is 125 - 175g daily, and these should all be in the form of complex carbohydrates (i.e. not sugar). The British and American diet commonly contains much more than this – one reason for our growing obesity problem.

How the body uses carbohydrates

The main function of carbohydrate is to provide easily stored and used fuel for energy. Most cells can only use a few simple sugars, the main one being glucose. Glucose is broken down within cells to make ATP to be used for energy. When we have enough ATP, glucose is stored as glycogen or converted to fat. Other uses of sugars include making the nucleic acids DNA and RNA.[169]

The **Glycaemic Index (GI)** of foods relates to the quickness that eaten carbohydrates get into the blood as glucose. A food with a high GI gets into the blood quickly, which means the pancreas must put out a big wallop of insulin to deal with the glucose. Then the pendulum swings and the blood sugar drops dramatically and you get cravings for more sugar, and thus the pendulum swings again. This generally puts pressure on the body, and can lead to mood swings in susceptible individuals. Some people's bodies seem to react to processed sugar (which is effectively pure glucose) as if it is more like a drug than a food. For these people, eating only complex carbohydrates – including potatoes and other things with a low GI – can be life-changing.[170]

Foods with a low GI are healthier and take less of a toll on the sugar balancing mechanisms of the body. Eating foods with a high GI consistently is one factor which can lead to diabetes, obesity, high cholesterol and heart disease. The concept of the Glycaemic Index was invented by Dr. David J. Jenkins and colleagues in 1981 at the University of Toronto. As mentioned before, carbohydrates that break down rapidly during digestion and quickly enter the bloodstream have the highest glycaemic indices. A lower glycaemic index suggests slower rates of digestion and absorption of the sugars and starches in the foods, and probably there-

---

[169] Nucleic acids are made of nucleotides. These are the largest molecules in the body, made of a nitrogen-containing base, a pentose sugar (do you remember what this means?) and a phosphate group.
 DNA is found in the cell nucleus. It is the genetic material that allows for protein synthesis and replicates itself before cell division. Its sugar is deoxyribose and its bases adenine, guanine, cytosine and thiamine. It forms the famous double helix shape.
 RNA is formed in the cytoplasm and copies part of the DNA to carry out its instructions for protein synthesis. Its sugar is ribose and its bases adenine, guanine, cytosine and uracil. Its shape is a singe strand, straight or folded.
[170] Kathleen DesMaisons *Potatoes Not Prozac, A Natural Seven-Step Dietary Plan to Stabilize the Level of Sugar in Your Blood, Control Your Cravings and Lose Weight, and Recognize How Foods Affect the Way You Feel.*

fore means the liver has longer to more effectively remove and process the products of carbohydrate digestion, creating lower insulin demand, better long-term blood glucose control and a reduction in blood lipids. The current methods use glucose as a reference food, giving it a glycaemic index value of 100. You can compare this to the foods listed below.

Low GI foods – less than 55

Peanuts, low-fat yoghurt, cherries, grapefruit, pearl barley, red lentils, milk, dried apricots, butter beans, fettuccine pasta, brown (wholemeal) pasta, apples, pears, tinned tomato soup, apple juice, noodles, white pasta, All Bran, chick peas, peaches, porridge made with water, oranges, white grapes, orange juice, peas, baked beans, carrots, kiwi fruit, brown rice, crisps, banana, raw oat bran, sweet corn, course grain bread, rye bread, course grain whole wheat bread and porridge from ground oats

Medium Glycaemic Index foods (56 to 69)

(You may include a few of these foods each day, but again limit portion sizes if you want to lose weight). Wholemeal bread, muesli, boiled potatoes, sultanas, pitta bread, white basmati rice, honey, digestive biscuits, cheese and tomato pizza, ice cream, new potatoes, tinned apricots, raisins, shortbread biscuits, couscous, pineapple, sweet melon, croissant, Ryvita and crumpet.

High Glycaemic Index foods (70 or more)

(Swap these foods for those with a low GI value or eat them together with a low GI food. Having a jacket potato with baked beans, for example, will lower the GI value of that whole meal). Porridge from rolled oats, instant porridge, mashed potatoes, jacket potato, all kinds of white bread, watermelon, swede, bagel, bran flakes, chips, all cereals containing sugar, sweeties, rice cakes, parsnips, ordinary white rice and sugar.

Fats or 'Lipids'

There are different types of fat. Important in the body are neutral fats and phospholipids, plus some others, like steroids and vitamins A, D, E and K. Fats are mainly used for energy production, and a little for construction.

Neutral Fats

Neutral fats are called **triglycerides**. They are very large molecules, and must be broken down into their building blocks before absorption. Fats are digested to fatty acids and glycerol then re-converted to triglycerides for transport in the lymph. The length of the fatty acid chain of a fat, and how 'saturated' with hydrogen ions, determines how solid a neutral fat is at a given temperature. Longer chains of **saturated fatty acids** are solid at room temperature (e.g. animal fats like lard). Shorter chains with double bonds between carbon atoms are what we call **unsaturated fats**. These are liquid at room temperature (e.g. vegetable oils like olive, peanut (mono-unsaturated), corn, soybean, and sunflower oil (poly-unsaturated)). Basically, a healthy and balanced fat intake is one in which we eat more PUFAs (poly-unsaturated fatty acids) and MUFAs (mono-unsaturated fatty acids) from vegetable and fish, and less saturated animal fats from meat and dairy products.[171]

The liver can make most of the fatty acids we need except for **linoleic** acid (from lecithin) and **linolenic acid**. Linoleic and linolenic acids are **essential fatty acids**, so-called because the body needs them but cannot make them – they must be eaten in the diet. Current thinking is that many of us are deficient in these essential fatty acids, and when we do eat them, they are likely to not be in the best proportion – we should have a higher proportion of 3s to 6s, and mostly people have too many 6s and not enough 3s. Essential fatty acids are long-chain polyunsaturated fatty acids from linolenic, linoleic, and oleic acids, being classed in two families: **Omega-3** and **Omega-6**. (There is also an Omega-9 fatty acid. Although the body needs this too it is classed as "non-essential" because the body can manufacture a little on its own from the essential fatty acids). The healthiest cell membranes contain a lot of omega-3 fatty acids which are highly flexible.[172]

Phospholipids

These are assembled in the body rather than taken in the diet, but are included here for completeness. They are modified triglycerides – being *di*glycerides with one phosphorus-containing group and only two fatty acid chains. Because of this they are uniquely 'di-polar', which means they have a non-polar end (the fatty part) and a polar end, the phosphorus-containing part.

Steroids

These are interesting molecules which are structurally different from fats but which are fat-soluble. The most important is cholesterol, ingested in meat, eggs and cheese, and a little produced by our liver.

Trans-fats – mad, bad and dangerous to eat…

Ultra-low fat diets full of processed 'low fat' foods are dangerous. Many companies are now removing **trans-fatty acids**, which are man-made poly-unsaturated fats found in some low-fat margarines and many processed foods. Trans-fats are taken up by the body and used to make cell membranes and tissues where naturally occurring poly-unsaturated fats would normally be used, and then they impair some aspects of cell function. They compete with

---

[171] Actually, this may not be true. A lot of the studies comparing the health benefits of saturated and unsaturated fats lumped saturated and trans-fats together thus invalidating the results. It is a lot more likely that trans-fats and rancid unsaturated fats are the main problems. In recent history there has been a move away from cooking with lard and butter towards cooking with vegetable oils, yet heart disease and others are increasing not decreasing (though of course this is likely only one of many factors). Consider also that Eskimos eat very high amounts of saturated fats and yet are very healthy, having much lower incidence of heart disease and other similar diseases. As an aside, skimmed milk is dangerous and amongst other diseases can lead to prostate cancer – a risk that is avoided with using whole milk products. Further, saturated fats may be more protective than harmful. The most likely thing is that fresh, organically grown or wild-crafted foods un-processed, not mucked around with in any way, are best. More on this later.

[172] It has been found that the composition of tissue and in particular of the nerve cell membrane of people in the US is different from that of the Japanese, who eat a diet rich in omega-3 fatty acids from fish. Americans have cell membranes higher in the less flexible omega-6 fatty acids, which appear to have displaced the elastic omega-3 fatty acids found in Japanese nerve cells.

normal fats in the body for enzymes, and replace normal fats and oils in **eicosanoid** formation (eicosanoids are fats used to make controlling substances including prostaglandins). It is now known that trans-fats raise levels of unhealthy, heart-disease-causing LDL cholesterol (low density lipid), and lower levels of the healthier high HDL cholesterol (high density lipid), as well as increasing triglyceride levels and lipoprotein. As well as increasing coronary heart disease, other health problems including skin problems, impaired brain and nerve function, and more tendencies to asthma and arthritis. It is these unnatural trans-fats which are the real problem, not simply saturated fats from animals. Check labels for 'vegetable fat' or 'partially hydrogenated' vegetable oil and aim to avoid these.

What foods contain fats

The most abundant are neutral fats. These can either be saturated fats in animal foods like meat, dairy and eggs, or unsaturated fats in seeds, nuts and vegetable oils. We also get cholesterol from the diet, mainly from egg yolk, milk and meat.

How the body uses fats

Neutral fats are the most efficient and compact way for the body to store fuels. Deposits are found largely beneath the skin. They also provide insulation from heat loss and protection from trauma.

Phospholipids are used in making cell membranes.

Cholesterol is the essential raw material the body uses to make vitamin D, steroid hormones (including the sex hormones and cortisol) and bile salts, as well as myelin.

Essential Fatty Acids – the Omegas

Essential fatty acids are used in the body to make important regulatory substances called **thromboxanes, prostaglandins and leukotrienes**. These are involved in blood clotting (thromboxanes), inflammation (prostaglandins & leukotrienes), womb activity, digestive function (both movement and secretion of enzymes) and regulation of blood pressure (prostaglandins). Eicosanoids are the essential fatty acids gamma linolenic acid (**GLA**) and ecospentanoic acid (**EPA**). Looking at the ways in which the body converts linoleic and linolenic acids into the fatty acids which serve as the raw ingredients for **eicosanoids** (prostaglandins, leukotrienes and thromboxanes) can give us useful information about the importance of essential fatty acids. We will take a look at these **Omega-6** and **Omega-3 pathways** here.

The **Omega-6 pathway** starts with **linoleic acid**, a substance which is found in many seed and vegetable oils (sunflower, safflower, walnut, corn and soya), as well as nuts, organ meats and human milk. Some linoleic acid is made into **arachidonic acid** (also found in quantities in meat, liver, kidney, egg yolk, and prawns), which is used to make those eicosanoids which have an *inflammatory* effect on the body, as well as being thrombotic (blood clotting) and increasing muscle spasm. Some Omega-6 fatty acids go to make *anti-inflammatory* eicosanoids *before* the inflammatory arachidonic acid is made. One type of Omega-6 which tends to end up as anti-inflammatory eicosanoids is *gamma*-linolenic acid (GLA), found in evening primrose oil, blackcurrant seed oil and star-flower oil. It seems to be the relative *amounts* of the starting materials eaten that will affect the ratio the body makes of anti-inflammatory to pro-inflammatory prostaglandins. If we eat more animal products, more pro-inflammatory prostaglandins seem to be produced. Of course, even if lots of vegetable oils are eaten rather than animal fats, both pro and anti inflammatory substances prostaglandins will be made – we need the inflammatory prostaglandins to keep the body properly repaired and healthy.

The **Omega-3 pathway** is about **linolenic acid** (found in linseed, hempseed, pumpkin and soya bean oil and dark green leafy vegetables). Only the eicosanoids with *anti-inflammatory*, anti-thrombotic and antispasmodic effects are made by the body from this pathway. In addition, **ecosapentanoic acid (EPA)** near the end of this pathway inhibits the conversion of arachidonic acid to the inflammatory eicosanoids because it uses the same enzyme. *So eating lots of EPA not only provides the ingredients for anti-inflammatory eicosanoids, but also actively reduces the pro-inflammatory ones our body can make.* EPA is one of the important active ingredients of fish oils. This is how they work to help inflammatory conditions such as arthritis, allergic conditions like eczema and asthma and gynaecological complaints: not only do they encourage the making of anti-inflammatory prostaglandins, but they block the creation of inflammatory ones. This Omega-3 pathway also acts to reduce blood clotting and therefore the risk of heart disease. As well as this, EPA is used to make the best possible quality flexible cell membranes, known to be important in the brain but no doubt also having an effect all over the body.

So the idea is to reduce the dietary intake of animal fats in favour of oily fish, and make sure your vegetable oil consumption isn't all sunflower oil, but includes linseed oil, as well as eating lots of leafy green vegetables.

To summarise, the Omega-3s always end up encouraging anti-inflammation, and the Omega-6s can encourage anti-inflammation or inflammation, whilst animal fats (from meat and dairy) encourage inflammation.

Western medical thinking has often been wrong about fat. The early idea was that the problem was with saturated fats, thinking they can clog up the arteries as fatty deposits called **atheromas** collect on blood vessel walls. This was seen as a major contributing factor in high blood pressure and heart disease. Also, excess fat in the body means more fat collecting around internal organs, which always need a bit of fat for protection. If a lot of extra fat accumulates around the heart, it must work harder. However, newer thinking is a little more complex than just avoiding all fats. We need to not simply eat less saturated fat (an idea which has led to a huge 'fat free' food industry, and, as discussed earlier, is almost certainly wrong, the harmful effects of fat being more likely due to trans-fats), but actually eat more polyunsaturated fats from vegetables with an emphasis on the Omega-3s. Remembering that this includes eating much more green leafy vegetables too, by which we can give the body ingredients for making more of the anti-inflammatory eicosanoids, thereby protecting it from coronary heart disease and other inflammatory conditions ranging from arthritis to endometriosis and other gynaecological conditions.[173]

Proteins

Proteins are the main structural materials of the body, also having the most varied functions of any molecules in the body. Proteins make enzymes, haemoglobin, the contractile proteins of muscle actin and myosin, immunoglobulins, hormones and more.

What foods contain proteins

Proteins make up most of the body, and this goes for animals too, so all animal and fish flesh is high in protein, as are dairy products such as milk and cheese. But plants are the alchemists of the earth, and it is they that originally make amino acids by fixing the nitrogen from the earth into the soil and taking it up to build into amino acids. If you think about it, cows eat only plants, turning grass into all that solid muscle. We can't do this, not because the amino acids aren't available in grass, but because our digestive system is not able to access them. [174] All the amino acids we need are in plants, but in order to get them, some attention to what we eat is needed. Vegetarians need to think about their food groups. There are basically three groups of vegetables: beans and pulses, grains, and nuts and seeds. To get complete protein from one meal, you need to eat two of the three groups together. In other words, peanut butter (nut) on bread (grain); rice (grain) and lentils or peas (pulse); humus – made of chickpeas (pulse) and tahini (sesame seeds). I'm sure you get the idea. Don't let this put you off vegetarianism: vegetarians definitely live longer than meat eaters, at least in the modern Western world.[175] Soya beans are unusual in that they contain all the essential amino acids. This is why tofu and tempeh are such useful foods.[176]

---

[173] To get to grips more with this important topic take a look at Ruth Trickey *Women, Hormones and the Menstrual Cycle*, and Dr Paul Clayton's *Health Defence*.

[174] There is a way of making a 'curd' from grass and stinging nettles that we can eat to access these amino acids. It's called 'LEAFU' and it involves a lot of boiling and skimming and pressing. You end up with a very dark green stuff that tastes a bit like seaweed and is highly nutritious. 'The basic principal is to juice lush leafy matter [not gone to seed] and heat the filtered juice just up to boiling point. The resulting green 'scum' you skim off and put in calico, or similar fine cloth and press slowly but very well to get all the fluid out [may take several hours]. You end up with the 'scum' turning into a dark green tablet which can be cut up and added to food. Equipment is the thing. There is still nothing I can recommend. However have a go with whatever you can come up with, and let me know how it goes.' Thanks to Michael Cole info@leafcycle.co.uk or leafudevon@hotmail.com

[175] "VEGETARIAN DIETS and LONGEVITY: A study of 11,000 vegetarian and health-conscious people followed for an average of 17 years found that they had an overall mortality level 44 percent below that of the general population." *British Medical Journal* 1996;313:775-79. From: http://www.earthsave.org/health/rxhealth.htm

[176] Plus it seems there is a protective anti-cancer effect from eating soya, at least in traditional ways such as in tofu and tempeh as is done in Japan. Levels of breast cancer there, for example are much lower than in the West. It's likely that soya milk which is a more recent invention is not so good. Of course, the Japanese also have a diet very high in Omega 3s, which no doubt has an effect also.

How the body uses proteins

Fibrous proteins include collagen, which is found in abundance in connective tissue including bones, tendons and ligaments, skin, arteries and veins – in fact everywhere in the body. Keratin waterproofs the skin, hair and nails. Elastin is what gives elasticity to ligaments and elastic connective tissue, allowing the lungs, the bladder and the arteries to stretch and recoil back. Finally, actin and myosin are the fibrous proteins responsible for muscle contraction and cell division, actin also being used for intracellular transport.

Globular proteins are also called functional proteins, and play crucial roles in almost all biological processes, consider the implications here of increasing microwave pollution. It has been observed that microwave pollution causes changes to protein production in cells and that these changes extend even to the cells' genes.[177]

Protein enzymes include salivary amylase and oxidase enzymes, amongst many others. There are transport proteins such as haemoglobin (transporting oxygen) and lipoproteins (transporting fats), plus many others. The plasma proteins, including albumin, provide osmotic pressure to the blood, as well as being either a base or an acid, thus keeping pH balanced in the blood. There are also protein hormones, such as growth hormone and insulin, and immune functioning proteins such as antibodies, complement proteins and molecular chaperones.[178]

Vitamins and Minerals

Vitamins are used in tiny amounts for growth and maintaining good health. They are not used for energy or building blocks, but mainly function as 'coenzymes' or parts of coenzymes. Coenzymes are substances which act with an enzyme to accomplish a particular task; For example, some B vitamins work as coenzymes in glucose oxidation. Vitamin D acts as a hormone.

Most vitamins are not made in the body and must be taken in food, except vitamin D (made in the skin in the presence of sunlight), and vitamin K (made by bacteria in the bowel). There are fat soluble vitamins (A, D, E and K), and water soluble (B and C). Vitamins are involved in an incredibly diverse number of activities in the body, from bone formation to skin and mucous membrane development and maintenance to blood clotting and anti-oxidation (the mopping up of free radicals, the by-products of oxidation, which cause tissue

---

[177] European Union Risk Evaluation of Potential Environmental Hazards from Low Frequency Electromagnetic Field Exposure Using Sensitve in vitro Methods. December 2004 – from WDDTY Vol 17 no 7 October 2006.

[178] The **complement system** is a cascade of chemicals which helps clear pathogens from the body. It is part of the innate immune system – however, it can be recruited and brought into action by the specific immune system. Small proteins circulate normally in the blood, and when stimulated they change to release cytokines, which attack the membranes of pathogens. Proteins in this system account for about 5% of the globulins in the blood.
Chaperones are proteins that help with the folding/unfolding and the assembly/disassembly of large molecules. When a large protein is being made, for example, chaperones prevent polypeptide chains from joining too soon into a big structure that doesn't function properly. **Enzymes** are catalysts. Most are proteins. They temporarily bind to one or more parties in a reaction, speeding up the reaction but not being changed themselves. Many of them need vitamins and minerals to be made.

damage and are implicated in cancer formation and aging).

Minerals are also needed in moderate amounts. These include calcium, phosphorus, sulphur, potassium, sodium, chlorine, magnesium, iron, iodine, zinc, copper, chromium, cobalt, fluorine, selenium and manganese. Some are needed only in minute amounts so are called 'trace minerals' or elements. However all are essential for functioning.

NUTRIENT	ESSENTIAL FOR	FOUND IN
Vitamin A	Vision, growth, reproduction and maintenance of healthy skin	Liver, fish oils, eggs, dairy products. Red, yellow, orange, and dark green vegetables and fruits contain alpha- and beta-carotenes, which are converted in the body to Vitamin A
Vitamin D	Proper formation and maintenance of bones and teeth	D-fortified milk and cereals, cod liver oil and naturally in the skin when exposed to sunlight
Vitamin E	Antioxidant action, defends cells against damage by free radicals	Vegetable oils, margarine, wheat germ, nuts, seeds and green leafy vegetables
Vitamin K	Blood clotting	Eggs, cereal and green leafy vegetables
Vitamin C	Healthy bones and teeth, wound healing	Fruits (especially citrus) and vegetables (especially those in the cabbage family)
Thiamin (Vitamin B_1)	Carbohydrate metabolism (energy production)	Whole or enriched grain products, fortified cereals, pork and organ meats
Riboflavin (Vitamin B_2)	Metabolism of protein, fat, and carbohydrates into energy	Milk and other dairy foods, organ meats and enriched and fortified grains
Niacin (Vitamin B_3)	Carbohydrate, protein, and fat metabolism	Poultry, fish, beef, peanut butter, legumes and enriched or fortified grain products
Vitamin B_6	Manufacture of amino acids and red blood cells	Fortified cereals, sweet potatoes, chicken and beef and liver
Vitamin B_{12}	Energy and amino acid production	Beef, milk, cheese and shellfish
Calcium	Making and maintaining bones, muscle and nerve function	Dairy products, leafy green vegetables and calcium-fortified foods (e.g. orange juice, cereals)
Iron	Carries oxygen in red blood cells to body cells	Meats, eggs and dark leafy vegetables
Phosphorus	Supporting tissue growth and repair, major bone component	Milk, meat, poultry, fish, eggs, legumes and nuts
Magnesium	Energy production and nerve function	Legumes, nuts, whole grains and green vegetables

Potassium	Nerve function and muscle contraction	Fruits, vegetables, meat, poultry, fish and milk
Folate	DNA synthesis; involved in making protein	Fortified cereals, enriched grains, leafy greens, legumes and asparagus
Zinc	Cell reproduction and tissue growth and repair	Meat, eggs, seafood and whole grains

What Happens in the Gut – Digestive Processes

The digestive or GIT (gastrointestinal) system consists of a long tube that goes from the mouth to the anus, with various 'accessory organs' which produce digestive enzymes (remember enzymes? chemicals which speed up or slow down chemical reactions) and other substances to help with digestion. Digestive enzymes affect reactions involving the breakdown of food and control of digestion.

The tube of the gastrointestinal tract is made of four layers. The innermost layer is of course epithelial tissue. The mouth and oesophagus have a compound epithelium, but the rest of the tube is lined with simple, columnar shaped epithelium, a single layer of cells, which is replaced every twenty-four hours. Beneath the epithelial lining, which secretes mucous and so is known as the **mucosa**, is a **sub-mucosa** layer. This is special to the gut, and contains enzyme producing glands as well as an extraordinarily complex network of nerves.

There are in fact so many nerves in the sub-mucosa of the gut that they are known as the **ENS (enteric nervous system)**. Yes, we really do have 'gut feelings': the ENS produces neurotransmitters just like those found in the brain. There are 100 million neurons in the gut. Every type of neurotransmitter has been found in the gut – in fact, it is here that 95% of our body's serotonin is produced (so much, in fact that it would poison us if it got into the blood). The main nerve controlling gut activity is the vagus nerve, but the gut can influence the brain via this nerve also. Even if the vagus nerve is cut, the gut continues to function and regulate its own activities. The epithelial cells of the gut wall make neurotransmitters, as well as the nerve cells of the submucosa.[179]

After the sub-mucosal layer is the **muscle layer**, made up of smooth muscle cells arranged in length-wise and cross-wise sheets all along the gut tube. In the stomach there is an extra layer going diagonally.

The outer layer is, as usual, **connective tissue**, supporting and protecting the whole tube. In places, this forms part of a special protective membrane called the **peritoneum**, a serous membrane similar to the pleura of the lung and the pericardium of the heart.

Digestion is said to be carried out in both mechanical and chemical ways. Mechanical digestion involves the physical munching and churning of food, both the obvious chewing

---

[179] Candace Pert discusses this fascinating subject in her book *Molecules of Emotion*.

and chomping which goes on in the mouth and the more hidden inner movements of the digestive tract. If you put your ear on a friend's tummy, you won't have to wait long before you hear some noises – evidence of the constant movements of the gut.

Chemical digestion is done by the digestive enzymes. These break down food by hydrolysis; that is, by the addition of a water molecule between each bond to be 'lysed' or broken, the opposite of 'dehydration synthesis'.

The *accessory organs* are the liver, gall bladder and pancreas. As well as producing bile to help with fat digestion, the **liver** also processes the end products of digestion, and stores things for future use. In fact, this amazing organ has more than a thousand known functions – and you can bet there are more we don't yet know about. So don't be fooled by its title of 'accessory organ': it is one of our most important and complex organs, and I've given it a chapter all to itself. The **gall bladder** is a small muscular sack found underneath the middle part of the liver. The gall bladder collects the bile the liver makes and concentrates it, storing it until a fatty meal enters the small intestine, upon which the gall bladder contracts and squeezes bile into the intestines to help digest fats. The other accessory organ is the **pancreas** which is crucial for digestive function. The pancreas makes gallons of digestive enzymes daily, as well as hormones involved in keeping the blood sugar balanced.

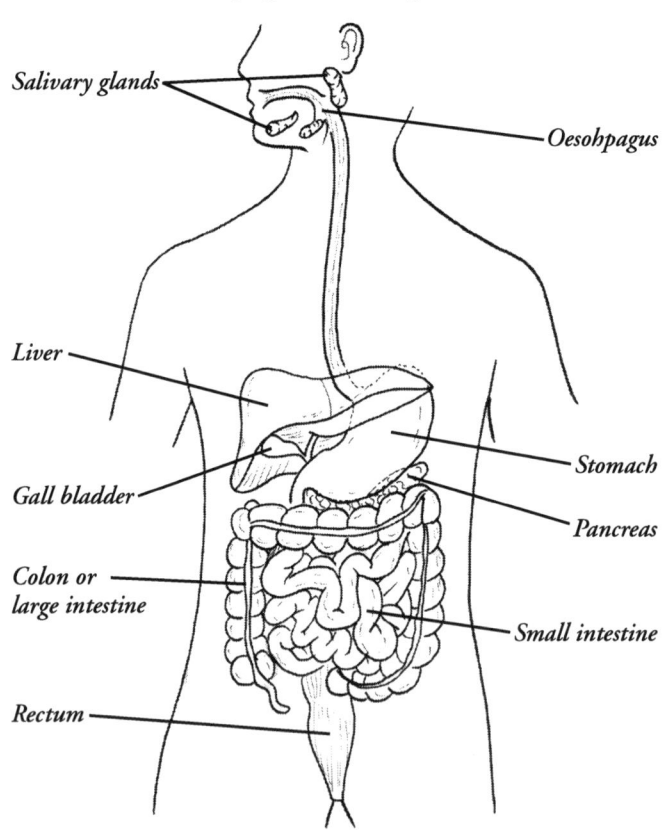

There are four activities in the digestive system: ingestion, digestion, absorption and elimination. In plain English this means eating food, breaking it down, taking into the bloodstream what we want and getting rid of what we don't want. In a nutshell, we eat and break down food into component parts by churning it up and mixing it with digestive enzymes, then (mainly in the small intestine) we absorb the bits we want. The rest stays in the tube, and in the large intestine we absorb water from it to make it solid then excrete out this unwanted matter as faeces. We will now take a look at the processes which go on in each part of the gastrointestinal tract, starting at the top.

The mouth

Chewing mechanically breaks down food. This 'mastication' involves the thirty-two teeth, the lips, the tongue and the muscles of the cheeks (called masseter and temporalis).

A few dentists are interested in looking at dental health in a holistic way – in other words, considering that problems in the teeth can be related to problems elsewhere. There is said to be a correlation between energy lines or meridians and individual teeth; one theory is that low level chronic problems, such as can ensue from a root canal with a small chronic inflammation persisting at the dead root of the tooth (and which may be difficult to feel because the nerve has been killed), can cause corresponding problems elsewhere in the body.[180]

Saliva is a watery fluid made and secreted by the three pairs of salivary glands (the parotid, sublingual and submandibular glands). Saliva contains salivary amylase which begins starch digestion, breaking down starches to the disaccharide maltose. About 1.5 litres per day of saliva is produced, being a mixture of water and mucous. Saliva also contains lysosyme, a disinfectant which lyses the cell walls of bacteria to destroy them. Production and secretion of saliva is under autonomic control (it happens automatically). Like all other digestive activities, it is stimulated by parasympathetic nerves and inhibited by sympathetic stimulation. This means that when we are afraid, we get a dry mouth. If you concentrate on keeping your mouth full of saliva, you can encourage parasympathetic action in your nervous system. There is a surgeon who operates without anaesthetic, using biofeedback mechanisms to help his patients stay in a relaxed state; one important thing is keeping the mouth full of saliva. A dry mouth increases sympathetic activity and therefore our sensation of fear (in other words, when you get afraid the fear dries out your mouth, and that in turn makes you more afraid). It seems if the mouth is wet we are less likely to become afraid and tense. Have you ever noticed yourself salivating with pleasure or anticipation? When hypnotists use hypnotism to enable a person to have an operation without anaesthetic, one important thing is that the person must keep their mouth moist at all times.

The presence of food in the mouth, as well as the smell, and even the thought of food, begins this reflex secretion. Swallowing begins as a conscious movement, then as the food

---

[180] What Doctors Don't Tell You, July 2008.

reaches the back of the tongue, a reflex automatic swallowing action takes over, continuing as a **peristaltic wave** in the longitudinal and circular muscle layer of the whole of the digestive tube. The first part of this is called the food pipe, or **oesophagus**.

The oesophagus

Peristalsis propels food along the alimentary canal; gravity is not required. Generally, it takes about one second per inch for swallowed food to reach the stomach.[181] The oesophagus is designed to withstand a certain amount of rough treatment: it is lined with compound epithelium and its mucosa produces a good layer of mucous with which to protect itself. At the bottom the oesophagus passes through the diaphragm, which helps to form a sphincter muscle – the cardiac sphincter (or lower oesophageal sphincter) – which should only allow food to pass down into the stomach (except if it should need to open to allow vomiting). If this sphincter stops working properly, a person suffers from 'reflux' of stomach acid into the oesophagus, which can cause a painful inflammation, known as reflux oesophagitis or heartburn. If the sphincter becomes badly incompetent, part of the stomach can herniate (protrude) through it. This is the very painful condition called hiatus hernia.

The stomach

The stomach functions as a reservoir. Although a continuous part of the tube, it can close itself off and form a bag by closing the cardiac and pyloric sphincters (the pyloric sphincter blocks the exit of the stomach into the small intestine). The stomach receives eaten food and mixes it with **gastric juice**, containing **hydrochloric acid**. Hydrochloric acid has the incredibly acidic pH of 1, which is so strongly acidic it would burn your skin if dropped onto it. Gastric juice also contains **pepsinogen**, mucus, water, intrinsic factor and gastric lipase. Gastric juice is secreted in varying proportions as a result of a local hormone called **gastrin** being released by the stomach's g-cells; gastrin is secreted when peptides are detected in food entering the stomach. Thus the amount of acid secreted varies according to the protein content of a meal and by the stomach being stretched.[182] Gastrin also increases movement in the stomach. This is a neat example of the way the digestive system controls itself. As well as being affected by outside stimulus (for example the nervous system), activity in each part

---

[181] Old herbalists in Britain used to do the 'deglut' test to check the speed of a person's peristalsis; the patient lies down, and holds a small amount of water in their mouth. The herbalist has a stethoscope over the patients' stomach, and looks at a watch with a second hand. The herbalist says 'go' and the patient swallows. The time it takes to hear a gurgle as the water enters the stomach is noted. If it takes much less than 7-8 seconds, it may indicate hypermotility in the GIT. If it takes much more than 8-9 seconds, it may indicate a slow peristalsis. This would not be used on its own as a diagnosis – more that it can give another piece of the puzzle.

[182] Interestingly, the acid secretion is actually controlled by gastrin causing histamine to be secreted, which then affects acid secretion. So taking antihistamines regularly can have an effect on your digestion. Also, the brain uses histamine as a neurotransmitter – it seems that it stimulates brain activity, making lots more glucose available for the brain cells, which we need in a tricky situation. This is why antihistamines make you drowsy.

often stimulates the next section to ready itself for action.

The pepsinogen is activated into **pepsin** by the hydrochloric acid, which also acts as a superior solvent to water. Pepsin must be made in its inactive form, since its function is to dissolve and digest protein, and as the body is made of protein. If it was made in active form it would simply digest the stomach cells as soon as they made it. When the pepsinogen and acid meet, the pepsinogen is activated into pepsin and begins protein digestion. The hydrochloric acid is also a strong disinfectant, killing ingested bacteria and parasites, and it also acts as the stimulus to secretion of **CCK** (**cholecystokinin**) by the duodenum, which in turn causes secretion of **bile** and **pancreatic juice**. To protect itself from the strong acid, the stomach lines itself with a millimetre thick layer of alkaline mucous.

Once the pepsin begins protein digestion – food is churned into **chyme**, which, within a few hours, enters the small intestine. Stomach emptying rates vary with different meals – carbohydrate meals empty sooner than protein and fat meals. Light fruit and vegetable meals may only stay an hour. Meals heavy on fat and meat could stay up to 6 hours. The rate of emptying is controlled by nerves and hormones.

The small intestine

The small intestine comprises three parts: the **duodenum**, **jejunum** and **ileum**. In an adult the whole thing is about six metres (twenty feet) long, and one inch thick. It has the same four layers as the rest of the gastrointestinal tract. The entire population of epithelial cells in the intestine, which has secretory cells as well as absorptive cells, is replaced every few days.

The muscle layer, or **muscularis**, of the small intestine carries out movements called **segmentation** as well as peristalsis (segmentation is as it sounds, a closing off of small segments of the tube at a time). It is in the small intestine that digestion is finished and most of the absorption of nutrients occurs, so it is perfectly designed for these processes. In the first part, lots of digestive juices are squirted into the duodenum to finish off the digestion of starches, fats and proteins.

The wall of the small intestine is folded again and again to give maximum surface area. There are big folds, and small folds called **villi**. Each **villus** contains a central lymph duct, called a **lacteal**, into which fats are absorbed into a network of capillaries that form part of the **portal circulation**. The epithelial surfaces of the villi send up tiny projections called **microvilli**, which further increase the surface area. This all means that there is a vast area of mucosa for digested nutrients to be absorbed by.

Looking at the small intestine in parts, there are three sections. The first is the **duodenum**. About 10 inches long, the mucosal walls here (as well as in the next part which is called the jejunum) produce two local hormones called **secretin** and **cholecystokinin** (**CCK**), as well as other regulating hormones. Secretin causes the pancreas to make and secrete a bicarbonate-rich fluid to neutralize the acid of the stomach,[183] and it also inhibits stomach functions, slowing things down there – basically opposing the actions of gastrin. CCK acts on both the gall bladder and the exocrine part of the pancreas[184], causing bile and pancreatic juice to be secreted. These enter the duodenum together at the **sphincter of Oddi**. However, CCK is also a neuropeptide: a neurotransmitter or brain chemical which works in the brain to stop us feeling hungry. CCK also has receptors in the immune system and spleen. It is probable that the effect of CCK on these is to quiet down the immune system: eating heavily generally does depress immune function, which makes sense as it lessens the chances of newly absorbed foods being treated as foreigners and triggering an immune response.

Candace Pert is one scientist who has done years of research on neuropeptides, or as she calls them 'the molecules of emotion'. There is a two way communication between the brain and the body, mediated by these small proteins for which receptors can be found all over the brain and body. This network of communication translates into our experience as memories stored in the body, and illness or disease being expressed in our emotions and in our bodies – and this is very much a two-way street.[185] As the ancient Chinese understood, strong emotions can affect our physical functions, but also if our physical functions are out of balance, these in turn affect our emotions.

As we have already discussed, the whole gastrointestinal tract has a vast and complex nervous system of its own, the **enteric nervous system** (**ENS**), in addition to its parasympathetic and sympathetic supply. Digestive processes are sped up by parasympathetic stimulation from the brain and slowed down by the sympathetic stimulation of the fight or flight response, but many of the processes of digestion are mediated by internal nervous control. The ENS completely regulates peristalsis, and other digestive functions are carried out without interference from the central nervous system. The particular relationship between the brain, emotions and gut functioning have long been recognized by some systems of natural healing, as well as in common understanding (think how many references there are to gut feelings, butterflies in your stomach, can't stomach it and so on).

Pancreatic juice contains enzymes to digest starch, protein and fat. Bile emulsifies fats. You can think of bile as being like detergent. Have you ever tried to wash up a fat-covered plate without washing up liquid? The water simply runs off the oil. This is because fats and oils like

---

[183] The 'intestinal neutralization equation' is important in maintaining the body's acid-base balance. It is what happens in our small intestine when stomach contents containing hydrochloric acid (HCl) enter it. The acid would eat into our intestinal wall and damage it, but the liver and pancreas make sodium bicarbonate ($NaHCO_3$) which enters the small intestine with bile and pancreatic juice and neutralizes the stomach acid into a very weak acid called carbonic acid.

Hydrochloric acid + Sodium bicarbonate = sodium chloride + carbonic acid
(Strong acid)   (weak base)   (salt)   (weak acid)

[184] Exocrine glands secrete into a local area of the body. Endocrine glands secrete into the blood, therefore their secretions (called hormones) travel all over the body and can have far reaching effects. The pancreas has two parts: an exocrine part which secretes digestive enzymes into the small intestine, and an endocrine part, secreting the hormones which control blood sugar into the blood (insulin and glucagon).

[185] Candace Pert *Molecules of Emotion*.

to stick together, but don't like water. What washing up liquid does is **emulsify** the fats. This means it gets in there and separates the fat molecules, encouraging them to mix with the water instead of sticking together. Bile basically does the same thing: it doesn't actually digest the fat molecules (i.e. break them down into fatty acids and glycerol), but it separates them out so the lipases – the enzymes which digest fats – have a bigger surface area to work on.

The other parts of the small intestine are the **jejunum** and **ileum**. Digestion is completed as bile emulsifies fats, and pancreatic juice containing proteases,[186] lipases, amylases and nucleases continue breakdown of food to its building blocks: proteins into amino acids, fats into fatty acids and glycerol, starches into sugars, nucleic acids into amino acids, sugars and phosphate.

Absorption of nutrients

No matter how good your guts are at digesting the food you eat, if you can't then absorb the nutrients into the blood, you will starve. Absorption occurs by passive and active mechanisms. The small intestine wall is folded many times, with villi and microvilli, to create a huge surface area. The nutrients are absorbed across the absorptive cells and enter either blood capillaries, or the lacteal (lymph duct),[187] in the case of fats. The blood capillaries join into venules which join into veins which join to form the **hepatic portal vein**. This is a major vein which goes to the liver, ensuring that any substances that enter the bloodstream go first to that amazing organ of detoxification.

Malabsorption

Malabsorption can result from anything that interferes with normal digestion: a problem with bile or pancreatic juice getting to the small intestine or damage to the mucosal lining, for example. The incredibly complex nature of the digestive processes means there are plenty of potential nutrition problems. Naturopathic medicine and nutritional therapies recognize a lot more complex nutritional deficiencies than does orthodox medicine, which really only considers the most enormous problems, like, for example, celiac disease (or gluten enteropathy). This is a disorder resulting when gluten, a protein from wheat, rye, barley and oats, is poorly digested and damages the intestinal villi resulting in diarrhoea, pain and malnutrition. Strangely, it seems orthodox medicine has not caught on fully to the importance of good nutrition – think of the food you get to eat in hospital!

---

[186] These are secreted in inactive form and activated by a hormone called enterokinase (sound familiar?). Just like the pepsinogen in the stomach being activated by hydrochloric acid.

[187] I wonder about the increased incidences of many cancers in meat eaters, as compared with vegetarians. Surely a high fat diet, eating meat and dairy products daily as many in the industrialised West do, clogs up your lymph system? There must be loads of fat in the last parts of the system, as it enters here before returning to the blood circulation. It seems likely that this extra load would make it harder for the lymphatic system to do its work of cleaning things up.

Leaky Gut Syndrome

Whole proteins are not usually absorbed. They are too big to cross the epithelial lining of the gut. Sometimes this lining becomes impaired and 'leaky', allowing proteins which would normally not have been absorbed to enter the blood. Strange proteins in the blood upset the immune system, which instigates an immune attack against them. This is how some food allergies and intollerances appear.

These are very common in infants as the mucosa is immature – probably deliberately to allow IgA (Immunoglobulin A) antibodies in breast milk to reach the infant's blood stream. Also, it is thought that some foods are hard to digest and therefore more likely to be a problem (wheat and dairy, for example). Once there is a problem with one food, the gut wall can be impaired and more foods become problematic. The problem is not so much with the foods themselves, or the immune system, as with the gut.

The Large Intestine or Colon

After the small intestine, the chyme enters the large intestine, or **colon,** which is about 1.5 m long. The colon begins at the lower right abdomen with the **caecum** (from which the **appendix** comes), then goes up and around the belly; the **ascending, transverse, descending** and **sigmoid colons**. Here in the colon is where water and any nutrients left are absorbed from the digestive waste, making it more solid. This waste is known as **faeces**. For the colon to work well, we need plenty of dietary fibre in our diet. Fibre used to be called **roughage**. It consists of the edible parts of plants which our intestine cannot digest and absorb. In the large intestine, fibre is fermented by bacteria to produce gases (carbon dioxide, methane and hydrogen) and short chain fatty acids (butyrate, acetate and propionate). These short chain fatty acids are absorbed and used by the epithelial cells of the gut wall for fuel, or passed into the bloodstream. On beginning to eat more fibre a person will often initially get bloated and suffer from gas (wind), but usually the bacteria in the gut soon adapt to the increased fibre and these problems decrease. It is essential for health to have a good colony of bacteria in the gut. There are different types of fibre and we need them all. This means eating a good amount of fruit and vegetables which contain 'soluble fibre', as well as whole grains and cereals which contain 'insoluble fibre'. Fibre helps to prevent constipation (especially insoluble fibre, when taken in with plenty of water), lowers blood cholesterol and maintains stable blood glucose levels (soluble fibre). A low fibre diet (such as is eaten by meat eaters who do not eat sufficient fruit and vegetables) is associated with bowel diseases like diverticulitis and even bowel cancer. The type of soluble fibre called **FOS** (fructooligosaccharide*)*, is a **prebiotic**, which is the food of choice for the healthy, helpful bacteria in the gut. Eating plenty of this helps to ensure a healthy gut flora (more below).

Some bacteria enter the large intestine at the caecum; although most should have been killed off by the various acids and digestive enzymes of the stomach and small intestine. These bacteria thrive in the bowel, which is a good thing, as they make B vitamins and most of the vitamin K we need for blood clotting. Some of them make gases called **flatus**, a variety of which can be pretty smelly! Most bowels make about half a litre a day of gas. This is increased depending on the diet.

Naturopathic medicine gives a lot of thought to what is going on in the bowel, to asking the question 'is there a healthy 'gut flora'?'. This is not an unusual type of margarine (!), but refers to having the right balance of the best bacteria in your gut. These are the same bacteria which make yoghurt from milk – **acidophilus** and **bifidobacteria** being the two main types. Good gut bacteria can be established at birth: what should happen is, if we are born in the optimum natural way, our head comes out right past mum's anus. Any residual faeces in our mum's bowel will have been squeezed out whilst we were being pushed out – so there will plenty of her gut flora hanging around at the entrance to our world. Then we get put to her breast, right next to her armpit which has a particularly high concentration of bacteria living there. Thus we get 'colonised' by the right bacteria: our mum's (assuming of course that mum doesn't have a problem with her gut flora). Having a good colony of the right bacteria living with us means there is less room for more undesirable, disease-causing bacteria to move in and create problems. Then breast milk, by far the best food for infants, promotes the growth of bifidobacteria.[188]

Problems here are very common. Being born in hospital with any difficulties often means we are immediately removed from our mothers, so we don't get that initial opportunity to be colonized by the best sort of bacteria. Antibiotic therapy, whilst sometimes essential for keeping us alive, knocks out the healthy bacteria of our guts as well as any pathogenic ones (broad spectrum antibiotics are the worst). Once the helpful bacteria are gone, there is the opportunity for less helpful ones to thrive, plus potentially problematic yeasts such as the Candida which causes thrush and is normally found living with us anyway, but can become a problem if allowed to grow too much.

A diet full of refined carbohydrates and sugar feeds this kind of problem. Hormone therapy such as the contraceptive pill and hormone replacement therapy (H.R.T.), commonly prescribed for menopausal women, also encourages the wrong sort of gut flora. Excessive flatulence – farting – can be a sign that our gut flora is not as good as it could be.

While eating the right kind of bacteria – like live yoghurt – can do us good, in itself it is not an effective lasting treating for poor gut flora. More effective is to feed our helpful bacteria what they like to eat. This will make them multiply and grow, crowding out the 'bad guys'. What 'good' bacteria in the gut like to eat are called 'prebiotics' – non-digestible oligosaccharides, mentioned above. These are the plant equivalent of fat – they are how the plant stores energy in a concentrated form. The two main ones are inulin and FOS or oligofructose. They are found in many plants, the best being chicory root, Jerusalem artichoke, leeks, onions,

---

[188] Bifido bacteria represent 95% of the bacteria in the gut of a breast fed infant, compared with 25% in a bottle fed baby – making breast fed babies much more resistant to stomach upsets and diarrhoea, Paul Clayton *Health Defense*.

wheat, bananas, grains and vegetables. The longer vegetables have been stored in cold storage, for example before ending up on the supermarket shelves, the lower their inulin content.[189]

When the faeces enters the **rectum**, it's incredibly sensitive stretch receptors trigger the **defecation reflex**. If circumstances are favourable the faeces may then leave the body via the anus. The defecation reflex is interesting, in that it can be over-ridden if the time is not convenient – ever had that experience of having to rush out early in the morning before you had time to empty your bowels, then found yourself on the bus or somewhere you couldn't follow the urge when it came? In ordinary circumstances, you can ignore the feeling – suppress your defecation reflex. Only trouble is, what tends to happen then is you have trouble going later when the facilities are available. Regularly suppressing the reflex can lead to problems with constipation.

Brown Gold

In rural China in the olden days, poo was of great value. Any passing visitor was strongly encouraged to make a contribution to the family's privy before leaving!

The toilets were all compost loos, not the water-guzzling systems of today, but dry toilet systems. The basic variety is just a big hole, to which cellulose like hay or straw or sawdust or cardboard is added along with all the poo and wee. Did you know that after only one year of hanging around, the excrement turns into top quality soil or compost? And after two years, any pathogenic bacteria normally found in faeces, such as *E. Coli*, have gone.

Nowadays permaculture people generally use 'humanure' on crops such as fruit trees rather than lettuce, but it is still regarded as one of the best fertilizers in existence.

It's interesting how much 'stuff' us modern humans have about poo. Many people are horrified by the thought of a simple compost loo, yet happily put not only enormous quantities of poo into the sea, but also all those brightly coloured smelly chemicals called 'cleaning' products along with it. Meanwhile, we make artificial nitrogenous fertilizers which take much energy to produce and are quite toxic in ways we are only just beginning to realise, to put onto our crops which need them because the soil is so depleted (from lack of proper composting!). It simply is not good homeostasis!

In classical Chinese medicine, the colon - or Colon Official - is known as the 'Official who brings Purity and Sparkle'. Without getting rid of the dregs, the leftovers, the rubbish, there can be no purity and sparkle in our cells and tissues. The Colon Official does not only operate in the bowel, but is the energy responsible for removing rubbish or waste from every cell in the body, and indeed from every part of the mind and spirit. A person suffering from a serious colon imbalance can smell really rotten; of rubbish or even of faeces.

---

[189] Dr Paul Clayton *Health Defense*.

The Peritoneum

Lining the walls of the abdominal and pelvic cavities and surrounding the abdominal organs is found a serous membrane similar to the pericardium and the pleura, made of a mix of connective and epithelial tissue. This membrane is called the **peritoneum**, and is a double layered membrane with one layer lining the walls and one layer snug to the organs. Between the two layers is a potential space called the peritoneal cavity.

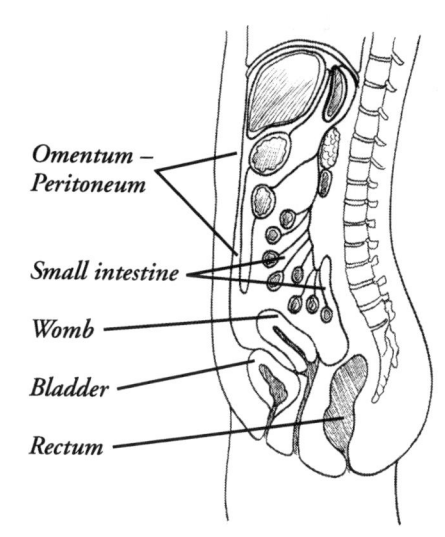

Development of the Digestive System

The very young embryo is flat and consists of three **germ layers** – layers of different types of cells – called the **ectoderm**, **mesoderm** and **endoderm**. These layers fold to form a cylindrical body, and it is the internal cavity of this which becomes the cavity of the digestive tract. This tube is closed at both ends to start with. The endoderm at the very front touches a part of the ectoderm called the **stomodeum** (meaning 'on the way to becoming the mouth'). These two layers, also called membranes, fuse, making the oral membrane which then becomes the mouth. A similar thing happens at the other end, with the endoderm fusing with the ectodermal **proctodeum** making the **cloacal membrane** which forms the anus. By the eighth week in the womb, the tube is continuous from mouth to anus and is open to the external environment at both ends. Soon after this the glandular organs – salivary glands, liver, gall bladder, and pancreas – bud out from the tube. They keep their connections to the tube, these becoming ducts opening into the digestive tract. Although the foetus gets its nutrients from the mother's blood via the placenta, its gut tube practices by swallowing amniotic fluid. This helps the development and maturation of the gastrointestinal tract. Sometimes things go wrong with the development of the gut, including cleft palate, cleft lip and tracheo-oesophageal fistula.[190] These are usually surgically corrected.

The newborn infant grows amazingly quickly, doubling its birth weight in 6 months. Its stomach is very small (about the size of a walnut) so it must eat little and often. Breast milk is the best food for a baby. The epithelial lining of the infant gut, as discussed with the immune system, is immature and much more 'leaky' than an adult gut. This is probably to allow the passing of the mother's antibodies, which are proteins, into the baby's blood. Many

---

[190] A fistula is an abnormal connection or tube or opening between two adjacent body tubes which normally are not connected. In this case, there is a connection between the oesophagus and the windpipe, which obviously can cause serious problems with breathing as milk can enter the windpipe.

health problems can come as a result of not being breast fed. To avoid likelihood of allergy development, a newborn should have only breast milk for the first six months, or longer if the child shows no great interest in other food and is developing well, and is best kept away from common problem foods like wheat, sugar, or cows milk until a year old. Of course any preservatives, colourings or other additives should be permanently avoided if possible.

The teeth start to grow when the baby is about six to seven months old, and come fully by about age two (although the back molars can be later), by which time a baby is eating an adult diet. Most children have a full set of twenty milk teeth by the time they are three. The milk teeth are pushed out by the permanent teeth growing up behind them, starting from the age of about five or six and finishing by the age of fourteen, by which time most children will have lost all their milk teeth and will have a full set of twenty-eight permanent teeth. At around age twenty, four more teeth usually grow at the back of the mouth – these are called the **wisdom teeth** and complete the adult set of thirty-two.

In old age the digestive processes decline.

A healthy diet?

Of course there is different opinion about what is a healthy diet, but I'm sorry to say the average general practitioner or family doctor is rarely a reliable source of knowledge about optimum nutrition. The standard British diet is not great: a preponderance of animal fats, wheat and sugar is not really a good recipe for health. It is strange that the current growing obesity problem in the UK comes as a surprise to anyone. It's really not enough to just eat five portions of fruit and vegetables a day – aim for more like ten. It's not rocket science, eating healthily. Basically, aim to cut out additives as much as you can and keep off drugs, including tea, coffee, alcohol and tobacco. Eat fresh foods, predominately vegetarian (vegetarians live about 6-8 years longer than meat eaters). Stick with 'whole foods' – this means unrefined brown rice, brown pasta and bread. Keep sugar to an absolute minimum.

Try and cut out wheat and dairy, give it at least a month then reintroduce one at a time, see how you feel. A lot of people feel better without them.

Drink mainly water. Bear in mind that fruit and vegetables contain lots of water. If you want the flavonoids from red wine, try grape juice instead or eat lots of red-coloured fruit and vegetables.

To anyone who says it's a boring diet, I'd say, why not try for a few months? you can feel so much better on good food that it soon becomes the kind of food you really fancy; feeling lethargic and low from a less healthy diet soon looks less appealing and interesting. If you need help with adjusting to a healthy diet, consult a nutritional therapist.

Here is something to consider about processed 'food', adapted from an editorial in the British Medical Journal (18 May 1996)[193] *about how the food industry resists responding to the need to reduce salt in processed foods now the connection with high blood pressure and heart disease is completely established:*

'The world's food and soft drink industry spent over £550m on advertising in 1994, compared with less than £5m on promoting fresh fruit and vegetables. In Britain, basic cooking skills are in decline as processed foods make up more of the average diet. To counter these forces governments will need to invest substantial resources in health education. The British government should be congratulated on the achievements of the Health of the Nation. But if it is serious about reducing premature deaths from cancer and heart disease it will need to ignore the voices of vested interest and listen to the advice of its independent expert advisors.'

Interrelationships

The digestive system delivers the nutrients required by every cell of each of the body's systems, so is vital to them all. The nutrients processed in the gut enter the blood or the **lymph** and are transported around the body by the **cardiovascular** system. Food is moved through the gut by action of its smooth muscle lining, and tone and condition of the **skeletal muscles** is involved in healthy bowel function. The diaphragm massages the abdominal organs and keeps them healthy, and forms part of the cardiac sphincter which stops food from moving up from the stomach into the oesophagus. The digestive system works with the **bones** under control of the **endocrine system** to keep calcium balance in the blood right. The endocrine and **nervous system** are very much involved in regulating the functions of the digestive system.

---

[193] EDITORIALS: Fiona Godlee *The food industry fights for salt* BMJ, May 1996; 312: 1239 – 1240.

Chapter Twelve

THE LIVER

The liver is a very large organ with over a thousand known functions. Don't worry; we won't discuss them all here! We will just look at some of the main ones.

The liver cells or **hepatocytes** are arranged in **lobules** around a central vein. Extra-leaky blood capillaries called **sinusoids** (or sinuses) run down to this central vein carrying blood from the **hepatic portal vein** and from the **hepatic artery**. Small **ductules** receiving the bile made by the hepatocytes run the other way from the blood and take the bile to the gall bladder.

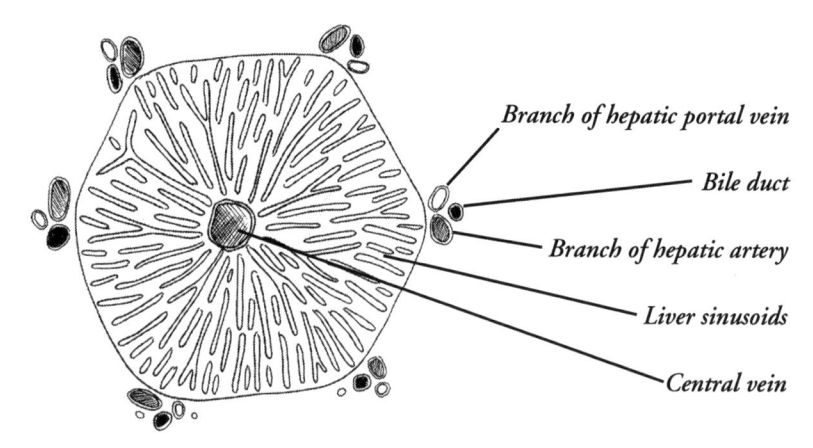

Branch of hepatic portal vein

Bile duct

Branch of hepatic artery

Liver sinusoids

Central vein

Creating bile

This is one of the main roles of the liver with respect to digestion. The liver lobules are specially arranged to secrete bile. Cells are arranged in a hexagon around a central vein, with a peripheral connection receiving incoming blood into sinusoids (very porous capillaries). This incoming blood is a mixture of arterial blood from the hepatic artery and blood from the hepatic portal vein that contains all substances recently absorbed from the gut. Hepatocytes secrete bile into small channels called canaliculi, which then join up to form the bile ducts. The bile flows in the opposite direction to the blood, to prevent their mixing. The hepatocytes get the ingredients of bile from the blood; these are water (97%), plus bile salts which are formed from cholesterol, some inorganic salts like sodium bicarbonate to make the bile alkaline, and bile pigments, which are made from the breakdown of haemoglobin from old red blood cells. Bile pigment is a water soluble yellow substance. It is what gives urine and faeces their characteristic colours, being either excreted by the colon or absorbed into the blood and excreted in the urine. If there is a problem in the liver blocking bile from entering the gut this results in jaundice, a yellow skin, due to the pigment building up in the blood, therefore in the skin. As well as having a yellow skin the person will have dark urine but a very light, putty-coloured stool;[194] the pigment is all in the urine, being water soluble and excreted by the kidney, but none is in the stool as it cannot get from the liver into the intestines. After the liver cells make it, the bile goes to the gall bladder where it is concentrated by water being removed from it, and stored until needed.

Some other functions of the liver

- Making plasma proteins. These include albumin, which provides the osmotic pressure of the blood, fibrinogen involved in clotting, and immunoglobulins for the immune system. Thus a healthy, well-functioning liver is crucial to immunity. Take a moment to consider the huge importance of this function, and the devastation in many areas of the body if something goes wrong with it.
- Making urea. Old amino acids which contain nitrogen are broken down in the liver and **deaminated**; the nitrogen which is poisonous to the body is packaged in a convenient water soluble molecule called **urea**. Urea is excreted by the kidneys in urine. Mixed with cellulose (for example, from cardboard), this makes wonderful compost – the nitrogen is returned to the soil for plants to use as they make amino acids.
- Detoxifying hormones, drugs and alcohol. The liver cells take alcohol and denature it. If your liver isn't working well, a small amount of alcohol will make you very drunk for a long time. This is what happens to alcoholics sooner or later. There are many special pathways in the liver involved in taking drugs and breaking them down – making them stop working, or putting them into an excretable form. This includes hormones[195] as well as exogenous drugs.
- Processing digestive products
- Storing iron and vitamins A, D, E and K
- Storing glucose as glycogen
- Making heat – due to all the chemical reactions going on there, the liver generates a lot of heat. This can be transported round the body via the blood.

The liver has a huge role in the regulation of metabolism. Some of these processes have already

---

[194] 'Stool' is the medical term for poo.

[195] Remember, the only way your stress hormones can be excreted whole is in tears – otherwise, the liver must deactivate them. So do your liver a favour: become a 'cry baby' today!

been mentioned, but as it is so important it is worth taking a more detailed look at it.

Blood sugar metabolism and its nervous and hormonal regulation

Only simple sugars are absorbed in the gut: glucose, galactose and fructose. The body likes glucose, so the liver converts galactose and fructose to this, and it is normally the only sugar in the blood. The brain *must* have glucose to make energy for its activities (skeletal and cardiac muscle prefer it too, but can use fatty acids instead).

The liver is known as the **glucostat** organ; it has a central role in keeping the blood sugar balanced. It stores glucose as glycogen when blood glucose is high, and releases it back into the blood as glucose later. The liver stores, as glycogen, one hundred times the amount of glucose as is found in normal blood. A hormone called glucagon from the pancreas causes glycogen to release its glucose into the blood when the blood sugar is low. (Muscle stores glucose as glycogen too, but cannot release it back into the blood; the storage is for its own use.)

The liver can also convert excess glucose to fats and proteins. When the glucose in the blood is low, the liver can *make* new glucose from amino acids and from fats, as well as from lactic acid (made in muscle during anaerobic respiration, or glycolysis). The making of new glucose is called **gluconeogenesis**.

Carbohydrate metabolism is controlled by the nervous system and hormones; nerve regulation is mediated in the hypothalamus. Low blood glucose (hypoglycaemia) a few hours after a meal leads to sympathetic arousal with release of adrenalin and noradrenalin from the adrenal glands. These substances, which are both neurotransmitters and hormones, act on the liver to cause glucose release from glycogen, and on adipose tissue to break down stored fat into fatty acids and glycerol. The heart and muscles then use fatty acids for energy, sparing glucose for the brain. Also hunger centres are activated, and the hypothalamus stimulates the anterior pituitary to secrete a hormone called **ACTH**[196] (which causes release of cortisol from the adrenal cortex), and growth hormone. These hormones act together to cause stores of energy to be released; glycogen is converted to glucose, triglyceride fats to fatty acids and glycerol. In addition, cortisol promotes the making of new glucose from amino acids in the liver. In addition to the catecholamines[197], cortisol and growth hormone, the blood sugar is raised by glucagon from the pancreas.

Metabolism of fat and its regulation

Remember that fats are made of carbon, hydrogen and oxygen and are actually very like sugars. There are two general types of fats – fuel and structural. The main fuel fats are neutral fats or triglycerides. The structural fats are cholesterol and phospholipids, used for making

---

[196] Adrenocorticotrophic Hormone, which we will be hearing much more of later.
[197] The catecholamines are adrenalin and noradrenalin, known in the USA as epinephrine and norepinephrine.

steroid hormones, vitamin D, myelin tissue, and cell membranes respectively. Fats are an ideal compact way of storing energy in a small space; they represent much more energy per gram than carbohydrates. Fatty acids can be oxidized to make ATP or to convert to amino acids, and glycerol can be oxidized or used to make glucose. Glycerol and fatty acids are stored in adipose tissue as triglycerides; more are stored when fatty meals are eaten. Under stimulation from catecholamines (e.g. adrenaline), growth hormone and cortisone, the triglycerides are broken down to yield fatty acids and glycerol into the blood. Fatty acids are then used by the heart and muscle as a fuel, thereby sparing glucose for the brain, and the glycerol part of the fat molecule is used to make glucose.

Conversely, *insulin* is the main hormone promoting fat formation, causing glucose to be transformed into fat and stored. There is also a hormone called **leptin**[198] which is involved in fat formation; it is made by fat cells and then acts on the hypothalamus to decrease appetite and to increase fat-mobilising hormones like thyroid hormone. A lack of leptin or its receptors could be a factor in obesity – too little leptin means your metabolic rate is lowered since thyroid hormone levels are lowered too. The body thinks times are hard if you have low leptin, as it will assume there isn't much fat because food supplies are low and will drop metabolism to make available energy go further. This is why excessive dieting can over time actually have the contrary result of people being unable to lose weight: the body goes into starvation mode and tries to hang onto to every calorie. Decreased leptin also increases appetite, making dieting more painful. People who are overweight and trying to lose weight need to be aware of this pitfall of severe dieting. Leptin levels are particularly lowered when carbohydrate intake is low – so don't drop these too much when dieting.

As we have seen, the liver is central to fat metabolism. It can store fats; it can convert glucose into fatty acids; it can convert glycerol to glucose and glycogen. It can also convert fatty acids into some amino acids and vice versa. The only thing the liver *can't* do regarding fats is make fatty acids into glucose. When carbohydrate supplies are low, the liver breaks down fatty acids to a substance called **acetyl CoA** (acetate) to use as fuel. If this is happening a lot, **ketone bodies** are formed. If ketone bodies are being formed, there is a smell of pear-drops on the breath. This happens in fever and dehydration; small children tend to get it very quickly without cause for alarm, but it also happens in untreated type 1 diabetes with potentially fatal results if unchecked – so if you ever smell that pear-drop smell on someone's breath, it's worth checking out what the cause could be (unless you just happen to be sat by them on a bus!).

The liver also forms **cholesterol**. Cholesterol is not used for fuel but for making things: steroid hormones (sex hormones, aldosterone and cortisol), vitamin D, the myelin sheath around neuron axons, and the waterproof layer of the skin (sebum). Cholesterol is also the main ingredient of bile salts that help digest fat. Cholesterol is eaten in animal products (egg yolk, liver, fatty meats, cheese), and also is synthesised by the liver. So, cholesterol itself is not

---

[198] From *leptos* – Greek word for 'thin'.

a bad thing – it is essential for life. Now there are understood to be different types of cholesterol in the blood:

HDLs or High Density Lipoproteins; these are considered to be 'good' cholesterol because they actually protect the body against cardiovascular disease. They are made of mainly protein, with a small amount of cholesterol.

LDLs or Low Density Lipoproteins; get the name 'bad' cholesterol. They are made mainly of cholesterol with very little protein and are the ones which have been associated with an increased risk of coronary heart disease.[199] LDLs accumulate more in the body when a person eats a diet high in animal fat and low in vegetable and fruit.

Metabolism and regulation of proteins

Over one hundred thousand different proteins are thought to exist in the body. There are twenty amino acids making them up, and the body can only make twelve of them from fatty acids or glucose; the other eight must come from the diet. Tissues need amino acids for growth, repair and normal turnover of cellular proteins; membrane receptors and most regulatory substances in the cell are made from protein.

As with carbohydrate and fat metabolism, the liver is central to protein metabolism. Here amino acids pool and are used to make liver and blood proteins (albumin, globulin and fibrinogen), as well as glucose, fats and energy (ATP). There is a second amino acid pool in the blood and a third pool in the tissue cells. As well as making all the non-essential amino acids, the liver can degrade proteins and deaminate amino acids to form urea, a detoxified form of ammonia which is water soluble and can be excreted by the kidney. Tissue proteins are normally not used for energy production except in times of starvation, and even then proteins of the heart and brain are spared.

Growth hormone and insulin promote the making of proteins during growth by increasing uptake of amino acids and synthesis of proteins in muscle and bone. Thyroid hormone affects protein formation in the heart, skeletal muscles, liver and kidney. Oestrogen (one of the female sex hormones) and androgens (the male sex hormones) cause protein synthesis in reproductive tissues. Cortisol also plays a role in regulation of protein metabolism in that it promotes protein breakdown in many tissues during stress and starvation, and in the liver it increases the uptake of amino acids and the synthesis of enzymes used for gluconeogenesis so more glucose can be made there.

---

[199] Technological medicine's answer to high LDL levels is the class of drugs called 'statins'. These have an impressive list of side effects however. A good alternative is to change one's diet and take in plenty of vitamin C to ensure our arteries have what they need to make the necessary collagen to repair themselves, as per Linus Pauling's method. You can look at http://lpi.oregonstate.edu/resagenda/about.html: 'The Linus Pauling Institute was established at Oregon State University in August 1996 under an agreement reached between OSU and LPI's antecedent organization, the Linus Pauling Institute of Science and Medicine (located in California from 1973 to 1996). The Institute functions from the basic premise that an optimum diet is the key to optimum health.'

Metabolic heat and metabolic rate

All the vital functions or work of the body require energy, got from oxidation of food to make ATP as discussed. This process of making ATP also generates heat, and in addition many of the functions of the body generate heat (e.g. the friction from muscle contraction and the electrical impulses of nerve conduction). This heat is not wasted but travels in the blood to maintain body temperature – like a central heating system in a house, in which the heat from the water boiler is transported round the house in pipes and radiators.

Basal Metabolic Rate or **BMR** is based on how much energy is needed to maintain the body at rest (lying down) in terms of the calorific value of food. It is considered to be about 2000 calories/day for the average adult. Metabolic rate decreases during sleep and increases during activity. Young people have a small body mass to surface area ratio, and therefore cannot store as much body heat, so need to eat more – they have a higher BMR than adults. As we age, we generally need to eat less as the BMR is reduced. Metabolic rate is increased by catecholamines[200], thyroid hormone, growth hormone, androgens and progesterone. Eating also increases BMR, as does absorption of foods – particularly proteins, which increase the metabolic rate by 30%. Leptin, which is produced by fat cells, also increases metabolic rate.

Regulation of body temperature, heat production and loss.

Normal temperature for humans (and other mammals) is 37° Centigrade. Metabolic heat is generated and travels in the blood around the body. Only the core of the body – the brain and internal organs – is maintained at 37°C. The limbs, in the absence of movement, have only arterial blood to warm them and tend to be at a similar temperature as the external environment – and therefore subject to frostbite. Skin plays a major role in heat regulation: it can retain and lose heat as needed. You may remember it does this through capillaries constricting or dilating and through sweating/water evaporation. Also, body hair and subcutaneous fat prevent heat loss. The hypothalamus of the brain has a thermostat which reads body temperature and initiates heat gain and loss responses in the skin, as well as causing us to shiver and engage in other activities such as huddling up, curling up, pacing, or lying down when over-heated.

Fever is a special case: toxins from microbes cause white blood cells to release cytokine hormones which reset the hypothalamic thermostat, setting into motion shivering and skin vasoconstriction to retain heat. As we have discussed, fever is a natural defense response – the heat kills off the bacteria. The body cools itself down after killing off microbes by sweating and skin vasodilatation. If a fever is too high (above 42.2°C, 108°F) the brain may be damaged.

---

[200] Adrenaline and noradrenaline.

CHAPTER THIRTEEN

WATERWORKS - THE URINARY SYSTEM

(THE KIDNEYS AND BLADDER)

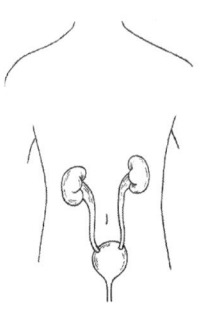

With the function of filtering the blood and excreting urea[201] and excess water from the body, the urinary system consists of two kidneys, two ureters, one urinary bladder and one urethra. The kidneys are found at the back of the body, in the top of the posterior abdominal cavity, tucked up right under the diaphragm on either side of the spine. They are protected by the ribs. If you put your hands on your back so that they are flat on the last few inches of your ribs, they will be right over your kidneys. If you gently tap your kidneys, they may feel a little sensitive; if so, it may be good to give them some love. Actually they need some love anyway, tender or not. It's a good practice to get in the habit of rubbing them every day and thanking them for all their hard work – you'll see why soon.

The ureters are tubes which come one from each kidney, and pass down the flanks to empty into the bladder which is found anteriorly (at the front) at the bottom of the abdominal cavity, just above your pubic bone when it's full. (Try poking around there when you have a full bladder – you will certainly feel it!). This system has two main responsibilities: water balance, and waste disposal.

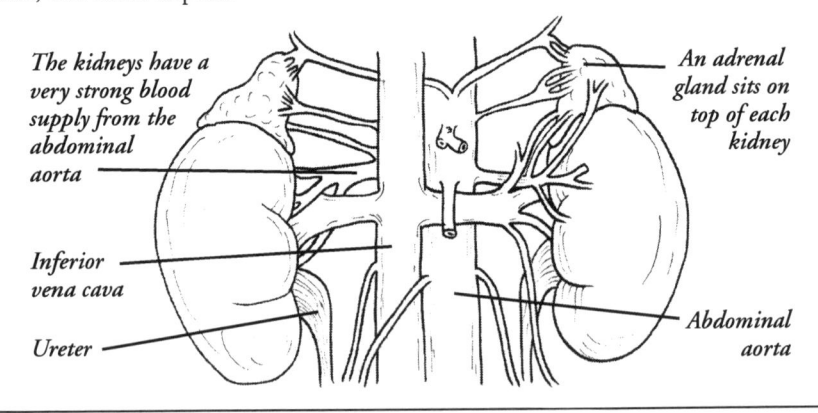

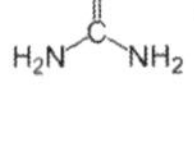

The kidneys have a very strong blood supply from the abdominal aorta

Inferior vena cava

Ureter

An adrenal gland sits on top of each kidney

Abdominal aorta

---

[201] This is urea, which is a nitrogen-containing water soluble substance made by the liver to allow the body to safely excrete nitrogenous waste from broken down amino acids.

The kidneys are simply incredible. Every minute they filter 125 ml of blood. In other words, in less than an hour all the blood in the body has passed through them. (No, I'm not taking the p...!). Each kidney contains many tiny tubules called **nephrons**. The nephron is the functional unit of the kidney. It is basically a tube which filters the blood. There are about half a million in each kidney – so obviously they are very small.

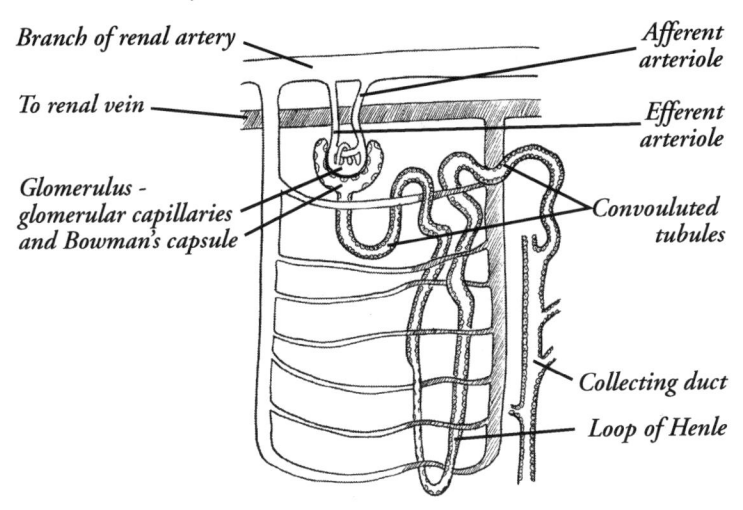

Branch of renal artery
To renal vein
Glomerulus - glomerular capillaries and Bowman's capsule
Afferent arteriole
Efferent arteriole
Convouluted tubules
Collecting duct
Loop of Henle

All small particles (not cells or proteins) in the blood pass out of the **glomerular capillaries** into the Bowman's capsule and thus into the convoluted tubules. Bowman's capsule is a kind of egg-cup shaped end of a long tube. The glomerular capillaries, a globular network of permeable tiny blood vessels, sit inside where the egg would go. **Bowman's capsule** continues as a tube which leads to the collecting ducts. Proteins and red blood cells are too large to pass out of the glomerular capillaries; therefore they are not normally found in the urine. Important things like glucose as well as varying amounts of water and salts are reabsorbed into the blood from the tubule. What is left (which contains any wastes or substances the body doesn't need) passes into the **collecting ducts** as urine, and from there out of the renal pelvis through the **ureters** (by peristalsis) to the bladder. The **urinary bladder** is a hollow, muscular, elastic sack which collects the urine until it is time to expel it from the body. During urination, the urine passes from the bladder through the internal and external sphincters, out of the **urethra** to the exterior. Almost all the action in the kidneys happens in the nephrons. At the end of these, urine has been formed and collects in the collecting ducts, then leaves the kidney in the ureters as urine.

Nitrogen is Plant Food

Urine, containing urea, a neat little package of nitrogen, is ideal fertilizer for plants. Did you know you can make wonderful compost out of cardboard and urine? Try it for yourself at home if you have a garden; get a crate and make drainage holes in the bottom, then stack cardboard in it, flat sides parallel with the sides of your crate. Add wee regularly – men can do this directly, privacy allowing! You will find that the cardboard (cellulose) will rot down and together with the urine make a fabulous and rich potting compost. Alternatively, pee on a straw or hay bale for a year. Open it up and you will find it changed into excellent compost.

Some plants[202] take nitrogen from the air and fix it in the soil so other plants can take it up and build it into amino acids. We eat the plants, or animals eat them and use the amino acids for building muscle, then we eat the animals' muscle (meat), and use the amino acids for all our protein needs. When we've finished with them, the liver breaks them down and packages the nitrogen as urea, which our kidneys excrete and which the earth needs as food.[203]

Urine Formation

We will now look at urine formation in a little more detail. It happens in three stages – filtration, tubular re-absorption and tubular secretion. It is with these functions of the nephrons that the kidneys eliminate nitrogenous wastes (the end products of protein metabolism – urea etc), and also regulate the volume, composition and pH of the blood.

Glomerular Filtration

Incredibly, *180l per day of filtrate enters the nephron tubules* – about 179l is reabsorbed (i.e. most of it). High pressure exists in the glomerular capillaries because the efferent arteriole which leaves each glomerulus is smaller than the afferent arteriole which enters it.

Due to this high pressure one fifth of the fluid flowing through the glomerulus is filtered into the Bowman's capsule. This is effectively 125ml/min.

A fairly constant blood flow is maintained through the kidney. Mainly this is achieved by the kidney regulating itself. According to need, and changing with variations in the general blood pressure, its own auto regulatory processes either constrict or dilate the afferent arterioles (the ones going in to the glomeroli), to decrease or increase the blood supply respectively. This means that no matter what is happening in the body as a whole, the kidneys can keep doing their work in a measured manner.

Tubular re-absorption

This is the process by which needed substances are reabsorbed from the tubules into the blood. Basically the filtration process allows all particles in the blood smaller than plasma proteins to pass into the tubules. Some substances are routinely completely reabsorbed (e.g. glucose).[204] Others, including sodium and water, are reabsorbed in varying amounts, thus their blood levels are controlled. The kidney tubules can reabsorb substances both passively

---

[202] Many legumes do this, such as clover, alfalfa and soybeans. Some trees and shrubs can also be used in a similar fashion, for example, the fast growing alder.

[203] We in the civilized West are so weird that we actually put our pee, along with copious, brightly coloured, smelly, chemical toilet cleaners, into the sea instead of back to the earth. The really weird part is we are brain-washed into thinking this is a 'cleaner' alternative…

[204] After all, peeing out glucose would be like throwing money away.

and actively. Some substances travel by diffusion and some need ATP activated carriers; some, including creatinine and drug metabolites, are not reabsorbed because they have no carriers, are too big, or are not lipid soluble.

Re-absorption of sodium and water is controlled in the distal tubules and collecting ducts by hormones which regulate the amounts kept in the body;

Aldosterone, which increases the re-absorption of sodium – and therefore water which always follows sodium around like a lost sheep. Aldosterone is made and secreted by the adrenal cortex.

Anti Diuretic Hormone which increases the re-absorption of water in the collecting ducts. **ADH** comes from the posterior part of the pituitary gland. There is a disease called diabetes insipidus, in which large amounts of very dilute urine are excreted, not related to fluid intake. This is caused by not having enough ADH, or by the kidneys not responding to this hormone. There is a diuretic drug called conivaptan which inhibits ADH formation and can cause diabetes insipidus.

Tubular Secretion

Tubular secretion is the way the kidney adds substances to the filtrate from the blood or tubule cells. In this way, urea, drugs (e.g. penicillin, which is too big to pass over the glomerular membranes, so must be excreted by secretion[205]) and excess ions are eliminated, and the pH of the blood is regulated by varying amounts of hydrogen ions being secreted into the tubules.

The **renin-angiotensin** mechanism exists to raise a dangerously lowered blood pressure, for example, as you might get if you lost a lot of blood suddenly in an accident. It is triggered by stimuli (including low BP and intense sympathetic nervous system arousal) which cause the 'Juxta Glomerular' cells to release rennin.

Renin is an enzyme which acts on **angiotensinogen**, made both in the liver and locally in the proximal convoluted tubule. Angiotensinogen releases **angiotensin I** which is converted to **angiotensin II** by **ACE** – angiotensin converting enzyme – which is associated with the capillary cells in various body tissues, especially in the lungs. (You may have heard of ACE inhibitors which are a class of drug used for high blood pressure. As the name suggests, these block this mechanism and therefore lower the blood pressure).[206]

Angiotensin II is a potent vasoconstrictor and activates smooth muscle throughout the body, raising the blood pressure. It also increases sodium re-absorption in the kidney tubules, and

---

[205] Pharmaceutical drugs are designed to withstand breakdown by the body, in order to exert as strong as possible effect for as long as possible. This means that 60-90% of any drug a person takes is excreted out of body into the environment, often by the kidney. Due to this, over the years there has been and continues to be a frightening and ever-increasing amount of pharmaceutical drugs in the water chain of the earth; antibiotics, female hormones oestrogen and progesterone, drugs for high blood pressure and antidepressants such as prozac to name a few. Worried? Don't lose sleep over it, but be aware of it and aim to minimize it!

[206] The most common side-effect with ACE inhibitors is a persistent dry cough. They can also cause a big fall in blood pressure when first used. Other less common side effects are kidney and liver problems, a type of swelling called angioedema, rash, inflammation of the pancreas, hay fever-like symptoms, sinusitis, sore throat, nausea, vomiting, indigestion, diarrhea or constipation and blood cell changes. (from BUPA website).

stimulates the release of aldosterone from the adrenals, causing still more sodium re-absorption in the tubules. Water follows sodium, so blood volume and therefore blood pressure rises. The afferent arterioles are less sensitive to angiotensin II than most body arterioles, including the efferent, so the glomerular pressure increases. Angiotensin II also stimulates the release of ADH and makes us feel thirsty by activating the thirst centre in the brain.

Regulation of concentration and volume of urine

This is basically done by varying levels of ADH (anti diuretic hormone) from the pituitary. In the absence of ADH, dilute urine is formed. This is the basic level. Then when ADH levels in the blood rise, the collecting ducts become more permeable to water, which then moves into the blood, consequently forming more concentrated urine.

Dehydration, diuretics and drinking lots of water…

There are interesting and contradictory theories about water and how much we need. It is common for holistic nutritional therapists to say that most of us are dehydrated: we don't drink enough, and what we do drink is dehydrating. For example, caffeine-containing drinks like tea and coffee are diuretic and make the body lose water, and also are experienced as toxins which need to be excreted, therefore needing extra water to clear them from the body. Alcohol and sugar drinks cause a similar reaction.

Then there are the toxic strains of modern life to contend with: air pollution, food additives and contaminates like pesticides, drugs, nicotine, foods experienced as toxins like wheat, electro-magnetic pollution and the big internal one, stress hormones. In order to excrete any toxin, the body uses water – remember, nothing moves in the body without it. The idea is that many people are toxic to some degree or other and are therefore in need of water.

There are variable amounts given for needed daily water intake. There's this thing about eight glasses a day which seems to be a bit of a myth. My nutritional therapist tells me that it's best to drink eight *pints* of water every day in order to restore the body to full hydration.[207] Try it yourself – though it does of course require many trips to the loo, some people do feel benefit from it very quickly *(although, if you have kidney disease this amount of water would be* **harmful***, and epileptics seem to get more fits if they drink lots of water, so this is not for everyone)*. Try taking one or two pints, half hot half cold, straight away as soon as you rise to get the ball rolling. Considering that at night your body can lose up to 1½ pints of water through breathing and sweating, this can sound like a reasonable idea.[208]

---

[207] Of course, you also need to get your omega 3 oils into you; fish oils or linseed tea (for recipe, Google or take a look at http://www.sustainablehealthsolutions.co.uk)…thanks Zoe!

[208] On the other hand, Israeli nutritional healer Sarah Hamo, who cured herself from cancer with radical diet change after being given months to live by the doctor, says that a person who has cleaned up their diet and takes no toxins in, eating a large amount of fresh vegetables and fruit grown organically, needs to drink very little water, and should only drink when thirsty. She says that the more we drink, the harder the kidneys must work, and herself drinks about 30 glasses of water **per year**!… Sara Hamo *The Golden Path To Natural Healing*.

When the body is dehydrated, it may do all kinds of things to try and set things straight. Sometimes it panics and tries to hold onto water, leading to symptoms such as oedema[209] and high blood pressure[210]. The orthodox treatment for these conditions will be diuretics, drugs which take water from the cells and force the kidneys to excrete it. Of course, if the problem is actually caused by dehydration this treatment will make the situation worse. Actually, a better treatment could be to start drinking more water. One 'side effect' of diuretics is dizziness and drowsiness. These are actually caused by the brain being dehydrated causing the cells to shrink. This can cause confusion which makes a person forget to drink or eat, exacerbating the problem and potentially even leading to death, especially among older people who may be isolated and have no one to keep an eye on what they eat or drink (in the modernized parts of the world that is – in many cultures, Elders are still highly valued and taken good care of).

Diuretic drugs work by making the body lose sodium, which water inevitably follows. Along with the sodium, potassium is lost. Depletion of potassium leads to weakness, fatigue and cramps in the legs. Other trace elements such as zinc and magnesium will also be leached. The effect of this may be more subtle, and therefore less easy to spot, but both are vital for our bodies health. Zinc is essential for healing, reproductive function, bone health and maintaining good blood sugar levels. Magnesium is the 'anti-stress mineral', helping the circulation and digestion: a lack of it can cause insomnia, depression, anxiety and fever.[211]

Interrelationships

The kidney is very obviously related to the **circulatory system** in that it is blood which is filtered by the nephrons, and the kidneys are very much involved in regulating blood pressure. Hormones of the **endocrine system** are largely responsible for controlling kidney activity; rennin controls body fluid levels and blood pressure and aldosterone controls mineral balance. The kidneys help stimulate **bone** marrow production. Together with the other excretory systems, the **digestive system** and the **skin**, the kidney cleans the body. The **liver** and kidney have a special relationship in that urea comes from amino acids broken down in liver, and the liver makes other toxic substances water soluble, so they can be excreted by the kidneys.

---

[209] Oedema is excess water in the tissue spaces. It will accumulate at the ankles when you've been standing, making them swollen, or the sacrum if lying down for a while.

[210] If the body holds onto water and it thus increases in the tissue spaces, the blood vessels may take more. An increased blood volume can cause high blood pressure.

[211] Nutrients like minerals in the soil in the UK are measurably lower by about 60% than they were fifty years ago. This is due to modern farming methods which take out more than they put back. This means we are all in danger of deficiencies. (1992 Earth Summit Report indicated that the mineral content of the world's farm and range land soil has decreased dramatically).

Chapter Fourteen

THE WIRING
THE NERVOUS SYSTEM

Overall control and co-ordination of body activities is, in traditional physiology, seen as being the realm of the nervous system and the endocrine, or hormonal system. The two systems are very much inter-linked and back each other up well: nervous control being incredibly fast but short-lived and hormone action being slower to happen but its effects lingering longer in the body.

The scientific medical model has it that the brain is in charge of everything, and is pretty much the most important bit of us, with the rest of the body being there as support for it. I find it rather enjoyable that in Chinese Five Element medicine, the nervous system/brain is not so important – as I've said earlier, it is the heart which is in charge of our life's purpose; the nervous system has the less important role of responding to danger and so keeping us alive! Eastern philosophies (such as Siddha Yoga) concur with this view.

Western thought also used to agree with this, thinking that the human was controlled by a little man or 'homunculus' which lived in the heart. It was after dissection of human bodies showed no such little man that the brain was elevated to supremacy.[212] The mainstream, mechanistic, view is that the brain is responsible for what we call 'mind'. This comes out of medicine's reliance on old Newtonian physics to explain the universe mechanistically. Interestingly, as quantum physics is incorporated into biology, more is discovered about what really makes us tick: the 'mind' is understood not only to be in the brain.[213] Emerging work on communication molecules throughout the body has led to the coining of the term 'bodymind' to describe our being.[214] The 'mind' is everywhere, a network or flow of communication equally in the tissues of the body as in the brain.

Then there is the issue of whether you think being alive is all there is to it: in other words, the material reality is all there is, or whether you hold with a reality that includes a Divine presence in the universe, and within each of us. Eastern philosophies talk about the Universal Mind being the underlying intelligence of everything in the universe, including our bodies and our human minds.

---

[212] Can you imagine the conversation "Oh bugger, no little man, I guess we will just have to tell 'em that spongy mess in the head is what controls the show, they are not going to like it"...

[213] Bruce H. Lipton *The Biology of Belief*.

[214] Candace Pert *Molecules of Emotion*.

Well, whatever you believe, we will now have a go at introducing and simplifying the functions of the human nervous system. A suggestion to ease your understanding of this complex system is to treat the following bits of information as a kind of jigsaw puzzle: I will present you with a whole lot of information about different aspects of the nervous system; like a jigsaw, imagine you are taking a look at the pieces, turning them face up and spreading them out before beginning to make the whole picture. Don't try to connect them until the end of the chapter, by which time I hope things will have begun to be clearer.

Nerve cells

The nervous system is all about information, control and co-ordination. Messages are transmitted and received from and to the brain and all parts of the body by special nerve cells called **neurons**.

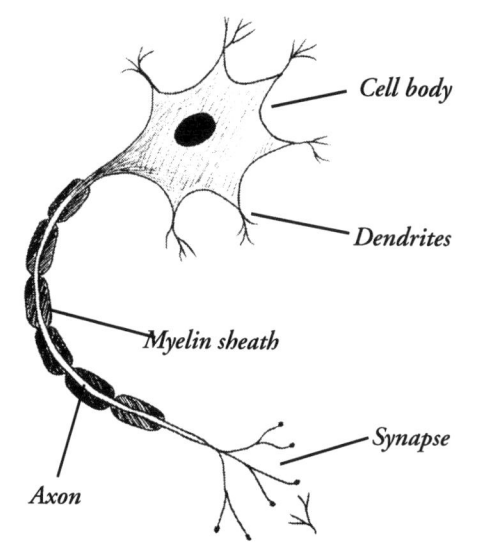

A neuron has a cell body, which contains the nucleus and usual organelles of a cell – mitochondria and so forth. Projections come off this cell body: **axons** and **dendrites**.

Axons convey impulses away from the cell body, and dendrites towards. Axons can communicate with other nerve cells, or, in the case of the end of motor nerves, with glandular or muscle cells, causing secretion or contraction. The projections, which may also be called the 'nerve fibres', are sometimes covered with an insulating substance called myelin.

Myelin looks white. It is a fatty material, which insulates the nerve fibres and hugely increases the speed of conduction of a nerve impulse along the fibre. If it helps you can think of it as being like the plastic covering the wire of an electrical appliance. Without the insulation the nervous impulse, which as you will learn is electro-chemical in nature, cannot travel in its usual way. Some neurones are designed to work fine without myelin, but those which are normally myelinated must keep the myelin covering in good shape in order to work normally.[215]

In the brain, a nerve cell may have connections with many thousands of other cells, creating an incredibly complex network of nerve fibres with an enormous number of potential

---

[215] People suffering from the auto-immune disease multiple sclerosis (MS) have a situation where their immune system is attacking the myelin sheaths of nerves. This means that the nerve can no longer work – the message cannot be properly carried. MS can affect both the motor nerves (doers) and the sensory nerves (feelers), so a wide range of problems can be experienced. For example, the persons' sight may be lost as the optic nerve is affected, or they may lose control over muscles and be unable to walk or use their arms.

'nerve pathways'. Because nerve cells are permanent – that is, not continually replaced throughout life – it was long thought that we are born with all we will ever have and these degenerate throughout life, making nervous system functioning a downhill affair. Well, it's true that we don't keep on making new neurons, and that brain cells do die off each year, but the good news is that actually throughout life nerve cells make new dendrites, creating more connections with each other. Deepak Chopra suggests this is a physiological expression of the increasing wisdom people may show with age, when the different parts of life and knowledge connect more and more.[216]

There are different types of neuron, depending on whether they convey sensory or motor information or both, and on where in the nervous system they are found. They all have the same basic structure of cell body, axons and dendrites, but with variations according to specific function. Here are a few examples:

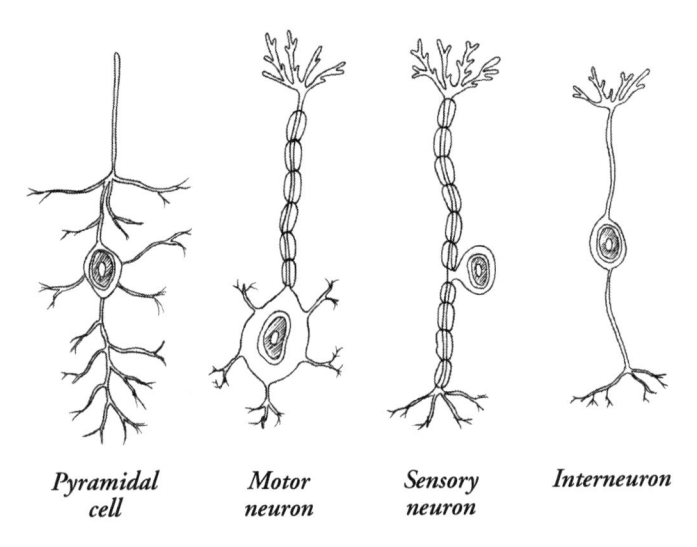

Pyramidal cell　　*Motor neuron*　　*Sensory neuron*　　*Interneuron*

The nervous system is *structurally* divided into **central** and **peripheral** systems. The central nervous system is the brain and the spinal cord. The peripheral nervous system is all the wiring, bundles of nerve fibres running to and from the central nervous system. *Functionally*, the nervous system can be separated into the **somatic** and **autonomic** systems. The somatic part deals with more conscious body stuff – what we feel from the skin and muscles – plus the so-called **special senses** like hearing and sight, and the deliberate movements we make. The autonomic system deals with the visceral[217] or unconscious stuff.

---

[216] Deepak Chopra *Quantum Health*.

[217] Visceral means guts or organs.

Nerve impulses

Another name for a nerve impulse is an **action potential**. It is all to do with the 'concentration gradient' of sodium and potassium ions. As you know, the cell membrane is selectively permeable and does not allow ions to completely balance out across it. Also there is a **sodium-potassium pump**, which puts three sodium ions out of the cell for every two potassium ions it lets in. This means that in its resting state, there is a slight increase of positively charged sodium ions *outside* the cell. These like to line up along the cell membrane, attracted to opposing negatively charged ions which line up on the inside of the cell membrane. This creates an electrical charge across the membrane that is called the **resting membrane potential**.

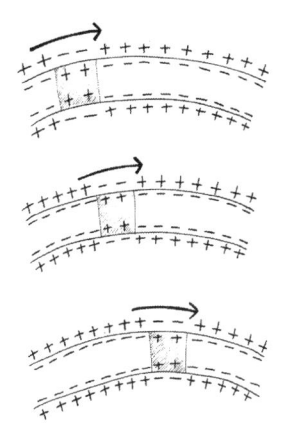

An action potential is a travelling wave of electrochemical ('ionic') excitation. In order for one to happen, there must be sufficient **excitement**. There is a threshold below which nothing will happen, but above which will trigger an action potential which is all-or-nothing; in other words it is always of the same magnitude. When a part of the membrane is excited, it becomes suddenly more permeable to sodium ions; the charged sodium ions outside the cell membrane suddenly rush into the cell as the membrane permeability alters, changing the electrical charge, making it more positive on the inside compared with the outside, opposite to what it is in the resting state. This is called **depolarization** of the membrane. This change in charge then excites the next bit of the membrane, causing it to become extra permeable to sodium and thus exciting the next bit of the cell, and so on, all along the membrane, like miniature waves on a beach. The potassium channels also open, but more slowly, so when they do, potassium rushes out of the cell (down its concentration gradient) and thus decreases the positive ions inside the cell, restoring the membrane to its resting state – this is called **repolarisation**.

Action potentials occur in nerve and muscle cells; skeletal muscle action potentials come as a result of stimulation by a nerve, and result in actin and myosin sliding over each other to shorten the muscle fibre. Action potentials in nerve cells occur when the dendrites of a neuron produce what is called a **graded potential** after being stimulated. There are protein channels in the membrane of the dendrites which are activated and opened by the graded potential, which causes ions to enter or leave the cell, changing the membrane potential – it can either depolarise the membrane therefore excite it in a way that could lead to an action potential, or hyperpolarise or inhibit it in a way which makes an action potential less likely to occur. So in order for enough stimulation to occur to lead to a full action potential (or nerve impulse), generally quite a lot of channels in the dendrites must be affected in an excitatory way.

More about synapses

When the action potential in a neuron reaches the end, it causes the release of a chemical called a **neurotransmitter**, which then binds onto receptors in the next neuron – this is called a **synapse**. There are also electrical synapses, a direct wiring together of neurons, where there are gap junctions through which the action potential travels straight though to the next neuron – these are quicker, providing better synchronization where needed. Synapses, then, are places where one nerve meets another. In the majority of cases however the nerve cells do not actually touch; rather there is a space between them called the synaptic space. As you know, what surrounds all the cells in the body is fluid, predominately water. Neurotransmitters are made in the nerve cell and stored in tiny 'bladders' called vesicles at the end of the axon. When the wave of electrochemical excitement reaches the end of the axon, the vesicles go to the cell membrane and release their contents into the synaptic space. The neurotransmitters scatter through the fluid between the neurons (across the synaptic space) and on coming into contact with the next neuron they bind to a receptor on its cell membrane. This begins an electrical response in the new nerve.

Neurotransmitters are peptides, or small groups of amino acids. They are made in the neuron's cell body and sent down to the end of the axon. In the central nervous system neurotransmitters may be excitatory or inhibiting. Our brains are awash with chemicals stimulating or soothing our nervous systems. There are at least a hundred peptides that are known to act as neurotransmitters. A chemical called **acetylcholine** is the main excitatory one for the nervous system, as well as at the neuromuscular junction. There are also inhibitory neurons, secreting neurotransmitters which calm down adjacent neurons, making them less likely to fire off an impulse. **GABA** (**GammaAminobutyric Acid**) and **glycine** are two inhibitory neurotransmitters. Other neurotransmitters include serotonin, dopamine, glutamate, aspartate, histamine, noradrenalin and adrenalin (norepinephrine and epinephrine), nitrous oxide and adenosine tri-phosphate (ATP).

Neurotransmitters work by bonding with a receptor, thus preventing another transmitter from activating that receptor, and affecting the membrane potential in some way either to lead to increased or decreased excitement. So different substances can affect how excitable or inhibited the neurons are. Like with so many things in life, the outcome is to do with the balance between one way and another – it is not so much black and white, but a shading of grey that we end up with. In terms of neurotransmitters, they can either cause an **excitatory postsynaptic potential (EPSP)** or an **inhibitory postsynaptic potential (IPSP)**, which cause a slight depolarisation or a slight hyperpolarisation respectively. In other words, an inhibitory neuron will cause **hyperpolarisation** (making the membrane potential more negative) which then makes it harder for another neuron to depolarise the membrane above threshold level and begin an action potential. An excitatory neuron will make the membrane potential less negative and therefore towards the threshold level needed to spark a full action potential. All of the many EPSPs and IPSPs of the many dendrites get added together, so to speak, and this decides the result.

The neurotransmitter binding effect is inactivated by either re-uptake of it back into the neuron, destruction of it by enzymes, or diffusion away from the receptor and out of the synaptic cleft. Synapses were thought to be the be all and end all of communication in the nervous system and beyond, but in fact there turns out to be more too it, since peptides and their receptors seem to communicate not just across the tiny synaptic gap but across vast distances (inches!). Peptides circulate in the body and find their target receptors all over the place, not just within the nervous system.[218] Communication within the body (and probably between bodies too) also relies on very subtle, quantum processes to do with light (protons) travelling through microtubules within the dendrites and neurons. This and other processes explain why thoughts do not arise in one discrete area of the brain and travel neatly around via neuronal pathways, across synapses from one neuron to the next, but instead arise everywhere at once. Quantum scientists figure that there is a kind of Internet of the body that allows simultaneous communication between all the neurons of the brain.[219]

Central Nervous System
Meninges
The central nervous system consists of the brain (also called the encephalon) and the spinal cord, which are surrounded and protected by **meninges**. The meninges are special protective membranes made of three layers: the **dura mater**, the **arachnoid mater** and the **pia mater**. The outermost layer, the dura mater, is very tough and strong. It is joined in places to the inside of the skull and the vertebral canal of the spine. The arachnoid mater in the middle is full of a delicate network of fibres and blood vessels. The pia mater is the soft membrane that is actually in contact with the sensitive brain tissue. Between the arachnoid and pia maters is found 'CSF', **cerebrospinal fluid**, which further protects the central nervous system by acting as a shock absorber. The brain is certainly more protected sitting in its cerebrospinal fluid than it would be if it was banging around in the skull without it. CSF also is found in holes in the brain called **ventricles**, and in the **central canal**, the channel which runs through the spinal cord and is connected with the ventricles. The ventricles of the brain are connected together by tiny canals, so the CSF slowly circulates throughout the central nervous system.[220]

Meningitis is an infection of the meninges. The reason it can be life threatening is that it causes an increase in production of CSF, therefore an increase in pressure around the brain. The skull and spine are rigid, so cannot expand with this pressure. It is the brain, delicately soft and squishy, that is pressed on, causing the terrible headache and other neurological

---

[218] Candace Pert *Molecules of Emotion*.

[219] These theories, of scientists Pribram, Jibu, Yasue, Hameroff, Scot Hagan, are beautifully elaborated in Lynne McTaggart's book *The Field*.

[220] Cranio-Sacral therapy works by correcting improperly moving cranial bones. If the bones of the skull are not moving against each other as they should, the circulation of CSF is affected, which in turn can affect anything in the body via the nervous system.

symptoms of meningitis. Because the brain is so squishy, permanent damage can be done to it by this onslaught of pressure.[221]

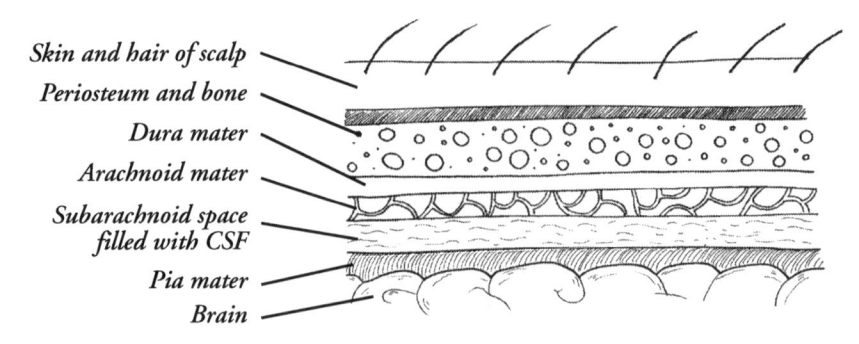

Skin and hair of scalp
Periosteum and bone
Dura mater
Arachnoid mater
Subarachnoid space filled with CSF
Pia mater
Brain

The Brain

The brain is known as the control centre. We are going to look at it only very simply. There are literally billions of nerve cells in the brain, all with their axons and dendrites. Parts of the brain look grey: these are cell bodies and unmyelinated axons (Agatha Christie fans will remember Inspector Poirot and his 'little grey cells'). Parts of it look white: these are myelinated axons, rapidly taking information to other parts of the brain. Each neuron in the brain can grow many dendrites, some of them having hundreds, which means that the possible combinations of connections between nerve cells is greater than the number of atoms in the known universe.[222]

One mechanism thought to be involved in memory is that any particular thought to do with learning or memory or moving a leg or speech or taste or anything, is associated with a particular combination of neurons firing, called a **nerve pathway**. Remember our 'membrane potential' from a few paragraphs above? Here's an interesting thing: the more times a particular pathway is activated, the more likely it is that it gets fired off by some stimulation; the resting potential of the membranes may change to make them more sensitive. In practical terms this means that the more you think a particular thought and use a particular nerve pathway, the less stimulus it takes to trigger that pathway off again and the more you are likely to think that thought. You can think of it like an old-fashioned record, the more the needle goes round, the deeper the groove. Although this is thought to be one of the ways that memory works, the exact mechanism is not clearly understood. However it could explain why any kind of learning (including that of anatomy and physiology which you are engaged with at this moment) requires repetition, repetition, repetition. This fact about the brain is definitely

---

[221] A friend of mine had meningitis as a young man. The headache was so bad he was banging his head against the wall. In hospital, a spinal tap (lumbar puncture, where a needle is put into the space between the pia and arachnoid maters in the lumbar region) was performed – as the fluid was drained away into the needle, he felt the headache go, from the top of his head downward.

[222] This wonderful titbit comes from Deepak Chopra's inspirational and fascinating book *Quantum Healing*, a highly recommended read.

worth dwelling on and contemplating; the more you think a particular thought or set of thoughts, the more you will think it. I am sure this is partly how affirmations[223] work. You might ask yourself, 'what are my habitual thoughts? Do they serve me? Would I like to change them or am I happy with their habitation of my head?'. You can make new positive pathways or collections of neurons that will be more likely to fire off than old negative ones.

Then there are all those neuropeptides and their receptors. Biochemical change at receptor level is the biochemical basis of memory. Cells make and re-absorb receptors all the time in response to their environment. Likewise, the cells can put peptides together very easily in response to need. It's true that our thoughts are affected by our brain chemistry, but it's also true that our thoughts affect our brain chemistry. We can use our thoughts to encourage our brains to make more favourable, 'feel-good', neurotransmitters. We can learn to accept all of our emotions and allow them free flow and healthy expression, which prevents them getting stuck – emotions are part of the communication system for our body and mind.[224]

The brain consists of the following parts:

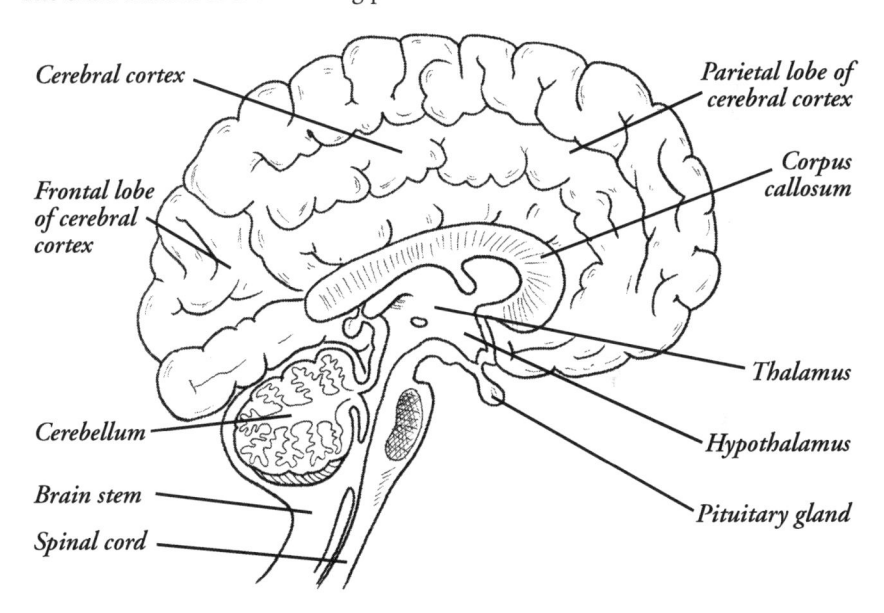

Cerebral cortex
Parietal lobe of cerebral cortex
Corpus callosum
Frontal lobe of cerebral cortex
Thalamus
Cerebellum
Hypothalamus
Brain stem
Spinal cord
Pituitary gland

The cerebrum or cerebral hemispheres

This is the seat of what is known as the 'higher functions': conscious awareness, memory, the special senses[225], speech, and conscious movement – it's what you are using right now to study

---

[223] 'Affirmations' are statements, always put in the present tense and in the positive, to contradict one's negative beliefs. You don't put an affirmation in the negative – 'I can't remember anatomy' – rather turn it around – 'I easily remember anatomy'. Affirmations need to be said hundreds and thousands of times every day. After all, you heard the negative stuff over and over again, and now you tell it to yourself over and over. They are of use only when you have identified a negative message you are telling yourself repeatedly – the point of the affirmation is to transform those messages. They can really work; try them for yourself.

[224] Candace Pert – *Molecules of Emotion*. By now you will realize that this book is a must-read!

and think about this information. It includes the motor cortex, where control of all voluntary muscles of the body originates, and the sensory cortex, where all sensations from the skin, muscles and joints end up. The cerebral cortex has four lobes: the **frontal**, **parietal**, **occipital** and **temporal** lobes. The frontal lobe is associated with reasoning, planning, speech, movement, emotions and solving problems; the parietal lobe with movement, recognition, perception of stimuli and orientating ourselves in space; the occipital lobe concerns itself with visual processing and the temporal lobe with hearing, memory and speech as well as emotion.

The cerebrum is divided by a deep cleft into the right and left **hemispheres**. Each side functions slightly differently. The right hemisphere is more associated with creativity, music and mathematics (which you might think was more to do with logic but apparently goes with the right hemisphere). The left hemisphere is concerned with logical thinking.
A bundle of axons called the **corpus callosum** connects the two sides.[226]

The cerebellum or 'hind-brain'

This is found under the occipital bone at the back of the head, and is responsible for co-ordination of movement and balance. Remember how muscle groups act together for smooth movement? As biceps in the arm contract to flex the elbow, triceps, the extensors, gradually relaxes to allow a smooth and controlled movement. It is the cerebellum which co-ordinates this.

The Thalamus

This is a large area of grey matter deep in the forebrain. It has sensory and motor functions. Almost all sensory information from the body enters it, from where neurons send it to the cortex, which lies above. It is the last relay site of sensation information before the cerebral cortex. The thalamus is also central to emotional experience. Easy then to understand the importance of touch to good emotional and mental development – without touch, the young human fails to thrive and may even die if the deprivation is extreme. All sensations of touch are received by the thalamus, which is also central to emotional experience.

---

[225] This term is used in physiology to refer to vision, hearing, smell and taste.

[226] Sometimes the corpus callosum is claimed to be bigger in women, though this has not been absolutely proven. It is also not proven that a larger one leads to more intelligence, though some say it is. The theory is that if the two hemispheres are more fully connected, our thinking is more connected too. Interestingly it seems that listening to certain kinds of music, like Beethoven, as a very young one, leads to development of a thicker corpus callosum (therefore possibly more intelligence.) Schizophrenic people, especially women, seem to have a particularly thick corpus callosum. (So we can conclude according to this research that people with bigger corpus callosums may be either more prone towards mental skills or mental illness, or possibly both!). Since the brain grows partly in response to how it is used, and boys in our culture may be particularly discouraged from free emotional and creative expression, it may be that this leads to the difference, though the difference is found in rats too. Perhaps the behaviour needed for successful rearing of young leads to its development. This is not proven in any way, more a philosophical aside. The whole area of gender difference is fraught with difficulties, since cultural conditioning and expectations begin at birth or even before if people know they are having a boy or girl. For example, researchers find that boy babies get a massive amount more attention than girls. Although some of the differences between men and women are physiological in basis, many are not and can vary considerably from culture to culture and time to time.

The Hypothalamus

This houses the thermostat, which sets the body's temperature. In an immune response, the thermostat will be turned up to allow the body temperature to increase to make a hostile environment for invading organisms. The hypothalamus is also the regulator of autonomic nervous and endocrine function. It controls the pituitary gland, which hangs from it like a pea on a slender stem, and which in turn controls release of many of the body's chemical messengers, or hormones.

The Amygdala

This is in the temporal lobe of the cerebrum, in that part of the brain located beneath the temporal bones of the skull. It is involved in memory, emotion and fear.

The Hippocampus

This is found in the medial (middle) part of the temporal lobe. It is important for learning and memory, particularly for converting short-term memory to permanent memory, and also for remembering where things are in space in the outside world.

The thalamus, the hypothalamus, the amygdala and the hippocampus are collectively called **The Limbic System.** The limbic system is considered to be the **emotional brain.** So you can see how closely related touch, emotion, memory, the endocrine system and visceral functions of the body are.

The Brain Stem

Found at the base of the brain is the brain stem, a kind of thickened spinal cord, which continues from it below. It contains the control centres for vital functions, such as the cardiac centre, vasomotor centre and respiratory centres. It consists of the three parts known as the midbrain, the medulla oblongata, and the pons varoli.

The Spinal Cord

The spinal cord is a continuation of the brain stem, and extends down the spinal column within the vertebral canal. It is as wide as a finger, and, like the brain, is surrounded by CSF and meninges which cushion it from damage. It consists of millions of nerve fibres, axons and dendrites, which transmit information between the body and brain. The nerve fibres in the spinal cord are grouped together in bundles called ascending (sensory) and descending (motor) tracts. The spinal nerves come off the spinal cord, with sensory fibres coming out of the posterior (dorsal) side and motor fibres from the anterior (ventral) side. These sensory and motor fibres join just outside the spinal cord to form the spinal nerves which are part of the **peripheral nervous system.**

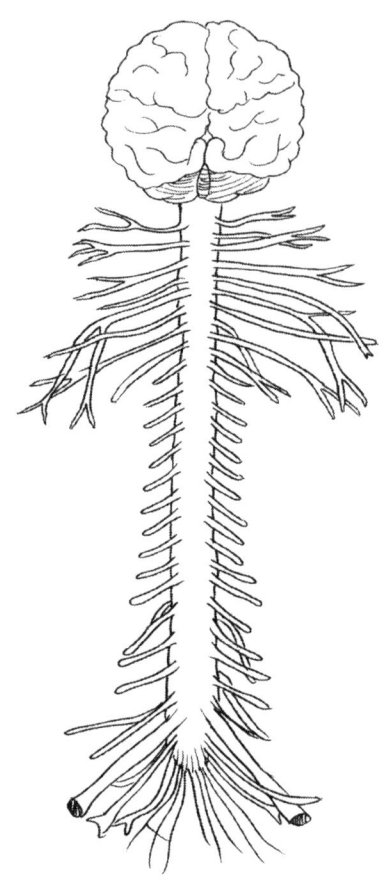

The Peripheral Nervous System

The peripheral nervous system consists of nerves and sensory receptors. A nerve is basically a bundle of many nerve fibres wrapped in connective tissue (a similar arrangement to a skeletal muscle being bundles of muscle fibres wrapped in fibrous tissue). Nerves are large enough to be seen with the naked eye, looking like thin white threads. They carry information from the brain and spinal cord to the rest of the body, including the arms and legs. The largest nerve in the body, comprised of many thousands of nerve fibres, is the **sciatic nerve**. It is about the size of your little finger at its widest.

The nerves of the peripheral nervous system are arranged in pairs coming off either the brain or the spinal cord. Twelve pairs of **cranial nerves** leave the brain and supply the head and neck, special senses (e.g., optic nerve, olfactory nerve), and parasympathetic supply to the organs (via the vagus nerve).

Thirty-one pairs of **spinal nerves** leave the spinal cord, supplying the skin and muscles of the trunk, arms and legs. Peripheral nerves may consist of motor fibres or sensory fibres, or more often a mixture of both.

Motor nerves convey impulses from the central nervous system to the body; these can be orders either for a muscle to contract, or a gland to secrete.

The motor system consists of command areas in the brain known as the **motor cortex**. From here, **descending tracts** go down the spinal cord, being the fibres of **upper motor neurons** bringing messages from the motor cortex. **Lower motor neurons** leave the spinal cord via the ventral or anterior horn via a particular spinal or cranial nerve to go to skeletal muscle, smooth muscle or gland. These are called 'effectors'.

Tone in muscles is maintained by constant firing of lower motor neurons, which the upper motor neurons inhibit or stimulate as necessary; hence when an upper motor nerve is damaged, we may see generalized muscle spasm and increased reflexes – think of a person who has had a stroke. However, when a lower motor nerve is damaged, we get flaccid muscles and absent reflexes.

Sensory nerves pick up information from sense receptors and carry it to the central nervous system. Sensory receptors have a structure that allows them to be excited by a particular kind of stimulus, such as light, pressure, or damage. These receptors can be exteroceptors, visceroceptors or proprioceptors. **Exteroceptors** pick up information about the outside world – like the sensations of the skin and the receptors of the special senses. **Visceroceptors** are in the internal organs and tubes of the body, and let the brain know about internal factors such as blood pressure or the level of carbon dioxide in the blood. **Proprioceptors** are found in tendons and joint capsules, and they give information about where the body is in space. Close your eyes for a moment – notice that you can still feel where you are, how your body is positioned. This is the sense of proprioception.

Sensory receptors can be classified in another way as mechanoreceptors, thermoreceptors, photoreceptors, chemoreceptors and nociceptors, sensitive to pressure, temperature, light, chemical changes and damage to tissues respectively. Over-stimulation of *any* receptor is painful, so all act as **nociceptors** at some time. The receptors are at the beginning of sensory nerves, which enter the spinal cord at the back (the dorsal root) and ascend to the brain. Some then synapse in the brainstem and some in the thalamus before ascending to the sensory cortex. Others go to the cerebellum.

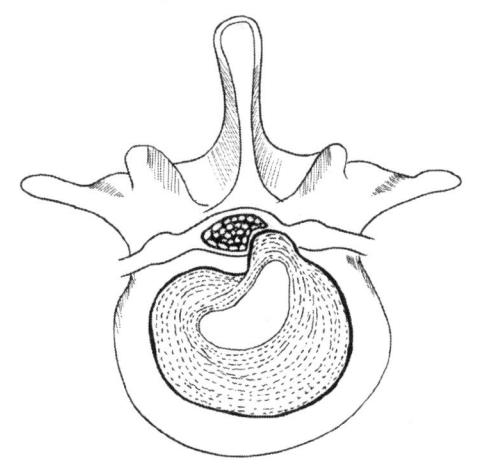

A common and well-known problem with spinal nerve roots is that caused by a **slipped disc**, which generally develops for a long time before it actually strikes. The intervertebral disc got thinner, compressed and weaker over time, until suddenly it is no longer capable of doing its job of supporting the spine. The rings of fibres in the cartilage that makes it up loosen, and the softer centre of the disc bulges out (herniates). Because there are strong ligaments to the front and sides of the vertebral bodies, and solid bone where the transverse process comes out at the back, the most likely direction for the disc to bulge is towards the sides and back (postero-laterally), straight into the spinal nerve. The herniated disc presses against the nerve root, and the resulting over-stimulation of the nerves within causes inflammation with horrible symptoms including pain, numbness, paralysis, pins and needles and so on.

The Autonomic Nervous System

This part of the nervous system, thought to be automatic and completely outside conscious control – hence the name – maintains and governs the vital functions of the body, such as breathing, circulation, digestion, heart rate and so on. There are two complementary parts of it, which work together to maintain homeostasis: the sympathetic and parasympathetic nervous systems. These work together in partnership; where one stimulates activity in a part of the body, the other sedates.

The Sympathetic Nervous System

The sympathetic nervous system provides the **fight or flight** response to stress. This means making the body ready to either fight or run away from something perceived as a threat to our survival.[227] Sympathetic nerve stimulation increases heart rate and force of contraction, ups the blood pressure, speeds up breathing, and diverts blood to the skeletal muscles and the brain, decreasing digestive and sexual activity.[228] The pupils dilate to let in lots of light so you can see well. Adrenalin (epinephrine) is released which mobilises the body's stores of glucose and fat and backs up the nervous action. It's all about mobilising the body's resources to act now.

It's easy then to see why our modern stresses are so dangerous to the body's wellbeing. How many times in your life has it been appropriate or even possible to either fight or run when you've felt stressed? For most modern humans, stress comes in the form of overwork and loneliness; perhaps due to parenting, long lonely days, trying to make ends meet to feed a family, caring for someone alone, or working in a competitive office environment.

The design of the body favours a strongly physical approach to stress, which should be short lived giving us time to rest and recover and rebuild our reserves. The stresses of modern life not only not require us to fight or flight, but are also relentless. They go on and on, without a break, without the chance to stop and recover in the parasympathetic mode. Of course, we developed a flight or fight response in the first place because at the time that's what we needed; perhaps over the years we will evolve a new response that is more appropriate to what we need now. Actually we do have lots of inbuilt healing mechanisms to help us recover fully from stress, which it is possible to learn to utilise more fully – more on this in chapter twenty-three.

So what is stress? In terms of our physiology, we only have one response to something we consider stressful: the fight or flight response. This is how we react, whether the stressor is an external event (like the appearance of an axe-wielding maniac, nearly getting run over by a bus, someone at work bullying us, a difficult deadline, a screaming toddler day in day out), or an internal event (like feeling bad about ourselves, or a thought about a past event that we haven't yet had the opportunity to heal from). Sometimes **stress control** is about reducing our stress intake and increasing relaxation; sometimes it is about changing our reactions to things, so our internal landscape becomes less stressful.

The sympathetic system is also called the **thoraco-lumbar system**, because the peripheral nerves for it come off the spinal cord in the thoracic and lumbar regions, creating what is known as the **sympathetic chain**. You can see that the sympathetic nerves come off the spinal nerves as soon as they leave the spinal cord, and form a chain by which they are all connected. The sympathetic response is an all-over affair; it's not local. It's like the alarm going off on the Starship

---

[227] It's a shame there isn't a 'flight, fight or diplomacy' response!
[228] You don't stop for a meal or a quickie when running away from a sabre toothed tiger...

Enterprise: it happens at all levels, in all parts of the system. It can vary in intensity, ranging from a mild yellow alert to a more serious orange alert or a full on red alert panic attack.

The fight or flight response shows beautifully the inter-linking of the nervous and hormonal systems for control of the body's activities. Sympathetic arousal involves the stimulation of nerves going to the adrenal medulla, which leads to the release of the chemical adrenaline[229] into the bloodstream. Adrenalin (and noradrenalin, its twin) is actually the neurotransmitter of the sympathetic nervous system, being released from the sympathetic nerves at their synapses and neuromuscular junctions. In the sympathetic response, adrenaline also gets into the blood and therefore travels all around the body, acting as a hormone, stimulating or sedating all tissues with receptors for it.

Think back to when you have had a shock: there is an initial jolt, which is the sympathetic nervous system waking up. Soon after, there is a building sensation of excitement or fear as the adrenaline enters your bloodstream and further increases the heart beat and turns up the fight or flight response. When the event perceived as a stress is over, the adrenalin reaction will fade. The liver takes the adrenalin out of the bloodstream and metabolises it into an inactive and excretable form.

If the stress response is prolonged, the body makes additional provision; the hypothalamus in the brain sends a chemical called a **releasing hormone** to the pituitary gland, telling it to release the hormone **ACTH** into the blood. When it passes through the adrenal cortex, ACTH (**adrenocorticotrophic hormone**) tells the adrenal cortex to release a hormone called cortisol[230] into the blood. Cortisol basically mobilises the stored energy in the body to provide increased blood sugar for all the anticipated activity – running, fighting and thinking. As an extra effect, cortisol is anti-inflammatory; it suppresses the inflammatory response which is part of how the body heals from damage; if you fall over running away from a sabre toothed tiger and twist your ankle, there's no point in it getting all swollen up and stopping you from running. The cortisol represses this response so that you can carry on and thus stay alive. Of course, running on your injured ankle will damage it more, leading to an even greater inflammation when you do finally make it safely back to the cave. (More on inflammation and healing in the pathology section later). It is this anti-inflammatory action of cortisone that has led to its widespread use in modern Western medicine as a symptomatic treatment to suppress inflammation.[231]

After a stress response, the body can reach **resolution**, in which case the sympathetic system is turned off in favour of the parasympathetic. However sometimes the stressful situation is ongoing, or perceived as such, and then the body responds with something called

---

[229] Adrenalin and noradrenelin to be exact, known in America as epinephrine and norepinephrine.

[230] Cortisol, cortisone and hydrocortisone are all glucocorticoid hormones made in the adrenal cortex, which also makes the mineralocortisoid aldosterone and some male sex hormone or androgen.

[231] You can easily see how there would be so many dangerous side effects from taking steroid hormone cortisone.

general adaptation syndrome, a chronically stressed system with the adrenal glands releasing what cortisone they can. In time, if resolution does not occur, **exhaustion** ensues.

Cortisol and the other stress hormones are damaging to the body. The liver must work extra hard to metabolise these additional toxins. However, there is a wonderful mechanism to help us recover and take the pressure off our bodies and minds when we are stressed – crying! In tears, we can excrete damaging stress hormones whole. This is the only way to get them out of the body without the liver first metabolising them. In other words, crying is the cure for being hurt, so get to it! It's time we reclaimed this wonderful healing process, for both men and women – after all, no-one would be so ridiculous as to say, 'be strong, hold on to your pee', or 'real men don't shit'. Actually it's a relatively recent idea that men shouldn't cry. For most of our history, men have wept as freely as women. It looks like this really stopped during the industrial revolution. Remember that tears are a brilliant way for the body to excrete the damaging products of stress, and start encouraging them in yourself and others.

If you don't cry enough, and the stress is ongoing and relentless, many physical problems can ensue. The most obvious and common are muscle tension, digestive problems and high blood pressure. The reproductive system can be disrupted, causing infertility, impotence, menstrual irregularities and menopausal difficulties. Tight muscles can in turn cause other problems including poor joint health.

There are three stages to General Adaptation Syndrome

The first stage of GAS is called **alarm,** and is the fight or flight response discussed above. Once the cause of the stress is removed, the body goes back to normal. If the cause for the stress is not removed, GAS goes to its second stage called **resistance** or **adaptation**. This is the body trying to provide longer-term protection. It refers to the **HPA (hypothalamic pituitary adrenal**) axis and secretion of cortisol by the adrenal cortex. If this adaptation phase continues for a prolonged period of time without periods of relaxation and rest, the result is fatigue, concentration lapses, irritability and lethargy as the effort to sustain arousal slides into negative stress. The third stage of GAS is called **exhaustion**. In this stage, the body has run out of its reserves of body energy and immunity. Mental, physical and emotional resources are empty. The body experiences "adrenal exhaustion". The blood sugar level decreases as the adrenals become depleted, leading to decreased stress tolerance, progressive mental and physical exhaustion, illness and collapse.

The Parasympathetic System

The counterpart to the fight or flight system is the **parasympathetic nervous system**, also known as the **rest-repose system**. This brings the body back to normal, relaxed functioning. It slows down everything except digestion and sexual functions, which it encourages. The parasympathetic system is also called the **cranio-sacral system** because its peripheral nerve supply is from the cranium and the sacrum.

This is the realm of deep rest and relaxation, and is undoubtedly the place where healing happens. All natural systems of medicine emphasise the importance of rest and relaxation in recovery. Indeed, until recently recuperation and convalescence were better understood by modern medicine too. This is not the case now, where being in hospital means being woken up at horrible o'clock in the morning, and often repeatedly through the night as well to have temperature, blood pressure or something taken. A stay in hospital is rarely a deeply restful experience. It seems that the current obsession with productivity – working away regardless of the cost to health or state of mind – is becoming worse and worse, encouraged by powerful suppressive drugs like anti-inflammatories and anti-catarrhals.[232] When you hear about people having days off sick, the figures are usually about how much money has been lost to business due to this illness. In fact the industrial revolution was fuelled by caffeine, and modern global capitalism carries on this proud tradition. The empires of Europe with the riches they generated from slavery made the industrial revolution possible. Tea was imported, and quickly became popular as it enables people to work more than they really have energy for, especially when sweetened with sugar grown by African people taken as slaves (in exchange for iron goods from the UK, for example) to the West Indies and made to work the sugar plantations.[233] Caffeine potentiates and mimics adrenaline in the body, so with its help we can fool ourselves that we have plenty of energy, when in fact we are running on empty. A useful way to think about caffeine consumption is that it allows us to borrow time from tomorrow. Not such a bad thing, as long as the day comes when we have a chance to rest to pay it back. Almost everyone, including our world leaders and governments, are keeping going on coffee and tea. I wonder about this: does it mean they are really in a state of constant sympathetic arousal? In which case it is no surprise that decisions seem to be being made that are totally about reacting in the present, rather than considering the impact of current actions on future generations.

Feeling exhausted when relaxing is an indication that the person has been running on their sympathetic system for some time, hence the typical scenario of a hard-working person going on holiday and getting sick. This is why many people prefer an action holiday – to really stop and unwind means to feel the true state of affairs in the body mind and spirit, which are exhaustion and the absence of reserves. This is not as much fun as the hyper state of adrenaline arousal. Adrenaline can be addictive.

When the parasympathetic system is operating, muscles relax, the mind slows down, and digestion increases. The body concentrates on digesting and absorbing nutrients and on building reserves for future contingencies. If there are no spaces in the stress, there is never an oppor-

---

[232] I'm sure there was an advert in recent years about a man who stays home with a cold losing his position at work to the man who took the cold-suppressing medicines and went into work...

[233] Interesting to realise that it was also the industrial revolution that entrenched the idea that men must not cry. You need to numb out from all sorts of feelings in order to be a 'good worker', or indeed a 'good boss'.

tunity to properly rebuild. Also, the immune system, being allied to the inflammatory response, is suppressed by the stress response. A diminished immune system has implications on all levels, from being vulnerable to infections to the more sinister lack of protection from cancer.

So the emphasis in natural medicine is on encouraging the rest-repose function: deep relaxation and rest, putting the whole being into a place where healing can happen. Massage practitioners and other body workers soon hear direct evidence that parasympathetic stimulation is happening – their clients' tummy rumbles increasingly as the person is relaxing! Actually, if a person has been years on a stressful adrenaline habit, they will probably feel tired and ill on beginning to relax. Remember, they are feeling the true state of affairs in their system, rather than the false energy felt from being on adrenaline. In time, as the healing progresses and the reserves are built up again, this will pass.

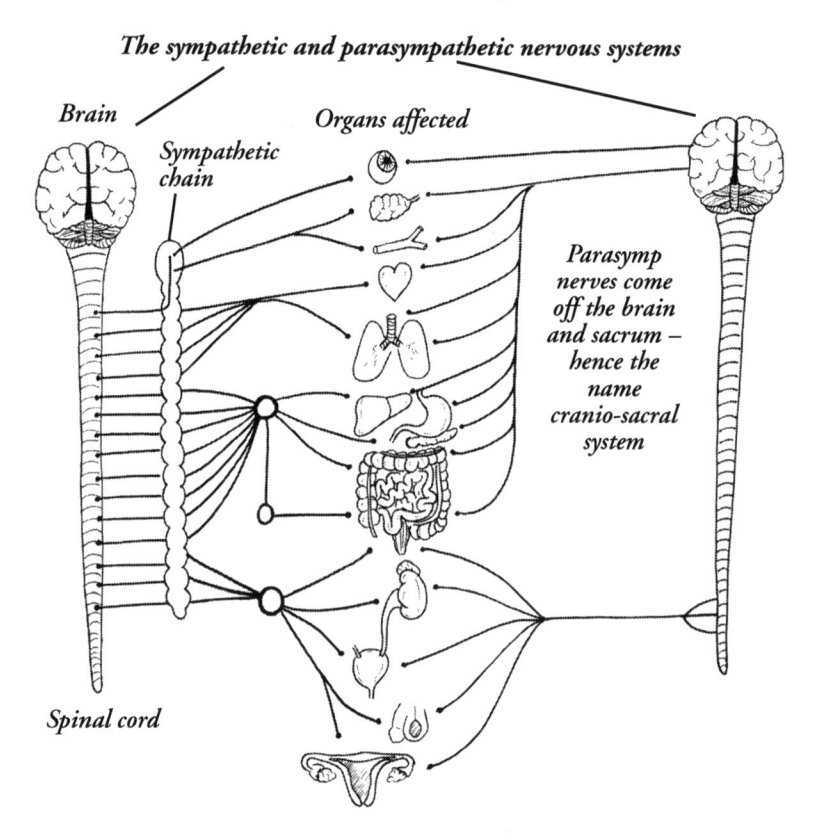

The sympathetic and parasympathetic nervous systems

Brain

Sympathetic chain

Organs affected

Parasymp nerves come off the brain and sacrum – hence the name cranio-sacral system

Spinal cord

Reflex Actions

Reflex actions allow for very fast responses to possible hurt. A stimulus from the outside excites a sensory nerve, which sends a message to the spinal cord. Here the sensory nerve synapses with a motor nerve to send an order for immediate action. This means that a reaction to a stimulus can come extremely rapidly, without the brain having to make a decision about what to do. One example is the knee jerk response, when a tendon is stretched suddenly, it will reflexly move to minimise that action. Another type of reflex is dropping something hot, or reacting to a danger when driving before being consciously aware of it.

Some reflexes can be overridden (e.g. drop it, it's hot! NO! I don't want to drop it, it's my favourite casserole dish, and I'll keep hold of it even thought it's burning me...). The knee jerk stretch reflex cannot be overridden.

The 'reflex arc' has five elements: sensory receptor, sensory neuron, integration centre, motor neuron and effector.

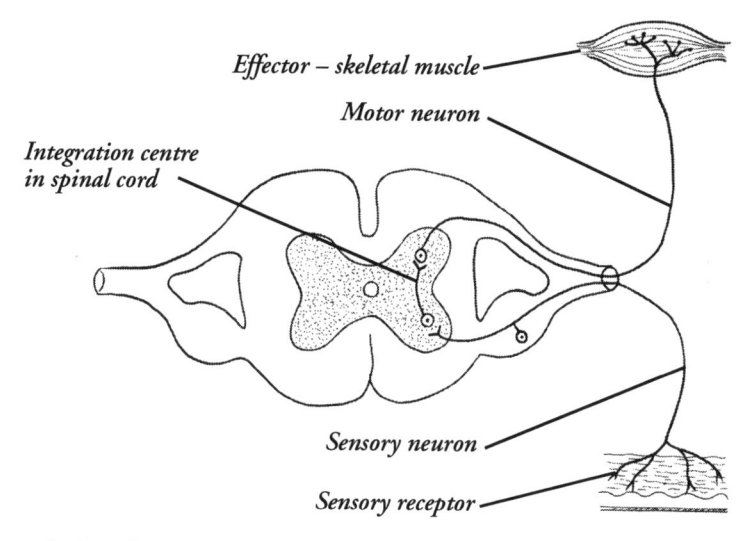

Interrelationships

It seems obvious that **all systems** rely completely on the nervous system for their proper functioning. The balance in the autonomic nervous system between its sympathetic and parasympathetic parts profoundly affects **all of the internal organs** therefore all of the systems. The nerves (like all other systems) receive the nutrients they need for repair and maintenance from the **circulatory system**. Toxicity affects the nervous system very quickly so it is particularly in need of all the eliminatory systems – **digestive**, **urinary**, **skin** and **respiratory**. The **endocrine** and nervous systems are completely intertwined.

CHAPTER FIFTEEN

GLANDS AND HORMONES
THE ENDOCRINE SYSTEM

The endocrine system is comprised of a series of **glands**, which secrete chemical messengers called **hormones** directly into the blood. It works with the nervous system to control and co-ordinate many body functions and maintain homeostasis.[234] Substances which act as neurotransmitters in the brain and as hormones in the blood are made in many organs and tissues. There is a constant two-way flow of information around the body which the endocrine system plays a part in.

Stephen Buhner says:

'Nineteenth-century medical practitioners were excited to discover powerful glands in the body that produced substances with marked impact on the body's functioning. These, while located at widely divergent places in the body, were grouped together in what they called the endocrine system...However it turns out that every organ in the body produces hormones, molecular substances that significantly alter physical functioning...There is, in fact, no such thing as *the endocrine system*, and contrary to most medical thinking, the heart is one of the major endocrine glands in the body.'[235]

No wonder it is easy to become confused with the endocrine system! As well as being a figment of our imagination, it is a beautiful and complex system of completely different hormones (which could be described as internal drugs) which regulate with amazing intelligence many functions of the body. Most hormones are peptides – small proteins made of amino acids. The steroid hormones are made from cholesterol.

Each hormone affects its **target cells** by altering cell activity – increasing or decreasing the rates of those cells' normal processes. Hormones generally can cause one or more of the following effects:

- Altering membrane permeability, or potential
- Stimulating the making of proteins or enzymes in the cell
- Activating or deactivating enzymes
- Producing secretory activity
- Stimulating cell division (mitosis)

Target cells for a particular hormone are those which have receptors for it on their cell

---

[234] As discussed in the introduction to the body, homeostasis relates purely to physical functions, especially the control of temperature, blood sugar and body fluids. You may like to re-read these pages.

[235] *The Secret Teachings of Plants* – if you read one book in your life make it this one!

membrane. The state of health of the cell membrane and condition of its receptors are crucial for its ability to respond to hormones or other biochemical signals. The actual amounts of hormones are miniscule; so small as to almost not be there. The tiniest fluctuations have massive impact on our physiology.

Most hormones are controlled by **negative feedback**. As discussed in our beginning chapters, this means that raised circulating levels of the hormone are detected by receptors, and this information is fed back to the gland, causing a reduction in the release of that hormone. The **positive feedback** mechanism is unusual in health and relates to specific big events such as childbirth, when more and more oxytocin is released as labour progresses.

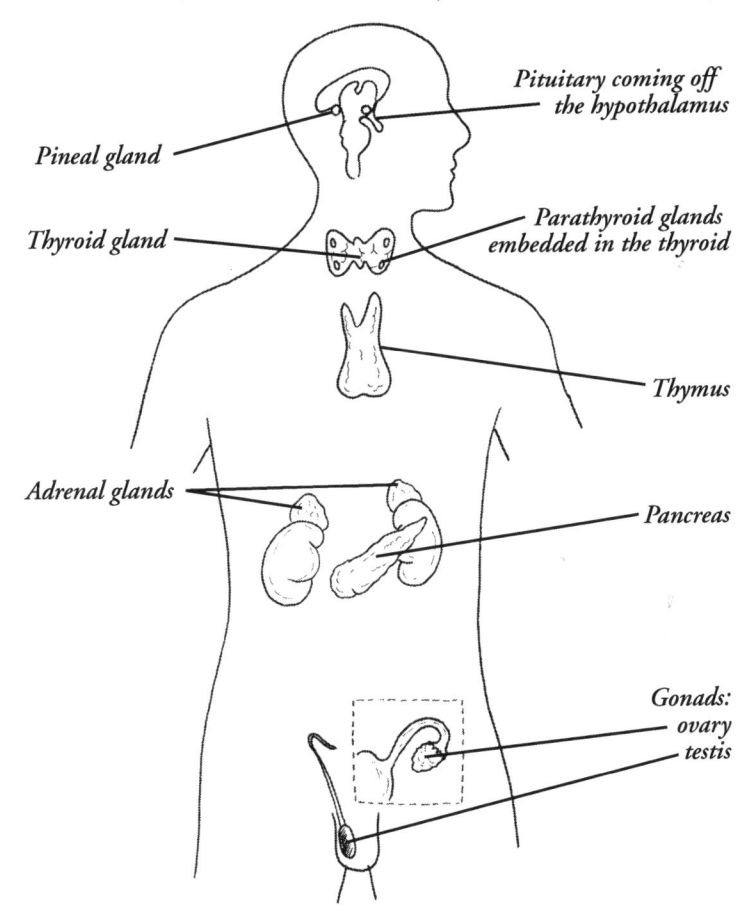

Control of Hormone Secretion

Many hormones are controlled via the nervous system. The hypothalamus controls the release of pituitary hormones by its own hormones, which are known as **releasing factors**. The pituitary hormones in turn cause the release of other hormones. The autonomic nervous system, especially the sympathetic 'fight or flight' response, also increases production of many hormones. As you will remember, it has big effects on the blood sugar hormones like cortisol, insulin and glucagon, as well as growth hormone, thyroid hormone and the other adrenal hormones.

Because of the wonderful complexity of the endocrine system, it is easy to become confused about it. Although the best advice is to study *one* gland at a time, here we are introducing the whole lot together... You might find that looking at imbalances helps as a way to learn and remember the actions of hormones.

A very interesting aspect of endocrinology is the strong relationship between hormones, neurotransmitters and emotions. As discussed already, there are great similarities between peptide hormones and neurotransmitters, with many substances acting as both. They are called 'neurotransmitters' when found in the nervous system and 'hormones' when secreted into the blood. These peptides are also produced by the white blood cells of the immune system. Immune cells, nerve cells, endocrine glands and many cells, tissues and organs throughout the body have receptors for them. It is useful therefore to see them as informational substances, by which means the trillion cell community that we are keeps in touch.

The purely mechanical view, which unfortunately seems to still be prevailing in the majority of the medical world, sees emotions as being caused by chemicals. This is a convenient belief for reliance on drug therapy, as it means logically there is no deep obstacle to treating emotional difficulties with chemicals. A different slant, the more holistic one, sees the dance of thought, feeling, and chemical expression as being a two-way street: our thoughts are continually affecting our chemistry as well as the other way around. Neurotransmitters and hormones are the chemical expression of our thoughts and main emotions, in turn affecting our thinking and feeling. This model is eloquently described by Deepak Chopra in his book *Quantum Healing*, Candace Pert in *Molecules of Emotion* and Bruce H. Lipton in *The Biology of Belief*.

The Pituitary Gland

The pituitary gland is a pea-sized gland attached to the hypothalamus of the brain, but it is in fact two glands – the anterior pituitary gland and the posterior pituitary gland. Together they are known as the **master gland**, as this controls many other endocrine glands. It makes a whole list of hormones, detailed below.

Growth hormone, which affects the growth and differentiation of cells and tissues, especially bone. Although it is obviously hugely influential in childhood, it is just as essential in adulthood since growth continues throughout life. Tissues are replaced routinely or when damaged, and this cannot be done without growth hormone. There are many other factors involved in growth also. Growth hormone has an important effect on protein, fat and carbohydrate metabolism. The effects of growth hormone are to make sure lots of proteins are synthesized; fat is broken down to be available for use in energy production, and blood glucose is maintained within the normal range (growth hormone tending to increase it). Under-secretion of growth hormone in childhood leads to the condition called dwarfism, in which mental development is normal but growth of the body is stunted. Over-secretion of growth hormone in childhood leads to gigantism. Later in life, over secretion results in the condition known as acromegaly, a painful condition where the bones in the hands, feet and skull grow abnormally.

Thyroid stimulating hormone (**TSH**) is released from the pituitary when the hypothalamus sends a releasing hormone. TSH goes to the thyroid gland to cause secretion of thyroid hormone.

Adrenocorticotrophic hormone (**ACTH**). Likewise having a releasing hormone from the hypothalamus, ACTH causes release of adrenal cortex hormones. It is one of the primary **stress hormones**, as discussed in the previous chapter on the autonomic nervous system.

Gonadotrophic hormones (luteinising hormone, LH, and **follicle stimulating hormone, FSH**) control activity in the gonads in men and women. FSH stimulates development of the ovarian follicles, and therefore the ova, or eggs, and production of oestrogen in a woman, and sperm production in a man. LH stimulates progesterone secretion in women and testosterone production in men.

Prolactin is responsible for milk production. It begins to be secreted during pregnancy, but the extraordinary high levels of female sex hormones floating around at that time stop it from working. On about the third day after childbirth, there is a sudden and dramatic drop in pregnancy hormones, allowing prolactin to go to work, filling the breasts with milk. This is known as 'the milk coming in', and, as anyone who's had a baby will know, results in breasts like massive melons that are so full of milk it makes your eyes water…

Melanocyte stimulating hormone stimulates melanocytes in the skin. These are the cells that make the pigment melanin, which makes our skins dark to protect us from the damaging UV rays of the sun.

The above hormones are all produced by the anterior pituitary, or **adenohypophysis**, at the front of the pituitary, which is made of glandular epithelial-type tissue. Inhibiting and releasing factors from the hypothalamus control their release and travel directly to the pituitary in connecting blood vessels. So the nervous system is involved in directing much pituitary, and therefore endocrine, activity.

At the back is the **neurohypophysis**, or posterior pituitary. This is made of nervous tissue, being a continuation of the brain. The following two hormones are actually made in the cell bodies of neurons in the hypothalamus and migrate down the axons, which end in the posterior pituitary, and are released into the body's blood stream when the nerve cells are stimulated.

Anti-diuretic hormone increases water re-absorption in kidneys.

Oxytocin ejects milk from the breast, and makes the uterus contract. The stimulus for its release is the sucking of the nipple – thus breastfeeding right after birth helps the uterus contract and expel the placenta[236] and for the months afterwards gets the uterus back into

---

[236] The placenta is a blood-vessel rich organ formed by the uterus to nourish and supply the developing foetus with oxygen.

shape. Oxytocin is a hormone which is involved with powerful bonding and loving feelings, important for establishing maternal bonding. It is secreted from within the brain and from the ovaries and testes as well as by the pituitary – a good example of an informational peptide.

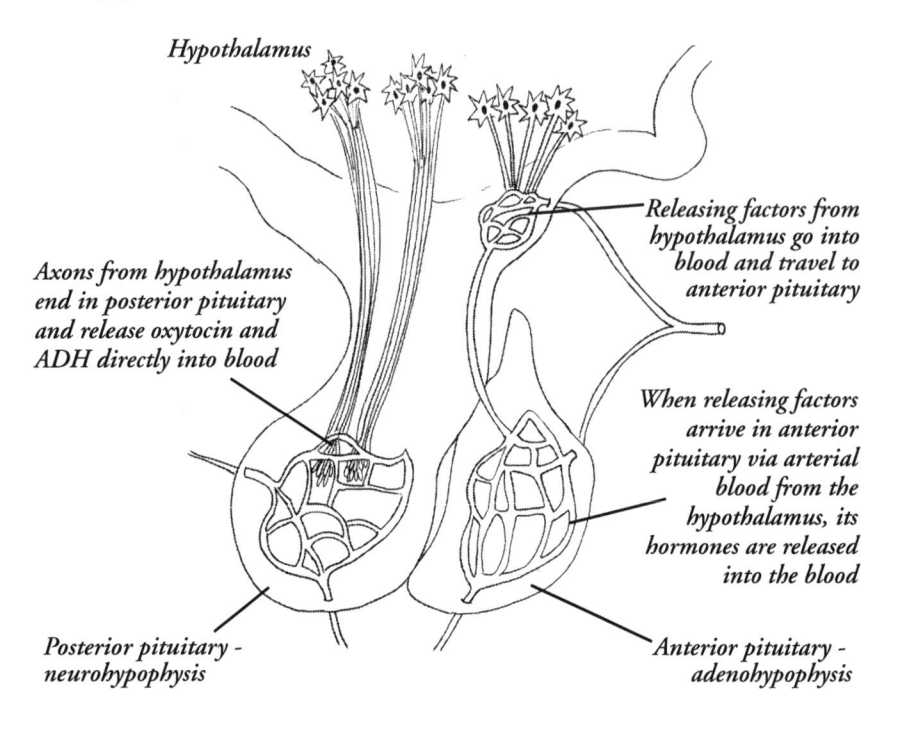

Hypothalamus

Axons from hypothalamus end in posterior pituitary and release oxytocin and ADH directly into blood

Releasing factors from hypothalamus go into blood and travel to anterior pituitary

When releasing factors arrive in anterior pituitary via arterial blood from the hypothalamus, its hormones are released into the blood

Posterior pituitary - neurohypophysis

Anterior pituitary - adenohypophysis

The Thyroid Gland

The thyroid gland is found in the front of the neck below the larynx (Adam's apple). It is shaped like a bow tie, with two wings either side and a narrow bridge or **isthmus** between them crossing the throat.

Thyroid hormones – **thyroxin**, or tetraiodothyronine, and triiodothyronine[237] – work on metabolism: they stimulate metabolic rate in cells and promote growth. They affect cellular differentiation, growth and metabolism – in other words, pretty much everything! It is thought that they increase the efficiency of ATP production by the mitochondria. T3 and T4 (as they are called) promote protein synthesis by acting on DNA, increase carbohydrate absorption rate in the gut, promote fat metabolism and encourage uptake of glucose by cells for energy production. It is likely that all the cells in the body have receptors for thyroid hormones.

The thyroid gland also produces **calcitonin**, which lowers the amount of calcium in the blood, in its 'C cells'.

---

[237] Having four and three iodine atoms each respectively.

Too much or too little...

Common symptoms of **hypothyroidism** (too little thyroid hormone) include lethargy, fatigue, cold-intolerance, weakness, depression, dry skin, hair loss and reproductive failure. If these signs are severe, it is called **myxoedema**. In the case of iodide deficiency, the thyroid becomes unusually large, and is called goitre.

Hyposecretion of thyroxine in childhood causes **cretinism**, retardation of growth and of proper development of the nervous system. (This condition would most likely happen in inland mountainous areas far from the sea, where salt was difficult to obtain and iodine levels in food were low).

It used to be that under-active thyroid was commonly caused by iodine deficiency – hence the use in herbal medicine of seaweed to treat it.[238] Nowadays this is much less common because table salt is usually iodised and most people have too much, rather than too little, salt. However under-active thyroid is now even more common. Often there is an auto-immune element to it.

Remember what we discussed in our chapter on cells? The health of a cell and the condition of its receptors are of vital importance. You can have a situation where a person has all the clinical symptoms and signs of an underactive thyroid, but their blood thyroid levels are normal when tested. This could well be due to a problem with the cells' receptors for thyroxin. The cell membrane being in poor shape could be to do with something as simple as dehydration, or a deficiency in the essential fatty acids of which the membrane is made.

Common symptoms of **hyperthyroidism** (too much thyroid hormone) are the opposite: the person is manic, anxious, nervous, an insomniac, has a fast heart rate, is heat intolerant, and often has eye problems which make the eyes bulge. It is called **thyrotoxicosis**. Menstrual irregularities are common with both under and over active thyroid. Untreated, both can lead to heart failure.

The Parathyroids

The parathyroids are four tiny glands embedded in the thyroid. They were discovered accidentally after removal of the thyroid gland for overactive thyroid led to terrible problems with calcium metabolism in the body. **Parathyroid hormone** works with calcitonin (also from the thyroid) to balance the blood calcium levels: it increases the calcium levels in the blood by increasing intestinal absorption, decreasing calcium secretion in the kidney tubules and increasing re-absorption of calcium from bone. Calcitonin (from the C-cells of the thyroid gland) does the opposite. Calcium is needed for proper muscle and nerve function, bone metabolism and the general well being of cells. There are no recognised diseases involving too

---

[238] It is dangerous to come off drugs for under-active thyroid. It is not possible to substitute herbs for hormone replacement therapy, and this should not be attempted.

much or too little calcitonin, although this can be present in many diseases. However too much or too little secretion of parathyroid hormone does occur in disease.

Too much or too little…

Too much parathyroid hormone can happen from a tumour of the parathyroids which secretes the hormone. It leads to abnormally high blood calcium levels, kidney stones and weak bones. It also occurs secondary to kidney disease. If the kidneys are poorly and not able to reabsorb calcium in the tubules, calcium levels will fall, leading to increased parathyroid secretion to try to maintain normal blood calcium. Calcium will then be taken from the bones.

Too little parathyroid hormone leads to a decreased concentration of calcium in the blood, which causes painful muscle spasm, known as tetany, and convulsions. The most common causes are surgical removal of the parathyroid glands and diseases like auto-immune conditions, which destroy the glands.

The Adrenal Glands

The adrenal glands sit one on top of each kidney. The adrenal medulla (in the middle) secretes **adrenalin** and **noradrenalin** (known as epinephrine and norepinephrine in the States), involved in the 'fight or flight' response, and the outer cortex secretes the **steroid** hormone, which regulate the body's use of carbohydrates, as well as salt and water balance. The steroid hormones are **glucocorticoids** (including **cortisone**), which affect glucose, fat and protein metabolism, as discussed earlier with metabolism in the chapter on the liver. The general idea is to mobilise energy stores to allow plenty of glucose available in the blood for cellular respiration, and in addition the suppression of the inflammatory and immune responses.

Then there are the **mineralocorticoids**. **Aldosterone** controls the re-absorption of sodium and water in the kidney. It increases re-absorption of sodium and increased re-absorption of water by the kidney tubules, therefore leads to decreased water and sodium in the urine and increased potassium excretion by the kidneys.

The adrenal cortex also produces a small amount of **androgens**, or male sex hormones. In women these become important after menopause, when the ovaries are no longer producing oestrogen, and a woman's muscle and fat cells can convert the adrenal androgens to oestrogen.

Too much or too little…

Too many cortex hormones are called **Cushing's disease.** The most common cause of this is 'iatrogenic' – caused by steroids prescribed by the doctor. Natural causes include either a problem in the adrenal cortex or a problem in the pituitary leading to too much ACTH secretion. The clinical features of Cushing's disease include high blood pressure, obesity of the trunk but wasted limbs, round 'moon face', thin skin and metabolic disorders like diabetes.

A deficiency of steroid hormones is known as **Addison's disease**. This most commonly comes after an infectious disease (like TB), or is seen as an autoimmune destruction of the adrenal cortex. It leads to lethargy, diarrhoea, weakness and cardiovascular disease.

Lack of aldosterone usually occurs together with too little cortisone in Addison's disease, but it can occur on its own. The resulting electrolyte imbalances and low blood pressure can be lethal, causing heart failure.

The Gonads

These will be discussed in more detail with the reproductive system. The gonads are the ovaries and testes. As well as producing the egg and sperm from which a new human grows, these have an endocrine function. The ovaries produce oestrogen and progesterone; the testes produce testosterone.

Oestrogen makes the ovum mature and keeps the skin soft and the hair in good condition, as well as maintaining other female secondary sexual characteristics. Progesterone is the pregnancy hormone, which prepares the uterus for pregnancy and maintains the pregnancy. Testosterone is the male sex hormone, which causes development of the genitalia and secondary sexual characteristics in males, and is involved with production of spermatozoa. Testosterone is partly responsible for libido in both men and women.

The Pancreas

The pancreas, as well as its exocrine function described with the digestive system, contains groups of cells called the **Islets of Langerhans,** which secrete insulin, glucagon and somatostatin. These important hormones control blood glucose levels. Insulin lowers blood sugar by transporting it into cells for use in energy production, and stimulating the muscle and liver cells to store it as glycogen. Lack of insulin is found in diabetes mellitus.

Glucagon is opposite to insulin: it stimulates the liver to convert glycogen to glucose and promotes gluconeogenesis, thus increasing the level of blood sugar.

The third hormone, somatostatin, is less known. It decreases the levels of both glucagon and insulin.

Too much or too little...
Insulin Deficiency – Diabetes Mellitus

This is a very significant disease for humans, with more and more people suffering from it each year. The symptoms of diabetes are being constantly thirsty, constantly needing to urinate, often feeling tired and lethargic and unexpected weight loss.

There are two main types of diabetes; type I and type II

Type I is also known as **insulin-dependant diabetes mellitus** or IDD. It usually begins in childhood or early adulthood, being due to destruction of the beta cells of the pancreas which make insulin, probably due to autoimmunity. The body is suddenly unable to make insulin. This leads to an emergency situation where the blood is full of sugar but the cells are starving, which causes the symptoms of diabetes: fatigue and weakness, tiredness and mental confusion, thirst, skin infections and urinary infections. The excess sugar in the blood is food for bacteria, which easily thrive on it, and the kidney can't keep up with reabsorbing all the glucose, so the urine also contains glucose.

This type of diabetes is treated by injection of insulin, which must be done at least three times daily for one's whole life. Later (more so if the diabetes isn't managed well) there is damage to the small blood vessels and nerves, with eye and kidney problems. Amputations are common due to losing sensation in the feet, and not noticing an infection taking hold until it is too late.

Type II is also known as **non-insulin dependant diabetes mellitus** or NIDD. This begins more slowly and is associated with our modern diet of excessive sugar and fat. It is the fastest growing disease in the world. It starts with an **insulin resistance** – that is, normal levels of insulin but insulin receptors which don't respond well – and then continues with insulin levels getting higher to try and get the receptors to respond, but the receptors carry on getting worse. The disease is often controllable by changing the diet. Strangely, I found that although it is stated that if you eat a high fibre, lots of fruit and vegetables and whole grains, low animal fat diet, you are much less likely to get diabetes, still eating sugar and fat are not seen as causes – this is because some people can eat like this and not get diabetes. In order for it to be an accepted cause, it seems that everyone who eats too much fat and sugar and not enough vegetables would have to get it. This doesn't make sense, as not everyone who smokes gets lung cancer but it is still a known cause. Obesity is seen as a huge risk factor, although not a cause. The naturopathic view is that the inability of the insulin receptors to respond is likely to be due to the massive and unnatural amounts of refined carbohydrates many people eat today, coupled with high fat and low fibre diets. This type of eating basically overwhelms the receptors which get tired and fed up of responding to insulin. Diabetes type II can lead to an insulin dependant form if not checked.

Too Much Insulin – hyperinsulinaemia

This is most commonly seen in type II diabetes with insulin resistance. More unusually it can come form a tumour secreting insulin. It can also occur in type I diabetics who take too much insulin. This leads to a radical drop in blood glucose levels which starves the brain of glucose and can lead to coma and death. The first signs of this serious situation are usually irrational or aggressive behaviour; relatives of insulin dependant diabetics learn to look out for this and know that it is essential to get some glucose into the diabetic who begins to behave in this way. Due to the extreme irrationality, this can literally involve having to sit on them and force sugary stuff into their mouth. If such a situation happens while they are asleep it is particularly dangerous, as coma and then death can result un-noticed.

The Thymus Gland

The thymus gland is found behind the sternum. It secretes a group of protein hormones called thymopoietins and thymosins. These are essential for the development of T-lymphocytes. The thymus gland is most active in childhood, later atrophying, although it does retain some activity throughout life.[239]

The Pineal Gland

The pineal gland in the brain is involved with cycles of night and day. It is found protruding from the roof of the third ventricle, in the diencephalon, which is close to the pons, the cerebellum and the cerebrum. The pineal gland is light sensitive.[240] One of the hormones it produces is **melatonin**. As the light decreases, it secretes more melatonin. It has some action in cycles of sleep and wakefulness. Melatonin inhibits the secretion of gonadotrophins from the anterior pituitary, and is involved in sexual development. The pineal gland also secretes the neurotransmitter **serotonin**. It slows down activity at puberty, and is often calcified in adults.

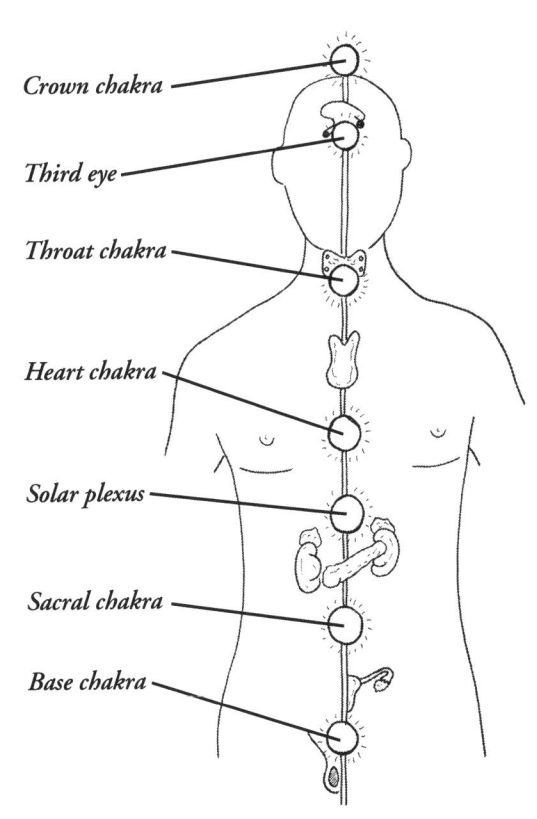

Crown chakra

Third eye

Throat chakra

Heart chakra

Solar plexus

Sacral chakra

Base chakra

Endocrine glands and Chakras

The Chakra system, which originated in ancient India, is about the life force or energy within the body and mind. It is said that everything in the entire universe, from the tiniest subatomic particle to the great spiral galaxies, are spinning wheels of energy. So also the chakras are centres of energy within us; they are wheels or disks of spinning energy based around the spinal column. Each chakra has a particular sphere of influence, and it is interesting that each can be correlated with a particular endocrine organ as well as with a concentration of nervous activity. There are different schools of thoughts on chakras and these systems may vary as to which chakra they relate to which gland. For example, the base chakra at the bottom of the spine is associated

---

[239] Don't forget to tap your sternum daily for a few minutes to stimulate the thymus and therefore maximise your immune system's protection.

[240] It is not light sensitive itself but it is fed information about light from the retina, via the suprachiasmatic nucleus.

with survival. Some put the adrenal glands with this chakra, some the testes. The second chakra, or sacral chakra, to do with sexuality and creativity, may be correlated with the ovaries and womb or the testes and prostate. The third chakra which is about our will and power in the world in relation to others, lies near the pancreas, but sometimes is given association with the adrenal glands. The heart is found at the centre of everything and is to do with our loving connection with ourselves, each other and all that is. The thymus gland lies here, with its protective immune activity and somewhat mysterious actions. The fifth chakra in the throat is to do with communication and creativity, with our voice and our outward expression of what is within. Wrapped closely around that area is the thyroid gland. A point between the eyebrows is the third eye chakra; in some systems it is associated with the pituitary gland, in others the pineal. The seventh chakra, called the crown, is sometimes associated with the pineal gland and sometimes with the pituitary gland. There are good arguments for both; it makes sense to put the pineal gland with the crown chakra as the crown is to do with our opening and connection to the heavens, to the light above, and the pineal gland is tied closely in with matters of night and day, light and darkness. On the other hand, because of the fact that the third eye is all about seeing - which is very much to do with light and dark - it makes sense also to put the pineal gland with the third eye.

Interrelationships

These are obviously everywhere, in terms of **every system** being at least in part regulated by hormones. It seems also that everywhere makes hormones too, with more being discovered all the time. As hormones are secreted into the blood, there is a special relationship with the **cardiovascular** system. The **digestive system** absorbs the raw materials for making them, the **liver** metabolises them once their job is done, and the **kidneys** and **bowel** then excrete the metabolites.

Chapter Sixteen

THE BIRDS AND THE BEES
(The Reproductive System)

This system is for the reproduction of the species. It's obviously very important. In fact, there is an argument that it's the most important system of all – that the entire organism has developed around the genes' determination to survive.[241]

It is a fascinating system, and not just because it's about sex! Men and women really have very similar bodies. We all have the same three hormones present in our bodies – progesterone, oestrogens and testosterone. These hormones are steroid hormones, being made from cholesterol like cortisone. In fact the body kind of mixes and matches them: cholesterol is made into a precursor molecule (called **pregnenolone**) which can then be made into either any of the sex hormones, or any of the adrenal cortex hormones. The actual amounts involved are very small – tiny fluctuations have a huge effect on us.

In a developing embryo, the genitalia look identical until two months in the womb, actually looking more female than male.[242] At this point, if the baby is male and has testes, they begin to secrete testosterone. The presence of testosterone makes the genitalia begin to develop, to look more male: the erectile tissue, which forms the clitoris in the female, and the inner labia, are elongated and join to form the penis; what will be the outer labia in a female join up to form the scrotal pouch which will house the testicles outside the body.[243] The gonads are similar in size and shape, and begin life in the same place, on either side of the lower abdominal cavity. The testes migrate through the inguinal canal – a tunnel through the abdominal muscles – in the last weeks of gestation.

The differences are tiny, yet hugely important for reproduction. You might be surprised to find that the significant difference between us is less to do with the appearance of the plumbing – known as the **genitalia** – than you might think. In fact, the biggest difference between the sexes can be seen in the functioning of the gonads. In a woman, all the eggs her ovaries will ever make are partially made while she is still inside her mother's body in the first

---

[241] Richard Dawkins argues this extraordinarily material approach to life in his book *The Selfish Gene*.

[242] You will find some great pictures showing the development of the external genitalia of female and male human embryos if you take a look at URL http://en.wikipedia.org/wiki/Development_of_the_urinary_and_reproductive_organs

[243] If you are a man, take a look at yours, if a woman, find a friend to let you take a look: you can see the seam down the middle of the scrotum where the two sides knitted together to form it.

months of gestation. This means that, in a way, our grandmothers have a big part in making us, and we all begin life inside our grandmother's body; the egg that we grew from was made by our mum's mum when our mum was growing inside her. What our granny ate, smoked, drank, as well as how she lived, her stress levels and nutritional status when she was pregnant with our mum, has an affect on our health and life. This is especially true if we are female, and it will also affect our reproductive lives – the primordial eggs in our ovaries were all made by our mother when she was carrying us.

In contrast, sperm cells are made daily by the testes. The tubules of the testes are made of a specialized layered epithelial tissue, which like all epithelial tissue is always dividing and growing and replacing its cells. When the cells reach the lumen of the tube they break off from the wall and stay inside – they are the sperm cells. Millions are made daily by the **seminiferous tubules** of the testes.

To me, this is the major reproductive difference. It is interesting how it mirrors the ancient Chinese concept of yin and yang, female and male energy: the yin is the constant, unchanging, still form. The yang is the changeable and adaptive form.

Before puberty male and female bodies are very similar, apart from the difference in the immature genitals of each. At puberty the sex glands become active under command from the pituitary. The sex hormones cause growth and development of the genitalia and development of the secondary sexual characteristics - pubic hair, armpit hair, breast development in women; facial hair and deepening voice in men.

It is the **gonadotrophic hormones** – **FSH** and **LH** from the pituitary – which stimulate secretion of oestrogen, progesterone and testosterone and make these changes, preparing our bodies for making babies; causing ovulation and menstruation in women, and sperm production in men.

Gender

For convenience, we will take a look at female and male reproductive systems separately. Many, but not all, human societies have been very rigid in attitudes to gender and the roles for men and women. Although these rigidities have been challenged to varying degrees in recent decades, there is still a lot of work to do to free us from the oppressive notions that surround gender. Strict ideas of what a 'real man' or 'real woman' is, plus distortions and disconnection from spiritual traditions, lead to many, many people feeling not quite right, due to not fitting into to these narrow definitions.

In biology, it turns out things are not as clear cut as all that. We generally think that there are two sexes, or genders, but in fact there is more variation than you might think. Individual women and men may have quite different levels of the male and female hormones, affecting the physiology and emotional makeup in all kinds of ways. Some people are born hermaphrodite – possessing both male and female sexual organs.

Sex is almost always determined at conception, by the sex chromosome part of our genes. The sex chromosomes are **X** and **Y**. **X** is known as the female and **Y** the male chromosome. This is because if there is a single **Y** chromosome present, maleness is the result. The absence of **Y** (and presence purely of **X**) leads to femaleness.

Usually the female germ cells (ova, or eggs), have two **X** chromosomes – **XX**. Sperm cells have either **XX** or **XY** - one **X** and one **Y**.[244]

When the egg and sperm meet, each gives one chromosome to the new person; so it is the sperm which determines gender more than the egg which is always female.[245] If there is a **Y** chromosome present, the male characteristics will develop. If no **Y**, it's a girl. Interestingly, it seems that a very small percentage of the time it is possible for an embryo to start as **XX** then within a few days lose a bit one of the chromosomes to become **Y**, so a boy develops.

Unusual numbers of sex chromosomes

Some people have extra sex chromosomes. These sex chromosome abnormalities are fairly common, only slightly less common than Down's syndrome (an autosomal problem – affecting chromosomes other than sex ones).

Some women are born with only one X chromosome – XO. These people are said to have **Turner's Syndrome**. They are usually short in height, and often have webbed necks, small jaws and high, arched palates in the mouth. The ovaries do not develop normally so they do not ovulate or develop the usual secondary sexual characteristics – they have exceptionally small breasts and are sterile. Nowadays they are given growth hormone when young to make them grow a little extra, and oestrogen after the age of puberty to encourage growth of breasts and menstruation, so that they appear relatively normal.

Then there are **metafemales**, or XXX females. These woman are usually taller than average as adults, with unusually long legs and slender bodies, but they otherwise appear normal. They have normal sexual development and are fertile, but are usually of lower range

---

[244] The chromosomes' names are given for their shape; literally, the X chromosomes look like an x and the Y like a y. I like to wonder about that extra bit on the X chromosome – if you take a quarter away from the X you get a Y. What is all that extra genetic information women have contained in the X chromosome? Is it responsible for our depth of intuition and wisdom, for some of the particular strengths of women? Or does it contain all sort of nutty stuff that can hold us back at times…Of course I am only playing with this: it is very difficult for us to really figure out the important differences of characteristic between men and women – the fundamental ones, rather than the culturally imposed ones. It is a good idea to keep an open mind in this area.

[245] Some animals, frogs for example, are known to be able to reproduce by parthenogenesis – the eggs divide and produce an embryo without fertilisation by sperm. In these cases the embryo would always be female and contain only the genetic material of the mother. Apparently parthenogenesis can be artificially induced in any animal ova, but the embryos do not develop fully. However, it is thought to happen naturally sometimes. Mostly this is thought to be impossible for humans – and it certainly has not been possible to induce artificially. However, there is an article at http://ourworld.compuserve.com/homepages/dp5/sex2.htm which claims there have been cases where at birth doctors have found there to be no physical way that sperm could have entered the womb due to obstruction (and quotes a lancet article), it mentions this could be due to parthenogenesis or vestigial, usually non-functional, male reproductive glands producing some semen and causing self-fertilisation. I am not sure how valuable the references in the article are, or whether the 1956 article has since been debunked, but it is an interesting area so I decided to include it anyway.

intelligence or may have slight learning difficulties – especially if they are XXXX or XXXXX, which can happen. This condition occurs in about one in one thousand female babies. It occurs more often in the children of older mothers.

Men sometimes have an extra X chromosome – being XXY or, more unusually, XXXY, XXXXY, or even XYXXY. This is called **Klinefelter's syndrome**. Men with this genotype are usually completely sterile, or nearly so, and the testes and prostate glands are small so they produce only small amounts of testosterone. These men usually have relatively high-pitched voices, asexual or more female body shape and breast enlargement, along with comparatively little facial and body hair. They are often a little taller than average, and are inclined to be overweight and have learning difficulties as children. Mostly they are ordinary enough in appearance to fit in to society with no problems. It is not uncommon for the syndrome to be discovered only during investigations for infertility. The symptoms are more extreme if more than one extra X chromosome is present. Again, it is more common in the children of older mothers.

Then there are the XYY men – the **supermales**. These men are usually tall and generally appear and act 'normal'. However they are producing high levels of testosterone, so in puberty they are usually slender and have severe acne. Most of these men are unaware of their condition as it has little affect on ordinary life and they are usually fertile. There is no convincing evidence, though some theories, that these men are more prone to violence and aggression.

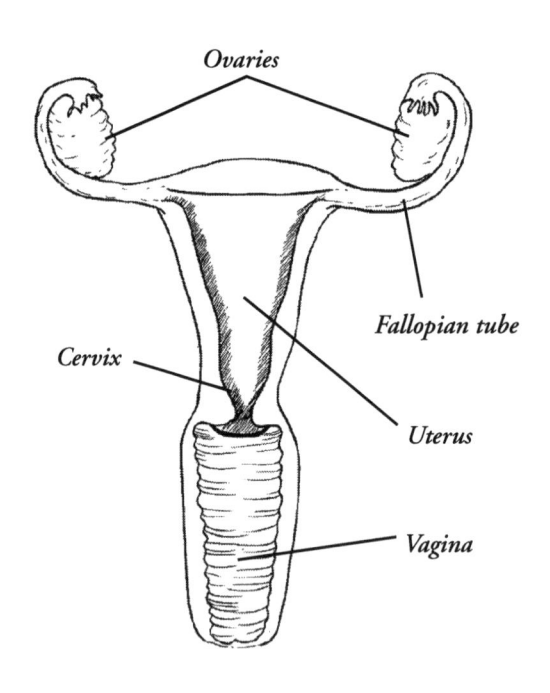

The Female Reproductive System

In women the **internal genitalia** are the two **ovaries**, two **fallopian tubes**, the **uterus**, and the **vagina**. The **external genitalia** are known as the **vulva** or **pudenda**.[246] There is the erectile tissue that is the **clitoris**, the internal and external **labia**, the **vaginal** and **urethral orifices**. Strangely enough, the clitoris was not mentioned in anatomy textbooks until relatively recently. Yes, really. Matter of fact, I don't remember it being mentioned in my sex education classes at school in the UK in the late seventies/early eighties. I hope things have

---

[246] Pudenda literally means 'that of which one ought to be ashamed'. It can refer to the external genitalia of either sex. Charming, eh?

improved in this area. As you will see from the section on development, the clitoris is related to the penis and is erectile – in other words, it becomes engorged with blood and highly sensitised during sexual arousal. It is possible for a woman to conceive a baby without sexual pleasure, and without the clitoris, but sexual pleasure is not possible without the clitoris.[247] I would argue that the presence of the clitoris in fact shows that sexual pleasure is a gift from the Gods – we just wouldn't have one at all if sex was just about making babies.

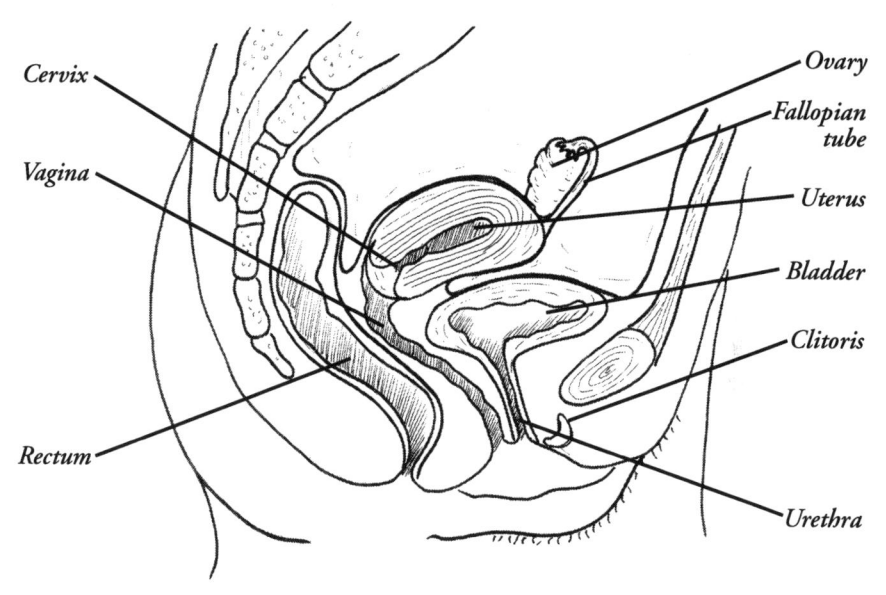

The ovaries produce hormones that regulate reproductive functions. **Follicle stimulating hormone, (FSH)**, from the pituitary causes the ovary to develop its **ovarian follicles**, each containing an immature ovum, or egg, at the same time stimulating the ovary to produce the hormone **oestrogen**, which keeps the skin soft and the hair in good condition, as well as maintaining other female secondary sexual characteristics. These begin to develop at puberty when oestrogen is first made and released by the ovary. The breast tissue is stimulated to grow and enlarge – before puberty, boys and girls have identical breast tissue. It is solely the influence of the female sex hormones which makes the breasts grow and develop. The other female **secondary sexual characteristics** include the pattern of female body hair and fat distribution which gives the female body its distinctive shape.

---

[247] 'What's the difference between the clitoris and the pub?...most men don't have any problem finding their way to the pub...' I thought long and hard (he he, no pun intended) about including this joke, as I generally don't like jokes which in any way belittle one group of people or another. Then I decided to leave it in, because if anyone – man or woman – reading this realises they don't know enough about this wonderful organ, the clitoris, then they need to increase their knowledge. Take a look at www.the-clitoris.com to get well informed.

All about oestrogen

There are three main oestrogens: oestradiol (which is strong and most active), oestrone (weaker than oestradiol) and oestriol (produced by the kidneys from other oestrogens, 80 times less active than oestradiol). The combined effects of these are usually what we mean by 'oestrogen levels'. As well as making the female secondary sexual characteristics and causing the maturation of the ovarian follicle, oestrogens influence the structure of the skin and blood vessels and the strength of the bones throughout life.

What oestrogen does is stimulate increased cell numbers wherever there are oestrogen receptors – for example, in the breast and uterus. It also stimulates each cell to make more receptors; so the more oestrogen there is, the more oestrogen-receptive cells there are, and the more sensitive each cell is to oestrogen. Some tumours are **oestrogen sensitive** – this includes some breast cancers as well as benign tumours[248] like fibroids, which are non-cancerous tumours in the muscle layer of the womb.

The ovaries secrete strong oestrogen each month after the period, peaking around ovulation then continuing until just before the next period, when production drops. But did you know that your body can also make oestrone from **aromatisation** of male sex hormones made in the adrenal glands. This process happens in the cells of the hair follicles, brain, skin and bone, but mainly in the muscle and fat cells. This is why after menopause, when the ovaries stop producing oestrogen, skinny women may have more symptoms of oestrogen withdrawal than those with a bit of padding. It's interesting that after menopause the metabolic rate slows, so the tendency would be to gain weight though one is eating the same amount. Nature's way of ensuring that post-menopausal women get enough oestrogen?

When getting rid of the strong oestradiol from the body, it is converted to two metabolites, one of which is 'good' and the other 'bad' (so called for being involved in some breast cancers). The liver removes oestrogen from the blood and puts it into the bile, where it passes into the intestines. Some of this is excreted in the faeces, but some can be reactivated by intestinal enzymes produced by gut flora, and reabsorbed into the blood. These enzymes are higher in a woman with a high animal fat, low fibre diet. This type of diet then means higher oestrogen levels in the blood.

In addition, there are also **xenooestrogens**, chemicals with strong oestrogen-like effects. All groups of man-made chemicals have some: detergents, pesticides, fertilizers and plastics. So the modern diet, combined with increasing pollution, is increasing oestrogen-dependant cancers and fibroids.

Phyto-oestrogens

There are many plants which contain oestrogens. These **phyto-oestrogens** have a weak oestrogenic effect. The interesting thing is that weak oestrogens will bind to oestrogen recep-

---

[248] Benign tumours are ones which do not spread to other places – those that spread are called malignant, and new tumours in other parts of the body which come from them are called **metastases**.

tors, stopping strong oestrogens from binding – therefore in pre-menopausal women plant oestrogens can protect from harmful excess oestrogen, and therefore potentially some cancers. Soya is one food full of plant oestrogens. In Japan, where a lot of soya is eaten, breast cancer is very rare (although soya probably isn't the only reason for this). In postmenopausal women, however, plant oestrogens provide a bit of oestrogen stimulus and can protect from symptoms of withdrawal like hot flushes, mood changes and even perhaps osteoporosis.[249]

Menstruation

Menstruation is the cyclical loss of the blood-rich lining of the uterus. Every month this lining builds up, ready to accept and nourish a fertilized ovum. If no fertilization occurs, the lining is lost, shed as menstrual blood.

The ovarian follicles develop in the first half of the menstrual cycle. At the end of this time the follicle is mature and ejects its ovum into the abdominal cavity. In the second half of the menstrual cycle, after ovulation, luteinising hormone (LH) from the pituitary makes the empty follicle mature into the **corpus luteum** (meaning 'yellow body'), which secretes progesterone. 'Pro-gesterone', literally 'for gestation', is the pregnancy hormone which prepares the uterus for pregnancy by causing thickening of the special wall of the uterus. If no conception occurs, then two weeks after ovulation the lining of the uterus is shed as menstrual blood. Menstruation occurs every month, from menarche in the early teens until menopause at age forty to fifty, varying from woman to woman.

Many cultures have understood menstruation to be a powerful time for women. In the words of Alexandra Pope in her excellent book *The Wild Genie*: 'menstruation is power – the power of knowledge, understanding and love of your own mind, body and soul, the nourishment and nurturing of the Feminine – The Wild Genie.'

It is certainly well worth reclaiming menstruation from the mire of weird ideas and disgust of women's bodies that came up with 'the curse' as a name for this most intimate and sacred of life's processes – without which none of us would be here.

Many tribal peoples have customs which dictate that a menstruating woman retreat during the bleeding time, or 'moon time'. Although some cultures have evolved to see menstruating women as dangerous, many see it as an extremely powerful and beneficial time. The First American (Native American) customs involve retreat to a 'moon lodge'. It is understood that a menstruating woman is the most receptive it is possible for a human being to be. The women go into the moon lodge, retreat, rest and dream. When they emerge, they look into their 'bowl' – the womb – and see what gifts have been given from Spirit. The gift might be a poem or a new recipe, or something bigger for the people, like a vision of where the buffalo are, where the hunters can find food.

I weep to think of the wisdom we in our modern culture have lost, all those gifts from

---

[249] Ruth Trickey *Women, Hormones and the Menstrual Cycle*.

Spirit from all the menstruating women. For us the idea is to ignore our period altogether - put on white clothes, go swimming or horse riding, whatever. No wonder menstrual problems are so very common.

The Goddess

The Old Ways of this island of Britain, like those of all places in all times of old, honoured the Goddess, worshipped her three parts which reflect the three stages of life of a woman, and the phases of the moon: the young woman is the Maiden, the new moon, a Goddess of spring, of fresh newness and innocence. Her colour is white.

Then comes the red blood stage of the Mother, the ripeness of the full moon, the woman and Goddess in her aspect of giving and nurturing the next generation.

With menopause, the end of menstruation, the woman enters the Crone phase. The Crone is the aspect of the Goddess who, with the dark moon, enters the underworld, moving freely in the land of the dead to collect wisdom and secrets not accessible by anyone else. The colour of the crone is black. White, red and black - the colours of the Goddess...

The Charge of the Goddess

Listen to the words of the Great Mother:
Once in the month, and better it be when the moon is full, then shall you gather in some secret place. To these will I reveal things that are yet unknown.

And you shall be free from all slavery.

Keep pure your highest ideal, strive ever towards it, let nothing stop you or turn you aside.

For mine is the cup of the wine of life, and the Cauldron of Ceridwen. Though I am known by a thousand thousand names, yet the whole round earth does venerate me.

I am the beauty of the green earth, the white moon among the stars, the mystery of the waters and the desire in the hearts of women and men.

Before my face let your divine self be enfolded in the raptures of the infinite.

And know the mystery - if that which you seek you find not within you, you will never find it without you.

For behold, I have been with you from the beginning and I await you now.

(*from* Doreen Valiente's *Charge of the Goddess*)

Women who live together generally will begin to menstruate together. It seems we communicate by **pheromones**, odourless volatile components of sweat which signal hormonal activity to each other. There is a belief that women who live without electricity and in sight of the moon generally will menstruate with the dark moon and ovulate when the moon is full. However, I could not find any research to corroborate this (I'd love to hear it if there is – info@holisticanatomy.com). More on the stages of the menstrual cycle follows.

Events of the Menstrual Cycle
Day 1-14 - the proliferative phase/follicular phase.

FSH and a lesser amount of LH from the pituitary cause the ovary to develop its ovarian follicles, each containing an immature ovum, surrounded by supporting cells. These produce oestrogen which in turn makes the ovum mature. Within the follicles, the ova develop. They begin as **primordial follicles**, then become a **primary follicle**, then **secondary follicle**, then mature (**Graafian**) follicle. It takes 90 days or more to go from primary to mature (ovulation, at day 14 of the menstrual cycle, is of secondary oocytes).

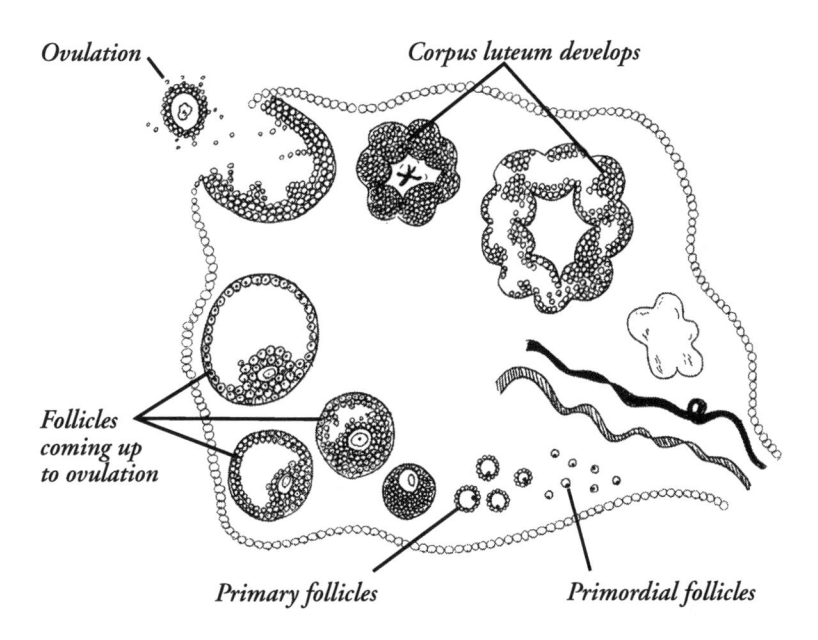

Ovulation

Corpus luteum develops

Follicles coming up to ovulation

Primary follicles

Primordial follicles

Ovulation - day 14

When blood oestrogen reaches a certain level, a **positive feedback mechanism** causes a surge of LH at mid cycle; in other words, the more oestrogen there is the more LH is secreted until it reaches the peak of the mid cycle crescendo. The surge of LH in turn leads to a huge surge in oestrogen, causing an egg cell (or primary oocyte) which is ready to develop further into a **secondary oocyte**. This secondary oocyte is **ovulated**: the follicle bursts and releases it into the pelvic cavity, the egg then usually being swept into the uterine tube by the wafting action of these fallopian tubes' ciliated epithelial lining. It is only when it meets a spermatozoa that it is stimulated to complete its development to yield one large **ovum,** which is ready for action and can join with the sperm to form a **zygote**. Or not...

Menstruation   *Proliferation phase*   *Ovulation*   *Secretory phase*

Progesterone

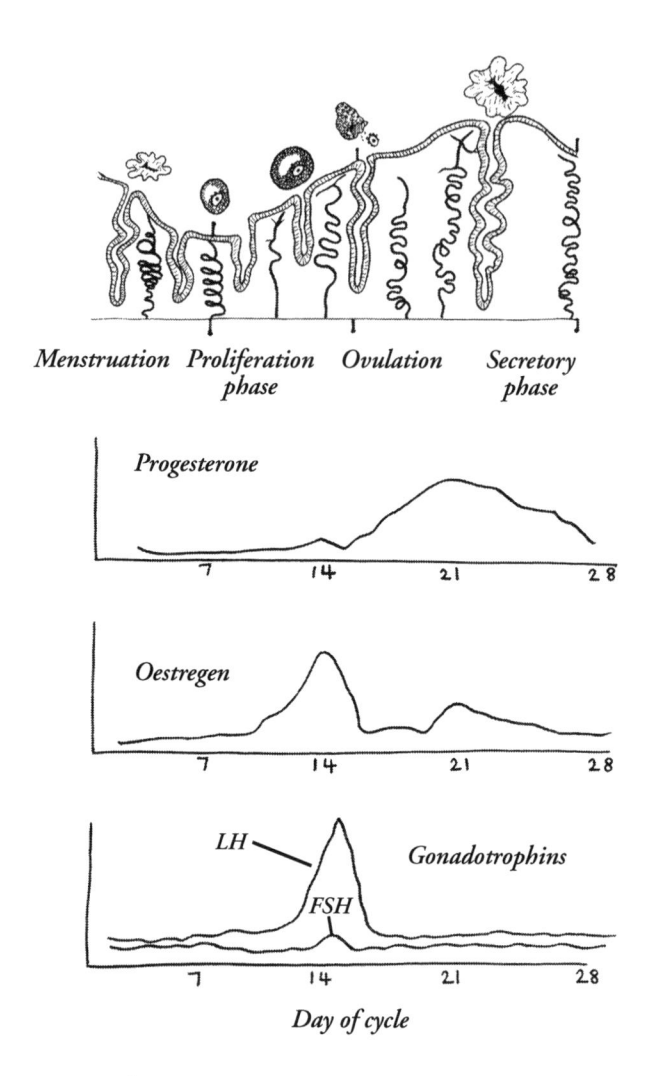

Oestregen

LH   *Gonadotrophins*   FSH

Day of cycle

Day 14 - 28 - Luteal or Secretory phase

In the second half of the menstrual cycle, after ovulation, LH continues to stimulate oestrogen production and also makes the empty follicle mature into the **corpus luteum**, secreting progesterone, the 'pregnancy hormone', which prepares the uterus for pregnancy by thickening the specialised wall of the uterus, the **endometrium**.

Rising levels of progesterone and oestrogen then inhibit the hypothalamic-pituitary gonadotrophic system (meaning that levels of luteinising hormone and follicle stimulating hormone, the gonadotrophic hormones, drop). If conception hasn't occurred the corpus luteum deteriorates and the ovarian hormones drop to their lowest levels before the cycle begins again. The last few days of this phase, if no conception occurs, are known as the **ischaemic phase**: the blood supply to the specially thickened wall of the uterus, the endometrium, is cut off.

Menstruation - day 1 -5 (beginning of follicular stage again)

If no conception occurs, then two weeks after ovulation the lining of the uterus is shed as menstrual blood. The first day of bleeding is called day one of the new cycle.

The hormonal cycle is controlled by positive and negative feedback interactions between gonadotrophic releasing and inhibiting factors from the hypothalamus, gonadotrophic hormones of the pituitary and the sex hormones themselves.

The Male Reproductive System

We will take a look at the men's bits now before moving on to what happens when the women and men get together. The male reproductive system consists of two **testes**, two **vas deferens**, **seminal vesicles** and **ejaculatory ducts**, the **prostate** gland, the **urethra** and the **penis**.

The testes are made of very long coiled **seminiferous tubules** which make sperm cells, or **spermatozoa**, under the influence of follicle stimulating hormone from the pituitary. LH, known in men as **interstitial cell stimulating hormone** (ICSH), causes the interstitial cells found amongst the seminiferous tubules to make testosterone, the male sex hormone.

Sperm cells

Spermatozoa have a head, containing genetic material and the ability to penetrate the ova, a middle section containing mitochondria for making energy and a tail which moves the sperm along. There are millions of sperm in one ejaculation, made every day. The sperm cannot move until the last part of their maturation which takes place in the **epididymis** tubules – the last part of the testes continuous with the seminiferous tubules before and the vas deferens after.

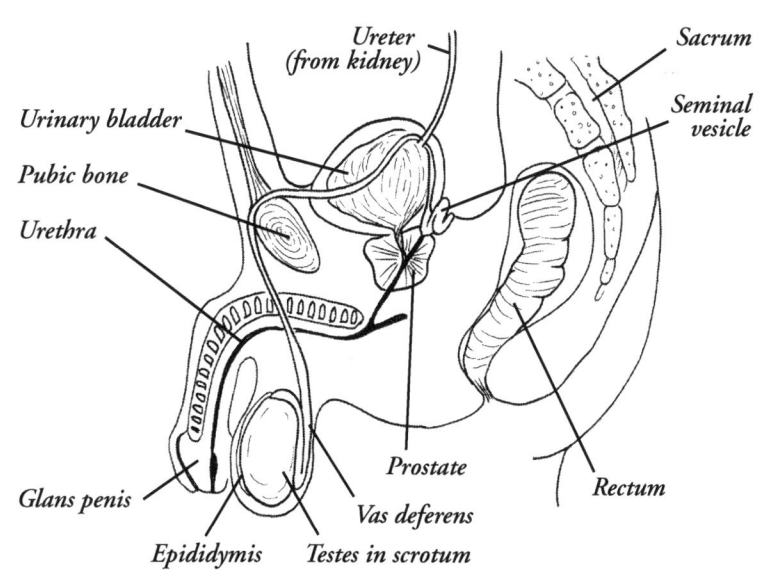

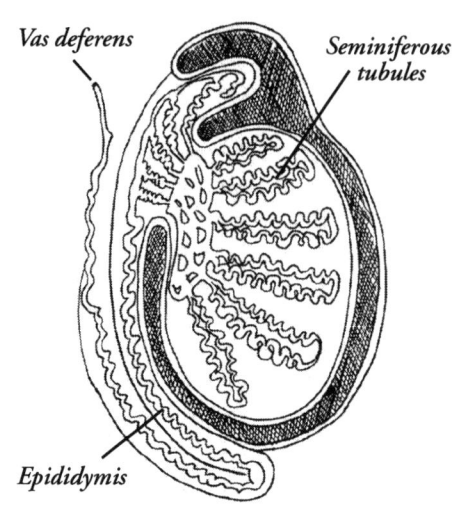

Testes

The testes hang outside the body in a sack called the **scrotum**. This gives the necessary lower temperature that spermatogenesis (making sperm) requires. The scrotum can be pulled up close to the body when it is cold by a special muscle, the **cremaster muscle**, or lowered down in hot weather, to maintain a good temperature for sperm production. If the testicles are repeatedly too hot – as occurs when wearing tight trousers, or sitting all day with a computer at waist level, lowered sperm count, and therefore infertility, can result.

A tube called the **vas deferens** carries sperm from the testes into the body, via the spermatic cord which passes through the **inguinal canal**, to the root of the penis. Much of the semen, or ejaculate, is produced by the seminal vesicles and the prostate gland. Ejaculate is 10% sperm, 60% and 20% secretions from the seminal vesicles and prostate respectively and 10% alkalines and mucus from the bulbourethral glands. The secretions include nourishment for the sperm, fructose, lipids and amino acids as well as vitamins B, C and zinc.*

Interestingly, there are actually different sorts of sperm

One **ejaculate** will contain a whole variety: first out are the sprinters, the sperms in good shape expected to make it to the egg and achieve fertilization. Next come two different sorts, apparently: 'dud' sperm which basically block up the female's tubes and stop anyone else's sperm getting in. Some researchers even say that one lot are 'killer sperm' which hang around and attack any other males' sperm that shows up (yes, really! Before any conclusions are drawn from this, it must be remembered that we are closely related to other mammals and therefore share many of the same design features, despite these being not strictly necessary for our own way of life… We have 42% the same genes as a banana and all that). More interesting is the effect of feelings, and pheromones, on sperm production. A man who hasn't seen his beloved for a while will increase his sperm production on reunion, but will not if he has casual sex with someone less important to him. This effect of the beloved's proximity can happen even when she is absent if he is exposed to her pheromones – researchers in pheromones do strange things like soak material in people's sweat and tape this onto the subject's top lip for so many hours a day. Mmm, charming!

The tissue which in a female embryo becomes the womb, becomes the prostate gland in a male. The **prostate** is found surrounding, and indeed forming, the first part of the urethra

---

* This is why it's good for men to eat pumpkin seeds which keep their zinc stores replenished.

as it leaves the bladder. The prostate makes important local control agents called prostaglandins, and adds nourishing fluid to the ejaculate. Its secretions are involved in the maturation and activation of sperm.

The prostate very commonly becomes enlarged in elderly men, leading to a compression of the first part of the urethra and therefore an interruption in bladder control. This common condition is called **benign prostatic hypertrophy**. Herbal and nutritional treatments can do a lot to prevent it becoming a highly troublesome condition. Cancer of the prostate is also common, being the third most prevalent cancer in men.[250]

Sperm is introduced into the vagina through the penis, consisting of columns of spongy, erectile tissue around the urethra. Although in men, the urethra is the common route for urine excretion and for ejaculation, these functions do not happen at the same time.

> Semen *is Latin*
> *for a dormant, fertilized,*
> *plant ovum –*
> *a seed.*
> *Men's ejaculate*
> *is chemically more akin*
> *to plant pollen.*
> *See,*
> *It is really*
> *more accurate*
> *to call it*
> *mammal pollen.*
>
> *To call it*
> *semen*
> *is to thrust*
> *an insanity*
> *deep inside our culture:*
> *that men plow women*
> *and plant their seed*
> *when, in fact,*
> *what they are doing*
> *is pollinating*
> *flowers.*
>
> Stephen H. Buhner [251]

---

[250] Incidentally, two separate studies published in February 2007 found a link between eating dairy products and prostate cancer. One was the CLUE II study, involving nearly 4000 men in Washington County, Maryland (Cancer Causes Control, 2007; 18: 41–50), the other an analysis of over 29,000 Finnish men taking part in the Alpha-Tocopherol, Beta-Carotene Cancer Prevention Study (ATBC Study the higher risk of prostate cancer (Int J Cancer, 2007 Feb 2; Epub ahead of print). When researchers looked at the individual dairy products consumed, they found that the risk was higher *only with low-fat milk*- not whole milk or any other dairy. In fact, whole milk had a slight—albeit statistically not significant—protective effect (Am J Clin Nutr, 2005; 81: 1147–54). Accessed 21/7/08 at URL http://www.wddty.co.uk.

[251] Reproduced with grateful thanks to Stephen Buhner from his outstanding book *The Secret Teachings of Plants*.

The Lord of the Wood - The God

There are Gods of the woods and wild places, with the form of the human male but with horns on their heads. Cernnunos is one - the man with deer's antlers on his head. Pan with the horns of a goat is another. Herne the Hunter is yet another name, and there are horned gods in every culture from Egypt to India. Christianity - along with the Romans - turned these Gods into devils when sweeping through Europe and overthrowing the local cultures and religions, so many people today know nothing of the power and beauty of the Horned One. He is truly a spirit of nature, Lord of the wood, untamed and wild, protector of the creatures of the forests and fields, sexy and passionately alive, full of life, forever untameable. He dies and goes to the Goddess in the underworld each year, to be born again at the winter solstice. (This is why the Christians put their 'God is born' festival close to that time of year).

Cernnunos

In this untidy mind I roam untamed by certainties, bewitched by sight and sound, by turn of thigh on summer's day, a sigh of awesome love in hillside vision.
I see long-booted dreams of this or that, I find I am free at times to feel the shivers of the web, the warp and wind, in pleasures of a sacred kind I find I am free.

In this unruly world of weaving truths, a maze of crissed and crossed mythologies, the Wyrd begins and ends in words.

The word of God,
unspeakable.
Honey-voiced he speaks
of husky love in moonlit noon,
heavy-hung with longing.

His need makes no promises -
he gives an endless self of
blood and grain and surging spring,
he is a promise.

Pip Waller

The Birds and the Bees

Sexual arousal in both women and men is mediated by the parasympathetic part of the autonomic nervous system – via sacral nerves. The neural response triggers vascular changes creating erection in the spongy body of the penis or the clitoris. A **positive feedback** situation leads to **orgasm** which is controlled by nerves and smooth and skeletal muscle. Orgasm is accompanied by spasms of the pelvic floor muscles. In men this is usually accompanied by ejaculation which is the reflex expulsion of semen from the penis. A kind of ejaculation sometimes happens for women too at the moment of orgasm.

In the words of Thomas Moore, in the introduction to his book *The Soul Of Sex*, "Sex is infinitely more mysterious than one usually imagines it to be and it is only superficially considered when we talk about it in the term of hormones and the mechanics of lovemaking." **

Sexual pleasure and arousal are complex areas involving hearts, minds and spirits as well as bodies. It is easy to get bogged down by the plumbing, seduced by the notion that knowing the right technique is the main part of the game. The best approach to sex is to realise there is no one true way, no one way for everyone. Sex can be engaged on in many levels. It is too big a subject to get deeply into here, other than to take a quick overall look at sexual intercourse which can lead to baby making, and the general stages of arousal and orgasm. Take a look at Thomas Moore's *The Soul Of Sex* to go deeper. Now, back to the plumbing:

There are four stages of physical response during sex;

Desire and arousal, also called 'excitement'. Basically, gettin' hot for it. All kinds of things can get us in the mood: smells, food, touch, clothes, thoughts. Genital tissue swells: the penis and clitoris become erect and the vagina widens. Lubrication begins in both men and women. Blood pressure and heartbeat go up. You start to feel hot.

The plateau phase. This is the increase in sexual excitement building up stronger and stronger and leading to orgasm. Lubrication increases at this time along with breathing, heart rate and blood pressure. Sexual flushing of the face and body often occurs and muscle tension increases. The penis swells, the testes draw closer to the body, the vagina lubricates more as the womb draws into an upright position. The lower part of the vagina (part of the pelvic floor known as the 'introitus') engorges to its limit. The breasts engorge especially the nipple, which makes them look less erect. The clitoris moves up against the pubic bone. Continuous clitoral stimulation is needed at this stage for a woman to come to orgasm. Plateau stage can be reached and moved back from several times before proceeding to orgasm – or may not lead to orgasm at all. The stimulation required can happen in many ways, not all of them involving the genitals. In rare and wonderful cases, mental stimulation alone leads orgasm. Ever had a 'wet dream'? mmmm...

Orgasm; 'le petit mort' or 'the little death' in French. Physiologically, men's and women's orgasms are pretty much identical. The pelvic floor muscles around the genitals contract rhythmically at a rate of about 0.8 of a second about 5-12 times or more. Women usually have more contractions. Female ejaculation – the release of a large quantity of lubricant – happens in some women's orgasms, but not all. At the point of orgasm, the cervix dips with each contraction – possibly into a pool of semen that was delivered right there...

Resolution and resting time, when the body slowly returns to its normal state. Blood pressure, heart rate and breathing drop to below normal levels, and then eventually go back up to normal. The cervix opens for about 20 minutes to allow for passage of sperm, then closes again. The whole body sweats. Tons of endorphins are released which make you feel goooooood. This stage can last for minutes or hours. For the majority of men, sexual pleasure or arousal is usually impossible at this time. The length of the resolution

---

** Thomas Moore *The Soul Of Sex*.

period varies from man to man, and is usually longer for older men. Woman however are more often able to go pretty much straight back between the plateau and orgasm phases several times.

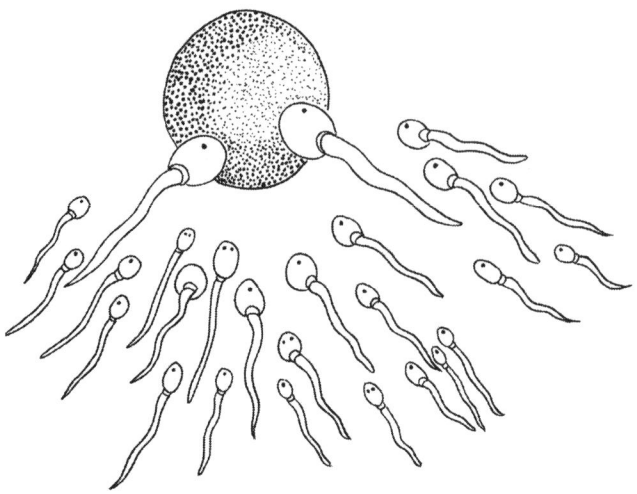

Often, (but not always, of course), sexual arousal with its erection of the penis and clitoris and lubrication of the vulva and vagina leads to sexual intercourse. During sexual intercourse - known as 'coitus' – the erect penis is welcomed into the vagina and both partners move, getting up some friction which builds the sexual pleasure. Usually during male orgasm ejaculation occurs and millions of sperm carried in the semen are spurted out of the urethra into the vagina. The sperm must travel all the way through the cervix and uterus and into the fallopian tubes to meet the egg. Fertilisation (or pollination...) occurs in the fallopian tubes.

Pregnancy - Fertilisation and development of the embryo

An oocyte (the proper name for an immature egg that is ready for conception) is viable for about twenty-four hours after ovulation. Sperm may remain viable in the female reproductive tract for one to three days. Assuming they meet at the right time in the right place – in the fallopian tube – conception can occur. The sperm must survive the so-called 'hostile'[252] (acid) environment of the vagina and become **capacitated** (which means fully ready for action, able to have a go at breaking down the eggs' outer layer). Many sperm must release the acrosomal enzymes stored in their heads in order to break down the ovum's outer layers. Thus although only one sperm binds to the egg's receptors, preventing other sperm from penetrating, really the conception is a joint effort. This triggers the final stage of **meiosis** by the secondary oocyte, and the sperm's and egg's **pronuclei** fuse to form the **zygote**. This is another piece of evidence which supports the concept that the important underlying drive of our nature is for co-operation rather than competition.

---

[252] One really wonders about some of the customarily used terminology...

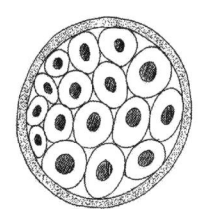

The **embryonic period**, lasting eight weeks, then begins. Firstly, the zygote divides and forms a ball of cells – the **morula** (meaning 'mulberry').

This becomes the **trophoblast**, which begins to secrete human chorionic gonadotrophin; and leads to the formation of a **blastocyst**. On arrival in the uterus at six days after conception this implants itself into the enriched endometrium the womb has prepared for it. Full implantation takes about a week. During this time the blastocyst has developed into a **gastrula** with three **primary germ cell layers**, and the embryonic membranes develop.

The three germ cell layers, from which all body organs will derive, are the **endoderm, mesoderm** and **ectoderm**: the ectoderm fashions skin and nervous system, the endoderm forms epithelial linings and the mesoderm forms virtually everything else. The very young embryo is flat and consists of the germ layers which fold to form a cylindrical body; it is the internal cavity of this which becomes the cavity of the digestive tract. It continues folding to form the rudimentary body parts.

By the eighth week we are 3 cm long (1.2 inches). All major brain regions are formed. The liver is disproportionately large and begins to form blood cells at eight weeks. Limbs are present. The skeleton is present as a cartilaginous blueprint and ossification begins. Weak, spontaneous muscle contractions appear. The heart and circulation is fully functional (the heart pumps by the fourth week). All body systems are present in at least a rudimentary form. Now begins the so-called **foetal period**, when we grow mostly in size, and refine the differentiation of organs and tissues.

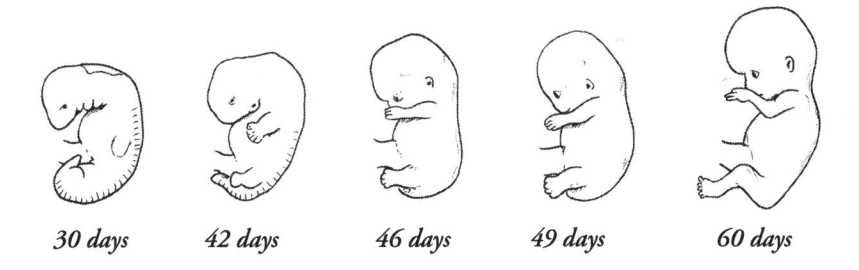

30 days   42 days   46 days   49 days   60 days

Drawn from pictures in David Sinclair & Peter Dangerfield's *Human Growth After Birth*.

Abnormalities in the embryo and foetus

It is thought that abnormalities in the embryo are responsible for many spontaneous abortions; the body has its own way of detecting and avoiding abnormal development. 'Genetic counseling' of parents known to carry inherited diseases is now established medical practice with the aim of avoiding genetic disease.

One example of this is Down's syndrome; the chance of having a child with Down's syndrome is about 1 in 100 in women who have previously had an affected child, and at least

1 in 50 in women over age 40, rising with age. The idea is to dissuade someone from going for it. Failing this, antenatal diagnosis is accepted practice: ultrasound scans are routinely given to women in the UK and these scans can detect some abnormalities in the foetus. In fact, sometimes scans wrongly show abnormalities when all is well and often do not show up abnormalities which are there.[253]

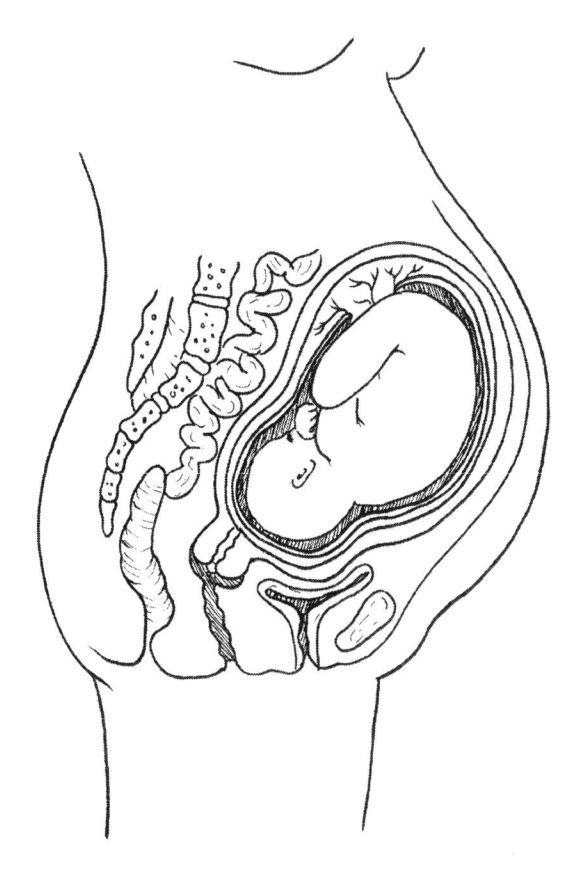

Countries differ in their thinking about the safety of scans. For example, in Italy five scans are done of every pregnant woman, but in the US obstetricians are advised by their professional body to only carry out scans when medically indicated. In vitro experiments show damage to cells when exposed to ultrasound. So far no problems have been found in vivo, but this does not mean there are none.[254]).

Maternal blood tests can reveal greater or lesser likelihood of abnormalities. These blood tests are given to all pregnant women in the UK, unless she declines them.

Amniocentesis is currently offered to all women over the age of thirty-five as well as to those who may carry inherited disorders. A small amount of amniotic fluid is removed around week fourteen to sixteen of gestation. Ultrasound helps to guide the insertion of a needle into the amniotic sac through the mother's abdominal wall, and about 10 ml of fluid is drawn off. The fluid will be checked for enzymes and other chemicals that serve as markers for specific diseases, and it will contain sloughed off cells from the foetus, which can be examined for chromosomal abnormalities. Abortion is offered when abnormalities are thought to be present. One in a hundred babies will die from problems

---

[253] The Lancet, 1998; 352: 1568-8, 1577-81. The inaccuracy of antenatal scans. Accessed from what doctors don't tell you website, www.wddty.co.uk

[254] www.wddty.co.uk site has summary of a lot of research which questions the safety of scans. Scans have been linked to lower birth rate, more premature births, more dyslexia in later life, and even more deaths. Even for serious abnormalities, the survival rate of babies when this has been picked up on a scan before birth is no better, and some studies show is even worse than when the baby wasn't scanned and the abnormality not detected until birth.

coming after amniocentesis – whether or not there was something 'wrong' with them. The main things found through this technique are Down's syndrome, anencephaly and spina bifida.

Chorionic villi sampling (CVS) is another test sometimes done. It involves suctioning off bits of the placenta – by a small tube inserted vaginally and guided by ultrasound. It allows testing at eight weeks, but is usually not done until after the tenth week. Like amniocentesis it is an invasive procedure that carries risk to the foetus and mother, for example, increased risk of finger and toe abnormalities.

What do you think about all this? When I had my son I thought about it a lot. I had had two miscarriages and two ectopic pregnancies, and thought I may never be able to have my own child, so you can imagine it had a particular impact. I decided against having any tests at all (despite being nearly forty therefore 'high risk'), because to have an abortion based on there being 'something wrong' with the child in the end sounds like fascism to me. I was surprised at how completely normal practice it has become – as if to question it at all is extreme or backward in some way. What effect does it have on a woman to abort a baby that her body has decided to carry regardless? What impact does it have on us, to know that we would have been murdered if there had been something considered 'wrong' with us?

Interesting questions – and not just for extremist religious groups, but for us all. There is a thing called the 'social model of disability', which basically says that people are 'disabled' not by their abilities, or lack thereof, but by the attitudes of the society they live in. How have we come to accept so readily the view that only a person who is productive is of value? Is the worth of a human life really measurable in terms of how we can 'fit in' to a society which is currently obsessed with amassing worthless treasures at the expense of the very planet we live on? I believe these ideas about who deserves to live and who doesn't are deeply wrong, and damage all of us.[255] If we were more balanced as a society there would certainly be a dramatic drop in the rate of abortions or people considering abortion, as well as in the birth of unwanted children.

When the baby is ready to be born

When the baby is ready to be born, the neck of the womb, or **cervix**, is opened up by contractions of the muscular wall of the uterus. This is called the **first stage** of labour, and it usually hurts quite a lot! When the cervix is fully open (called '**10 cm dilated**'), the uterus contracts rhythmically to push the baby out (**the second stage of labour** – which also stings a bit). As you know, the anterior pituitary hormone oxytocin is the stimulus for labour. During pregnancy, the hormone relaxin has been secreted in large quantities, causing the softening of the body's ligaments and connective tissue. This allows more openness in the joints, and later on helps to soften the cervix.

After the baby comes out, the placenta is expelled – this is called the **third stage of labour.**

---

[253] When thinking about this and researching, I looked into the disability rights movement. I found a lot of great stuff on the internet, including a lovely piece called 'if Down's people ruled the world', about what the world would be like. It is lovely, and eloquently illustrates the goodness and worth of these great people. www.nads.org if you'd like to see it.

Most British midwives have rarely (or even never, if they are relatively new) seen a natural third stage, since the third stage is automatically 'managed' by the injection of an oxytocic drug. The trend in modern, orthodox medicine when it comes to childbirth is generally to 'manage' it to the hilt. This has mainly come from the sadness of stillbirth and death of some mothers in labour, and wanting to minimise such deaths as much as possible, but unfortunately it has led to routine interference when none is needed. In fact, delivery of the placenta is a normal part of the process and usually will proceed without a hitch if left to happen. If the baby is put to the breast soon after arriving, its sucking of the nipple will increase contractions in the womb and help to push out the placenta. A mother is also able to feel a contraction happen and then push to expel the placenta. The contractions do not just stop the minute the baby is born.

There are many wonderful books about childbirth (see bibliography or just take a look in a good bookshop) and the importance of a natural and gentle arrival when possible, and also about how medical intervention early on in the labour process leads to more and more intervention being necessary, so I won't bang on about this too much. Just a little bit!

What about the pain?
Firstly, for most women labour hurts, and it hurts a lot. But what is this problem our culture has with pain? We are today conditioned to think that pain is a terrible and unbearable thing, and that we should have drugs immediately to prevent feeling any of it at all. And yet pain is definitely a part of a normal life, and the body and mind have mechanisms for dealing with it. Our perceptions of pain are actually a construct of our body and our mind, not something inflicted on the body that our body has to counter. Having a knife stuck in the body is what we have to counter, pain is just the messenger boy, and the messenger boy of our bodies' own choosing. Of course, pain still hurts, but our resistance to it hurts even more.

On the purely physical level, when we are in pain our cells make endorphins, the body's own natural opium, which is a very powerful pain reliever. During labour, which generally gets increasingly painful as it goes on, endorphin levels rise accordingly. If pain relieving drugs are used early on in labour, this natural process is interfered with, so more drugs are needed. Incidentally, breathing against resistance, in other words, in a forced way through your mouth, in and out, as you might when running, increases endorphin production. So getting with the breathing exercises in preparation for labour makes a huge amount of sense.

If you manage not to have any drugs, which unless things are going abnormally wrong is definitely within the capabilities of any woman, as soon as the baby is out and the pain stops you feel fine – tired, but with it and not drugged. This goes for the baby too. Since everything in your blood gets to the baby, he or she receives a good dose of all the drugs you take (though it is thought that gas and air leave the mothers bloodstream very quickly so very little if any gets to the baby).

Pethidine, the anaesthetic most commonly used during labour in the UK, gets into the baby's system and leaves them drowsy and sedated on birth, which can affect their ability to latch on well and take to feeding. An epidural leaves you more or less numb from the waist down, so you have no pain but also no feeling to assist you to push your baby out, which then opens the way to venteuse and forceps – implements to pull the baby out which can damage the baby, and in extreme cases even cause death.

I said I wouldn't bang on, so I won't, except to say one thing about elective caesarians: Chiropractics and naturopaths (as well as enlightened paediatricians like Michel Odent who pioneered water births) have long expounded on the importance of a natural birth for proper development of various reflexes. In actually coming down through the birth canal and pushing our way out, important developmental stages are followed. One of these is illustrated by research looking at elective caesarians – in other words, not an emergency life-saving operation, but a decision to have a caesarean at an appointed time, not waiting for labour to start in the natural way.[256] Babies born by elective caesarian have a higher mortality (death) rate than babies born naturally.[257] There is also a much higher level of respiratory distress in such babies – thought to be because hormones like prolactin released in huge amounts during birth help the final maturation of the lungs.[258] Also the squeezing out through the vagina compresses the lungs and pushes out the fluid which they contain before birth, this being an important part of their development.

When the milk comes in

Over time the uterus shrinks back. Oxytocin, the pituitary hormone which expels milk from the breast, is secreted in response to the nipple being sucked. This hormone also causes the uterus to contract. Thus breast feeding is good for the mother's body as well as the baby's, as it encourages the uterus to shrink down and tones it up after the work of carrying and giving birth to the baby. When the baby first suckles, it gets **colostrum** from the breast. This is a nutritious fluid filled with antibodies. After a few days this is replaced by milk, which is also full of antibodies. This is called **the milk coming in**, and it happens after a huge drop in pregnancy hormones with the placenta being gone. The new mum experiences it as a few hours of extreme emotions – crying, anger, and general ahhhhhghh! This happens at the same time as one's boobs become melon-like as they fill to bursting point with milk. What an experience!

There is a lot of weird stuff about breasts in our modern cultures: in the UK breast-feeding is absolutely not the norm, and it is not always possible to comfortably breast feed in public – yet every newsagent shop has magazines and newspapers full of pictures of young women's breasts on display. Breasts are supposed to be a particular size and shape for optimum

---

[256] I heard that one advert for these in Brazil, where they are extremely popular, read, "keep your love passage honeymoon fresh".

[257] Birth 2006; 33175 An analysis of nearly six millions births makes it look as if caesarean babies are nearly three times as likely to die within their first month of life as naturally delivered babies.

[258] Arch Dis Child 1997; 77: F237–8.

beauty[259], leading to more and more women having breast implants. If you have had this type of surgery you are usually unable to breast-feed. (Some implants are better than others in this respect).

Since breast feeding is so vitally important to give a person the best possible start in life, it is worth mentioning again here some of its advantages: breast fed babies are protected from infections of all kind, some of which are life threatening. Breast fed babies have much less atopic (allergic) disease. Breast fed babies are less likely to die from cot-death or SIDS (sudden infant death syndrome). Breast fed babies grow faster, and become healthier adults, with less allergies and easier access to their full intelligence – one study showed an 8 point increase in IQ of people who were breast fed compared with not. Breast fed babies get more close contact and warmth from their mums, and bonding goes better and is more intense. There are also great gains for the mother. The breast feeding helps the mother's body to get back to normal, and women who have breast fed have a reduced risk of breast and ovarian cancer before menopause, and osteoporosis after menopause. The LaLeche League is great for information about breast feeding.

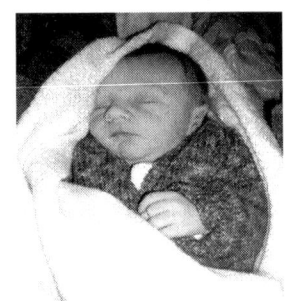

During childbirth stress hormone levels are enormously high in both mother and baby. In fact, it takes up to about six months for the baby's stress hormone levels to drop. This is one reason why new babies cry a lot – they need to release this stored up stress. The best way to help them is to cuddle them lots, keep them close, without too much excitement to aggravate them more, but allow them to cry while you hold them and gently reassure them that they are doing fine. Most babies seem to need to cry for about an hour a day or more, and definitely more if they experienced a difficult birth.[260] They really don't need to by shushed for every little noise they make. Imagine how you would feel, if you were trying to tell your loved ones how you were feeling and they kept saying 'shhhh', trying to distract you or shoving something in your mouth…

Menopause

The menopause is the cessation of menstruation and the end of the childbearing years. This happens usually somewhere between the ages of 40 and 50, sometimes unusually early in the 30s or later in the 50s. The ovaries stop producing oestrogen and progesterone, the remaining follicles atrophy (shrink) and no more eggs are ovulated. The uterus shrinks and atrophies, vaginal epithelium thins and there is some drying and keratinisation (hardening),

---

[259] And it's not only breasts. Did you know that there is now a growing trend of women having plastic surgery to improve the appearance of their genitals? Seriously, the surgeons have pictures of what the ideal pussy looks like: you can have a bit trimmed off here, or added there, so you can reveal yours with pride…

[260] Althea Solter *The Aware Baby*.

the vagina changes from acid to alkaline, breast tissue atrophies. Menopausal symptoms of oestrogen-withdrawal can include hot flushes and sweats, insomnia, nervousness and irritability, depression, poor memory and concentration, loss of libido and vaginal dryness, joint pains, headaches and palpitations.

This all sounds a bit grim, taken as it is from the medical model of menopause. There seems even to be a tendency to see menopause as a disease, an unnatural situation, given the modern practice of offering hormone replacement therapy (HRT) to every menopausal woman. In fact, for many women menopause is a powerful initiation into a new phase of life.[261] The child-bearing years are done, one is liberated from the possibility of pregnancy, which can free up enjoyment of sex now contraception doesn't have to be considered. In traditional societies who honour women and Elders, an old woman is a person of wisdom, a person to look to for counsel. White hair is a sign of wisdom – not something to be hastily covered up with dye to give an appearance of youth.

Good nutrition and herbal medicine, as well as any therapy which improves balance in the body and minimizes stress, can go a long way towards making menopause a positive experience with few symptoms. After menopause oestrogen is entirely obtained from conversion of androgens (made in the adrenal glands), which is done by fat and muscle cells. Thus stress will massively increase problems – the adrenal glands being tired from high production of steroid hormones. Medical herbalists often treat women suffering from menopausal distress with adaptogens – herbs which support the adrenal glands – such as liquorice and borage.

Interrelationships

The reproductive system is fundamentally related to **all systems** in that the whole body comes from reproduction. The **cardiovascular system** is very important, being crucial in sexual function (erection) and in bringing the needed nutrients for reproductive function. These nutrients come from food taken into the body and processed by the **digestive system**. In men there is a particularly intimate relationship with the **urinary system**. Sexual function and regulation of reproductive activity is mediated by the **nervous** and **endocrine** systems.

---

[261] Lesley Kenton *Passage to Power – Natural Menopause Revolution* is a great book to help with the reclaiming of menopause as a powerful natural phase.

CHAPTER SEVENTEEN

EXPERIENCING THE OUTSIDE WORLD

THE SPECIAL SENSES AND TOUCH

Sight

Sight can be seen as the most dominant human sense, with over 70% of the body's total sensory receptors being the special light-sensitive cells of the retina of the eye. The eye is incredibly complicated. What follows is an attempt to simplify this amazing part of the body, but further study is definitely advised if you want to deepen your understanding.

There are three layers to the wall of the eyeball – which is literally shaped like a ball. The outer layer is tough fibrous tissue – most of it is called the **sclera**, which you can see as the 'white of the eye'. This is the layer that holds the eye in shape. Over the coloured part of your eye, called the **iris**, is found the **cornea**, continuous with the sclera but see-through and more bulgy.

The middle layer of the eyeball is the vascular layer, which is full of blood vessels. The part of this at the front is the iris, which can be seen through the transparent cornea and gives the eye its colour.

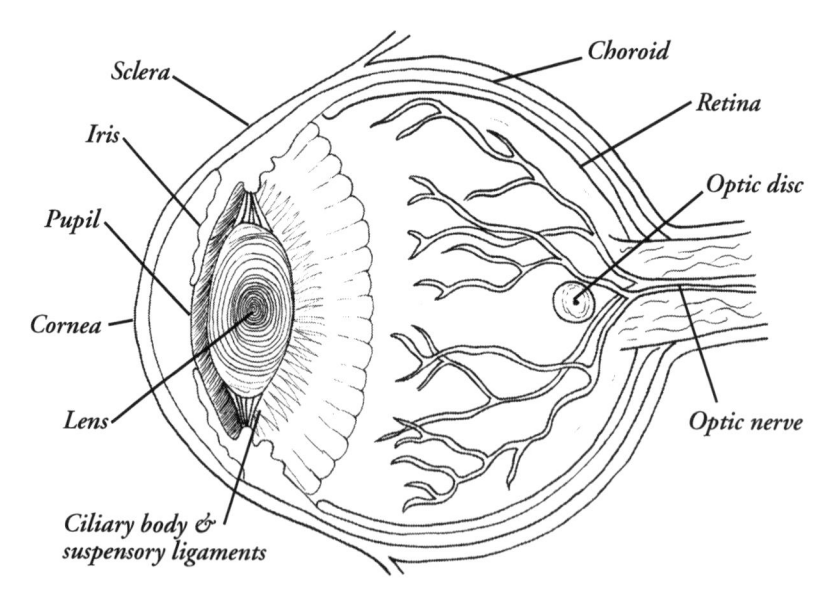

Iridology

Iridology is a diagnostic method which uses close examination of the iris of the eye to reveal areas of dysfunction in the body. Each area of the iris relates to a different organ or body part; and certain kinds of marks or discoloration are interpreted to mean particular problems. The general appearance of the iris is also important – for example, if you study people's irises you will see that they look like cloth or material, with fibres woven together. They range from being very tightly woven like silk to very loosely woven like hessian. Iridologists interpret this to reveal that person's basic constitution. A very tight weave means a very strong constitution; a very loose weave means a weak constitution. Some herbalists[262] would use this information to judge what kind of dosage and length of treatment to give; a person with a weaker constitution needs lower doses of medication given over a long period of time, and cure could be expected to take some time. Someone with a stronger constitution can take higher doses and more heroic measures, the body may throw up a strong healing crisis[263] and cure may happen more quickly.

Iridology is generally dismissed as hocum by orthodox medicine, although interestingly some iris changes are recognized as revealing pathological changes – for example, a white ring around the edge of the iris, called a 'corneal ring' usually indicates high cholesterol levels if seen in a younger person, though is considered a normal sign of aging in an elderly person (when it is charmingly called a 'senile' ring!).

Continuous with the iris and behind it is the **ciliary body** to which is attached the **lens** of the eye (via **suspensory ligaments**). The lens is literally like a lens of a magnifying glass or pair of spectacles; it can be moved forward and back as needed to focus the light which enters the eye onto the inner layer of the eye, the neural layer. This is the **retina** which contains the visual receptors. These photosensitive receptors are all connected to the **optic disc** at the middle of the back of the eye, which is the beginning of the **optic nerve**, carrying impulses to the brain. The optic disc visually makes a blind spot as it contains no light receptors.

There are various kinds of light. For us humans, our receptive range is called the **visible light range**, which doesn't included ultraviolet and infrared light. If something is either emitting light, or lit by light in our visible range, we can see it because the light enters our eyeball through the cornea and shines on the retina. On the retina are two types of receptors, **rods** which are light sensitive and can operate in dim light, and **cones** which need bright light and are colour sensitive. The rods and cones are excited by light, and this excitement is passed as a nerve impulse up the optic nerve and eventually to the visual centres of the brain, which then make a picture for us from the information received.

---

[262] Not all medical herbalists are trained in iridology, but those trained by the Self Heal school are. They may be members of the AMH (Association of Master Herbalists), as well as other herbalist associations or institutes.

[263] A healing crisis is the name given to the phenomenon by which the body, mind and spirit throw off something that is causing an illness and resolve it like a boil coming to a head. Healing crises may be many and varied. They could include things like a very high fever which finally turns, a chronic inflammation which becomes acute and then resolves, a skin disease which flares up then leaves and an emotional outburst like the crying that naturally accompanies grief and sadness and washes the pain away.

On the outside of the eyeball, where it is open to the elements, there is a thin mucous membrane called the **conjunctiva**, which folds back on itself to make the pinky-red layer you can see at the corner of your eye or if you pull your lower eyelid down.[264] If this gets inflamed it produces lots of sticky mucous which gums up your eye. This is called conjunctivitis. Babies are more susceptible to it, but luckily there is a very good cure for it – breast milk. All you need to do is squirt some milk in baby's eyes or into a dish and then bathe the eyes with a very soft cloth.(Breast milk is also good for pimples and nappy rash).

As mentioned above, the lens can be moved by muscles to be in the best position to focus light on the retina, depending on whether what we are looking at is close to us or far away. In some of us, this mechanism does not work perfectly, and we then need glasses to help us see properly. When you can see close up but not things in the distance, this is known as being 'short-sighted'. The opposite, being able to see distant objects clearly but not close ones, is called being 'long-sighted'. Long-sightedness happens to most of us as we age, hence older people find themselves holding things further and further away to read them, until the arms can't keep up and reading glasses are obtained!

Although medicine has gone the route of corrective glasses for sight problems, and drugs or surgery for other problems, there are ophthalmic specialists who have developed more holistic approaches, which usually involve a mixture of optimum nutrition and eye exercises.[265] The late Dr Stanley Evans of the Nutritional Health Eye Centre in Lowestoft, Suffolk, was one ophthalmologist who spent years in Africa and cured many eye problems, including cataracts and glaucoma, with a dietary therapy.[266] Short sightedness can sometimes be improved with eye exercises. It is usually due to weakness or poorly functioning muscles around the eye. Wearing glasses makes this problem worse, as the eye becomes lazier. The Bates Method is based on the work of late ophthalmologist Dr William Bates who did extensive research in the late 1800s, and combines eye exercises with nutritional advice.[267]

This is in no way to denigrate the amazing advances of modern medicine, which can do miraculous things when it comes to the eye: work in this field is truly amazing. Anyone with an eye problem should certainly straight away consult an eye specialist, even if you intend to follow a holistic route also – don't delay as time can be of the essence in treatment of eye disease.

There are a few other interesting bits to mention, like eyebrows, eyelids and lashes, which protect the eyes by keeping out sweat, bits of dust etc. Near the eye lids are special glands

---

[264] By the way, if you have plenty of oxygen in your blood, the conjunctivas look richly red. If they look pale, it could be a sign of anaemia.

[265] Often I think to myself, can it really be true that modern medicine is so blocked to so many ideas that seem simple common sense to most of us? Surely I have a warped notion of things, and really they are just understandably on the alert against quackery? Then I remember Dr Allinson – remember him, his wholemeal bread 'with nowt taken owt'? In the early nineteen hundreds he was a doctor who said people should eat fibre for their bowels to work properly. He was dismissed as a quack by the profession, so he left medicine and set up as a baker instead…

[266] Accessed 21/7/08 at URL http://www.wddty.co.uk .

[267] *The Bates Method* by Peter Mansfield describes this work.

secreting sebum which lubricates the eyelids. In the lateral part of the upper lids are found the **lacrimal glands**, which produce the all-important tears. When one cries, some of the tears spill out, and some drain down the **nasolacrimal duct** into the nose – this is why a good cry makes your nose drip, and causes you to sniffle. Tears wash the eye and also contain substances which destroy the cell walls of bacteria (lysine). Crying tears because of onions, or because something is in your eye washes the eyes clean. These tears are different to those we cry when we are hurt – be it physically or emotionally. Then our tears contain stress hormones, all the substances our bodies produce in large amounts when we are stressed.

Hearing

The ear is the organ which gives us hearing and provides the ability to balance. The structures of the ear are able to translate vibrations in the air (sound) into nerve impulses. The bit of the ear that you see is called the **pinna**.[268] This leads into the external auditory canal. At the end of this canal is found a membrane called the eardrum, which completely separates it from the middle ear beyond.

The middle ear is a cavity in the skull usually filled with air. A tube called the **Eustachian tube** connects it with the top back of the throat (the **nasopharynx**). This tube allows the pressure in the middle ear to stay equal to the pressure outside the body, so being equal on both sides of the eardrum. When you go up high or down low and your ears 'pop', this is the pressure equalizing via the eustachian tube. You can help this process by sucking, yawning or swallowing – so in an airplane when ears are feeling the pressure change, sucking a sweet or yawning can help with discomfort, or for a baby, putting it to the breast.

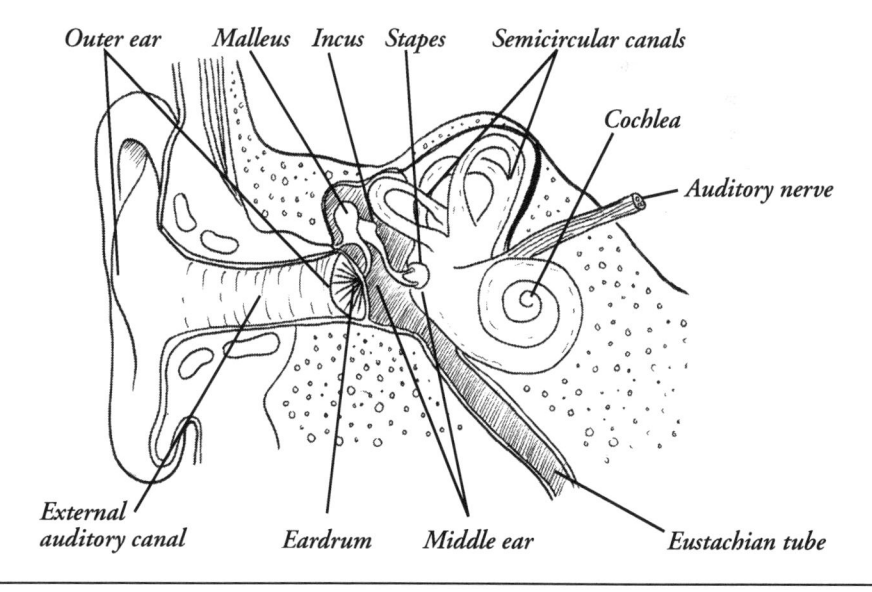

---

[268] There is a form of TCM (Traditional Chinese Medicine) which uses acupuncture points on the pinna to treat all the organs in the body. This auricular acupuncture is effectively used especially to treat addictions and stress.

In the middle ear three little bones called the **ossicles** are found. These are named the **malleus**, **incus** and **stapes** – hammer, anvil and stirrup, due to their shape. They are joined together and to the **eardrum**, and vibrate as the drum vibrates. At the far end they are attached to a membrane opening into the **inner ear**, where the vibrations are transferred to fluid in the **cochlea**, which is full of sensory receptors which respond to these vibrations. Thus nerve impulses are generated which travel to the brain via the **auditory cranial nerve** where they are interpreted into sounds.

There is also a part of the inner ear called the **semi-circular canals**, also fluid filled. As we move about, the level of fluid changes in these canals. This information is conveyed to the brain and used to help us know where we are in space and to maintain our balance.

In both the cochlea and the semi-circular canals there are tiny hair cells which get moved about by the vibrations in the surrounding fluid, and it is the movement of these hairs which stimulates the sensory nerves of both hearing and balance. Loud noises which cause massive vibrations in the ears, like machinery in a factory or loud music with a heavy bass beat, damage these fine hair cells. This damage is permanent and causes deafness.

Deafness is very common in older people, so most of us think that hearing loss is a natural part of aging. But actually in less developed countries, where there is a lot less noise, there is a lot less hearing loss in the elderly – most people do not experience it at all. So environmental factors must be a huge part of hearing loss. Loud noise may be the biggest culprit[269] – think how loud the cinema is nowadays. Next time you go to the pictures, try wearing earplugs. You'll still be able to hear, and your ears will be protected a little. By now you will not be surprised to hear that nutrition plays a part also. In fact, good nutrition can actually protect one against hearing loss from loud noises. High doses of vitamins A, C, E and magnesium – in other words, antioxidants – were found to do this in an animal study in 2007.[270]

Sometimes the nerves of hearing are damaged, by viral, vascular, hereditary or other causes. One controversial treatment for this is a **cochlear implant**, a surgical implant into the cochlear which receives and transmits sound to the hearing centers of the brain. Like all surgical procedures, this carries certain risks, including infection. 10% of children and 5% of adults experience complications from this treatment.

There is a movement called 'deaf liberation', the crux of which is to define deaf people as a linguistic minority, having their own culture and community, rather than as 'disabled'. The social model of disability is used: this is a way of seeing *society* as something that disables people, rather than the disability itself, by not setting up the world in an accessible way. There is diversity in the deaf community in terms of views on cochlear implants. Some see them as a form of eugenics and genocide of a people, as a very dangerous and experimental surgery.

---

[269] There are also some drugs which can damage the ears and cause impaired hearing, including some antibiotics, calcium channel blockers, the Pill and HRT and anaesthetics.

[270] Yamashita D, Jiang HY, Le Prell CG, Schacht J, Miller JM, Post-exposure Treatment Attenuates Noise-Induced Hearing Loss. Neuroscience 134: 633-642, 2005.

This camp would view deaf people who decide to get a cochlear implant as giving in to the oppression against deaf people and valuing hearing more than deaf culture. Others see cochlear implants as a choice much like laser eye surgery and are of the opinion that it is simply a high tech hearing aid used for enjoyment and further access to sound but does not affect one's status in belonging to deaf culture.

It's interesting to think about how our culture has developed to be a primarily visual and auditory one: television, cinema, radio, video games, and the usual way of being taught – being lectured to, mean that our sight and hearing are used a lot more than our other senses. This undoubtably has an effect on the others, which are more acute in peoples who live in different, more natural, ways.

Taste

Taste is known as **gustation** and we have the **gustatory receptors** to thank for it. There are about ten thousand of these arranged in **taste buds**. They are sensitive to chemical stimulus. The dissolved substance must enter a pore in the taste bud to come in direct contact with the receptors. We are able to detect four tastes with the four different types of receptor which are found in different parts of the tongue. These are the sweet taste (at the tip of the tongue), bitter (at the back), sour (the middle sides) and salty (the front and front sides).

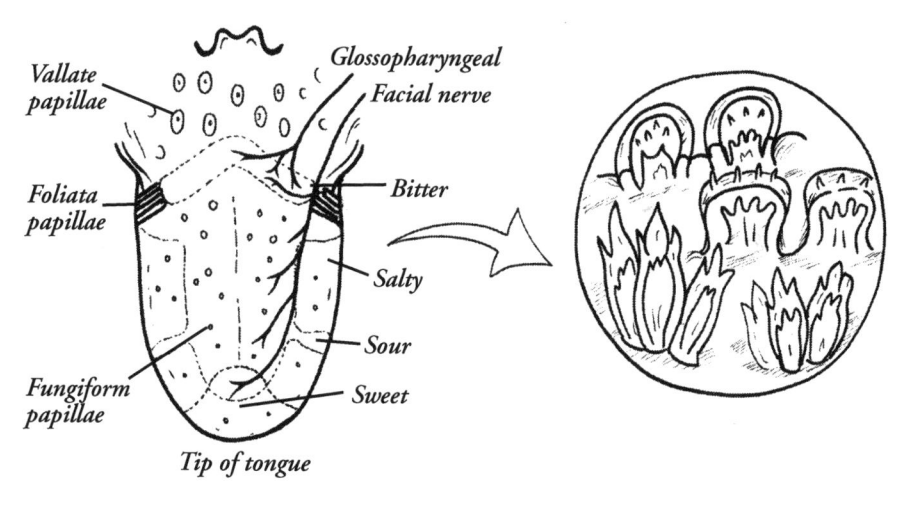

Interestingly, Chinese medicine classically describes five tastes, one for each of the elements; these are bitter, sour, sweet, salty and pungent – pungent being things like garlic, onions and chilies. Actually the pungent taste is due to irritation, activating the nociceptors, from the mildly damaging effect of the hot substance on the delicate mucous membrane of the mouth.

The sense of taste is quite dependent on our sense of smell – if we lose the sense of smell, we are not able to taste satisfactorily. You have probably experienced this yourself when you have had a blocked up nose from a cold.

Some taste buds become less sensitive to tastes the more we bombard them, especially the salty ones. The more salt you have, the less you taste and the more you want. If you cut salt out entirely, everything tastes bland for a while. But soon the taste buds will wake up and become more sensitive to variations again. It's worth trying this if you are a heavy salt eater, as excess salt is definitely bad for us in that it can put up the blood pressure, and therefore put strain on the heart – as you will remember from the chapter on the cardiovascular system.

When the bitter taste buds are stimulated, there is a reflex stimulation via the brain of digestive processes. Taking a bitter tasting drink a half hour or so before eating therefore primes the stomach to receive food by increasing acid production there, and stimulates the liver and gall bladder to release bile. This is the reason for 'aperitifs' – drinks to take before dinner, which are flavoured with bitter tasting herbs. 'Bitters' are used in herbal medicine to stimulate and encourage digestion. Herbs which are soothing to the stomach, on the other hand, are often sweet tasting – marshmallow root, liquorice and milk vetch being three examples. The sweet taste is the taste of the mother, of the earth, and is the first taste we experience in life with our mother's milk.

Smell

We get our sense of smell from **olfactory receptors** in the roof of the nasal cavity. A specialized epithelium there contains many receptors which are attached by fibres that pass through little holes in the ethmoid bone up into the **olfactory bulb**. Here the main nerve tracts are found, which on stimulation relay messages directly to the brain.

The ends of the dendrites of the **olfactory receptors** in the epithelium of the nose form tiny hair like projections or **cilia**, which are kept covered by a thin layer of mucous. Chemicals in the air we breathe are absorbed by these olfactory hairs and stimulate a nerve impulse.

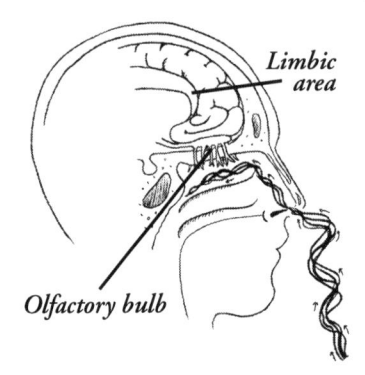

Unlike all the other sensory information the brain receives, the olfactory nerves pass straight to the cerebral cortex (all other sense information passes through the thalamus and synapses a few times before reaching the cortex). This makes our sense of smell the most direct of all our senses. It is considered to be the most 'primitive' – meaning the oldest. The part of the brain that interprets smell, the olfactory bulb, is part of the limbic system[271] – that part which deals in memory and emotion – so an odour can trigger a memory or a feeling very strongly.

Limbic area

Olfactory bulb

Students can utilise this mechanism by always having a particular smell about when studying, which can then be taken into an exam situation. (Essential oil of rosemary is ideal for this purpose, as it has a stimulating effect, increasing circulation to the brain.)

---

[271] You will recall that the limbic system receives all information from sensation at the body surface, and is associated with pain and pleasure and all aspects of emotion. It works closely with the hypothalamus to maintain homeostasis.

Volatile oils

Aromatherapists work with volatile or **essential oils**. These are oils that are found whole in plants and easily evaporate – i.e. are volatile, which means they give their molecules to the air. This is what gives plants their aroma. Essential oil molecules are absorbed by the skin and mucous membranes of the body, and are transported in the blood whole, to be excreted largely by the kidneys, lungs and skin. Thus when you smell an essential oil, it not only tickles your olfactory apparatus to create a nerve impulse, but in addition it is actually absorbed across the olfactory neuron's membranes and so passes directly into the brain.

Touch
(not considered a 'special sense', but a 'general sense')

There are six main sensory receptors in skin, each responding to a different kind of touch. The receptors, once stimulated, send their electro-chemical message to the cerebral cortex, which interprets the information so that we experience it consciously.

Free nerve endings are the most widely distributed. These respond to light touch, pain and temperature. They go through the dermis right up into the epidermis. Stroking and rubbing a place we have just banged reduces the amount of pain we experience. This is explained by the 'pain-gate' theory. The pain-gate theory describes how we can block sensations of pain by rubbing the place it hurts, because touch messages travel faster than pain messages. When both are simultaneously detected by the free nerve endings, the touch sensations arrive at the brain first, blocking the pain ones. A free nerve ending looks like the end of a motor nerve.

Meissners' corpuscles are oval and filled with highly coiled dendrites. They detect light touch and are found in the lips, the palms of the hand, the soles of the feet and the genitals. Each corpuscle is half in the dermis and half in the epidermis.

Ruffini's corpuscles contain collagen amongst the dendrites and react to pressure and stretching of the skin. They are found in the dermis.

Pacinian corpuscles in the dermis are sensitive to vibration. They are especially dense in the fingers, genitals and bladder.

Root hair plexus is a nerve ending attached to the roots of the hairs on the skin. As the hair moves the root moves and this stimulates the root hair plexus.

All six touch receptors are attached to sensory nerves, which join together in a sensory fibre and leave the skin to head for the central nervous system.

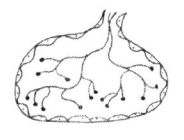

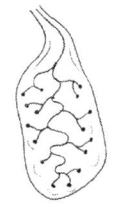

Ruffini's ending   *Pacinian corpuscle*   *Merkel's disc*   *Meissner's corpuscle*

Touch is essential for proper emotional and physical development. Young people who are not touched become withdrawn, do not grow well physically and may even die.[272] Remember that the limbic system, which is the key part of the brain involved in emotions, pleasure and pain, receive all information from sensation on the body surfaces. So, whether we are touched with love and intelligence, respect and sensitivity to our needs, or with violence, disrespect, carelessness and clumsiness, the part of our brain which deals with emotion gets to hear about it and interpret it straight away. You will not be surprised to hear that modern research is proving the benefits of touch. For example, premature babies who are massaged grow nearly 50% more than ones left alone in an incubator, despite eating no more. Also, children between the ages of seven and ten from families who do lots of wrestling and physical play feel much more confident in themselves and better about their bodies.

It's really very simple – keep your young ones very close to you and cuddle them all the time when they are newborn, then carry on being close for the rest of your lives.

---

[272] Some charming research in the 1950s with baby monkeys showed that a total lack of touch leads to death in infants. A lack of proper touch in infant rats and monkeys has also been shown to increase anti-social and stressed adult individuals. Personally, I find it staggering that anyone should feel the need to prove that infant people need very close contact with their parents by cruelly experimenting on animals.

Chapter Eighteen

FROM NEWBORN TO ELDER - DEVELOPMENT AND AGING

A BRIEF OVERVIEW OF DEVELOPMENT FROM INFANT TO ADULT

There are enormous changes involved in the growth and development of a human. It is not just a case of the addition of more cells and tissues to become bigger: there are changes in the form of the whole body, as well as in the form of its organs and systems, and there are equally huge changes in aspects of its functioning.

Sometimes material is added (like bone and fat), but sometimes growth involves the death of tissues and cells. For example, the thymus gland, which is large and active up to 6 yrs of age then gradually degenerates. Orthodox Western texts say that in adults the thymus has little function; indeed it can be almost entirely replaced by fatty tissue, but perhaps this little function is still important. Consider the ancient Chinese practice of tapping the sternum daily to promote longevity. Perhaps tapping, a kind of massage, stimulates the thymus and encourages a slowing of degeneration, or a maximisation of the little function that is left. Remember that the thymus is involved in activating T-cells to make them specific for a newly-come-across antigen – a type of influenza for example. T-cells are also key in the body's destruction of cancerous cells. For us to live long into old age we need the immune system to continue to be capable of responding to new challenges as well as keeping us clear of cancer.

At other times growth involves complete replacement of tissues; for example the milk teeth being replaced by permanent ones, or bone being laid down on its cartilaginous blueprint, then continuously being re-absorbed and made again. Growth takes place throughout life, in many tissues of the body (epithelial tissue being among the most **labile -** meaning that it is always growing and being replaced).

Phases of growth

There are four phases of growth of the body.[273] At first, in the embryo, we begin to grow mainly in size, without much attention to development of function. This merges into a second phase (which begins as we enter the foetal stage in the second month in the womb) when there is equally growth in size and differentiation of functional activity. This phase

---

[273] David Sinclair and Peter Dangerfield *Human Growth After Birth*.

continues throughout childhood and ceases at maturity with the attainment of adulthood, in the late teens or early twenties. During adulthood a third phase occurs, being mainly to do with maintaining functional activity, with growth supporting and allowing this, and repairing loss from wear and tear. The last phase occurs in old age, when growth no longer keeps up, cells are lost without replacement and functioning may become less efficient as a result.

There are very interesting cultural differences in attitudes and expectations around aging, and there is evidence that our beliefs about aging and the type of life we lead have major impact on the rate of our deterioration. The actual causes of aging are not known, though it is known to occur in all species of vertebrates in a similar manner as it does in us. Aging can be speeded up or slowed down by various things, but not stopped. In the end, death awaits us, and this is as it should be, as new humans come to take our places. (Cultures that have retained their knowledge that everything that dies returns and that there are dimensions outside of physical reality do not have quite the death phobia that the modern West does).

Patterns of growth

Not all systems of the body follow the same pattern of growth. The respiratory, digestive and excretory systems keep the same relative size during growth compared to the rest of the body. The skeleton also behaves in this manner, but some body systems follow different growth curves.

Lymph nodes and other lymphoid tissues grow rapidly in childhood and are at maximum size by the age of puberty. Then a process of regression and degeneration occurs, so at the age of twenty there is much less lymph tissue present in our bodies than there was at the start of puberty. As we have discussed, this is particularly obvious with the thymus gland.

The **central nervous system** and the organs of special sense, along with the skull which houses them, grow so rapidly in childhood that they reach about 90% of their adult size by the age of five or six. At the age of twelve, a child's head is almost the size it will be as an adult. After this the growth of the nervous system is much slower than that of the rest of the body. It used to be thought that nerve cells do not regenerate at all, that it was all down-hill in terms of the nervous system and aging, but this is now known to be untrue. It is certain that we can follow activities which keep the nervous system functioning well, including keeping on thinking about new ideas, learning new skills, practicing meditation, and keeping our emotions flowing freely.

Puberty brings particular changes to the **gonads**, thanks to the gonadotrophic hormones from the pituitary and the sex hormones, oestrogen, progesterone and testosterone. These changes include the development of the secondary sexual characteristics as well as maturation of the reproductive function, as outlined in chapter sixteen. Oestrogen and testosterone are also the stimulus for closure of the cartilaginous growing plates of the bones.

Many things affect growth and development

There are factors which are important both before birth, and even before conception, and during childhood and beyond. Nutrition is of paramount importance. Not only must we have supplies of enough proteins, carbohydrates and essential fats for building and energy, but trace elements, vitamins and minerals are also essential.

Altitude affects growth: high altitudes retard it. Oxygen deficiency for other reasons has this effect also (for example, caused by congenital heart defects and severe asthma). Poverty is another factor inhibiting growth due to poorer nutrition being available, but also disease and emotional factors: we do not grow without love. Children growing up in homes without love may suffer in all kinds of ways, one of which is 'psychosocial dwarfism', where they literally do not grow. Many manage not to grow even if injected with growth hormone. If these children are given love, they will begin to grow and catch up with others of their age group.[274] Emotional trauma locked in the bodymind can interfere with healthy growth and development.

Antenatal poisoning such as from alcohol or other drug consumption by expectant mothers also stunts growth and impairs development; some of the effects of this do not show up until much later in life, and even may be seen most strongly in the next generations.

Interestingly, and not surprisingly to students of Chinese medicine, there is a large amount of evidence which suggests that growth in height is faster by 2 - 2½ times in the spring and summer than it is in the autumn and winter (on the other hand, growth in weight is faster in the autumn than the spring; this makes sense: we need to stock up for winter).

Descriptions and definitions of aging

In a way, aging (known in medi-speak as **senescence**) begins at maturity, a stage on the pathway to death. Just as growth follows different curves, so does aging.

Cells and tissues show some changes: for example, nerve cells look different with age. However, the idea that they die off at a steady rate is now disproven; some areas of the brain-stem are now known to retain their numbers well into old age. Also, a nerve cell of an older person who has continued to learn will have countless more dendritic connections with its neighbours than in youth. Generally the brain, along with other cells and tissues, tends to dry up (to keep well in life we need to stay juicy! On a physical level this means keep hydrated by eating lots of fresh fruit and vegetables and drinking water, and make sure to consume plenty of essential fatty acids).

Bones often lose density (osteoporosis), therefore becoming more easily broken. Healing is generally slower – probably due to impaired blood supply and nutritional deficiency.

Hearing degenerates – peak hearing is at age ten, apparently – though you will have understood from our discussion on the special senses that modern life is responsible for a much more rapid decline in hearing than was the case for our ancestors, and is the case in less developed societies. The other special senses are also impaired, including vision, smell and taste. Consider, is this partly because we don't really pay attention and fully use all our senses?

---

[274] Deepak Chopra's *Quantum Health*.

Often elders are excluded from ordinary life in our modern culture, plugged into the TV with very little meaningful connection or communication happening. Is it any wonder that many of them give up listening or looking out?

Memory and the ability to learn can be observed to be less efficient already in early adult life than in childhood; on the other hand this is not true of everyone. If one's mind is kept free of accumulated emotional distress, the memory tends to work much better.

There are changes in the **cardiovascular system**, also; calcium and fatty deposits can build up in the blood vessels, leading to increased blood pressure, making the heart work harder and wear out sooner. **Anaemia** is common in the elderly. This may be due to insufficient replacement of old red blood cells, but the fact is that many old people have a diet grossly deficient in iron and other essential nutrients. Lymphocytes are also less in number.

Lymphatic system/immunity, as discussed above with development, is one of the earliest to show changes, which are seen in the thymus gland, lymph nodes and spleen.

The Respiratory system has reduced capacity due to stiffening of cartilage and therefore less movement in the joints of the thoracic cage. This interferes with breathing and allows secretions to accumulate in the lungs. Also the elasticity of the lungs is diminished, so vital capacity is diminished due to reduced emptying. These changes manifest as shortness of breath, inefficient oxygenation, liability to infections (bronchitis and pneumonia) and fibrosis of lung tissues. Yoga and meditation practices which encourage deep breathing will minimize the likelihood of this happening.

In old age the **digestive processes** decline in a few ways; the teeth are often impaired or gone, the production of saliva is decreased and the stomach is less elastic so is unable to stretch to take in a large meal. Appetite may remain however, and this can be annoying for the elderly person. Impaired nervous control may disturb the defecation reflex. Peristalsis is slowed, causing constipation, and the colon has more little pouches in it – called diverticular – therefore diverticulosis (when the little pouches get inflamed and painful) is more common. The sizes of the liver and pancreas are reduced (although the aged liver is capable of regenerating as is that of younger adults). These factors, together with the all too common social isolation, and difficulty getting about and therefore difficulty shopping and cooking, mean that many of our elders are undernourished. This impacts in turn on all the other systems.

The urinary and reproductive systems: the kidneys become smaller and less efficient, therefore blood levels of urea, sugar, creatinine and uric acid rise. One in three men after the age of seventy have some impairment of the prostate gland, and there are changes in the testes and hormone secretion; although fertility may be retained well into old age. Menopausal changes in women lead to a fall in oestrogens secreted by the ovary, which affects the whole of the system: the uterus shrinks and atrophies, vaginal epithelium thins and there is some drying and keratinisation, the vagina changes from acid to alkaline, and breast tissue atrophies.

The endocrine system: there is a decline in production of hormones by the thyroid gland, adrenal cortex and the gonads.

The skin thins, loses subcutaneous fat and is markedly less elastic. Healing tends to be less efficient in the elderly – it takes longer, and scar tissue is less strong. There is a decline in Meissner's corpuscles (the receptors in the skin which respond to light touch), and so the sense of touch is impaired. Hair loss on the skull is widespread in men, although more hair grows in the nostrils and ears. It is not known why this is. Fingernails grow more slowly and often become brittle and liable to cracking. I think that it is possible or even probable that this is due to deficiencies rather than 'normal' aging.

Not all a disaster...

It makes a bit of a grim read, doesn't it? Especially for us raised in the modern materialistic culture, which idolizes the external appearance of things and values youthful looks more than the beauty of wisdom and age. Many of our assumptions and even experiences of aging are due to our cultural beliefs and attitudes. This really is true. Many experiments have shown that the actual physical signs of aging can be reversed by a change of attitude. It has been found that markers of physical age such as space between the joints of the fingers, eyesight and hearing will improve when people act and talk as they did when they were younger and more actively involved in life.[275]

It is also found that meditating leads one to age more slowly. Robert Wallace did a study in 1978 looking at biological age in meditators. The assessments for biological age Wallace used were blood pressure, acuteness of hearing and close vision – the ability to see near objects, such as the written word. These are markers known to deteriorate with age. Wallace found that the meditators were five to twelve years younger in biological age than they were in chronological age (the five-years-younger group had meditated for less than five years; the twelve-years-younger group for longer than five years). It seems that the deterioration of age involves a certain amount of choice! A study done in 1980 in three old people's homes near Boston, USA, compared the effects of learning transcendental meditation, practicing a typical relaxation technique and learning creative word games to keep the mind sharp. On testing after practicing for a while, the meditators scored highest on markers for mental health, blood pressure and learning ability. But the most amazing thing was that three years later, one third of the residents had died, but not one single meditator...[276]

As we enter more deeply into old age and therefore get closer to death, we begin to enter more into the realm of the spirit.[277] It can be said that as Newborns and Elders we are closest to God, having just come from Spirit, or being closer to going back to Source. Our modern

---

[275] Deepak Chopra *Unconditional Life*.

[276] Deepak Chopra *Quantum Healing*.

[277] Rudolph Steiner spoke and wrote about this, as he did about all the stages of life.

culture is confused about age, about wisdom, and about death – it seems we will do anything to claw back an extra few years, months or minutes of life, so great has our fear of death become. Yet there is no getting out of life without death for any of us, and this fearful avoidance and denial of it becomes a fearful avoidance of life itself.

> *Gray hair is a crown of splendour;*
> *Is attained by a righteous life.*
> – Proverbs 16:31

How about going grey? The pigment-making cells of our hair gradually die off, and the hair becomes white, grey or silver. Have you noticed how few people today have grey hair? It looks to me like an epidemic of covering up. I am beginning to go grey myself now, so this is a topical issue for me! I know that most hair dyes are poisonous – polluting for the environment and actually toxic for us, being absorbed into the body through the delicate skin of the scalp. A study in 2004[278] showed a definite link between using hair dye long term and lymphatic cancer. This is not surprising, as you will remember from our toxic toiletries discussion in the chapter on skin that almost all mainstream toiletries contain at least one carcinogenic chemical.

In most cultures, white hair is a sign of wisdom. The modern world however has lost respect for the past, and looking around it can seem that we have few Elders and a lot of old folk, since many people spend a lot of their life concerned with amassing material goods and little else. It's not easy to learn true wisdom, and to grow closer to spirit naturally, if one is focused on looking young, still being able to get it up and keeping up with the world news (or the latest soap operas…). I'm pleased to see the initiative called 'The Elders' – Richard Branson and Peter Gabriel's idea to gather some 'global Elders' to help with global problems. The Elders are Nelson Mandela, Desmond Tutu, Ela Bhatt, Gro Brundtland, Jimmy Carter, Muhammad Yunus, Graca Machel, Kofi Annan, Lakhdar Brahimi, Fernando H. Cardoso, Mary Robinson and Aung San Sui Kyi. They are promoting peace and human rights worldwide and are going on missions to places experiencing difficulties to offer the help of their wisdom and experience in conflict resolution. See www.theelders.org to find out more.

---

[278] Yale University (2004, February 17). Hair Dye Use Increases Risk Of Non-Hodgkin's Lymphoma. *Science Daily*. Retrieved July 15, 2008, from http://www.sciencedaily.com /releases/2004/02/040217072523.htm

Chapter Nineteen

INTERRELATIONSHIPS
How the Systems (and Everything) Interconnect

Although we have looked at the body systems separately for ease of study, in fact none can properly function without all of the others. We are a whole, not the sum of our parts. Each system is the only one capable of carrying out its particular functions, and all the systems depend on the good functioning of the others for a smooth ride. When things go wrong in one system the effects are felt everywhere.

We are not composed of separate systems working together like the parts of a machine to make a whole machine operate well. We are alive, dynamic and completely connected – not just the different parts within us, but we ourselves are a part of the universe, connected in countless ways to all that is. Have you heard of the 'butterfly effect'? This is the idea that the flap of a butterfly's wings in one part of the world may ultimately cause a tornado in another – a small change somewhere leads to a chain of events which eventually leads to huge changes. It is not that the butterfly's flapping actually produces the tornado, but certain details of weather can be affected, in a chaotic (unpredictable) manner, by the butterfly, and therefore, of course, by very many other factors.[279]

We will begin in this chapter by looking at the body then begin to consider extending our view beyond. There is a holistic philosophy of dis-ease that sees illness coming in a particular system or part of the body according to the emotional or spiritual struggles we are having. I am including briefly some of these ideas – not to be adhered to rigidly but for interest's sake.[280]

How the systems interrelate

Most of this has been said at the end of each chapter, and here is connected as a whole.

It is obvious how connected to the muscular system the **skeleton** is: muscles are attached to bone, cross joints, rely on the framework of the skeleton for movement, and need the calcium in the blood (reserves of which are stored in bones) to be at the right level for proper functioning. Too little calcium in the blood leads to **tetany** – spasm in the muscles. Too much, and the muscles are over-relaxed.

The bones are deeply involved with the cardiovascular system: blood cells are produced in

---

[279] This comes from the work of Edward Lorenz, American mathematician and meteorologist who did pioneering work on chaos theory.
[280] Louise Hay *Heal Your Body A-Z*.

red marrow, and an imbalance of calcium affects the heart, as well as all the other muscles. Too much calcium in the blood affects many systems, as calcium deposits are laid down on bone, and in the kidneys, blood vessels and other organs.

Nerves make muscles contract to move the skeleton, and each bone has its own extensive nerve supply. It is the digestive system which provides nutrients for making bones (e.g. calcium, phosphorous and boron, as well as the glucosamine used for repairing cartilage). The skin makes vitamin D from cholesterol and sunshine, which is then used for bone production. There is a deep relationship between the skeletal system and the kidneys, which help stimulate production of bone marrow, while the endocrine system controls calcium balance partly by re-absorption and laying down of bone. In terms of the reproductive system, oestrogen is involved in maintaining bone density.

Bones, being ruled by the planet Saturn, are about structure and authority, so problems here can be to do with our relationship to authority or with how comfortable or safe we feel with the structure of our life and the universe.

Muscles are completely reliant on nervous stimulation for movement and tone. Muscles depend on the digestive system to get glucose for energy, which they store as glycogen (as does the liver). Hormones are involved in the control of this process. It is the digestive system which provides nutrients for muscle growth – the amino acids for actin and myosin production. Muscles also need oxygen for making ATP therefore getting energy to contract – this comes to them courtesy of the lungs and circulation.

The skin has important muscles (the pili erectors, which make our hair stand on end) in its dermis, and these are moved by the nervous system. It has a very rich blood and nerve supply. It makes vitamin D for the bones, and has a very small part to play in breathing. If the skin is not able to properly control temperature, all the systems can be affected. Think what it would be like in an office with no heating, or a broken boiler that wouldn't turn off – without a good temperature, it is impossible to work well. If all the pores are blocked, we die because it seriously messes with the body's thermoregulation. Hormones affect the skin strongly – causing acne when in excess for teenagers, or dryness in deficiency for menopausal women. The skin relies on good digestion to receive all the nutrients it needs for its constant renewal and repair.

The skin can reflect our relationship between our inner and outer selves. It protects who we are, our sense of individuality and self-hood. Sometimes skin problems like eczema are to do with irritation and anger, something burning us up being expressed in the skin. In holistic terms it is quite a good thing for disease to come out in the skin in the sense that it is very superficial – much more serious to have a problem which goes deeper into our underlying organs.

The cardiovascular system is clearly intertwined with the respiratory system, as the blood carries oxygen and carbon dioxide around body, and to and from the lungs in the pulmonary circulation. The lymphatic system works together with the blood circulation to provide drainage at tissue level of fluid and waste. Immunity is so intertwined with the blood circulation and white blood cells as to be completely inseparable. The circulation being the main transport system, it carries hormones, nutrients from the digestive system, and waste products. Blood brings glucose and oxygen to muscles and all other cells for energy production. The kidney filters the blood and keeps it clean. Blood cells are made in bone marrow, and the blood brings oxygen and nutrients to the skin, hair and nails.

Blood and the circulation are of the Fire element, therefore there is a strong association with our ability to feel and express joy and the other emotions freely, in positive ways. Our heart beats the rhythm of the cosmos, is the place we are connected to the love of and in the universe.

The marriage of **lymphatic** and cardiovascular systems has been discussed above – one cannot function without the other. In the digestive system, the lymphatic lacteals in the villi of the small intestine help fat absorption. Lactic acid and urea formed in muscle cells is drained away in lymph. Movements of the muscles and pressure changes in the thorax to do with the musculoskeletal system are key for movement of lymph. Louise Hay says that problems in the lymph system are reminding us to keep the mind focussed on the important things in life – love and joy. Holding on to fluids may be about holding onto someone or something from the past. The immune function part of the lymphatic system is involved with proper functioning of all systems since it protects everywhere in the body from external threat and from internal toxins and abnormal growth. The liver is key in making immunoglobulins and protecting from toxins and foreign substances with gain access to the body via the digestive tract. Our emotions, the endocrine system and immunity are so closely intertwined that even modern medicine is beginning to take a look with its psychoneuroimmunology.[283] Beliefs about our vulnerability can give us colds and 'flu, as can being overwhelmed with mental activity and confusion. Anger and irritation which isn't being satisfactorily expressed and resolved can lower immunity and therefore come out as an infection.

All body cells require oxygen, brought into the body by **the respiratory system**. Thus all of the other body systems rely on it. There is an especially intimate relationship between the respiratory system and the cardiovascular system. By its function of detoxing the body the respiratory system further helps all cells of the body. In Chinese medicine, lungs are of the Metal Element, therefore to do with what is really vital, valuable and important when all has been stripped away. Because of this association with respect and value, the lungs are also involved in the expression of grief – grief being what we feel when we lose something we value. When we breath deeply we are inspired – we take in life. Problems with the lungs may be to do with not valuing or respecting ourselves, not feeling able to take in life or grief which we are struggling to fully accept – which means feeling it deeply.

The digestive system has links to all systems, as the whole body needs nutrients. In addition to this, the cardiovascular system transports nutrients around body. Digestion is controlled and aided by hormones. Lymphatic lacteals in the villi of the small intestine are needed for fat absorption. Glucose from digestion is used by muscles to make energy, and

---

[283] Never mind red lorry yellow lorry, try saying psychoneuroimmunology three times fast...

muscles in the gut wall do the peristalsis which pushes food along. As we have said, all digestive organs have a very rich nerve supply. The digestive system works together with the bones, the endocrine system and the kidneys, to keep the calcium balance in the blood right. This is needed especially by the muscular and nervous systems for their proper functioning. The digestive system, along with the kidneys, lung and skin are essential for excretion. Remember the 'enteric nervous system'? This system is so richly supplied with nerves that it is completely and swiftly affected by nervous tension and fear. Indigestion can mean we are having problems digesting and assimilating our experiences.

All the systems are related to the **nervous system** in some way. For example, breathing is controlled by the brain, and the brain needs a constant supply of oxygen, so the nervous and respiratory systems are interdependent. New research suggests that a lack of oxygen from breathing problems may be the cause of memory problems, attention deficit and learning and behavioural problems.[281] The cells of the immune system are sensitive to neurotransmitters, with some white blood cells producing them themselves. The lymphatic system is involved in detoxification, so keeps the blood clean; the brain is very sensitive to toxins. The endocrine system is controlled by the hypothalamus. Many hormones affect the brain and moods/emotions. The gastrointestinal tract has so much nerve supply it has its own brain – the enteric nervous system. The nerve cells of this ENS make neuropeptides, with a huge effect on mood. The skin is so full of receptors it is considered to be a sense organ in itself.

Sympathetic and parasympathetic nerves supply all the internal organs of the body and the skin. The nerves do maintenance and repair with nutrients from the digestive system brought to them via the circulatory system. When toxins build up in the body the nervous system is very soon affected, so the kidney, bowel, liver, lung skin and lymphatic systems which work to keep the body clean are crucial to allow good nervous system functioning.

The nerves are about communication, so problems with them can reflect difficulties we might have in this area.

The nervous system works intimately with the **endocrine system** to maintain homeostasis. The pituitary gland is particularly linked to the hypothalamus, which controls it. Hormones are carried in blood to target organs. Digestion relies on hormones from the stomach, small intestine and pancreas. As for the reproductive system, hormones govern it – for example follicle stimulating hormone (FSH) and luteinising hormone (LH) controlling sex hormone and gamete production. The mind-body link may be to do with control issues and balance.

The **kidneys** are related to the circulatory system in that it is blood which is filtered by the nephrons, and the kidneys are key in controlling blood pressure. Hormones control kidney activity – renin controls body fluid levels and blood pressure, and aldosterone controls mineral balance. The kidneys help stimulate bone marrow production. Urea comes from

---

[281] Journal of the American Medical Association, 2007; 297: 2681-2 via www.wddty.co.uk

amino acids broken down in liver.

It has been argued that all systems exist to allow **reproduction**. Certainly to make a baby all the systems are required, to keep at least the mother's body going in a healthy way through nine months of gestation. There are special links between this system and the endocrine system, which controls its cycles and activity, and the nervous and circulatory systems which are intimately involved with sexual activity and sensation.

Stress, fear for the future and unconscious aversion to being a parent can interfere with reproductive function. Sexual difficulties often come from guilt and shame about sexual love, anger at a present or past lover or unresolved abuse issues. Problems with the genitals or reproductive organs may be associated with shame and guilt about sex and beliefs about punishment.

The Interconnectedness of All life

We can't discuss interrelationships without at least a brief consideration of the mind and the spirit, and indeed the entire universe. Of course, the dominant culture of the West and many of its citizens does not believe in this kind of interconnectedness. If you have been indoctrinated with our modern separatist view, try to suspend it for a moment and allow the following snippets on this vast subject to blow your mind wide open.

Electromagnetic field of the earth

As we will explore in Appendix B, so-called 'primitive' people – those who follow the Old Ways of the earth – take it for granted that we humans are connected with all that is, an integral part of a magnificent and mysterious whole, where all are affected by each other. Thus we have immense power to affect our universe, and at the same time we are ourselves are affected.

Actually, this isn't so far-fetched. All of us living things work on a circadian rhythm of 24 hours, a cycle of night and day, with various biological activities following a clock which is in sync with the Earth's rotation around the sun. We also have other rhythms in the body; half weekly, monthly, and yearly ones, for example. Most of the functions of our body systems are affected, and the most amazing thing is that the synchronizer of it all is not within us, but is external: from the sun and the planets.[284] For example, big solar storms in space change the electromagnetic field of the earth. One dramatic manifestation of this is that rates of heart attacks are increased – the most heart attacks occur within a day of a solar storm. Another researcher, M.A. Persinger, found that unsettled and changing weather in space leads to higher numbers of attempted suicides, nervous disorders and epileptic seizures.

There are different energies in different places on the earth. The modern term used to describe the stress caused by earth energies is 'geopathic stress.'[285] This is not a new idea, as

---

[284] Franz Halburg did a lot of this research. See the chapter 'The Right Time' in Lynne McTaggart's *The Intention Experiment*.

[285] The section which follows, on geopathic stress, was kindly written by Lucy Harmer. I suggest you consult her book *The Art of Space Clearing and Intuitive Feng Shui* (published in French *La Purification de l'Espace* Jouvence Editions 2003, to be published in English by North Atlantic Books, March 2010). www.innerelf.com

Nostradamus (1503-1566) wrote:

'Where plants perish and animals are absent, there you should not live, the place is unhealthy. You will experience disharmony and lose your poise. However, when you find the place where happy, vital and healthy people live and many old folk are in good health, then stay there, you will soon do without medicine or a physician. The mysterious forces of the Earth will make you healthy.'

The historian Plutarch (125BC-45BC) also noted that:

'Men are affected by streams of varying potency issuing from the Earth. Some of these drive people crazy, or cause disease and death; the effect of others is good, soothing and beneficial.'

In the West, these currents are often called 'ley lines'. They are known as different forms of Earth energy, created by the natural electromagnetic fields that emanate naturally from the earth. Some of these planetary energy networks can be harmful to humans, such as the *Hartmann* network, which is like a circuit that runs both longitudinally and laterally about every two metres from North to South and East to West. The *Curry* network is composed of diagonally running currents that cross on a North-East/South-West and South-East/North-West axis. These networks of earth energy can be felt to a greater or lesser degree anywhere and they can provoke geopathic stress. They can be felt more strongly if there are morphological distortions on the Earth's surface, and where the two different currents cross the stress is intensified.

Geopathic stress is caused when the earth's natural energy rising up is distorted and becomes unstable. Ley lines can become magnified, unstable or distorted by underground streams, mineral concentrations, tectonic movements, fault lines, underground cavities, railway lines or motorways, tunnels, construction projects, mines, excavations and anything else which causes a shock to the earth. Even pylons and street signs can cause geopathic stress if they are badly positioned.

There are also terrestrial rays that are beneficial to human health. These are yang currents known in the West as *Schumann* waves. Unfortunately, these waves have trouble moving through modern construction materials such as concrete, with the result that they are very weak in large urban areas.

Geopathic stress can cause insomnia, irritability, colds, chronic fatigue, headaches, anxiety and, over the long term, even serious chronic illness such as cancer. Every single person suffering from cancer or a sleep disorder to whom I have given a consultation, has slept with his/her bed over a geopathically stressed area where two or more currents crossed. Fifty percent of women who sleep on a nodal point or area where the currents cross (i.e. where the geopathic stress is acute) over a long period of time are unable to conceive. Geopathic stress is now considered as one of the principle factors in 'Sick Building Syndrome'. The most common indications of geopathic stress are usually resistance to medical treatment, a feeling of being constantly run-down and exhausted, anxiety, nervousness, depression, loss of appetite, insomnia, restless sleep, feeling cold, cramps, chronique fatigue, mild headaches and backache and tingling in arms and legs. Geopathic stress does not cause an illness as such, but lowers your immune system, so you have less chance of fighting any illness. It prevents your body properly absorbing vitamins, minerals and trace elements from your food and decreases your resistance to environmental pollution, thus increasing allergies.

To reduce geopathic stress, there are a few options. Earth acupuncture is an effective remedy but the effects must be verified regularly to be sure that the stress has not returned. To perform earth acupuncture, ask the guardian of the place to show you the healing points or use dowsing rods to discover them. Then place copper or iron earth acupuncture pins (like stakes, sometimes with a crystal attached) into the ground in order to neutralise the effects of geopathic stress. Follow your intuition as to which method to use.

Simply placing your bed in a non geopathically stressed area is the best possible remedy! An easy book on how to detect and avoid geopathic stress is Rolf Gordon's *Are you Sleeping in a Safe Place.* (www.rolfgordon.co.uk).

There are also some materials that are useful in protecting against geopathic stress, such as cork or tatami, which can be placed under beds, especially if the geopathic stress is due to underground water. There are other insulating materials such as mineral sheets that can be used to protect against other causes of geopathic stress and these would be recommended by a good dowser or feng shui consultant.

If you suffer from a lot of geopathic stress, you can purchase a *Raditech* – a device that you plug into an electrical socket. The device activates certain minerals by applying a small electrical current, thus neutralising some of the effect caused by geopathic stress. The new devices are much more effective and emit far less electromagnetic radiation. Most people's well-being increases dramatically but some of my clients have reported only a slight benefit. If you are interested, I suggest that you buy a device that offers a trial period.[286]

Influenced by our environment

You are probably not aware of all the different factors which influence you in your home and place of work, nor the impact they have on your life. Some of these influences (of which most are now scientifically proven) are: the psychological impact of colour; visual art; ornaments; electromagnetic fields (or EMFs) and micro-wave pollution emitted by computers, televisions, microwave ovens, mobile phone antennae, etc; geopathic stress; the gases emitted by building materials; the physical and psychological effect of clutter; the location and orientation of a place; the spatial arrangement of furniture; air quality; lighting, and so on.

The art of Feng Shui deals with these things and more. The official definition of Feng Shui, as given by the London Feng Shui Society is: "Feng Shui is the practice which consists of analysing the influence and the interaction between people, buildings, and the environment in order to promote a better quality of life."

---

[286] For more information and to purchase a Raditech go to www.dulwichhealth.co.uk

Some of these influences, such as geopathic stress, EMFs, microwave pollution and lighting, can give rise to certain health conditions, such as depression, miscarriages, hyperactivity in children, insomnia, irritability, colds, chronic tiredness, headaches, anxiety, and even in the long term, serious illnesses such as cancer.

Feng Shui rebalances and corrects the energy flow within a place in much the same way that acupuncture works on the body's meridians. When energy is circulating freely, every aspect of your life will be enhanced, your health, your relationships, your job, etc. The aim of Feng Shui is to re-establish any lost sense of balance by improving your surroundings. It can bring about a deeper sense of harmony and well-being in your home or place of work.

There is an integral part of Feng Shui, space clearing, which aims to free a place of old emotions, the memories encrusted in the walls, and to raise its energy level by creating a sense of harmony with the inhabitants. Space clearing cleans out all the thought forms and negative patterns of behaviour which have been left behind by past occupants and which can have a considerable impact on the lives of the people who've moved in. The energy of a place is partly created by the traumas, events, moods, etc, which have taken place there. Every time a strong emotion is felt by someone in a particular place, part of its energy is deposited on the walls.

Sometimes the memories anchored in the walls or the emotional imprints of a place simply don't reflect the hopes and aspirations of the person living or working there. If you feel emotionally blocked or you sense a certain heaviness in your home or workplace, if everything you try seems to turn out badly, or if the projects you undertake don't seem to move ahead, the space definitely needs clearing.

Space clearing clears out the past and releases all emotional imprints, energy cycles and any useless constraints relating to the history of the space. It raises the level of vibration and helps you to manifest your most heartfelt desires. It brings more light and astral energy into your home or workspace so that you can experience a better quality of life.[287]

Connected with nature

Edward O. Wilson wrote of 'biophilia' in 1984. He said that humans have evolved together with all other life on earth, and our intimate involvement with nature is essential to our thriving. Stephen H. Buhner writes eloquently of this in *The Secret Teachings of Plants*:

'And without this bonding, what is life? What is life without this exchange of soul essence between the human and the wildness of the world? Tasteless food in some dusty and empty place rising in geometric precision out of an empty plain. A mathematical life forced into place by bulldozer and concrete and Man. And what are we then but abandoned and crumpled newspapers, stories without meaning, blowing down some wind-swept, darkened street?'

---

[287] This section, on Feng Shui and space clearing, like the previous one on geopathic stress, was written by Lucy Harmer.

Connected to each other

As well as being connected with everything else, we are deeply connected to each other. Countless experiments have proved what we really already know – that we communicate across space, 'know' things about each other, and can 'see' events at a distance. For example, Dean Radin's experiments from 1997 showed that people being sent healing intention react to it in a physiologically measurable way, and that the more connected two people are, the stronger this effect is. People can become connected in this way quite quickly. If two people attempt to connect mentally, their brain waves and their heart rhythms move into sync together, in an entanglement called 'entrainment'. Luckily, it seems that the healthiest rhythms take the lead, bringing the other person into sync with them.[288]

Then there are some interesting 'twin studies'. For example, the 'Jim Twins' from Ohio, USA. These were separated at birth and only met at age 39. Both were called Jim (named by their adoptive parents), both had a dog they named Troy, they had done similar work and had married twice, first to a Linda then to a Betty. They drove the same car and holidayed on the same stretch of Florida beach at the same time every year. Several pairs of twins have died at the same moment. For example, Peg was killed in a car crash when the steering column entered her chest. Her twin Helen woke up at the same time with chest pain, and died on the way to hospital. The scientist Percy Semour makes a case for these twins being 'entrained' – a large scale version of the entrainment of particles described by quantum physics.[289]

Then there is the phenomenon of 'remote viewing' – travelling outside of the body to 'see' things which are elsewhere. Of course, to shamans this is quite an everyday activity. But interestingly, the remote viewing process was developed by researchers at Stanford University under contract to the American government for the use in intelligence collection. In autumn 1996, the CIA released information on this so-called "Star-gate program"; official confirmation was given that the government had, for twenty-five years, trained and used psychic spies to observe targets in the Soviet Union and elsewhere. Paul H. Smith, a retired Air Force major, says "practiced, experienced viewers can access a target nearly 100% of the time. This doesn't mean they get all the data they were looking for. They retrieve information indicating that they were 'there.' However, these experienced viewers regularly obtain extremely accurate, often error-free information from the target." This subject of course is a whole book in itself, (or even many books. You might try Percy Seymour's *The Third Level of Reality* and Stephen H. Buhner's *The Secret Language of Plants*). There is ample evidence, out there and in here, about our interconnectedness.

---

[288] Lynne McTaggart's *Intention Experiment* has brought together much fascinating research in this area, and presents it in a very readable way.

[289] Percy Semour *The Third Level of Reality – A Unified Theory of the Paranormal.*

Mind-body connections

Then there is the power of the mind. What we see is what we get – and we seem to have a tendency to see what we believe, and filter almost everything else out. There is a lovely story in Deepak Chopra's *Quantum Health* about a woman in a lot of severe abdominal pain who had an operation for what were suspected gallstones; when they opened her up she was riddled with cancer, so they just closed her again without being able to do anything. Her daughter, told that there was nothing that could be done and that death would be imminent, asked that her mother not be told, in order that she gets some enjoyment from what little life was left to her. The woman was told the operation was a success. Some time later, she turned up to see the doctor, completely healthy and said 'Doctor, I was so sure I had cancer back then. When I found out it was only gallstones I was so relieved and determined to live my life to the full.' Many studies have shown that people's beliefs about their health and illness has a significant effect on recovery. We will take a deeper look at this in chapter twenty-three.

You can see I have just touched the tip of the iceberg here. There is so much to say on interconnectedness because basically life is an ever changing interconnected flux. What conclusions can be drawn from the few bits I have selected to try and open this subject up are left to you, and will no doubt be affected by many interconnected factors about you and your life: what you believe, how connected you feel with yourself and others, how aware of the magnificent beauty and power of nature and how much of that beauty and power has been lost and is continuing to be lost, and your relationship to Spirit, to name but a few. There is much to be gained from expanding our awareness of connection.

Enjoy your explorations.

Chapter Twenty

DROPPING THE ROBE - DEATH AND DYING

Normally the body, this web of interconnected functions and structures, is kept together by homeostatic mechanisms. If one or more vital functions or parts of the body are lost or damaged, homeostasis cannot be maintained and the whole individual will die. This can happen suddenly or slowly; from injury, trauma, starvation or dehydration, and aging. On the cellular level our bodies are always in a state of dying and regeneration, and many of our cells are replaced constantly throughout life. After the body dies, some cells remain alive for up to several days afterwards. Life and death are not as clearly distinct as we might think.

Spiritual traditions – that is, pretty much all systems of thought in the world, with the exception of modern Western science – consider that death is the severing of the spirit from the body. Hence the title of this chapter, which I have borrowed from the very beautiful cultures of the First Americans (Native Americans). To *drop one's robe* is simply to let go of the body, the robe the spirit has worn for this lifetime (the good red road, that which we travel in the body), and move on to the blue road of spirit.[290]

The spirit is the animating force of the body, which can be particularly seen in respect of the heart and lungs: keeping the heart beating and the lungs breathing – the two vital movements which all other functions depend on for immediate survival. When the spirit leaves, the heartbeat and breathing cease. Most cultures also consider that the spirit continues to inhabit the body for a time after physical death; it does not leave straight away, but takes time to go. Traditional funeral rites are often about helping the spirit to leave and enter the 'next world' fully and not get trapped here as a ghost.

I found it interesting that in all of the physiology books I have looked at, there is nothing about death. Of course, physiology is the study of the functions of a living body, but still, since death is certainly coming to all of us, I find it surprising that it is not a topic generally covered. Sogyal Rinpoche, a Tibetan Buddhist Master, on first coming to the UK, was shocked at the absence of thought about death in our culture. In Tibetan Buddhism it is customary to consider one's own death, to meditate on it and prepare for it, certainly from

---

[290] Jamie Sams *Sacred Path Cards.*

adulthood on.[291] In many cultures death, as an integral part of life, is something all will be familiar with. In modern British culture, we do not speak of death, even with the dying. We can be ninety years of age and still be concerning ourselves with the minutiae of life, without ever giving a thought to our death, which we know must be growing closer.

Our dying people are kept out of sight in hospitals or hospices (if they are lucky). During Victorian times the current trend of solemn, buttoned down funerals began; people strive not to 'break down' – not to express their grief publicly.

Contrast this with almost every other culture, where if a dead person doesn't get a really good send off, which includes a lot of wailing and releasing of tears and grief as well as a rousing celebration of life, the job has not been done properly. For example, the Dagara people of West Africa consider that many tears are needed to wash the deceased's spirit over to the next world. The Dagara also recognize the importance to the living of expressing grief fully – a funeral is an opportunity for everyone to cry and release their feelings of loss publicly, together with everyone else. This is the time for all grief to come out, not only about the person who just died, but about all the loss we will experience as living humans. The Dagara rightly understand how dangerous a human being who cannot cry is.[292]

Contrast this with unfortunately all too common happenings in the UK; when someone cries at a funeral they often apologise for 'breaking down'. If someone is not ready to get fully back to the party very soon after their loved one dies, they are considered to be stuck or in need of jollying along. There is a trend of prescribing tranquilizers or antidepressant drugs for a person unable or unwilling to suppress the expression of grief. We have evolved a culture of seeing suppression of grief as strength, and the expression of it as weakness, to the detriment of our physical, mental and spiritual health. It is very likely that the two world wars of the twentieth century hardened this pattern – there simply was too much grief and no time to feel it and recover fully from it.

Modern medicine measures success rates by how long a person lives – for example, the 'five year survival rate' in cancer treatments. Sophisticated machinery can keep people alive or resuscitate a person who actually died. Designer babies are being made to provide a sibling for a child with a disease who can be kept alive with organ or bone marrow transplants. We will do anything to buy a few more years, a few more months, a few more days. It looks like we have a bit of a death phobia. There are probably many reasons for this. One is that so many of us are so full of unexpressed grief we cannot bear to go near the subject of loss; another, that if the material body is all we believe to exist, and with which we are completely identified, then the end of it means complete annihilation.

So, consider this – one day, you and everyone else you know is going to die. This could happen in a variety of ways. In the UK, one in three of us will die of heart disease. This

---

[291] Sogyal Rinpoche *The Tibetan Book of Living and Dying*.

[289] From Malidoma Patrice Some's book *Of Water and the Spirit*.

could be a heart attack or a stroke, killing us immediately or leading to a slower journey towards death. One in three of us will die of cancer, which can take weeks to years to die from, and can vary from being relatively pain free to being excruciating agony.

What feelings does this bring up for you? It is worth considering the reality of our death, not to get all morbid and obsessed about it but to bring us right up to the reality of life and the present moment, and to put into perspective what is important and what is not important. One thing about death, and about grief, is it sure shows us what matters. All the superfluous stuff is stripped away. We can step up to the moment with dignity, with courage and even with humour, and accept it as the last great adventure, opening our hearts to each moment.[293] We can let go with grace when the time comes, instead of trying anything to buy another few moments, weeks, months of life without regard to the cost of this to our earth or to future generations. When we are driven by fear we are missing out on being fully here, being fully able to enjoy our lives. We may as well sit back and enjoy the ride. We can let go of our loved ones when it is time for them to move on, rather than wasting our last precious time together in pretence and desperate holding. Many spiritual traditions emphasise the sense of being aware of death to inform our lives, although very few are about 'judgement' when it happens. Maybe this Christian version of what happens has put our culture wholesale off going willingly into death, by scaring so many generations with hellfire and damnation!

We can be more scared of things when we don't understand what is happening, so one remedy is to find out more about the process of dying. Another is to go for life and truly live it, opening to each moment in trust, love and awe at our great good fortune to have any time in an amazing human body on this beautiful earth of ours.

The Process of Dying

Let's take a look at what happens to the body of a person who is going through the process of dying. Deborah Singrist, in her book *Journey's End - a Guide to Understanding the Dying Process*, describes the changes that take place during dying as occurring in four dimensions – physical, mental, emotional-social and spiritual.

The body shuts down and physical changes happen with circulation, metabolism, breathing, lung secretions, elimination and the senses. What may be abnormal in the living becomes normal in dying. Death is an experience that comes to each person in a unique way, and it happens to the whole person, not just the body. Pain and suffering, like comfort and healing, can occur in any part of a person - not just the body. In fact the opportunities for growth in the emotional, social and spiritual areas are tremendous, even though the body is slowing as the person gradually lets go.

---

[293] My lovely proof-reader Patch Mendes told me a story about a Hopi man who had lived as a clown, making his people laugh all his life. He faced his death well and his last wish – his last joke – was to ask that his dead body be thrown from a building in the town. Everybody laughed… (if anyone knows any more of this story I'd love to hear it, it would be good to honour the man with his name.).

There are many physical signs of dying. The circulation slows as the blood pressure drops and heart rate slows, so hands and feet may feel cool or cold to the touch. The fingers, earlobes, lips and nail beds may show signs of this diminished circulation and look bluish or light grey. When death is very near, the feet and knees may look mottled – blotchy purple colouring appears. With reduced circulation, the vision may be blurred.

The body no longer needs lots of energy and the digestive system is slowing down, so appetite for food – and later for fluids – lessens. As eating and drinking slows the body becomes naturally dehydrated, making the dying person sleepier and less aware of pain and discomfort. Nearer to the time of death, a fever is common.[294] Secretions in the lungs thicken and gather in the lungs or back of the throat, making breathing sound moist and congested – the 'death rattle'. Usually this does not bother the dying person as they come closer to death. All kinds of changes in breathing happen – to the rate, rhythm and depth. There might be periods of not breathing for up to half a minute or more, or breathing may alternate between being slow and shallow, faster and deeper.

As the kidneys and bowel eventually stop working, and with dehydration, a smaller amount of urine is produced and is dark in colour, and bowel movements become less common. If the bowels do not move for three to four days, this can cause great discomfort.

Hearing is the last sense to go, so it makes sense to always assume a dying person can hear you, even if they are unable to respond. Gentle touch is always a great way to communicate and to make sure the dying person knows you are there. Close to the hour of death, the skin may feel moist.

Mental and emotional changes also happen during the dying process. With the slowing of circulation and breathing, the brain receives less oxygen. This, together with physical pain, fear or metabolic changes in the body can cause restlessness and agitation and occasional or constant confusion. Levels of alertness and awareness may rise and fall. A dying person's attention begins to turn inward, lessening awareness of surroundings. Some people may fall into sleep so deep they cannot be awakened.

Then there are emotional and social factors. Many dying people wish to review their life, looking back in search of meaning and fulfilled purpose. There are often regrets to be felt, forgiveness of self and others to be given, good-byes to people and places to be made. The living can help the dying by being prepared to listen and share in these processes.

Whether a person is religious or not, spiritual considerations are often present when one is dying. People consider the meaning of life, of hope, suffering and death. Old losses coming up and being grieved, revisiting the past and forgiving it and the people who have hurt us are common activities for someone who is dying. It is not unusual for a dying person to experience a vision of someone who has already died, or a spiritual or religious figure. Dreams of one's ancestors are common.

---

[294] Perhaps we are particularly warmed by Tatewari's love on this part of the great journey.

Each person dies at the right moment – for some this may be surrounded by others, for some, alone. Some people seem to hold off or bring on the moment of death, dying just after someone from out of town arrives, or after an important anniversary.

What happens to the body after death

After death, the body changes still more. Sometimes the bowel and bladder open and empty immediately. Within four hours, the skeletal muscles become stiff – this is called **rigor mortis**, the 'stiffness of death' in Latin. Usually the face stiffens first and the hands and feet later. Maximum stiffness develops in twelve to forty-eight hours, depending on the temperature around the body as well as other factors.[295] What happens in the muscles is that ATP runs out as the circulation stops bringing oxygen and glucose to the cells. The muscle cells do not all die straight away – they can continue anaerobic respiration and make some ATP, but eventually will be unable to make more. Do you remember that ATP is used by muscle cells to unlock the contraction of actin and myosin, energizing them for the next contraction? So without ATP, and also with calcium ions leaking all over the place within the muscle cells, the myofilaments cannot be unlocked, and the muscles become and remain strongly contracted.

Rigor mortis only wears off as the cells and tissues begin to decompose. Without normal maintenance, the lysosomes in the muscle cells escape and begin to dissolve the actin and myosin, so unlocking the tension. This is the beginning of the process of **putrefaction** – the decomposition of the body after death. Putrefaction is the dissolving of the body by its own enzymes and bacterial action. The body is gradually changed into its chemical components of gases, liquids and salts. Soon after death bacteria invade the tissues. These are bacteria which in life were normally present in the gut and the lungs. They prefer anaerobic conditions, so as oxygen is straight away absent after death they quickly multiply. The hotter it is the quicker decomposition occurs. Bad smelling gases are produced as the body liquefies. All in all, a decomposing body does not look or smell great, and the dead are therefore best removed from the vicinity of the living before putrefaction becomes advanced. This is no doubt the reason most religions which evolved in hot countries insist on a quick burial. Sometimes normal putrefaction does not happen, and a variation called mummification happens. This only happens in conditions of dryness of heat, when air can circulate – for example, in the desert, or in a chimney. Instead of rotting away, the body shrivels and is converted into a leather-like mass of skin and tendons surrounding the bones. Internal organs may be decomposed, or occasionally preserved. Newborn infants are small and sterile, so more commonly mummify. As you probably know, the ancient Egyptians preserved the bodies of some of their dead by using processes which encouraged this phenomenon.

Student doctors in the UK and US dissect dead people in their first year of study to assist in the learning of anatomy. Consider that medical students, like the rest of us in the West,

---

[295] For example, a starving person has less stores of glycogen in the muscles to use in respiration; therefore rigor mortis will set in more quickly.

will have been protected from death and may never have been close to it before. The experience of dissecting a 'cadaver' has the most profound impact on them. Medics are expected to put on a face of not being too bothered by death. Medical students will begin to come into contact with ill people, some of whom will be terminally ill. The dissection of cadavers and involvement in autopsy does not really prepare students for interaction with the dying.

Until recently, many medical schools also had 'dog labs' where students practiced operating on dogs – as well as learning about anaesthesia and dissecting a living, breathing, bleeding body, the dogs died on the operating table, therefore exposing the students to death. This process has recently been dropped from most medical schools.

Often in the second year of medical training, the students participate in an autopsy – the dissection of a dead person in order to determine the cause of death. In Britain the law states that any person who dies without having seen a doctor in the preceding two weeks who can confirm cause of death must be given an autopsy.[296]

As a student of herbal medicine I visited a morgue with a group of fellow students. One of the people being dissected was a ninety-six year old woman who had died in her sleep. Because she was healthy and not 'under the doctor', she had to be given an autopsy according to the law! It turned out that she had died from a massive stroke – half of her brain had turned to liquid. This kind of death, most definitely from 'old age', is the kind many people wish for. It is a shocking but valuable experience to be in the presence of death.

Death in a Nut

*(This story is from the great Scottish traveller storyteller **Duncan Williamson** who died in 2007. I learnt it from the book Death in a Nut by Eric Maddern and Paul Hess,[297] and repeat it here with grateful thanks to them all).*

Once upon a time there was a boy called Jack who lived with his mother in a cottage by the sea. Jack helped his mother tend the vegetable garden and look after the goat and chickens. He loved to walk on the beach and collect driftwood and other interesting things. One day he got up and his mum was still in bed – he went into her and she was very sick and pale in bed. 'I'm very ill, Jack. I think Old Man Death will come for me soon!'. 'O no, mum, please don't say that – I couldn't bear to do without you, I'd be all alone in the world.' 'I know, Jack, it's hard for you. But you're young; you'll get married and have your own family. I'm sorry, but I'm so tired, I must sleep now.'

Jack went off to the beach, devastated. As he walked along by the sea's edge, he saw an old man coming towards him, carrying a scythe. It was the Grim Reaper – Old Man Death himself. As he got close to Jack, he asked 'do you know the way to the cottage by the sea?' and Jack said, 'that's my mother's cottage. You can't go there!' But Death said, 'she is ill and in pain, she needs me. It's her

---

[296] This is in order to eliminate foul play.
[297] Eric Maddern and Paul Hess *Death in a Nut*.

time to go.' 'No!' shouted Jack. You can't take my mother.' And he took Death's scythe and snapped it in two. 'You've done it now' said Death, and they began to fight. But the strange thing was, every time Jack hit him, the old man got smaller and smaller. Soon Jack had him in the palm of his hand. He found a hazel nut the squirrels had eaten, and stuffed Old Man Death's head first through the hole and into the nut, then plugged the hole with a stick. There he had him – Death in a nut! Jack threw the nut as far as he could out to sea. 'There. You won't get my mum now!'

When Jack returned home, his mum was in the kitchen making scones. She said a wind had come through the cottage and left her feeling fine. 'Why don't you fetch some eggs for our breakfast, Jack? So Jack went off to find the eggs, without telling his mother about Old Man Death.   When she tried to crack the egg on the side of the frying pan, 'clunk!' it went, and wouldn't break. 'Clunk, clunk, clunk.' She tried again and again, but the eggs would not crack. 'How strange' she said. 'The eggs have all gone off. Go and get me some vegetables from the garden and I'll make some soup for dinner.' So Jack brought in some leeks and carrots and turnips. But when his mother tried to slice them, the knife slipped straight off, as if they were frozen solid. 'But we haven't had a frost for months'. 'Ok then, you'll have to kill the cockerel, and we'll have him for dinner instead' said Jack's mother. So Jack caught the cockerel and tried to wring his neck – but no matter how he tried, the neck of that cockerel kept unwringing itself! He took the cockerel in to his mum, and she chopped off his head. The head came off – then flew right back on the cockerel's neck again! Again and again, Jack's mother tried to kill the cockerel; but he simply would not die.

'How strange!' said Jack's mother. 'Well, go to town and buy some chops for supper from the butcher' and she gave Jack half a crown, and off he went. In the town, Jack saw a big crowd of people in the Square, but he ignored them and ran into the butchers to ask for his chops. But the butcher had none. Every time he'd tried to kill a cow that morning, the cow had jumped right up again. Jack told him about trying to kill the cockerel – 'you tried to kill one, well I tried to kill ten!' exclaimed the butcher. 'It is all very strange – it's as if nothing will die!'

At that, Jack realised it was something HE had done. He ran home and told his mother all about putting Old Man Death into the nut. 'O dear, Jack,' said his mum. 'You shouldn't have done that. We need Death to live – you better go and find that nut and let him out!' So Jack went and walked along the beach, looking for the nut. He was tired and hungry and cold, and he walked for three days and nights searching for the nut. In despair, he sat by the water's edge. Suddenly he saw it – the nut! He picked it up and pulled out the plug. Out came the Grim Reaper, and as he came out he grew back to his full size. 'You thought you could be rid of me, that without me there would be no troubles in the world. But without me, my boy, there can be no life.' He asked for his scythe, and Jack told him 'my mother made me mend it. It's by our house'. So they went up to the cottage and Jack handed Death his scythe. The Old Man tested the blade with his thumb and said 'you've done a good job Jack. And because you've been fair with me, I'll leave your mother alone for a while.' And he disappeared.

After that, Jack's mother lived to a ripe old age, and when Death finally came for her, Jack didn't mind so much, because he had learned that without Death there can be no Life.

The grieving process

It is not only those people who are close to the dying person who grieve. The person dying also undergoes the grieving process to some degree or other, depending on their feelings about their life. As we near death, receive catastrophic news, or go through some type of life-altering experience we go through various stages of grief. Elisabeth Kübler-Ross defines five stages of grief. These steps don't always come in order, and are not always experienced all together by everyone, although Kübler-Ross observes that a person will always experience at least two of the stages.

The five stages of grief

- *Denial* – it can't be happening to me. It must be a mistake.
- *Anger* – Why me? It's not fair, someone is to blame.
- *Bargaining* – if I do this, it won't happen. Let me live to see my child grown and I'll (do whatever) in return.
- *Depression* – extreme sadness, lack of motivation or desire to fight anymore. When one melts into this, the big healing tears come with the feelings of loss.
- *Acceptance* – at last comes the feeling that this is the right time; all is well, I accept.

Meditation on death

As I have said, in many cultures it is the norm to be very aware of death, and to meditate on ones own inevitable death in some way. In Stephen's Levine's book *Who Dies – an Exploration of Conscious Living and Conscious Dying*, many ways of working with pain and impending death are presented with compassion and great humanity. You might like to try for yourself a taste of something of the sort.

Sitting comfortably, your body supported and having taken care to ensure no interruptions, begin by breathing in and out, in and out. Be aware of your body, its sensations, its aches and pains. You are your body, but you are more than your body.

Be aware of your mind, your thoughts: fast or slow, fleeting or persistent. Watch your thoughts. You are your thoughts, but you are more than your thoughts. Who is watching your thoughts? Become the watcher.

Think about your life with compassion and love. Think about your parents. You are their son or daughter – but you are more than that. Think of your children, your family. You are a parent, a spouse. Think of your work. You are a .... But you are more than your work. When you retire, you still live.

Who is it that will die?

Near Death Experiences

Near death experiences are experienced by about 10% of people who come close to death. The kinds of things people experience are traveling down a dark tunnel towards a bright light, seeing their own body from above, experiencing vivid memories, entering another world and meeting loved ones, gods, angels, spirits. Some people have mystical experiences of melting into the oneness of the universe. Materialistic scientists (i.e., those who do not accept the existence of the Spirit) say that all these experiences can be accounted for by the disorganized activity of the dying brain. This argument does not convince those who have had the experience, or the many people who believe that the soul has an existence which does not depend on the body. Some people who have had a near death experience have seen details of the hospital ward or accident scene which, being unconscious, they could not have seen with their physical eyes. Skeptics say that the brain changes the timing of these events to make the person feel they happened after the clinical death, when in fact they happened before. Helen Graham's book *Soul Medicine* begins with a description of what happened to her sister's friend who was struck down by a mystery virus and lay in a coma. Doctors said she was brain dead and would not survive long off intensive care and life support, but soon after she was moved to a normal ward she recovered consciousness. She had experienced being out of her body. She knew things she could not have known about things that happened as she lay in coma – like knowing a nurse had had a new haircut – she could not have seen the old one while she was awake. She also knew things no-one else yet knew, like the fact that her daughter was pregnant and that she would give birth to a girl.

MRI scans of a dying person have never been taken, to see exactly what happens in the brain and body. To a tribal person living with experience of an Ancestral tradition, all this speculation is hilarious – the existence of the ancestors is not taken on blind faith or on the threat of punishment from some distant god or religious authority, but is directly experienced throughout life.

Religious Attitudes to Death

What follows is a totally oversimplified in-a-nutshell look at death from various religious perspectives. Again, each one could be a book in itself and to really penetrate the mystery of it all would take longer than any of us have got in this life. Please be very sure that I have missed out much of importance in my clumsy attempt to give an overview of religious attitudes to death.

Buddhists see death as the breaking apart of the material which we are made of, and as an awakening to our true nature. The dying person's state of mind is of great importance. After death, we may return to the human world, or enter a pure world of bliss, or if we achieve enlightenment, merge with the ultimate nature of mind. Having said that, there are many different schools of Buddhism each with different takes on death. We can't really understand death from a Buddhist perspective from the outside, partly because Buddhism has a very deep take on who we really are that is completely different to our Western way. We are both the self and not the self; there is no abiding self. In a sense, 'you can never die because you were never born'. Then there is the matter of not being able to grasp Buddhism with the intellectual mind to further complicate things…

Christians believe that if you embrace Jesus Christ as your 'saviour', you will go to Heaven, and that a time will come when Christ returns to earth and all true believers will be fully resurrected in the body. There is 'a time to be born, and a time to die' (Ecclesiastes 3:2). Anyone who has not embraced Christ goes to Hell, so missionaries try to 'save' everyone.

Hindus believe in reincarnation; you die, and your spirit leaves the body but will return again in another body. So death is not a calamity but a natural process of the soul. After death, a person may take the path of the sun and merge with the light, not returning to a body. If a person takes the path of the moon, she or he returns to a new body, the status and fortunes of this next life depending on his deeds and actions in his life, and whether her children performed proper funeral rites. Hinduism believes in many heavens and hells, and many Gods and Goddesses being an expression of the great Divine. Hindus cremate the dead in order to help the release of the soul. Hindus in mourning do not celebrate festivals for a period of time as a mark of respect. This gives the mourners time to fully grieve before returning to normal life.

Judaism sees death as natural, and as giving meaning to life. Since Hashem (literally 'The Name' – so called because the name of G-d is considered too holy to say or write in Judaism) is ultimately just, the afterlife must give ultimate justice and redress any apparent unfairness about life. In Paradise we finally understand the truth of Hashem. Hell is a greater distance from God, heaven is to be with God. Judaism does not believe a Jew will go to heaven and a Gentile to hell, rather that individual ethical behaviour is what's most important.

Muslims gather round to comfort the dying. Burial happens as soon as possible. The body is laid on the right side, facing Mecca. A person faces judgement from Allah on death. The family of the dead must pay debts as soon as possible, and maintain close and courteous relationships with each other. Prayer and supplication for the deceased is essential, along with visiting graves – the living should remember death and the day of judgement. Only true believers have a chance of Paradise, therefore it is important to spread the religion.

The Old Ways of **shamanism** or **paganism**, where they still exist, usually consider reincarnation to be what happens; the soul or spirit leaving the body after death. It is possible for a spirit to be stuck in this world – this is a ghost. The correct funeral rites are essential to take care of and help the spirit in its journey. Spirits often will return to the tribe for future lives. Without proper funeral rites we do not return to the same place – we can be born into any different tribe or culture (this is what has happened to almost all of us, and is the reason we can feel drawn to a completely foreign culture, even feeling more at home with it than with our own). Some souls remain in the next world, and will give what help they can as our Ancestors. Our Ancestors need our love and offerings, and we absolutely depend on their love and support.

SECTION TWO
HEALTH AND DISEASE

There are many models of health and disease in the world. In these three chapters we will look at the basics of orthodox Western pathology, then further explore what 'holistic' can mean and then take a brief look at mind/body medicine and healing. For those interested in systems which take a completely energetic view of health and disease, appendices A & B introduce the energy-based models of shamanism and the five element system of classical Chinese medicine.

CHAPTER TWENTY-ONE

A BRIEF INTRODCTION TO WESTERN PATHOLOGY

Western pathology is basically an understanding about what is going on in the tissues when things go wrong. It is brilliant in its way; it has taken the art of looking at the physical, molecular level of the body to figure out exactly what is going wrong in a particular disease to a fairly deep level, in a relatively short space of time. Enormous breakthroughs in physiology have occurred over the last hundred or so years, and more knowledge is being uncovered all the time. However, at present, it has a great weakness which can mostly be traced to its failure to incorporate quantum understanding of the nature of matter and energy into it's theories, remaining wedded to the Newtonian perspective of man and universe as machine.[298]

Causes of Disease

Some diseases are classified as being **organic** – these are the ones where it is possible to see a definite change in the tissues and cells, for example, ulceration or inflammation. Some diseases are not possible (yet) to 'see' in this way – these are called **inorganic disease**. There was a time when most were lumped into a strange category called 'all in the mind', which at the same time seemed to mean they didn't really exist. As physical imaging and other diagnostic techniques have become more sophisticated, and more understanding of the physiology of stress has emerged, things have been changing. There is an attempt at moving towards holism developing in orthodox medicine (at any rate, they certainly try and use the word a lot!); any good anatomy, physiology and pathology textbook, for example, now takes a look at how the systems interrelate rather than simply looking at them as separate areas.

Having said that, the most common way of classifying diseases is in terms of the body system which they primarily involve. This means there is a tendency to compartmentalize pathology. The health services are also compartmentalised – you will see one doctor for your leg, another for your gut – and still another for your shoulder. Joined up medicine has not arrived quite yet. Of course GPs (general physicians) are by definition generalists. And while, say, kidney disease is classed under nephrology, specialists will be aware of the affect of, and

---

[298] Bruce Lipton *The Biology of Belief.*

effects on the rest of the body, and while cardiovascular pathology may come under a different department the patient will be referred. There have been articles written in the medical field of the need to more closely integrate the different services for someone with kidney disease, so there are joins there. It is perhaps more the case that as a whole orthodox doctors are unaware of the more subtle interactions – for example of diet, stress and lifestyle – only taking gross imbalances of these as being of any importance.

The problem with Western medicine is not with pathology; it is more with the fact that it tends to see the first line changes in tissues as *being* the disease. A list of 'causes' reveals not a deep probing into whys and wherefores, but more a series of 'hows'. For example, one cause of disease is inflammation, but inflammation as a cause of disease (and there are very many inflammatory diseases) really just describes what is going on in the tissues. As we discussed in the chapter on the immune system, it is possible to take a very deep look at the causes of infection in terms of looking at the terrain – the condition of the body – but the current orthodox line is that viruses, bacteria, fungi etc. (the mediators of infection) *are* the cause.

The body is seen as a machine. This is, as John Ball says in *Understanding Disease (a Health Practitioners Handbook)*, both its strength and its failure. No one questions the brilliance of Western medicine in life-saving situations – when you are smashed up in an accident it can put you back together and keep you alive so you can heal, or in extreme acute illness, it can keep you alive until your body can figure out righting things. It is in chronic illness where its weakness lies, and in over-treating acute illness, which would have been self-limiting, thereby causing problems for the future. Also it uses medicines which, while they may affect the particular 'target', are largely incompatible with the body, working to control a part of it rather than working with it, hence causing damage elsewhere. This is the classic mistake of treating the symptoms rather than the cause.

Here is a list of causes of disease, into which it is possible to categorize most orthodox diagnoses:

Infections are one classic cause of disease; micro-organisms like bacteria, viruses, fungi, yeasts, parasites have got into the body and are using it as a host, causing problems to it. Louis Pasteur, the father of modern microbiology, said on his deathbed, 'le terrain c'est tout' (the terrain is everything), meaning the state of the body decides whether you get ill. The micro-organisms are only taking advantage of an already weakened system. Unfortunately, modern medicine has disregarded this gem in favour of seeing the microbes as the enemy to be killed at any cost.

Immune disorders, including auto-immunity, allergies and cancer. Cancer can be considered as a failure of the immune system, because with so much cell replication going on all the time in the body, mistakes and mutations are inevitable – so the production of cancerous cells occurs normally within us. If our immune system is happy and functioning well, these cells will be quickly disposed of before they can make a nuisance of themselves.

Auto-immune diseases involve the immune system launching an attack on parts of oneself and allergies involve the immune system being too aggressive in dealing with harmless substances the body comes in contact with.

Trauma, or physical damage to organs and tissues. This can be mechanical trauma, like being run over by a bus or being slowly damaged by repetitive work, or chemical trauma such as happens from environmental toxins like coal dust, asbestos, smoke, pesticides and food additives.

Stress. Yes, it's official, Western pathology can see that some diseases are caused by stress, and many are aggravated by it. You will recall from our section on the sympathetic nervous system how systemic our reaction to stress is.

Nutritional factors, including malnutrition from lack of food and diseases caused by too much of the wrong sort of food. It's interesting that we have now in the West many people with the problem of obesity who are also malnourished,[299] in the sense of lacking in vitamins and minerals and other essential nutrients.

Iatrogenic: a 'doctor induced' disease – that is, caused by the treatment used for another disease. Iatrogenic disease includes problems which come from side effects of drugs, medical mistakes and accidents, and things like picking up an infection in hospital. For example, a person may be given steroids for asthma and develop osteoporosis as a result. The osteoporosis is an iatrogenic disease. Iatrogenic disease is between the third and first cause of death in the USA, and between the third and fourth in the UK.[300]

Congenital and inherited disease: This includes a wide range of abnormalities ranging from Down's syndrome and Turner's syndrome, to haemophilia and sickle cell anaemia. Also, many diseases seem to run in families, so have an inherited factor, including eczema, arthritis and some cancers. There is a school of thought popular now that puts everything down to genes – if we can isolate the gene responsible for an illness and change or eradicate it, we can conquer that disease. It is very likely that our genes give us the propensity to one type of illness or another, however this does not mean that the genes are 'causing' that disease. Genes themselves are turned on and off by environmental triggers. Most diseases still seem to need environmental triggers of some kind to manifest.

Degeneration: the aging process, wear and tear. An interesting area, since so much of aging is culturally dependant and strongly interwoven with our beliefs and feelings. Some very interesting research has been done showing that the signs of aging, including joint thickening, poor eyesight, hearing loss and decreasing memory, can be reversed under circumstances which change a person's attitudes and focus. Also good to remember is that two

---

[299] According to Terry Pratchett this is due to the rider of the apocalypse called Famine having to be more creative in the Western world – see Terry Pratchett and Neil Gaimon's *Good Omens*!

[300] According to Dr. Barbara Starfield of the Johns Hopkins School of Hygiene and Public Health, 250,000 deaths per year are caused by medical errors, making this the third leading cause of death (after cancer and heart disease) of Americans. This research was published in the Journal of the American Medical Association in May 2007.

people may have the same level and type of degeneration, for example, worn away cartilage in the hip joint; whilst one person is in terrible pain and cannot walk, the other hardly has any symptoms at all. Symptoms and signs are not necessarily closely related.[301]

Of course some diseases are very tricky to fit into these classifications. Western pathology has a great category called 'idiopathic disease' – this is a disease having an unknown cause or mechanism. Sometimes problems come about from lifestyle, like pressure sores and wasting in people who are very sedentary. Mental and psychological 'diseases' are often seen as being completely different and separate from physical diseases by orthodox medicine, whilst at the same time the trend is to assume biochemical changes are the cause of everything. I explore this further in chapter twenty-three.

Various disease states

Western pathology focuses on changes in the tissues that come about in disease states – hence a **pathologist** is someone who studies diseases. The term also refers to those people who cut up dead people to examine their tissues and organs to see why they died. Other more holistic systems of medicine usually focus more on what has happened in order to allow the diseased tissue state to arise than on the condition of the tissues themselves.

Various disease states that can be observed in the tissues of the body include such things as inflammation, cell damage or death, and abnormal cell growth. Cells can become swollen and look cloudy, can actually die and break down completely, can abnormally accumulate fat, and can atrophy (that is, shrink in size or number if the word is referring to tissues). One very simple example of atrophy is what happens to skeletal muscles which aren't used. When you break your leg and it is in plaster for weeks without you weight-bearing on it, it will be noticeably smaller and more flaccid than the other leg when the plaster is taken off. Below we will take a closer look at inflammation, which is one of the most universal cell and tissue responses to problematic circumstances.

Inflammation

Many diseases involve inflammation. Inflammation is interesting because, although it often causes many if not all of the symptoms of a disease, it is in itself an important part of the body's healing mechanism. When tissues are damaged or infected, white blood cells are attracted to them in large numbers. First come the neutrophils and then the granulocytes, both releasing their chemicals to encourage and increase the inflammatory process (histamine, prostaglandins and others). These cause the capillaries to dilate and become more permeable, allowing protein-rich fluid containing nutrients and building blocks for repair to

---

[301] A symptom is something you feel and report; a sign is something which can be seen or measured by another. For example, pain is a symptom, swelling is a sign.

leave the blood and enter the tissues, along with many white blood cells which will be able to fight any infection and clean up debris from damage. This fluid also dilutes toxic or harmful substances. The swelling also slows down the spread of infection as clotting factors in the tissue spaces turn the whole thing into a gel, making it more difficult for micro-organisms to move freely. This is the underlying mechanism behind the swelling you get when you bang your knee, for example.

The classic signs of inflammation are:
- **Swelling** (from extra fluid in the tissue spaces).
- **Heat** (blood brings heat, so with the extra activity going on things heat up).
- **Redness** (extra blood in the area).
- **Pain** (from the pressure on nerve endings caused by the swelling).
- **Loss of function** (well, it hurts and it's swollen, so you can't use it as normal).

You can see that although it causes troublesome symptoms for us, inflammation is in fact one of the body's most important healing mechanisms: without it, healing does not happen well. Research has shown, for example, that people taking anti-inflammatory drugs have significantly slower healing time for broken bones. The research hasn't been done on other healing times, but it is logically likely that all healing times are slowed down by anti-inflammatories (in fact, sometimes healing is deliberately slowed down by application of steroid anti-inflammatory drugs, for example, in certain eye operations when it is important that healing happens slowly).

If all goes well, this inflammatory activity means any infection is soon got under control, and any damage is repaired with new cells and tissues. Then hoards of phagocytes (first neutrophils and basophils, then macrophages) that have entered the area clean up all the debris. Remaining white blood cells return to the blood and gradually the tissue returns to normal. This is called 'resolution'. Sometimes the body is not able to resolve the situation, and a chronic inflammation is set up. Sometimes an open sore, an ulcer, forms. Sometimes there is a lot of pus (an attractive mix of dead and alive bacteria and white blood cells!) which needs to be discharged from the wound for resolution to occur.

Infection is a common, but not the only, cause of inflammation. Trauma also causes it, and the naturopathic view is that build up of toxins in the body is a common cause, with the inflammation seen as the bodies attempt to remedy things. Many chronic illnesses are basically inflammatory, including arthritis, asthma, eczema and coronary artery disease (which causes heart attacks).

Various states of inflammation are occurring all the time in the body. They are largely mediated through chemicals called **eicosanoids**, which also mediate their resolution. Remember this from our discussion on essential fatty acids in the chapter on nutrition and diet? Basically, animal fats are used to make the pro-inflammatory eicosanoids, and essential fatty acids – from fish oils, nuts and seeds and green vegetables – are used to make the anti-inflammatory ones. The diet of our ancestors contained a lot more oils and fewer fats. The modern diet is quite the reverse, so most of us are pushing our bodies more towards inflammation than away from it. Changing the diet away from animal products and towards vegetables and fish can tip the balance back and lead to the end of a chronic inflammation.

One way for the body to resolve a chronic inflammation is to turn up the inflammatory response back into an acute phase – all the extra activity can help resolution. Traditional treatments which use this route of healing include deep heat, mustard plasters, and stinging an inflamed joint with nettles; an old country cure for arthritis involved rolling naked in a bed of nettles in the springtime (although one hopes they covered their genitals first at least!).

The phagocytotic white blood cells will always try to keep any infection inside themselves. You can get a situation where monocytes will be infected, not be able to destroy the invading organism, but keep it inside them. A bunch of infected monocytes can be surrounded by a bunch of normal ones, and sometimes even the whole thing is then further walled off by a connective tissue capsule. This can happen in TB of the lungs, when a 'granuloma' like this forms, keeping the TB separated from the rest of the body, while still not able to be rid of it. Such a situation can remain for many years, until at a time when the immune system is low, it is not able to keep it controlled and the infection breaks out and spreads through the body.

This is a very extreme example, but actually 'low grade infections' of all kinds can exist in the body for years. A very common focal point for these is the mouth – a niggling tooth, for example. Also viruses like the herpes family can linger in a dormant state then flare up into an active infection at times of stress – this is the cause of shingles, cold sores and genital herpes.

Diagnosis and Symptoms

Many diseases are named with an impressive sounding Latin name which in fact is merely a description of what is happening. Yet we are generally conditioned to be reassured by such diagnoses (or scared by them depending how bad it is). Generally it makes us respect the practitioner more if they give us a nice little tag for our disease – especially if we can barely pronounce the name. You go to the doctors with an illness, and you walk away with a disease! Ah, it's bronchitis – the tubes of the lung are inflamed; aha, it's irritable bowel syndrome – the guts are not working properly but no ulcer or growth or abnormality in the tissues can be found.

Diagnosis is generally about gathering enough information about symptoms and signs to get an accurate picture of what is going on and come up with the right label. There are of course some uses in having the label: it may be possible to get a fairly accurate picture of what is going on in the body and what can be expected if things don't alter. The expected course or progress of a disease is called the **prognosis**.

Symptomatic treatment

Most treatments in orthodox medicine are deemed successful if they effectively eliminate the symptoms of disease. On the other hand, holistic systems see symptoms as being not the be-all and end-all, but the warning light on your car; if the warning light goes on when you are driving your car, do you stop and disconnect it then drive on, happy that the light is no longer on? If so, you will not then be surprised when some serious problem occurs. Yet we have gone along with the simplistic idea that if a drug has got rid of our symptoms, the problem is gone – even though the drug may cause other conditions, and do nothing to eliminate the cause of the initial problem. Thus iatrogenic disease thrives.

!!!RED FLAG CONDITIONS!!!
(meaning, symptoms never to ignore)

Depending on your level of training, this will be more or less known knowledge for you. Many holistic systems of medicine have complete methods of diagnostic and treatment that do not refer to pathological tissue states at all. However, the holistic therapist or healer needs to be thoroughly aware of those 'red flag' conditions for which a person is best referred immediately to their physician. Without this, it might be safer to have the practice of always referring every prospective patient for a medical check-up of symptoms before agreeing to take them on. Sometimes the sledgehammer of orthodox medicine will save a life when an imbalance has moved far into the tissues, or a person does not have the strength or resource to effect changes quickly enough to mobilize their innate healing ability. This does not mean that the person would not also benefit from treatment by a holistic system at the same time, however.

Below is a list of such red flag symptoms and signs – not a comprehensive list, but a beginning. The practitioner is always best to be on the alert to the possibility of serious disease.

- Abnormal bleeding – although by no means always indicative of serious disease, and it is not necessary to whip up fear in your patients about this,[302] bleeding in an unexpected place should always be investigated. This includes bleeding from the vagina which occurs outside the normal menstrual cycle, bleeding from the rectum (unless it is known that the person has haemorrhoids or 'piles', which should also be investigated if the bleeding is prolonged or excessive) and blood in the urine, as well as coughing up blood or blood in vomit.
- Stools which look like black coffee grounds – this indicates the presence of partly digested blood from higher up the gut.
- Loss of appetite/increased appetite.
- Sudden weight loss without dieting .
- Weight gain when dieting.

---

[302] Unless carrying out 'emotion testing' in the way of the five elements! See Appendix A.

- Sudden change in bowel habit – although a person with IBS (irritable bowel syndrome) may have constant changes in bowel habit without any sinister implications, bowel cancer can show itself with a change in bowel habit. Be very suspicious if a person who has usually been regular experiences rapid and lasting changes without there being any major change in their diet.
- Unexplained vomiting.
- Lumps and bumps can be cancer, although not necessarily. Of course, if you agree with Dr Hamer[303] about emotional shock and conflict causing cancer, you might think it not to a person's interest to fall into the hands of the orthodox system! At the same time, let's say the cancer was caused by emotional shock or trauma, unless you can give that person sound advice on how to effectively remedy the situation, telling the person that may be worse than useless. No matter what your thoughts about cause, you would be on very shaky ethical and legal ground if you did not refer someone who had an unidentified lump. It always the person's individual choice to decide what to do, should it be found that cancer is indeed present.
- Difficulty in swallowing which can be (but isn't definitely) caused by a tumour.
- A headache which began gradually and got worse and worse and doesn't go away, or any other kind of pain like this.
- Exhaustion and tiredness which do not very quickly respond to your treatment – common medical causes (excluding overwork, stress, depression and lack of sleep!) include anaemia and under-active thyroid, but more sinister underlying disease is possible.
- Changes in sleeping patterns.
- Interrupted vision of any kind, or pain in, around or behind the eye.
- Persistent cough or breathing difficulties.
- Waking up in the night unable to breath or in paroxysms of coughing, then feeling better for sitting upright (this can be due to heart failure).
- Failure to produce adequate urine.
- Constipation which does not respond to treatment – after not opening the bowels for a week, a person can become very ill.

There are others of course. It is worth repeating here to make sure it sticks that any ill person should be seen by a ***fully trained professional*** and that signs and symptoms can be easily confused or overlooked. Remember that a little knowledge can be a dangerous thing and don't let your ego get carried away thinking you know more than you really do. At its best orthodox medicine *is* lifesaving.

---

[303] http://www.newmedicine.ca

Chapter Twenty-two

TOWARDS A HOLISTIC PARADIGM

A paradigm is a world-view, a belief structure. There are quite a few to choose from, although you wouldn't think it from what is available in the mainstream. We usually get quite attached to our own, and very easily think it is the only one. In fact, we usually don't even see it as a 'paradigm'; it's just how things are. If we do recognize it as a paradigm, we like to think it is the only sensible one. Here we will begin to explore the various shades of the meaning of holism. This is intended as an introduction, a call to arms – or at least, to thinking. I am not answering all the questions here, but rather aiming to develop our concepts of what holistic medicine can mean. There is a lot of dilution going on of the meaning of 'holistic' as mainstream medicine tries to incorporate holistic ideas into its practice. This is good and worthy and will probably lead to less suffering for people being treated within that system; at the same time we need not settle for this dilution as if it meant that there is nothing much more to it.

Deeply holistic paradigms can challenge our existing belief structure if we are educated in the West – as I have said, Western orthodox medicine is unique in the world for not considering the spirit. Spirit is a difficult thing to define – yet somehow, we know what it means. One great description I have come across came via my teacher Eliot Cowan,[304] world renowned healer in the Five Element tradition:

Think of where your body has been today – all the movements it has made from when you woke up to the present moment. Even if it's early in the morning, your body will have been active all the time in one way or another. Now think of where your mind has been – where you have ranged in your thoughts. You will see that the movements of the mind so far exceed those of the body, that really there is no way for the body to keep up with the mind – the mind is too fast for the body to grasp. Well, your spirit is to your mind what your mind is to your body – the mind simply has no way to grasp the spirit, the spirit is too vast, too fast, too beyond, for the mind to get more than a now and then glimpse of it. Yet many of us have had experiences where we came close to feeling things in our spirit – highs, peak experiences, moments of deep peace, deep joy, connection, serendipity.

Thomas Moore also writes eloquently of the soul or spirit in his books.

---

[304] To find out more about Eliot Cowan's work you can take a look at *Plant Spirit Medicine – The Healing Power of Plants*.

Causes of disease

For most systems of medicine in the world, the spirit is in charge, healing must happen *in* the spirit and healing comes *from* the spirit. At heart, holism says that a person is a whole, and also is a part of the greater Whole. Because we are deeply connected both within ourselves and with everyone and everything else in the universe, all these influences, within and without, affect us. You are your body, but you are more than your body: your thoughts and feelings affect your physical reality far more than you may realize. You do not exist in isolation: your relationships, from the beginning of your life to the present, have formed and continue to form you. If your family is sick, you are affected. If your community is sick, you are affected. If your society is sick, you are affected.

As we said above, infections are one classic cause of disease; one would think this would be a straightforward case, micro-organisms like bacteria, viruses, fungi, yeasts or parasites (nits, worms), have got into the body and are using us as a host, causing problems to us. But go a little deeper, and you will want to know – what happened to upset our balance so that micro-organism got in and caused trouble? If you get a bunch of people and literally paint cultured cold virus directly onto the membranes in their nose, only a minority of them (20%) will get the cold.[305] You cannot change this figure by giving them wet feet or blowing cold air down their backs. It seems quite a low figure, doesn't it? (Although there is reasearch that shows gettings chills can double your chance of catching a cold).

Louis Pasteur, the father of modern microbiology, said on his deathbed, 'le terrain c'est tout' (the terrain is everything). In other words, it's not the infectious organism that causes the disease, but the condition of the person affected. Unfortunately, Pasteur's followers were already excitedly rushing off on the path of finding something to kill the invading organisms, and this is the path which orthodox medicine is still stuck on. The result of all this is MRSA and other 'super bugs', an increase in allergies and other signs of impaired immunity, plus the as yet unknown effects of pharmacological pollution.

Do you get a cold if someone with one sneezes on you? Why is that? Is your immune system really so low – is it to do with what you eat, with high stress levels? Why are you stressed? Is it from your life now, or because emotional trauma in your childhood has left you more vulnerable to stress? Is it simply because you believe you will get a cold? Is it because you really need a few days in bed to rest and take stock? Is it that your immune system is in good enough shape to throw up an acute illness, to help you detox…creating a fever and lot of copious mucous is one way to give your body a good clear out? In other words, is it a sign of weakness to get this cold, or a sign of strength?

To be truly holistic, a physician or healer must make space to think about and try to understand all the factors operating on a person's life (whilst realising that, at least on the conscious level, we can never understand everything, and that understanding is not the only

---

[305] Deepak Chopra *Quantum Health*.

source of healing). Even on the apparently straightforward physical level, we can ask what is going on in each organ and system of the body. The traditional case history of modern medicine includes a 'systemic enquiry' into just this.

To take a detailed medical history of a mature adult will usually take *at least* fifty minutes, and often turns up some things which a naturopath or herbalist will connect. Let's take, as an example, a person who has osteoarthritis (wear and tear of the hyaline cartilage causing inflammation and pain). The orthodox treatment for this will be drug therapy – anti-inflammatories and pain killers, which all have varying degrees of side effects.[306] A medical herbalist or naturopath who spends an hour or more taking a full case history [307] finds that the person is also constipated and has a poor circulation. Constipation leads to build up of toxins in the body, which can lead to inflammation of the joints. You will remember that cartilage has no direct blood supply of its own to carry away toxins, getting its nutrients from the synovial fluid and underlying bone. Bowel function can be improved and the circulation stimulated by herbs, exercise and massage. These things, added to removal of toxins from and addition of good quality nutrients to the diet, will have a huge effect on the person's symptoms. A naturopath may use chiropractic or osteopathic techniques to balance the bony and muscular body, creating a better alignment – poor physical alignment puts extra pressure on joints and can cause damage. Release of muscular tension around a joint reduces compression and therefore decreases damage and encourages regeneration of the cartilage.

So even looking purely on the physical level, you can see that one can attempt to be holistic, rather than simply acting to stop the symptom without addressing the cause of a problem. Then there is the emotional and spiritual level to consider.

A five element practitioner or a homeopath might take more like two hours to take a detailed history, which will include emotional history, the highs and lows of ones life, likes and dislikes – an attempt to feel into the spirit. Stephen H. Buhner[308] brilliantly describes the technique of using the heart as an instrument of perception – literally feeling into the physical, mental and spiritual reality of another person to 'diagnose' where and how things aren't right. Shamanic practitioners use the dream journey and trance state to gather information about the spirit of their patients.

So as you can imagine, there are many questions for the holistic therapist to consider. What are people eating? How are their stress levels? Do they have families in good shape, time to spend with loved ones, children, and friends, time to play and have fun? Do they have safe affordable places to live, a life free of worry? Do they have access to good, clean water? What

---

[306] A person with osteoarthritis which has been found on x-ray is usually told that the condition is irreversible and nothing can be done for them.

[307] Which might be done even in the medical model, but which is no longer used by GPs who have about 5-8 minutes for each consultation.

[308] *The Secret Teachings of Plants.*

about residues of pesticides and artificial fertilizers in water and foods? Food additives? What about air pollution? Toxic build up in the environment of chemicals in toiletries, paint, clothes dyes, furniture, drugs? Do people have a feeling of being connected, of belonging, of a meaningful purpose for their lives? Is a person's work meaningful, useful, and contributing to the good of the whole? Are they treated with love and respect, are they valued, at work and at home? What is at the heart of their problem? Where is their heart at?

These questions and more belong in a discussion of holistic health. You can I am sure already see that for most of us, there are not positive answers to these questions. Holistic medicine, taken as far as it can go, cannot simply mean adding on a nice 'treatment' to existing orthodox healthcare – although this is not to dismiss the value of lying in a darkened room being rubbed while nice tinkley music plays!

Society's imbalance impacts on our health

One weakness of the 'new age' paradigm is its failure to take on the general problems of the dominant cultures – there is an idea that if we can get everything right for ourselves this will be enough. Well, we can get most things right for ourselves over time, but to go for total healing, global healing is needed, and this means radical change in the way societies are set up. A truly holistic medicine, for example, could never be driven by hunger for profit as are the pharmaceutical companies, which drive and fund most research into medicine.

If you are thinking holistically, can you really use a treatment to save one person's life that will create pollution and damage many others', including generations to come? This is a very difficult question, and I am not suggesting there is a clear-cut answer, but it is a question worth asking. At what price are we prepared to save one life, and why? Is our inability to accept death actually creating more death in the future?

Pharmaceutical pollution

Pharmaceutical drugs are designed to be stable in the body, to not easily break down, for stronger and longer lasting effects. They are 55-90% excreted whole in the urine. Tap water in cities is recycled over and over from sewage plants, and filtration systems are not set up to remove pharmaceutical substances. Therefore, antidepressants, anti-convulsants, anti-cancer drugs, antibiotics, HRT, steroids, statins and drugs for high blood pressure have all been found in measurable amounts in tap water in cities. It is not known how the increasing numbers of these drugs in the world's water table will affect us – or all the creatures of the earth and seas, from bacteria and single celled organisms up. When streams were tested at random in the US, 80% were found to contain some antibiotics, steroids, synthetic hormones or other common drugs.[309]

---

[309] Study conducted in 1999-2000 by the U.S. Geological Survey (USGS).

Lynn Roberts, leader of a Johns Hopkins team that began a study to determine the scope of pharmaceutical pollution in the United States, says "This is an important new research area. Over the past few years, scientists in Europe have found pharmaceuticals in natural waterways, sewage treatment effluents and even in drinking water. Yet until this year [2003] there have been virtually no scientific studies examining this issue in the United States. It's important that we begin to look at this because there are many ways in which pharmaceuticals in the environment could produce undesirable effects on aquatic organisms or even humans."[311]

And this is just the drugs. The whole of technological medicine also pollutes heavily by the waste it produces – incineration of disposable plastics, and radiation waste, for example. Stephen H. Buhner's excellent book *the Lost Language of Plants* has a few chapters detailing this important area.

We are experimenting with the Earth, with our children and our children's children, by pouring huge quantities of toxins of all kinds into the environment. Contrast this to the attitude of many First American tribes – considered 'primitive' by our 'civilised'[312] society, these people have a philosophical outlook which makes it one's duty to consider the effects of any action on the next seven generations.

So environmental and ecological concerns must be a concern of the healer. A person can control what they put into themselves in the way of toxic food and drink and drugs. But we do not have the choice to keep away from harmful environmental pollution. Once toxic substances which do not biodegrade are in the world's water, they travel everywhere. Some of them have been found in the fat of polar bears at the North Pole. It begins to look as if some kind of political activism is necessary on the part of physicians and healers. Society needs to be changed in order to allow for peak health of us all.

While we are on the subject of changing society, let's consider one major social factor which has a huge impact on health and life expectancy worldwide. Poverty is the main killer in a lot of the world. Infectious diseases can take hold most aggressively in people whose immune systems are weakened from lack of adequate nutrition and from stress. Poor people in rich countries do not have access to the same quality of food (organic, for example). Cardiovascular disease, the biggest killer in the developed world, is particularly high in people of African heritage living in northern industrialized countries. People of African heritage are up against particularly vicious racism. These facts are related. I will say more on emotional stress and high blood pressure in the following chapter on emotional causes of disease – actually, once you start talking holistically, you will see it becomes more difficult to separate everything into neatly labelled topics…

---

[311] Lynn Roberts is an associate professor in the Department of Geography and Environmental Engineering of John Hopkins University, Baltimore USA.

[312] Mahatma Gandhi, when asked what he thought of Western civilization, responded by saying 'I think it would be a good idea'.

There is also a stress in witnessing the oppression and abuse of other people. What is the price we pay here in the rich North, knowing that our wealth is built on the extreme suffering and poverty of the economic South? Interestingly, the shamanic or energetic view would be that we are affected by the energy of this even if we are personally unaware of the facts – we are all connected after all.

I don't want to bang on too much here (on the other hand, why not, it needs banging on about); just to make the point that a person's inner harmony and access to full healing will be impaired in a grossly imbalanced society such as our own. This is not to say that there are not wonderful things about all societies. But there is a conspiracy of silence, it seems, when it comes to really taking a look at the reality of modern globalisation and capitalism and the price paid for it. A helpful perspective to take is one where we do not blame any group or individual – including ourselves – for the ills of today, instead seeing that societies have a way of perpetuating themselves due to the way people are brought up to fit into them. The more correct perspective is that the enemy is the oppressive unbalanced society itself, not any particular group – not even those groups that look like they have all the power. It is the society which needs to be changed, transformed.

People get hurt by the imbalances in our society. Look at individuals to see the imbalances of society writ small, and look at society to see the imbalances of individuals writ large. The people in power, the people in oppressive situations over other people, were not born wanting to hurt others – any more than we are born wanting to be hurt. Rather we are hurt in myriad ways in our upbringing, and learn to acquiesce with it over time as the only way we can figure out to behave. Due to our acquired imbalances, we continue to act in ways which support the unwholesomeness of our society. This applies to those in power as well as those currently in the oppressed position; history is full of examples of people overthrowing tyranny then setting up a new tyranny in its stead. Change must be more fundamental, and involve us all on a deep level. 'We must be the change we wish to see in the world'.[312]

Research

We need to do research in medicine because it is so full of misinformation and bullshit that it might be helpful to figure out what really works and what doesn't; what should be kept, what adapted and what abandoned. Old ideas that never really worked, new ideas that never really worked: each can become established practice which people are very loathe to let go of. The danger is there for so-called holistic or alternative therapies too.

Research models currently held up as good practice within medicine do not serve holistic health ideals well. The 'gold standard' of orthodox medicine is the double-blind placebo-controlled trial, or randomised controlled trial.

---

[312] Mahatma Gandhi.

People in a randomised study are divided into two groups, one given the active drug and one a placebo - a drug which has no expected treatment value and which looks and tastes as close as possible to the active drug. The people are allocated either active drug or placebo by a code usually generated by computer. The idea is that this randomisation makes up for any variation in each person's illness (like differences in severity or duration of symptoms), so allowing successful statistical evaluation of any difference between the two groups. The "double-blind" bit is that everything possible is done to make sure that neither the patient nor the researchers know which drug (active or placebo) each subject is receiving. The idea is that this ensures that the beliefs of the patient or researcher about whether or not they are getting 'the real thing' do not interfere with the results.

This one size fits all approach does not lend itself to herbal medicine or homeopathy, for example, which use a highly individual approach to prescribing. A trial in 1998 on Chinese herbal medicine for IBS showed improvement in two groups, one receiving standardized treatment and one individually tailored treatment. After sixteen weeks there was no difference between the two groups, but on follow-up fourteen weeks after the treatment ended, only the group who had received individualized treatment maintained improvement. This is a good example of evidence of the value of holistic, individual treatment which aims to treat underlying causes of disease – taking longer to resolve, but with lasting benefits.[313] Yet it was widely reported as showing that off the peg herbal treatment is as good as individualized treatment, because the longer term effects were not considered. It is not easy to design a randomized controlled trial to really investigate individual treatment. Research within complementary medicine is looking for new or adapted research models which can more effectively test holistic medicine.[314]

Other research paradigms are developing which can more properly measure the effectiveness of natural therapies.

One of these is 'narrative research'

Narrative research is basically about valuing and gathering people's stories about their experience. It is a fairly new research area in nursing where it is recognised that many human factors are important – medicine cannot simply be reduced to a one-size-fits-all treatment strategy divorced from people's experience. As Dr A M Carson [Head of School, School of Health, Social Care, Sports & Exercise Sciences North Wales Education Institute, Wrexham] told me:

'Narrative research is a co-operative enquiry that aims at developing and enhancing practice. It resists simplistic techniques, and instead proposes a holistic and organic process where all persons involved in the enquiry have the opportunity to become more conscious of who they are and what they are doing. While standard methodologies aim at the articulation of an objective or subjective reality, narratives want to develop a self-reflective critique of these

---

[313] Benoussan A et al. Treatment of irritable bowel syndrome with Chinese herbal medicine. JAMA 1998; 280:1585-9.
[314] Ally Broughton. Herbal Thymes December 2007; pages 29-30.

realities. As such, narrative research is never neutral about its aims and practices, but tries to define these practices in an ethically coherent way.'

What is 'ultimate health'?

A key part of holistic health paradigms is a definition of health. What is it? Holistic systems do not define health as the absence of disease. Mostly, a model of a fully healthy human is given: full of energy and zest; feeling connected and happy; more accurately deeply contented, with our lives and with our well-functioning bodies; interested and involved in many things, with a deep sense of the rightness of our existence and the goodness of the universe; enjoying work and play in a balanced manner, with healthy relationships, balanced diet and exercise programs; taking care of our planet, knowing our deep connection with each other and with all life; working to restore, and then to cherish and wonder at the awesome splendour of nature.

For most of us, this is not how we feel a great deal of the time, though we may not have a labelled 'health condition' defined by modern medicine. The drug companies (and cosmetics companies, food companies, and, well, everyone!) are trying to cash in on how bad we feel by inventing more and more 'conditions' requiring 'treatment' – drugs for 'personality disorders' and to boost sexual performance to extreme levels, for example. This is ignoring the cause of our problems. So what can 'holistic' paradigms offer regarding 'treatments' – what can we do to feel better, to reclaim our human birthright of zest?

The next chapter takes a deeper look at emotional considerations, how emotional hurts affect us and what can be done to fully recover from past hurts. After this are two appendices which briefly discuss two holistic models; the five element system from classical Chinese medicine and the shamanic perspective. These are by no means the only valuable methods, simply the examples of completely holistic systems which I know most about and can therefore present intelligently. They are also of particular interest because there is a strong emphasis on placing the person into the context of family, community and society – with a viewpoint that sees the imbalances in the family, the community and the wider society impacting heavily on the individual – rather than a model which sees people as being somehow inherently flawed and prone to illness and unhappiness.

CHAPTER TWENTY-THREE

EMOTIONAL HEALTH – MIND BODY CONNECTIONS

Human beings are emotional beings. We have all sorts of feelings all of the time. It is fair to say that most of us struggle with emotions, one way or another. Many human societies have evolved in such a way that emotions, the effects of them on the body, mind and spirit, and how to improve problems in this area, are poorly understood. This is certainly true in the UK, where displays of emotion are not encouraged – even crying at funerals doesn't seem to be general practice nowadays. Many of us are uncomfortable with emotions, our own or anyone else's. Some of us are numb to our own feelings, cut off from knowing what we feel, even to the extent of thinking we don't have strong feelings at all. Some of us feel awash with emotion and struggle to contain it, often being labelled ill because of our strong feelings.

In fact, this medicalisation of human emotions is becoming increasingly widespread as the greedy drug companies seek to find ways to turn *everyone* into a customer.[315] The trend in psychiatry and in the so-called 'mental health' system is to look to biological or genetic causes for mental disturbances, and advertise products for them as if these biological causes have been found, when in fact they have not.

"When ...psychiatric interest groups promote a theory or treatment for depression, its aim of selling psychiatry is often beclouded by scientific trappings...citizens...are unlikely to protest 'they're trying to sell me shock treatment and drugs...', or 'they're trying to get me to pay medical doctors to solve my psychological and spiritual problems.'" [316]

---

[315] Are drug companies really so bad? Perhaps. But here's a thought; to be holistic there is the need to heal conflict, and this no doubt must include the conflict that is felt between alternative and mainstream. if we view big pharma as an enemy, that in itself harms us by generating fear; if we are scared of chemicals that also harms us, it also means we are in some way disconnected from the source, ultimately it is ok if we become a little bit poisoned, we are still one with the Divine. The thing is, as soon as we see big pharma as being bad, we create an us-and-them scenario, it makes us both separate of into our separate camps, until there is a valley between us and we are stood on top of our opposing mountains with cannons pointing at each other. The question is how to make peace with something that can be harmful, how to steer others away from that harm while not creating conflict or fear, and how to portray this in a book...Thanks to Mark Jack for this great contribution.

[316] Peter Breggin *Toxic Psychiatry – Drugs and ECT: The Truth and the Better Alternatives* page 183.

It might surprise you to learn that hardly any psychiatrists actually train in any kind of psychological talking therapy, or even counselling.

"If you are educated in the humanities or have a few good self-help psychology books, and if you like to think about yourself and others, you may have more insight into personal growth than your psychiatrist does...If you have also shared feelings and personal problems with some of your friends, then you may well have more experience and practice in 'talking therapy' than your psychiatrist." [317]

It seems the profession as a whole, along with a lot of others, would prefer to blame 'faulty' people for their suffering instead of take on the reality of how much we hurt ourselves, our children and each other with our lack of emotional awareness and with the oppressions which operate within our society. There are, however, many psychiatrists and psychologists who say very clearly and convincingly that the research evidence to support the theory of mental illness having a biological basis – and therefore logically being treatable with chemicals – simply does not exist[318] (to say the whole field of psychiatry is based on no evidence what-so-ever is a huge thing to say; I am paraphrasing Peter Breggin here who has been a psychiatrist in practice for many years. Check him out.[319]). Conversely there is much evidence about how traumatic events in a person's childhood and the effects of oppressive cultures impact on mental health.

The stress factor

Many people are increasingly aware of the importance of our emotions to health and disease. It is now widely recognized that 'stress' causes disease. You might like to take a read of the nervous system chapter again; when something is perceived as stressful, the body is stimulated to get ready for flight or fight (the sympathetic response) and the relaxing, healing, restoring aspect of ourselves (the parasympathetic) is suppressed. The stress response is about action now – do something quick to get out of danger. It is not favourable to reflection, to feeling the complexity of our deepest feelings, to figuring out deeper meanings, meditating on the meaning of life or planning for the future in a rational and connected way.

So far so good – I don't need to spell out again how the changes in the body which come about during the stress response, maintained long term, will take a toll on the body and even lead to serious disease. Our modern societies are incredibly stressful; fast-paced and furious, with little time for rest and recuperation, the balance is definitely tipped towards the sympathetic and away from the parasympathetic for most of us. In addition, the kind of activities many of us are engaged in, characterised by a lack of involvement in the body and over-use

---

[317] Peter Breggin *Toxic Psychiatry – Drugs and ECT: The Truth and the Better Alternatives* page 20.
[318] Peter Breggin *Toxic Psychiatry – Drugs and ECT: The Truth and the Better Alternatives*.
[319] http://www.breggin.com

of the cognitive, brain-based intellectual view of the world leads to a loss of heart coherence. Coherence is a term used to refer to connection, harmony, order and structure within and amoung systems. Physiological coherence refers to the ways in which the whole human body communicates and stays in alignment with itself and with outside forces. Heart coherence is this phenomenon as it occurs in the heart.

Here it is described by Roland McCraty in a monograph called Physiological Coherence from The HeartMath Institute (2003);

"It [coherence] is the harmonious flow of information, cooperation, and order among the subsystems of a larger system that allows for the emergence of more complex functions. This higher-order cooperation among the physical subsystems such as the heart, brain, glands, and organs as well as between the cognitive, emotional, and physical systems is an important aspect of what we call coherence. It is the rhythm of the heart that sets the beat for the entire system. The heart's rhythmic beat influences brain processes that control the autonomic nervous system, cognitive function, and emotions, thus leading us to propose that it is the primary conductor in the system. By changing the rhythm of the heart, system-wide dynamics can be quickly and dramatically changed.

We use the term 'coherence' in a broad context to describe more ordered mental and emotional processes as well as more ordered and harmonious interactions among various physiological systems. In this context, 'coherence' embraces many other terms that are used to describe specific functional modes, such as synchronization, entrainment, and resonance. Physiological coherence is thus a specific and measurable mode of physiological functioning that encompasses a number of distinct but related phenomena. Correlates of the physiological coherence mode, which will be considered in further detail in this monograph, include: increased synchronization between the two branches of the ANS, a shift in autonomic balance toward increased parasympathetic activity, increased heart-brain synchronization, increased vascular resonance, and entrainment between diverse physiological oscillatory systems. The coherent mode is reflected by a smooth, sine wave-like pattern in the heart rhythms (heart rhythm coherence) and a narrow-band, high-amplitude peak in the low frequency range of the HRV power spectrum, at a frequency of about 0.1 hertz."[320]

If the heart is in charge as it was designed to be, the brain entrains to the heart's electromagnetic signals. But when we lose touch with natural environments and become top-heavy, living in our heads rather than our hearts, the heart entrains to the brain and diminished heart function results. As Stephen Buhner describes,

"Increased heart coherence and heart/brain entrainment has shown a great many positive health effects. Increased heart coherence boosts the body's production of immunoglobulin A...also produces improvements in disorders such as arrhythmia, mitral valve prolapse,

---

[320] Accessed from the internet July 2008 URL:http://www.heartrelease.com/coherence-1.html

congestive heart failure, asthma, diabetes, fatigue, autoimmune conditions, autonomic exhaustion, anxiety, depression, AIDS, and post-traumatic stress disorder. In general, in many diseases, overall healing rates are enhanced. One specific treatment intervention study, for example, found that high blood pressure can be significantly lowered within six months – without the use of medication – if heart coherence is re-established. And as heart/brain synchronization occurs, people experience less anxiety, depression, and stress overall." [321]

Heart entrainment is basically about bringing relaxed, aware attention to one's heart, and to the feelings one gets from observing one's environment, rather than living in a point somewhere in your forehead. When a human being is in a natural, wild environment, with many different things to take our attention (meaning more a feeling kind of attention, not a thinking kind of attention), this state emerges naturally. So holistically thinking, to create balance, ultimately we do need to change things in our societies, to set things up so that there is a lot less stress for everyone, and more natural and wild environments to experience what it is to truly live.

More healing mechanisms

So let's consider something: think of the incredible elegant complexity of the body, with its amazing homeostatic mechanisms. If stress is so bad for us, such a killer, wouldn't we have inbuilt recovery mechanisms to help us off-load its dangerous effects? Good thinking; because, yes, in fact, we do. One of the most important things for us humans is to connect – as described above, we need to connect with ourselves, with our hearts, but we also need each other. Talking, sharing feelings, showing our feelings with beloved others, is necessary for human health. Let's take a look at what having our feelings means.

Crying, laughing and other ways of getting feelings out

We have already discussed one of the most powerful healing mechanisms for the human mind and body – weeping. Crying tears is one of the main ways the body can rid itself of toxic hormones which will damage the body if allowed to accumulate. Yes, the liver can metabolize them so that the kidneys and bowel can excrete them, but how much better just to excrete them whole in our body fluids? We can do this not only in tears but also in sweat and saliva.[322] These very physical processes are part of the emotional discharge mechanisms we have, which are there to allow us to completely recover from hurtful or stressful situations.

Another great way of discharging emotion is laughter. Re-evaluation counselling[323] figures laughter to be the main way people can discharge the emotions of embarrassment and shame,

---

[321] *The Secret Teachings of Plants.*

[322] Remember the thing about having a dry mouth building up feelings of fear? If they are not out, they're in. Producing saliva full of stress hormones means those internal drugs which will lead to more feelings of fear are being excreted instead of getting into the blood to whip up the fearful stress response.

[323] Which began in the 1950s and is now practiced by thousands of people in 86 countries of the world. You can find out more on www.rc.org

light fears and anger. Deeper fears and hurts are discharged by shaking, sweating and crying, anger by flushing and sweating; physical tension and pain by yawning. Talking about our experiences is also an essential part of recovering from past hurts. It seems that when we get hurt in any way, if we don't get to use the inbuilt healing process of discharge to recover from that hurt at the time, the hurt will linger in our mind and body until such time as we get to feel it. Basically, to feel is to heal.

Norman Cousins wrote his book, *Anatomy of an Illness*, in 1979, describing his experience of curing himself after he had been given six months to live when suffering from an extreme form of arthritis. He decided to die happy, and spent all his time watching great comedy movies and laughing. Instead of dying, he recovered and was back at work after six months. He describes laughter as 'internal jogging'.

Cardiologist Dr Michael Miller of University of Maryland found that laughter expands the blood vessels and increases blood flow to the heart by 22%. After laughing, there are significantly lower levels of cortisol and adrenaline. Laughter has also been shown to increase production of natural killer cells, B cells, helper cells and immunoglobulins, some of which effects remain for hours after a good long laugh. This would back up the observations of re-evaluation counselling (also called co-counselling because it is a peer activity), which comes from the experience of thousands of people as they learn to reclaim the healing process of emotional discharge and together laugh, cry, sweat, shake and yawn away the residues of stressful experiences.

Some studies have found that laughter also helps to relieve pain and even to reduce blood sugar and protect the kidneys in diabetics. The Gesundheit Institute in Virginia, founded by Dr Patch Adams, a doctor and a former clown, uses laughter as its main therapy.[324]

What about anger?

Anger deserves a brief word here as it is one emotion many of us have difficulty with, at least in the UK, where it is not considered 'good form' to express it, and as a consequence many people are full up with old unreleased anger and do not know what to do with it, whilst at the same time it spills out as road rage and suchlike. Anger is an energy – of stress, in physiological terms. It is meant to give us the thrust to act, to get out of the threatening situation we find ourselves in. As I have already mentioned, one crucial aspect of the unhealthy impact of stress in our modern lives is that we get all dressed up with no place to go with it; something happens to make us feel threatened and the body naturally has a 'flight or flight' reaction; yet we have to just sit there and take the pressure. We must learn ways to push the feelings down, and so this way anger and frustration can build up in us over the years. Anger is discharged from us using angry, forceful sounds and movements, heat, sweating and tears.

---

[324] See What Doctors Don't Tell You vol 18 no 9, Dec 2007, about what research has shown the benefits of laughter to be.

To give yourself some space to release some of this energy you might like to try using your voice forcefully on a daily basis; try shouting into cushions if you are living somewhere you can't shout without freaking out the neighbours. Punching cushions is good too, or hitting the bed or sofa with a baseball bat or suchlike. If you start to feel very hot you'll know that anger is discharging from you.

Primal Therapy

Dr Arthur Janov pioneered Primal Therapy in the 1970s and since then his Primal Training and Treatment Centre in Venice, California has researched the effects of deep discharge (the full feeling of old emotional wounds and the expression of this pain by tears, sobbing, shaking and screaming) on thousands of people. Janov's premise is that many people are hurt very early on in life by birth trauma and by not having our needs met as very young ones. This 'primal pain' is repressed, being too difficult to feel at the time.[325] Janov goes so far as to say that if we had felt it as tiny ones, we would actually have died from its magnitude – for a newborn infant, to have no one looking after us is fatal. Repressed pain does not go away, but lingers in the body and mind. When a person learns to go back early and re-experience past hurts, crying like a baby – hence the 'primal scream' – the old hurts can be fully discharged with wonderful effects. Janov's research has shown that these effects can be measured physiologically by changed levels of stress and sex hormones, a dropping of high blood pressure and fast heart rate to normal levels and improvement in immune function.[326] It is not uncommon for people to grow and mature in ways that were previously held back. For example some women's breasts may develop more, or some men become broader in shape, more hairy or deeper of voice.

The bodymind [327]

A whole mind-body medical discipline is emerging - called 'psychoneuroimmunology' or PNI - around the definite links between the mind and the immune system. Candace Pert's *Molecules of Emotion* is a great introduction to this, as is Deepak Chopra's *Quantum Healing*. Psychoneuroimmunology is a way for science to understand that the mind becomes the body, and vice versa, through myriad connections of the chemical network of communication that continuously runs both ways between brain and body, emotion, thought and physical function.

---

[325] Re-evaluation counselling would say that as young ones we would have tried to discharge it with crying and so forth, but most babies are stopped from crying with dummies (pacifiers), over-eating or 'trained' out of it by simply being left to 'cry it out' – which means effectively that the baby gives up on anyone caring enough to come and pushes the feelings deep down.

[326] Dr Arthur Janov *The New Primal Scream – Primal Therapy Twenty Years On*.

[327] The term bodymind was first proposed by Diane Connelly and reflects the understanding that the body is not separate from the mind. (Candace Pert's *Molecules of Emotion*).

There is plenty of research that shows positive thinking and a happy attitude are good for your health. The difficulty for many people is how to actually change one's mental habits and get free from the old hurtful ones. Certainly reclaiming the discharge process is a great place to start; these old hurts need to come out so they can stop messing us up. Otherwise, positive thinking and affirmations and the like may serve more to push the painful stuff further in, with damaging effects on our health. So, lots of laughing and, if you are in good enough shape to listen well to another person, check out www.rc.org for your nearest re-evaluation counsellors. If not, look for a therapist who knows the value of, and encourages, emotional discharge like crying – rather than one who wants to teach you how to push it down more effectively! This includes steering clear of all counsellors who recommend anti-depressants to their clients. If they are doing that, they obviously don't have trust in the healing power of their therapy – which may be with good cause!

"Even in a full-time lifetime general practice of psychiatry it's possible to offer help without ever starting a patient on antidepressants. Depressed people don't tend to hurt themselves when they have a good relationship with a therapist and some hope of improvement. I try to help individuals experience their feelings, to understand the sources of their despair, and to overcome their hopelessness, while providing a caring, morale-building relationship and guidance towards more effective ways of living. Often this involves the client learning new, more positive values and a more daring, creative approach to life. Nor do I think that I am more effective as a therapist than many others in the field. There are no 'great therapists', only great clients…" [328]

It's simple in a way – we need to give ourselves and each other permission to feel our feelings without censoring them or pushing them down. The complicated bit of this is that for most of us we have been pushing them down for so long that there is a bit of backlog to clear – lots of old feelings hanging around so long that we might not even know what they were about to start with. They are poisoning us and need to come out and be released.

Meditation

We need to somehow change what our minds are focusing on. A good way to learn to take charge of your mind and your thinking is to learn meditation. Transcendental meditation (TM), which involves repetition of a mantra in time with the breath whilst sitting quietly, has been the subject of over six hundred research studies. Regular meditation has been shown to increase creativity and intelligence, improve memory and perception, sharpen concentration, increase EEG coherence of brain functioning, reduce stress in several ways, improve the health and reduce the negative effects of aging, improve relationships and self confidence, and even improve productivity at work and decrease crime, conflict and violence.[329] Yes, really. A

---

[328] Peter Breggin *Toxic Psychiatry – Drugs and ECT: The Truth and the Better Alternatives* page 211.

[329] www.t-m.org.uk has references for many of these studies. They make a fascinating read.

project was undertaken in the 1970s to get 1% of the population of 24 different cities meditating, and compare crime rates in these cities compared with 24 similar 'control' cities (which didn't have 1% of the population meditating). Crime rates dropped in the meditating cities in the year targeted, which was 1972, as well as in following years.[330]

What we believe is what we get

We need to change our minds, because our beliefs and our thoughts shape our lives and our health. Take the placebo and nocebo effects, for example: if we believe we will get better from a treatment, then we will, even when the treatment has done nothing. If the doctor who we trust tells us nothing can be done and we are sure to die – that is what tends to happen. Deepak Chopra's *Quantum Healing* has great stories about both of these effects.

This subject of mind-body medicine is of course fit for several books at least, and a lifetime study. So I hope I have whetted your appetite a little and encouraged further investigation. I am sure that much more disease than we realize is due to emotional trauma trapped in the body. There is a huge resistance in the West to taking this on – orthodox medicine, along with many citizens, has taken the 'we don't know what causes this' approach to life's problems. We do not want to or know how to take responsibility, and we are provided with many ways to numb out from feelings.

Then there is another problem: if disease is caused by emotional difficulties, does this mean it is a person's 'fault' when they get ill? I hope that my presentation in this area in no way encourages this kind of incorrect approach, which is singularly lacking in compassion. To make things as clear as possible, what I am saying is we get hurt – just that. We get hurt, and do not have the help we need to fully recover. The biggest reason most of us get hurt is due to the huge imbalance in our societies and the oppressive patterns running throughout it. It's not our fault we got hurt, we didn't ask for it, we would much rather it had not happened. But it did, and these hurts make us sick, whether we believe they do or not. That's the bad news – the good news is it is possible to heal from them completely, in various ways, most if not all of which (from where I'm standing) seem to involve the discharge process in some way.

Cancer as a manifestation of emotional trauma

There is such a resistance in mainstream society and medicine to taking this on that those who champion it are ridiculed and even persecuted. One such is Dr Dirk Hamer, prosecuted in more than one country for his pioneering work with people with advanced cancer. This was despite his very high success rate – such that the public prosecutor (Wiener-Neustadt in Austria) had to admit that after 4 to 5 years 6,000 out of 6,500 patients with mostly advanced cancer were still alive.

---

[330] The Transcendental Meditation program and crime rate change in a sample of forty-eight cities, Journal of Crime and Justice 4: 2545, 1981.

Dr Hamer developed testicular cancer after his son was shot dead. He wondered if his son's death was the cause of his cancer, and began to investigate. He looked at over 15,000 cases of cancer and always found the following characteristics to be present, which he termed the 'Iron Rules of Cancer':[331] These state that cancer starts with a serious shock experience, creating trauma and conflict that manifests in the psyche, brain and then a particular organ. He identified themes of trauma and says each type shows a change in activity in a part of the brain, corresponding with the organ where the cancer has manifested. He claims to be able to show a direct relationship between these, with the cancer improving as the brain lesion reduces and the trauma is resolved. He photographs the brain with Computed-Tomography (CT) – the problem area looks like the surface of water after a stone has been dropped into it. Later on, if the conflict becomes resolved, the CT image changes, an oedema develops, and finally scar tissue.

Apparently, Dr Hamer can accurately diagnose illness – including diabetes – from looking at someone's CT picture. He can also do this with the emotional conflicts that person experiences. The organ focus of a particular brain change reflects our subconscious associations – and interestingly these seem to be very much in keeping with five element philosophy. For example, biological conflicts involving water (also other fluids, such as milk or oil), lead to kidney cancer,[332] fear of death to lung cancer and mentally swallowing a bigger chunk then we can digest to stomach or intestinal cancer. Dr Hamer believes that most secondary tumours are caused by the cancer-fear or death-fear resulting from the patient given the cancer diagnosis or a negative prognosis. Another 'nocebo' effect.

Of course, some people are full of cancer everywhere by the time they are diagnosed, which doesn't seem to fit Hamer's theory. Hamer says that secondary cancers, if not caused by the stress of the initial cancer, are caused by other unresolved traumas rather than being related directly to the initial tumour. Hopelessness and despair create chronic stress, which prevents healing of all types. Dr Hamer's healing programme includes finding what the original emotional shock experience was and making sure it is being healed. Sometimes when a tumour is found in someone, it is already dormant and the person has healed from that crisis – but the shock of medical intervention can make that tumour, or another one, grow. If the original conflict is still active, any means to resolve it should be taken; emotional healing therapies, meditation, embracing the grieving process fully if there has been loss. Hamer argues that the worst thing we can do is take tranquilizers or antidepressants for shocking events, as these interfere with our proper healing process.

---

[331] Actually this name puts me off somewhat – it certainly seems to imply a rigidity of approach.

[332] Perhaps there will be an increase in kidney cancer soon, what with global oil and water supply issues.

The following is taken from the Internet:[333]

The New Medicine of Dr Hamer

By Walter Last [Rescued web page — March 2004]

'Hamer regards all diseases as consisting of two phases, initially with active conflict followed (if possible) by a healing phase that reverses the conflict program. He does not call them diseases anymore but rather special biological programs. In all he is stated to have worked with over 31,000 patients and found his theories confirmed in every single case without exception. Hamer claims that overall the New Medicine has a 95% success rate with cancer. Siemens, the manufacturers of the CT equipment have independently verified the existence of the Hamer Herds in the brain…Nevertheless, Dr Hamer faced exceptional persecution. Under German law the right to practice medicine can be withdrawn if the doctor has diminished mental abilities. This law was used in 1986 by a German district court to withdraw his right to practice. As proof of Hamer's inadequate mental condition the court stated that he was not willing to retract his theories and swear allegiance to the principles of orthodox medicine…he was incapable of converting back to the principles of orthodox medicine: he tried to convince a group of prominent professors of the correctness of his theories only one month before the court case! One year later the same court requested a psychiatric assessment of his mental abilities, which Hamer refused. A court-appointed psychiatrist, without ever seeing him, diagnosed him anyway as being a psychopath. In 1997 Dr Hamer was arrested and jailed for 18 months under an obscure natural therapy law introduced under Adolf Hitler to suppress Gypsies. His crime was that he had given free health advice to some individuals who had asked him for his opinion. The public prosecutor had openly stated that all means must be used to remove Hamer from society.'

Medical heretics beware!

There are serious criticisms of Dr Hamer and his work. It is not easy to tell from researching this whether he is a saint or an evil quack – both are equally unlikely. It seems that many people who consult him have been through orthodox cancer treatment then been written off – nothing further can be done for them. My thinking is that he is certainly onto something, but that the reality is that it is not easy for a person to get to the bottom of, and resolve, their deep-seated emotional conflicts and pain, not even when they are well. To do this whilst seriously ill with cancer would not be any easier. Therefore I expect there is a gap between the theory and understanding which can be gained with the scans of Dr Hamer, and the actual practice and ability of people to resolve their issues in time to halt advanced cancer. However, it is certainly true that vested interests

---

[333] Accessed July 2008 from URL http://www.hbci.com/~wenonah/new/hamer.htm.

within medicine will go to great lengths to punish those who go against the accepted norm – particularly if that person is a medical doctor. Traitors are worse than the established enemy!

Above all, it is all about feeling our feelings. It's when we push them down and deny them that they make us ill. Feelings are not illnesses – they are normal human responses to our situation. It gets complicated for most of us because we have a lifetime of pushing them down behind us; when we stop, all sorts of old feelings come up, the origin of which has probably been forgotten. Although it can feel unbearable to feel them, feel them we must if we are to regain our full humanness. The unbearable becomes bearable when we face it together. The final word goes to that wonderful and brave psychiatrist and psychotherapist Dr Peter Breggin, who's book *Toxic Psychiatry* is one of the most important books ever written in this field:

"*...the vast majority of people overcome depression without resort to any mental health services. They do so by virtue of their own inner strength, through reading and contemplation, friendship and love, work and play, religion, art, travel, beloved pets, the passage of time – all of the infinite ways that people have to refresh their spirits and to transcend their losses.*" [334]

---

[334] Peter Breggin *Toxic Psychiatry – Drugs and ECT: The Truth and the Better Alternatives* page 211.

Appendix A

A BRIEF INTRODUCTION TO FIVE ELEMENTS/CLASSICAL CHINESE MEDICINE: A COMPLETE HOLISTIC SYSTEM

The Five Element system is a complete system of medicine. Classical Chinese Five Element medicine was brought to England in the 1970s by J.R. Worsley who had travelled widely in China. Its foundations were laid down over 2000 years ago in ancient China.[335] Why I am including it here is that one of its great differences from other systems is that symptoms are treated by the practitioner with benign indifference – a diagnosis cannot be made by reference to symptoms at all!

Of course as patients we don't treat our symptoms with benign indifference; but the Five Element view is that, as part of nature, we are capable of being in complete balance and health, and when things go awry there are signs which a skilled practitioner can read – changes in the sound of our voice, our colour, our body odour and the emotional tone of our lives. The diagnosis of our particular imbalance is made on these parameters and not on any symptoms of illness. This is in complete contrast to modern Western medicine, which is largely focussed on symptoms.

Like all other systems with their roots in ancient times, the Five Element system is derived from a close study of nature. At heart, it understands that Spirit is at the root of health; that most imbalance causing disease originates at the level of Spirit. In this chapter I am attempting the merest introduction to the Five Element system, which is an amazingly complex and elegant paradigm. In my descriptions of elemental imbalance here I am mainly emphasizing the way they manifest in the emotional and spiritual spheres, rather than the physical. If you are drawn to further study there are excellent books on the subject, as well as courses to learn how to become a five-element practitioner.

The elements themselves

The Chinese word which has been translated as "element" really means something more like 'phase' or 'movement'. The elements are great cosmic forces which shape everything in the universe.[336] You can think of the elements as being like the seasons.

---

[335] Professor J.R. Worsley *Classical Five Element Acupuncture Volume III - The Five Elements and the Officials*.
[336] Nora Franglin *Keepers of the Soul – The Five Guardian Elements of Acupuncture*.

As I write this midwinter approaches; outside it is icy cold and beginning to get dark already, though it is only 3pm. The trees are bare, the landscape bleak. The energy of the earth has gone deep below. Nothing is happening on the surface. Even though the Christmas mayhem is approaching, there is a pull to go quiet, to go within, to do little, to sleep more.

This is not a time for action, for doing, but for being. This is the time of Water; rain washes the land clean, snow and ice freeze us into immobility. The colour is black or dark blue, the black of night. Water is Life, more than any other element – any desert dweller knows this. The absence of Water brings certain death – therefore the emotion of water is fear; fear having the function of keeping us alive. Water is always changing and moving, from rain to ice to snow, even from the stagnant pond it is moving as it evaporates into the air to come down as rain on a far off mountain. There is a mystery to water – where does it come from? Life comes, just as the spring emerges from the earth, out of some great mystery, the original Source.

After this phase of darkness and quiet, of conserving and resting, comes the next – the spring, the time of growth. Everything will erupt with green; a magnificent orchestrated medley of growth. This is the Wood element – like a tree, it contains all the others within it; water is drawn up by the tree, which is made of wood. It takes the heat of the sun to make energy and it grows with its roots in the earth, from which it takes the precious minerals or metals. More than any other element, Wood is the element of healing; of the growth of regeneration as well as development. Wood is upward-moving, surging, vibrant. Wood is determined to grow to its full potential and will push through obstacles which impede on its progress. Thus the emotion of Wood is anger; the emotion which arises in us when our growth is thwarted, the emotion which we can use to assert our boundaries. The colour is green.

When the prolific growth of the spring, of adolescence, is over, we reach a period of maturity with the energy of summer. Everything is at its peak. Plants are in flower, attractively drawing insects and bees to them. As days lengthen and grow warmer, we come outside and are drawn to each other, to play and laugh and party. This is the energy of Fire – expansive and connecting, the warmth of joy and love, fun and laughter. The red energy of the Heart.

Towards the end of summer, the grass is yellowing and the flowers have turned to fruit. The Indian summer or harvest time of berries and fruits and nuts shows the bounty of the Earth element, which is all about nourishment and sweetness. Our Mother Earth gives us all that we need for survival; she nourishes us at her sweet breast throughout our lives. The Chinese gave the Earth element the colour yellow because of the rich yellow earth of their fertile places.

Then comes a time when the weather changes; a fresh cold sharpness is felt in the air, and we breathe deeply, feeling its purity and quality. Autumn is here, the time of winds and falling leaves, a time when all will be stripped away but the bare essentials. This is the time of Metal, with its energy of worth and quality; the precious metals and minerals which plants drew up from the earth will be returned as vegetation dies down and rots away. Metal is the element of purity – and so has the colour white.

And so the wheel will turn as the water of winter comes again to wash the land clean.

These Five Elements exist within us all, each having spheres of influence and controlling functions in our body, mind and spirit. The elements manifest within us as personalities – known as 'officials' – who are in charge of various areas. For example, the Water Officials are the Kidney and the Bladder, in charge of the control and storage of fluids. But do not make the mistake of thinking that the officials are just another name for the organs you now know something about; they are this, but they are much, much more. It's best to literally imagine them as people, a great gang of highly skilled and honourable wise ones who are running the show – a kind of spiritual Numbskulls![337]

Whilst we all have all the elements within us, we also are all born with one particular mix of elements which is uniquely us, and which shows where our greatest strengths lie, what is the calling of our soul. One element will predominate – though there is an element within an element, and an element within this and so on, so the complete picture has depth and complexity. Our main element will be revealed by the way we most relate to the world, and because of this, because it is the one we are most 'out there' with, it is also the one most vulnerable to hurt. When we get hurt the wound happens first in our main element, causing an imbalance. For most of us, this happens at a very young age – even pre-birth, due to the gross imbalances within our society. This 'original wound' is known as the 'causative factor'; from it all of our problems originate and can be traced back to.

Because we are part of nature, nature shows our need in natural ways, which become more and more obvious to the trained eye. Each elemental disturbance shows itself in the sound of our voice, a colour that comes to certain areas of our face, a type of odour, and a particular flavour of emotional imbalance.

Elemental emotions

Emotions are central to our existence. The Five Element system has it that a human being is an emotional being, that we are *always* experiencing the world through our emotions. If we are in balance and harmony (which few of us are), we feel appropriate emotions according to the situation.

The general emotional tone for a balanced person is a deep contentment or joy, a feeling of connection to all things and rightness with the world and our existence in it. Interestingly, this is what Candace Pert, neuroscientist, also suggests – that our natural state is happiness.[338]

Although our natural state is happiness, there are five emotions which will rise and fall within us on top of this basic happiness depending on what is happening. If something happens to impede our growth, then anger naturally arises – giving us the impetus to remove

---

[337] British people of a certain age may remember a comic book that had a story about the Numbskulls – funny little men who live in your head and run the various operations of your body.

[338] Candace Pert, *Molecules of Emotion*.

the obstacle and continue our growth. Of course for British people there is a general cultural imbalance here, as we are in a society which really frowns on anger. The joke is, in New York, if someone steps on your foot, you say, "get off my foot"; in London, if someone steps on your foot, you say, "sorry"!

When your desires are fulfilled, you feel joy – not the same as the deep joy which underlies it all, but a more frothy happiness to do with satisfaction of some want. When someone is in need, the natural emotion to feel is sympathy – the emotion of the mother tending to her hurt child. 'There there, poor you, tell me all about it' – actually in Britain we don't encourage sympathy much either – the famous stiff upper lip!

There is a feeling of respect in the presence of that which we value, and when we lose something we value, the natural feeling is grief.

Finally there is the emotion which is very much connected to feeling alive – fear. Fear is what helps to keep us alive, since it warns us to react to danger.

You can think of the emotions as being like doors – one must always be open, and when one is open the other four are closed. We feel one at a time, and when we are in balance we are able to move with ease from one to another. When imbalance is present, something goes awry with this mechanism. For some people, it's as if one door is stuck permanently open, and there is only one emotion they feel no matter what the circumstances. For others, one door is locked closed and they simply cannot go there no matter what. For most of us, it is as if there is only one emotion that we most come alive in, though we can go in and out of the others a little.

Diagnosis of the causative factor

We are all moving more in and out of balance throughout our lives. Here follows a very brief introduction to how we uncover a person's causative factor, or 'CF'. As a general rule, the more imbalanced a person is the more extreme the signs described below. This is not to say however that a balanced person is like a bland empty page – when in balance each element has its particular beauty and strengths; the particular gifts we bring to the world are expressed through the power of our elemental makeup.

People with what is known as a 'Wood CF' look green, smell rancid, have a voice which shouts or has emphasis, or else lacks all shout, and may be stuck in anger, or unable to express appropriate anger at all. You have probably come across someone like this, who sounds furious even when they are asking you the time, or conversely someone who tells you about the most terrible outrage against them but is unable to feel the slightest hint of anger (o yes, the doctor took off my good leg by mistake, but never mind he did a great job…).

Fire people are red or often 'lack of red' – pale, or grey. The odour is scorched; the sound is that of laughing or a lack of laughing, the emotion joy, or a lack of joy. One extreme example is a person who tells you with hilarity about how last week they lost their job, got evicted from their house and were diagnosed with terminal cancer. The opposite extreme is the person who talks with absolute flatness about the wonderful holiday they just had.

For Earth people, the colour is yellow, the smell is fragrant, the voice has a singing quality to it and sympathy is the emotion that will be pronounced or absent. An imbalanced Earth person might be always looking after others, stuck in permanent sympathy. On the other hand, they might be completely unable to understand the suffering of another.

For Metals, the colour is white, the smell is rotten, and emotions focus around weeping and issues to do with loss or grief, or with a sense of value. Some people are stuck in grief, unable to move on from loss. Others are spiritually impoverished, unable to value anything enough to feel any grief at losing it.

Water people are blue or black, smell putrid, have a groaning voice and may be stuck in fear, or unable to feel fear at all and go after extreme situations in order to feel something.

The smells are interesting. It is not a person's armpits or feet or whatever we are talking about – it is a general overall odour that characterizes us. The smells have a quality, a feeling. When I smell the Wood smell for example, it's like a punch – I feel an upward movement in my head. Sometimes it really does smell like old oil. Sometimes it would be better described as 'green'. The Fire smell can be quite spicy, sometimes smells like freshly ironed linen sheets, or can be like anything scorched – even quite unpleasant like burnt rubber. I feel it in my head also, but it moves in all directions, not just upwards. The Earth smell I feel down in my tummy, a warmth. Sometimes a person smells so fragrant it's like they have perfume or aftershave on when they haven't. The fragrant smell, like all of them, can be anything from lovely to revolting, sickly and cloying. The Metal smell, rotten, can be like old rubbish or even like poo. But it can also be like gentle rotted down compost or leaves in a wood. I feel it like a heavy or low sensation in my throat and the front of my body. The putrid smell of Water is sharp and acrid, almost chemical in nature, like ammonia. It can smell like brackish water or like sweet urine.

Don't assume, however, that we can all be easily categorized; it's safe to say there are probably about a billion different types of each causative factor. You can't stereotype people, and knowing a person's CF does not mean you know anything else about them. What it reveals is what a person most needs at the deepest level to restore them to health.

As I have said, symptoms are not at all useful in making a Five Element diagnosis. This is because each element feeds the next, and is in relationship with the others. Thus if the winter is too mild and the spring too dry, the summer and harvest time will suffer.

'Anything can come from anything' is the Five Element motto when it comes to symptoms. A Fire person might have all of their symptoms in the Earth element and no apparent problems in Fire. The diagnosis can only ever be made on sound, colour, odour and emotion. The elements are expressed in the body via the officials. These officials are a team, working together to make the whole body, mind and spirit function well. Each one has unique areas of responsibility, and each is the only one who can provide that service to all the others. So if one is very sick, all can suffer in different ways. Each element manifests as two officials, but the element of Fire has four. These come in two pairs and take care of the functions of Fire in quite different ways.

The Twelve Officials

The Water Officials are the Bladder and the Kidney. The Bladder is 'the official in charge of the reservoirs and reserves of fluids.' Fluids must be stored to be on hand when we need them, otherwise they are not of benefit. The Bladder Official is in charge of this – is in fact the only official who is even remotely capable of storing fluids of any kind.

This applies to all fluids in the body, not just urine and water but blood, lymph, tissue fluid, tears, sweat, synovial fluid, cerebrospinal fluid, sexual fluids – even including hormones which are found always in the blood and body fluids. (The bladder in the body is not in charge of all fluids physiologically speaking. Do not try and correlate this all physiologically; this is a completely different system). Qi (the energy of life) itself is a fluid – in the sense that it flows through the body, mind and spirit. We always need it, and must always have reserves from the unpredictability of life. It is the Bladder Official who maintains these reserves, thus giving us adaptability – the ability to move with the flow of events. If we don't have reserves, we naturally feel afraid: how will we survive in a crisis? We can be literally paralysed with fear. The biggest way to deplete our reserves is by overwork, making this a chronic imbalance of the whole of modern society, in which overwork is the norm. The modern world relies on caffeine to fuel unrealistic and unsustainable workloads. Caffeine exhausts the Water Officials – by allowing us to work more than we have energy for. A good way to relate to caffeine is to realize that in using it, you are borrowing time from tomorrow. Eventually, it must be paid back. Overwork is often motivated by fear, so in fact it is a vicious circle, fear leading to overwork leading to depletion of reserves, leading to fear.

The Kidney is called 'an official who excels through ambition and cleverness' and has a lot to do with our intellect and mental clarity. The Kidney is like a spring emerging from the earth – it harbours our Ancestral Qi, which is kind of like the sand in our hourglass – at the moment of conception, we get ancestral Qi from our mum and our dad. We will use up this Qi throughout our life, and when it is gone we die. We can never get any more of it, but we can use it up at faster or slower rates, depending on how we live. Throughout our life we also get Qi from the Earth Mother, through eating, and the Heavenly Father, through breathing.

The Kidney, as controller of fluids, is in charge of cleansing in our body, mind and spirit. The emotion of Water is fear, and one aspect of this is *awe* – the fear we feel when we come face to face with something huge and mysterious. The aspect of the Kidneys and the Water element of bringing forth life is awesome – mysterious, impenetrable, cannot be made sense of. The Kidney Official is the only official capable in any way of controlling fluids.

The Wood Officials are in charge of growth processes; the Liver is the architect, who makes all the plans for everything in the body, mind and spirit. The Gall Bladder is like the building contractor, who makes the day to day decisions to do with carrying out the plans of the architect.

Nothing can happen without a plan. Someone must have the vision, the foresight to figure out what to do in any eventuality. This is the job of the Liver Official, who holds the vision and the blueprint for our lives on the grand scale as well as the everyday. Think of the incredible energy of growth seen in our bodies during childhood. The Liver controls it all. Then, when physical growth is over, growth must continue at the same powerful rate in the mind and the spirit throughout our lives. The Liver in good shape is capable of making plans with strength and flexibility. The Liver is also the detoxifier, and as such is overloaded by drugs and alcohol. If our Liver Official is in poor shape, we may be stuck and unable to see any way out of an intolerable situation, unable to plan – or we may be rigid and bound to over-planning everything, trying to control every aspect of our lives and the lives of others. The Liver Official makes all of the plans for the body mind and spirit – it is the only official capable of making any kind of plan.

The Gall Bladder Official is like an air traffic controller, sitting in isolation and thinking carefully to make the decisions necessary to orchestrate and execute successfully the plans of the Liver. To do this, it needs a certain purity. It is known as 'the upright official of decisions and judgment'. It coordinates all the other officials and pairs of opposites – the right and left, upper and lower, front and back. It is related to order and orderliness. If impaired, we might find it difficult to decide things, or have poor judgment. Or we may be rigid and judgmental, with an obsessive over-concern for purity, unable to tolerate disorder. On the one hand, feeble decision makers, on the other obsessive over-planners. Habitual lateness can be a Gall Bladder thing; to do with difficulty organising and coordinating enough to be on time, or it can even be a kind of covert aggression – anger being the emotion of the Wood Officials. As you've probably guessed, the Gall Bladder is the only official even remotely capable of making any kind of a decision…

The Fire Officials are different in that there are two pairs of them – one pair is the Heart and Small Intestine, one the Heart Protector and the Triple Heater.

The Heart is the Emperor, the Supreme Controller, in ultimate charge of guiding us to fulfil our Divine purpose or destiny. Remember that the names of the officials originate in ancient China; then it was seen that the role of the Emperor was the representative of the Divine on earth. He stayed in his palace, protected from everyday affairs, meditating and focusing on God in order to be able to receive Divine guidance regarding the destiny of China. So our Heart Official is kept in splendid isolation, protected from occupation with everyday affairs, to allow her or him to remain in contemplative connection with the Divine and guide us wisely on our journey through life.

The Heart is helped out particularly by two officials – its twin the Small Intestine is the official food taster – 'the Official in Charge of Separating the Pure from the Impure'. Nothing passes the Emperor's lips that hasn't first been tasted by the Small Intestine, to ensure no poison gets to the Heart. Remember that the officials are operating on the level of the mind and spirit as well as the body – so all ideas and all energy which come our way are received by the Small Intestine, who then decides whether to let them in or not – whether they are pure or impure. Consider the huge amount of information we modern humans are subjected to: junk mail, newspapers, the internet, the television. All of this information must be sifted through by the Small Intestine to decide if it is of value for us to take in and digest or not. You can see how this official can so easily be overwhelmed these days – like an overworked clerk, sometimes it is made ill and even simply gives up because of the terrible burden of work put upon it. This can be a very serious situation because without a well-functioning Small Intestine Official, a person becomes completely unable to discern, to tell the difference between right and wrong. One way this shows up might be a person who keeps having terrible relationships, choosing the wrong people to be with – because they are literally unable to tell what would be good or bad for them. On the physical level, if the small intestine Official is not well, you might have a person who, although they eat a very good healthy diet, is poisoned and toxic because the Official absorbs everything that should be excreted; or is malnourished because the Official is unable to absorb anything at all.

Extremely, you even have 'sociopaths' and people such as paedophiles who are so confused that they try to get adult love from children. In the Five Element view, they are not monsters to be punished, but people in such a terrible state of imbalance that they cannot tell what is good or bad – people who are in great need of healing. The Five Element system says that people are and behave only as the condition of their Officials allows them. The small intestine official is the only one that can distinguish right from wrong, pure from impure.

The other pair of Fire Officials is the Heart Protector, known as the 'Official in Charge of the Pleasures of the People', and the Triple Heater. These are two officials who do not really have equivalents in terms of organs, although the Heart Protector is sometimes called the Pericardium, and sometimes Circulation/Sex – its two areas of physical functioning.

The Heart Protector is the second official with the express job of protecting the Heart Official. The best way of doing this is to have an open loving heart and have a lot of fun! The Heart Protector loves a party, and loves to connect in a loving way with others. It is this function of warmth and joy which is able to afford our Heart the best protection (remember the research we discussed about laughter being good for your heart?).

Most of what we think of as heart disease is in fact a problem with the Heart Protector failing to do its job. It's ironic that when we get hurt, we can have the tendency to shut down, to avoid getting close again in case we get hurt some more, when this is the very worst thing we can do in terms of looking after our Heart. When a person's Heart Protector is not working well, we can feel the most terrible vulnerability, feeling the slightest casual unkindness like a blow to the heart.

The Triple Heater is like the heating engineer – it keeps the warmth (and Qi) circulating evenly around the body mind and spirit, keeping everywhere at the right temperature for all the officials to function well. You can feel it directly on the body by feeling the 'Three Jaios' – place a hand on the belly below the umbilicus, above it, and over the heart, comparing the temperature in each area. They should be pretty much the same, neither too hot nor too cold.

The Triple Three Heater is known as 'the Official of Balance and Harmony'. It is responsible for the principle of 'warming up' – not just physically, but mentally and emotionally. Think of an orchestra warming up to get in tune with each other, or a party which warms up to be a whole, rather than separate individuals – this is the province of the triple heater. On a mental and spiritual level, when the triple heater is not working you might see a person who blows hot and cold, incredibly enthusiastic one minute and cold and un-caring the next. Someone may be unable to maintain relationships, or indeed any project, for lack of continued enthusiasm.

Since the Earth element is about the bounty of our Mother Earth and about nourishment, naturally the Earth Officials are those in charge of receiving nourishment – the Stomach – and of transporting this sweetness throughout the being – the Spleen/Pancreas. So if our Earth Officials are in good shape, we are well nourished and have a deep sense of security. If not, we may be voraciously hungry, unable to get what we need, deeply insecure, angry and vicious at our lack, or smothering and over-nurturing to compensate for our lack.

The Stomach Official is the 'official in charge of rotting and ripening' – just as the physical stomach receives food and digests it ready for the small intestine to absorb, the Stomach of the mind and spirit receives ideas, experiences and energy and digests them, make sense of them, so we can fully absorb them. In this way the Stomach is about understanding – chewing over our life experiences and making sense of them. Without a balanced Stomach, we might worry endlessly; chew over the same thoughts again and again without satisfactory conclusion. We may be unable to properly understand our experiences; and in extreme cases even be cut off from reality.

The Spleen Official can be simplified as having a fleet of little yellow lorries (trucks) which transport everything around the body, mind and spirit; nourishment, blood, nerve impulses, energy, everything. When the Spleen Official is not working, we see signs of stuckness on the one hand, and over-activity on the other. Memory may be poor, as it is the moving function of the Spleen which is responsible for bringing the memories from their storage place to the forefront of the mind. Nothing can move without the Spleen Official.

Finally the Metal Officials – the Lung and the Colon. These are responsible for maintaining purity in the body: the Lung brings in the pure, rarefied energy of Heaven, the energy of quality and respect and all that is worthwhile in life; the Colon removes the waste and the dross, and in this way maintains purity and sparkle in every cell of our body and our being.

A person with a problem with the Colon Official gets polluted, negative, literally 'full of shit'. Sometimes a person might be filthy in their body, their home, their language. Sometimes the opposite is seen, an obsessive cleanliness. Some people become champion grudge-bearers – a kind of mental or spiritual constipation. Others may show the imbalance with an obsession with status and worth, a need to impress.

The Lung Official is about worth and quality, and is what allows us to take in essence and quality. So an imbalance may be seen as an inability to receive a complement and expression of appreciation of one's worth. In Chinese medicine the skin is known as the 'third lung' – so problems with the lungs may be seen in the skin quality.

Five Element treatment protocol

Actual treatment within the Five Element protocol involves much more than strengthening the causative factor, important though this is. There are, for example, blocks to treatment which must first be addressed. There is something called 'aggressive energy' which is a serious and unnatural condition which untreated will eventually result in death. This condition can be detected by subtle changes in the pulse. There is also something called 'husband-wife imbalance' which can cause terrible symptoms in the body mind and spirit – and is also detected from the pulses. Then there is 'possession' – an invasion of the mind and spirit by some foreign entity. Risk factors for this condition include underlying poor health, terrible emotional or physical shocks, drug and alcohol abuse, amongst others. You can see that it could well be fairly common in today's world! If possession is suspected, a practitioner treats this first before doing anything else, as it will completely block all healing otherwise.

The above is, as I have said, just the briefest introduction to the Five Elements. To study them completely is a lifetime's work. I'm repeating this to make it absolutely clear that there are many, many important things missing from this chapter, that it is not pretending to do anything more than skim the surface. If you want to learn more, there are excellent books and courses on the subject.[339] You can get Five Element constitutional treatment as acupuncture or as Eliot Cowan-style Plant Spirit Medicine.[340] I definitely advise trying it for yourself: it will transform your life in ways you can't even begin to imagine.

---

[339] Angela & John Hicks *Five Element Constitutional Acupuncture*, J.R. Worsley *Classical Five Element Acupuncture*, Nora Franglin *Keepers of the Soul.*

[340] To find a PSM practitioner in the UK and Europe: http://www.plantspiritmedicine.org.uk or in America http://www.bluedeer.org/psm.html
To find a Five Element acupuncturist www.sofea.co.uk www.acupuncture-coll.ac.uk http://www.fivelement.com

APPENDIX B

SPIRITUAL CAUSE OF DISEASE; THE SHAMANIC PERSPECTIVE:

At the close of this book I'd like to say a little about the ways of our Ancestors, the Old Ways, the ways of the Earth and of the ancient Gods of this planet of ours.

The shamanic paradigm, common to all indigenous cultures throughout the world, sees the universe as being a whole, completely interwoven entity. Everything is alive and has energy, or a 'spirit', and all things are connected. We live in constant relationship with everything; our family, tribe, community, society, the animals and birds, insects, all creatures, also the spirits of nature, plants, the land, fire, air and water. The idea is to be in harmony with all, that disease – dis-ease – comes about when the energy or relationship between a person and themselves, their community or their environment is not right.

There are ways for a person to live in right relationship; Ancient ancestral traditions involve detailed knowledge of how to live thus, as well as having an effective treatment system for when things go wrong, including those kind of emotional and spiritual diseases for which modern Western medicine is at best ineffective, and at worst (and all too often) downright destructive.[341] In this appendix I will give a short overview of the shamanic perspective.

Everything that exists is made of energy. This physical reality of ours to which we are so attached is one aspect of this dream of life, but it is not as solid as we believe. There are other realities too, known as the spirit world, the other world, the next world, the world beneath the water; what Michael Harner calls 'non-ordinary reality.'[342] We can access the realm of non-ordinary reality through our night-time dreams and through waking visions. There are many methods for connecting with non-ordinary reality, often involving drumming, rhythm and song, dancing and the burning of sacred herbs.

Michael Harner researched shamanic cultures throughout the world after having a profound shamanic experience when studying a tribe as an anthropologist. Instead of dismissing his experience, he realized something real had happened and began to look into it, to try to understand it. Finding that rhythmic drumming is an integral part of most shamanic

---

[341] Peter Breggin's *Toxic Psychiatry*, describes the barbaric Western treatment of such dis-ease eloquently.
[342] Michael Harner *The Way of the Shaman*.

practices throughout the world, he undertook research on the effects of this on a person's brain waves and found that the effects are to put the brain into theta waves – a trance state. It's interesting that dance music (trance, acid house, techno to name a few types) uses drum beats of the same frequency as shamanic drumming.

In indigenous cultures, everyone knows that dreams are real and important. Everyone dreams. Our Ancestors, spirit guides, animal spirit helpers, angels; all can come to us through our dreams, giving us the help and guidance we need. To keep the clearest spirits coming through, there are ways to purify and cleanse ourselves, and to protect ourselves from negativity.

In intact indigenous cultures, people all have initiations to identify them strongly to the spirits, to ensure their rightful place in the tribe.[343] These initiations are essential to growth and maturity. Contrast this with what we get here: some 'career advice' and maybe an eighteenth or twenty-first birthday piss-up… Without initiation, a person does not easily become a proper adult and grow spiritually throughout life. Thus we have a society with many old people but very few Elders – and a lot of furious young people who know at a very deep level they are being short changed.[344]

Although everyone dreams, there are those who are called to go much deeper. These are called Shamans, Seers, Diviners, Medicine Men or Women, Witch Doctors[345], Sangomas. The word in common usage now to identify them is 'Shaman.' This word comes from Siberia. Since it is now fairly common to refer to any of these medicine people as a Shaman, I will do so here.

A Shaman is one who has been called to something extra – to deep work with the other realms. It is not a glamorous calling; it involves much hard work and sacrifice. Most people in indigenous cultures do not seek it out, as it is not an easy path at all. The Shaman really belongs to the Spirits, and to their community; it is a life of service. The shamanic perspective is that all disease involves some kind of problem with non-ordinary reality. Broadly speaking we can say there are three types of problem which manifest in illness:

A person can have lost some of their vital force, energy, spirit or soul – this is called **soul loss**. This can cause depression, tiredness, depletion, confusion, a sense of not feeling all there, and other problems. The remedy is called 'Soul Retrieval'.

Secondly, a person can have some energy attached to them that doesn't belong to them, is not theirs. This is called an **intrusion**. It can involve daggers of negative energy which have

---

[343] Malidoma Some *Of Water and the Spirit*.

[344] There is a great organisation called the Mankind Project which recognises this problem and offers powerful initiations into manhood for men. www.mkp.org.uk
It has a sister organisation, Woman Within, offering initiations for women. www.transitionseurope.com

[345] Witch Doctors in Africa traditionally helped people who had been harmed by witches, who are people who practise negative or dark magic. However in the UK in recent years the word 'witch' has been reclaimed by those who seek to practise the old pagan ways of this part of the world, and does not mean a person who practises the 'dark arts' as they are called in Harry Potter…

been thrown at us, or us holding parts of someone else's energy which we've taken from them unknowingly, or more seriously, what are called 'entities' getting attached to us. Entities seem to have a life of their own, and they suck on our life force to survive here. The biggest one I have ever seen was in a casino; it was as big as a house, and was involved in sucking people into gambling addictions. Entities are often involved in addictions. Some seem to be big globs of the energy of negative emotions, nasty happenings. You can often feel the unpleasant vibe or energy in a place where horrible things have happened. Intrusions can manifest as pains in particular parts of the body, feeling dirty or yucky, bad dreams, fear and even in feeling like something is in there with you. The remedy is called 'Extraction'.

Thirdly, there are problems with our **Ancestors**. Ancestors are an essential part of all indigenous traditions. Our Ancestors have passed through here before us, and want to help us. Our love and honouring of them feeds them, nourishes them, and shows them where we are so they can help us as much as possible. Think for a few minutes about your own family; do you know the names of your grandparents and great-grandparents? How do you feel about your family line? Are you proud, ashamed, angry, disappointed? Can you feel the love and support of those who came before you, or do you feel disconnected from your roots? Are you aware of unfinished business amongst your Ancestors? Is there trouble which has been passed through the generations? What are your strengths from your Ancestors? These are important shamanic questions. Remember that no matter what else your Ancestors did or didn't do, they survived, and because they survived, you are here, with this most precious life.

In some traditions[346] the word 'Ancestor' includes all the spirits who are helping you, which would also include the Gods.[347] There are Gods and Goddesses of everything – Fire, Water, the Earth, the Stars, Rice, the Forest, Mountains etc. It is possible to offend the Gods by not honouring them. On the other hand, having them on your side is a good idea. I'm very conscious as I write that this is all seen as superstitious mumbo jumbo by the dominant culture in the West. We don't seem to have a culture of 'as you sow, so shall you reap' any more. Our actions have only physical consequences. Yet the more I have become immersed in shamanic practices and ceremony, the more I have experienced the power of working in this way. Honouring and praising your Ancestors, including the Gods, gets results!

Shamanic healers may remove intrusions and banish entities, bring back lost soul parts, and help to restore good relations with the Ancestors. Some kinds of healing can be thought of as 'household shamanism' – the kind of safe shamanism that everyone can have access to. Shamanic journeying falls into this category. The shamanic dream journey is an easy and safe method for anyone to learn to deepen their connection to the spirit world, and to become aware of helpers and allies. The journey is in your spirit. When journeying, the body is made

---

[346] For example the Xhosa tradition of Southern Africa. To find out more about this tradition see *Sangoma* John Lockley's website www.african-shaman.com

[347] Those who have issues about the word 'God/s' may think of them as being powerful natural forces.

comfortable and things set up so as not to be disturbed by the telephone ringing and so forth. The journey feels at first as if it is happening in your imagination – like a visualisation. At its best it becomes more like a dream – a powerful waking vision, in which you are fully participating, which you are not controlling but are making decisions within.

A person may journey to meet their 'power animal' for example. Having a strong connection to a power animal is seen as crucial by most tribal peoples. In fact, some say if your power animal is with you, you can't die! Animal spirits are usually found by journeying to the 'lower world' which is accessed by going down a tunnel from this world (the middle world). It's a bit like Alice going down the rabbit burrow, and coming out into a completely new world where different rules apply. Different animals offer us different 'medicine'. For example, hedgehogs are protected by their spines, so are able to be innocently friendly and playful. Foxes are cunning and good at getting around un-noticed. Badgers are very fierce and protective, and also like to dig up roots – which makes them herbalists, healers of the body. Eagles and kites and other large birds of prey can fly very high, and have excellent eyesight – so they can see far, see the whole picture, take us high into the spiritual realms.[348]

You get the idea. Animals are, of course, our Ancestors – probably in the genetic sense as well as the shamanic sense. They love to help us. Plant spirits also are keen to help. In fact, everything we need for our physical survival comes via plants. This fact is hidden from most of us in the modern world, but it's true none the less. Plants are extraordinarily generous to us and love us despite our poor treatment of them. We can look to them for all kinds of help; help with our minds and spirits, with restoring harmony to our bodies, as well as with our basic survival needs – food, shelter, warmth, oxygen production. Plant spirits are traditionally accessed via the lower world, as well as directly in the middle world by hanging out and tuning in with them.[349]

Allies and spirits in human form can also be safely connected with by the lay person. These may be met anywhere, but often in the 'upper world' – the heavenly realms, which one gets to by going up from the earth in one's spirit body. Of course, if you just go up, you get to space and other planets. To get to the upper world, you must pass through a barrier, which often appears as a kind of membrane (this membrane does not exist in ordinary reality – you won't crash into it while flying a plane. You need to be travelling outside of your body in the realm of non-ordinary reality to encounter it). Once through the barrier, you are in the upper world, a weird and wonderful place full of all kinds of landscapes.

It is also possible to travel in non-ordinary reality in the 'middle world' – you can go in your spirit body to visit friends, to look for lost objects, to do distant healing, to check over the energy of a place or person, to see if your expected visitor is nearly arriving, to check your

---

[348] There are various books on animal medicine; Jamie Sams *Medicine Cards*, Lucy Harmer's *Discovering Your Animal Spirit* (*Apprivoisez votre animal totem*, Jouvence editions 2006 out in English next year) contact www.innerelf.ch
[349] Eliot Cowan's *Plant Spirit Medicine* is a good start. Also Elizabeth Brook's works.

car has not been stolen…the shamanic journey has many possible applications.

Household shamanism can and should be practiced by pretty much everyone. We all benefit from having our lives enriched by direct personal contact with our guides, allies, and Ancestors. Some people are called to take things further, and this is where it gets tricky for us modern people. Traditionally, deep shamanism would only ever be undertaken by one with a calling, who would then follow an arduous and dangerous training programme usually lasting for years with a teacher who had in turn been fully initiated in an ancestral tradition that had its roots in the beginning of time. This is deep shamanism, and some paths still remain unbroken. However, nowadays many of the ancestral traditions have been lost. Certainly our own northern European ways were scattered years ago, by the Romans and later by Christianity.[350] This means that most of us have no access to proper shamanism, anchored to an ancient lineage. Many people today practice shamanic healing without having been initiated in an ancestral tradition (myself included). There is a place where this is ok – there is some middle ground, between everyday household shamanism on the one hand, and the dangerous and very powerfully effective deep shamanism on the other. It is important to recognize the limitations of this, and for the shamanic practitioner who is not affiliated to an ancient tradition to be aware of these limitations and difficulties. Shamanic practices are only partly about techniques. Mostly, they are about building power. No matter how powerful an individual may be, this is as nothing compared to the power of an ancient and unbroken lineage.

I hope this has whetted your appetite to find out more about shamanism. These ancient ways are an important part of our human existence, without them we are seriously in trouble. There are some excellent books in the bibliography for further study, but the best thing to do is put the books away and spend as much time as possible in nature. If you are interested I encourage you to learn to journey. You can do this alone, but also find a course or workshop to attend and learn in a group – much more fun as well as being safer and more effective.[351] Enjoy the journey!

---

[350] There are traditions left here, such as the way of the Bee Masters and Mistresses. See Simon Buxton's book *The Shamanic Way of the Bee*.

[351] You can check out my website www.thedreamingbutterfly.com and Lucy Harmer's www.innerelf.ch as well as looking for the Sacred Trust who offer lots of great workshops. Open your heart and pray sincerely to find the right teacher and place for you to learn, and you'll find it.

BIBLIOGRAPHY

Here below is a list of the books/sources I have found useful. If you want a traditional anatomy and physiology textbook I suggest you go to a shop with a big selection and take plenty of time to browse until you find one that is accessible to you, and provides the depth of information you require. First come books, magazines and papers alphabetically, then websites.

I have starred *** my favourite, even life-changing, books, to make sure you don't miss them.

1   A.D.T. Govan/P.S. Macfarlane/R.Callander *Pathology Illustrated* (second edition Churchill Livingstone 1986).

2   A.W. Priest and L.R. Priest *Herbal Medication – A Clinical and Dispensary Handbook* (C.W. Daniel Co. Ltd, UK 1983).

3   Alan Philips *Dispelling Vaccination Myths, an introduction to the contradictions between medical science & immunization policy* (Prometheus, 55 Hob Moor Drive, Holgate, York YO24 4JU 2001). *** *You can buy this booklet from Helios Homeopathic Pharmacy, 01892 537254*

4   Alexandra Pope *The Wild Genie- The Healing Power of Menstruation* (Australia. Sally Milner Publishing Pty Ltd 2001). ***

5   American Journal of Clinical Nutrition, (2005; 81: 1147–54). Accessed 21/7/08 at URL http://www.wddty.co.uk. About link between eating low-fat milk dairy and prostate cancer: CLUE II study, involving nearly 4000 men in Washington County, Maryland (Cancer Causes Control, 2007; 18:41–50) and Alpha-Tocopherol, Beta-Carotene Cancer Prevention Study (ATBC Study the higher the risk of prostate cancer (Int J Cancer, 2007 Feb 2; Epub ahead of print).

6   Andrew R. Biel and Robin Dorn *Trail Guide to the Body: How to Locate Muscles, Bones and More* (Books of Discovery 2005).

7   Angela Hicks & John Hicks *Five Element Constitutional Acupuncture* (Elsevier Ltd 2004).

8   Anita Petek-Dimmer (2002) *Does Systematic Vaccination Give Health To People?* Accessed at URL http://www.whale.to

9   Archives of Disease in Childhood 1997;77:F237-8. *Respiratory distress in Caesarean babies.*

10 Aretha Sulter *The Aware Baby – A New Approach to Parenting* (Shining Star Press 2001). ***

11. Dr Arthur Janov *The New Primal Scream – Primal Therapy Twenty Years On* (Abacus 1991).
12. Benoussan A et al. *Treatment of irritable bowel syndrome with Chinese herbal medicine.* Journal of American Medical Association 1998;280:1585-9.
13. Birth 2006;33175 *Caesarean babies nearly three times likely to die within their first month of life as naturally delivered babies.*
14. Broughton, Ally *Herbal Thymes* December 2007; 29-30. Research in herbal medicine.
15. Bruce H. Lipton *The Biology of Belief: Unleashing the Power of Consciousness, Matter and Miracles* (Mountain of Love/Elite Books, California 2005). *** One of the best books I have ever read. ***
16. Candace Pert *Molecules of Emotion* (Simon & Shuster, 1998).
17. Christopher Menzies-Trull *Herbal Medicine – Keys to Physiomedicalism Including Pharmacopoeia* (Christopher Menzies-Trull 2003).
18. Dr Dale Layman *Physiology Demystified* (McGraw-Hill Companies 2004).
19. David Sinclair & Peter Dangerfield *Human Growth After Birth* (Oxford University Press 1998 6th Edition).
20. Deane Juhan *Job's Body – A Handbook for Bodywork* (Station Hill Press Inc., Barrytown, New York 12507. 1987).
21. Deborah Sigrist *Journey's End – a Guide to Understanding the Dying Process* (Lifetime Care publishes it and the cost is $4, includes shipping. It can be ordered by: phone: Hotline: 001-585-214-1415 www.LifetimeCare.org *Journey's End*, 3111 S. Winton Rd. Rochester, NY 14623-2608).
22. Deepak Chopra *Unconditional Life – Mastering the Forces That Shape Personal Reality* (Bantam Books October 1991). ***
23. Deepak Chopra M.D. *Quantum Healing – Exploring The Frontiers Of Mind/Body Medicine* (Bantam Boooks USA 1989/1990). ***
24. Edda West (2003) *Is Fear of Fever Hurting Our Children?* Accessed at URL http://www.vran.org
25. Elaine Marieb *Human Anatomy & Physiology 6th Edition* (Pearson Education Inc. Publishing as Pearson Benjamin Cummings 2004).This is my personal favourite in terms of a very detailed and in-depth A & P book.
26. Eliot Cowan *Plant Spirit Medicine* (Swan.Raven & Co. 1995). ***
27. Elizabeth Brook *A Woman's Book of Herbs* (Women's Press Ltd 1992).
28. Eric Maddern and Paul Hess *Death in a Nut* (Frances Lincoln Children's books 2005).
29. Fiona Godlee *The food industry fights for salt* Editorial in BMJ, May 1996; 312: 1239 – 1240. Accessed at URL http://www.bmj.com
30. Graeme Tobin *Culpepper's Medicine – A Practice of Western Holistic Medicine* (Element Books Ltd. USA 1997).
31. Grandgirard, A, Bourre, JM, Julliard, R, et al. *"Incorporation of trans long-chain n-3 polyunsaturated fatty acids in rat brain structure and retina."* Lipids 1994; 29(4): 251-58.

32 Heinz R. Pagels *The Cosmic Code: Quanutm Physics As The Language Of Nature* (Simon & Shuster New York 1982).

33 Helen Graham *Soul Medicine - Restoring the Spirit to Healing* (Newleaf 2001).***

34 Helen M. Langevin & Jason A Yandow *Relationship of Acupuncture Points and Meridians to Connective Tissue Planes* (The Anatomical Record [Newanat.] 269:257-265,2002).

35 James Lovelock *Gaia: A New Look at Life on Earth* (3rd ed., Oxford University Press. [1979] 2000).

36 Jamie Sams *Sacred Path Cards – The Discovery of Self Through Native Teachings* (Harper Sanfransisco 1990). ***

37 Jamie Sams & David Carson *Medicine Cards - The Discovery of Power Through the Ways of Animals* (Bear & Company 1988).

38 John Ball *Understanding Disease – A Health Practitioners Guide* (1990 C.W.Daniel Company Ltd , 2005 Vermillion). A must have for anyone in practice who wants to understand the language of orthodox medicine and what is happening in the tissues of a person with a given disease.

39 John Upledger *Your Inner Physician & You – Craniosacral therapy and Somato-emotional release* (North Atlantic Books 1997).

40 Journal of Crime and Justice 4:2545,1981. *The Transcendental Meditation program and crime rate change in a sample of forty-eight cities.*

41 Journal of the American Medical Association, 2007;297:2681-2 Lack of oxygen from breathing problems linked with poor memory, attention deficit and learning and behavioural difficulties. From www.wddty.co.uk

42 Joyce Withers *The Virgin Stones* (Temple DPS Ltd 2002).

43 Kathleen DesMaisons *Potatoes Not Prozac, A Natural Seven-Step Dietary Plan to Stabilize the Level of Sugar in Your Blood, Control Your Cravings and Lose Weight, and Recognize How Foods Affect the Way You Feel* (Simon & Shuster London 2008 [new edition]).

44 Kathleen J.W.Wilson OBE & Anne Waugh *Ross and Wilson Anatomy and Physiology in Health and Illness* (Churchill Livingstone Eight Edition 1996). Another favourite, good for looking up pathologies system by system.

45 Leslie Kenton *Passage to Power – Natural Menopause Revolution* (first published Ebury Press 1995, then Vermilion 1996). ***

46 Louise Hay *Heal Your Body A-Z The Mental Causes for Physical Illness and How to Overcome Them* (Hay House 1998).

47 Louise Hay *You Can Heal Your Life* (Hay House Inc. 1994).

48 Lucy Harmer *Discovering your Animal Spirit* (published in French "Apprivoisez votre Animal Totem" Jouvence Editions 2006, to be published in English by North Atlantic Books, May 2009). www.innerelf.com

49 Lucy Harmer *Shamanic Astrology* (published in French "Les 12 Animaux Totems de l'Astrologie Chamanique" Jouvence Editions 2007, to be published in English by North Atlantic Books, May 2009). www.innerelf.com
50 Lucy Harmer *The Art of Space Clearing and Intuitive Feng Shui* (published in French "La Purification de l'Espace" Jouvence Editions 2003, to be published in English by North Atlantic Books, March 2010). www.innerelf.com
51 Lynne McTaggart *The Field – The Quest For The Secret Force Of The Universe* (Harper Collins 2001). ***
52 Lynne McTaggart *The Intention Experiment* (Harper Collins 2007). ***
53 Lynne McTaggart *The Vaccination Bible* (What Doctor's Don't Tell You 1998).
54 Lynne McTaggart (Ed) *The Medical Desk Reference* (What Doctors Don't Tell You 2000).
55 Lynne McTaggart *What Doctor's Don't Tell You A Review of conventional medicine and safer alternatives*. Monthly, various issues www.wddty.co.uk
56 Malidoma Somé *Of Water and the Spirit – Ritual, Magic and Initiation in the Life of an African Shaman* (Penguin 1994). ***
57 Marlo Morgan *Mutant Message Down Under* (HarperCollins /HarperPerennial 1991, 1994). ***
58 Michael Harner *The Way of the Shaman* (Harper and Row 1980).
59 MLA University Of Illinois At Urbana-Champaign (2000, April 12). *Study Of Rats' Brains Indicates Brain Continues To Grow After Puberty*. ScienceDaily. Retrieved March 2, 2008, from http://www.sciencedaily.com/releases/2000/04/000406091914.htm
60 Nora Franglin *Keepers of the Soul – The Five Guardian Elements of Acupuncture* (School of Five Element Acupuncture 2006 www.sofea.co.uk).
61 Pam England & Rob Horowitz *Birthing from Within* (Partera Press New Mexico 1998).
62 Paul Blakey *The Muscle Book* (Bibliotek Books 1992).
63 Dr Paul Clayton PhD *Health Defense – How you can combine the most protective nutrients from the world's healthiest diets to slow aging and achieve optimum health* (Accelerated Learning Systems Ltd Bucks UK 2001). ***
64 Paul Pearsall *The Heart's Code: Tapping the Wisdom and Power of our Heart's Energy: The New Findings About Cellular Memories and Their Role in the Mind/Body/Spirit Connection* (Broadway Books, New York 1999).
65 Percy Seymour *The Third Level of Reality – A Unified Theory of the Paranormal* (Paraview Special Editions, 2003).
66 Peter Breggin *Toxic Psychiatry – Drugs and Electroconvulsive Therapy: The Truth* (London 1993 Harper Collins). ***
67 Peter Mansfield *The Bates Method* (Vermillion 1994).
68 Professor J.R. Worsley *Classical Five Element Acupuncture Volume III - The Five Elements and the Officials* (Publ J.R. & J.B. Worsley 1998).

69. Rebecca Chalker *The Clitoral Truth – The Secret World At Your Fingertips* (Seven Stories Pr 2002).
70. Dr Robert O. Young *Sick and Tired – Reclaim Your Inner Terrain* (Woodland Publishing 1999).
71. Roland McCraty *Physiological Coherence* (monograph - The HeartMath Institute 2003). Accessed from www.heartrelease.com/coherence-1.html
72. Rolf Gordon *Are you Sleeping in a Safe Place?* www.rolfgordon.co.uk
73. Ruth Trickey *Women, Hormones & the Menstrual Cycle - Herbal & Medical Solutions From Adolescence to Menopause* (Allen & Unwin 1998, 1999, 2000).
74. Sara Hamo *The Golden Path To Natural Healing* (The Natural House Publishing, Jerusalem 1990).
75. Shakti Gawain *Creative Visualisation – Use the Power of Your Imagination to Create What You Want in Your Life* (New World Library 2002).***
76. Simon Buxton *The Shamanic Way of the Bee* (Destiny Books 2004).
77. Simon Mills & Kerry Bone *Principles and Practice of Phytotherapy – Modern Herbal Medicine* (Churchill Livingstone 2000).
78. Sogyal Rinpoche *The Tibetan Book of Living and Dying* (Rider, An imprint of Random House UK Ltd 1992, and Harper San Francisco in USA).
79. Stephen H Buhner *The Lost Language of Plants – The Ecological Importance of plant Medicines to Life on Earth* (Chelsea Green Publishing, Vermont 2002).*** Essential reading ***
80. Stephen Harrod Buhner *The Secret Teachings of Plants – The Heart as an Organ of Perception In the Direct Perception of Nature* (Bear & Company 2004 Vermont). ***Essential reading***
81. Stephen Levine *Who Dies – an Exploration of Conscious Living and Conscious Dying* (Gateway Books 1995). ***
82. Su Fox and Darien Pritchard *Anatomy, Physiology & Pathology for the Massage Therapist* (Corpus Publishing 2001).
83. The Princeton Review *Anatomy Colouring Workbook* (Second Edition. Princetown Review Books 2003).
84. Thomas Moore *The Soul of Sex* (Bantam 2003). ***
85. Viera Scheibner *Vaccination. 100 years of orthodox medical research shows that vaccines represent a medical assault on the immune system* (New Atlantean Press. Santa Fe, NM. 1993).
86. Yamashita D, Jiang HY, Le Prell CG, Schacht J, Miller JM, *Post-exposure Treatment Attenuates Noise-Induced Hearing Loss.* Neuroscience 134: 633-642, 2005. About antioxidants as treatment for noise-induced deafness.
87. Dr Yubraj Sharma *Vaccination – controversy, Safety and Side Effects.* Positive Health July 2003 Issue 90 (Positive Health Publications. Bristol).

Websites

1. **www.darkfieldmicroscopy** About looking at living blood with a special type of microscopy.
2. **www.mnwelldir.org/docs/history/biographies/louis_pasteur.htm** A history of Louis Pasteur.
3. **www.ourworld.compuserve.com/homepages/dp5/sex2.htm** David Pratt *Virginal Reproduction* 2003. About parthenogenesis.
4. **www.t-m.org.uk** For referenced studies about meditation.
5. **www.en/wikipedia/org/wiki/Development_of_the_urinary_and_reproductive_organs** Shows pictures of developing foetal genitals.
6. **www.sciencedaily.com/releases/2004/02/040217072523.htm** Yale University (2004, February 17). Hair Dye Use Increases Risk Of Non-Hodgkin's Lymphoma.
7. **www.cheniere.org/books/aids/ch5.htm** About French scientist Louis Kervran, working on elements changing to other elements.
8. **www.hbci.com/-wenoah/new/hamer.htm** Walter Last *The New Medicine of Dr Hamer.*
9. **www.african-shaman.com** About Sangoma John Lockley.
10. **www.breggin.com** The wonderful Peter Breggin's website.
11. **www.mkp.org.uk** The Mankind Project, initiation for men.
12. **www.nads.org** American site of National Association for Down's syndrome.
13. **www.rc.org** About re-evaluation counselling.
14. **www.theelders.org** About Global Elders.
15. **www.t-m.org.uk** For referenced studies about meditation.
16. **www.transitionseurope.com** Woman Within, initiation for women.
17. **www.ccst.co.uk** About craniosacral therapy in the UK.
18. **www.upledger.com** About John Upledger and craniosacral therapy.
19. **www.bluedeer.org** To find a plant spirit medicine practitioner in the US.
20. **www.plantspiritmedicine.org.uk** To find a plant spirit medicine practitioner in the UK.
21. **www.acupuncture-coll.ac.uk** To find a five element practitioner in the UK.
22. **www.sacredfirecommunity.org** About sacred fires and Tatewari.
23. **www.vran.org** About fever and vaccinations.
24. **www.nimh.org** National Institute of Medical Herbalists, finding a herbalist in the UK.
25. **www.rhs.org.uk** Royal Horticultural Society, about trees and climate change.
26. **www.innerelf.ch** Lucy Harmer's website, about Feng Shui and space clearing.
27. **www.thedreamingbutterfly.com** Pip Waller's site offering shamanic courses.
28. **www.lhmeridian.co.uk** Lorraine Horton's site for Meridian School of Massage in Birmingham.
29. **www.manchester.ac.uk** About essential oils active against MRSA.

30 **www.drpaulclayton.com** For nutrition expert Dr Paul Clayton.
31 **www.btinternet.com/~andrew.murphy/asthma_buteyko_shallow_breathing.html** About Buteyko breathing for asthma.
32 **www.leafcycle.co.uk** About Leafu, protein food from grass and nettles, from Michael Cole.
33 **www.sustainablehealthsolutions.co.uk** For recipe for linseed tea.
34 **www.dulwichhealth.co.uk** To buy a Raditech, a device to help reduce geopathic stress.
35 **www.newmedicine.ca** About Dr Hamer's controversial cancer theory and treatment.

ACKNOWLEDGEMENTS

First I would like to give heartfelt thanks to those whose words I have directly quoted

Peter Breggin *Toxic Psychiatry – Drugs and Electroconvulsive Therapy: The Truth.*

Stephen H Buhner for words from *The Lost Language of Plants – The Ecological Importance of plant Medicines to Life on Earth* and *The Secret Teachings of Plants – The Heart as an Organ of Perception In the Direct Perception of Nature.* Particular thanks to Stephen Buhner for allowing me to reproduce his wonderful poem *Semen* from *The Secret Teachings of Plants.*

Sara Hamo *The Golden Path To Natural Healing.*

Deane Juhan *Job's Body.*

Bruce H. Lipton. *The Biology of Belief: Unleashing the Power of Consciousness, Matter and Miracles.*

Lynne McTaggart *The Field – The Quest For The Secret Force Of The Universe* and *The Intention Experiment.*

Thomas Moore *The Soul of Sex.*

Deborah Sigrist *Journey's End – a Guide to Understanding the Dying Process.*

Eric Maddern *Death in a Nut* (not exactly quoted, but very close to Eric's version of this story).

Roland McCraty *Physiological Coherence.*

Lucy Harmer *on Coupe Feu, geopathic stress, Feng Shui and space clearing.*

Dr A M Carson Head of School, School of Health, Social Care, Sports & Exercise Science NEWI, Wrexham, *on narrative research.*

Lorraine Horton of the Meridian School of Massage, Birmingham, *on skin rolling, and for her encouragement and support.*

Hilary Butler (The Immunization Awareness Society) *for her collection of references about fever.*

Walter Last *The New Medicine of Dr Hamer* from www.hbci.com/~wenonah/new/hamer.htm

Manual Lymphatic Drainage UK *for their words on manual lymphatic drainage,* from www.mlduk.org.uk

Michael Cole *for his information about Leafu, protein food from grass and nettles.* leafudevon@hotmail.com

Then there are the many others who have helped me in all kinds of ways, and without whom this book could not have happened

- A huge thank you to my very dear friend and all-round wonder woman **Rachel Lloyd**, whose lovely drawings have made the book a million times better – and thanks to her lovely baby son Joseph who has slept enough to allow her the time to do them.
- Huge thanks to **Andy Garside**, the fabulous designer who quite literally turned up on my doorstep at exactly the right moment and has made this look like a proper book. (www.andygarside.com).
- Warm love and gratitude to my dear sister **Lucy Harmer** for believing in me, funding me, and helping me out in so many ways I can't imagine what I'd do without her.
- Thanks to my lovely son **Alex Whetstone** for putting up with me slaving away at the computer early in the morning, and for getting on with playing without me to allow me to write this; thanks also to his dad **Miles Whetstone,** my mum and dad **Sheila** and **David Waller,** and **Hugh Newton** for spending time with Ali while I work.
- Warm love and thanks also to my natural mother **Kate Harmer** for reading this in its early stages and encouraging me, and for all your other help over the years. It means so much to me that you are in my life.
- I couldn't have done it without **Patrick Mendes**, my funny, gorgeous and very particular proof reader, who has brightened up my life this summer as well as taught me all sorts of things, not only about colons and semi-colons. Gratitude and warm love to you, Patch, and to **Tatewari** for sending you along, and generally blessing me in countless ways.
- Thanks to the wonderful **Mark Jack** who helped me with checking for mistakes and inaccuracies and contributed with a lot of warmth and humour.
- Grateful thanks to **Anja Saunders** (nee Dashwood) who founded the Academy of Natural Health in London, and **Gillian Cleary** who founded the Blarney Acupuncture and Reflexology Centre in Cork, Ireland, both of whom gave me a start as a teacher of Anatomy and Physiology.
- Thanks to **Richard Ashley** (Fash), for his photos of the sea and the power station at Warrington, and to **Lynn Amanda Brown** for her wonderful photo of a sacred fire (on the cover).
- Thanks to the lovely and clever **Anna Dowding** for the final proofread, and to her gorgeous boy Joshua for letting her do it.
- Last but by no means least, thanks to all my **students**, who have taught me such a lot over the years, and to all of the **colleagues** and **friends** who have taken a look at the book at various stages along the way and given me feedback and encouragement to continue on; without that I probably wouldn't have made it to the end.

INDEX

Abdominal cavity **6**,144,179,185
Abnormal bleeding 244
Abnormalities in the Embryo 195
Abortion 195-197
Absorption of nutrients 19,**129,131**
Acetylcholine 154
Acidophilus 133
Acids and bases 17,20
Acquired immunity 95,103-105
ACTH .... *see Adrenocorticotrophic hormone*
Actin and myosin .17,18,38,**62-64**,122,123,153,218,231
Action potential 153-154
Active transport 26,27
Addison's disease 174-175
Adenohypophysis .... *see anterior pituitary*
Adenoids 97
Adenosine diphosphate .... *see ADP*
Adenosine triphosphate .... *see ATP*
Adipose tissue 35,140,141
ADP 21,22
Adrenal cortex...140,147,163,164,171,**174-175**,179,215
Adrenal Glands...9,79,140,164,169,**174-175**,178,184,201
Adrenal hormones 174-175
Adrenal medulla 163,**174**
Adrenalin 140,154,162,**163,174**
Adrenocorticotrophic hormone 140,163,171,174
Aerobic respiration 18,**65**,66
After death 231-236
Agonist 66
Airway resistance 111
Albumin 17,18,80,82,123,139,142,**174-175**,220
Aldosterone 141,147-149,163
Allantoin 49
Allergies 99,103,104,132,200,123,239,240,247
Aluminum 16,104
Alveoli 8,82,97,**108-111**
Amino acids **17,18**,20,22,**122**,139-142,144,146
Amniocentesis 196-197
Amoeba 24
Amygdala 159
Anabolism 5,14,22,116
Anaemia **83**,204,214,240,245
Anaerobic respiration 18,**65**,140,231
Anatomical position 50,56
Anatomical terms 50
Anatomy of the heart 75
Ancestors 2,93,104,230,235,236,275-279
ANF – atrial naturetic factor 79

Anger ... 199,218,219,221,234,**258-259**,266,267,268,271
Angiotensinogen 147
Anions 15
Antagonist 66
Anterior pituitary 140,**170-172**,177,197
Antibiotics 2,98,104,133,147,206,249
Antibodies 18,30,84,**102-104**,123,132,135,199
Antidepressants 147,249,260
Antidiuretc hormone 147-148,172
Anti-inflammatory 5,71,99,120-122,163,242,243
Anti-microbial 41
Antioxidant 88,124
Antipyretics 96,98,100,101
Aorta 70,75,75,78,144
Apocrine glands 44
Appendicular skeleton 50,56
Appetite increase 244
Appetite loss 141,222,230,244
Arachidonic acid 120,121
Arachnoid mater 155,156
Arms or 'upper limb' 56
Aromatherapy 219
Arsenic 16
Arterioles 70,73,148
Artery **70-73,75**,81
Articular cartilage 55,58,69
Articulations 57-62
Ascending (sensory) tracts 159
Ascending colon 132
Asthma...45,104,111,114,**115**,120,121,213,240,242,257
Atheroma 71
Atlas **52-53**,60
Atoms 11,13-18,88
ATP ...18,**21,22,24**,26,27,30,38,64,65,154,172,218,231
Auditory cranial nerve 206
Autism 98,104
Auto-immune disease 151
Autonomic nervous system 161,167,169,171,192,256
Axial skeleton 50,55
Axis **52,53**,60
Axons 141,**151**,152,156,159,171
B vitamins 21,72,88,123,132
Babies 41,50,97,104,110,111,133,158,180-183,
                196,199,200,204,210,228,259,280,281
Bacteria 2,4,5,19,21,**23-24**,83,90,94,102,106,117,
            123,127,129,**132,133**,134,143,176,205,231,239,
                                        242,247,249
Bad cholesterol 120,142
Ball and socket joints 60

Basal cell carcinoma 46
Basal Metabolic Rate 143
B-cells 102
Benign prostatic hypertrophy 191
Bifidobacteria or bifidus 19,133
Bile 20,120,126,129,130,131,138,139,141,184,208
Bile ducts 138
Bile pigment 139
Bile salts 20,120,138,141
Biophilia 224
Birds and the Bees 192
Bladder ....see urinary bladder
Blood 37,82-86
Blood clotting 10,20,21,**84**,120,121,123,124,133
Blood groups 84-85
Blood plasma 37,71,82,139
Blood pressure 71,72,79,**80-81**,86,87,147
Blood sugar 117,126,140,175
Blood vessels 70-73
BNF - brain naturetic factor 79
Body cavities 6
Body Systems-an overview 7-9
Bodymind 150,213,259
Bone 37,47-61,124,170,173,218
Bone formation 21,42,**48**,123
Bone healing 49
Bowel 123,**132-134**,137,243,245,248,252
Bowman's capsule 45,46
Brain 9,18,32,130,150,151,**156-159**,160-
                        162,166,170,172,213,220,256,262
Brain stem 113,**157**,159
Breast feeding 50,103,107,133,135,136,199,200,204
Breast tissue **183**,201,214
Breathing ...65,74,90,**107-115**,161,162,198,214,245,270
Breathing difficulties 220,245
Bromine 16
Bronchi 108,109
Bronchioles 108,109
Bruce Lipton iv,18,22,24,25,30,238
Burns 45,46,91
Bursa 60
Butterfly effect 217
Caecum 132
Calcification 37,49
Calcitonin 172-174
Calcium 14,15,36,37,47-49,**124**,172-174,217-218
Calcium carbonate salts 47
Calcium levels 60,173-174
Calcium phosphate 37,47
Calpol 97,98,100
Canaliculi 138
Cancellous bone 47,59
Cancer 21,46,90,99,104,105,119,122,132,
                        137,148,166,176,185,191,200,216,
                        222-224,226,228, 229,239, 245,249,261-263

Candace Pert 27,125,130,150,155,157,170,267,281
Candida 106,133
Capillaries 70,**73**,**79-80**,90,97,109,110,113,
                                    129,131,138,241
Capillary beds 73,74,79
Carbohydrate metabolism 124,**140**,170
Carbohydrates **17-19**,**116-118**,133,176
Carbon 16
Cardiac sphincter 128,137
Cardiovascular System 8,**69-88**,217-218
Carpal bones 56,60
Cartilage **36**,58,59,69,99,248
Cartilaginous blueprint 36,48,49,195,211
Cartilaginous growing plates 36,212
Cartilaginous joints 55,**58**
Catabolism 5,**14**,22,116
Catecholamines (also see adrenalin) 140,141
Cations 15
Causative factor 267,268,269,274
Causes of Disease 238-239,247,250,252
CCK (cholecystokinin) 129-130
Celiac disease 131
Cell membrane **24-27**,34,119,153,154,169,173
Cell reproduction 31,125
Cells 23-33
Cellular memories 76,283
Cellular respiration 21,30,65,107,174
Central Nervous System 152,155
Cerebellum 66,**157**,**158**,161
Cerebral hemispheres 157-158
Cerebrospinal fluid 155,270
Cerebrum 157-159
Cernnunos – Horned God 192
Ceruminous glands 44
Cervical vertebrae 52
Cervix 53,**182-183**,193,194,197
Chakra system 177
Change in bowel habit 245
Chemical 3,14,17
Chemistry **11-22**,116,157,170
Chemoreceptors 161
Chest cavity 6,74,111
Chicken pox 105
Childbirth ....see labour
Chinese medicine 5,41,65,78,82,82,86,107,134,205,
                        207,213,219,237,253,**265-274**
Chlorine 15,16,124
Cholesterol ...20,71,87,117,119,**120**,138,140,**141-142**,
                        179,203,218
Chromium 124
Chronic bronchitis 114
Chorionic villi sampling 197
Chyme 129,132
Cilia 34,62,109,208
Ciliary body 202,203

Ciliated epithelium	34,109
Circulation	8,**69-88**,110,129,195,**218-219**,274
Classical Chinese Medicine	78,134,237,253,265
Clavicle	51,56
Clear layer	43
Clitoris	179,**182-183**,**192-194**
Clot formation	45,71
Clotting response	71
Cobalt	16,124
Coccyx	52,53
Cochlea	205-206
Coenzyme Q10	87
Coenzymes	20,**21**,123
Collagen fibres	4,36,45,47
Collecting ducts	145-148
Columnar epithelium	33
Compact bone	47,48
Complement proteins	18,123
Complementarity	3
Compound epithelium	33,37,125,128
Condyloid joints	60
Conjunctiva	204
Connectedness	1,2,14,29,225-226
Connective tissue	4,6,18,**34-38**,47, 63,71,91,123,160,197
Consciousness	12,14,23,79,157,235
Constipation	132,134,214,245,248,273
Control of temperature	9,97,159,168
Convoluted tubules	145
COPD - Chronic obstructive airways disease	114
Copper	16,124,223
Cornea	202-203
Corpus callosum	157-158
Corpus luteum	185,187,188
Cortisol	20,120,140,142,143,**163**,164,165, **174-175**,179
Cortisone	see cortisol
Cough	34,98,104,109,112,114,245
Cranial nerves	160
Cranium	47,**50-51**,58,164
Cremaster muscle	190
Crying	96,164,199,203,205,254,257,258-260
CSF	see cerebrospinal fluid
Cuboidal epithelium	33
Curry network	222
Cushing's disease	174
Cutaneous membrane	37
Cytoplasm	4,5,24,28,29
Darkfield microscopy	85
Deafness	206
Death	236,240,241,249
Death and Dying	227-236
Death rattle	230
Deepak Chopra	32,152,170,215,247,281

Defecation reflex	134,214
Dehydration synthesis	17,19,126
Dendrites	151-156
Deoxygenated blood	70,76,77,109
Deoxyribose	19,20,117
Dermis	35,36,**42-45**,209,218
Descending (motor) tracts	159
Descending colon	132
Detergents	17,40,184
Development and aging	211-216
Development of the Embryo	194
Diabetes insipidus	147
Diabetes mellitus	175-176
Diagnosis and Symptoms	243
Diaphoretic	101
Diaphragm	**6**,**7**,**111**,114,115,128,137
Diastolic pressure	80-81
Diet	84,87,**116-125**,132,133,**136**,142,148,176,184, 214,239,242-243,245,248,272
Dietary fibre	132
Dieting	141,244
Digestion	5,**116-137**,149,161,164-165,208,219-220
Digestive enzymes	125-127
Disaccharides	19
Disease	94,100,102-106,130,213,222,237-280
Diuretic	27,81,147-149,171
Divine Will	78
DNA	18-20,24,25,**29-31**,54,117,125,172
Dopamine	154
Down's syndrome	181,195,197,240
Drainage	89-93
Drinking lots of water	148
Drug addiction	28
Drugs	28,71,81,87,90,100,136,139,142,147-149, 165,173,198,206,228,240,242,249,**249-250**, 253,271
Duodenum	129-130
Dura mater	155-156
DVT – deep vein thrombosis	84
Ear	44
Eardrum	205-206
Earth acupuncture	223
Earth energy	222
Earth Mother	107,270
Earwax	44,96,**205-206**
Eccrine glands	44
Ectoderm	135,195
Eczema	45,121,218,240,242
Edward O. Wilson	224
Effector cells	102
Eicosanoids	20,**120-122**,142
Eicosapentaenoic acid – EPA	120-121
Einstein	12
Elastic fibres	35,36,44,71,72
Elastic tissue	36,48,59,71

Elders	149,201,**214-216**,276
Electric fields	12
Electrical synapses	154
Electricity	12,186
Electrolytes (salts)	15,16,45
Electromagnetic fields	79,222,223
Electrons	13-16
Elements – chemical	14
Elements – five	265-274
Elimination	19,41,59,127,229
Embryo	135,179,181,190,194-195,211
Embryonic period	195
Emotional brain	159
Emotional health	65,254
Emotions	106,113,130,157,158,170,199,210,212, 219-220,**254-264**,267-269,277
Emphysema	110,114
Encephalon	155
Endocrine glands	9,130,168-178
Endocrine system	9,44,60,88,137,149,159, **168-178**,220
Endoderm	135,195
Endoplasmic reticulum	4,29,30
Endothelium	71,73
Energy	11-12
Enlarged lymph node	92
Enteric nervous system	125,130,220
Entrainment	225,256-257
Environmental pollution	223,250
Enzymes	14,**22**,123,125
Epidermis	35,39,**42-43**,93,209
Epididymis	189,190
Epiglottis	108
Epinephrine	*see adrenalin*
Epithelial tissue	4,**33-34**,70-71,109,125,135,180,211
Erythrocytes	*see red blood cells*
Erythropoietin	83
Essential fatty acids	25,**119-120**,173,213,242
Essential oils	40-41,219
Eustachian tube	205
Evolution	2,23
Excretion	5,132,174,191,220
Exhaustion	164-165,245,257
External auditory canal	205
Extracellular fluid	5,25,26,80
Extracellular material	4
Eye	40,96,**202-205**,245
Eye problems	173,204,245
Facilitated diffusion	26
Faeces	**132-134**,139,184
Fallopian tubes	34,62,**182**,**187**,**194**
False ribs	55
Fascia	35,36,**63-64**
Fascial unwinding	64
Fat soluble vitamins	21,123
Fats	19,86,88,**118-121**,129,130-131,**140-142**,242,243
Fatty acids	18-20
Fatty deposits	71,87,121,214
Female Reproductive System	**182-189**,**200-201**
Femur	51,57
Fertilization	185,190
Fever	**94-102**,141,143,247
Fibroblasts	32,36,45
Fibrous joints	50,58
Fibrous proteins	17,18,123
Fibrous tissue	**36**,57,63,160,202
Fight or flight response	130,**162-164**,169,174
Five Element medicine	265-274
Five stages of grief	234
Flat bones	48
Flatus	133
Flavonoids	71,136
Floating ribs	55
Fluoride	40
Fluorine	16,124
Follicle stimulating hormone	171,180,183,188,189,220
FOS	*see fructooligosaccharide*
Free nerve endings	209
Fructooligosaccharide	19,116,**132-133**
Fructose	19,140,190
FSH	*see follicle stimulating hormone*
Funny bone	56
GABA	154
Gaia Hypothesis	28
Galactose	19,140
Gall bladder	4,6,126,130,**138-139**,208,270
Gametes	31
Gamma linolenic acid – GLA	120,121
GammaAminobutyric Acid	154
Garlic	40,41,207
Gas	*see flatus*
GAS	*see general adaptation syndrome*
Gastric juice	128
Gender	158,180-181
General Adaptation Syndrome	164
Genes	25,30,179,181,190,240
Genetic counseling	195
Genetic material	20,29,30,31,117,181,189
Genitalia	175,179,180,182
Geopathic stress	221-224
Germ theory of modern medicine	94
Germinative Layer	43
Gestation	179,180,185,196,221
Gliding joints	60
Globular proteins	17,18,123
Glomerular capillaries	145-146
Glomerular Filtration	146
Glomerulus	145-146

Glucagon 130,140,170,175
Glucocorticoids .... *see cortisone*
Gluconeogenesis 140,142,175
Glucosamine 36,59,218
Glucosamine synthetase 36
Glucose 10,**18-19**,140,175-176
Glucose oxidation 21,123
Glucostat organ 68,140
Gluten 131
Glycaemic Index –GI 117-118
Glycogen 10,14,18,19,22,65,68,116,117,139-141, 175,218,231
Glycolysis 18,65,140
Goddess 83,**186**,192
Gods 12,183,192,235,236,275,277
Golgi apparatus 29,30
Gonadotrophic hormones 171,180,188,189,212
Gonads 6,9,25,169,171,175,179,212,215
Good cholesterol 142
Graded potential 153
Grandfather Fire – Tatewari 44,88,98
Granular layer 43
Greater trochanter 57
Grey hair 216
Grief 203,218,219,228,-229,234,268,269,288
Grieving process 234,262
Growth 6,33,42,123,124,170,172,**211-216**, 218,266,271
Growth hormone 18,123,140,141-143,**170-171**, 181,213
Gustation – taste 87,107,156,158,207,208,213,234
Gustatory receptors 207
Gut flora 132-133,184
H.R.T. 133,173
Haematocrit 82
Haemoglobin 17,**82-83**,**112-113**,139
Hair 40,**42-44**,123,143,175,180,182,184,201,209, 215-**216**
Hair follicles 37,40,43,184
Hartmann network 222
Haversian canal 48
Hay fever 99,147
HDL cholesterol 120,142
Headache 81,98,155-156,245
Healing mechanisms 32,162,242,257
Hearing 158,**205-207**,213,215,230,240
Heart 7,8,35,38,**75-79**,80,**86-87**,**88**,120-122,142, 178,195,219,225,227,245,248,**256-257**,258, 266,271,272
Heart attack 86,229
Heart disease 35-36,71,71,**86-88**,117,119-122,142, 228,272
Heart protector 272
Heavenly Father 107,270
Heavy metals 88,92
Hepatic artery 138

Hepatic portal vein 131,138
Hepatocytes 138
Herbal medicine 5,97,101,173,201,208,252
Herne the Hunter .... *see Cernnunos*
Hiatus hernia 128
High blood pressure 71,72,**81**,**86**,121,136,147,149, 174,249,250,257,259
Hinge joints 60
Hippocampus 159
Histology 23
Holism 238,246-253
Holistic 12,28,34,42,45,50,127,148,170, 204,217,218,241,244,**246-253**, 265
Homeopathy 101,252
Homeostasis 1,4,**9-10**,161,168,208,220
Homocysteine 72,88
Hormone 9,168-178
ACTH .... *see adrnocorticotrophic hormone*
Horned God .... *see Cernnunos*
Horny layer 42,43
Horse chestnut 74
Human consciousness 12,14
Humerus 51,56
Hunger 10,35,140
Hyaluronic acid 5
Hydrochloric acid 95,96,128-131
Hydrogen 14-20
Hydrolysis 19,126
Hyoid bone 50,109
Hyperactivity 104,224
Hypertension .... *see high blood pressure*
Hyperthyroidism 173
Hypoglycaemia 140
Hypothalamus 97,140,141,143,**151**,**159**,163, 171-172,189
Hypothyroidism 173
Iatrogenic disease 240,244
Ileum 129,131
Ilium 52,57
Imbalances in a society 24
Immune system **94-106**,123,130,135,139,151, 166,170,211,220,223,239,240,247,259
Immunity .... *see immune system*
Immunoglobulins 17,**102**,**103**,122,139,219,258
Incus 205,206
Indigenous cultures 275,276
Infections 96,99,100,104,106,166,200,239,243,247
Inflammation 20,45,58,59,106,115,120,121, 161,163,203,238,239,**241-243**,248
Ingestion 127
Inguinal canal 179,190
Inherited immunity 103
Innominate bones 57
Insulin 9,18,106,117,118,123,130,141,142, 170,**175-176**

Integumentary System .... *see skin*
Interconnectedness of all life 221
Intercostal 111,113,115
Interferons 95
Internal environment 15,**28**,95
Interneuron 152
Interrelationships 46,60,68,88,93,106,115, 137,149,167,178,201,217-226
Interstitial fluid 5,10,80,90
Intervertebral discs 54,58,161
Intervertebral foramen 53
Intrinsic beat of the heart 78
Iodine 16,124,172,173
Iodine deficiency 173
Ions 15
Iridology 203
Iris 202-203
Iron 16,82-83,124,139,214
Irregular bones 48
Ischium 52,57
Islets of Langerhans 9,175
J.R. Worsley 265,274
Jejunum 129,131
Joint capsule 38,58-60
Joints 38,**57-60**
Juxta Glomerular cells 147
Keratin 18,43,44,123
Keratinocytes 39,43,95
Ketone bodies 141
Kidney problems 99,176
Kidneys 99,144-149
Klinefelter's syndrome 182
Labia 179,182
Labour 10,58,169,171,**197-200**
Lacteals or lacteal vessels 90,93,219
Lactic acid 65,140,219
Lactose 19,116
Langerhans cells 39,95,96
Large Intestine .... *see colon*
Larynx (Adam's apple) 36,50,87,88,**108-109**,257,258,266,272
Laughing 257,258,260,268
LDL cholesterol 120,142
Lead 16
Leaky Gut Syndrome 132
Left atrium 76-78,109
Left ventricle 76-78
Legs (lower limb) 57
Lens of the eye 203
Leptin 35,141,143
Leucocytes .... *see white blood cells*
Leukotrines 20
Ley lines 222
Ligaments 18,34,36,47,**57-60**,71,91,123,161

Limbic System 159,208,110
Linoleic acid 119-120
Linolenic acid 119-121
Linus Pauling 71,142
Lipids **19**,116,**118**,190
Lipoproteins 18,123,142
Lithium 16
Liver 7,14,18,19,20,32,68,72,96-98,106,118-120, 124,126,**128**,**138-142**,147,149,163,164, 184,195,208,214,257
Liver lobules 138
Liver Official 270-271
Location of Organs 7
Long bones 47,**48**,58
Louis Pasteur 94,239,247
Low blood pressure 81,175
Lower limb .... *see legs*
Lower motor neurons 160
Lumbar vertebrae 52-53
Lung compliance 111
Lung volumes 112
Lungs 8,34,36,37,41,76,77,**107-115**,147,199, 209,214,219,227,230,243,273-274
Luteal/Secretory phase 188
Luteinising hormone LH 171,180,183,188,189,220
Lymph 89
Lymph capillaries 90
Lymph nodes 8,37,**89-93**,212,214
Lymphatic movement 90
Lymphatic System 8,37,**89-93**,95-102,114, 131,214,219,220
Lymphocytes 91,102,106,177,214
Lymphoid tissue 32,37,91,97
Lynne McTaggart 2,11,14,31,33,79,88,105,283
Lysosomes 29,31,231
Lysosyme 127
Magnesium 16,87,88,124,149,206
Malabsorption 131
Malaria 83,99
Male Reproductive System 189-192
Malleus 205-206
Maltose 19,22,127
Manganese 16,124
Manual lymphatic drainage 91
Master gland .... *see pituitary gland*
McCraty 79,256,284
Measles 98-99,103-105
Mechanoreceptors 161
Meditation 212,214,215,234,**260-261**,262
Medulla oblongata 159
Megakaryocyte 84
Meiosis 31,194
Meissners' corpuscles 44,209
Melanin pigment 39
Melanocyte stimulating hormone 171

Melanoma 46
Melatonin 177
Membrane potential 15,27,153,154,156
Membrane receptors 27,142
Memory 78,**156-159**,201,208,214,220,
                                                          240,260,273,282
Memory cells 102,103
Meninges **155**,159
Meningitis 105,155-156
Menisci 58,60
Menopause 174,184,185,186,**200-201**,282
Menstrual Cycle 44,122,**185-188**,244
Menstruation ....*see menstrual cycle*
Mental health 215,254,255,264
Mental illness 158,255
Meridians 5,64,127,224
Merkel's cells 44
Mesoderm 135,195
Metabolic heat 143
Metabolic rate 22,141,**143**,172,184
Metabolism 5,**14**,**22**,**140-143**,172,173
Metacarpal bones 56,57
Metafemales 181
Metatarsal bones 57
Microcosm macrocosm 24
Microvilli 129,131
Microwave pollution 22,123,224
Feng Shui 221,223-224
Midbrain 159
Middle ear 205-206
Milk coming in 171,199
Mind 33,150,157,215,220,226,235,246,254-264
Mind-body connections 254-264
Mineral oil 40
Mineralocorticoids 174
Minerals 20-22,87,**123-125**,149,223,240,266
Mitochondria 2,4,18,21,29,**30**,65,171,189
Mitochondrial Eve 30
Mitosis 31,33,41,168
MMR 104
Molecular chaperones 18,23
Molybdenum 16
Monosaccharides 19
Mother's milk 208
Motor nerves 9,161,160
Motor neuron 152,167
Mouth 50,125,**127-128**,135,207,243
MRSA 41,247
Mucous 34,96,109,125,127,128,129,208,247
Mucous membrane 21,34,108,123,204,207
Multiple sclerosis 106,151
Mumps 99,104-105
Muscle contraction 15,18,27,38,63,**64-65**,123,125,143
Muscle tissue 4,5,**38**,66,72,87

Muscles 38,**62-68**,152,158,162,164,218
Muscular System 62-68
Myelin 20,120,141,151
Myocardial infarction 86
Myosin ....*see actin and myosin*
Myxoedema 173
Nails 18,**43-44**,88,123,219
Narrative research 252-253
Nasal cavities 108
Nasopharynx 205
Naturopath 94,248
Naturopathic medicine 131,133
Near Death Experiences 235
Negative feedback 10,169,189
Nephron 145,146
Nerve cell 38,64,65,119,151,154,213
Nerve fibres 20,151-152,159,160
Nerve impulses 153,205,206,273
Nerve pathways 152
Nervous system 150-167
Nervous tissue 4,23,**38**,171
Neurohypophysis 171,172
Neuron ....*see nerve cell*
Neuropeptides 130,157,220
Neurotransmitters 27,79.125,140,**154**,157,
                                                                 168,170,220
Neutral fats 19,118,120,140
Neutrinos 13
Neutrons 13
New biology 24
Newtonian physics 150
Nitrogen 9,16,17,20,24,117,122,139,144,145,146
Nocebo effect 262
Nociceptors 161,207
Noradrenalin ....*see adrenalin*
Norepinephrine ....*see adrenalin*
Normal temperature 143
Nose 36,48,9596,108,205,207,208,247
Nucleic Acids 20,117,131
Nucleus 4,13,19,20,25,29,82,117,151,177
Nutrients 8,19,28,30,42,58,70,116,129,
                                                    131,132,137,149,165,219-220,248
Obesity 86,117,136,141,174,176,240
Occipital bone ....*see occiput*
Occiput 52,158
Odontoid peg 53,60
Oedema 80,91,149,262
Oesophagus 109,125,128,135,137
Oestradiol ....*see oestrogen*
Oestriol ....*see oestrogen*
Oestrogen 61,142,147,171,174,175,180,
                                                  181,183,184,185,188,200,201,212,218
Oestrone ....*see oestrogen*
Old Ways 4,186,221,236,275
Olfactory bulb 208

Olfactory receptors 208
Omega-3 ....*see essential fatty acids*
Omega-6 ....*see essential fatty acids*
One-way valves 74,90
Oocyte ....*see ova*
Optic disc 202-203
Organ location ....*see location of organs*
Organelles 3,4,23,29,83,151
Organs 1,4,6
Organs of elimination ....*see elimination*
Orgasm 192-194
Osmosis 26
Osmotic pressure 18,26,123,139
Ossicles 206
Ossification **48**,195
Osteoarthritis 58,248
Osteocytes 49
Osteoporosis 185,200,213,240
Ova 171,181,187
Ovarian follicles 171,183,185,187
Ovaries 6,99,116,174,**175**,178,**179-184**,200
Overview of Aging 211-216
Ovulation 180-189,194
Oxygen 8,14
Oxygen debt 65
Oxygenated blood 76,77,109
Oxytocin 10,169,**171-172**,197,199
Pacemaker 77-78
Pacinian corpuscles 44,209
Pain 41,46,86,87,91,131,161,198,199,203,208,
            209-210,226,229,242,245,248,258,259,263
Pancreas 117,126,129,130,135,140,169,175-176,273
Pansalt 87
Papillae 42,207
Paracetamol **97-98**,100,101,104
Parasites 83,99,129,239,247
Parasympathetic nervous system 164-166
Parathyroid glands 169,174
Parathyroid hormone 173-174
Particles, subatomic 3,13
Patella 48,57
Pathogens 90,94-96,104,123
Pathology 3,95,**238-245**
Pelvic cavity 6,187
Pelvic girdle 50,57
Penis 179,183,**189-191**,192-194
Pentoses 19
Pepsin 129
Pepsinogen 128-131
Pericardium 37,**77**,114,125,135,272
Periodic Table 14
Periosteum 36,**47-48**,57,59,63,156
Peripheral nervous system 152,**159-160**
Peristalsis 62,**128-130**,145,214,220

Peristaltic wave 128
Peritoneal cavity 135
Peritoneum 135
pH **17-18**,110,113,123,128,146,147
Phagocytosis 5,27,92,95,97
Phalanges 48,51,57,60
Pharmaceutical Pollution 80,249,250
Pharynx 108,109
Phases of growth 211
Pheromones 44,186,190
Phospholipids 20,24,25,118-120,140
Phosphorus 119,124
Photoreceptors 161
Physics 3,11-12,14,150,225
Physiological Coherence 256,284
Physiology 1-4,9-10
Phyto-oestrogens 184
Pia mater 155-156
Pineal Gland 79,169,**177**,178
Pinna 205
Pituitary Gland 79,147,157,159,163,**170-172**,178,220
Pivot joint 60
Placebo effect 100,252,**261**
Placenta 171,197,198,199
Plasma proteins 18,**80**,82,123,139,146
Platelets or thrombocytes 84
Pleura 37,77,**108**,**110**,125
Pneumothorax 110
Pollution 22,81,90,123,148,184,223-224,227,249-250
Polysaccharides 19,116
Pons varoli 159
Portal circulation 129,131,138
Positive feedback 10,169,187,192
Posterior pituitary 170-172
Post-menopausal women 201,184
Potassium 14,15,16,25,**27**,87,**125**,153
Power animal 278
Prebiotics 133
Pregnancy 58,91,171,185,197-201
Pregnenolone 179
Prickle cell layer 43
Primal Therapy 259
Primordial eggs 180
Progesterone 143,147,171,175,180,185,**188**,200,212
Proliferative/follicular phase 187
Proprioception 161
Prostaglandins 20,**120-121**,191,241
Prostate gland 189,190,214
Proteins 17-18,122-123
Protons 13,155
Psoriasis 45,99,106
Psychiatry 254,255,260,263,264
Psychoneuroimmunology 219,259
Puberty 32,177,180-183,212

295

Pubic symphysis	57,58
Pubis	51,57,58
Pulmonary capillaries	76,82,**109-110**
Pulmonary disease	114
Pulmonary embolism	84
Pulmonary veins	76,78
Pulmonary ventilation	111
Pulse	8,76,78,81,86,274
Pupil	202
Pus	90,242
Putrefaction	231
Pyloric sphincter	128
Pyramidal cell	152
Qi	82,107,270,272
Quantum physics	3,11,14,150,225
Radial pulse	8
Radial tuberosity	56
Radius	51,56
Red bone marrow	47,57,82,102
Red cells or erythrocytes	82-83
Red fibres (of muscle)	66
Red Flag Conditions	244-245
Reflex Actions	166-167
Reflex arc	167
Religious Attitudes to Death	235-236
Renin-angiotensin	147-148
Reproduction	6,25,179-201
Reproductive System	179-201
Research paradigms	12,251-253
Respiratory centres	113,115,153
Respiratory membrane	110
Respiratory System	**107-115**
Responsiveness	5
Resting membrane potential	15,27,**153**
Rest-repose system	164-166
Reticular tissue	37
Retina	202-204
Ribs	51,55
Right lymphatic duct	89
Rigor mortis	231
RNA	19,20,29,117
Root hair plexus	209
Rudolph Steiner	95,215
Ruffini's corpuscles	209
Sacroiliac joints	57
Sacrum	51,54,57,149,164
Saddle joints	60
Saliva	**127**,214,257
Salivary amylase	18,123,127
Salivary glands	126,127,135
Salt	15,81,**86-87**,88,136-137,173,174,208
Salts	see electrlytes
Sara Hamo	94,148
Scans – ultrasound	87,196-197
Scapula	51,56,66
Schumann waves	222
Scrotum	179,189-190
Sebaceous glands	40,43,44
Sebum	40,43,141,205
Secondary sexual characteristics	175,180,181,183,184,212
Segmentation	129
Selenium	16,124
Semen	181,190,**191**,192-194
Semi-circular canals	206
Seminiferous tubules	180,189,190
Sensory nerves	9,151,160-161,206,209
Sensory neuron	152,167
Sensory receptors	41,66,160,161,202,206,209
Septum (of heart)	76-77
Septum (of nose)	108
Serotonin	125,154,177
Serous membrane	77,110,125,135
Sesamoid bone	48,50
Sex	42,183,190,**192-194**,172
Sex chromosomes	181
Sexual arousal	192-194
Sexual intercourse	194
Shaking	158,159
Shamanic journey	277-279
Shamanism	12,236,**275-279**
Shampoo	40,43
Short bones	48
Shoulder joint	50,56,60
Sick Building Syndrome	222
Sight	202-205
Sigmoid colon	132
Silicon	16
Simple diffusion	**26**,27
Simple epithelium	33
Sino-atrial node	77
Sinuses	108
Sinusoids	73,97,138
Skeletal muscles	62-68
Skeletal System	62-68
Skeleton	36,48,**50-57**
Skin	33,35,39-46
Skin conditions	45,91
Skin rolling	35
Skull	50,58
Sleeping	113,223,245,284
Slipped disc	161
Small intestine	126,129-132,271
Smell	208-210
Smoking	34,74,86,114
Smooth muscle	**38**,62,72,90,109,125
Sneezing	96
Social model of disability	197,206

Sodium	15,16,25,27,153
Sodium chloride	*see salt*
Sodium lauryl sulphate	40
Somatic nervous system	152
Somatostatin	175
Soul loss	276
Soya	120,121,122,185
Space Clearing	221,224
Special senses	202-210
Specific acquired immunity	*see acquired immunity*
Sperm	30,31,62,171,**180-181,189-191,194**
Spermatogenesis	190
Spermatozoa	*see sperm*
Sphygmomanometer	80-81
Spinal canal	53,155,159
Spinal cord	159-167
Spinal nerves	159-160
Spinous process	53
Spirit	16,79,95,185,186,192,226,227,235,**246**,265,276
Spongy bone	*see cancellous bone*
Sprain	59
Squamous cell carcinoma	46
Squamous epithelium	34,42
Stapes	205,206
Stephen Buhner	70,77,79,168,191,256
Sternum	50,51,55,56,58,177
Steroid hormones	20,120,141,**168**,174,201
Steroids	118,119,174,240,249
Stomach	125,126,**128-129**
Stratified epithelium	34
Stratum corneum	*see horny layer*
Stratum germinativum/basale	*see germinative layer*
Stratum granulosum	*see granular layer*
Stratum lucidum	*see clear layer*
Stratum spinosum/malpighian	*see prickle cell layer*
Stress	65,79,86,96,139,148,149,162-166,200, 205,240,245,255-257,260
Striated muscles	62
Stroke	71,72,81,84,87,160
Strontium	16
Subclavian veins	89,90
Subcutaneous fat	19,35,39,**42**,143
Submucosa	125
Sucrose	19
Sulphur	16,124
Supermales	182
Supreme Controller	75,78,271
Surface tension in the alveoli	111
Surfactant	111
Suspensory ligaments	202,203
Sutures of skull	50,58
Swallowing	108,109,127-128,245
Sweat	37,41,**42,44**,257
Sweating	41,46,97-101,143,148,258
Sympathetic chain	162,166
Sympathetic nervous system	162-164
Symphytum officinalis	49
Symptomatic treatment	163,244
Synapses	154-155
Synergist	66
Synovial fluid	**58-60**,248,270
Synovial joints	38, **58-60**
Synovial membrane	**58-60**,106
Systolic pressure	80
Talc	40
Talking	109,255
Tarsal bones	48,51,57
Taste	207-208
Taste buds	207-208
Tatewari - Grandfather Fire	44,88,98
T-cells	102,211
Tears	96,139,164,205,234,259
Teeth	127,136
Temperature regulation	10,143
Temporo-mandibular joint	50
Tendons	18,36,63-64
Testes	175,179,**189-190**,193
Testicles	*see testes*
Testosterone	171,175,179,180,189,212
Thalamus	157,**158**,159,161,208
Thermoreceptors	161
Thirst	8,148
Thoracic duct	89
Thoracic vertebrae	52,54,55
Thoraco-lumbar system	162
Thorax	6
Thromboxanes	20,120
Thymus Gland	102,169,177,178
Thyroid hormone	27,141,142,143,170,**172-173**
Thyroid stimulating hormone	171
Thyrotoxicosis	173
Thyroxin	*see thyroid hormone*
Tissue fluid	*see interstitial fluid*
Tissues	33-38
Tone in muscles	65,66,160
Tonsils	97
Touch	41,42,44,58,59,**209-210**
Toxic 'skin care' products	40
Toxins	16,34,40,83,90,93,96,97,105,220,240,242, 248,250
Trace elements	149,213,223
Trachea	108-109
Trans-fats	119-120,121
Transitional epithelium	34
Transverse colon	132
Transverse processes	53
Tri-iodothyronine	*see thyroid hormone*
Triple heater	271,272,273

Tubular Re-absorption 146
Tubular Secretion 146
Turner's syndrome 181
Twins 225
Tylenol .... see Calpol
Types of bone 47-48
Ulna 51,56,58
Ultimate Health 253
Ultra violet light 39
Ultrasound scans 196
Upper motor neurons 160
Urea 139,142
Ureters 144-145
Urethra 144-145,183,189,190-191
Urinary bladder 6,10,34,**144-145**,183,189,191
Urinary System 144-149
Urine 139,145-149
Urine Formation 146
Uterine activity 20
Uterus 171,175,**182-183**-188,194-201
Vaccinations 16,103-106
Vagina **182-183**,191,193-195
Vanadium 16
Vas deferens 189-190
Veins 70,71,73,**74-75**
Venous return 68,**74**,88,90,114
Venules 70,74
Vertebrae 48,**51-55**,106
Vertebral body 53
Vertebral canal .... see spinal canal
Vertebral column 6,**53-54**
Vesicular transport 27
Villus 129
Viruses 5,92,97,101,**239**
Visceroceptors 160,162
Vitamin B12 83,124
Vitamin C 71-72,74,124,142
Vitamin D 20,21,42,61,123,124
Vitamins 20-21,123-124
Volatile oils .... see essential oils
Vomiting 96,128,147,245
Vulva 182,194
Water 5,8,14-15,148-149
Water balance 8,144,174
Weight 135,184
Weight loss 175,244
Western Pathology .... see pathology
White Blood Cells 83,95
White fibres 66
Wind .... see flatus
Wireless technology 18,22
Wisdom 152,201,215-216
Wisdom teeth 136
Yawning 205,258

Yellow marrow 47,48
Yin and yang 1,180
Yoga 49,114,150,214
Zero Point Field 11,13
Zest 11,253
Zinc 16,124,125,149,190
Zygote 11,31,194-195